DIRTY TYCOONS

DIRTY TYCOONS

KING OF CODE-PRINCE CHARMING-WHITE KNIGHT

CD REISS

FLIP CITY MEDIA INC.

King of Code

Prince Charming

White Knight

Barrington isn't a real place and these folks aren't IRL people. If they seem real I've done my job, but it's still a coincidence.

Infinite thanks to the K's for their help with research. If there are mistakes or misinterpretations of coding, quantum physics, the dark web, or reality itself, that's on me.

KING OF CODE

Things don't have to change the world to be important.

— STEVE JOBS

4U7H0R'5 N073

AUTHOR'S NOTE

Though there are a few towns called Barrington in the United States, my Barrington is a made-up place. The lack of state or geography is intentional. Barrington is everywhere in America—and nowhere specific. The troubles there reflect small-town concerns many communities share, and it's going to take me a few books to unpack it all.

To that end, I tried to strip the residents' dialect of a specific region, but one might show up. That's unintended.

I want to tell the story of your town, no matter what town or city you call home.

Though I'd love to assure you that I was successful in this (or any) endeavor, I have no way of knowing until it's too late.

I hope you enjoy the book—wherever you're from.

I

Steve Jobs. Bill Gates. Jeff Bezos.

Kings. Emperors. Rulers of kingdoms they built with their own hands. Their own sweat. Nobodies who clawed their way to the top with sheer grit.

Everett Fitzgerald. Even my buddy Fitz is a king.

Rockefeller. Carnegie. Ford. Vanderbilt.

They changed the world.

I'm about to become one of those guys.

Decades from now, they're going to talk about what I'm about to release into the world. Where I thought of it. What I ate for breakfast. How I got here. I worked harder, thought bigger, drilled deeper. I changed myself from the inside out to get here.

Today, I am granted meetings with kings.

In thirteen days I, Taylor Harden, become a king of kings.

I I

There's going to come a day I don't have to fuck in the supply closet. One leg over my shoulder, the other dropping off the side of the table, naked enough to get the job done, but clothed enough for waistbands and shirttails to get in the way. I hadn't fucked in a bed in four years. I didn't see my apartment for weeks at a time. I'd showered at the gym until we bought the QI4HQ and warehouse, then I put a shower stall in my office.

"Harder," she grunted in the dark. "Fuck me harder."

I gave it to her. A stream of filth left her lips, and I parried with more until we were both reduced to syllables. Then, nothing but the need to get back to work.

We rustled our clothing back on.

"Did you set up the cage?" I tucked in my shirt.

"We made it presentable last night. Jack needed to clean his shit."

Jack. I loved him like a brother, and he could cut code like a motherfucker, but he'd left a Tech World packing slip on his desk when the *NY Times* had done their profile on me. The photo Greeked when it was enlarged. Lucky him.

"Raven, I don't want a repeat of—"

"There's not going to be—"

"I mean it."

"Taylor." Her voice had moved to the door. "Everything's going to be perfect this time. I promise."

She opened the door before I could remind her that I was the one who decided what was perfect and what sucked.

III

"Why four?" Keaton had asked in my studio, years before. His English accent made him sound perpetually disgusted by my arrangements, but he'd insisted on seeing the shithole I lived in so he could feel sorry for me. I'd gone white hat and starved while he'd stayed black hat and thrived. His shirt cost more than my rent.

"Why four what?" I sat in the desk chair in front of my machine. It was the only other chair besides the one he'd bent his six foot four inches onto. He took up half the damn apartment.

"You're naming the company QI4. Q is quantum. I is intelligence. Why four?"

"I liked the way it sounded."

He finished his beer and got up to put his bottle in the recycling. He did it slowly, as if he wanted to fuck with me. He'd been an asshole since high school. Keaton Bridge, aka 41ph4 W01ph (Alpha Wolf if you don't speak l33t), had taught me the art of the dark web, where identities, guns, and drugs were traded in glorious, unindexed chaos.

"Seventy million," he said.

I was glad I hadn't dressed up to meet him because I almost pissed myself.

"But..." He trailed off intentionally for effect.

"But?"

He leaned his ass on the kitchenette counter and folded his arms. "You clean your ass up. You look like a bloody slob."

I ran my fingers through my hair. I hadn't had it cut in months. It was straight-ish when short, but when it got below my ears, it started curling. My beard was short, and my skin was olive but sallow from lack of sun. I'd lost weight, missed the gym for forever, my clothes hung off me.

"At least I don't look like a politician."

"Seventy million," he repeated, reminding me I was in no position to insult his suit. "In Bitcoin."

Oh, fuck him. He couldn't pay me in an underground, digital currency to finance my above-board venture.

"Dude. Come on. How am I going to exchange that?"

"Dude," he mocked me flatly. "I'll help you."

"I'll never get a government contract."

"*We* will. It'll just take time."

"We?"

"I'm tired of living in the shadows."

"Whoa, whoa, I said 'silent partner.' I don't need someone coming in, telling me what to do. Not even... before you even say it... not even the 'Devil of the Dark Web' or, no, *especially* not the devil."

"You'll have control, Taylor. It's all you. I'll never even show up at the office. But my investment will essentially reveal Alpha Wolf's identity, which will serve my purposes and clear the way for the exchange."

I tilted my head right then left as if I was letting resistance drop out of my ears. It was a moment to breathe. I'd expected worse when I asked him for seed money. I'd figured he'd drop a couple hundred grand I could tuck away in expenses while I tried to line up real capital.

Now he wanted to be the capital. Talk about a gift horse. I was looking right in its mouth and wheeling it into the gates anyway.

My phone had encrypted channels with all my primary contacts, including Keaton. As I was walking out of the hall closet after Raven, it rattled as he messaged me.

<Good luck today. Don't fuck it up.>

<You should be here to take some credit.>

<Credit is one thing I don't need.
Keep the receipts off the desk.>

Raven looked great walking into the hall after she'd just demanded I rip her apart with my cock. I had no feelings about her whatsoever, and that lack was mutual. Working sixteen-hour days in the same office meant we fucked each other or didn't fuck at all.

This was why I didn't hire women, besides the fact that they turned nerd IQ points into premature ejaculations. I usually wound up fucking them. But my lawyer had said to hire one, pay her well, and not fuck her. I'd taken two thirds of his advice. Raven had needs, same as I did. She was so anti-drama, anti-emotion, she practically had a dick.

"Check on Jack." I closed the door to the supply closet. "He's a fucking slob."

"The room will be clear."

"It better be."

"Yes, El Presidente." She threw the snark over her shoulder when she was already halfway down the hall.

I went the other way and pressed my thumbprint into a pad by sealed double doors.

A robotic voice came from the speaker. "Name."

A name would have been too easy. None of us used it. I used song lyrics.

"I don't give a fuck, chuckin' my deuces up."

A slot opened, and I put my phone into it. The slot closed. I had a mechanical watch, a Langematik that had set me back twenty grand, which was a deal, I promise you. It wasn't digital, so it didn't need to be checked before entry.

Green light. I burst into the Faraday cage, which was spotless and windowless. The walls, floor, and ceiling were lined with copper mesh that would stop all manner of motherfuckery. The room had no internet. No signal entered or escaped. Not even the drip-drop of electromagnetism from monitors. I'd put copper wire cages around the coding pit and the small factory on the floor below where engineers built the chips and boards.

I'd put full-spectrum lighting on both floors. It dimmed as it went dark outside and projected season-appropriate nature scenes on three walls. The rows of monitors were manned by the best coders on two continents. Three if you counted Giorgo, who had been born in Italy but trained in India. Above them was a huge screen rolling code.

I watched it roll. It didn't look like C++, Java, or anything seen before because I'd rewritten the rule book.

It was beautiful.

I got up on the platform in front of the screen and faced the thirty-three guys sitting at their computers. "Jack!"

He spun around. He was in Silicon Valley chic: a Nirvana T-shirt, jeans, and sneakers. I was the only one wearing a suit, but then again, I was the only one in charge. Fuck Zuck and his sweatshirt and sneakers. I was rewriting the rules.

"That fucking picture better be in your drawer."

He snapped up the picture of his nephew, threw it in his drawer, and slapped it shut.

"Lock it." I didn't wait for him to fuck with the key. "Everyone."

The last five of them turned away from their screens and trained their attention half on me. The usual ADHD cases who couldn't switch tasks easily. I waited. These guys were my people, my tribe. From the least social to the blabbermouths, we understood each other. I knew how to give them what they needed.

"Do not put it past journalists to 'accidentally' open your drawers to look for an emergency tampon. Do not put it past them to look at your cables or 'unintentionally' hit your spacebar to drop the screensaver. Do not think for one second that they didn't bring someone with a photographic memory. Shut the machines down. Name. Rank. Year of hire. How fucking pleased you are with your stock options. If you're not, you're going to have to take a deep breath and talk to Raven."

I got a little laughter. Women scared nerds. Another reason to keep them out of the cage. I wanted my guys to feel safe.

"As a reminder. You can neither confirm nor deny the following." I held up a finger. "The existence of a third quantum logic gate." I held up another finger. "The transverse micro kernel system." A third finger made a W. "Machine code translation circuits." I put my hand down on the railing and pushed off it. "The only thing you can confirm with utmost certainty is that no one currently living on planet earth can hack Quantum Intelligence Four. And that, men, is because you have perfected this thing to within an inch of its life. You know it's going to change the world. Your code is going to be inside the machines of every company in the world, and that's nothing compared to the day we scale and it's in every home, on every phone, in every chip manufactured in every factory in every country. That's you."

I paused to let that sink in and leaned on the railing as if I was whispering in their ears. "After today's announcement, everyone's going to try to get in here. Beware social engineering hacks. We cannot defend against those inside the system. People will hand you thumb drives, cables, whatever. Strangers are going to ask you for your pet's name… which you can't use as a password, but they'll try."

"Who can have a pet?" Deepak shouted. "We live here!"

Laughter followed. Deepak could drop a joke. He was as much a partner as Keaton, and he was going to be a rich man.

"In fucking paradise, Deepak Das Banerjee. But you get my point. Don't pick up shit in the parking lot. Beware pretty girls… and boys, David." I pointed at him. "Beware of mail. Cameras. Your own phone can be used against you if you let a girl in a bar put her number in it." I took a pencil out of my pocket and held it up. "If any of you need one of these to write down a number, let me know. Because in thirteen days, at GreyHatC0n, New York, we are going to offer five million dollars to anyone who can get into Quantum Intelligence Four, and you…" I pointed at Joe, who'd never had a girlfriend.

He pushed his glasses up.

"You." I moved to Laurence, who had a weird facial tic. "You." Roger. High-functioning Asperger's. "You." Grady. Social anxiety. "You." Thom. "You." Perry. They all lit up when I pointed at them, and the energy in the room was about to burst. "You're all going to be the sexiest guys in the room."

Cheers. Exactly what I was looking for. I checked my watch, but I knew what time it was. Showtime.

"Gentlemen." I held up my hand, and they quieted. "Shut your machines down. The six of you who are staying, put your smiles on. The rest of you can take a powder. *Wired* has arrived."

I V

ired had brought seven people. Four women and three men. By the time I was out in the lobby, they'd surrendered their cell phones, Fitbits, and smart watches. They'd submitted to a pat down from security and gone through a scanner we'd bought from the same supplier the TSA used. They'd agreed to use our recording equipment and had already familiarized themselves with it.

Mona Rickard scribbled in her little pad. She'd brought her own pencil. It was thicker than the ones we provided. I let it slide when I saw her grip was tangled and unusual. She needed it, and getting a transmitter into solid wood was a project a Boy Scout would have had trouble with.

"Five million," she said, a brown curl bouncing and swaying as she wrote. "For anyone or only people registered at GreyHatC0n?"

"Anyone," I replied. "Worldwide. We'll accept a remote hack. Welcome the attempt, actually. I hear that on the big day, teams are logging in from Râmnicu Vâlcea. That's in Romania."

"Yeah. Thanks. I know. I wrote a piece on Hackerville."

So they'd sent me a girl who at least knew something. Chalk one up for *Wired*.

"The Quantum Four code isn't even based in binary," I continued. "The circuits are built on three-dimensional thinking."

"QuBit. One, zero, random."

"Exactly. When the machines are released to Oracle next year, they can open them up and try to reverse engineer, but they won't. Even the client can't breach it."

"You wouldn't be the first to make that claim."

"If the casing is cracked, the boards self-destruct. They sink and melt."

"And production is here, in California?"

"The machines are made here, on site. We have a plan to scale when we can guarantee security."

The team followed Raven and me to the double doors leading to the Faraday cage. I stopped in front of them and faced the *Wired* team.

"Do you have way to ID the winner?" Mona asked, her diamond engagement ring jogging back and forth as she wrote.

The team got into the elevator as I answered.

"We do," I said. "A masked audit of all compliant commands. Non-compliant are going to look like shitstain on a wedding gown."

I explained nothing. If *Wired* sent anything less than their most technical writer they could fuck themselves. I wasn't wasting my time teaching her how to read metadata. She was going to have to ask one of the guys in IT.

"You have a protocol. And metaphor noted." She looked up and flipped her brown curl away from her eyes. "You're pretty sure of yourself."

"I'm sure about these guys on the other side of the door."

"I hear it's all men."

"I hire the best regardless of gender."

"And all the best had dicks?"

Someone on her team snorted with laughter. The elevator doors opened, and I led the group to the cage doors.

"Google hires all the girls," I said.

"I'm sure." She folded her pad and pencil against her chest and smiled. We saw right through each other, but she couldn't print what I wouldn't say.

"We'll be going into a foyer between the world of Wi-Fi signals and EMPs. Kind of like a lock room in the space station."

"I'm ready if you are," Mona said.

I tapped the panel outside the cage.

"Name."

"I don't give a fuck, chuckin' my deuces up." I chanted the song lyrics flatly.

The door unlocked with a clack.

"Suck on my balls, please," a pipsqueak with the notepad said from behind Mona.

She spun on him like a schoolteacher. "What?"

"I had enough," I added, and Mona gave me a wide-eyed stare. "I ain't thinkin' about you."

Pipsqueak tipped his pencil to me. "Beyoncé"

I winked at him and opened the door. I didn't look back at Mona to see if she'd gotten over it. They piled in. I closed the exit behind them.

"We're ready. Behind these doors is a room sealed against Wi-Fi. There's no internet connectivity. All the electrical outlets route through a secure panel. Quantum Intelligence Four is pure virgin code."

It bleeds when breached.

We said that a lot around the conference room table, but not in front of Mona Rickard.

I opened the doors. My coders stood. On the screen I'd just stood in front of, and on the walls that usually displayed nature scenes, were the scrolls of masked code as it would appear on the Tor site. They were the only light in the room. I laid my hand on the one machine we'd left on. It was in a mini-Faraday and was responsible for the screens.

"What you see here"—I indicated the men in the room—"are the best coders alive today. And on the walls is QI4's code. It looks like nothing because it's masked, and it's going to continue to look like nothing unless someone gets in."

"Which won't happen." Deepak came from behind his desk with a big white smile. Charming fucker. He'd have no trouble getting laid once he had a minute to wink at a girl.

He held his hand out to Mona, and she was about to shake it when his smile melted like solder on a hot iron. His hand froze between them. I followed his gaze to one of the projections.

The code wasn't masked.

ASCII flew down the roll. Then—

"Binary?" I whispered and stepped toward the wall. There was no binary. QI4 circuits didn't work that way. "Shut it down!"

Scrambling. Clicking. Keys unlocking drawers where safepasses were stored. My glands opened like circuits for sweat, hormones, fight or flight, firing neurons in the face of a breach I didn't have an algorithm to process.

"Shut it down!" The scream rattled the top of my throat.

Jack was the first to have his passkey out, but before he could type in a command, the entire system went dark with a sigh of hard drives winding down.

We all stood in the dim, windowless room.

The air crackled with silence broken only by the sound of Mona's pencil looping over paper, like someone woken in the darkness, writing down the details of a nightmare.

V

WITTER

@Wired
Ex Black Hat hacker Beezleboy creates
the unhackable system. Until it's hacked.

@gizmodo
That time you bragged about the
unhackable system and someone…

@nytimes
Oracle Inc. may delay system
upgrades in the face of QI4 breach.

@hackerbitch
Beezleboy got pwnd. Always a
fucking pussy. #QI4choked

@git-up
Finally. Someone he couldn't screw

by snapping his bitch fingers.
 # tool # douche # QI4choked

@anon_00110001
@hackerbitch
He's the fucking King. What did he
make you choke on?

@engadget
Did someone just climb the
Everest of exploits?

@hackerbitch
@anon_00110001
Careful – your douche is showing.
 # QI4choked

@anon_00110001
@hackerbitch
Temporary setback. Your most useful skill is
tweeting with your legs in the air.
 # QI4rulz # stackslut

@shelly-code
@beezleboy363636
That, my friend, is the taste of crow.

@hackeropz
Rumored QI4 hack may be part of a
bigger stunt. Don't write off @beezleboy363636
& Alpha Wolf yet.

@hackerbitch
@anon_00110001

080 114 111 110 032 104 097 115
032 114 117 105 110 101 100 032
121 111 117 013 010

@anon_00110001
@hackerbitch
Not impressed by ASCII. Pron is nectar. You
can't even get a job that doesn't require
kneepads #QI4rulz

@DeadBeefCafe
Anybody seen @beezleboy363636?
Tor's quiet. His account's dead. Is he
hanging from his belt in the closet?

V I

his is how a guy ends up in a windowless room full of
computers, wearing nothing but his jockeys. He kicks
everyone out. He locks the doors. He looks for code fingerprinting. He
spends a long time—the lighting change he programmed tells him it's
just about twenty-eight hours—finding nothing. He takes a shower to
clear his head. In the middle of it, with soap in his hair, he realizes he
could check the core dump for clear text. Rinsing his hair doesn't even
occur, and drying off will take too long, so he puts his underwear on
while he's walking back to the cage. It sticks to him like a wet T-shirt
sticks to tits. He sits down and searches everything.

There isn't much to see until there's a squeak of the door opening
behind him, and he spins his chair to see who it is.

"How did you end up…?" Deepak held out his hands, incredulous over
how I looked.

The full-speed-ahead train of my thoughts runs through how I ended
up in a windowless room full of shattered computers, sitting in front of
my laptop, wearing nothing but my jockeys.

23

"Your dick hard?" I spun back to my screen.

"Yeah. I'm going to fuck you in the ass if you don't let everyone back in here."

"No one's getting in until we know who did this, or they're going to do it again."

"What the fuck, Taylor?" He pushed a smashed computer with his toe.

I'd trashed four in a deliberate, organized way and couldn't find a chip out of place. Then I lost my shit and smashed monitors against whatever edge I could find. Then I found it. A dongled chip with a quarter inch antenna right in the board.

"The poison pill was in the monitors. Five of them." I pushed the one nearest my foot toward him. A 27-inch screen with a lightning fast GPU. We didn't have the facilities to make our own monitors, so we bought them like normal people.

Deepak saw it right away and picked up the green board. "Motherfucker."

"Said that right."

"What was it talking to?"

"It had to be transmitted to something coming in and out of the cage. I found a power strip in reception with a receiver in it. Another fucking mail order. Never again."

Deepak spread the monitor guts on the table next to me and examined them closely. "We're a young office. We had to buy shit to set up. We had to buy a coffeemaker too. We can't open up everything and check for receivers."

"We do now."

"Did they come from the same place? The monitors and the power strip?"

"No. It's a fucking mess. I can't make a connection. Monitors through TechWorld. The power strip was Amazon. The coffee maker was some artisanal company in Seattle."

"You checked the coffee maker?" He stood up from his inspection of the monitor.

"It was clean. Look at this. I'm in the poison pill now." I pointed at a little chip in the GPU I'd hooked up to my laptop, then at the screen.

"Anything?"

"The complete Sherlock Holmes."

"Really?"

"Really. He's fucking taunting me with it."

Deepak looked over my shoulder. My hacker had pasted the entire library of Sir Arthur Conan Doyle in the comments, and I had to go through every word.

"Have you considered it could be one of our guys?"

"No."

That was out of the question. I paid them well and treated them like princes. They each had a stake in making this work, and they each cared about what we were doing. Whatever it was—worm, virus, hack from God—it had locked me out. I could see the size of the box my life was in, but I couldn't open it. I hadn't connected offsite backups because we were off the grid.

It wasn't anyone on the team. I trusted them, and not a line of code got pushed to the source without me looking at it.

It was me. I'd been complacent. I'd let all their work get destroyed. I'd failed them. They relied on me to lead them, and I'd let them down.

"You all right?" Deepak asked.

Fuck it. Guilt was taking up time and energy. I was running low on both.

By accident, I laid too much weight on the page down key and forwarded to the middle of a completely different section. I was about to go back when I saw slashes. I hadn't seen slashes anywhere else, then I noticed the digit at the beginning.

> *9 I beg* that y*ou will look upon it*
> *not as a battered billycock but as*
> *an in*te/ll/ectua/l/ q*roblem*.*

"Look at this." I pulled the paragraph onto the big screen in front of the room.

Deepak stood before it with his arms crossed. He was best when he had a problem to solve or a journalist to charm.

"Isolate the odd ones," he said.

I'd already done it.

9gtyue/ll/tn/l/qm

"He needed the q," I said. "So he misspelled problem."
"What if the slashes aren't for the letters?"
"Other options? Numbers?"
"Three Ls?"
"Or ones. Leet style."

9gtyue3tnqm OR 9gtyuetn3qm

We stood in front of the green letters on the black background, arms crossed.

He tilted his head a little.

I paced away and looked quickly.

He looked at it from the side.

I squinted.

As if we had the same neurons, Deepak and I always thought with one mind. This time was no different.

"Eleven digits. Geohash coordinates," I said. Geohash was a newer version of latitude and longitude that split the world into a grid and gave each box a code.

"God, please let it be Tahiti. I want to go to Tahiti."

We didn't have internet in the cage, but I had a geohash database inside it. I called it up, and the cached satellite picture came on the big screen. All grey. The coordinates were inside a water mass.

"Lake Superior," I said. "Change the three in the second string."

"Done." It came on the screen in a split second, and it was land.

"No white sand beaches." I folded my arms over my bare chest, looking at the pin. The coordinates fell on a big building in a little town in the middle of nowhere. "Where are we?"

Instead of answering, Deepak contracted the map until the surrounding area was in the frame.

Nothing.

Freeway.

Train tracks.

Farms.

An interstate.

A nameless tributary.

Nowheresville in The Great State of Nowhere, USA.

"Do you think…?" Deepak said.

"Yeah. I think he left it so I'd come looking for him."

"What are you going to do?"

"Go looking for him."

"Put on some pants first."

I was already out the door.

VII

Fucksville, Nowhere—aka Barrington—didn't have an airport in a one-hundred-forty-mile radius.

That wasn't true. They had a dirt landing strip for crop dusters. I'd passed it on the way. What a shit hole. If I'd chartered something to land there, I would have announced my presence before I even took off.

I wasn't a big fan of Caddys. I drove a Tesla. Caddys weren't a thing in San Jose, but it was the best car they'd had at the airport rental terminal. The girl behind the desk swore by it, hand on heart, eyes rolling with remembered pleasure, and I had to say, though it handled like a cruise liner, it drove like a spaceship.

As I passed into town, the sign said the population was 1,209, but there was a fifth space before the one, as if there used to be ten thousand more people.

The terrain was pre-winter blight. Post exploding fall colors and pre winter sting. Brown, leafless, scrubby. The sky was overhung with grey, but with no discernible clouds, as if a screen of dullness hung between the earth and the heavens.

No way the dude who hacked QI4 was in this town. This was a pitstop on the way to some big reveal that would either be humiliating or expensive.

I was a target. A betrayer. I'd gone from black hat to white hat. I'd created a system to thwart them and bragged about it. I was the Everest of the hacker world. They wanted to get me because I was big, I was a challenge, and I was there.

I pulled into a little parking lot in front of two stores. A restaurant and a grocery store. It was the first commercial zoning I'd seen since passing into town.

When I got out, I had a weird feeling I only got when I went to Scott's Seafood with Fitz. Everyone looked and pretended not to. The room got one eighth quieter. They nudged each other, looked halfway around, pretended to take selfies so they could see over their shoulders.

This was the same—but different. Obviously. Because Fitz and I going to Scott's was normal. My being in flyover central to find a hacker was crazy.

I went up the wooden steps to a restaurant called Barrington Burgers. It was closed. I looked at my watch. It was one o'clock on a Saturday. I cupped my hands around my eyes and looked in the glass door, angling to see through a slit in the blinds.

Looked all right at first glance. Homey little place. Chairs were pushed in but weren't upside down on the tables. Maybe it was dinner only?

Then I noticed the alcohol was gone from behind the bar. The plants were dead. Sugar packets were strewn across the wood floor, shredded and balled in a light dusting in the floorboard slats. Only the white packets were ripped. The blue and pink packets were untouched.

Mice. Rats, maybe. Smart fuckers. I wouldn't have touched that other shit either.

"You looking for someone, mister?"

I turned toward the voice behind me and my god. The prettiest things hid in the most unlikely places. Long, wavy blond hair that reached breasts hidden under a flannel plaid car coat that was cut for men. Jeans. Cowboy boots. No makeup. Wide, full lips with a crease in the bottom one. Angular nose. Freckles. Eyes that went from brown in the center to blue at the outer ring.

She looked away, a little pink in the cheek. Tucked her hair behind her ear. The diamond in her lobe had to be a carat and a half. It looked as real as she did.

"No one in particular," I said. "I was thinking of staying the night around here."

I actually hoped I wouldn't have to, but no one who could hack me *lived* here, and I needed a place to drop my stuff.

"Oh, uh. There's a hotel on Oakwood." She pointed in a general direction. Her hand was fine, delicate, with white tape around three finger joints.

I took out my phone. She stared at it. Were they still using flip phones in Nowhereville or something?

"Do you know what it's called? I can look it up."

"The connection isn't great around here. You just go right out of the lot. Go for about a mile and a half, and you'll see a gate onto Oakwood. Take that until you see it."

"What's it called?" I could GPS the name more easily than stare at my odometer.

"Bedtimey Inn? But like I said, the connection's pretty spotty around here." She jerked her thumb behind her toward the little convenience store. "I'm helping out at the grocery. Want to call from there and see if they have any room?"

"I'll just drive over."

She barely moved, but I could tell I'd snubbed her by refusing her offer.

"I'm sure you know what you want." Her eyelids fluttered. Her lashes were blond at the tips and darker at the roots.

Strange looking girl. Beautiful and exotic. Just a touch younger than me. Her nipples were probably the palest pink fading into bronze at the center. Or the other way around. I wanted to know.

It was the wanting that tweaked a thought, a memory, a flash of déjà vu. It tapped a turtle's shell, and though the animal heard the tap, it didn't come out.

"Do I know you?" I asked.

"Um, did you go to Montgomery High?"

"No."

"Do you work at the distro center off the interstate? I sub there sometimes."

"No." I couldn't help smirking. The notion that I was from here, working at the distribution center off the interstate, was ridiculous, and I couldn't hide it. "You just look familiar. But I've never been around here before."

I almost asked her if she'd ever been to Silicon Valley or suggested we'd met at MIT, but why push it? If someone that beautiful had ever left Barrington, she never would have come back.

"Okay." She folded her bottom lip in thought, and I knew where the crease had come from. It was so much sexier as the result of a habit than a genetic detail. "You sure you don't want to call first?" Another thumb jerk toward the little grocery store.

"I'm good."

A shiny blue pickup pulled up in front of the store. She waved at it. A guy in a baseball cap rolled the window down to give us a short wave and a dirty look that may have all been in my head. He looked to be in his late twenties, but hard twenties, with skin the product of sun and tobacco. A hound leaned over his lap and stuck his head out, giving a bark when he saw us.

The girl turned back to me. "Bye, then."

"Bye."

She took two steps down to the lot, blond waves flapping like Old Glory on a fall day.

"Do you have a name?" I called to her.

She turned and walked backward. "Harper."

"Harper." I said it more to myself than her.

She didn't ask me my name but went to the truck, gave the dog a pat, the guy a couple of words, then bounced up to the store. I flipped the key to the Caddy around my finger, watching her. When she disappeared, Baseball Cap opened the car door, watching me. The dog poured out and ran up the steps to the girl.

Harper.

I waved to the guy in the cap. He went toward the grocery store after his dog without waving back. I got in the Caddy and turned the key, but though I laid my hand on the gearshift, I couldn't move until I said in the car what I couldn't say outside.

"Wow."

VIII

*R*eception was worse than spotty. No hotspot. Data didn't work until it did for five seconds, then my phone would buzz so hard with back notifications I thought the casing would break.

I pulled into the motel parking lot. Two long stories. No cars. Unlit soda vending machine and a snack machine with nothing in the spirals. The office door had a coded realtor's key box on it.

So much for the locals knowing where to find a hotel. I plucked up my phone. No signal, but I could see what had come in. I ignored everything but Deepak on our cloaked and encrypted message stream.

<How's paradise?>
<By the way, the geohash puts you
in the Barrington Bottling Plant.>

"Don't tell me." I scrolled down. "It's—"

<It's closed.>
<OK, so obviously you're in a dead
spot. Oracle wants a meeting. We're
going to have to resell the whole thing

to them.>

"We have to close the hole first. Then GreyHatC0n." I was talking to myself in the front seat of the car. I never talked to myself. I was too secretive for that.

*<I'm on board for that, but we gotta
fix it and prove it at GHC0N.>*

> *<Agree. Coverage spotty here. Fucking
> wasteland. Set up Oracle meeting. Call
> Dan at Walmart. Tap me if anything.>*

The crunch of tires on gravel made me look up from my phone and roll down my window. A claptrap Chevy with a rusted-out bottom pulled up alongside the Caddy. At some distant point in the 1990s, it had been either dark blue, forest green, or some shade of grey. The hand-tinting on the windows was buckling and cracking, leaving clouds of transparency on the glass.

The passenger window rolled down slowly, with an uncomfortable grinding noise, revealing the blonde from the grocery store.

Harper.

"Hey," she said. "I called, and it turns out they closed."

"Apparently."

"Sorry. I don't stay in the hotels."

"Not your fault. I should have listened."

She acknowledged my apology with a smile. "I can take you somewhere else."

"Actually." I ended the sentence. I didn't want to ask this across car windows. I opened the Caddy door as much as I could without denting the Chevy and slid out.

She took the cue and got out of her car. We met by the taillights.

"Actually?" The wind caught the edges of her hair, sending blades out in a corona around her face. I gripped my thumbs in my fists. She folded her hands in front of her.

"Do you know anything about the Barrington Bottling Plant?"

She gave me half a laugh that was as good as an eye roll but wasn't. I got the impression eye-rolling was beneath her.

"Why? It's cl—"

"—osed. I know."

"You want to buy it? It's up for sale if you can pay the back taxes."

"I'm not in the market for a bottling plant. I just… you know…" I put up one hand in surrender. "I'm a lousy liar. So I can't make up something plausible, but I can't tell you either."

"Okay?"

"Can you take me to it?"

"Are you going to cut me into little pieces when we get there?"

"Uh, no."

Her eyes narrowed. "Do you intend any harm to me at all?"

"No."

"Are you going to come on to me?"

"No, but if *you* want to come on to *me*—"

"I don't."

"Too bad," I said.

"You really must be a lousy liar."

"Truth is easier. You're safe. Promise. I'll keep my hands in my pockets."

"We take my car."

"Deal."

She pulled out so I could open the door. When I closed it and she smiled, for the second time, I had the nagging feeling I'd seen her before.

I X

*S*he drove as if her Chevy was starving and the asphalt was its single food source. We passed a house in the rolling brown plains every thirty seconds. Some were in worse shape than others, but none looked occupied.

"You have a name?" she asked.

"Taylor."

"Taylor what?"

Did I want to answer that? I wasn't famous (yet). The odds that revealing my last name would endanger me were slim, but I was habitually close with information.

"Why are all these houses boarded? Oh, wait." We passed a set-back two-story with a car in the drive and a dog tied to a tree. "Not that one. But the rest."

She shrugged, flipping her hand off the wheel for a second. "Barrington closed, uh… I guess nine years ago? Give or take, so there wasn't anywhere to work. Folks moved or died eventually. No one's going to buy a house where they can't find a job so… here we are."

A big brick box crept over the horizon, closer than it should have been, as if it had sneaked up on us and whispered, "Boo."

"Why did you stay?" I asked without thinking.

"This is my home."

I was glad she couldn't see my face because my mouth was closed against a ton of shit I didn't say. Like, *you could model anywhere,* or *you're staying for your boyfriend, aren't you?* Which was followed by weirdly compulsive offers to dump him and come back with me. She'd said about ten words to me, half of them questions about whether or not I was a serial killer, yet I wanted to hear her voice again and again.

"Your parents from here?" I asked so she'd talk again.

"My family goes way back. Most left, but my sister and I stayed. I can't really see living anywhere else."

That seemed like a huge failure of imagination.

We got close enough to see the barbed-wire-topped chain-link fence around the factory. The yellow warning signs became visible as the road got rutted, but we were still a quarter mile away. The car rocked, and Harper had to slow down to a less death-defying speed. I opened the window. Vs and Ws of screeching birds headed south.

She stopped in front of a yellow-and-black arm blocking the road, next to a boarded-up guardhouse.

"Okay, you have to drive." She put the car in park. "When the thing goes up, you have to go through fast."

"Okay."

She got out, and I slid over.

She pointed at me through the window. "Put it in drive. You have to go right away. I mean it."

I put the car in drive. She nodded and gave me the thumbs-up.

Disturbing a nest of crickets or cicadas or some other noisy, hopping bug, she reached around the base of the arm and did something I couldn't see. The yellow-and-black striped arm jerked up violently. I went through.

Barely. I hit the gas and sped through. The back of the car was scarcely past when the arm slammed down with a high-pitched squeal.

"Jesus."

Hair flying behind her, she crossed in front of the car, giving me two thumbs up.

Yeah. That deserved a thumbs-up. My life was falling apart, but that had been fun.

She got in the passenger seat. "Great. Take this to the gate. Then we can get out and walk around."

"Can you get me inside?"

I had no reason to go inside, but it wasn't as though I had any idea what I was looking for anyway.

"That's why we're here, right?" Like a tour guide with nothing better to say, she pointed toward a bank of tall reeds to the left. "River's over there. I live just on the other side."

She smelled like ozone, the buzz of the air before it rained, crackling with the pressure of something about to happen as it pushed against the few seconds preceding it.

"Pull over here." She directed me left, around the chain-link fence and away from the parking lot.

The factory was predictably huge. Red brick. Big windows behind steel grates. What had once been graffiti dripped from as high as a kid's arm could reach, as if it had just been melted by cleaner but not wiped away. *BARRINGTON GLASS WORKS* stretched across the top in chipped green paint.

"This thing steers like a bumper car."

"How does a bumper car steer? Pull over by that concrete slab thing."

"It slides when you turn, like it's got no relation to the actual world. And it shimmies left." I put the car in park. "Is this even safe?"

She got out without answering. I rushed to follow her, taking the key out of the ignition as she ran her hand along the length of the fence. It rattled like chains.

"Wait up." I jogged after her. "Where are you taking me?"

"To the back."

"You're not going to cut me up into little pieces are you?" I handed her the car key.

She smiled slightly as she took the key. Just enough to let me know she was considering it.

"So, you came into town in such a rush, you didn't figure out where to stay. Can't tell me why you want to get into an old bottling plant. Got on a snazzy jacket." She whipped around the corner. "Driving a rented Caddy. Those are really nice shoes, and you don't even care that they're getting full of dirt."

"I have money. Never said I didn't, Miss Diamond Earrings."

She stopped short by a gate with a lock. "Tell me what you want here."

As far as I was concerned, I'd been the picture of patience and charm up until that moment. I hadn't pushed her to help me. I'd been nice. I hadn't freaked out half as much as I wanted over the fact that a trapdoor had opened up under my life.

"Are you done helping me?" I asked.

"If you're not here to buy the place?"

"I told you—"

"Everett Fitzgerald's talking about buying it so…" She drifted off as if I could infer the rest.

The Fitz I knew was eccentric, brilliant, two generations from royalty. I couldn't believe he'd ever heard of Barrington Glass Works. Not for a minute. Fitz was in the business of eliminating traffic and solving world peace. Not bottling.

"Since when?" I asked.

"Heard about it a month ago from a realtor in Doverton. He needs it to build the personal helicopters is what we think. He's coming in three weeks to look at it." She glistened with excitement. "When I first saw you, I thought you might be scouting for him."

"I'm not."

She shrugged, clearly disappointed.

"I'm not going to hurt you or the property. I'm not going to buy the plant. I'm not going to do anything you expect. In an hour, I'm going to be a crazy story you tell your friends. Are you going to let me in or not?"

"No."

My patience was held together with scotch tape, and it was getting loose. "Why not?"

"I don't have the code." She tilted her head toward the padlock. It was the size of a box of pushpins and had a row of buttons.

"Okay, you know what? This was fun. But I could have done it myself. I could have driven here with my GPS, parked at the guardhouse, walked here, and been in the same barrel of shit as I am now. No, I would have been better off because I would have had a car. So, no, I don't want to cut you into little pieces. It's not my thing. But my

God, if I were a cut-a-girl-into-little-pieces kind of guy, this would be the day I started."

She raised an eyebrow. Daring me. She was *daring me* to cut her into little pieces, which wasn't even on my list of shit to do.

"Let me see this." I got my hands on the padlock.

It attached the ends of a heavy chain, which was wrapped around the poles of the gate. It had a code, which meant it could be cracked, right? I took out my phone to check the Tor boards. Maybe someone had a master code that worked.

No signal.

"Is this the only gate?"

"As far as I know."

"Do you have tools in the trunk? A hacksaw? Stick of dynamite?" I looked at the top edge of the fence. There was a break in the barbed wire. Maybe I could get in there. I hooked my fingers on the chain link just above my head.

"No."

I didn't believe her, but I didn't think tools would do it either. I also didn't believe she didn't know how to get in. There was enough graffiti to account for a hardware store full of spray paint.

"Rebecca or Carlyle would have the key, I guess. She's the realtor over in Doverton, and he does security for everything around here. We can call them if we go back."

"Yeah. No. Don't worry about it."

I took out my pocketknife and pinched out the awl. I didn't have time to pretend a normal way in was going to work, nor did I have the patience to explain a hundred times why I wanted to get into an empty factory.

I lifted the weight of the lock and looked under it. Three pinholes. One bigger than the other two. "Those earrings? They platinum?"

"White gold." Her veil of suspicion didn't obscure her curiosity enough to silence her.

"Can I borrow one?" I asked.

"Excuse me?"

"It's white gold, so it's hard enough that I won't bend it." I held out my hand. "If I break it, I'll replace it. But I won't break it."

She thought for a second, looking me up and down as if scanning my complete character. Either liking what she saw or accepting my shortcomings, her hands went to her ear. When she looked at the tall reeds, her hair blew back. Her neck, her jaw, those earrings. I wanted to mark her right at the base of the curve and the center of the length of her throat.

I didn't even have time for the fantasy, much less charming it into reality.

Two pieces of jewelry sat in her outstretched palm. The diamond post and the backing.

I reached for the post. "Thank you."

She closed her hand before I got it. "What do you think is in there?"

This girl.

"Someone left something for me in there. I don't know what it is, but I'll know it when I see it."

"Who?"

"Someone who wants to screw me. I don't want to be screwed. I want to get him before he gets me, but I have to follow along until I can make a move. Is that enough of an answer for you?"

She opened her hand and let me pluck out the post.

I was extra careful with the post, making sure to push and not bend. The lock popped open.

"So," she said when I handed her back the earring, "you're a thief?"

She couldn't know it was a trick question because she didn't know where I'd been and what I'd done.

"I like to know how things work. Once you know that, you can do anything."

She put the dirty earring in her pocket. I couldn't tell if she believed a word I'd said. It didn't look good for me though. I wouldn't have trusted me if the situations were reversed.

I hooked the lock over the fence and opened the gate. I gestured for her to go in. "Are you coming?"

She held her chin up and crossed through. I followed, leaving the gate open, and we went toward the building. As we got closer, the sheer magnitude of the place got very real. In the vast emptiness, it had looked to scale, but against the size of actual humans, it was titanic. The warehouse windows had survived the closure, some even looked new. The grass and brush were trimmed. We came to a sealed metal door set over a steel staircase to the second floor. The door was painted black. Shiny, as if it was new.

"We bottled beer and soda," she said. "The syrup and soda came from all over, but the glass bottles were too expensive to ship, so we made them here."

"Bottles have been plastic since forever."

"Yeah, the soda went away a long time ago. We did beer, then there was just nothing. All the bottling went to Mexico. The work just shrank and shrank."

"Are we going to have to get past another lock to get into the building?"

"Why do you think I'd know?" She laid her hand flat on the brick that was red in a space between turquoise washes. The touch was loving, as if the building was a pet elephant.

"I have a feeling you know more than you let on."

Her head made a sharp quarter turn. Surprise. Insult. Truth.

"Let's not play games," I said. "Like I said, I'm here to look at something and get the hell out. And I'm sure you have things you have to get back to. So, if you want money to get this over with—"

"I don't want your money."

Of course. Miss Diamond Earrings wasn't interested in money.

"Well, if you want something to get this done fast and get me out of here, just say it."

She wanted something. Something specific. The way she folded her bottom lip in half. The way she wouldn't look at me. There was so much more than simple, stubborn pride at work.

"What time is it?"

I shot my arm forward to hitch my cuff high and checked my watch. It was mechanical and got slow a few seconds every day. She peered over my forearm to see, and I was suddenly embarrassed to have such an expensive thing in Barrington.

"Almost two."

She crossed her arms and tapped her finger on her elbow. "I'm going to take you in because, yeah, I brought you this far and now I need to get going. But first..." She held out her hand. "Your wallet."

"My what?"

"I need to make sure you're not going to steal something or trash the place or whatever."

"No."

I wasn't giving her my wallet. It would take her a second and a half to find out my full name, Google me, and spread the word all over Twitter that I was in Nowhere, USA, a day after the bottom had fallen out of QI4. I didn't want to answer questions. I didn't want to give the guy who'd broken my life any more attention.

In a half second of clear signal, my phone buzzed repeatedly. An hour's worth of notifications were coming in. I had to look at them. They might be a way out of here.

I walked to the gate as if my no had been the final word. It wasn't. I was bluffing.

<I can't find you on the map. Are you
in a dead zone?>
<Where the fuck are you?>
<There you are.>
<You're right on top of it. Inside the
big building. Factory. Managed by Carl-
Ten Security LLC. Let me do some social
engineering on it.>

<Cracked gate code already.
Need doors. I see keys, not codes.>

On a whim, I asked another question.

<Need intel on girl living here. Mid
20s. Harper. No last name avail.>

<Anything else?>

<Nothing. I got a whole lotta nothing>

The signal dropped. Who knew when it was coming back? What was I going to do now? Go to the hotel in the next town over and try to get into the building legally? By asking nicely? I hated asking nicely.

Harper sat on the metal steps with the toes of her cowboy boots hooked behind the step beneath her. If I was going to be out of here by nightfall, morning at the latest, I needed to find whatever I was supposed to find. The longer I waited, the more I lost control of the QI4 narrative.

My fucking wallet. Driver's license. The real one. Credit cards with the company name. Gym membership.

Fine.

I walked to her. "You can get me in?"

"Yes." She crossed her heart, kissed the fingers that had committed to the cross, and flicked them at the grey sky.

I tossed her my wallet.

She plucked it out of the air. "Thank you."

"Let's go then. No fucking around."

I stood beneath her and watched as she flipped my wallet open and did forensics on it. Jesus Christ.

"Can we go?"

"Taylor Harden. That rings a bell."

"There was a singer with the same name," I lied.

She saw right through it. This was why I only lied through a computer screen. As long as no one could see my face, I could get away with anything. When I was a teenager, the screen had offered me a comfortable anonymity since my emotions showed all over my face. I'd gotten better at controlling my shit later in life, but lies were still hard.

"Platinum card?"

"You said you didn't care about money."

She pocketed the wallet and skipped down the steps. They clanged under her. Her hair swung as she traversed the side of the building and turned around to the backside and a rutted, overgrown parking lot with cracking yellow paint indicating eighteen-wheeler-sized parking spaces. A loading bay.

She clambered up a short metal stair and motioned me to follow. Next to the bays stood a human-sized metal door. She pushed the handle down and opened it.

"You're fucking with me."

"You coming or not?"

I didn't move. She shrugged and walked in, letting the door slam behind her. I pushed the handle down and pulled. It opened. Motherfucker. I'd given up my wallet without checking all the entrances. Unforced errors under pressure. I was smarter than this, and she was smarter than I'd expected.

X

*A*n eerie darkness hung over the place. Everything was gone. Offices empty. Halls strewn with beer cans and blankets. Walls dotted with circles of black cigarette ashes. She walked so fast I could barely keep up, but it wasn't as if I knew what I was looking for.

She pushed open wide fire doors into a concrete-floored room the size of a big-league infield. Light poured through the windows. There was stuff everywhere. Crushed boxes. Piles of shredded tarp. Plastic bags. I heard the squeak of rats.

"Here you are." She stood in the center of the room with her arms out.

"Here I am." Wires hung from the ceiling. A few ballasts were left, hanging crooked and bulbless. On the verge of a massive hack, it's easy to get excited and make a mistake. Accuracy is everything. I slowed down and looked at every single object. Every bit of wall space. "Where's the machinery?"

"Sold. It's just a shell. Globalization sucks."

Jesus. As if she understood anything about it.

"That phone you got would cost four thousand dollars without globalization."

"This?" She took out her phone as if it had germs and she had an immune deficiency.

"The complexity of making things can only be affordable with either automation or cheap labor. Trust me. I know."

Pocketing the phone, she nodded, rocking her cowboy boot heel on the concrete. "You know what I know? I know people. I know this town. I know Marty Luman. He's real smart but didn't go to college because he could make a good living here. Now it's too late. I know everyone in the Shover family because the entire town fed them when they lost their insurance and went broke paying for their daughter's leukemia treatments. I know Wally Quinn, who got so depressed when this factory closed that he shot his entire family then shot himself. Everyone who had two nickels to rub together left and took their chances someplace else, and I miss them. I miss all of them. These people are real. They're my friends. This whole town was built around this factory, and when Earl Barrington struggled to keep it open, we all struggled with him. So I don't give a shit about this phone because I got no one to call anymore."

That gorgeous bottom lip quivered.

"What happened to the kid?"

"What kid?" she spit out.

"Leukemia kid? Shriver."

"Greta Shrover died."

"I'm sorry."

"Whatever." She tossed me my wallet. The throw was good, but I wasn't expecting it, and it wound up open and facedown on the floor. I scooped it up. "Are we done here?"

Was I done? What was I looking for again?

"There's nothing to steal, and I didn't bring my bulldozer. So if you don't want to walk around with me, you don't have to."

She turned her back to me. "Fine."

Finally free, I could make short work of this.

I bounded up the steps to the second floor. It was divided into two big rooms. They had less junk than the first floor but were just as useless. I checked every room, every scrawl on every piece of garbage, every mark on the walls. Nothing.

I wasn't worried. Not yet. But I was getting ready to worry.

Third floor. The ceiling was a little lower, and there was no production room. Halls and office after office after office with cots, bags of garbage, broken heaters, a gas generator, a tent, sleeping bags. The stench was distinctly human. It didn't take long to see what had been happening on the third floor, but checking every single room and finding nothing boiled my raw anxiety until the shell of my denial fell away.

I was running out of places to check.

In the back, I found an open elevator shaft.

Up it, I heard Harper say, "Taylor? You all right?"

"No, I'm not all right."

Her head appeared from the first floor. "Why not?"

"Because I came a long fucking way and there's nothing here."

"What are you looking for?"

What would be the harm of telling her at this point?

"A message." I was shouting, and my voice bounced off the walls of the shaft, making me sound even angrier. Good, because that was how mad I was. "A cryptic, serial killer breadcrumb left by a fucker who stole something from me. And I'm not trying to insult you, but you wouldn't know it if you saw it."

"Did you check the roof too?"

"No, I did not check the fucking roof."

I didn't wait for her to answer but stalked back to the hall and up the stairs. The exit to the roof said, EMERGENCY — ALARM WILL SOUND. It was cracked open already.

Slapping the door open, I burst onto the cracked tar of the roof. The grey sheen had melted away, leaving a blue sky and blasting sun. Was the message in the scenery? Walking the perimeter, I could see clear to the horizon. A slope here, a cluster of buildings there, a city far enough away that it was a handful of grey Legos. Harper's shitty non-color Chevy sat on the other side of the fence. Past the tall reeds flowed a slate waterway too big for a stream and not quite a river. A single house peeked over the trees on the other side of it. The top shingles were pocked with newer, brighter patches. It loomed like a haunted mansion with a piebald roof.

What the fuck was I supposed to find?

I checked my phone. No signal. Nothing. What kind of black hole in the center of the country was this?

Fuck this.

I paced to the edge of the roof because even though I said, "Fuck this," with every step, I couldn't leave a single stone unturned. Was I supposed to see something on the roof or in the view from the roof? Was there a basement? Maybe I was supposed to be in the basement? I wasn't leaving until I figured it out. I'd crawl into one of those sleeping bags for the night if I had to.

I wasn't coming back here to do again what I should have done the first time. No way. The next time I got on a plane, I was going somewhere that actually existed with victory in one pocket and the world in the other.

I could see the interstate and a billboard for a topless place. In the other direction, an ad for the closed diner I'd passed on the way in. Nothing. No message on the horizon. None on the roof itself. There was so much graffiti on the walls that I walked right over the spray paint underfoot.

"Hey!" Harper called from the doorway leading to the roof.

I looked at her and saw the red writing at her feet. The foreshortening flattened the scrawl, making it readable.

```
IF (beezleboy cooperates) {
decryption occurs
/*087 101 108 099 111 109 101 046*/
}
ELSE {
engage humiliation protocol
/*083 116 097 121 032 097 119 104 105 108 101 046*/
}
```

As she walked toward me, Harper said, "We should—"

I held my hand up to stop her from stepping on the message, then I put it together and wanted her and a million others to trample the code until it disappeared.

I touched a red letter. It was dry. A pebble had gotten painted on. I put it in my pocket.

"We should go." She completed her thought even though she was distracted by the writing. "It's going to be cold tonight."

"Sure."

"Is this what you were looking for?"

"Yeah. I think so."

"Does it mean something?"

Did it? I knew what she meant, but I asked myself a different question with the same words. Did it mean something? Did I have to obey? Did I have to believe? Did I have to trust?

"The numbers inside the stars are ASCII text. It says, 'Welcome.' The next part is where the guy I'm looking for calls me by a code name I have on the internet. Says… see right here it says *if*? If I cooperate, I get something I want, and everyone laughs at me if I don't. Last line between the stars says, 'Stay a while,' which is real cute. Because the longer I stay, the more likely I am to be an even bigger loser and have the world laughing at me."

"Huh. That's weird."

"He wants me to think he's in Barrington."

"Interesting."

"Do you know a guy who knows stuff like this? Computer code? You might not recognize it—"

"Don't know a guy like that."

"He might be in IT security, or he might be a kid who stays inside a lot and plays video games."

"Nope."

"He could be really young."

She shrugged. "I have to go."

Everything I'd ever built could crumble, and she was shrugging. Great. She took off, not even looking to make sure I was following. Bounding down the steps, hair flying, she wasn't wasting any time. I chased her down the dirty stairways and outside.

"Wait up!" I called.

She didn't slow down, going to the other side of the gate, and she waited there for me as if I was a kid she wished she hadn't taken to the supermarket.

"I'll take you back to your car." She slammed the gate behind me and picked the lock off the chain links. What was her deal? "There's another hotel about twenty-five miles down the interstate. Or the country club in Doverton might have a room."

She knew something. She had to. She was trying to get rid of me so she could... what? Talk to the dude?

"I can't go that far."

"Why not?" She yanked the lock to make sure it stuck and headed for the car.

Because I'm afraid of leaving the geohash.

Because there's something on your mind.

"I have the feeling I'm supposed to stay here."

"Really?" she called over her shoulder before she got in the driver's side.

"Really." I jogged to catch her, putting my hand on the top of the door. "And I'm kind of stuck." I bowed to see in the open window.

She rolled her eyes and shook her head. "Yeah. You are."

She turned the ignition over, and I hurried around the car and hopped in the passenger side. We regarded each other for a minute. Her eyes were a sample of every single iris color in the human genome. She broke our gaze to pull forward and stopped the car at the striped arm.

"Your turn to get the gate up," she said.

I didn't know what switch she'd hit back there or if there were wires I had to cross. I didn't know if there was a key or a code. But I sure as hell wasn't going to sit there and tell her to do it. I wasn't going to puss out on a challenge. Because that was what it was. Flat out.

"Fine."

I got out and looked behind the box. It was everything I'd expected. A tangle of dozens of indistinguishable wires. Worse, they'd been painted white as if on spite. Two had to touch to make the arm go up. Four had been stripped.

She pulled the car up to the edge of the gate. The arm would swing up then down. If I did something wrong and sent it down early, it would land on the car—or her. I was frustrated as hell and a little pissed off at her for daring me to figure out how to do what she already knew how to do, but I didn't want to hurt her or bang up her car.

When I touched two of the stripped wires, the arm buzzed but didn't move.

Mathematically, the presence of four stripped wires made me less likely to find the combination. Three would have made it easier. I would have found the green wrapping, which would have been the ground wire, and eliminated it as a possibility.

I scratched the white paint off one.

Blue.

"Do you need help?" she called.

"No!"

The next wire was blue too.

"I got it," I added.

But I didn't, because the third wire was blue, which should have meant the fourth was the ground wire. But I checked anyway and it was blue as the sky. Either there was no ground wire, or they'd run out of green, or they didn't give a shit and never grounded the wiring.

I touched two more wires and a ball of light appeared. The copper ends of the wires went on fire.

"Do you want me to tell you what to do?" Harper asked from a mile away.

"I said I have it."

"You don't sound like you have it."

I didn't have it. I didn't have it at all, but fuck if I was going to admit it.

"You have to—"

"I said I have it!"

Getting out from behind the box, I stood by the gate and faced the car.

She leaned out the window like a fucking know-it-all. "You don't want me to tell you?"

She was smirking as if she knew damn well I was in over my head. Well, what the brain couldn't puzzle through, the body could correct with brute force.

"No."

I bent my knees and wedged my shoulder under the bar. My guess was that the gate had some kind of broken locking mechanism, which was why it slammed down so quickly. Which meant if I straightened my knees, it would rise with me.

"What are you doing?" she asked. "If you can't figure it out, just say so."

"So." I straightened my knees, and my shoulder picked up the gate. It was heavy, and it hurt like fuck, but it went.

"Shit." She pulled the car forward, but the gate tapped the top of her windshield. "I'll pull back and you can drive…"

Fuck that. I got my hands under the gate and nudged myself back toward the pivot point at the box. The changed angle would bring the other end of the gate a little farther up. It got heavier and harder to move as the pressure from the fulcrum increased.

It lifted and the shitty little Chevy passed through. I dropped the arm. My shoulder was unhappy, but my feet moved fast to get in before she took off.

"You have a really massive ego," she said, getting onto the highway.

"All the wires were the same color. Who does that?"

"Wires?"

"You have a different name for them out here?"

"You didn't see the switch?"

The switch? There was a switch?

"You didn't see the switch." She changed from question to statement.

"I guess I didn't."

She tried not to smile at my utter ineptitude. The force of her will against the strength of her instincts tightened the muscles around her mouth, twisting it into a wave form.

"It's cute the way you're trying to save my really massive ego." I had to smile, and so did she. "But you're going to hurt yourself like that. Go ahead, laugh."

She laughed, slapping the steering wheel. I laughed a little with her. Just a little.

XI

*S*he had gone into tour guide mode on the way back to my car. This is this, and that is that. Here's where I drank beers with my friends. Here's my high school. Here's Bobby Droner's place. He went to Iraq and didn't come back, etc., etc.

I listened carefully for an IT guy, a kid going to college, a computer engineer, a thief who'd found a way into the liquor store safe, a teenager who spent too many hours in front of video games. Names flew by me, and I caught what I could. But none of them was my hacker.

The only thing that kept me nodding was the knowledge that there would be an end to all this. When we entered a desolate square of empty storefronts and a post office, my phone buzzed.

Note to self: *The dead zone is live when the wind blows from the south.*

<Oracle meeting. Next Tuesday on
the Redwood campus.>

<I'll be done by then.>

<Good. Next. Harper Barrington.>
<Daughter of Earl Barrington. Owner

of the factory in the geohash coordinates.>

That explained the diamond earrings and how she knew which door of her father's old factory to open but little else.

<College records? She's smart.>

<Jack's on it.>
<You all right out there? You
didn't fuck her, did you?>

She had her wrist on the top of the wheel, hair blowing across her face. I hadn't fucked her, but man oh man, given the right time and place, a better situation? If my life wasn't in a spray of broken pieces at my feet?

<Nah.>

I had more to say, but the signal dropped and our messages self-destructed, as they were programmed to do.

"Good news from home?" Harper asked at a light there was no point in stopping for.

"Yeah. Hey, where's the nearest hardware store?"

"We just passed it."

I felt for the little red rock in my pocket. "Do they sell spray paint?"

"Yeah. Why?"

I held out the pebble. "I wonder if they'd tell me who bought this color recently."

Her reaction was the reason for the question. Would she look trapped? Would she confess she knew who it was? But as she turned the corner to the hotel, and before I could observe her expression, I saw my car. The conversation about who in town bought and sold spray paint became a big fat fucking joke. My rental car was covered in a red compliment.

NICE CADDY

"Fuck!" I got out and headed for it. The trunk was open slightly, as if the vandal hadn't snapped it closed all the way. Probably broke the lock. This was going to cost a fortune. Big damn inconvenience. I might as well just buy them a new fucking car. I didn't even like Cadillacs.

I noted the similarities in color and that whoever had coded the roof couldn't be the same guy who'd insulted the make of my rental. Besides the obvious subtlety of the roof message and the blunt ignorance of what was on the car, the E on the roof had been done with careful, straight lines. The E in NICE looked like a backward three.

"Wow." Harper had her hands stuffed in her pockets. "This kind of thing never happens."

I opened the trunk.

"Bullshit."

My bags were intact, though shuffled around from the drive. I looked beneath and between them, in the corners and under the carpet.

"Damnit."

My laptop was gone. I slammed the trunk closed and it popped open a few inches, as it was when I'd found it.

"Fuck you too." I cursed at the trunk but it didn't seem insulted.

I muttered obscenities, getting into the driver seat, door open, one foot still on the pavement as I put the key in the ignition and turned. Nothing happened. Not even a *whrr whrr*. Not even a *click*.

Harper got in front of the car and wedged her fingers in the hood. "Can you pop this?"

"You are a cliché of a cliché," I said.

"What?"

Fuck it. I wasn't explaining the word cliché or how the small-town girl who knew her way around a car was so unlikely it was obvious.

I popped the hood and joined her at the front grille.

"Well, doesn't take a rocket scientist to see your battery is gone." She slapped the hood down before I could get a better look. "My friend Orrin owns a garage. He'll give it a tow. Until then—"

"You knew the code for the gate the whole time."

"I'm sorry?"

"You grab me the minute I get into town and send me to a hotel you know damn well is closed. Then you follow me, all surprised, and take me to the fucking factory. And who suggested the roof? You. I was ready to go and then, 'Oh, try the roof,' because you might miss the big, fat fucking message."

I stepped toward her, and she stepped back. I didn't want to be threatening, but let's face it, I did.

"You knew the code to the lock, didn't you? If I couldn't pick it, you knew it."

"I don't know what you're—"

"You know exactly who he is."

"Who?"

The innocent act was cute. Real cute. Once I got to the bottom of this, I was going to fuck the cute right off her.

"Just take me to him, Ms. Barrington."

Her big, multicolored eyes got even bigger, and that crease in her fucking lip got deeper when her mouth opened in surprise. She recovered so quickly I doubted I'd seen it at all.

"I go by Watson."

"Since when?" I glanced at her finger. No ring.

She put her hand in her pocket. "You know my name. So?"

"Explains the earrings. Your father owned this town."

"And?" Her back was against the car, and I was six inches from her. "I don't own anything. The state owns the property for back taxes. And these were my mother's earrings. Sorry if I'm not allowed to have them."

"Take me to him." I was up in her face because fuck her explanations.

"I don't know any guy."

"Fuck you don't."

A car pulled up. I didn't look at it. In my world, cars passed all the time. I didn't look away from her defiant face or her chest heaving under the plaid jacket.

"I told you," she said.

"You *lied*."

"I did not—"

The wind went out of me. The world got swept into a whirl of color. Pain flashed through my back. A dog barked and growled.

When my vision cleared, I recognized his face. The guy from the truck outside the grocery store. He smelled of cigarettes and wintergreen gum. He pushed me up against the Caddy by my throat so hard that my back was arched against it and the only parts of my feet touching the ground were my toes.

"Orrin." Harper's voice came from my right, about five miles away. "He's all right."

"I don't like the way he was talking to you."

"Yeah, well." Her hand curved around his bicep. "He's from California."

"Aw, shit." He dropped me like a wormy sack of flour. I fell to my knees, rocks sticking in my palms, humiliated. "Why's he here?"

"Car broke down."

"Huh. Well, I can take care of that." He yanked me up by the collar until we were face-to-face. "I'm going to take your car to the shop. Give it a look. In the meantime, you are going to treat this lady like the queen she is. You understand?"

I breathed in the affirmative.

"Where's he staying?" Orrin asked Harper.

"I'll keep him at the house."

"Aren't you nice."

"You know us. We take all comers."

He got in my face. "I'm driving."

"I can take an Uber." This dipshit, backwoods, broken-down *Deliverance* shithole town without decent signal didn't have Uber. I knew that. But even though I kept my mouth shut for a living, I couldn't keep it shut in front of this guy.

He pushed me into his truck. "As far as you're concerned, I'm Uber."

The pressure on my chest disappeared when he let me go, and I found my footing. Adjusted my jacket. Despite all logic to the contrary, my pride was intact. My value was lodged firmly between my ears. I'd been beaten up by knuckleheads more times than I could count. And that was saying something.

"Now that you two are best friends," Harper said, "let's go. I'm getting hungry."

XII

*O*rrin drove and Harper followed. He didn't say why she followed to her own house and he wasn't taking questions. That was what it was. His dog, a bloodhound named "Percy, short for Percival" licked my cheek raw from the backseat. I scratched his neck.

"You like dogs?" Orrin asked.

"Love them."

"You got any?"

"Nah. I work twenty-hour days. Once things slow down, I'm getting one. Two, maybe. This a bloodhound?"

"Ridgeback. Runt of the litter but can still chase a rabbit halfway down a hole."

"Bet you can," I said to the dog, who ate up the attention, dropping a big slobber on my shoulder. It was all right. A dog knows when you like him, and if he likes you, he lets you know back. You didn't need to decode them.

We pulled up in front of the house I'd seen from the roof of the factory. I knew it was the same from the piebald roof. Victorian with original windows, warped wood, wraparound porch. It was pale yellow with trims in five different colors. The paint was so cracked and dulled I couldn't tell if the color combination had been an attempt at period authenticity or if they'd just used what they had. It would have been worth a fortune in Northern California.

The front yard was well-trimmed, with grass that was green and lush. The rosebushes were flowerless and thorny. The hedges were perfect. Five other cars were parked on the dirt patch to the left of the house, in the shade of the setting sun. Orrin put the truck at the end, behind Harper's car, which was still clacking as it cooled.

"Thanks for the lift," I said.

"You mind what I told you."

I nodded, but maybe I wasn't emphatic enough.

I was halfway out the door when he grabbed my shoulder. "Percy likes you, and that counts for something. But not everything. If I see you get like that with our Harper again, you and I are going to have more than words."

Our Harper? While I appreciated his protectiveness, I was curious about who was included in *our*. "I think that's more than fair."

The dog stepped over my lap and poured out before running up the side porch steps, where a woman waited to pet him. She was in her late twenties, no makeup. Short, curly blond bob. Jeans and an apron.

"Orrin," she said, "you staying?"

"Nah. Mal's cooking."

She eyed me. "You must be Taylor." She held her hand out, and I shook it. "I'm Catherine. You're welcome here."

"Thank you."

"Harper's in the kitchen if you want to say hello."

Behind her, Harper already stood at the screen door. She was diffused behind the ripped screen, wiping a bowl with a dishcloth.

"Hey," I said.

"You made it."

"I thought he was going to dump my body in the river."

"The river woulda killed you if he didn't." She pushed the door open halfway and stood to the side so I could get into what looked like a mud/laundry room.

As soon as I crossed the threshold, I was assaulted by the sound of people. Children. Pots banging. Parents shouting. China clacking.

"What's the occasion?"

She headed for the kitchen, and I followed, practically tripping on two toddlers, one running with a clean fork in each hand.

"Same occasion as always. People need to eat."

I checked my packet sniffer for signal. Nothing on data and no random Wi-Fi.

"We're partying like it's 1999," I grumbled.

"What?"

"Nothing."

We crossed a few rooms, and I peeked into others. They were spotless but bare to the floorboards. No furniture. No rugs. On the walls, between the sconces, were hooks, wires, and pale rectangles where pictures used to be.

The kitchen hadn't been updated since the seventies. Three women and a girl of about seventeen fussed with steaming pots and running water. Harper took a bowl from a woman who wasn't a day under ninety. She had a bandana around her wrinkled forehead and bangly bracelets on her thin wrist.

"Mrs. Boden, this is Taylor."

"Nice to meet you." Her handshake was firmer than I would have guessed possible.

"Likewise."

With her free hand, she pinched the scruff on my chin, which had just grown to a pinchable length. "Oughta do something about this. You look too French Resistance. And they couldn't free Paris without help, you know."

Harper broke in. "Carmen, Juanita, Beverly"—she pointed at each woman then the high schooler—"Tiffany. This is Taylor."

They each greeted me. I repeated their names so I'd remember, and Tiffany blushed and looked away when I did. Harper slapped me with her dishtowel as if I'd tried to seduce the girl, then she stuck her head into the hall before I could deny it.

"All children in the house! Wash your paddies!" She brushed by me. "You too."

A line of kids stomped past on their way to a sink and soap. I stood at the kitchen faucet and pushed up my sleeves. Harper stood next to me.

"This the usual no-occasion crowd?" I asked.

"Sometimes. You staying tonight? You're welcome to."

I didn't know what I should do. I felt trapped, but I wasn't. Not really. There was a hotel and a country club one town over, apparently. They probably had Wi-Fi. I could help Deepak track down our hacker from there, or I could make some calls to soothe buyers.

I could make it look good enough to stabilize the deal but not fix it. I couldn't walk into that meeting with conviction. I wasn't that good a bullshitter. My confidence came from doing things perfectly.

"I have a lot of work to do," I said.

True. But also false. I had work, but without a connection, I couldn't do shit.

"Orrin will probably have a new battery in it in the morning." She handed me a towel.

I shook off my hands. She had the loveliest smile. I had to remind myself that I could do both of us more harm than good. She was too sweet. Too sharp. Too blond.

Sideways to the sink, I dried my hands. "Who would take my battery?"

"Thieves?" She washed her hands.

"Very funny."

"Fresh batteries are worth money, which people here don't have a lot of. I'm not condoning it—"

"Or the spray paint, which was just mean."

"Or the spray paint." She dried her hands.

Everyone was out of the kitchen but us.

"Which was the same color as the painting on the roof. I'm thinking it's the same person. Or people."

She looped the towel around a drawer handle. "Even if I knew…" Which she did. I'd have bet my balls on it. "I wouldn't tell."

"Harper, I want you to know, if it's some kid crying for help, I'm not an animal. Actually, I just want to know how he did what he did."

"What did he do? Besides maybe rip off your car battery?"

"He hacked into a system, a computer system I'm developing. Whatever he did, it was really difficult. Really well-timed. The execution was perfect. Guy like that doesn't belong in jail. I'd probably hire him."

I couldn't decode what happened with her face. Surprise opened it a little, and I saw anger and happiness at the same time. Before I could pin it down, it was gone. She kept looking at me, and I kept my attention on her.

"Harper!" Catherine called in a singsong.

"Let's eat." She turned away and went into the dining room.

DINNER HAD BEEN LOUD, messy, and pretty delicious in a not-too-complex way. Men appeared from the yard when the food was out. We had stew in chipped bowls. The silverware was real silver, and the water glasses were canning jars. Folding chairs set next to white, plastic picnic chairs around a card table. I remembered most of the names. The kids were lively and well-behaved. Harper sat next to me.

When I was asked where I was from, my answer elicited questions about the weather, gas prices, and state taxes.

What I could gather from them was that the factory closing had hit them hard, but Catherine, who blushed when mentioned, had been the town caretaker ever since.

"I remember when she sold the dining room set we should be sitting on right now," a weathered man named Neil said. "My wife wanted to throw herself on it when they loaded it onto the truck."

"It was so nice." Beverly shook her head slowly. "How much did you get for it?"

"Enough to pay down Phil and Dina's mortgage. And worth every cent." Catherine stood and started taking plates, ending the discussion. "Harper made bonnet cookies this morning. Who's ready?"

The kids clamored to pick up every dinner plate. The dining room descended into chaos again.

"Bonnet cookies?" I whispered to Harper, catching the scent of the air before it rained.

She turned to me, and we were face-to-face in the middle of a crowded room. "There are so many eggs in the recipe. When my great-grandmother was a girl, they wouldn't fit in the bag. She put them in her bonnet on the way home."

"That's nice." I said it to fill space, watching the flickering changes in her expression. I didn't know if I should kiss her or grill her until she revealed who'd hacked me. Maybe I could do both.

❦

ORRIN HAD BROUGHT my bags in from the car. Everyone had said it was nice to meet me and left. I turned my back, and Catherine had somehow folded herself into the walls. The house fell into a dark stillness.

Harper led me upstairs, flicking on lights with loud *clacks* from old switches. The steps creaked like nobody's business.

"How old is this house?" I asked.

It was the smallest of small talk. But the house felt haunted, and that seemed like a relevant data point to proving it wasn't.

She stood at the top of the stairs with her hand on the banister. "Nineteen eleven. You look freaked out."

"Me?"

"You."

"I don't freak out. I have nerves of steel."

"Want a tour?" she asked at the head of the hallway. Two short halls went east-west, and a longer one went north-south. All were as bare as the lower level. "There's not much to see."

"That would be great."

"I figure it'll ease your mind." She put her hand on a knob.

"I'm not freaked out."

"Sure." She flicked on the sconces. The room we entered had a cot, a two-drawer dresser, and peeling wallpaper. "This was my room when I was a kid."

"Where do you sleep now?"

She was already out a door on the other side of the room. "This is a linen closet. It's between two rooms. They all are." Shelves. Towels. Sheets. A bulb on a wire. "This was my mother's room." There was a pause where I thought of asking a question, but she moved on before I could get a word out.

She strode through the room without stopping, clacking the switch behind her. "My sister's room."

It looked as though someone actually slept there. A half-open armoire had clothes in it, and the sheets on the full-sized bed were fresh but mussed.

"Catherine?"

"Yup."

She continued. We wound up in one of the short halls. A stairway led up to a door at the top. Framed pictures hung on the stairwell walls. I hadn't seen a single thing on the walls yet, and I slowed down to look.

"We keep the bodies up there." She waved me toward her. "Come on."

She blew through old maids' quarters, a narrow back stairway, three more closets, two bathrooms with toilets that hissed and sinks with separate faucets for hot and cold, a library full of books, and the only comfortable-looking chair I'd seen since entering the house. Every room was clean. Every one had the absolute minimum amount of furniture. None had a decorative element that could be moved without ripping off a part of the house.

"The master suite is the nicest." She opened the carved mahogany door a few inches. "You're not allergic to mold, are you?"

"Nope."

"Good." She opened it all the way.

It *was* the nicest, biggest, and it did smell of mold. A chandelier had hung in the center of a ceiling that seemed just a little higher than the rest. It had a mural of delicate flowers preserved under a layer of dirt. The hardwood inlay on the floor was in a chevron pattern, with a wide border of darker wood. Past wide French doors, a balcony looked over the black night of nowhere.

"It is nice. I don't see the mold. I can smell it but not see it."

She pointed at water damage on the wall. "It's worst on the bathroom side. There's a mushroom that grows out of the wall every year."

"That's not mold. It's—"

"Fungus. I know. We have both."

"The mismatched shingles are above this room?"

"Yeah." She opened the French doors to the outside.

"But there's a third floor?"

"Not over this half of the house."

She walked out onto a balcony that I wouldn't have trusted to hold the weight of a kitten. But she did, so I joined her.

The autumn air was cool and breezy. The interstate banded parallel to the northern horizon, invisible until headlights drifted along it like fireflies. Below us, light from the downstairs windows landed in the first few yards of the property. At first, I thought I was looking at a pit of snakes, but it was thorn bushes. Hundreds of branches were tangled together in a mass of sticks and rose hips.

Harper put her elbows on the railing, crossed her ankles, and stuck out her ass. What a work of beauty it was. I had to stop myself from slapping it as I passed.

"How far back does the property go?" I asked.

"To the river." She pointed straight back.

The river, if I could tell correctly in the moonlight, was a little more than an eighth of a mile away, where the reeds and a line of trees broke up the sightline. Above and beyond that was the roof of the factory.

A light flicked on in the house, and my instincts tracked the movement back to the yard and the tangle of thorn bushes. I didn't say anything, but she followed my gaze down below. The bushes took up about as much space as my first apartment in San Jose. The rest of the property to the river was trimmed and landscaped.

"We like it that way," she said. "It blooms in the summer."

"I wish I could see that." I did want to see it. Summer was on the other side of the next year, but I wanted to see it.

"The room next to this one is nice." She jerked her thumb toward another set of French doors on the other side if the balcony. "You should crash there."

My elbows joined hers on the railing. "I'm sorry about before. I was frustrated."

"Next time I won't be so nice about it."

"Really?"

"I can knock a guy's balls so fast he won't even know it until he screams soprano."

I laughed.

"I'm serious. Wanna try me?" She put her hands up and tried to look severe. It didn't work. She rotated her hands, angling the fingers, one knee up, mouth exposing her fight teeth.

I laughed again.

"Don't test me, stranger," she growled.

"Stranger?" I put my hands on hers. "We've shared a meal." I laced my fingers in hers, and she let me. "I've met your family and friends." I pulled her close. She let me do that too. "We broke into a building together."

"We're practically best friends," she whispered.

"The minute I saw you, I thought you were beautiful." I let my lips brush hers, and they crackled with ozone. "I could barely even speak."

"I don't believe you."

Drawing my lips over her cheek and down her neck, I felt the vibration in her throat when she moaned. I didn't want to rush, but I didn't have a lot of time.

She might tell me the hacker's name in the morning, when she was careless, maybe a little ashamed, wondering if she'd see me again.

Which was possible. If everything worked out with QI4, if I found the hacker and got this thing off the ground, I might get involved with a beautiful creature from a foreign land.

"Believe me," I whispered. "I'd never lie about something like this."

My lips found hers. When she spoke, I felt them move. "You're staying tonight though? The car."

She wanted it. Her voice was soaked in it. I could seal the deal in three to five minutes.

"I'm staying tonight."

"Good."

Lips at the side of her mouth, fingers stroking her neck, I asked, "Do you like to fuck, Harper?"

A little vowel sound escaped her lips. I was too close to see her expression, but her voice told me I'd gotten where I wanted to.

"I think you're beautiful. I want to see you naked. I want to make you come with my mouth. I'll make it last a long time." I paused. She didn't pull away. "I'd love to bury my cock in you until you come again. And again. And again."

Her breath fell heavy on my cheek. I pulled back to get a look at her face to see if she was horrified or turned off.

Her lips were parted and wet. Expressive and open. I kissed her.

I couldn't tell if she kissed me back.

She pressed her face into mine, but her lips weren't moving or responding. Not that my dick cared either way. It just knew I was smelling and tasting her. It felt me pull her body into it and burst into a raging erection before I had my tongue fully in her mouth.

Her arms stayed around me, but she didn't move any more than her tongue.

I disengaged completely. I wanted to seduce her, but I didn't want to take what wasn't offered. I'd overplayed my hand. Shit.

"Sorry," I said.

"No, it's fine."

"I misread your signals."

"You didn't!" She kneaded her hands together. Her eyebrows made an inverted V.

I wanted to believe her. On that balcony, she had a sincerity that went deeper than it had all day. Maybe I'd caught her by surprise, or maybe that was how they kissed out here.

"Well, thank you then." I reached behind the French doors and hoisted my bag over my shoulder. "Can I get into this room from here?" I pointed at the adjacent set of doors.

"Yeah. Sure. I, uh—"

"I really should get to bed."

She got in front of me. "I'll put sheets on it."

I hadn't known her for more than a day, but her desperation surprised me. She didn't seem the type. She was acting as if my attention had higher stakes than a less-than-satisfactory kiss. Of course, I could have been misreading her the way I had a second before. Which she denied. Which meant I wasn't misreading.

The snake ate its tail.

I spoke tenderly and took her hand. In that moment, she seemed too vulnerable for careless courtesies. "I'll do it. You've done enough to help me today."

"It's not a big deal."

"I'll feel bad if you do it." I squeezed her hand and let it go. "The linen closet is off the bathroom?"

"Yeah."

"Okay. Thank you. I'll see you in the morning."

"Okay."

I still wanted to seduce her, fuck her, get the name out of her. That strategy was on life support either way. Outside the strategy, human to human, I wanted to tell her something that was true.

"I meant it. You're really beautiful, Harper."

"Yeah, well… I know." She said it as if I was telling her the sky was blue. No embarrassment or fake humility. It was what it was.

"Hey, uh, you have Wi-Fi?"

"Yeah, the router, the thing with the antenna?" She wiggled two fingers at the sky. "Kind of old and spotty. You can get cellular in the backyard sometimes."

"Thank you."

"Good night."

"Bye."

I went into the adjacent room and snapped the door closed. The door to the master suite closed a few seconds later. I was alone.

XIII

J found the light switch. Two frosted glass sconces hung on either side of the bed, lighting the ceiling and casting the rest of the room in diffused light. It was as bare as the others. I put sheets on the metal-framed twin bed and got in the shower.

It had been a long fucking day. I had no way out of town, and I was in a mansion without a couch. My hacker wanted me to stay, and I was getting the fuck out of here. I'd pay the rental car company whatever they wanted once the battery was in as long as I could get on a fucking flight.

But Harper.

The moments before that kiss.

When her skin tingled under my lips.

She'd made me so fucking hard.

And I was again. Just thinking about it made blood rush to my cock. I ran my hand over it.

There had been something inexperienced about the kiss. As if she'd wanted to but didn't know how and nerves had kept her from going with her instincts. Was she that innocent? When I stripped her down, told her to sit on the bed, and stared at her naked body, would her chest break out in hot pink? When I gently asked her to lean back and spread her legs so I could see her pussy, would she hesitate? When I said I wanted to see her touch herself—

I grunted and came before I could finish the fantasy, shooting my load in the cleft of a cracked tile.

I finished washing myself, put on sweat pants, and plugged in my phone. A cone of lines appeared in the corner of the screen.

Live Wi-Fi. If she was right, it would be on and off.

Password protected. PassCrack, an app I'd developed and sold for Bitcoin donations back in the day, didn't work. WarWalk didn't either. It looked like a simple WEP but obviously wasn't. Weird. Even in Silicon Valley, which was riddled with IT guys, one of those would have worked.

A human sound came through the walls. A woman crying. More than crying. Wailing uncontrollably. I stood. Harper? No. There was a lightness in it. A crispness. Harper was throatier. The cries came from everywhere. Right, left, downstairs. For a second, they seemed to come from the balcony. Then the crying drifted away.

Seduction was out. As much as I wanted to fuck that girl, and I *really* wanted to fuck her, this place was crazytown. The internet made the world small enough to find the hacker from home, without risking my sanity. I could fuck Raven anytime.

Raven's not going to be half as good as Harper.

That was my inner predator talking. Raven was fine. I had to focus on getting Wi-Fi.

I had one last toy in my toolbox. An offline app I had been dicking with when I was bored and missing the old days. I'd developed it to pick stocks, and it had lost everyone money, but repurposed, it was a decent password finder. I ran it.

Boom. I was on. Notifications flowed in.

The crying started again—but closer.

Ignore it.

All previous messages from Deepak had self-destructed, but the new ones flowed, decrypting with my fingerprint on the device.

<Jack gets a bonus for this.>
<Tap me when you're on.>

<You're on.>

*<Everyone in the cage is getting a
bonus. What did he find?>*

<We should get on voice.>

<Can't. Close quarters.>

<Fine.>
<Harper Barrington also goes by Harper Watson.>

He uploaded a picture. The resolution was shit, but the smile was
Harper. The girl in the picture had dark hair. She was a little rounder.
Standing on Vassar St., in front of Building 32, with its metal façade that
was designed to look as though it was in a constant state of collapse.

I knew 32 well. Computer science. The AI lab.

<Is that her?>

<Harper Barrington's blonde>

<Try this one>

Another picture came up. She had on a knit hat and pinched her
bottom lip between two fingers.

<That's her>

Did she have a boyfriend who was studying at Stata?

Well, no, she had the books. *The Visual Disp—* was clearly visible
when I stretched the photo.

"Display of Quantitative Information," I said to myself, finishing the
title. "That's not even coursework, Harper. What are you doing?"

<Same girl>

I flipped between the two. Yep. Same girl. Take the dark hair out of the equation, and there she was.

I couldn't remember her. I lived in a world where the smartest men in the world gathered and were too awkward to make it with the small percentage of fuckable women. Women had always been easy to get into bed, but I'd never fucked her. Not a blond her and not a brunette her. I was sure I wouldn't have forgotten it.

> *<Was she there when I was?*
> *I'd remember this girl>*

The crying got louder and stayed consistent.

<She was a freshman when
you split>

How many girls at MIT were that hot? You'd think my dick would at least have a little recollection. The photo of her had self-destructed already, but the cognitive consonance of her paired with MIT had imprinted the photo on my mind. It was her. Harper Watson. No bell was rung, except for the Sherlock Holmes story in the scattered code comments of the poison pill.

Watson was a really common name, but the connection was made.

> *<She couldn't have hacked us.>*

I typed the statement but didn't hit Send. He'd ask why I thought that. My answer was simple. I knew all the female hackers with the skills to pull this off, and she wasn't one of them. I sent the message.

NO CONNECTION

The Wi-Fi had dropped. Reconnecting didn't work. I ran the hacking apps and my network protocol analyzer to check for available signal. As a despairing female wail rattled the walls, the packet sniffer did its job.

SCRAMBLER PRESENT

A chill immobilized my spine.

She'd seen I was on the Wi-Fi and cut me off.

No.

The name. Watson. Sidekick? Why not Sherlock or Holmes? Was I reading into it?

Maybe the signal had just dropped.

For all she knew, I was watching porn or checking email. Or could she see my conversation? It was encrypted end to end, but if she was good enough to hack QI4, nothing was safe.

I swung my legs over the bed and went into the hall in bare feet, shirtless, sweat pants hiked up over the right knee but not the left.

The crying was louder in the hall and seemed to be coming from every doorway. Harper had taken such a roundabout tour and there were so few markers that I was lost.

Not that I knew what I was looking for. A sound besides crying. A light in the wrong place. The smell of ozone.

"Ow!"

I picked up my foot, leaned on the wall, and looked at the bottom of my big toe. I plucked out the splinter, but once I started walking again, I realized I hadn't gotten all of it.

"You need to redo these floors," I grumbled to Harper as if she was in front of me and I had the authority to tell her what to do with her house.

Taking my hand off the wall, I noticed I was close to the stairwell up to the third floor. I favored the toe as I climbed quietly. Too quietly. Every floorboard in the house groaned and squeaked, but not the stairs to the third floor. They were as worn as a 1911 staircase and as quiet as if they'd been built yesterday.

She didn't want anyone to know when she was going up here. Because I knew for shit sure, by the time I hit the top of the stairs, that she was behind that door. When I saw the photos at the top of the stairwell, I was even more sure. It was dark, but my eyes adjusted. It was her. Graduation cap. Braces. Clear, dewy skin and freckles. Prom. Satin dress and diamond earrings. Receiving an award. I couldn't see the

details of the award, but she was blond again. She was blond in all
of them.

I put my ear to the door, pressing against it until the crying inside the
walls disappeared and all I could hear was the sound on the other side.

Clicks. Tons of them. She was typing like a fiend.

That was why she had tape on her fingers.

My God. It was her. Harper had hacked QI4.

What was with the kiss that wasn't a kiss?

What about the message on the factory roof?

And the name?

Why change it?

Had she been married?

How had she gotten the poison pill in the monitor?

Was she still married?

More than the name and the comfortable possibility that a man was
involved in the hack, the thought of her having a husband didn't sit right
with me.

I leaned on the door, listening to the pattern of the keystrokes. No
waiting. Straight typing. Not waiting for a response from someone on
the other side of the wires.

The spacebar made a different sound. I pressed my ear to the door.
How often it was hit told the story. Coding and English had a different
spacebar cadence.

A husband belied her tight innocence, and though none of it fucking
mattered, I became momentarily obsessed with the idea that she was
married. Maybe her rigidity was guilt. Maybe Mr. Watson was in a
faraway desert war or making a living in another part of the country. He
could be dead.

I forgot to listen for the spacebar patterns. I didn't notice when the
keys stopped clicking at all. All I noticed was the change in gravity as its
force went from beneath my feet to beneath my head as I fell. I got my
feet under me in two steps, tumbling into the room when the door was
opened.

Standing straight, I whipped around to find Harper with her hand on
the doorknob.

"I knew it!" I said even though I'd known nothing until three minutes before.

She yanked the door all the way open, teeth grinding, throat mid-growl. Her skin was lit by the whitish-blue of flat-screens, and the finger she pointed at me was wrapped with white tape. "Get out!"

"How did you do it?"

"I don't know what you're talking about."

We circled each other like boxers in a ring. Behind her was the door, a desk, three monitors scrolling code, an ajar bathroom door. The monitors were flowing C++, a deep web database for a retailer, and a Tor chat. Following my gaze, she hit a key, then another, and the screens went dark.

"How did you get into QI4?"

She turned back to me, and we circled each other again. "Fuck you."

"Are you married?

We stopped circling.

"What?"

I didn't know what had come over me, and it didn't matter. I didn't care if she was married or not. I needed her to give me my life back.

The utter stupidity of my question forced me to step away from my surprise and hostility. She'd hacked me. Fine. We had work to do. She and I.

But I kept losing focus.

She was that smart.

In that body.

Under a sleeveless ribbed tank, she was braless. Her nipples were rock hard. Her gym shorts rode low, giving me a peek at the smooth skin of her belly. If I kissed it, I'd be close enough to smell her.

"Watson. Harper Watson. Who is Mr. Watson?"

"Wait. Let me just…" Her eyes drifted over my face, down my naked torso, landing between my legs.

I was wearing sweat pants, and I was very, very hard. Of course. The body always betrays the mind.

She crossed her arms, covering her nipples but hiking her shirt up a little. "I'm not married."

"That's good to know. Um, this is a surprise, but—"

"Why? Because I live in flyover country or because I'm a woman?"

"Yes."

"You are fucked up, Taylor Harden. You were always fucked up."

"Always fucked up?" She locked her jaw against another word, so I filled in. "Did I know you from MIT?"

Her eyes flickered. I knew more than I was supposed to, and it unnerved her. Good.

"IHTFP." She unlocked her jaw enough to hiss the campus acronym for *I hate this fucking place.*

"I didn't… we didn't…"

"No. We didn't. I was a freshman. You were fourth year, and you never came back after Christmas break."

I scanned my mind again, narrowing the parameters to the years before I left. Brunette Harper still wasn't there, but the photos hadn't lied.

"You had dark hair. Why?"

"No one takes blondes seriously."

"No one takes… what?"

"I know how it goes in tech. No one takes women seriously. We're unemployable, unfinanceable, useless. And a blonde? All blondes are good for is sucking dick. I've been around Tor sites. As a guy. I know how you assholes talk. I know what you think."

Deny. Set yourself up as an exception.

"I'm sorry." I wasn't. But whatever. I needed to get off the subject and onto more important topics, like what the fuck we were going to do about this mess. "First of all, I want to say… the hack? Wow." I slow-clapped. I couldn't tell if she appreciated my admiration at all, so I stopped. "How did you—"

"Fat chance."

"Excuse me?"

"I'm not telling you shit."

I'd never met a hacker who wasn't a show-off. Telling the community *how* you breached a target was ninety percent of the exploit's fun.

"Harper, you exposed a serious vulnerability. I'm willing to offer you a lot of money."

"Too late."

There wasn't a hacker on earth who didn't want to give the gory details of their exploits. At least none I knew, but they were all dudes. This was another planet.

She just needed a little prodding.

"It was Jack's receipt on the desk. You run it through a sharpening algorithm? So you could see what we were ordering and from where? How did you intercept the monitors? The distro center outside town is Amazon. We got it from a store in Denver."

Her face didn't change. That told me more than any expression. The effort to not signal acceptance or rejection was harder code than subtly answering without saying anything.

She wasn't telling me shit.

"What do you want?" I asked.

She turned toward the monitors and tapped her fist against her mouth, but she didn't say what she wanted. I got the sense she never would.

"Why did you bring me here?" I asked gently because she held all the cards and her exploit wasn't going as planned. That much I could tell.

"I didn't think you'd come here."

"Why leave the coordinates then?"

"I thought you'd send people, like law enforcement or the news or *anyone*. I thought then everyone would see what's happening here and feel sorry and understand and do something. But you didn't, and now I don't know what to do."

Like a soundtrack, the crying in the walls rose again. It had more of a sad, weeping quality and less of a wailing despair.

"That's not you," I said.

"It's not."

"Who is it? Catherine?"

"She's sensitive. She gets like this a few times a week. Her heart breaks for everyone but herself."

"Who's she crying for today?"

Her throat expanded and contracted as she swallowed. The monitors made her eyes white at the edges. She was thinking, but I couldn't tell what was on her mind.

"Here's what you're going to do, Taylor Harden." Her gaze went over my body again.

My boner was gone, so her gaze lingered just above my waistband. I realized that though her expression was sexual and hungry and I liked sex as much as the next guy, I had no power in the relationship. The feeling wasn't pleasant.

"Go back to your room. Rest up. We'll talk tomorrow morning."

"No. We talk now."

She spun the Herman Miller chair to face her. Twelve hundred dollars new. The most expensive piece of furniture in the house.

"Good night." She sat and swiveled herself in front of the bank of screens.

"Now, Harper."

She acted as if I hadn't spoken at all. With her back to me, she was still and calm. One screen came to life, asking for a password. The others stayed black, and I could see her reflection in them. She was crying, but somehow, she held her body still.

"Close the door on the way out," she said without a hitch in her breath. I'd never seen a woman with such control.

She didn't want comfort. Offering it could only make the situation worse. I had to do what she'd asked. What choice did I have? I opened the door, noticing the deadbolt for the first time. I could pick that if I needed to get back in.

"Taylor?" The sexy, innocent girl who was suddenly more terrifying than any guy I'd ever met. Even crying, she was scary.

"Yeah?"

"I have a scrambler on your cellular data. And you won't be able to get into the Wi-Fi again. I plugged that."

"You're fast."

"Yep."

I had nothing left to say. I wasn't going to stand there and beg for an answer.

When you have no negotiating power, you have to use the only leverage you have.

You walk away.

XIV

My father was a licensed contractor. He'd inherited the business from his father and assumed I'd take it over at some undefined future time. He bought property, fixed it, sold or rented it. He renovated and rebuilt houses if he liked the owners. It wasn't unusual for my father to work Saturday and Sunday, miss dinner, come home with a beard after being gone for days at a time. I'd never met a man who worked harder for every penny he had, and for me and the citizens of our little world, he had plenty.

My mother stayed at home with me and my little sister until she started school, then Mom kept the books at my dad's business and brought us to the office after school and on weekends. She'd always been good with numbers, but at one point, she stopped using the calculator because it slowed her down. Once Dad ascertained that she hadn't made a single mistake, he thought Mom's genius was her most charming trait and bragged incessantly.

Once Mom started working, Dad started taking me to jobs. If I was old enough to hold a wrench, I was old enough to tighten elbow joints. I learned everything he taught me, and I learned a lot of stuff he didn't.

He talked to my mother differently than he talked to me, and his tone with her in the office was different than his tone at home. He spoke to the guys who worked for him differently than he spoke to my mother. When he took me to the bank, his body language talking to the guy in the suit was different than the lady behind the glass.

And always, always, always, he was in charge. My dad had a very small kingdom in the state of New Jersey. He didn't have a big name or millions of dollars in disposable income. We didn't have servants or an army. We were regular people.

But he was a king.

So in sixth grade, when they took me out of St. Thomas and put me in Poly Prep, I was in for the shock of my life.

I had everything I needed, but there were people with more. Much more. People who didn't work as hard. People whose power wasn't *earned* but inherited or lucked into.

A year at Poly cost more than double the national average income. I didn't learn that until much later, but I knew at the time that something was off. The kids at Poly were different in ways I couldn't pinpoint. They didn't really know what their parents did for money and spent no time thinking about it. They didn't know how to fix things and didn't know how to find out. And Dad was different around their parents. Still confident but louder, brasher, less astute.

It was as if he didn't know how to crack their code.

He didn't know how to crack Mom's either.

Just as I was settling in, the stress of the money, the culture, the missed signals snapped her. She cleaned the house. Redid the books from the past two years. Accelerated every plan and activity.

She was manic, and she was everywhere. Bake sales. Theater department treasurer. Substitute statistics teacher.

Then she was depressed, and she was nowhere, and her room smelled of sweaty sheets and unbrushed teeth.

I swore to myself it didn't affect me. I swore I had it under control.

And I did—as long as I was on land.

Gov (short for Governor, I kid you not), my best bud in that first year, invited me out on his dad's sailboat for the weekend. In the first few hours, pulling out from the dock on Wiggins Park Marina, heading down the Delaware River and out toward the bay, the taste of salt and the thrust of the boat put me in high spirits. Gov and I talked about the kids in school, the sights on the banks of the river, and fantasized about the size of the fish we'd catch.

As the Delaware Bay fell away and the dark fists of landmasses grew smaller on the horizon, I grew uneasy. Following Gov, I did some tasks below deck, got ready for lunch, and stayed calm.

But it was out there. I knew it was out there.

Gov and I were in the front of the boat, watching the lap and curl of the water around the tip of the boat. He left me there so he could pee or eat or answer his father's call. With a sandwich in one hand and a can of Coke in the other, I was alone.

Utterly alone.

I didn't have a landmass to orient by. The horizon was an endless circle around a spotless, treacherous sea. The sky was a flat blue, and the boat was nothing, nowhere, the finitely small about to be crushed by the infinitely large.

The sky had weight, and it pressed against my chest. I was being snuffed out of existence as if I were no more than an offensive insect sliding on the curves of a pure white bathtub. I had to get out, but I was hemmed in by the indifferent sea.

Gov said I threw up. Maybe that part was seasickness. The rest was a good old-fashioned panic attack.

I pretended to laugh it off later, but inside, I never wanted to feel that insignificant again.

In Barrington, with the sound of crickets outside, I didn't just think about defeating Harper. I was distracted by the huge, unchanging physical landscape. Human instability. The breakdown of the small while the infinite spaces above could crush me with indifference.

I had to remove all emotion. Breathe. Keep the panic at bay. I had to break down my judgments and preconceived notions so I could see the code and only the code.

What could Harper want? Not a job. She hated me. Money? Capital? Power? Bragging rights? Sex?

She could have had any of those things by asking, but she hadn't asked. I went through her reactions to everything I'd said and done, but I hadn't been trying to figure her out all day. I'd been looking past her instead of at her.

I was rusty.

I kept thinking of her polychrome eyes, her ombré lashes, the crease in her lower lip. The body she'd hid behind a plaid coat was tight and feminine. Her tits alone distracted me for an hour.

And the hack.

When I could get my mind off her body, I went back to the hack.

She'd found her way into a closed system. I doubted it was a social engineering hack. Had to be a pure exploit. God damn. I wanted to hire her, fuck her, kill her, and decode her.

After she released QI4.

I didn't know how long it would take to patch the flaw she'd found, and it was more important than ever to do GreyHatC0n to prove the system was secure. I'd increase the prize. Lengthen the time.

Then I was back to the tits.

The eyes.

The code.

Dad.

How she did it.

When I could get out.

Of course a woman did this.

What did she want?

Crickets.

Tits.

Eyes.

Code.

Time.

Dad.

How.

IF (beezleboy decodes Harper) {
he will be king
/*and the king will own his subjects*/

}
ELSE {
the king will break
/*and the king can never break*/
}

XV

$\mathcal{I}$n the kitchen with the sun barely up an hour, Catherine didn't look as if she'd been crying all night. She looked bright and happy. A T-shirt with an eagle and an American flag peeked out from under her apron. She served me as if I was a king, but I didn't feel like one. I felt like a lazy guest.

"So, Mr. Harden," Catherine asked as she poured me a second cup of coffee. I stood by the counter rather than sit in the dining room. "What are your plans?"

I wondered if she knew what her sister was up to or if I was supposed to know that she knew. I wasn't going anywhere without answers, and I needed answers before I got back home.

"I think I'll be taking off this afternoon." I hid behind my coffee cup. "Some house you have here. Harper showed me the master suite." I put down my cup. "I couldn't tell if the ceiling was plaster fresco."

"It's enamel on tin."

The stairs creaked, announcing Harper well before she arrived.

"That saved it from water damage," I said.

"That's what Reggie said."

Harper, despite not crying all night as far as I knew, looked worse than her sister. Hair askew. Eyes puffy. Dragging her feet as if she didn't

85

have the energy to lift them. She didn't say a word to me as she picked up the coffee pot and poured a cup. She drank it black, cupping her hands around the mug.

"Good morning!" Catherine said. "I got eggs if you want some."

"No, thank you." She spoke into her cup, watching me over the edge.

"Good morning," I said.

"Good morning," she replied flatly.

Voice drained of emotion + intense look over cup = Catherine doesn't know what's going on.

Catherine went into the pantry, humming.

"How'd you sleep?" Harper asked.

"Like I was awake. You?"

"Slept like a rock."

Surprise her. Don't let her get her footing.

"Did you enjoy it?" Sleeping was the text. Fucking was the subtext. I put it on the side of a barn where she couldn't miss it.

"It's just sleep." She poured more coffee, avoiding eye contact. "Not exciting."

"What would you rather be doing?" I put another target on the side of the barn. I was getting to her. She put sugar in her second cup. No one did that. People picked the way they took their coffee and stuck to it. What was next? A caramel macchiato? Was she flustered? Or was she trying to tell me something about how unpredictable she was?

Catherine returned with cans of beans. Harper and I looked away from each other as if we'd be caught doing something we shouldn't.

"Can you give me a lift to Orrin's?" I asked.

"Oh," Catherine chimed in, "if you're going that way, can you bring Trudy Givney something?"

"The shop opens at ten," Harper grumbled.

"Perfect," Catherine chirped. "I'll get you an envelope."

Harper's attention lit on a stack of red-and-blue-swirled bowls on the counter.

"What are you doing with Grandma's bowls?" Harper asked.

"Oh, Rebecca can get—"

"No!" she barked. "You're not selling those. Put them back. Put them back right now."

"Harper, we talked about this. They're meaningless objects."

"Put them back, or I'm going to break them!"

Catherine paused while Harper's face went into a rigid adulthood that directly contrasted her threat to smash things rather than lose them. I was about to offer money for the bowls. Good money. Whatever they wanted.

"Here." Harper put her cup down and reached under her hair to her ear. "Take these. Sell them. Give the money to whomever." A quick tug to the other ear got the second diamond out. She handed them to her sister. "I don't even like them anymore."

Catherine took them without a moment's hesitation. "Thank you. It's Alejandro. They picked him up for shoplifting, and if he doesn't make bail—"

"I know. They keep him in jail."

"He's just a boy."

Harper nodded, and Catherine hugged her.

"I can help if you want," I interjected without thinking. "I have money. Just not here right now."

"We have it." Catherine patted my arm and left the room. The stairs creaked.

Harper poured more coffee with one hand and rubbed an earlobe with the other.

"Do you think that was weird, or was it just me?" I asked.

"You should have seen when she tried to sell the silver teapot." She handed me a cup. "She doesn't get it about maintenance. If she'd sold everything and invested it in something, she could help Alejandro now and his brother in ten years." She blew on the coffee. The surface flickered like a pitching ocean.

"And what you're doing now, bringing me here, that's maintenance?" I asked.

She sipped her coffee, thinking too hard. Maybe she was out of her league too. "I was supposed to be showing the world what was happening here. I wanted Everett Fitzgerald to see it before he came, and I know you know him. I want you to tell him about the bottle works." She shifted her cup around in her palms. "I didn't hack you for personal reasons."

Bullshit. Everything was personal. Even this. Especially this.

"Whatever I do to you won't be personal either."

She smiled and put her cup down. "Want to tell me what you're going to do to me? I'd like to be prepared."

"Exactly what you did to me."

She came to me and put her hands on my chest, drawing them flat down to my waist. "So you're out to ruin me? I like the sound of that."

She couldn't mean what it sounded like. No sane human would go to such trouble to get laid, but her expression oozed desire. So she wasn't sane, and neither was I. My mind was a seesaw with sex on one side and fear on the other. The fulcrum was curiosity. Once it was satisfied, I'd know whether to fuck or run.

I grabbed her wrists but didn't move her hands. "Is that all you want?"

I tried to sound amenable, and maybe I fooled her into thinking I'd believe anything she said, but I listened and assumed she was lying.

"More or less. You were pretty prolific at MIT. All the girls talked about how good you were."

"That's flattering."

She bit her lower lip and let it pop out slicked and wet. "I'm not as good."

"Girls don't have to work as hard."

She tensed like a two-by-four holding up an archway. If I'd had a caliper to measure the rage in her face, it would have stretched open as far as Frieda Gallen's legs.

She picked up her cup and straightened her spine. "We work twice as hard for half as much, and you know it."

"Not to get laid."

She spit out a laugh. Inside it was a long story she wasn't going to tell me. "I worked pretty hard to get you here. I might as well get something out of it."

"You can't get some redneck to fuck you?"

She slammed her cup down, spraying sticky black coffee all over the place. If it burned her hand, she didn't show it, and if the mess bothered her, she didn't take a second to clean it up. Her face went from stone-solid rage to soft humor.

"I ain't never fucked no city boy before." Her accent was overdone to the point of comedy.

Catherine blew in like a ray of fucking sunshine. Harper took her hands off me and wiped the spill off the counter.

"Got it!" Catherine sang, handing Harper an envelope. "She'll be at the coffee shop."

"I can do it later."

"Come on. I'll buy you a hot chocolate." I flicked her mug.

"I have to help Catherine."

"No, you don't," her sister said. "Just go!"

Harper gave me a look of death before she acquiesced. "Let me brush my teeth, then we can go."

XVI

The shitty Chevy went pretty fast for a car that looked as if it had been abandoned in a corn field. The seat rumbled and purred under me even though the plastic upholstery was cut into a foamy yellow wound. I cranked the window open and leaned my elbow out, angling my righthand fingers to rest on my forehead and chin.

The two-lane blacktop was pretty smooth, but the storefronts we passed were empty, boarded, broken, with sun-faded signs for a diner, a thrift store, fashion, sewing supplies, and pets. The necessities remained. Groceries. Pharmacy. A local bank with a name I'd never heard of. Liquor. A convenience store whose main convenience seemed to be lottery tickets.

"This the main strip?" I asked Harper.

A strand of her hair whipped out her open window. "Yeah. It's shit. I know."

"I didn't say that."

She stopped at a sign, though no one was coming in the other direction. The flapping strand dropped to her shoulder. "It's hard for people to run a business when no one's buying. Sew-Rite only stayed open until last year because Bonny lives in the back. Still does, but she's got no money to put stuff on the shelves." She pulled forward. In a block,

90

we were at the edge of town, cutting a hard right onto a pocked light industrial area.

"Why'd you come back? From MIT?"

"I live here."

"You didn't graduate." It was a question and a statement at the same time. If she'd graduated, she wouldn't have come back to Shitsville.

"Neither did you."

I was sure the situations were different. I'd had enough to live on from a trust Mom had set up in one of her moments of medicated lucidity. It was barely enough to live on, so I'd moved into a San Jose garage to reinvent circuits. Harper knew the story. Everyone did.

She wasn't going to answer a direct question. She wasn't going to be cornered by an inquisition. I was going to have to stir her until what I needed to know was kneaded into the conversation.

"You going to finish someday?" I asked.

"Are you?"

"I'm waiting for an honorary degree." I joked—but not really. "They only give them to you when you don't need them anymore." I paused as she pulled in front of a corner diner. "Like everything, I guess."

She glanced at me and slapped the car into park. "My father got sick." She spit it out as if holding it back would be permanent. "He started coughing, and then it was blood. He could have afforded an army of people to take care of him, but he only wanted Catherine and me. He didn't trust anyone in town. Genny Reardon's a nurse, and Dr. Therro at least could have helped with the medicine, but he thought they'd let him die because he closed the factory."

"Did they hate him?"

"They loved him." She slammed the car into park like a statement. "They wouldn't have let him die. Even though he did. Lasted three months after I got home."

"And you didn't go back? To MIT?"

"Couldn't leave my sister." She opened her door. "Let's go. I'm hungry."

SHE ATE a half-pound cheeseburger (rare) and a plate of fries (overdone) like a hostage. I knew she had food. She wasn't starving. She just had a healthy appetite.

"You have a hollow leg," I said.

"Here you go, hon," Trudy said, setting another pink milkshake in front of Harper while addressing me. "You having anything else, mister?"

"Taylor," Harper said around the last mouthful of burger.

She'd introduced me to Trudy when we'd arrived but made no other conversation about the envelope or what the fuck I was doing there. Trudy seemed to be the same age as Harper, with a little more makeup and several dozen fewer IQ points.

"Taylor, then." Trudy had a thick down-hominess that seemed forced and overdone, but I was starting to think it was genuine. "You staying around, Taylor?"

"No," Harper snapped before I could answer.

"That's too bad. Well, it's nice to finally see our Harper with a member of"—she dropped her voice to a whisper—"the stronger sex, if you know what I mean."

"I—"

"Trudy! Jesus!"

Trudy wagged her finger at her friend. "We don't talk like that in my mother's place. It's just unexpected, and you'd be crazy to think we weren't all wondering about him."

"I am crazy." Harper picked up her milkshake. "The check, please?"

"Nice to meet you." Trudy smiled and went behind the counter.

"Wow," I said once she was out of earshot.

"Forget everything she said."

"I'm wowing at you. You were kind of a bitch."

She slid the half-empty milkshake away. "If she was so happy I was walking around with a member of 'the stronger sex,' she wouldn't have looked at you like you were a meal ticket."

"And what am I to you?"

"Oh, fuck this." She leapt out of her seat and snapped the check out of Trudy's hand.

"Hey, I got it."

Before I could get my hands on my wallet, Harper had put the envelope and a twenty under the check and smacked them both down on the counter. She walked out without looking back.

"Harper!" I caught up with her and wedged myself between her and the driver's side door. "You're upset that I'm leaving?"

"No. I'm not."

"You spent a ton of time and energy getting me here, and now I'm picking up my car. You're upset. Don't lie."

"I'm upset because…" She took a deep breath. "I'm frustrated. Trudy went to school with me. She was knocked up in eleventh grade by Robbie Bonnacheck. She's lived with her mother since then, working two jobs and barely pulling in shit, so what does she do? She gets bored when she's twenty and lets Tim Breaker knock her up with a daughter who, by the way, is really, really cute, but my God… she can't afford to feed these kids. So now? She's twenty-four, and that money is for prenatal care because she's too fucking stupid to take birth control."

"Is that why you don't have kids?"

"I'm different."

"I'll say."

"And you know what really pisses me off? I love her, and I love her kids. I love the assholes who don't even think of using a condom and fuck their own selves up in exchange for ten minutes of… I don't even know."

I was about to say something. Add a little filler that had all the markings of compassion and empathy. I had neither emotion for stupid people or bad decisions, but for Harper, I had it.

"You don't even know?"

Her jaw clamped like a vise. "Just get in."

I got in, and she took off.

"You don't care, do you?" she asked.

"About?"

"Our troubles. You're not telling anyone."

"Can we stop this? Just for a minute?"

"Stop what?"

"The bullshit."

She let that hang in the air as she drove. I tried not to look at her, but it was hard. Even in profile, her expression changed by the second.

Making another left, she drove past an open chain-link fence. The driveway led to a cinderblock garage wide enough for three cars. One of them was the Caddy. A big dog barked. Piles of red-brown car parts hung from a huge shed with a roof but no walls.

"I'm not lying." She parked the Chevy between the shed and the garage.

"Tell me the truth, and I'll make phone calls about Barrington. I'll tweet it out. Everyone will know."

I didn't convince even the most gullible part of myself. She shook her head and laughed.

"Logic error," she said, unlocking the doors. "In exchange for media attention, you want me to admit I'm lying, but if I'm lying, I don't care about the attention."

The fall hurts when a guy's knocked down a few pegs.

She was still lying.

From the garage's shadows, Orrin came out of an interior door with a guy in cheap chinos and a yellow polo. Percy padded behind, happy at his master's heels. The rattle of a chain link snapped me to a much bigger dog making the racket. A ninety-five-pound bruiser was hurling itself at the fence it was trapped behind.

"You just want your shit back," she muttered.

"Well, yeah. I know what I want, and I did what I had to do to get it. You're a hacker. I can't figure out why you didn't just take the money you needed."

"You mean steal?"

"Yeah. Take. Steal. It's not any different."

She spun in her seat as if she couldn't hold back another second. "It *is* different. I don't steal. I don't cheat. I do things fair and square."

"Are you fucking with me? What kind of moral gymnastics did you have to do to convince yourself hacking me was fair and square?"

"You'd never do something for someone besides yourself. But you needed to get hacked. You're a little shit. You're every problem with the world."

"And now you're no better. Do you miss the moral high ground?

Because you left it as soon as you locked my system. Is the weather different down here? Or is it actually the damn fucking same?"

"I am not you. I care about people. All you care about is you. Not even you. All you care about is what people think of you."

"You don't know me."

Of course she didn't. She had no idea what I was thinking or feeling. She'd just made a bunch of assumptions. The fact that all of them were right notwithstanding, she'd built a composite picture out of thin air. I was allowed to get pissed about that.

"You targeted me because you don't like me, but you didn't make anything." Percy's barking got closer, but I had more to say. "You created nothing. You stole what someone else made, and you're holding it for what? What do you want to give it back?"

"I'll give it back." She let that sink in. "When I have what I want."

She crossed her arms, tapping her finger against her bicep. Her nails were naked, and she didn't have a stitch of makeup over her freckled nose. The highlights in her hair had been kissed by the sun, not the salon. So easy to take for granted. So easy to underestimate.

"How much do you want?" I tried to sound nonchalant. People had fraught relationships with wealth, so I never said "dollars," "cash," or even "money" during a negotiation.

"If I was after money, you'd be broke already."

She spoke truth. She could have done something much simpler and more profitable. But she hadn't. I still wasn't sure what she wanted. She kept me on shaky ground, and I was starting to think it was on purpose. She was hacking me, and I didn't have any defenses against her attack.

XVII

At one point, my mother had decided to clean my room down to the plaster. When I got home from school, all my shit was in the driveway, and she was painting the walls.

Clearly, she was in a manic phase. Clearly, she couldn't be reasoned with. I was supposed to let her do her thing and make sure she was safe.

But yellow?

I'd been powerless then too.

When she spoke about yellow paint day, even years later, my mother said the look I gave her broke through the mania long enough for her to stop painting and move to the next project. It was the only thing she'd ever remembered mid-episode.

"If I was after money, you'd be broke already."

After Harper said that, I must have given her the same look, and it must have come from the same place of powerlessness. Because I didn't accept that I was ever helpless, and the existence of a situation where I didn't have choices or options tasted like a mouthful of dimes dipped in shit. I spit it out.

"When I'm through with you, you're going to wish you'd killed me."

I'd broken through her tough-chick performance. She opened her car door and slipped out as if stomping toward the garage was proof of anger, not proof of a defensive position. I got out after her with every intention of driving home some point or another. I'd forgotten what we were talking about, but I was going to hurt her until she cried, and I wasn't going to give the smallest fuck about her feelings.

Which I did.

But I didn't.

Maybe a little.

Two steps in front of me, she turned toward me with her finger out as if she had a point to make and I gave a fuck what it was.

Which I did.

But I didn't.

Not even a little.

"Do it," I growled. "Sell off my code, and I will come after you until this town is a wasteland. Do you understand me?"

"Fuck you."

"Do you un—"

"Hey, Harper." Orrin's voice cut the wind just as Percy got his nose under my hand.

I petted him without thinking. Orrin pinched a lit cigarette between two grease-streaked fingers. Right behind him stood the guy in his fifties with the yellow polo, chinos, and clean hands. Despite the conservative costuming, he was tattooed with clock gears and pierced, his black hair whirling in the wind. His name, Johnny, and a corporate smile of a logo were embroidered over his left tit.

"Hey, Orrin." Harper was all perk and smiles, as if we hadn't spent the last five minutes threatening everything we each held dear. "Hey, Johnny!"

Johnny kissed her cheek, which was more than Orrin had done.

"Mr. Harden," Orrin said.

"Thanks for working on the car." I pointed at the Caddy sitting in the garage. "The hood's still up. Is it working?"

"Just fine."

"They call you Hard-on in school?" Johnny asked, proving that inside, he was more tattoo than polo.

"Yes. Yes, they did."

"You punch 'em? Or did you cry?"

"I fucked their girlfriends."

With every circuit in my brain, I mustered up the will to not look at Harper to gauge her reaction to what I'd said. I had little to gain from knowing it and everything to gain by acting as if I didn't care.

Johnny, on the other hand, whooped a laugh of surprise and delight. He stuck out his hand. "Nice to meet you."

"Same." I shook his hand.

"Welcome to the Capitol of Crap." He swung his arms wide. "Citizens too stupid to leave, and those that left are too damn cowardly to stay."

Orrin shook his head. "Don't mind him. He—"

"We're the salt of the earth's what they say. Them in power, with the money. They stroke us. Jerk us off with some bullshit about how hardworking we are. Tell us we're the real America. Like we're stupid. Them fucks set man against man so we can feel like winners, but let me ask you." He held out his arms and stepped back. "Do I look like a winner to you?"

"Jeeze, Johnny," Harper interrupted. "Can you—"

"If you want to win something," I said, "we can get in a fistfight."

Johnny whooped another laugh, falling into a deep, wet coughing fit. Even Orrin chuckled as we walked back to the garage.

"Well, not too many men alive can shut up old Johnny," Orrin said. "This is a nice car." He laid his hand on the chassis. "Regular battery doesn't fit. I had to order one special, then I called the rental company because they'd shit themselves if they thought an unlicensed guy was touching the engine. Let them know what was happening."

I turned away from the car. Across the road sat a corrugated tin building with boarded windows and a *Restaurant Supplies* sign swinging in the wind.

In the foreground, Harper leaned on her car with her arms crossed, talking to Johnny.

"Did they say when the battery was coming?"

"Tomorrow or next day."

Was that enough time to get Harper to release QI4? It was going to have to be.

"Here." I reached for my wallet, feeling the little red pebble in my pocket as Percy sniffed my balls.

"Sit," I said, and he did. "Good boy."

"Pay me when the work's done."

We shook on it, and Percy trotted back to the garage behind Orrin. When I got back to Harper, Johnny was headed for his truck.

"Am I taking you to the airport?" she asked.

This was her way of getting me to go home and tell everyone about Barrington? That was the exact opposite of what I was going to do.

"How do you know I won't just call the FBI?"

She crossed to the opposite side of the car. "What would all the hackers say if you narked on one of their own?"

"GreyHatC0n's in eleven days." I leaned over the roof of the Chevy. "We have a challenge running on day one. It's worth a lot to me to plug this hole. You could do a bunch of things with that money. Buy furniture for the house." I squinted at her in the bright sun.

"You think I went to all this trouble to buy a sofa?"

"Get help for your sister."

Her jaw tightened, and her eyes narrowed. I'd hit a nerve. She went from pensive to sharp in a split second. Behind her, the big dog *uhf uhffed*.

"Small business loans," I continued, "scholarships for the kids you were talking about. Supplies for the school. Whatever."

She leaned over the other side of the roof, tapping the hollow metal. "I know you don't come from money, Taylor. Not real money."

"So?"

"Money, real money, is about maintenance."

"Are you blackmailing me or asking for a job?"

Orrin watched from the office door. Harper gave him a dismissive jerk of her chin. He went inside.

I placed the pebble from the rooftop code on the roof of her car. "This is the same color as what's on the Caddy. You were with me when the car was vandalized. And maybe this is a town of coders, but it's not. You wrote on the factory roof. So who fucked up the car?"

"Maybe the hardware store's got one shade of red." She didn't even believe that.

"Sure, Harper. Whatever. Or you can tell me what you want? I'll give it to you, and you give me my life back. But tell me something I'll believe."

She laced her fingers together and tapped the pads of her thumbs. So much of her story was in her hands. The nails were cut short, and she'd taped her fingers again, but now I knew why they were wrapped like a hacker's.

"If you want me to take you to the airport, I will," she said.

"If I want you to unlock QI4 first?"

"You'll have to wait."

Progress. Too bad it didn't matter. She was nuts, and I was walking a tightrope with her.

*M*y situation was precarious, unusual, unprecedented. I couldn't tell if I was making a mountain out of a molehill or seeing the molehill from so close that it looked huge.

Harper had wondered if I was going to cut her into little pieces because she was imagining me in sections.

My phone was charged, and I got a moment of signal from the balcony overlooking the thorn bushes. Something was getting through the scrambler, or she'd turned it off.

Fuck encrypted texts. I called Deepak.

"Dude," he said without so much as a hello. "Where have you been?"

"It's her. Harper. The girl from MIT. She did it."

"Why?" His voice cracked. He was exhausted.

"Plight of the working man. She wanted to draw attention to the recession. Whatever. I'm coming back."

"How did she do it?"

Below me, the thorn bushes wove together like a square of steel wool. A bent and cracked white picket fence held the bed to shape.

"I don't know."

"And you're coming home?"

I almost called him crazy before I told him I was coming home for shit sure, but he deserved an explanation. "There's something off here. It's like a cross between *Children of the Corn* and *Wicker Man*."

"Are those movies? I'm more of a Bollywood guy."

"Creepy. It's creepy."

"Oh. Well. In that case, come back. We'll just tell the guys to find another job. Our clients will understand—"

"Deepak—"

"—why it's so important for you not to be in a creepy place."

Was he shouting? It was hard to tell with his voice so shredded.

"You don't get it."

"I get it, my friend. I fucking get it." He'd never taken this sharp a tone with me, and for that reason alone, I shut up. "You're in a new place with someone who has it out for you. Taylor Harden is a target and feels bad. Boo-hoo. Now get over it. You've had it easy your whole life."

"Wait a minute. I worked my ass off."

"But your head's buried in it. Creepy is working your ass off for *nothing*. You worked your ass off for *something*."

I could have argued, but I couldn't have argued with his intensity. We were going to have a long, hard talk over beers when I got back.

"Fuck you, Deepak." That was as close to capitulation as I intended to get.

"You too, baby."

The line of the factory roof was solid brown against the horizon. A V of birds headed south along it. If I showed my face in the office without QI4 in one piece, I was going to be a laughingstock. Distance insulated me.

"I'm coming back as soon as I figure this out, and I'm not playing into what she wants. Make sure no one talks about where I am."

"They don't know."

"Not a word to the press. No exposure. Nothing. My whereabouts are unknown."

"Agreed."

I peered into my room. Empty. Door closed. I did the same with the master suite. Empty.

"Can anyone hear you?" I whispered.

"I just got home. I live alone."

Just got home? He'd probably combed through hardware and code for twenty-four hours or more.

"You're working hard for something."

"Make sure of it."

I ended the call just as Harper came onto the balcony from the master suite. She had a disturbingly self-satisfied look that I wanted to kiss right off.

"How's everything back home?" She leaned her hip on the railing, arms crossed, indicating the phone I'd left facedown on the railing with a quick twirl of her finger.

"About as wonderful as you'd expect. I left a full complement of guys with their limp dicks in their hands."

She smirked. "That imagery is so appealing."

"Does it make you nervous, at all? Being out here with me? The guy you're in the process of fucking over? I could pick you up and throw you off this balcony right now. Leave you in the fucking thorn bushes." I'd never threatened a woman with violence before, and the threats came out of my mouth so easily I scared myself a little.

Harper didn't seem half as nervous about it as I did. "Who would unlock your system then?"

"I've cracked harder cases than you, miss."

I was a little closer, my finger pointed right at her like a punctuation mark. She looked away. Now she was nervous. The idea of violence didn't faze her, but the idea of being outwitted went right to the core.

"I didn't think you'd actually come." She touched my elbow, just brushing along it.

The normal reaction to being touched by an enemy would have been to pull away, but her electrical current didn't throw me back. It created a closed circuit between us.

Luckily, my right hand knew what my left was doing.

I grabbed her arm with my other hand and held it there. "What do you want?"

"A lot."

"What?"

"In five years? A house on the lake and a kid or two. Short term?" She put my hand to her chest. I was never going to get a straight answer. She was crazy and fucking gorgeous and too smart for her own good. All those things at once.

I was trying to put all the pieces together. She tilted her head, and I tilted mine. She leaned in a little, and I leaned with her as if I could hear her better. I was curious what she wanted short term because a clue to my fate was there.

"Short term I'd just like to—"

I leaned a little too far, brushing my phone off the railing. I grabbed for it. It bounced off my fingers, twisting in the air, off the back-porch overhang, spinning faster and away into the thorn bushes below.

"Fuck!"

I wanted to choke her, but it wasn't her fault. It had been my elbow leaning too far left.

I ran downstairs, past Catherine puttering in the kitchen, and stood at the edge of the thorn bed. It was bordered by a two-foot-high white picket fence. The thorns went to the top of it and not an inch past it.

When I tried to part the brambles where it looked like the phone had fallen, I was rewarded with blood from two slashes.

Harper was right behind me. "Let me call you!"

"You know my number?"

She slid her finger over the glass. Of course she knew my number. I leaned over the bed.

"Is it ringing?" she asked.

"Fuck!" It wasn't ringing. There was no light. No buzz. No nothing. "Is it ringing on your end?"

She put the speaker on. Half a ring then a cut to voicemail.

"Shit." It had hit the wall and the ground from the second story, but the way it had smacked the porch overhang had probably had an impact.

"Maybe it just shut off when it fell?"

Her optimism was fucking touching. I didn't hold out much hope that it would ever work again.

"I'm gonna hack the shit out of whoever stole my laptop," I grumbled, scanning the bushes for an opening. "They won't be able to buy a pack of gum again." I walked around the perimeter, cursing myself for leaving it in the trunk.

Having circumnavigated the entire area, I crouched, trying to catch a glimpse of my lifeline to my world. The branches were so thick I could barely see an inch into the depths.

"Can we get in there?" I asked.

"I guess I can see if one of the guys can come by?"

"When?"

"Tomorrow afternoon, probably?"

I couldn't tell if she was sincere. Couldn't read her. Didn't know if she was full of shit or if "the guys" weren't available in the morning because no one did anything in a hurry. Didn't matter. Every word out of her mouth was a lie.

Fuck it.

Wasn't like it could ring anyway.

"Tomorrow, phone or no phone, you tell me what you want. I'm not staying around here without clarity on what I have to do to get my code back. If you won't give it to me, well, they can all laugh at me. I don't care. I will walk right out onto the interstate if I think you're wasting my time."

I didn't wait for a cute excuse or a snotty word. I couldn't tell up from down. I couldn't be sure if I'd pushed the phone over the edge or if she'd made sure I knocked it over.

Didn't matter. I was done with Harper Barrington and her bullshit.

XIX

For years, I called her Schrödinger's mother.

Quantum logic is often explained by the simplified version of Schrödinger's paradox. There's a cat in a steel box. You know it's there. You can't see it, hear it, or measure it, but you can show its placement. Is it living or dead?

It's both.

And neither.

A star, an atom, a mother with bipolar disorder—can be measured only by placement or mass, never both. Unsurety, in-betweenness, constant movement, randomness, the potential of all things to be in either one place or another, in one state or another, was the heart of quantum mechanics.

It was also the heart of my mother, who had become more and more unstable as the years went on. I eventually stopped calling her Schrödinger's mother because that would have made me Erwin Schrödinger, who created the puzzle to disprove the physics I believed in.

How's Mom?

Moving constantly.

Should I come home for Christmas?

Dad. Come home for Dad.

I did. When Mom was manic, she buzzed and spun around Dad. Her body was active, and her mind was focused on everything yet calm. When she was down, her body was in one place, usually bed, but her mind was elsewhere.

Harper was volatile and erratic. Or was she? I couldn't predict her any better.

Catherine had told me she was at the distro center working a night shift. My phone had gone over the balcony as if Harper had timed it so she wouldn't have to deal with the repercussions. As if having dinner with Catherine and whomever else showed up (Trudy and her kids, Orrin's wife, another family whose names I didn't remember) would calm me before bed.

I went to her bedroom door, seeing what kind of lock she had. I could open it, but it would be loud. Catherine saw me, and I couldn't seem to disappoint her by breaking into her sister's room.

So I waited until she went to bed, which never seemed to happen.

I watched the moon cross the frame of the window, imagining all the ways I could hack her if I just had my laptop.

Harper came back before Catherine was out of the way.

Harper was making me dependent on her, and someone in the town was in on it. Someone had spray painted the Caddy. Maybe there was an odd-shaped battery in there, but even if it would take a few days to be delivered, I was sure Orrin wasn't going to put it in and let me go until Harper had what she wanted, whatever that was.

Catherine was about ten minutes into shaking the walls with her sorrow when I thought I heard my phone ring outside. It was a little after midnight. I looked over the balcony and convinced myself I could see the phone's dim blue light in the bushes. But the illusion stayed longer than the time a phone would ring, and the sound of it melted into the mix of the wind and Catherine crying.

Piece by piece, I'd lost control over my life.

Right before I fell asleep, I wondered if I was going to die in Barrington.

The next morning, I got out of the shower to a steamed-up mirror. I found a note that only showed up when the mirror was fogged.

102 101 122 122 111 116 107 124 117
116 040 123 124 101 124 111 117 116

Decoded, it said "Barrington Station."

She was lucky I could read octal or she would have been waiting there a long time.

X X

No one downstairs. The house had two states: full of people or deserted. I poured coffee and tried to think clearly.

Barrington Station.

Couldn't Google it. Couldn't locate it on satellite. There was phone on the wall. It was a beige box the size of a bag of coffee with a curly cord. I had no idea what to do with it.

When I picked up the handset, I discovered a clear plastic circle set into the base piece. The spiral cord connected the handset to it.

I had to pause for a second. I'd seen this in movies. Right. Finger. Turn. Wait. No problem. But who to call?

Numbers were scratched on the wall in pen, pencil, a few scratched through the yellow paint to the plaster beneath. Some had names above and some didn't. It was like a living record of every number ever spoken through that old phone.

Car service. Right. They'd know.

I dialed. How people watched that circle tick around every time they wanted to make a call, I'd never know.

"Matt's Car Service," the female voice answered.

"Hi, I'd like a car to Barrington Station."

109

"Sure. You know that's closed, right? Next best bet is Doverton."

"It's fine if it's closed. That's where I'm going."

"Where we picking you up?" The dispatcher didn't seem to care one way or the other. She was just trying to get the job out.

"I'm not sure of the address." I'd never felt so incompetent. I could practically see her roll her eyes. "The Barrington house. The mansion. It's on a dirt road off… I'm not sure."

"I know it. You'll be in front?"

"Yeah."

"Fifteen minutes."

She hung up. I waited.

AGAIN, I'd done Harper's bidding. Again, I'd come like a dog when called.

The cab driver was a Middle Eastern dude with a short beard. Ahmed. He looked to be in his twenties and about five foot five. He pulled over on a nondescript patch of road. A pair of square wooden stakes stuck out of half-buried concrete blocks. The station sign must have been there.

"Barrington Station!" he said.

"Can you wait for me?" I handed him cash.

"I have another pickup." He handed a card over the front seat with the change. I took the card and left the rest in his hand for a tip. "Call and someone will come."

"I don't have a phone with me."

"You got fifty cents?" He pointed at a payphone ten feet in, a relic from the days when people needed to call a cab from the station.

"It works?"

"I know it does. Trust me. Fifty cents. You need two quarters?"

"No. I have it. Thanks. Hey—" I stopped myself halfway out the door. "What if I wanted to go to the airport?"

He laughed. "Airport? Hundred forty miles?"

"How much would it cost?" I didn't ask because it mattered but so he'd take me seriously.

"You call dispatch, okay?"

"All right."

I got out, and the car took off. I was alone in the middle of nowhere. Then I realized she could have left that little note at any time for any reason and I'd chased it like a puppy playing fetch.

The grass was knee-high, and leaves crunched underfoot. The trees were half-covered in red and brown leaves hanging on for dear life.

I walked perpendicular to the road and came to cracked pavement. Following it, a building appeared soon after. Red brick with green shingles, boarded windows, and poured concrete slab, it looked as if it had never been a major station. The archways had decorative stones over them, as if someone, at some time, had given a shit. I passed through the arch, into the station, through to the other side. The slab dropped off into grey gravel that led to rusted tracks.

I went into the station again. The floor was concrete. The walls were painted white under layers of graffiti. A locked door led behind the boarded-up ticket window. I scoured every surface for a message but found nothing.

Outside, I stepped onto the tracks. Facing north, they disappeared around a sharp turn. The fall leaves clicked in the wind, and the grass rustled with the movements of small animals. Rats. Squirrels, maybe. Groundhogs, if they had them out here. The clouds moved across the cyan sky so steadily I could have set my watch to them. Nothing else moved. Nothing else made a sound. I was locked in position, listening for changes as they snapped neatly into the continuity of time.

"It's amazing what you can do despite the obstacles." Harper's voice cut through a daydream I didn't know I was in the middle of. She came toward me from the north, walking on a track with her arms out for balance.

"You really work too hard to make a point."

She wore mirrored sunglasses I hadn't seen before. She dropped off the rail onto the ties. She wore a blue shirt under her open plaid car coat. It was unbuttoned, and her bra was red. The velvet swell of her tits curved into a sweet divot between them. Not too wide, not a straight, dark line. Just right for running my tongue over.

"I figured, since we're stuck together," she said, "we'd make the best of it."

"No. That's not what you figured." I overacted in the reflection of her sunglasses. I had to look *bigger*, but holding my arms out and talking louder didn't change the optics. "You're showing me more despair. I get it, okay? This sucks."

What did I see in her glasses?

A tiny man looking down her shirt.

I hadn't even realized I was doing it.

"Do you remember Lucy Park?" she asked.

"Sure, I do."

Lucy Park had been a sweet little Korean girl I'd done a first-year P-set with. She hadn't had much experience with men before we started it. By the time the quarter was over, she could take my entire cock down to the balls.

"She was a TA in my Calc 2 class. Married. Going for her PhD."

"Glad to hear it."

"She said you taught her how to fuck."

What the—?

The clouds moved at the same speed across the sky.

Calm down.

"We were both adults."

Had Harper dug something up? Was I going to wish she'd done no more than hack my system? Was she trying to ruin my life even more?

"She said you taught her what men like."

"I like grown women. I like them wet, and I like it when they want it. So if you're going to make up a story that I assaulted her, you got the wrong guy."

The line of her mouth curved a little, stretching the bottom crease. Her face was no more than a half smile and two miniature Taylors in the reflection of her glasses.

Crossing her arms, she unbuttoned the blue shirt. Her red bra was simple, unpadded, with a hook in the front. The thin fabric did nothing to hide her hard nipples.

"I was worried this would be uncomfortable." She unhooked the bra. "But that was stupid of me."

"Whoa, whoa."

My hand was doubled and huge in her lenses. The bra fell away. Her tits were round, velvet, crested with soft pink.

"I have something you want."

"Seriously?" Confused, irritated, disoriented, yet unable to keep from looking at her tits. The way they were proportioned against the curve of her waist. The shadow the sun cast on her belly. I stepped back, either to get away from her or get a good look at her. I wasn't sure which.

"You want QI4 back. And I need something from you."

I'd never been plied with sex before. Sex was casual and fun. She was using it to disorient me, and I didn't like it. Not one bit.

I advanced on her, taking her breast with my right hand, closing in on the nipple as I took her mouth with my tongue. I was merciless on her tit and her lips, biting and pinching my annoyance. I pushed my cock against her.

When I pulled away, two of me looked back.

I ripped the sunglasses off her and threw them on the ground. Her blue-ringed irises stared back at me. If I looked close enough, I was in the pupils.

Fuck her.

I abused her nipple, twisting until her mouth opened a little.

Pain or pleasure? Both?

"I don't like being manipulated," I hissed through teeth that wanted to bite her again. "You didn't hack me just to fuck me." Leveraging her hips, I pushed my erection against her.

She shifted so her clit felt me. "Teach me." Her breath was hot and damp. "Teach me how to do it."

I let her nipple go and grabbed the whole breast. I wanted to come on it. Paint it with my semen. Run my fingers through it and shove them down her throat. "Why?"

"Each thing you teach me, I'll release—" She gasped as I moved against her. "I'll release part of QI4."

"Tell me why."

"No."

I bit her lower lip. That lying little crease. She squeaked in pain, and I made her suffer before letting go.

"You have men here."

"I don't want to be fucked like a princess."

I took her chin in a hand still warm from her breast. "Why? You'll waste what I teach you on them anyway."

She pushed me so hard I nearly fell back. Good. She should be mad. She should be as pissed off and horny as I was.

"Now you listen to me." She bent slightly at the waist, as if she was ready to attack. Her tits went from objects of desire to objects of power. "You're going to do what I'm asking you to do. You're going to take as long as you need to. Teach me how to kiss for your boot loader. You'll get your master boot sector back when I can use my hands. Your object code when I can suck a cock. And the source code is released when I know how to fuck."

"You're crazy."

"I am. I'm out of my fucking mind. I'm nuts from seeing my friends die. From my sister crying all night. From these fucking drugs everyone drives a hundred miles to get. The filth in the water and the air's fucked my brain so bad I can't even think straight."

No. Her shouting, her tension, her growling conviction, told me… no.

Yes, but no. I was sure she was telling the truth about the things she saw, and I was sure she was unhappy and upset about the deterioration around her. But she wasn't crazy. I wasn't even sure she was truly as desperate as she wanted me to think she was. Maybe she was three steps from actual crazy desperation and she could see it coming, which would make her smart, shrewd, and very sane. She was what my grandmother would have called "crazy like a whorehouse priest."

I knew I'd deal with the priest; I'd just never thought I'd be the whore.

I held up my hands, stepping onto the track as if standing a few inches taller would make a difference.

The rail vibrated underfoot.

"What you're asking? It's crazy. But you're not," I said. "So I need to know why. I need to know what kind of plan I'm playing into."

"Did you ever need to know a woman's reasons for fucking you? What's the difference now? You do what you'd do if we met in some bar in SanJo. I do what I'd do if I was feeling charitable."

"That's a real achievement in compartmentalization."

The rail tremors underfoot sharpened, increasing with the faraway rattle of an engine.

"Trains still running on this line?" I asked.

"Yeah. Freight."

The tremors increased, and the steady silence was broken by a rumble. She didn't move her shirt down; it stayed bunched above her tits, tangled in her bra.

"They just pass Barrington?"

"At a hundred miles an hour."

I stepped off the rail. I wasn't in the mood to get run down. Standing close to her, she was a few inches taller, but still not taller than me.

"You can hear it," I said softly. "Same as I can."

"I know when to get off."

"Fine." I turned my back on her.

One step. Two. Was she getting off the rail? Was she really crazy? The rumble got louder, punctuated by clicks and clacks.

Basic stopping distance equals velocity squared over two times the coefficient of friction times the acceleration = unknown variables=tonnage, grade, maintenance, which means even best case, the train needs half a mile to—

Fuck this. When I turned to run toward her, she was still on the track. I grabbed her arm and yanked her away as the train came around the turn. I pulled her to the station as the freight train flew by. Without her sunglasses, I could see the determination in her eyes.

I'd lost a game of chicken. The simplest zero-sum game in the lexicon. Too simple for either of us.

"You just proved exactly nothing," I said.

"I grew up here. I told you I knew when to move." She buttoned her shirt without hooking her bra. "But you still felt the need to save me. See? You're not a total asshole. But that's *me*. So let's pretend this is about you and me. Just us. Not about Barrington or the people in it."

"I'm not touching you again."

"Yeah. All right. Sure." She stepped back, swaggering. "You need a lift back?"

Of course I did, and she knew it. But fuck her. I wasn't getting into a car with her.

"No."

"Suit yourself." She left the station and disappeared into the trees, ass swaying like a lure.

A few seconds later, her Chevy pulled out from the cover of the trees and onto the two-lane blacktop. Then she was gone.

XXI

Turned out I didn't have two quarters. I had ten credit cards, a twenty, and an emergency fifty-dollar bill jammed into the corner of my wallet. It was just as well. I had no idea where Harper had gone, and I needed a minute to think before I ran off half-cocked.

Walking on the shoulder in the direction Harper had driven, I tried to get my head around her offer.

I'd been pursued before. I wasn't so much of a predator that I only fucked what I chased. But this girl was insane. She'd gutted my life so I'd teach her how to fuck? It would have been easier to fly out to San Jose and shake her little tits at me. Sell those earrings for a nice hotel room.

My mind slid into the possibilities inside a hotel room, and now that I had full visual on the tit situation, I could get really detailed about it.

In every fantasy, Deepak texted to say there was no problem. We were ready to roll with GreyHatC0n. Without his messages, I couldn't touch her. Not even in a fantasy hotel room.

The route was a single lane in each direction, weaving through a lightly wooded forest. Not much traffic in the first hour. Three cars going in my direction and one coming the opposite way. I didn't put my thumb out for the first hour of walking, and only one truck slowed down to ask where I was going. The guy looked like a traveling salesman in a cheap suit with a passenger seat loaded with fast food bags. I waved him on.

I missed my phone.

How was Deepak going to contact me to tell me how fucked up it was that I couldn't sacrifice a little sex with a beautiful girl to save the company? How was I going to imagine the incredulity on his face when I told him how hot she was? That under normal circumstances, I would have taken her twelve ways from Tuesday? And she didn't want a commitment. Just a crash course in how to please a guy, with the first lucky guy being me.

Despite the fact that Harper had the keys to a lock I needed opened, she freaked me out. I didn't trust she'd do what she promised.

And it didn't matter.

Man, her body.

And the way she let me kiss her. Like she was receiving the kiss. That was what it was. She was learning it as I did it.

The buzz and rumble of a car coming from behind me woke my mind up to the pain in my feet and the time of day. The sun was getting low in the sky, and I was just going to have to stick out my thumb.

The SUV passed with the driver staring at my thumb and me. Then two more. I must have gotten to a more used part of the road. All the cars had local plates. All the drivers were women. If I was a woman, I wouldn't have stopped for me either.

The forest broke, and I was walking along open plain.

The rumble of a motorcycle cut the air as it passed. A motorcycle with a sidecar. I stuck my thumb out even though the back of a motorcycle or a deathtrap sidecar weren't what I had in mind. The bike stopped. The driver wore a leather vest that should have scared me, but I was tired and hungry. The back graphic said *Lord Of Rust* in old English lettering and had roses twined around the chemical formula for oxidized iron.

Odd. Odd in every way.

The ninety-five pound *uhff*-ing dog was in the sidecar with its tongue lolling. Johnny swung his leg over the seat, and we met in the space between us. His corporate polo was gone in favor of a T-shirt that said, "Horologists Take Their Time."

"Nice afternoon for a walk," he said. "Unless you don't wanna get robbed by a bunch of broke motherfuckers with tattoos."

"You gonna rob me?"

"Shit. I ain't no motherfucker." He smiled to let me know he wasn't offended. "Where you headed?"

"The Barrington place. I'm headed in the completely wrong direction, aren't I?"

He shrugged. "Depends how much walking you're fixing to do. Nobody picking up hitchers these days. Even nice white boys."

"Why's that?"

"Double murder a few months back. They found the guy, but everyone's skittish."

"Was he a nice white boy?"

"Yep. Nice haircut and an Oxycontin habit. Started like a regular robbery then went all wrong. Cops couldn't figure out if the hitcher was a bigger moron than the driver, but there was plenty of stupid to go around that night. I don't know what gets into people. They get a gun and have ideas. Gonna be a hero. Prove something. Shoot a guy who's high on painkillers in the knee and think the pain's gonna stop him from turning the gun back on you."

"Great story. Really."

"I have more."

I looked up the road, then back down it, then at the dog in the sidecar.

"Come on." He clapped me on the shoulder and stepped backward toward the bike. "I'll take you back if you don't mind sharing a sidecar with Redox."

"Redox?"

"Yeah, the—"

"Oxidation reduction process. Dude."

"Kids are gone, so a guy's gotta have hobbies, right? Mine's science." He pointed at me then at the dog. "This here's a nice city boy," he told Redox. "That's a fancy jacket, and it ain't gonna hurt you. Be good."

"Does he bite?" I asked.

"'Course he bites. No point otherwise. Your other option is to ride bitch with your arms around me, but you'd have to kiss me first."

I got into the sidecar. Redox was in the middle of the seat, and from the way he looked me straight in the eye, he had no intention of moving for a white boy in a nice jacket. I squeezed in where I could. Johnny handed me a black military helmet and took off back toward town.

XXII

Johnny made a stop at the gas station, and I got to the register in time to pay for his cigarettes and some beef jerky. He spent a bunch of time talking to the guy behind the counter about off-gassing pipes and toxins. The guy laid his hands over his plaid-stretched gut and nodded. I got the feeling Johnny was like the town idiot, except he was really the town savant.

"You know Harper went to MIT, right?" he said.

"Yeah," I replied. "She's pretty smart."

"We was all proud of her. Then she came back for that fuck of a father. He shoulda croaked faster. Done us all a favor."

"Harper said everyone loved him."

"Feed them enough barbecue, and they'll love you."

"I'll remember that."

He tossed me the black helmet. Redox hadn't budged.

"Is the Barrington place far?" I asked.

"Let's get something to eat first."

"I'm buying."

"Damn right, you are."

He took me across three empty parking lots and a light industrial service road behind an abandoned brick structure. We landed in a dark

121

bar right out of a movie. It smelled of stale beer and cigarettes and sounded like treble-heavy speakers and clicking resin pool balls. There was no sign out front.

Johnny pointed at a seat at the bar and introduced me to Kyle, Damon, Reggie, Curtis, and Butthead. A mug of beer and a shot of something amber appeared at my elbow.

"You were up at the Barrington place last night." Damon pulled on his long goatee.

"This is the California guy Harper found." Reggie handed me my shot and held up his own. I was apparently expected to drink it.

"Found?" I said.

"Knew each other in college, ain't that right?" Johnny added.

"Those girls pick up strays where they find 'em," Kyle said. "They're all right."

Damon grumbled something behind his beer.

"Crazy broads," Reggie added, smiling as if they were his own special crazy broads.

Kyle shook his head and threw back his shot, leaving wet hair on his handlebar moustache. Butthead, whose four hundred pounds were at least twenty pounds sideburn, shook his head as if he didn't have to say a word out loud. They all understood each other in glances and half sentences.

I threw back my drink. Wild Turkey. Maybe. It burned, but I liked a little burn now and again. I cooled it down with a gulp of cold, pissy beer. It was good, and a new shot was in my hand a second later.

Damon raised his. "To the Barrington girls."

Sure. I'd drink to that.

"What the fuck's that on your wrist?" Johnny asked me, clicking his beer mug on my Langematik.

"Fucking watch."

"How much that set you back? Thirty large?"

"What the—?" someone behind me exclaimed.

"Not telling."

"Oh, shit! He ain't telling!"

Everyone laughed. I didn't think it was funny.

"It was a steal." I wanted to show them I was shrewd. "My dealer found a guy who didn't know what he had, and I grabbed it."

"What you do for a living out there in Cah-lee-fornia?" Johnny stretched out the word to mock it. He was the leader of this crew, at least for the night.

"I'm a hacker." Which was partially true but most easily stated and threatening enough to make my balls look a little heavier.

"A hacker?"

"Holy shit!" Butthead exclaimed. "So you, like, get into people's computers and steal?"

"Yes and no—"

The gang argued about what hackers did, their feelings about us, how cool or not cool the entire idea was, and whether or not hacking made you a man or a pussy.

"Hack me!" Damon took out his phone. With his long goatee and huge holes in his ears, he could have been transplanted into the San Jose hipster scene in the blink of an eye.

"Are you serious?" Butthead tried to talk sense into him, but Damon waved his phone at me.

"Fuck it. Hack me right now. I ain't got nothing to steal. Fuck it. I want to see."

"Nah." I denied his phone. Once I touched it, it was mine.

"Do it, motherfucker."

"No."

"You ain't shit. You mean you can't."

The group went up in *awws* of resignation when I shook my head. They really thought I couldn't. No one had doubted me in years, and suddenly my balls were featherlight.

"Fine," I said, taking Damon's phone. I pressed the volume and home keys at the same time. "Give me that safety pin." I pointed at a row of them on his jacket, and he pinched one off.

"You need the passcode to… oh shit."

I didn't have my own device, which would have cut my hack time in half. But there wasn't much I couldn't do once I was into his phone, which only took a second. Then I downloaded a piece of code I'd developed to do a particularly neat trick. A few taps, and his life opened her legs for me.

"Your One US Bank password is 123123? Are you trying to get robbed?"

"What the—?"

"You have $423.34 in there. I'll leave you the twenty-three dollars. You're welcome."

Voices of amazement and awe, which I bathed in. I was a sucker for this shit. I didn't need or want his four hundred dollars but his esteem. Their esteem. I didn't know them, but these guys made me feel like a king.

Butthead had his phone in his front pocket. I tapped it with Damon's to connect them. It was so easy it was a joke.

"Butthead," I said, "your Twitter password is 'titties,' all lowercase. So's the America First Bank checking and the—"

"I like titties. What can I say?"

"Kyle."

"I know my passwords, thank you." His voice was resonant and serious. What it suggested clearly was "I believe you're a hacker. You can stop now."

I gave Damon his phone. "Do a factory reset and protect yourself, would you? All you guys. Long passwords, all different, numbers, letters, symbols. All right? Stop fucking around."

"Tell you what, California Boy," Kyle said.

Shit. This wasn't going to end well. Nothing that started with "tell you what" and ended with something besides your actual name ended well.

"You beat me at eight ball, and I'll give you my bike." Kyle pointed out the window at a shiny Harley. "You lose, and I get that watch."

It was a fair trade if only the objects were considered. Except I could buy a new watch in a minute, and his bike was probably a bigger investment for him.

"I can't take your bike," I said.

"You think you're gonna win?"

"I know I am."

"Man, you are all balls, kid."

"Might be so. But I can tell the time on the wall. What are you going to do without your ride?"

"Fuck it." He slapped down his empty mug. "Don't care. Come on."

He grabbed the shoulder of my jacket and "helped" me up. Someone tossed me a stick, and I caught it. Chalk came half a second after, and I snapped that out of the air with my other hand.

I really didn't want his bike, and I liked my watch, but I could risk it to give these guys a rude awakening. Because math. Physics. And I was just tipsy enough to not care about getting the shit beat out of me. Loose enough to think landing in the hospital with a pool cue up my ass would get me enough sympathy from Harper to release my system.

Yeah. The shots had gone right to my head. Kyle put another Wild Turkey on the table rail.

"Do you fucking people eat?" I asked.

Butthead shouted over the music, "Johnny! Get Mr. California a burger! And get two for my fucking belly." He turned back to me with a smile. "Yeah. I'm fat, and I don't give a shit."

I took out my wallet and gave him my credit card. "Then get three. I don't give a shit if you're fat either. But change your passwords. Make them longer and put in a number or something."

"You're all right for a California freak." He took the card.

"You're the nicest fat fuck I ever met."

I must have been drunk to say that, and everyone else must have been drunk to laugh so hard. Kyle started the rack. Damon pushed him away and accused him of cheating. Kyle cursed at him. Johnny pushed them both away, said something about even odds of a stripe or a solid falling, and rearranged the balls. Once the rack was set, it was determined that the guest broke. The eleven landed.

"So how you like that Harper?" Kyle asked.

She's nuts.

"Nice girl." I circled the table, doing geometry in my head. I could land the nine and set up the next four shots. I wouldn't take his bike right off the bat, but I wouldn't lose either.

"You stay in the house last night?"

I sank the nine and had a perfect set up for the ten.

"Yeah. Side." I leaned over, took the ten. I wasn't drunk enough to miss the twelve in the side pocket or the setup for the fifteen in the corner.

"She show you Barrington hospitality?"

The balls clicked, and the fifteen made it, but the fourteen wasn't lined up like I'd wanted. Because… what was Kyle talking about? Was he implying I'd fucked her?

"Food was good. Mattress was lumpy."

"She made you forget about that though. That's my guess." He leaned on his cue and winked.

I looked at him over my cue, still sliding it over my thumb. "She's a nice girl."

"Sure is."

I had a lot going on in my life. I was responsible for the employment of dozens of people, and my life's work, the work they'd all slaved over, was being held hostage by a crazy woman who'd threatened to sell it. I was in Nowhere, USA, without a car or a cab. My phone was broken and imprisoned by thorns. I was going to get the shit beaten out of me if I wasn't careful.

But when he implied that Harper was some kind of easy whore, I was ready to tear shit up. I was aware that she'd taken her shirt off in an abandoned train station and begged me to fuck her, but that was me. The thought of her fucking these guys—or any guy, if I was being honest with myself—boiled the bourbon in my blood.

I took my shot, and the fourteen dropped in the corner. "She's a beautiful girl." I paced around the table after the thirteen, which hung on the edge of a corner pocket. "And smarter than anyone in this room." I leaned over and sank it. "Including me."

I was complimenting her to get the guys to talk, maybe tell me if they were in on her plan, but that didn't mean I was lying.

"Me too," Johnny said. "Just saying."

"She's too good for this shit." The thirteen sank like a body over a waterfall, and the cue ball bounced left, tapping the eight. It dropped into the side pocket. "Too good to be stuck here. If I were her, I'd do some desperate shit to get out."

I laid my stick across the table and held my hand out to Kyle.

Ruefully, he pulled on the silver chain that made a U at his waist and isolated a key.

"You don't know this town well enough to say that." He snapped off the key. "We're her people."

"That may be so." I still didn't want his bike, but in the seconds that passed, I decided I'd give it to Harper as payment for their shitty rutting. "But she's yours too."

Kyle slapped the key in my outstretched hand and grabbed it tight. I braced myself against what I thought was next. A punch. A flip. Any act of violence I had coming for shooting off my mouth in the backwoods.

"I don't need you telling me what the Barrington girls are." He looked at me closely, inspecting every pore, every hair, every flick of my eyes.

I looked back at him with the same directness, funneling my inexplicable anger in his direction. "What are they?"

I wanted him to say it so I could get this over with. His face cracked, and lines appeared around his mouth when he smiled. It was as if I'd said something that relieved him.

"They're us. That's all there is to it. They're good girls. Good people. And if you respect them, we respect you." He let my hand go.

I put the key on the rail. They'd been baiting me, trying to get me to say something dirty or cruel about Harper and her sister. Fuck them and, also, good for them.

"Who's going to win you your bike back?" I asked.

"One of my people." He tossed the cue to Reggie.

XXIII

*I*n the dream, I was eating her pussy. It was dry, but I was eating that shit as if it was my last fucking meal. Her legs clamped tight around my head, squeezing and squeezing and squeezing, until I said her name right into her cunt.

"What?" Her voice was clear, as if her thighs weren't around my ears.

"Harper." My voice was flat and toneless in sleep.

"You're going to wear it out."

The dream ended. I was left with a headache and a dry mouth.

I didn't want to open my eyes. If I did, I was either in the hospital or in the Barrington house. Maybe I was in Butthead's house. Or Kyle's. Maybe I was lying on the pool table.

But where I wasn't was my own bed or the couch at QI4HQ. Nope. I was definitely still in Shit City and batshit crazy Harper Barrington/Watson was right next to me with her freckles and her strawberry-shortcake tits.

"Water," I croaked like a frog.

"Right next to you."

Keeping my eyes closed, I reached to where I'd remembered the night table was in the room I'd slept in.

"You're more likely to knock it over like that."

Damn. That meant I was leaning in the right direction, which meant I was in that same room. Fuck.

"And anyway, that's the wrong side," she added.

Different room? Okay. I reached out with my left hand. My knuckles found cool plastic.

"For the love of Pete." Her exasperation was cute in a psycho kind of way.

The cold container was put right in my palm. It was short. I opened my eyes. Everything was a mad blur except the water container I held three inches from my face. It was a purple-and-yellow sippy cup with clowns biking around the sides.

"You don't have to pick your head up this way," she explained.

I closed my eyes and put the bottle to my lips, sucking on the end like I'd sucked her hard little clit. I remembered it had been a red-painted pebble.

Or not.

That had been a dream. Right.

"Thank you."

"There's something for your headache if you can reach it. Or I can get it for you."

"I got it." I gave up sweet darkness and opened my eyes for real, blinking the blur out. The ceiling was painted in roses. "You put me in the moldy room."

"Closer to the stairs. You were heavy. Butthead's not in great shape, you know."

I got up on my elbows. I was dressed. I knew that much. A blanket was thrown over me, hiding my dream-induced boner. When I turned to Harper, my neck hurt. She was in a white wicker chair, one knee folded with her bare foot up on the edge. Her arms wrapped around the bend in her leg, and her fingers laced together around her calf. I couldn't read her expression.

"Thank you," I said. That hurt too.

"You still drunk?"

"A little."

"Kyle said you could still hit bank shots better than you could stand."

"It's math." I scooped up the three brown pills on the night table. "I can do that drunk."

"Apparently. You were the proud owner of half the Harleys in town until about midnight."

"I don't ride." I washed down the pills with sippy-cup water and flopped back on the pillow. "They can keep them." I put my arm over my eyes. My Langematik was gone. "Where's my watch?"

"You played nine ball with Johnny. Mistake."

Right. Math + Sobriety > Math / Drunk.

"Those guys are a bunch of assholes. I don't know how you stay here."

I meant it as a compliment, and she read my sarcasm like a pamphlet on guy-speak.

"They're all right." Her voice was bathed in warmth and pride.

"No, I mean, yeah, sure. They're fine. But I can't get the hell out of here, and I don't even live here."

"You should really think about my offer. I'm a great student."

"You're a terrorist."

"I'm desperate. There's a difference."

I moved my arm and looked at her. "Why?"

"Why is there a difference?"

"Why are you desperate?"

She got up, leaned down until her hair brushed my chin, and whispered so close I could hear the wet pop of her tongue on the roof of her mouth.

"You haven't been paying attention."

She quickly kissed me and walked out before I even felt it.

XXIV

I'd gotten where I was from paying attention. Her town was desperate. The guys in the bar last night were desperate. They stank of it. Their jokes were laced with it. They were uneducated, unemployed, and stuck. But Harper had money, beauty, and talent. Maybe the headache was keeping me from seeing what she wanted me to see.

Maybe that was all I had to do. See her problem. Then she'd release my system and kick me out of her fucking house. Maybe she'd marry one of Johnny's kids and make smart babies.

Yeah. No.

Harper didn't need to marry anyone right now.

My reaction was so quick I couldn't question it until I was entrenched in refusal. Obviously, from a completely impartial standpoint, she was too good to be stuck here. I didn't need to want her myself to know that. Staying here and making babies with a guy in a trucker hat was a betrayal of her potential. As opposed to (me) someone with resources (me) and a valid passport to take her around the world (me).

Not me, obviously. I wasn't interested in crazy. I wasn't even interested in a relationship.

But someone *like* me.

The room swam when I sat up, and the knife in my head jabbed hard when I stood, but I wasn't so hungover that pissing in the bed was an option. By the time I'd emptied my bladder, I had my balance back. My eyes cleared, and I could see the wiry mushroom growing out of the ceiling. The paint it grew from was probably full of lead. I put my dick away, washed my hands, and tried to walk out. But the mushroom bothered me. It had a long stem and a small, cone-shaped head. I pulled it, but the plaster put up a fight. A chunk of dusty white grit came off, leaving rocks and dust on the toilet tank. But a string of mycelium stayed attached. I pulled again. Another line of plaster came off.

"Shit." I dropped it and let it hang from the fissure. That was going to bother me more than if I'd just left it alone.

"Mr. Harden?" A female voice came from the bedroom.

Catherine stood in the doorway with her hands folded over her chest. She was so sweet and unassuming in an apron and dress. Like a real throwback to an earlier time. The exact opposite of her sister. I wondered how much she knew about what Harper was up to.

"Yeah. Hey, thank you for putting me up again."

"It's not a problem. I was making eggs. Did you want some?"

"Hell yeah."

She smiled. She liked being useful. I could tell that much. "Any preference?"

"Any way you make them. But if it doesn't matter to you, fried is fine."

"How many? Three?"

I could have eaten a dozen. "Yeah. That would be great. Thanks." She was about to leave when I stopped her. "Catherine?"

"Yeah?"

"Where's Harper?"

"Running errands. Be down in ten if you like your eggs hot."

CATHERINE HAD EGGS, coffee, toast, and bacon ready on the kitchen table. I washed up in the sink.

"I made a mess in the bathroom."

"What was it?"

"The mushroom was making me crazy."

She laughed. "Reggie plasters over it at least twice a year."

I rinsed, wondering what a person would have to do to make Catherine angry. "I can spackle it up."

"Really? Well, you can see if there're any tools in the shed." She handed me a towel. "When are you leaving, Mr. Harden?"

She didn't sound cruel or rude. Her tone barely moved.

I wiped my hands, wishing I had an answer. "I keep trying to."

The eggs were still warm. I tried not to shovel them, but I was starving.

"I want you to think about taking Harper with you." Catherine sat across from me, cradling her coffee mug.

Did she know her sister was a hacker? Did she know her sister was inches away from ruining me?

"Excuse me?"

"She's dying here, and she won't leave. The longer she stays, well, you know what happens."

She didn't know. She thought Harper was just her smart sister.

"To be honest, I don't know what happens."

"She made it to twenty-five without having kids. Most girls around here start at eighteen. She's going to be an old maid like me unless she finds a man who can match her." Catherine didn't look as if she'd hit thirty. Hardly an old maid. "I think where you are, she might find happiness."

In Silicon Valley, a girl like Harper would get swooped up like a steak in a wolf's den. She'd have her pick of rich and talented men. The fact that what she'd done to QI4 would make her a talent commodity was an oddly secondary concern.

"She can go where she wants."

"No, I mean… you could introduce her around. Be her friend."

My reflection stared back at me from the black surface of my coffee. "I could. But where I'm from, no one really likes me. Right now, my company's under attack, and outside the people who work for me, everyone thinks it's funny, or cool, or they're somehow vindicated. The whole world watched me burn, and now you know what they're disappointed about? Not that my creation crashed. They're disappointed that they won't get to be the ones to take me down. They won't get the glory. Someone beat them to it. So I'd love to help Harper, but if I brought her back with me, they'd hate her too."

"I doubt everyone hates you."

"Believe it. I can show you tweets that would make your hair turn red."

She blew on her coffee and sipped it. Tapped the edge. "She's had a rough time."

"I know."

"When our father died, she was supposed to take time off school and go back. But our mother…" Catherine shook her head pensively. "She took a mortgage out on the factory, defaulted first chance she got, and left with everything. Just. Gone."

"I'm sorry."

She waved as if it was old news. "There was a man involved. Of course. Had been for a while. She was waiting for our father to die so she could leave."

"So you started selling furniture."

She smiled at some foolishness then sighed. "I hear someone has a problem… if all I have to do is give them an antique to sell, I give it to them. That's all they'll take. An object or work. No one accepts a handout."

"It's a big house. That's a lot of problems."

"It is." She gathered the plates and brought them to the sink. "And there are more. Always. The furniture's gone, and I'm running out of projects around here."

I couldn't imagine her sacrifice. Richest girl in town with a father who owned the primary place of employment reduced to poverty by her own mother.

"Do you have tools around? Hand tools? Stuff like that?" I asked.

"In the shed out back. We've loaned a lot out and sold some, but the basics should be there."

"Okay, to your first question, I don't know when I'm leaving. Harper and I have some things to work out."

"What things?" Her voice was all hope wrapped in surprise.

"Just things. Let me fix that hole in the wall first."

XXV

I found the shed to the right of the thorny bed of bushes. It was a rotted-out mess. The door nearly came off when I opened it, and dozens of crickets jumped whenever I moved something. How did these women decide what got attention and what didn't? Was it money? Time? Materials?

The tool bench was tidy but dirty with disuse. Some of the metal jar tops screwed into the ceiling had glass jars of nails threaded in; some were just circles waiting to be used. This had been someone's special place. They'd kept pictures of boats, model planes, vintage cola signs, and wooden boxes that probably held treasures I had the curiosity but not the courage to open.

A hole in the roof had let water in, rusting everything. A hoe with the grey handle. A sledgehammer with the handle half broken off. A pair of pliers screamed in a permanent open state.

I found a box of old scrapers crusted in plaster. I found three containers of joint compound. I could only get one open. After working past an inch of dried crust, I found a pocket still wet enough to use.

Back upstairs, I scraped off the mushroom and plastered over the crack, laying the compound on as smoothly as I could. It stuck and shifted on the cracking plaster, and I ended up with a larger patch than I wanted. Eradicating the mushroom meant ripping out the mycelium, which was probably in the wood on two of the walls and the bedroom adjacent. No one had time for that.

"Taylor?" Harper's voice came from the open French doors.

I checked my watch, but it was gone. Once I was on the balcony, the breeze cooled the moisture on my skin. The sun came in at an angle, and I was a little hungry.

Harper looked up from ground level, shielding her eyes from the sun. Her hair was in a loose ponytail at the back of her neck.

"What are you doing?" she called.

"I'm not leaving until you give me what you took, and the mushrooms were making me crazy. They grow behind the walls. It's… unnerving."

"Unnerving?"

I gripped the railing. *Are you doing this or not?* "Come up here, Harper."

I'd decided. I was doing this.

I pointed toward the doors on the other side of the balcony that led to the room I'd slept in the night before. I did not say please, and I did not ask a question. One of us was in charge, and it wasn't her. Even if she had the keys to my life on the little ring in her head, this wasn't working if she was the one calling the shots.

I washed my hands in the mycelium-free bathroom by my room. No time for a shower.

The stairs creaked. A pressure grew behind my balls because I knew what was coming.

She stood at the end of the hall, hand draped on the bannister. Branches of hair had escaped her ponytail and dropped to either cheek. I pointed at a spot on the floor in front of me. She scratched a spot on her neck, which was unremarkable except for her hand. It looked as if it had been rinsed in light blue paint and scrubbed. The tinge was in the corners of the nails and the deep lines in her wrist.

"Come into my room and close the door," I said.

"You're all sweaty."

"You want to do this or not?"

If I had been trying to scare her, I'd failed. She practically skipped into the room.

"Close the door," I commanded again. She did it. "I want to set the rules right off."

"Okay."

"You won't tell me why you want this or why you went to all the trouble, but if you're trying to trap me into marriage or some shit—"

She laughed derisively. "Yeah. No."

My feelings were not hurt.

Nope.

Not one bit.

"Condoms." I put up a finger. "Every time."

"Yes."

I put up a second finger. "Don't come to me with emotional attachment. I'm not interested."

"Me neither."

My third finger made a W. "This has to be done in nine days. If it's not, I'm leaving, and I'll just deal with the consequences."

"It won't take longer than that. I told you. I'm a really good student."

"All right. Let's get this show on the road."

I dug my thumb into my other palm absently, thinking this might not be a bad way to spend a few days. QI4 would be back, Deepak would spin it into a learning experience; we'd work on manufacturing our own goddamn monitors and BIOS. I could just go back to the way things were. That alone was enough to give me serious wood.

"Take your clothes off, Harper."

XXVI

I'd never seen anything like it. She *was* a good student. Good like the kid who raises their hand highest, shakes it, bounces, and says, "Ooh ooh!" until they're called on. She dropped her jacket like a bad habit and attacked her shirt buttons with enthusiasm.

"Okay, okay," I said. "Hold up."

"What?" She was frozen with her shirt on one shoulder.

"Slow down." I dropped into a chair, crossing my legs and watching.

She tossed her shirt on the floor. Then her bra. Bent to slide her pants down. Deliberate. Slow. Authentic.

By taking away the cover of kisses and close bodies, I intended to make her uncomfortable. Punishment for what she'd done. Hack my system. Humiliate me. Put everyone on my team in jeopardy. Lure me hundreds of miles away. Use me.

And for all of it, never tell me why.

She was naked in front of me. Smooth and pale, hair over her shoulders so I could see her shape from top to bottom, her rounded tits, her curved waist, the bald triangle between her legs. The tiny slit at the bottom was the focus of all my attention. I couldn't have solved for x and looked at it at the same time.

"You shaved." I asked a question by stating the obvious.

"Men like it. No?"

"Some do. Some don't."

"What about you?"

"How you keep yourself is your business. There aren't any rules."

"Ah."

"A guy will let you know."

I got near her and let the backs of my fingers run over her nipple. My body pushed up against my mind, saying, *Now now now*. But the moments before the first time, before sex with whomever, they were worth savoring.

She licked her lip and looked at me with an utter guilelessness that was so sexy the pressure to get my dick in her became unbearable. Fucking her would be so easy. Giving her a tip or a trick, nailing her, bending her, and making her come over and over. So easy.

But I had my pride. "Kneel on the bed."

She did it, and I tapped the edge of the foot.

"This is awkward," I said. "You're blackmailing me, you won't tell me why, and I still want to fuck you."

"You're a complete fucking douche, and I still want to fuck you."

I held my finger up to her face. "Keep talking like that, and I might start to like you."

A smile crept across her face. She confused the fuck out of me, but I liked her. I hated her. I was angry at her. I was afraid of her. And still, I liked her.

Letting weight fall against her bottom lip, I leaned into her until I could feel her breath on my chin.

"The moment before a kiss is important," I said. "You need to savor it."

"Okay." Her eyelids fluttered.

"Never rush." I heard her swallow. "Lips first. Keep it loose." I brushed ours together, and she shuddered. I had full wood already. "Light. Gentle to start."

I kissed her top lip then below. She tasted like river water and rain. I flicked my tongue into her mouth quickly, and she gasped.

"Has no one ever kissed you before?"

"Not like this."

"Open your mouth, just a little, and play against me. Make me work for it."

Her jaw moved against mine. I played her lips and tongue, tasting every millimeter, every fold of skin and membrane, getting inside her just a little until I pried her open and owned her.

She groaned into my mouth, laid her hands on my stomach, and brought them down to my waistband. She unlooped my belt. "Is this right? That I'm going for it? Or should I wait?"

"If I wanted you to stop, I'd move your hands. Same for you."

"I'm not good at cues." She nodded and slipped the belt from the buckle.

"You're doing fine."

"When I was a kid," she said, "they thought I was slow. I said weird things. The other kids didn't like me because I didn't relate like a normal person. Teachers hated me because I'd start to answer a question then ask another question they couldn't answer before I finished. They thought I was too stupid to finish a thought. I'd start a sentence in class and get distracted by all the things in my head I didn't know. So I'd just stop talking." She opened the belt and got her fingers behind my top button.

"Don't stop." I wanted to fuck her. Needed to. But I wasn't talking about her getting my dick out. "Telling me. Don't stop the story."

"My grades were terrible. If I hadn't been rich, I would have been special ed. But my parents made sure I was with the 'normal' kids." She took her fingers off my pants long enough to make air quotes.

She popped my jeans button. I took a hard breath. I had to listen to her, or I was going to blow my load.

"I didn't get picked on for the same reason. Everyone was afraid my dad would come down on them at the factory. But one teacher, Mrs. Prescott, she started asking me questions, and when I paused, she asked me what I was thinking about instead of getting annoyed."

"People with high IQs have a hard time socializing."

She made quick work of my fly buttons. "Yes. And that plus everyone being scared of me? That's why I don't know how to do this."

I took her by the wrist and kissed her hand.

"You know how." I put each finger in my mouth, sucking until it was wet.

Her breath got quicker. Her every-color eyes widened.

"When you stroke me, it's better when your hand is wet." I lowered her hand to my cock. That worked. "Gently at first."

The head of my cock felt like a full balloon. I slid my fingers down her belly.

"Spread your knees."

She leaned on me to keep her balance, and I touched the wettest cunt I had ever touched in my life.

Shit. I was going to lose it. I pulled away.

"What?" She looked as if I'd slapped her.

I pushed her down. "On your back."

The best part of sex is the moment a girl's legs open the first time. It's hot when she's naked and her tits are at full attention. But that moment, when a girl shows me where she's most vulnerable…

She lay before me with one hand over her belly and her ankles crossed. I was at her feet, returning her stare.

"How am I doing?" she asked.

"Great." A little pressure on her thighs and her legs opened like a flower.

"So what I was just telling you?" she said.

Her clit was hard and wet, and when I touched it, she stopped talking.

"About you being socially awkward?"

"Yes, I—"

When I slid my finger in her, two things happened at once.

One: she came.

Two: a ring tightened around my knuckle.

I moved with her and yanked out as she was in mid-arch. It was cruel, but I was shocked out of the moment.

She was left in a puddle of skin, breathing heavily, and I knew she was wondering if that was how it was supposed to go.

"You didn't tell me," I growled harder than I should have.

"I was about to!" Her hair looped all over her face.

"You have to tell a guy before you even get your clothes off."

She scrambled onto her knees and put her fists on her naked hips. "Well, that's a rule you don't get a second chance at."

"How are you a virgin?"

"I just told you how."

"Between Mrs. Prescott and MIT, you couldn't get laid?"

Naked and shameless, hands still on her hips. "Have you noticed everyone steers wide of me and my sister?"

The guys had tried to get me to admit I was fucking her, and when I hadn't, they'd seemed good with it. Better than good. Kyle had seemed relieved.

"You got cooties or something?" I asked.

"My father's dying wish was for them to 'protect' us. Me especially. Fact that it was years ago hasn't changed anything."

"Protect you from what?"

"Getting hurt. Casual sex. Pregnancy. We're like prize cows. Damon's been trying to get in my pants since high school. Johnny broke his finger in sophomore year because he caught us behind the grocery store. That was that." She slapped her hands together.

"Every guy at MIT wasn't trying to get you into bed?" I buttoned up. Fun times were over.

"They could try. Sure. But I—" She stopped herself and balled her fists at me.

"What?"

"Nothing."

"I just had my finger in you. We're past 'nothing.'"

She got off the bed and snatched up her pants, finding the waistband. She put them on without the underwear.

"None of them were like me. Bunch of guys who could barely talk to a woman, and when they did, I felt like a redneck piece of trash." She fastened her fly as if she could just as easily have ripped it to shreds. "And stupid me. There was this one guy who was the worst of them." She isolated the collar of her shirt, stretching it as if she was going to put it on. "On the first day, he stood next to me in line in the Forbes Building. One of his friends got in front of me, and I was too timid to say anything. But this guy called his friend a fucking jerkoff and told him to get in line…" She wrestled into the shirt. "No one else talked like my people here, but he did. I saw him around and tried to be near him, but he didn't notice." She interrupted buttoning the front to snap her fingers. "Then I had to come home."

"Honestly? Can I say something *honestly* without you destroying my life?"

"Sure. Why not."

"If I'd noticed you, I would have fucked the shit out of you."

"Thanks. I think."

"And if you were in SanJo when I staffed... I might have hired you. But the 'wanting to fuck you' thing would have been a problem."

Her jaw tightened, and her face hardened as if she didn't believe me.

"That's not comforting," she said.

"I didn't say it to comfort you."

"You need to fix that, Taylor. You need to grow up and stop letting your dick run the show. It's pathetic."

I'd been told that before, but her disgust sent the message right into me. I was ashamed. Deeply ashamed. I carried my cock as if it was the president of the company, and I didn't make any excuses for it, but now I wanted to curl into a ball and think about all the decisions I'd made because of where I wanted to stick it.

I'd thought I was making sure the workplace was appropriate, but what I'd done was make it safe for the impulses of the least appropriate person. Me.

And... Raven. Of course I'd made sure there was one consenting partner in the office just for me.

Nice leadership. Real nice. I didn't blame Harper for being disgusted.

"Yeah. Well. I guess, when you put it that way, you're right."

Her mouth got narrow and tight, folding hard in the center crease. She opened the night table and took out a pen, biting the cap off as she came toward me.

I let her take my hand and twist it until my forearm was up. She wrote a string of numbers on it while clamping her teeth on the cap. Four digits in, I knew what it was and tried to stay still and quiet until she finished.

4920616d20736f20736f7272792c2062757

42074686973206973206e6f74206f6665722e

"Thank you." I felt ridiculous for thanking her.

She must have felt the absurdity too. She put the cap back on and pulled out her phone.

"I have to go to work," she said, tapping on the glass. "Keep your nose clean." She tossed the device on the bed faceup. The contact was QI4HQ, and it was ringing.

"You had me on speed dial?"

She walked out without answering.

I was shaking as I read off the last letter to Deepak.

"Got it." He read it back to me.

"Close the Faraday cage before you put it in. And assume we're being monitored."

He dropped his voice. His breath had the cadence of a man walking quickly. "Someone's here. He's taller than I thought he'd be. He knows where my mother lives… in Rangpur, for fuck's sake."

That was Keaton. Six-four and as imposing as an all-knowing monolith.

I wasn't surprised my shadow investor had shown up, but I was alarmed. I'd assumed I'd be there to fend him off when the time came. Deepak didn't have the tools or testosterone to keep Keaton away. "Stall him."

"Easy for you to say. Where did you find this guy?"

"Tor, where else?" I lied.

"Great. Fucking great." He paused. I felt everything he wanted to say because I knew him.

"He's not scary," I said.

Deepak grunted.

It was my responsibility to say what needed saying with the

knowledge that Harper might be listening. I had to take what I knew about her and decide what she cared about. "He's putting on an accent to scare you. Did he mention MI6?"

"In passing."

"He's not British Intelligence." I couldn't leave it there. Deepak and I didn't lie to each other. Not outright, though I'd omitted plenty. "Not officially, but…"

But what?

It was a bad time for omissions. And what scared Deepak might also scare Harper. Not a bad thing.

"He knows people," I added. "He's done… work."

"Work?"

"Work. Just…look, that's Alpha Wolf, okay?"

"*OhGodohGod*. Taylor, what did you get me into?"

Before I could devise a smart answer that would both soothe Deepak and scare Harper, the voice on the other end got deeper, with an English accent sharpened for maximum impact.

"Beeze Taylor, my little protégé. You're calling from a well-cloaked number."

"Apparently."

"Are you enjoying yourself?"

I sat on the floor with my heels angled against the wood. "Weather's great where I am."

"Where are you?"

"In the United States. I'm not running away with your money. You know that, right?"

"You're too much of a pussy to steal from me. It's your incompetence that surprises me."

"Let's skip the niceties, okay? I'm going to fix this. We're going to be ready for GreyHatC0n. Period."

"Your sidekick's typing something into what appears to be the only working machine in this useless little cage you have here. Could it be a hexadecimal string? How quaint."

Keaton was never the positive and supportive type, but he stood by me when things got rough and was loyal to a fault.

"It's up!" Deepak cried from somewhere close. "It's booting!"

A cheer went up from the guys.

I didn't realize how tense I'd been until the anxiety dropped off me like a coat. It was over.

What was I going to do about Harper?

The question wasn't a new source of anxiety but a new source of possibility. My thoughts were unfiltered, unguarded. The walls between the compartments of my life fell away, and the impossible bled into the possible.

Take her with.

Stay here

Long-distance relationship

Hire her

Make her fucking president

New division

No sex

I'm the boss

Just business

All sex

Find her something with a friend

Do not let this girl out of your sight

You can have her

You win

You lose.

I could parse it all. Figure it out. Make a decision.

But from the other side of the phone, Deepak shouted. "Fuck!"

"Oh, dear." Keaton sounded bemused, which I'd learned was a way to keep from getting angry.

I'd seen Keaton angry only once, when he'd found out the FBI flipped me on the credit card hack. I hadn't turned on him, but he'd lost an opportunity. It wasn't pretty.

"What's happening?" My unguarded moment was frozen into a minute.

In the background, Deepak was shouting *fuck* over and over at a machine-gun tempo.

The phone dinged in my ear. A message.

"Take a look," Keaton said. "And let's be clear—I'm not leaving until I've protected my investment. And you. Even if it hurts."

The phone went quiet. No Deepak. No white noise from the guys in the cage. Harper's phone received the photo. It was a picture of the cage's big screen. Black but for five words at the bottom.

Enter decryption key to boot:

She'd said she'd give it back in four sections. I should have believed her.

I didn't know how long I sat there with my head between my knees, trying not to cry like a little bitch.

XXVIII

The next morning, it was my father's voice that got me off the floor. In my head, clear as day, he told me to stop feeling sorry for myself. No problem ever fixed itself, and this one wasn't any different.

I had her phone in my hands. What more did I need?

Trying to use the same hack I'd used on the Barrington guys, I came up against a solid security protocol. She'd walled off everything so she could make the call for me. I couldn't see what she had on there. I couldn't even see her phone book. I tried to get past it but wound up frustrated.

"Fuck this." I tossed the phone on the bed and got in the shower.

Harper had unlocked the QI4 boot loader. I didn't know what else I'd expected. The agreement was bigger than what we'd done. Teach her how to please a man, not stick a finger in her and make her come in three seconds.

The water wasn't hot enough. I turned the knob. I needed to burn this shit right out of me. Man up. She wanted to fuck. What was the problem? Why even hesitate? I'd used and been used by women since I was in my teens. I'd made deals and exchanged favors. Sure, I'd felt as if

I had more power in those transactions, but so what? Harper and I were just another negotiation. This didn't have to be any different.

Which meant what? Three more turns in the bedroom? I could do that. Bang it out by tomorrow. So to speak.

I put on my jacket, brushed my hair, and got myself looking like a sore thumb in this shithole. But I was as far away from crying like a bitch as I'd ever been.

From the top of the stairs, I heard Catherine in the dining room, chatting with other women. Maybe the same crowd as had made dinner the night before. I didn't hear Harper's voice. I backed up and stood at the foot of the stairs to the third floor. The door was closed. I went up and pressed my ear to the wood. Nothing on the other side. Not a keystroke or a breath.

So.

A choice.

Was I Taylor or Beezleboy?

I'D BEEN ENROLLED in Poly for about a week when I realized I didn't fit in. Cliques had already been established, and rich kids were thick with them. Not every parent wanted every kid in their mansion, and not every kid wanted every other kid ogling their seven-hundred-dollar shoes.

I'd thought we were rich. But guess not.

Keeping my nose clean wasn't that hard. At that age, I couldn't get far enough away to see the pattern of class and cruelty. I was back to being a lonely kid, far away from my friends and my neighborhood. Out of my depth and out of my league. My dad told me to buck up, and my mother wouldn't get out of bed. She just cried on the days she didn't have the energy to fix everything.

I was sitting alone in the cafeteria when Keaton found me. He was two years older, but since I'd skipped third grade, he was only one year ahead in school. In maturity, he was at least decade older.

"You're in my JavaScript class." He shoveled down a plate full of string beans. He was the first vegetarian I'd ever met.

"Yeah. I like it." I'd been pushed ahead in math and science and was borderline remedial in reading.

"It's shit."

"But it's easy."

"You want to learn some real stuff, you come to my house on Saturday." He pushed a card across the table. Name. Number. Address on my side of town.

"I'll ask my mom."

He snorted. Didn't say another word to me for the rest of the meal.

XXIX

$\mathcal{H}$acking is about technology, coding, and knowing people. It's also about the mechanics of the world. Keaton taught me that with few words, and I lived it. I knew how a toilet worked. The physics of chairs. How to make moonshine and beer. The world became one giant hack, full of things that needed to be understood so they could be broken to my advantage.

Once her phone went to sleep, I couldn't reopen it. It was locked tight. Unlike Damon and the guys, she knew how to protect her device from attack.

But she wasn't around, and her system was just up a little flight of stairs.

There's not much to picking a lock once you get the feel for it. There had been an awl in the Barrington shed toolbox, and I had a tie clip I didn't care about, so I bent it open. After listening for movement and hearing nothing, I was in Harper's office in three minutes.

I closed the door behind me. The stairs wouldn't creak, but her windows faced the front of the house. I'd see her shitty Chevy coming up the driveway.

Tapping the spacebar did nothing. She'd shut her system down when she wasn't at it. Good girl.

I hit the power button. The floppy disk drive (yes, the floppy drive) croaked to life, and the fan spun. While it booted, I opened her drawers.

Hackers distrust computers for good reason. We're big fans of pencil and paper with their eternal compatibility and geographical security. Harper was no different. Her desk drawer was full of scraps of paper, analog office supplies, and wooden pencils. A girl after my own heart.

That being the case, I ignored what was inside the drawer in favor of what was hiding under it.

I pulled the drawer all the way out and felt along the bottom panel. Flat wood all the way to the back…until I came to a ridge. Something stuck in the seam between the bottom and back panels. I flicked it with my fingernail, felt it give a little, then got under it and slid out a little green notebook.

Sitting at her desk chair, I flipped through. Calculations and drawings for a tiny circuit I recognized as the poison pill she'd left in the monitor at QI4. Seeing the drawings, how she did it with a soldering iron and a cut board from a cheap cellphone, I started to sweat. My face got hot. Was it anger or embarrassment? Was it the fact that she'd done what anyone could have?

No.

This was special.

She's special.

And she did you a favor.

The pain in my chest should have decreased when I saw the details, but it got worse. The simplicity and scale of the design couldn't have been reverse engineered, and I had to give her credit. With very little to go on, she'd cracked open what I'd sealed tight.

What the notes didn't tell me was how she'd gotten into the monitors or how she'd gotten a signal past the Faraday cage. It didn't tell me where she'd hidden the transmitter that went into and out of the cage often enough to move pieces of data.

Most importantly, it didn't tell me why learning how to fuck like a pro was on her virgin radar.

I brushed my hand under my nose and smelled only soap. I'd washed the sweet scent of her off my fingers.

Taylor Brian Harden
023-56-1029 5/29/88
Camden, New Jersey.
Cooper's Poynt El. Grad '01.
Poly Preparatory HS. '05 MIT '05-'08

M-Julie Kips 078-11-1876
F-David Harden 173-63-1850
Mar 07/12/85, St Paul Episc.
923 N. Jordan Rd. 08103 856-365-2289

Ella Susan Harden 09/05/91
Cooper's Poynt El. Grad '05. Camden HS. '09
Rutgers MBA Bus Admin '13
084-55-6570 Mar. Quentin Mitchell
04/23/13 034-15-2230

Pets - Goldfish - Irving d. 6/99.
Sib. Husky - Jamesey d. 10/02

Fiona Messing '05 Donna Grettin '05
Brenda Svenka '06 Carolyn Borlyn '06
Katrina Yu '06 Franziska Popp '06

She was good. Organized. Tight and unemotional. After the social
security numbers of my entire family, the addresses, the names and
deaths of every pet I'd ever owned, the women in my life took up pages.
Some of it had been culled from interviews and articles. Some from
rumor. My family's socials had been pulled from some dark corner of the
internet. The picture of me that had been stuck in the pages was on
photo paper. Eighth grade graduation. Green cap and gown. An A+
nerd. I flipped to the back.

Grace: Let's hang out this summer. - Taylor

Grace Kensington hadn't taken even one of my calls in the months before high school, but a year ago, to support an opiate habit, she'd sold a bunch of Taylor Harden mementos on eBay in anticipation of my upcoming fame. Photos. Yearbooks. A Christmas card. I'd bid up the price of the yearbook with two fake accounts and bought it for far more than it would ever be worth.

I ripped the page out and stuck the picture back in. I didn't care about my info. None of it would get Harper anywhere. But she had too much on my family. She'd done her work a little too well.

I put the notebook back in the seam and put the drawer back in. I yanked on the bottom one. It was locked. I jimmied it open with a paperclip from the top drawer.

The computer was finished booting. The monitor was still black, and the boot code flowed up the screen in greenish characters, ending in a C-prompt.

C:\

Old school DOS. Nothing fancy. Not a bell or a whistle in sight. It didn't ask for anything because the user was supposed to know what to enter. How many password fails before the system locked completely? Didn't matter. I could deal with that.

The bottom drawer was full of shit, but I knew what I was looking for. I looked under manila folders full of old bills, a sweater, a half-used box of pens, and found a floppy disk with BSD labeled in blue pen.

I stuck it in and rebooted, holding down F5 until…

Bypassing System Files…

And there it was. I checked the index, added a few programs to the config and autoexec files, and had access to everything. The machine hummed, waking up a more user-friendly OS.

I scanned the files and found one called QI4, but it was just a collection of articles about the system. A personal profile of Beezleboy. I found a subfolder with the incorporation papers and a deeper subfolder with two links to blogs about Alpha Wolf, aka Keaton Bridge.

Otherwise, nothing. Nothing hidden. Nothing protected. I knew where to look for shit a user didn't want found, and she had nothing. None of it. Either she was a genius or... well, there was nothing else to say. She'd left me with a lock I could pick and an empty computer.

Chrome hooked up to the web right away. Worked fine from up here, proving she was scrambling signal to isolate me.

Jesus. She was using an AOL address.

All right. This was pure bullshit.

I found Tor, the most popular browser for the dark web, and opened it. I went to the most recent page and got an eyeful of a Chaxxer conversation between @TheWatsonette and @Flow_Bro.

And it was filthy.

I scanned it quickly so I wouldn't get any harder than I already was.

*/Your pussy is so wet. You squirt
into my mouth when you come./*

> */I can take your whole cock down my
> throat. Shove it all the way in until
> I'm kissing your balls./*

/Spread your cunt apart and.../

> */I'm ready for you, my Prince./*

Oh, fuck that. I couldn't read another word, and so much for not getting a hard-on. I rode a wave of jealousy, then a swell of rage, into a trench of sorrow. She wasn't completely innocent, but she didn't talk like this to me. Not that I would have minded. But I was confused. I couldn't fit all of it into my head. My finger inside her. Her eager sexual authenticity. The membrane gently squeezing my finger.

Sitting up straight, I pretended I was reading someone else's account. Some strange woman I'd hacked. Someone I didn't care about.

/You like when I call you a whore./

The chat ended there. She'd left. Which was good because I wasn't reading another word. My pretense shattered.

What was she doing? She didn't have to talk to this @Flow_Bro guy, if it was even a guy. Was she looking for achievement points to please him? Was that what this was about?

The reality I had lived with for the past few days was shaken. I had to see her. Touch base. Make sure she was still Harper. Not quite innocent, not quite jaded. Dirty talker, maybe. I didn't know.

Why didn't I know?

Why did it matter?

It mattered. I didn't have to know why. I only had to know what *was*. Was the cat alive or dead? Why it was in a fucking box was irrelevant.

Voices came from the second floor. I wasn't ready to admit I'd broken into Harper's room, so I shut down and tiptoed to the door, hearing a male and female voice.

"Where is he?" The guy sounded a little pissed off.

"Upstairs. Johnny, leave it be."

"What's going on with him?"

"What do you mean?" Now Catherine seemed a little pissed herself.

"Cath, don't pretend you're not a grown woman."

"Don't ask questions I don't want to answer."

"You want her getting hurt?"

"It's time for you to go."

The voices became indistinguishable murmurs, then the two of them appeared in the front drive, stopping by Johnny's truck to talk. He had on his yellow polo shirt and a blue zip-front jacket that hid his tattoos.

My ride was in the shop, and I was in the middle of nowhere. Was I going to sit around and wait for Harper to come back? Read more of her dirty talk? Putter around the kitchen?

No. None of it.

I slid onto the stairwell and used my tie clip to lock the deadbolt behind me, then I took the stairs two at a time until I was in the front yard. Catherine was coming back toward the house, and the truck was pulling forward.

"Johnny!" I knocked on the back of the truck, and he stopped.

Leaning into the passenger side window, I asked, "You going to the distro center?"

"Yeah."

"Is Harper there?"

"I think she's filling in a shift."

"Can you take me?"

He leaned back as if he was trying to see the entirety of what I wanted. "She's working."

"I'll wait." I pulled the handle, but the door was locked. "Look, I don't have a phone. I don't have a car. So if that means I sit and wait, I sit and wait."

Johnny glanced at the clock then clacked the locks open. "I'm not going to be late on your account. She'll likely be on break in an hour."

I climbed in. The car smelled of dog and baby powder. Johnny turned onto the narrow highway. Pictures of children and young adults hung from the visors and rearview.

"Your kids?" I asked.

"What do you want with Harper?"

"Nothing."

Johnny huffed and got onto the interstate, speeding up to the limit. "Your lie stinks worse than a dog's asshole."

"I'm trying to not get my fingers broken, if you don't mind."

"She told you about that, did she?"

"You didn't ask for my opinion but—"

"Sure didn't."

"She's a grown woman. She can make her own decisions."

He didn't talk for a while, and I had nowhere to go with my statement. The long, yellow distro center came up on the right like a giant hunk of cheese in a puddle of parking lot. We slid off the exit toward it. A line of yellow trucks steered onto the interstate like sticks of butter on a conveyor belt.

"I'm not saying I did everything right in my life," Johnny said. "But if I see a bonehead like Damon trying to make time with her, or that asshole Lawrence, you can trust me one thing: I'm stopping it."

He turned down a wide driveway. Two food trucks were parked on either side of the road. One with tacos, one with burgers and fries. Plastic tables and chairs ringed the backs of the trucks. Beyond them stood the yellow guard tower.

Johnny stopped behind the taco truck and unlocked the doors. "I'll tell her you're here."

I opened my door but didn't leave. Not yet. "I don't need your permission, so I'm not asking. I'm telling you that Harper and I might or might not do whatever the fuck we want."

He leaned over so far I could smell lunch on his breath. My fingers ached. I bent them into fists.

"If you do," Johnny said, "you better get her out of this shithole."

Was he demanding I marry her? Jesus, I just wanted QI4 back in one piece and maybe a few spins around her body to get it. I couldn't promise anything except that I *wouldn't* make her or Barrington my responsibility.

"She'll do what she wants." That seemed noncommittal enough while still being true. She would do what she wanted no matter how fast I ran or how far behind I tried to leave her.

XXX

By my calculations, her lunch hour should have fallen around 6:40 p.m.

I sat. I stood. I paced. I kicked cans. A shift came out, lined up, and went back in. I helped the guys behind the taco truck haul the garbage onto a pickup. They gave me a container of pozole and a little white plastic spoon to eat it with.

A horn hooted from the yellow building. For a few seconds, nothing happened, then people started streaming toward the trucks.

Reggie came out in his yellow polo with an ID card hanging from a lanyard. I sat with him and a few other guys in yellow shirts and lanyards, talking about baseball and this dude Donnie's garage renovation. When their half hour lunch was up, Reg said he'd tell Harper I was waiting for her, as if it was totally normal for a guy to hang out in the middle of nowhere, waiting for a girl. They gave me a wave and went back through the gate, and I waited alone again.

I checked the time on my wrist, but my watch was gone. I was nowhere, never, without a buoy to navigate to. The only thing to do was wait.

KEATON HAD LED me down to his parents' basement and snapped the deadbolt behind him. We were in a concrete room with a washer and dryer, hanging shirts, and an ironing board. The circuit breaker door didn't close all the way.

"What's your dad do for a living?" I asked.

"Mossad." He smiled a little. "CIA sometimes. He's a quadruple agent. A freelancer."

The look on my face must have been pure horror because that was what I felt. We were red, white, and blue; apple pie; *e pluribus unum*.

Keaton laughed and clapped me on the shoulder. "I'm joking. Man, you should see yourself."

He brought me through the laundry room to his inner sanctum.

"Where's your accent from?" I changed the subject.

"Mother Russia," he said with a thick Russian growl. "I have as many accents as I want."

The inner room was finished with grey industrial carpet and a black leather couch. A huge flat-screen with gaming cubes sat on one side of the room, and on the other was a bank of computers.

"Donna Breckenridge," he said. "Let's talk."

I shrugged, leaning over to look at the ASCII chart pinned to the wall. "Nothing to talk about. We held hands, then she pretended I didn't exist."

"And Ryder nailed you at lunch."

I'd gotten a nasty "accidental" elbow in the ribs that still smarted.

"Unrelated." I ran my fingers over the keyboards. We had computers at school, but my parents couldn't afford to get me a laptop of my own.

"False." He pulled out a chair. "Women are all about getting you to do things. Ryder's in my grade. He's been dating Donna and talking to Jennifer Paige. Donna sees him talking to Jennifer and uses you to make him jealous. Ryder's a dumb twat, so he did what dumb twats do. Gets on you to prove a point. Jennifer gets scared. Donna's vindicated. Ryder's back in her pocket. Done."

He was right. I knew it in my guts.

"You want to get her back?" Keaton asked.

I shrugged. "She's not that hot."

"I don't mean 'get her back.' I mean payback."

My heart hadn't been shattered or anything, but I was curious about what he had on his mind. "Sure?"

"Have you ever heard of the dark web?" He flipped on a computer. The hard drive whirred and clicked.

"No."

"Sit down. You're going to love this shit."

I sat down, and he taught me everything. I loved that shit.

BETWEEN THE YELLOW shirt and the direct sunlight, her polychrome irises seemed paler. Her hair had escaped the rubber band. The flyaways looked like gold solder wire.

"What do you want, miss?" I asked nonchalantly from my new home in a white plastic chair. "This is my spot."

"Lunch?"

"I've had the pozole and a burger. Both were good. I noticed the Hispanic people eat at the burger truck by about the same ratio as the taco truck. White people are about a seventy-three / twenty-seven in favor of the burgers. I've seen one black person all day."

"What did they eat?"

"She brought her lunch."

"Can't blame her. This stuff starts to wear on you."

"What are you having?" I asked, standing. "I'll buy."

She sighed. "A burger, I guess. I'm not feeling tacos."

"Tacos? Fuck that. They have a menu that takes up the entire side of the truck. Have you tried the pozole?"

"I don't even know what that is."

I shook my head and leaned down so I could whisper in her ear. "How to fuck is the least of what you need to learn."

She elbowed me. "You're such a jerk. You still haven't apologized for freaking out."

"I'm sorry." I led her to the taco truck. "Now that you know the social norms and I know your fragile condition, I'm sure it won't happen again."

"I guess I can't blame you. I'm a statistical outlier."

"I love it when you talk dirty."

I ordered her the pozole, but I wasn't thinking about statistics or soup. I was thinking about the dirty talk I'd seen on her Chaxxer account, which I wasn't supposed to know about since I'd boot loaded her machine and broken into her room like a thief.

She took the soup with both hands, and we sat down.

"Thanks for the boot loader decryption," I said. "And your phone."

I slid it over to her. She let it sit. Her breath rippled the surface of the soup as she blew on it. "Have you ever heard of the Stockholm Syndrome? It's when a hostage sympathizes with their captor."

"Never had it." I swirled the straw in my hot horchata. "Stockholm's cool though."

"You have it bad. You're thanking me for giving you back what's yours and apologizing for sex I made you have."

"You aren't making me do anything."

She spun her soup around the container, avoiding eye contact.

I bent over the table, trying to get her attention. "Harper?"

She put her spoon on a napkin. A pool of red soup soaked into it. "I know you want to think you have control, but I am making you."

"Does that get you off or something?"

"Not really."

The hooting from the factory whistle echoed over the plain. Break over.

"Shit," Harper exclaimed before shoveling her soup. "I have to get back." She spoke between gulps.

Our time was over, and I remembered why I'd come.

Dozens of yellow shirts lined up to return to work. No one paid any attention to Harper and me at the little table. Now was the time to find out if The Watsonette was an alternate personality or a part of her I hadn't dug up yet.

"Tell me something," I started.

She answered with an *mmm* between mouthfuls.

"How are you going to suck my cock later?"

She froze, swallowed, glanced around for eavesdroppers. I shook my horchata, looking at her over the edge of the Styrofoam cup.

"I… uh…" She cleared her throat. Folded her bottom lip.

"You know why guys like to watch a good sucking? It's our dirtiest part going into a girl's beautiful mouth. She's letting it happen. Making it happen. My dick in her fucking mouth."

She put her pozole down and looked at her phone. She was going to have to run to get to work in time. I needed a dirty phrase or two that matched what I'd seen on Chaxxer, but she tapped on her phone with one hand and folded her lip with the other.

I wasn't fooled by her attention to the phone. She heard every word.

"I'm going to watch," I continued. "As my dick disappears into your face."

She put the phone on the table, glass down. "I've been practicing," she said, eyes finally on me. "With things. My fingers. A Coke bottle. I can get your whole cock down my throat until I'm kissing your balls."

There she was. The Watsonette.

My next move was obvious. Call her a whore and see how she reacted. Did she leave the chat or hang around?

But I couldn't. The word wouldn't leave my lips. "You'd better get back to work."

She tapped the phone with her nails. "I just told my supervisor I ate bad pozole and I'm not coming back."

"And now you want me to put my dick in that dirty mouth?"

"Yeah."

The way everything she said made me smile had to be the Stockholm Syndrome.

"I like you, Harper."

She didn't say anything. Her eyes were huge. Her demeanor was calm, and she didn't say a fucking word.

"I want to know why. Of everything, why this?"

"Ever have a goal, Taylor?"

"Don't get me started."

"I have a goal, and it's through you. You'll live. You'll walk away and be fine."

"And you? Will you be fine?"

She smirked from one side of her face. "Oral and you get the object code back."

"You tell me how you did it. Then you suck my dick, then the decryption code."

I couldn't believe what I was saying. It was all win for me, but I felt as though I'd never bargained for anything as hard in my life.

She leaned back in her chair and crossed her arms and legs. "I like you too."

I crossed my arms, leaned back on cheap plastic chair legs, and crossed my ankles. Now we were fully crossed. No one was going anywhere.

"How did you transmit signal out of the cage?"

She shook her head slowly and stood. "That's not on the table." Scooping up her soup container and my empty cup, she dumped them into the garbage. "Wait here."

She went past the gate and into the parking lot, showing her ID card to the guard as she went. I was alone again. Her Chevy came out of the gate soon after, and I got into the passenger seat. She drove onto the interstate.

"The poison pill had an antenna," I said. "Too short to send far."

"Didn't have to."

I hadn't expected to hear that. As if she could see my discomfort, a smile twitched her lips. Hackers loved nothing more than recounting an exploit. As much as I didn't want to give her the satisfaction of telling me how she'd done it, I needed to know.

"Just tell me. If your exploit isn't part of the deal, there's no deal," I said.

"I never met a guy so unwilling to get a blow job."

"I never met a woman who wanted to give one for your reasons. If I can even figure your reasons out. Which I can't."

She got off the interstate and took a couple more left turns than rights. I was sure she was trying to disorient me, but that was easier said than done. Eventually, she pulled past an opening between two beige-painted cinderblock walls, past rusted hinges and a couple of wrought-iron strips bent into the shapes of an alien alphabet.

It was a place of weird contradictions, like a toy graveyard or an abandoned arcade. Wood rectangles the size of my railroad apartment in San Jose were set in a grid. Brightly painted cracked flowerpots, broken swing sets, a brand new but disconnected screen door. A twist of lead pipes coming out of the ground. One had a valve and spigot.

The fact that I couldn't see it right away after my father taking me to so many job sites was embarrassing. It wasn't until we slowly passed a tractor trailer wheel filled with thriving tomato plants that my brain put the pieces together. We were in an abandoned trailer park.

She stopped in the spotty shade of a tree and put the car in park. "This was my father's last project."

"Looks like it didn't go so well."

"He made money. Trust me."

We got out. It was chilly, fall weather. The trees' leaves hung like laundry from the branches. When the wind blew, dozens fell like brown scrap paper.

She spun a few feet from me and held out her arms. "Ready?"

I wasn't. My dick was, but I wasn't. "How did you get signal out of the cage?"

"Are you sure you want to know?"

"Very sure."

"Then you'll show me?"

"How to suck a dick better than a Coke bottle? Yeah, Harper. It'll be my pleasure."

She looked down slightly. Bit her lip. Prelude to a lie? Or a closely held truth? "You want a lot for not much."

"I want everything. And I'll pay everything for it."

"Yes. You will." She whispered it like a filthy promise.

Fuck her.

Fuck her for being so in control. Fuck her for being so beautiful and intense. Fuck her for fucking up everything. Fuck her for scaring the shit out of me.

I took her by the back of the head and kissed her, not to tell her how much my body wanted to fuck her or how much I needed to get control of this negotiation, relationship, deal, plan, whatever, but to decode her. In the kiss, my anxiety was soothed. Her lips were honest. The groan in her throat told me she had less control than she thought. Her tongue yielded. She had barriers, but in that kiss, she told me she wasn't a stone monolith.

When I pulled away, she gasped.

"I could spend the entire day kissing you," I said. "But that's not why you brought me here, is it?"

"No. It's not."

Was she disappointed? Yes. I decoded that much as well, and I relished it. I had to do what she wanted. I didn't have to pretend to like it, even if I wouldn't have been pretending.

I undid my belt. "You're going to suck my dick. You're going to take the entire thing down your throat, and you're going to swallow whatever I give you. Is that what you're after?"

"I want to learn how to do it right."

"Don't worry about that. You're going to learn."

Opening my pants, I got my dick out. I was so hard it hurt. She knelt in front of me, knees in the dirt. When she laid her eyes on my cock, I thought I'd burst right there. I turned her chin upward.

"Open your mouth."

She did, just enough to fold the crease in her lower lip.

"So you know how to open your throat?"

"Ahh." She made the noise people made for the doctor.

I put two fingers on her tongue. "Press the back of your tongue down while doing that." I slid my fingers down her throat as far as I could.

Her eyes scrunched shut. Her stomach heaved twice.

"Hold it down," I said, and she got control of her gag reflex. "You really have been studying." I took my fingers out, letting her breathe.

"Thank you."

Why didn't I get the dirty talk? Why did Flow Prince or whatever get it and all I got were the innocent polychrome eyes?

"Tell me what you're going to do."

She opened her mouth and slapped it shut. "I..."

"Yes?"

"I'm going to suck your dick. I hope you like it."

I laughed. Who could help it? Her courtesy was disarming even when it made me question everything I'd seen on her screen. Even when she was holding me hostage.

"Assume I'll like it and say it again. Say it..." I paused, realizing the right way to approach it. "Say what you'd say if you were typing it and you couldn't see me."

She put her hands on the backs of my thighs, bringing me that much closer to her mouth. "I'm going to suck you until you come in my mouth."

"You know how a news reporter says things?"

"Am I too much like that?"

She was, but complaining would get me nowhere.

"Do this. Say it real seductive. Too seductive."

She tilted her head and puckered her lips, letting saccharine syrup mixed with heavy musk fall from them. "I'm going to suck your dick."

I held my laugh in the back of my throat. "Now do the news reporting with twenty percent of that second try."

"I'm pretty sure you know what I'm going to do already."

"You want to learn to do this or not?"

Deep breath. Eyes closed. She put her hand around the base of my cock and opened her eyes to look up at me. "Fuck my face, Taylor. Fuck it hard."

My dick throbbed in her hand, and for a moment, just a moment, I lost the ability to speak. I had to clear my throat before I responded. "Gold star."

"Yay."

Yay? Who made this woman? What cruel god put together the sweetest traits with this level of joyful filth? I'd never met anyone like her. I didn't know if I'd said that to myself before, but I was sure I'd say it again. She was a complete original.

"Put your lips at the tip."

She did what I told her.

"Lick the drop off. The tip and behind it, right here? That's the most sensitive part. Now put your hand around the base. Open. Say *ah* and press the back of your tongue down. Right. Breathe through your nose as long as you can. Open. Good."

I pushed her head down, and she bobbed on me. Fuck. I usually guided a girl and let her guide me, but this was ridiculously hot. She took every instruction, every correction, as if her job was at stake.

"Pull away when you need a break. Lick the sides and start again."

She did and took me deep again. A blade of hair stuck between her lips and my dick. I pulled it away and tucked it behind her ear. I could come in that hair. I could blow into her mouth the next time the wind blew the leaves down, but that would give her all the control, and I had something to prove.

I wanted information more than I wanted an orgasm.

"Put your hand around it." I nudged her head away, and she looked up at me with my dick in her fist. "The signal. How did it transmit?"

"You want to know now?"

"Now."

She rolled her eyes and licked the taste of my cock off her lips. "The poison pill transmitted to an object that went in and out of the cage. A little bit at a time. When the object was outside the cage, it transmitted to a Pwnie Express item in reception."

"We found it. The power strip."

"Right. It had a router in it." She held up two fingers to show me the miniscule size of the router. "It transmitted back to the object and brought information back. Once I figured out how to lock you out, and when *Wired* was coming, I told the Pwnie Express when to encrypt and how to decrypt, and it told the object." She moved closer, and I couldn't help but touch her face. She was a work of art. Her hack was as gorgeous as she was, and both made me angry and humbled at the same time. "The object went in and told your system what to do."

I stroked her cheek with my left hand and grabbed a fistful of hair with my right. "What's the object?"

She put her hand over my left wrist and held it. "Not yet." Defying the force of my hand, she pushed toward me, flicking her tongue over the head of my aching cock.

"Tell me, or I'm making you swallow."

She answered by opening her mouth, and I replied by fucking it.

"I'm going to come," I gasped. But I had to teach her, not just come in her mouth. "A guy should tell you. And you don't have to swallow for anyone else, but for me, because you won't tell me the… you take—"

Too late. I blew it all, and she took it. When I looked down, her face was knotted.

"Swallow."

She closed her mouth and swallowed, shaking her head like a puppy. "Ugh, I hope I can get used to that."

I ran my thumb along the corner of her mouth, wiping the moisture away. She was lovely. "Why would you have to? Who are you doing this for?"

"Myself."

"Really?"

She straightened her hair, and in the instant before she got on her feet, I felt her desire to answer fully and completely. Tell everything. A moment of weakness, maybe. Or I could have been misreading her.

By the time she stood, the moment was gone, and she was a hacker, a terrorist, my captor, and she was withholding information I needed.

"The decryption code." I put my dick back in my pants. It was still sensitive.

She folded her bottom lip, deep in thought. I waited. Zipped. Buttoned. Tucked.

I didn't want to be too transactional. I didn't want to come in her mouth and ask for payment. Maybe I was a bigger pussy than I thought. She was the one who had turned a blow job into a negotiation.

"I didn't expect you to come here," she finally said.

"And?" I fastened my belt. Was my voice hard? Sharp? Too bad. This was business.

"I need to generate it. Let's get back."

We got in the car, and she took off, eating road like a whale eats krill.

"We skipped a hand job," I said. "We need to go back and get that done."

She perked up. "You're halfway there."

"Yeah."

She was right. I was halfway. The point of no return. Too far away from home to quit and too much a stranger in Barrington for comfort.

XXXI

When we got back, she ran upstairs without a "give me a minute" or a "wait here." I was like a piece of furniture in a furniture-bare house. My fingers twitched. I wanted to talk to Deepak, touch that old life, connect to the person I knew I was. Even if it meant being reminded of my failure to protect my work, I wanted to be the person I'd spent a decade building.

I made coffee and brought up two mugs.

Harper's door at the top of the stairs was open. Was it an invitation?

"Harper?" I put my foot on the bottom step.

She appeared in the doorway above me. "You were in here."

"I was."

"Like what you saw?"

Was she talking about breaking into her room? Or opening her computers? Or seeing her notebook?

"Maybe."

"Coming up here is cheating."

I took a step up and put my next foot above. "Really? You didn't tell me that."

"I shouldn't have to. I can't let this slide."

"What does that mean?" I could smell her. Smell the room. Feel the pressure of her presence on my dick. I put the cups on the bottom step and started up to her.

"You're going to forfeit getting the decryption today."

"What?" I froze halfway up.

"Play fair."

"I do. You—"

I had some choice words for her as I bounded up the rest of the stairs. Just as I got to the top, she slammed the door in my face. The lock clapped shut.

"Do not fuck with me, Taylor." The door muffled her voice. She was right on the other side. Inches away.

"I'm a hacker. I hack. I get into things. You can't put this door at the top of the stairs and think for a minute I'm not going to come up here."

"What did you see?"

I didn't want her to know. I had no idea what kind of leverage I had, and until I did, I wasn't telling her anything. "Your room. Again."

"And?"

How much was I willing to give? "The elastic on your panties is wearing out."

"What *else*, Taylor? Do not even think of lying to me."

Do not even think of lying to me? Who fell back on that?

Someone who was fishing, that was who. I was the one with leverage. She had no idea what I'd seen, and she wanted me to tell her.

And the fact was she wanted something from me that I didn't have to give her. So she could hang on to the Harperware decryption for now. At some point, she was going to want me to teach her something else.

"If you need me," I said, stepping down one, "I'll be around."

I hopped down the stairs without hearing a reply.

XXXII

I looked over the balcony at the thorn bed. My phone didn't light up, and I didn't hear it. Even if I got it out of that mess, it would be useless.

I went through the other doors, to the master suite. Flicking the light on, I craned my neck to look at the ceiling mural with its vignette of pink flowers. It looked Victorian enough, but in the lines, I could see a touch of 1980s.

Catherine came to the doorway with a tray. "You didn't come down to dinner."

"I forgot. Sorry."

"Barnard came by to see how you were getting on."

"Barnard?"

"A large gentleman." There were no tables. She put the tray on the floor. "Fuzzy hair."

"Butthead?"

"If you must."

Well, I'd certainly stepped in it. That was what I got for not asking his real name.

"And Orrin called. He said to tell you the battery's coming in the morning. Your car will be ready."

A car. So simple, yet… everything. A car equaled an option. I'd been short on options until just then.

Catherine pulled her cardigan around herself. "We never fixed this room because I didn't want the ceiling ruined."

"You can fix the mycelium without ruining the ceiling. It's tin."

She looked at it dreamily. Harper was her exact opposite. Catherine had rounded edges and a soft voice. Her sister's edges were going to gut me.

"This was my room," she said. "Daddy gave it to me when he and Mother moved to separate rooms. Those flowers? He had them put in for me when I was having a hard time. Look, over here." She pointed toward a dim corner.

I looked at what she told me but didn't see what she saw.

"Those open roses with the leaves up like that? In a V?" she said.

"Yes. It's…" Weird? Off? Not flower-like?

"That's Harper."

I got up on tiptoes as if the extra two inches would help.

"She was always running around," Catherine continued.

I could see it when I stopped trying to make it a flower in my head. The petals of the rose next to her made a skirt that flowed in the wind, and the beige center of the flower was a little girl's face. The more I looked at it, the more it looked like Harper.

"And I was always trying to get her to stay still and read or pay attention or do anything."

The leaves of the rose next to Harper were around her sister, and looking at it, squinting, I saw Catherine's face in the details. She stopped looking up, and I did as well. We regarded each other in the yellow light.

"A lot of things happened in this room. A lot of tears under these flowers," she said.

"I know why you don't want it ruined."

"Do I bother you at night? People say they can hear me cry all over the house."

"I haven't heard it," I lied.

"I keep saying I'll stop."

"It's your house."

"I'm not upset about not having anything left. Or the conditions I live in, compared to what it was. I wish I'd lost it all sooner."

"Why?"

"The thing about money, Mr. Harden, is that it burdens you with expectations. You get this impression that everything you do matters to other people. And it's not true. Everything doesn't matter. Only some things matter, and those things have to be attended. But the rest?" She shook her head. "I'm being cryptic. I loved a boy who didn't have any money. My parents, and this was the only thing they ever agreed on, they found this unacceptable. He disappeared."

"Is he alive?"

She shrugged. "I don't know. My father had the ceiling done to cheer me up."

I smiled. I couldn't help it. The irony was unavoidable.

Catherine saw it too. She smiled and waved as if swatting the entire thing away. "I should have taken it down, but I still like it."

"You're a masochist."

"I am. Now. Your soup is getting cold. When you're done, leave the tray in the hall."

"I can—"

"No arguments."

I tried to argue anyway, but she left with a wave.

I didn't eat much. My brain was calculating.

I wasn't halfway home. Not without the second decryption code. Was it easier for me to get the Caddy, go back to California, and deal with my shit? If she wasn't going to shell out what she'd promised, I didn't have to hang around and provide services.

And the ability to leave gave me leverage. I could leave, or I could stay, depending on whether or not she produced the decryption code.

But I was leaving.

The decision to go back to the familiar calmed me until I fell asleep.

XXXIII

In the morning, Harper was nowhere to be found. There wasn't a peep from behind the locked door, but there was a new lock. As if that could stop me.

I'd pick it when I had something to look for in there. I'd pick it so hard it would blow out the jamb.

Catherine was AWOL. Everyone was. The house was cold and empty. I made myself a peanut butter and jelly sandwich and looked out the back window, onto the thorn garden.

A dog barked from the front. I shoved the last bite in my mouth and met Percy on the porch. Orrin got out of his truck.

"Found you," he said. "Your phone's dead."

"Yeah. I know."

"Harper said you were sleeping."

Percy licked my fingers then stuck his nose in my ass.

I pulled him away and stroked his neck. "Where is she?"

"Over at the glass works." He pointed toward the backyard and over the horizon.

It didn't matter where she was anyway. Not at all.

"I'll get my stuff," I said. "And I'll get the car out of your shop right away."

"Came to tell you about the car. The battery was four hundred dollars."

"No problem, I—"

"Then the damn rental car company came and towed it. I didn't have a chance to even get the battery out of the box. And I can't return it. Fucking *policies*."

I was cut off from another route the fuck out of Barrington, and this dude was worried about a few hundred bucks. "I need a ride to the airport. I'll give you the four hundred for the battery and another four hundred for the lift."

Percy barked as if he thought it was a great deal.

"I gotta open up the shop."

"Later, then." Maybe I sounded desperate. I didn't care.

"Might be able to get you a ride tomorrow. Everyone's over at the works, scrubbing down for Fitz. Word is he's coming around to look into buying the works building."

Harper had mentioned him a million years ago, on the roof of that same factory. I knew him I could call him up and tell him the citizens of Barrington were good people but shithouse crazy, if I had a phone.

"I have to go." I'd already turned back toward the house. I was distracted. My brain was sorting through puzzle pieces. Harper. Fitz. Barrington. QI4. *Silicon Valley Magazine*'s "Most Eligible Tycoon of the Year."

"I'll come around tomorrow," Orrin called behind me.

"Sure." I didn't know if he heard my mumbling. Nothing was clicking, but I knew the pieces fit.

I went right through the house and upstairs to pack.

Past the river reeds, maybe a quarter mile back, I could see the top of the factory. Men were up there, five, maybe six, moving in and out of sight. They weren't meandering or fucking around. They had a purpose to their movements.

I went back up to my room, which had a better angle on the factory. The people on the roof moved slowly, bent down, got up. Harper had spray painted code lines up there. A coded message that put me on notice. I was going to be humiliated.

I smiled. I couldn't help it. Fuck her. I wasn't giving her an inch I didn't have to. I was going to get my fucking boot decryption and be done with her.

A female form walked onto the roof. Long, wavy hair, too far away to discern blond from brunette, but her arm went up and touched her face. I could see her, in my mind's eye, folding the crease in her bottom lip.

XXXIV

The factory wasn't far as the crow flew. I had no idea how to get across the river or what other manmade barriers were between the Barrington mansion and Barrington Glass Works. Without satellite or GPS, there was only one way to find out.

Past the bed of thorns, patches of pines huddled amidst a grass flat. From above, I hadn't noticed how well tended they were, with moats of dirt around the base of each trunk. Spring birds chirped. Cicadas screeched. The sky above was a huge dome broken by the receding mansion and the trees I passed. I came to the tall reeds, which were taller than they'd looked from above. A dirt path opened up, and the sound of the trickling river joined the sounds of birds and insects behind me.

There was a smell. A not very river-ish smell. The reeds closed around the path until it was a foot wide, then it crooked hard right, then hard left, onto a wooden bridge.

The river was the source of the smell. I pulled my hood around to my face and covered my nose. A white sign on a rusted chain swung across the entrance to the bridge.

CONTAMINATION ADVISORY

Avoid contact with soil and river sediment. Use soap and water to wash river water and sediment off skin completely.
United States Environmental Protection Agency.

I wasn't going back to the mansion. Fuck that. I went under the chain and crossed. The bridge itself was on concrete pilings, and the whole thing was in pretty good shape. The painted metal rail was worn at the top where people would put their hands, but I kept my hands in my pockets. The wood boards creaked but were solid enough.

The river looked like any other river, not that I'd seen hundreds. The water wasn't brown, and there wasn't a ton of garbage floating in it. The reeds grew tall. A weeping willow bent over the stream on the other side. The tree didn't look good. Otherwise, there was just the smell.

A four-foot-wide corrugated metal pipe ended at the shore. It was dry inside. Whatever had flowed from the factory into the river no longer flowed, but the toxicity remained.

I ducked under the chain barrier on the other side. It had the same contamination warning.

So much for that.

The factory was in my sightline. The graffiti had been reduced to no more than a tinge of color. Some was a light blue wash that matched Harper's fingernails from a few days before. Cars were parked on both sides of the chain link, and the gate was open. Huge twenty-foot dumpsters were lined up against the walls. I jumped when glass crashed from inside one.

A man waved to me from a window-sized opening on the third floor. "Sorry!"

I waved back and went in the same door Harper and I had used last time.

Where there had been desolation before, the place was abuzz the second time. People everywhere. Talking in groups, pushing brooms, dragging black plastic bags, wiping down the walls. I waved to Reggie and Kyle, who were throwing garbage out the window, then I ran up the stairs, two at a time, to where I'd last seen Harper's figure against the sky.

She pushed a broom across the roof, moving red-stained liquid into the drain. She stopped, moved the broom quickly over an area to scrub, then pushed again.

"You're too good to push a broom all day."

"Wrong." She didn't look at me. "No one's too good to push a broom."

She swept hard, sending a wave of frothy red water away. The semicircle right behind the broom was bare for a split second, and I could see how much her work had faded.

I was in her way. The red water lapped against my shoes. They'd be ruined. She pushed the bristles against my toes, and still, I didn't budge.

"Taylor." She leaned on the handle.

"What?" I crossed my arms.

"You're in the way of the drain."

"I'm leaving today."

She tapped the bristles on the tar, keeping her eyes on the little red splashes. "How?"

"I can still get a cab. I can get a lift. I can walk thirty miles to the next train station. You can have one of these guys tie me down. I know at least some of them are in on it. I don't know who, but it doesn't matter. You're trying to brainwash me for when Fitz shows. I don't know if you're going to play on our relationship or try to get in his jock. But I'm out. I have enough problems. I'll get past your lockdown on my own."

She leaned on the handle again, finally making eye contact. "It's just a mess in here."

"Who'd buy it in this condition? Not a guy like Fitz. He's an OCD case about business. He'd only buy a spotless factory in a spotless town."

"So? We read up. We're smarter than we get credit for."

"Good on you. You don't need me anymore." I got out of her way and headed for the door.

"I don't want to sell QI4," she said, and I had to stop to listen to the rest. She knew how to keep me, that was for sure. "It's wrong to sell it." She kept sweeping. "It's one thing to lock it and make you pay to unlock it, but selling it to someone else is just wrong. But I will. I can get a lot of money for it."

Keeping cool was probably the hardest thing I'd ever done. I could barely stand the thought of my code being inaccessible. The thought of it going to someone else made my hands hot. "You do what you have to."

"Bummer though."

"You're going to have to figure out the 'maintenance' part that's so important to you."

"You're bluffing."

She was in control. I'd forgotten that as a kind of survival instinct, but when she reminded me, I was hell-bent on not showing her how much it bothered me.

"Maybe. But you're in a world of shit yourself." The bite in my voice didn't make me sound tough. It sounded like overcompensation. A presentation of aggression from a man with no power. If I'd felt in control coming across the river, I didn't on the factory roof.

"If you finish the job with me, you'll get your system back."

"You already broke one promise."

The last of the red water went down the drain. On the west side of the building, old furniture and garbage crashed to the ground amid the grunts and shouts of the men hauling it out.

"I don't know why I'm here," I said. "I don't understand what you want or why. Why the sexual favors?"

She picked up a heavy bucket that sloshed when lifted. "They're for me, okay? Everything I told you is true. The reasons you were brought here. All true. But the sex stuff?" She went to another patch of graffiti on the ground and plopped the bucket down. "That's for me. I got everything I could out of online bullshit. Stupid dirty talk with strangers. I'm done with it. So yeah, there's a little revenge in there, but that's the deal."

"You know, when you lie, your nose looks like it points up a little more."

She dunked the broom in the bucket and scrubbed the spray paint. "Stay or leave. Let me know what you decide."

She gave no guarantees, no promises, offering around a deal so ambiguous and unenforceable I didn't know where I stood from one minute to the next. I couldn't measure her. She was movement, not mass. All options and potentialities, but no answers.

The sky over the roof was a dome of clear blue, like a ceiling with limits. It promised that if you went high enough, you'd touch it. It lied. It was an illusion of the finite.

I got off the roof before it pressed me into a dot.

XXXV

"**Y**ou know what they're doing to you? They're setting you up. They're telling you your life might be shit, but at least you're not him. And you, they're telling you he's out to get you. And you two fucking idiots believe it."

I heard Johnny's voice echo through the second floor as I came down the metal steps. He had a hand on a shovel by a pile of debris, and the other hand pointed at one of the Hispanic dudes I'd seen at the lunch area, while he yelled at a guy with a yellow bandana.

"I'm so sick of your paranoid bullshit." Bandana pushed Johnny's shoulder. I'd met him the same night I'd met Johnny, but his name escaped me.

"Who benefits? Ask yourself." Johnny was undeterred. "You? Have you benefitted one bit from thinking you're better than Florencio?" He pointed at the Hispanic dude. "Cos when you do that, he's not gonna rise up with you and crush them fuckers at the bank. He's gonna come against you. You dumb shits are too busy fighting between yourselves to fight together."

"I can't stand this *pendejo*." Florencio grabbed a broom that had fallen on the floor and got to sweeping. "But you're worse."

"You!" Johnny pointed at me.

"What?"

"When you rich fucks talk to banks, you talk about this shit, right? Don't fucking lie."

"No. We just talk about money." I got close enough to see his wrist. My watch sat on it like a twenty-thousand-dollar game of nine ball. Johnny's tattoos were all gears and numbers. I got the feeling he'd known exactly what it was worth when he'd made the bet. Seeing him wear it bothered me. "Nice watch."

"They're out for us." Johnny turned his full attention to me. Bandana flipped him off and dragged his bag to the window. "Make us fight so they can take the spoils."

"You know you're crazy, right?"

"Sure, I'm crazy. Seeing what I've seen will make you that way. They have all the money, but if we worked together, they couldn't stand against us. This 'anyone can make it' bag of shit they sell us keeps us complacent. Makes us blame ourselves. Bullshit. Pure bullshit. Ask anyone here. All worked hard. Now we can't see a doctor. Can't drink the water. Can't give the kids an education. Don't tell us we didn't work hard, and we're not the only ones. And once you see it? Once you see what happened to us, you start to think, oh my God, is that what they been doing to black people this whole time? And yeah. Shit changes, and you go fucking crazy." He pushed his shovel. The debris was heavy, and he put his weight behind it. "Now we're cleaning up for—"

He lurched back, crying out in pain and dropping his shovel.

"Johnny!"

"My back!" He fell to one knee, hand just above his butt. "God damn it!"

I caught him, but there wasn't much I could do.

"Oh, for the love of fuck, John-boy!" Kyle came out of the woodwork and held up his friend. "This is your lazy ass."

"Help me over to the steps."

We guided him over as he grunted and winced the entire way. A woman ran over to help.

"Johnny, you done it again." She had the exhausted impatience of a woman who'd committed herself to a real pain in the ass.

"I'm fine," he complained.

We put him on the step. It was the only place to sit.

"Take it easy," the woman said. "We can't afford you to miss work."

Kyle pulled off his hat and scratched his scalp. "If we want to paint this floor on Saturday, we gotta clean it up today."

"I'll shovel his shit," I said.

"No, no, no," Johnny protested.

"Yes, yes, yes," Kyle said. "Be a nice break from your ranting and raving."

"I'll carry my own weight." Johnny started to get up, but he cringed and flopped back down.

"I tell you what," I said. "I shovel your shit, and you give me back my watch."

He shrugged and shook his wrist as if he really liked my watch and didn't want to give it up.

"Oh," the woman said. "This is your watch?"

"It's mine now," Johnny said. "And California here won't last an hour doing actual work."

I picked up his shovel. "I'm Taylor. This is my watch. And my back's in great shape."

"I'm Pat," the woman said. "Shovel for my husband, would you? He doesn't need another watch. He only has two wrists."

I nodded to her and turned to Kyle. "What are we doing?"

Kyle showed me the piles of shit and where they went. Then I spent the morning pushing garbage across the floor, into bags, and down the chute. Someone brought music. Fights broke out over "angry white guys screaming," "your bumpkin bullshit," and "taco Tuesday tunes." No one seemed to get deeply offended, but the insults flowed equally between everyone. They were joined by a common goal—seduce Everett Fitzgerald with a spiffy factory.

I didn't think Fitz would be moved by a clean floor as much as a cost-effective deal, but it wasn't my job to save them from disappointment. I didn't say much because breathing was hard enough. Shit was heavy, and I had a point to prove. I didn't have the energy to spare on anyone's musical taste.

By the time lunch was announced, I was a mess of sweat and I smelled like a landfill. Card tables and grills had been set out in the parking lot with ceviche, burgers, asada, and hot dogs. Children ran underfoot in a never-ending game of tag.

"Get away from the river!" Catherine roared at one of them, her gentleness turned to fire.

The kid in question froze then spun away from the tall reeds.

"She's got a wild animal inside her," I said to Harper, who had just straddled the bench next to me with a plate of tacos.

"Yeah. With the kids especially."

"Thought you were over tacos?"

"I changed my mind." She tilted her head to get a taco to her lips. Hair dropped over her cheek and threatened to dive bomb into her lunch.

I flicked it back and over her ear. She had the taco in her mouth when her eyes went a little wider in surprise. The gesture was too intimate. I knew it before I got the hair all the way over.

Harper wasn't the only one looking at me as if I'd just shit my pants. I couldn't swear every single eye was on me, but Catherine and Johnny, who was flat on his back in the bed of his truck, had their heads tilted our way.

"Sorry."

She spoke around her chewing. "I'm sorry, actually."

"Really?"

The afternoon wind was picking up, and she pulled another lock of hair out of her mouth before I could.

"Yeah. We have a deal. You put out, and I didn't pay up."

"Way to make a guy feel like a whore."

She shrugged. "You'll live."

"Well, I'm sorry I broke into your room… but not really."

"You know the saying about the snake?"

"The one that bites you because… what did you expect? It's a fucking snake?"

"That one." She faced into the wind, blowing her hair away from her face.

I took the last bite of hamburger. A triangle of tomato fell out and landed on my shirt. Harper took a napkin out of her pocket and wiped me.

"Stop." I took the napkin. "This is the cleanest thing that's touched this shirt all day."

She smiled, chewing a wad of taco in one side of her mouth. She had a charming, unself-conscious efficiency about the way she chewed her food and spoke volumes with her expression at the same time. She was an open book written in a code I was just starting to understand.

I could have watched her eat for a long time, but a cry came out from the second floor.

"Barrington ladies!" It was Damon, who I'd seen in passing by the dumpsters. His tattooed arms leaned on a second-floor ledge, and the sun made two reflective dots on his sunglasses.

Harper shaded her eyes and turned his way. Her body was curved to click into what mine wanted. It was like math. Only exact figures balanced the equation.

"What?" she called.

"The office is locked," Damon shouted.

"So?"

"Did Daddy give you the key?"

The word *daddy* had a venom I hadn't heard all day. It burned with acidic meaning and was thick with leisurely intent, yet it was subtle enough to pretend you didn't hear it.

"I'll be right up!" Catherine called back. She was as sweet as always but with an edge of impatience, as if she was telling Damon not to fuck with her.

Harper sighed as Catherine walked away with a ring of keys. "I'd better go too." To me, she said, "You finish eating."

When she walked away, her ass swayed and her hair flew in every direction. With her curves and the way she moved them, I had no choice but to follow. I could eat later.

XXXVI

*H*acking real life was at least as good as finding weaknesses in code. Once Keaton and I had learned how to pick a lock, opening doors became as much of an addiction as building profiles. We'd find a single piece of information about a person, tack it onto another piece we found on a Tor site, grab a birthday from social media, uncover an address from the mortgage rolls. We skimmed just enough to not get caught, only buying things where our marks bought things. I didn't excuse it. I knew it was wrong, but I did it anyway.

Until the pure code hacks, which were sexier, more difficult, and got the most esteem from the boys in the hacker forums.

I hacked my dad first but didn't take anything. The pure rush was being able to do it. I had power over him. In retrospect, that moment where I looked at his bank account without him knowing was the moment I became a man.

Life was a problem to be hacked. It was never about money. It felt good.

As soon as I saw Catherine struggling with the dozens of keys on the ring, I wanted to cut the shit and hack the problem. But Damon, Harper, two other guys, and myself just watched, quickly alternating between impatience, anticipation, hope, and disappointment, in that order.

I knew the lock, and I knew the type of key. It would be a Kwikset with the three triangle cutouts on top. But she went through every single one.

"Come on, princess." Damon's face was clammy, and he kept rubbing his hands on his jeans.

"Hang on." Catherine isolated a silver key. The last one, and it was a Kwikset.

Anticipation, hope, impatience, disappointment as the key didn't turn the lock.

She dropped the ring.

"You are so useless." Damon scooped up the keys and gave them to her.

I didn't know Catherine, but I wanted to punch Damon.

Harper snapped at him before I could react. "There're no loose Fentanyl bottles in there, if that's what you're after."

"Fuck you, you rich little cunt. You don't know shit about—"

He had me at *cunt*. I had the advantage of surprise, pushing my forearm against his throat and his head against the dirty wall. "What did you say?"

The pressure on his esophagus didn't temper his hostility, which was fine with me. I wasn't ready for the apology Harper deserved.

"Who the fuck are you?"

"Taylor." Harper's voice, behind me. Far, far away.

"Don't talk to her like that."

He pushed me hard against the opposite wall.

"Damon!" Catherine, miles away.

"You push a broom and think you're one of us?"

In a split second, Damon and I were locked hand-to-face-to-shoulder-knee-in-stomach-defense-offense-defense-offense. He had worked with his body his whole life, putting me at a disadvantage, but he wasn't just fighting me. He was fighting whatever made him sweaty and shaky.

Damon's friend, whose name I never learned, just lit a cigarette. Catherine and Harper worked as a team, splitting us. I wound up against the wall with Harper's hand on my chest.

I pointed over her shoulder at Damon. "I'll pick this lock if you leave now."

"You pick the lock?" Damon sneered. "Bullshit."

"Get out of here," I sneered back.

"I get it. Money sticks to money. Fine. Fuck it. Pick the fucking lock."

"Just wanted to mop the fucking floor." Damon's friend regarded the tip of his cigarette then flicked off the ash.

I held my hand out for the keys. Catherine dropped them into my palm. I flicked through the club member cards, snapped the thickest one into the right shape, and was in the office in thirty seconds. There was nothing but an overturned desk and empty shelves. Huge windows looked out onto the halfway-clean factory floor.

I stepped out of the way and let Cigarette Man kick his wheeled yellow bucket through the doorway. Damon made a point to brush against me on the way out.

I almost shoved him, but Harper vise-gripped my arm. I snapped out of it.

"You dropped a bunch of stuff." She pointed toward the hall floor.

I picked up my wallet, a pen, and the napkin she'd used to wipe tomato off my shirt. It had fallen open, revealing a row of numbers written in marker.

"You really should pay better attention," she said softly. "You almost threw it away. And I wasn't writing it again."

"Thank you."

"It's—"

"I need your phone again."

She handed me the black rectangle. When it hit my hand, it woke up. I saw the wallpaper. Harper from just below, with her blowing hair, indecisive eyes, and the factory outlined against the blue sky behind her. She looked powerful, confident, the muse for a revolution.

"Oh, the code." She took the phone and hit the glass with her thumb. "Here."

She handed it to me, the photo safely tucked behind the keypad screen.

I wasn't scared. Not that. But something closer to freaked out.

And not at her.

At myself. At how easily I handled her power over me and how badly I wanted her at the same time.

"I'll use the one in the house."

"Suit yourself."

I kissed her without thinking then ran, but I had to make a stop at the lunch tables first.

XXXVII

Kyle scrubbed down the grill with a wire brush as everyone packed up the paper plates and leftover food.

"Kyle, I need you to watch Harper." I told him what had happened with Damon outside the office.

"Saw him leave a minute ago. Probably getting a fix. But I'll keep an eye on her."

"Thank you."

I ran back to the house, pounding over the bridge, through the reeds, past the thorn garden, napkin crumpled in my hand, until I got to the kitchen, which looked like a culinary bomb had hit it. This must have been lunch central. I picked up the receiver and stared at the clear plastic circle.

What was Deepak's number?

My grandmother had made fun of me one Christmas because I didn't know any of the numbers in my phone. She then recited every number she'd ever learned. By the end of dinner, we were singing the number my mother grew up with. Grandma still lived there.

I dialed. It took forever.

"Hello?"

"Grandma?" She was pretty deaf. I had to yell. "Hi, it's—"

"Taylor?"

"Yes. Do you—"

"What are you doing all the way out there?"

"What? I—"

"The caller ID says you're—"

"Gram. Do you have my work number?"

That's right. I didn't even know my office number.

"Do you know you're on the news?"

I was on the news? I wasn't much of a news watcher and usually picked up what was happening by following media on Twitter. I hadn't seen a TV in the house, and when I'd seen one in the bar, it had been on sports. So, no, I didn't know I was on the news.

"What are they saying?"

"Your computers didn't work."

"They work, Grandma."

"And you disappeared. Your partner. The Indian—"

"He's from Bangladesh." Why did I bother correcting my grandmother? She was close to eighty. She needed to be happy more than she needed to be correct.

"He was on *Morning Joe*. He said you were fixing it, but Maria Bardono didn't believe him. Said you were running away with everyone's money. Said you were a criminal. And I said, that's the last time I watch you, Mr. Morning Joe. My grandson is no thief!"

She was sweet and loyal, but I'd been a prolific thief and digital trespasser since before her dotage.

"When did they say that?"

"Yesterday. But today Joe had a different guy on. Said you fixed it. I liked him, this second guy. Real handsome. Had a nice confidence on him and an English accent."

She had a short memory for boycotts and a sharp eye for authority.

"Was it Keaton? The second guy? Keaton from Poly? Do you remember him?"

"Oh, I remember that boy. Could be. The tall one, right? Are you coming back here? Or going to California? Roger from the deli usually saves me the pig's feet if you want me to make them."

"I don't think I can."

"Just tell me if you're coming."

Talking to Grandma had always been a commitment of time and patience. I was short on both.

"I will. Do you have my work number?"

"Your what?"

"My work number. I know. You were right. But—"

"You always ate them when you were little. You were the only one."

"I know. I'll come see you, Gram. Do you have—"

"It's just pork, I said a hundred times. You believed me."

"I did. And you were right. Do you—"

"Give me a minute. I'm getting the book out. I'll have Roger save them for you. He gets a side of pork second Tuesday of the month."

I banged my head on the doorway molding.

"Just tell me ahead, or that bitch on Chestnut gets them," she said.

"Okay."

"All right. Let me look. These letters get smaller all the time. B. E. G. Harden is H. H. H. Here you are."

She read off the number. I snapped a pencil from a busted mug and wrote it on the wall.

"Thanks, Gram. I'll come visit. I promise."

"You better. I'm going to be dead soon, you know."

"You have another twenty years. Easy."

"Maybe, you little shit." She said it with an abundance of affection and humor. "Maybe."

We said our good-byes, I made promises I intended to keep if I ever got out of the middle of nowhere, and I hung up. I dialed the front desk at QI4. I should have been able to get Deepak's extension right away, but naturally there wasn't a touchpad. So I had to wait until a receptionist picked up. Then I had to identify myself, prove it, and growl like a lion before they'd give me Deepak.

"Where have you been?" he asked right away.

"Shithole, USA, with no phone. Do not ask."

Calling the middle parts of the country a shithole was as natural as pissing standing up. Until that moment. In the shitholiest kitchen in Shithole, USA, I stopped feeling a fundamental truth in the word. The people here were all right, and they were mopping a factory floor to keep the town alive. That said a lot about the place. I was going to take that back—but not now. I read the code to Deepak.

KDQwOCkgNTU1LTEyMjY=

"I'll head down to the cage," he said. "This is base64. Did you translate it?"

I hadn't even thought to look at how it would translate. "In my head? No." I searched for something to write on besides the wall. "I'll do it on a piece of paper if you can't."

"Hang on. I'll do it on my phone."

I heard the sounds of the office as Deepak walked through it. Ronald's loud conversations about "this girl gamer on Twitch." The hiss of the servers. The bird soundtrack in the hallway. The universal *ding* of the elevator.

I felt something I didn't recognize at first because I'd never felt it before, but when the elevator doors in my office whooshed closed for Deepak, I realized what it was: I was homesick.

Deepak laughed and got back on the phone. "You know what it is?"

"What?"

I heard the elevator doors open.

"Our phone number." Deepak rattled off a string of Bengali when the ID pad asked for his name.

"She's such a fucking card," I mumbled as if I was annoyed, but the truth was she was being thoughtful. She knew I couldn't get my phone. She knew I'd have to use a landline. She knew I wouldn't have shit memorized. So she gave it to me, knowing that I'd be able to scratch out the answer but not knowing I was in too much of a hurry to do it.

"She?" He interrupted my warm feelings. His chair squeaked, and computer keys clicked against the muted stillness of the cage. "Is it Harper Watson?"

"Who? No."

Yes, but no. He wasn't allowed to know about her yet. I didn't want her accused, and I didn't want Keaton flying his ass out here to torment her or scoop her up. Nope. I wanted her to myself. She was mine. All mine.

That makes no sense.

"Jack checked on her. Did you know we interviewed her?"

"For what?"

"The cage. To replace Walter."

My skin tingled. My breath stopped. My brain went into complete shutdown while I tried to remember every woman we'd interviewed.

I couldn't recall a single one.

But how many had been that hot? You'd think my dick would at least have a little recollection.

"I'd remember."

"You were looking at your phone the entire time, but sure. You might remember her score on the coding test though."

The test was a beast, and my guys in the cage were the best. None of them had scored under ninety percent.

"What was it?"

"Perfect. But, your dick."

Was that true? Had I forgotten a perfect score? I mean, yes, I didn't hire women. Very few small operations did. When I was as big as Google, I'd take the risk. Until then, I couldn't afford a lawsuit or an HR debacle. Couldn't deal with a work slowdown when we were hosed constantly. And the guys in the cage? We didn't have a pill to manage the awkward social reflux.

"What the hell was Keaton doing on TV?" I asked, changing the subject. A group must have gathered around Deepak. I could hear the guys goofing off.

"He called off the Oracle meeting. Someone traced the blockchain and yada yada—he was unmasked." *Tap tappa* of keys. "Why can't we get you on video?"

"I'm on a landline. And bullshit. He wanted to be unmasked."

A group cheer went up from the other side of the line.

"It's up!" Deepak shouted. "'Enter decryption code to boot OS.' Like a boss."

"Two more," I said quietly.

I was in two worlds, thinking with two minds. The feel of her body and the comfort of my real life. Getting between her and Damon because she needed me. A way in. A path I was unreasonably afraid of losing.

But I didn't know her. I only felt her in places I hadn't thought I had. I didn't know why she was doing what she was doing. Why she kept me here. Why she wanted me to teach her the fine art of fucking. If she just wanted vengeance for not getting a job, she would have stolen my system and sold the decryption keys to the highest bidder. So there was something more.

And Keaton was making a move. He was loyal and trustworthy, but not always in the way you expected. He'd be the first to do some damage to QI4 in the service of what he thought was the greater good. He'd act unilaterally and inflexibly.

I'd gotten mono in high school. Worst three weeks of my life. While I was laid up, some script kiddie trying to make points doxxed my personal email, address, name, and birthday. His name was Nelson, and he'd gotten the info simply. He knew me personally and just posted shit from the school directory as if he'd cracked my ID.

Turned out that, besides making points, Nelson was a little twisted out. His girlfriend had mono too. She'd given it to me. Or I'd given it to her. We'd never know who had it first.

Once Keaton found who doxxed me, he erased Nelson's ID from the face of the dark web and wiped out his parents' bank accounts, all while I couldn't get out of bed.

I wouldn't have done that, but Keaton wouldn't undo it. He was Alpha Wolf, and his decisions were not under review. A hacker was only as good as people's fears, and if he let shit slide under his watch, he had no way of maintaining respect.

What was he after now? Why was he coming out of his shell? I wasn't there to tell him to stop or to plead for Harper. I was laid up in Barrington with an analog illness, and Keaton was home and assuming we'd been attacked by a hostile entity.

And weren't we?

Wasn't Harper just another bad actor after an exploit?

Why did she deserve anything less than the most painful response? She'd publicly humiliated us, and she needed to be dealt with. Anything less would be a show of weakness.

I jumped when the phone rang. Not with the usual long rings you hear in old movies. This was a quick European *bring-bring* with pauses between.

Back when phone phreaking was a thing, changing the ring was a fun trick to pull.

Ha-ha.

I picked up the handset. "Keaton."

He was in what sounded like a crowded restaurant. "Hello, Beez."

"Dude. You're pulling call data from the office?"

"You're calling from a landline. How convenient."

Convenient because the location wasn't cloaked. Was I being stupid or subliminally intentional?

"Listen to me," I said.

"No. You listen to me."

I would not be shut down. Not after all the work I'd put in. Not after coming this far. But the back door opened behind me, and a gaggle of women entered with groceries. They were chatting, laughing, plopping bags on the counter.

"Barrington?" he said, having tracked down the phone number in five seconds. Fuck.

Catherine patted my cheek then kissed it. "Hello, Taylor."

"Thank you for helping!" Juanita kissed my cheek too.

I was sure Keaton could hear it. Shit, this was embarrassing. Mrs. Boden gave me a wet one. If Harper came and kissed me on the mouth, I was never going to get Keaton to look me in the eye again.

But she wasn't with them, which was strange.

"What the hell is going on over there?" Keaton asked.

I went into the dining room, stretching the cord around two doorways until the coil was pulled straight. "I don't know what you have planned, but you have to run it by me first."

"You're a non-actor as far as I'm concerned. You're taking too long. Did you find him?"

"I did. I'm getting it unlocked. Just—"

I was met with rage.

"You're *asking* for decryption? Waiting for it? Like a patsy. Like a *n00b*. No. We don't wait. We take. This is what you never got. We take what we want and destroy people who get in our way."

"Keaton, I have this."

"So do I."

"How? Can you tell me how?"

"I don't work for you."

That was true. It had been made clear at the outset. Money flowed at his discretion. We weren't partners, but I wasn't the boss either. And now that he had physical access to the cage, it was too late to cut him off.

"I'm not saying you need my permission. I'm querying the exploit," I said.

I heard a car door slam on his end. A luxurious *thup* that shut out noise from the street. "Someone in this company brought a device into and out of the cage. Yes?"

"Yes. It communicated with a loaded power strip in reception."

"Did you find out who it is?"

"No."

"Once I find out, I'm going to grind them under my heel. Then I'm going to make it easy for both of us. You're going to destroy the man who tried to destroy us, then Barrington is going to be thrust into the dark ages."

He didn't have to tell me the gory details. Revenge and chaos were what he did. That was the kind of person he knew. His family's friends broke things for a living. He could fry the power plant, the water supply, or the sewer filtration without breaking a sweat. He didn't have to touch Harper to do it.

"What if I get the codes before you start breaking shit?" I didn't know why it mattered to me that he didn't destroy Barrington, but it did.

"At the rate you're going?"

"You find the mole there. I'll take care of shit here. Like a team."

"Get me the codes. All of them. Until you do, I'm going to protect you. I'm going to do what you won't do yourself."

Could I warn Harper? Would it matter? Without knowing his plan, what would I warn her about?

Why was I setting myself against my entire life to protect her?

"Fine."

I was about to walk back to the kitchen to hang up, but Keaton said, "Taylor."

I stopped halfway between the kitchen and dining room as two teen girls came through with dishes and flatware. They giggled when they saw me. The red-haired one blushed hot pink.

"Yeah."

"Remember why you started this. You wanted to change the world."

The click and scrape of the girls setting the table got far away.

"Are you there?" Keaton asked.

A little girl with one pigtail half out came into the dining room with a big pitcher of water.

Red Hair took the pitcher and flipped the one intact pigtail, saying, "Go fix your hair, muffin."

"I'm here," I said.

The pigtail was half out because the little one had been cleaning the walls of an abandoned factory all day. And why would a child do that? Everett Fitzgerald was coming to town, and they were all working toward a common goal. That was why I cared. I wanted to see if they could do it.

"She sounds young for you," Keaton said.

"That's not funny."

He paused. Keaton didn't fill the air with words if he had nothing to say or if he needed to take a moment to think. "Something's just become really clear to me…"

"I'll call you when I have the next code."

"You were always a sucker for pussy, Beez. I knew one of them would get to you eventually."

He hung up.

The kitchen was in full swing. All four burners had pots, and every bit of counter space was covered with someone hacking away at a vegetable.

I didn't give a shit about Barrington. I didn't care about Harper, her family, her friends, her father's fucking factory. I could have passed a polygraph stating I didn't give a shit about anything but QI4 and a tight circle of people, none of whom were in this little factory town, dammit.

"What's wrong?" Catherine asked.

"I don't care!" I barked the lie that revealed itself more the more I repeated it.

I cared.

God dammit. I cared.

The hustle in the kitchen stopped for a second. Catherine took me by the elbow and led me into the pantry.

"Catherine, really," I said. "I'm sorry. I'm fine. I was thinking about something else."

"Do you need to go home? I can get someone to give you a ride."

I breathed a rueful laugh. I should have asked her in the first place. I'd have been home already. But it was too late. Keaton knew where I was and that there was a woman involved. And I cared.

"I need Harper."

I didn't mean I *needed* Harper. But it didn't matter what I meant anymore.

"I can call her."

I didn't need a nursemaid, and I didn't need favors. Catherine had enough to do without me worrying her about a threat from Keaton. She didn't need to worry about me or my whining either. Harper and I could take care of it.

"No. I'm fine. Never mind."

She reached into her apron and plucked out a car key, dangling it between us. "She's helping Pat at the store for a couple of hours if you want to pick up a few things."

That must have been the store where she and I had met a hundred years before.

I took the key. "All right."

"I'll get you a list."

I was left in the half-empty pantry with its peeling shelf paper and scalloped molding.

Note to self: you're not going to put anything past that woman.

XXXVIII

I felt blinded by my location. The miles between my company and me were almost as bad as the lack of digital communication.

I had to go back to Cali. Had to get out of here. Had to warn Harper. Had to help the company, myself, this woman who was in the process of destroying me. Had to find out how this knot of facts would turn into a noose and leave me swinging on Main Street.

P&J, as it turned out, was indeed the grocery store Harper had been minding when I'd arrived. I wondered if she'd made it a point to be there, knowing I'd be coming in that way.

She had. I knew it as well as I knew my own motivations. She was too smart to leave that to chance.

Pat was behind the counter. Not Harper. I grabbed the things off the list and dropped them on the belt at the only checkout.

"Thanks for helping out today," Pat said as she rang me up.

"No problem. You were there all day too, and you're right back to work."

She shrugged. "Gotta get done if you want your carrots."

"Have you seen Harper? She's going to miss a really nice dinner."

"She's over at our place. Our modem's been on the fritz. She's the only one that can fix it since our youngest went off to school."

"Ah."

"Eleven seventy-two."

I gave her twenty, and she made change.

"I don't have my phone." I took the coins. "And I need to talk to her. So, can I borrow…"

I stopped myself. Asking for a home address was weird enough. Asking so I could chase a woman down was weirder. I'd have to ask to use the store's phone.

"You can just go over there. I hear you're pretty handy with computers too. She might need some help."

"Yeah. True. Hey. I was wondering something," I said, using all my powers of nonchalance. I was pretty sure they were inadequate. "How did you all find out Everett Fitzgerald was coming to look at the plant?"

She smiled, leaning against the counter. "Well, so interesting. Harper told a fancy commercial realtor over in Doverton he was looking for a space. Said she talked to someone she knew from when she was at college who happened to work for him. Fanny connected the dots."

"It's lucky the agent in Doverton had those kinds of connections."

"Fanny knows just about everyone."

I could accept that as the official story, but unofficially, no.

"Did you talk to Fanny?" Too direct. I backpedaled. "I mean, did you send her a fruit basket or anything? It would be pretty cool if it went through."

"Harper took care of it. Those kinds of connections, you only get them in college."

"I'd have to agree."

We chattered aimlessly as Pat bagged. She had three smart children she was extremely proud of. All were away. Temple. Duke. Northwestern.

"You cannot believe what these places cost."

"I can imagine." I'd used the second of Keaton's Bitcoin infusions to pay my student loans. He'd thought it was funny that I still owed people money when I knew how to hack a bank and take thousands in such small increments I wouldn't get caught.

"We couldn't put up anything for tuition," Pat continued. "The house isn't worth squat. Johnny can only fix so many clocks, and the grocery store margins are pretty tight. I don't even want to think about the debt they're gonna have."

I wanted to employ her children without even knowing what they did. I had an impulse to employ the entire town as if it had cast a softening spell on me.

"Don't. They'll work it out."

She gave me directions. I thanked her, took my bags of groceries, and headed over to Oxalis Street. The layout of the town was becoming clearer. The main strip that Harper had taken me past was a few parallel streets from the civic center. Post office. Library. City clerk.

A cluster of houses grew around a closed train stop. Following Oxalis Street around it, I found Pat and Johnny's place. I parked in front of the narrow, white-shingled house with a porch and a rusted swing in the front yard swinging in the late afternoon sun.

A dog barked, but no one answered the door.

"Who is it?" an impatient male voice came from the end of the driveway.

The drive was grass with two dirt stripes leading to a one-car garage. A circa-1970s Mercedes covered in boxes and tarps took up one side. Benches and tables took up the rest. The carriage doors were open, and Johnny was leaning over a brightly lit table with magnification goggles.

"Hey, Johnny," I said. "Have you seen Harper?"

He stood straight with difficulty, as if his back still bothered him. "Went home. Fixed the wireless and left."

I should have gone, but I couldn't help looking at the table as he laid his tweezers down and pushed the goggles up on his head. The table was lined with butcher paper, and an open clock sat on it. Gears were arrayed all over the table with pen circling them in groups, labeled with arrows, or placed on tea saucers.

"Where's my watch?"

"Close by."

"Johnny, you're pissing me off."

He shrugged. "You took off after lunch. There are guys still there cleaning. The trade was the watch for a full day of work. Not half a day's work for a really nice piece you lost fair and square."

I was going to lay into him. Keaton had made me feel like half a man, and now this asshole was halving the difference again. I wouldn't be taken advantage of. I was lost and trapped and worse for the wear, but that watch was mine.

"You look like you're about to blow a gasket." He got off his chair and buckled from a back spasm. Instinctively, I reached out to help him, walking him to a beat-up green couch.

"Where's the watch?" I asked when he was settled.

"Where I can't get to it right now."

"I want it now."

"Don't worry, Cali-Boy." He shifted until he was settled in the cushions. "Things will go to shit if we know what time it is or not. Fancy watch ain't gonna save nobody."

Maybe he was right. Maybe I shouldn't get a whole watch for a few hours of work, and maybe everything was going to shit. Maybe I couldn't save the world or Harper or myself. But I couldn't use that as an excuse for not trying.

XXXIX

It was getting dark, but I found the way back to the Barrington house easily. Nothing to it. I had the lay of the land already. I drove around the back and put the car where I'd found it.

Mrs. Boden, wearing a different color bandana on her head and the same bangly bracelet, came to the back porch with the red-haired teen.

"About time!" the older lady shouted.

"Is Harper back?" I asked, handing the bags to the blushing redhead.

As if summoned, Harper came through the swinging door, keeping it open so everyone could get past. She looked at me through the screen.

"You coming in?" she asked.

"We need to talk."

"Did the decryption key work?"

The door slapped closed behind her as she came out, and we were alone. The way the setting sun hit her cheeks made her glow, and the strands of gold hair at the edges looked translucent. She belonged on a postcard.

I kept forgetting she was holding me hostage. I kept forgetting I needed to think strategically. I had more at stake with this girl than I'd ever had with another.

"Did you doubt it would work?"

"Not really. I'm just making conversation."

"What are the thorns about?" I pointed at the thorn bed that had eaten my phone and went down the stairs to the yard.

She came after me. "Don't you have these where you're from?" She snapped a dry twig off the end.

"Roses? Yes. Impenetrable, groomed thorn bushes in our yards? No."

"It's not normal to give the gardeners in town something to do?" We walked around the perimeter.

"You are not normal."

"It still blooms in spring. It's really nice. You should see it."

We were at the back end of the yard, where the very top of the factory's roof cut the horizon.

I took her hand, pulling her to a stop. "Harper."

"Taylor?" Her hair flew in her mouth when she turned, and she drew her finger across her cheek to get it out.

What was I supposed to tell her again? That I knew we'd interviewed her. That I didn't give her the job despite her having a leg up on everyone else we saw.

But was I contrite? Accusatory? Was I just going to relay information? What did I want out of her after I told her I knew?

"Thank you for helping today," she said. "If you'd asked me when we met, 'Would Taylor Harden help clean the factory?' I would have said, 'No, not for any reason.' But there you were. Pushing a broom. Scooping up shit. Not being an asshole."

"My watch was at stake."

"Yeah. Whatever. You can say what you want to keep your reputation as a shithead intact."

"I have a reputation as a shithead?"

"You know you do."

I did know it, and I reveled in it.

She faced me and put her other hand out. I took it, holding both hands between us. I couldn't help it.

"Well, you guys are such a bunch of sad sacks I had to help. And let me tell you, every guy in Barrington has a little asshole in him. Trust me. I've played pool with them."

"I want to say…" She stopped herself as if she really didn't want to say. "Let's get together tonight and get you another decryption code. But… saying this is stupid." She bit her lip.

"Say it anyway."

"The sooner you get four codes, the sooner you leave."

I looked at our hands so I wouldn't have to look at her.

"I'm not sure if I want that," she said.

Was she playing some kind of game? No matter how many ways I peeled this onion, I couldn't get to the center. Was she after my heart? Had she changed the fucking rules?

I had feelings for her I couldn't cope with, but if she was going to start moving the goalposts, I would lose my shit. I couldn't do this dance. Not with Keaton walking around the cage like a specter.

I let go of her hands. She was turning my head inside out, and all the pieces were dropping to the ground.

"You have a buddy on Chaxxer." I'd started, so I had to finish. "I saw it on your screen."

Her eyes went a little wide, and her throat moved as she swallowed hard. She didn't have to confirm it. She knew what I'd seen.

"So?" She planted her feet far apart as if daring me to knock her over. "What's it to you?"

"More practice? Like me? The way I'm practice?"

"I like you better."

"Don't sweet-talk me. You've been telling how many guys on Chaxxer how hard you can suck the—"

"Shut up, Taylor Harden! You just shut your mouth."

"A few years ago, we met a guy on the dark web who was a big fan of my partner. He was no one then. Keaton was Alpha Wolf; this guy called himself Beta Wolf. Just for shits. 'Flow' is 'wolf' backward, and if the B in 'bro' is a beta?"

"When did you figure it out?"

"That Fitz was Flow Bro? That you've been talking dirty on Chaxxer? Or that you were the one to get him to come to Barrington?"

She blinked too long, and her expression went slack as if she was looking inside her own mind. Calculating. I could see her making connections, but what connections?

I wanted to know—for all the obvious reasons and one not-so-obvious reason. I wanted to know *her*. Not just why she was lying but how.

"I can sell him a factory," she said. "Or I can sell him a package. A place to make things and a girl who gives him what he wants, how he wants it."

"How did you find out he likes it dirty?"

Her expression changed a dozen times before she spoke. "Does it matter? I hacked him. He's a man. He's a rich asshole from daddy's money. He wants to be worshipped. He wants a few holes to stick his dick in, and he wants to be told he's got powers no one else has. You guys are all alike. You want to be treated as though you're gold-plated. Well, I got news—you're not. Not him. Not you. Nobody. We're all made of blood and electrical currents. All of us. And we all have a code in our neurons where a guy like Fitz can be tricked into doing the right thing. So, yeah. He's filthy, so I learned to be filthy. But it's got to work in the real world. You're teaching me to fuck so I can seduce him. If I can make him love me, he'll buy the factory. He'll hire us. He'll save us."

"You're crazy."

I'd made the observation before, but behind the thorn bush, something else stirred. She was crazy, but I wanted her. My cock pushed against my pants for her. Her insanity was rubbing off on me.

"You can be in or out." She got her finger in my face. "But you're in because I hacked you too."

I grabbed her wrist and wrested it away from my face. "No, Harper. You're crazy if you think I believe it. You're too smart for such a stupid plan."

There wasn't a bit of insecurity in her eyes. How could she be so confident?

I couldn't counter with the facts, couldn't tell her he wouldn't do what she wanted, because I was halfway to falling for her myself.

Maybe that was her gift.

Fuck this.

I was here to get shit done.

Shit was getting done.

Jamming my hand in her waistband, I made a fist around the fabric and twisted her jeans, tightening the crotch. She leveraged herself on my shoulders.

"When he walks away from you," I said, "come to me."

Her button-fly popped open when I pulled the sides apart.

"What are you doing?"

"Free lesson."

Her gaze went from hard to liquid in a heartbeat, and her hands went to the lump in my pants, stroking through the fabric.

Was it real? Was she faking it?

Pushing her pants down, I got my fingers on her soaking-wet pussy. Can't fake that.

I crushed her lips on mine, tasting her tongue, biting her with a vengeance that made her squeal. I was going to fuck her right there in the dirt. Half dressed, wrestling under the darkening sky, I was going to tear her apart.

She had my dick out, and my face was buried in her neck as she stroked it. There was no expertise in her movements, but the ache in my body responded as if she did everything right.

"Give me your hand," I said, taking it before she could offer it.

I kissed the tips of her fingers, sucked them, left a trail of saliva across her palm. She gasped in surprise and arousal. I'd get to that later. But for now, I took her thumb in my mouth and sucked hard.

"Oh, I didn't…" After another gasp, she finished, "I didn't know that could feel so good."

I put her slick hand on my erection and paced her. "The head's where the nerve endings are. You have to…" She ran her thumb along the back. "Do that."

She watched my expression with her big, multicolored eyes, taking in my every reaction like a learning machine.

She's learning how to fuck someone else.

I'm fine with that.

I wasn't fine with it. The pressure was building as she jerked me off. It got harder to think. The firewall between my jealousy and what I allowed myself to think was under attack. I put my hands on her cheeks and pressed her face to mine until I felt her breath on my lips.

"You don't… ah…"

Say it.

Do not say it.

Do. Not.

"You don't have to do this."

"Should I suck it instead?" Her voice was soft and suggestive.

She'd misunderstood. I could have corrected her, but I was about to lose it. I lifted her shirt and let loose on her belly, burying my face in her neck, her ozone smell, the air before a storm.

"Harper." I groaned it. The longing in my voice was audible.

I'd been jerked off before, but this time I was in a weakened state. Not because of the orgasm. Those were a dime a dozen. Another bit of chemistry was at work. Some new variable had been added to the algorithm.

She pulled away, holding her shirt up so it wouldn't get sticky. Under her white bra, her body dripped where I'd marked her with my DNA. I could only see the top of her head because she was looking down, moving her unbuttoned jeans away.

When she looked at me, her hair was a wheaten nest and her grin was a conspiracy of desire against logic. As if we were in on something together. As if we were partnered on an epic hacking exploit.

That was it.

I changed my mind about everything.

"Stay there," I said, taking a wrinkled hankie out of my back pocket. "It's the guy's job to clean you up." I kneeled in front of her and wiped her off. "Any guy that doesn't clean you off, you get rid of, you hear? He's not worth you."

It was getting dark, but when I looked up at her, I could just about see her face. The wind blew from the direction of the river, covering her like window blinds. She shook her head. The hair came off her face, falling to one side.

"You got that?" I said. "It's things like that that you have to watch for."

"I got it. He wipes me off."

"He worships you."

I kissed her where I'd marked her, running my tongue below her navel, pulling her jeans to her knees. I kissed the fronts of her thighs as she ran her fingers through my hair.

"He worships me."

She was wearing boots. I could have waited for her to get it all off, but I needed to taste her.

"He treats you like a queen." Pulling her open, I got my tongue on her clit.

"Oh my God." Her knees bent, giving me better access.

Without a wall or a bed to lean against, we fought a losing battle with gravity and physics. We fell into a tangled pile on the ground with my head between her legs, her pants and boots still on, her fingers gripping my scalp. We were feral animals, and I wanted to eat her alive.

I reached up to touch her face. My fingers slid into her open mouth. Her breathing got hard and fast, and the taste of her got clearer, sweeter, more raw. I covered her mouth so the people in the house wouldn't run out to rescue her.

She came in the dirt and scraggly grass, pushing my face between her legs as I pushed my hand harder on her mouth.

"Wait. Wait, stop," she muttered behind my hand.

Even when she tried to wiggle away, I kept on, lightening up so it wouldn't hurt, but I wanted another. One for her. One for me.

Her second orgasm flipped us over. My hand fell away from her mouth, and she straddled me with her jeans behind my neck. Her back arched. I held her to me until she stopped moving.

"Please." She was practically weeping. "No more."

I let her go. She shifted back but couldn't untangle herself completely without help. Her jeans had slid lower and were completely wrapped around the boots. My body was between her legs, with one hand over my head and one trapped by the jeans.

"Oh, dear," she said. "I think we're stuck."

"Think of it as coding praxis. One step at a time."

I rolled until I was on top of her, more or less, holding myself up with my free arm. I kissed her cheek then her lips.

She flicked her tongue over my chin. "That's what I taste like."

"Yes. And I want to tell you something."

I'd never told a woman anything like I was about to tell this one. So I paused and considered it. Thought hard. Swapped words around. It had to be perfect, but I kept changing what that meant.

"I think I need to take a boot off." She shifted and stared at the dark blue sky.

"No. You need to stay still for a minute."

She moved her face from the sky to me. "Okay. I'm still."

"You and I." Nothing I'd prepared was right. I threw it all away. "We don't have to be against each other. We can be…"

Be what?

Partners?

Something simply more?

Or less?

I wasn't ready to define what we were. I wanted to define what we weren't.

"You don't have to do this," I continued. "This thing with Fitz. It's bullshit. You're making it up because it's a stall for the real reason."

"What's the real reason?"

"You want me."

"Oh, God, you have to stop believing your own PR."

She bucked her hips, flinging me to the side. I wrestled her back down with one arm.

"There are too many steps." I held up one finger with my free hand. "You come up with the hack of the century to—one—lure me here"—two fingers made a V—"so I could train you to fuck"—I put the W in her face —"so you can seduce a guy into reopening the factory. And that's two steps right there." Four fingers. "You want to tell me how that plan makes any sense?"

"It makes sense." She growled from deep in her chest. "We've tried Congress. We've tried the law. We spent money we didn't have sending people to talk and talk and talk to businesses. We're still dying here. The only thing that makes sense is getting a human man to do what human men do."

I twisted, pulled, held her in place while I bent my body through the space between her legs and her jeans. Kneeling in front of her in the dark, she was an odd-shaped silhouette in the twilight.

I growled at her, "Human men *fuck shit up*."

She rolled onto the balls of her feet and stood, naked between her waist and her calves. The house lights cast a glow on the top of her body while the thorn bed made twisted shadows over her stomach. I could smell her pussy.

"You know what?" she said, leaning over to loosen her pants from her boots. I reached out to help her, but she swatted me away. "My reasons and my sense aren't your business. Your business is getting your code back."

She slid her underwear up, covering her delicious pussy smell. I remembered I was on my knees with my dick out. My first impulse was to lash out at her. Hurt her. Bring her down to her knees. But a little voice mentioned that hadn't worked with her yet and trying it again would be the definition of insanity.

I stood. "You're better than this."

She spit out a laugh and shimmied her jeans over her hips. "Don't sweet-talk me, Taylor. It's not going to work."

But it had already worked. Her tone was more pliant.

"I should have hired you."

"So you remember?"

I didn't, but I didn't want to admit it any more than I wanted to lie about it.

"When I heard you had an opening, Catherine scraped up the money for a flight," she said. "One night in a hotel. I aced the fucking coding test. You made some comment about 'fitting in with the culture' and didn't listen to my answer."

"So this is revenge?"

She walked along the back of the thorn bed, her boots crunching against the dirt path. One side of her was lit by the golden light from the house, and when she turned toward it, I could see her profile.

I couldn't run away. Couldn't fire her or ignore her. I was so angry and powerless the most hurtful things didn't seem hurtful enough. And as much as cutting her down would be the definition of insanity, I wanted to shame her. Cut her down. Make her cry.

"All I'm saying is…" I paused as if hovering my finger over the send button.

She stopped and looked at me, daring me to press it.

Fuck it.

"You don't have to be such a whore."

I don't know what I'd expected. She walked briskly to the house, taking big steps, ran up the porch stairs, and let the door slap behind her.

Her taste lingered on my tongue. I rolled it around with the word I'd used to break her and failed.

XL

*H*arper wasn't at dinner. I ate with everyone, made small talk, helped clear the table while watching the driveway for her car. I had a beer with Orrin and Butthead on the porch. It seemed like the best vantage point to watch for Harper to come back.

She didn't.

Percy looked at me with sad brown eyes and a drooping tail as if he felt sorry for me. When I scratched his neck, he laid his head on my lap.

"My God, son. What happened to you to make old Percy give you comfort?"

"Did half a day's work in a factory. Nearly snapped me in two," I deflected.

Butthead belched. Orrin laughed. Harper still didn't show up.

The fucking send button. It needed to be locked before a guy called any woman a whore, especially Harper Barrington aka Watson, who was just about as far from a whore as a woman could be.

Or she was a complete whore and I didn't care.

Maybe the question wasn't about her. Maybe the question was about why I thought I had to ask myself who a woman slept with and why. Or why it mattered. Or why some behaviors were good and some were bad, because I'd done some shitty stuff people could get on my ass about.

I didn't know what I thought about anything anymore. I was all turned around. These guys out here? A guy who let himself be called Butthead as a sign of affection and Orrin, who'd nearly taken my face off because he didn't like how I was touching Harper? Were they involved in what she was doing? Did they see some greater good?

I couldn't imagine they'd allow my voluntary abduction, but there were so many moving pieces to this puzzle I didn't think any one human could do it alone, no matter how smart and capable.

"How did you guys find out Fitz was coming?" I asked.

"Fanny the realtor," Butthead said. "Over in Doverton."

"She's pretty connected." I finished my beer. Debated having another. I wasn't pleasantly buzzed. Just slow and tired.

"I thought it was the Badger," Orrin said.

"The Badger?"

"Mayor. He looks like a fucking…" Butthead waved it away as too obvious. "But nah. He stopped bothering to even leave town after we couldn't get Pepsi to move in."

"Yeah." Orrin sipped his beer.

Whatever part in it they had, I believed they didn't know Harper was talking to Fitz on Chaxxer.

"You spray paint the Caddy, Orrin?"

"Why you asking?"

"You were around that day."

"You think *he* did it?" Butthead laughed. "Dude, that was me. All me."

"What did you do with my laptop?" The anger was a transparent wrap around the hope that I'd get it back.

"Harper's got it."

"Did she say why you should do something so fucking stupid?"

His laughter clanged to the floor as if I'd cut a chain of tension. "Nah. Just said it wasn't a big deal and it was a joke on some rich guy. Said to make an E into a three to pretend I was an uneducated rube, and, you know, she kinda got me going. But you're all right. I don't feel good about it."

Apparently, it was okay to victimize some people and not others. People you knew and liked, you left alone. Strangers, especially ones who fit a certain mold, were crimes waiting to happen. I was mad at the idea of a Butthead, a guy whose morals operated on a vector. But to his face I couldn't be, because I suffered from the same relativism.

"How did she know I was coming?"

"Internet." He shrugged and hid behind his beer.

"Same as how she knew Fitz was coming?"

"Told you that was Fanny," Orrin interjected.

"Fuck, Bernard," I said before finishing my beer. "I'm surprised you wrote 'Nice Caddy' instead of 'titties' all lowercase."

"I had to stop myself. Harper's a lady."

I must have been drunk, because I laughed, and Bernard aka Butthead laughed with me. Even Orrin got that look an older man gets when he has to reluctantly admit the kid got off a good one.

I went to bed on my thin little mattress and stared at the cracks in the ceiling. The noise lessened downstairs. Doors opening and closing. Water pipes rattling. Chatter. Children. I hadn't been around that many children since I was a child myself.

When everyone was gone, Catherine started crying.

If Harper came back, the sound of her would have been lost in the chaos. I needed to apologize or tell her it didn't matter or something. I needed to tell her I meant it, and I didn't. We could do this together.

She doesn't have to —

—maybe she wanted to —

—she's not a fuck-for-riches type —

—you don't know her —

—you know she's a decent person who —

—has been on Chaxxer —

—but she doesn't have to —

Around and around it went.

She was gone too long. Way too long. She could have been lying on the side of the road or in trouble or miles away at some rapist's second location.

I got out of bed and started putting pants on when there was a break in the wailing through the walls. I could hear better. A sound from the hall was coming through, then Catherine started again, and it was gone.

Was it clicking?

Pants on, I went into the hall and stood at the foot of Harper's stairwell.

Definitely clicking. She was at the keys.

I stayed at the bottom of her stairs, listening. Was she typing filthy things? Was @Flow_Bro calling her a slut? Or a whore? I'd done the same to hurt her feelings, not get myself off. Did that make me a better or worse person than him?

My bones ached. She could be doing anything up there. Re-hacking me. My brain could barely complete a thought except that she was safe at home, not twisted in a knot on the side of the road.

Bursting into her room, no matter the reason, was going to make it worse.

I crawled into bed and let the crickets lull me to sleep. Not even Catherine's crying could keep me up. I thought I'd slept for a few minutes, but when I woke, the crickets were done and the moon had moved across the sky into the frame of the French doors. Catherine had quieted.

A dark figure stood over me silently. The moon caught the blond edges of her hair.

"Harper?"

She didn't answer, but her shoulders shook, and she swallowed so hard I could hear it. I sat on the edge of the bed.

She held out something. It glinted in the moonlight, clattering to the mattress when she dropped it in the space between my legs.

"My watch." I looked at it but didn't see much but a dark circle. The ticking vibrated against my fingers. "Thank you."

"You have to know how to ask Johnny for things."

"Yeah." I put it on my wrist. The ticking was louder than my heartbeat, but barely. "I'm sorry about what I called you. I knew it would hurt you."

"Sometimes I feel like I'm a stranger here. In my own hometown. It's always been that way. Then I drag you here. It's been less than a week, but I have moments with you where I feel like you and I, we're strangers, but it's temporary. Like there's about to be *knowing* between us I don't have with anyone else. And then you're so cruel."

She sniffed. Her shoulders hitched. She pressed her fingertips against the insides of her eyes.

"But I have it coming," she said. "I know I do. I fucked with your life. I'm still fucking with it. You don't owe me anything."

What did she want? Besides returning my watch, was there something else?

"What brought you down here?"

She shrugged, waving in the general direction of her room, her computers, her Chaxxer account. "I wasn't in the mood for bullshit."

"So you came to *me*?"

She coughed a short laugh. "Go figure."

Turning to the moonlight, raising her hand as if she wanted to say things she couldn't, her breathing got thick and shallow. When she blinked, tears were displaced onto her cheeks.

I wanted to ask her where my laptop was, but it could wait. Everything that kept us apart could wait. She needed me more than I needed answers.

I leaned on an elbow, swung my legs back on the bed, and held my hand out to her. "Come on."

"I can't." She was fully crying. Not as unreservedly as her sister, but her voice was wet and broken.

"Clothes on. No sex. I won't even get hard."

She laughed a little and stepped forward. "Yes, you will."

"All right. I might get hard." I turned back the covers. "Come on. It's warm."

Tick-tick-tick, my watch counted the time it took for her to decide.

Knee first, then hand, then shoulder and last leg, she crawled into bed and turned onto her back to look at the cracked ceiling and the bald, dark light bulb.

Everything about that was wrong. I put the covers over her and was overcome with tenderness. It overrode all my good sense. All the brain power I'd wasted and some that I'd used. She was the enemy. She had my life in her hands. She was the reason I was trapped. If I wanted to get what I needed from her, I had to keep my distance.

All those things were true.

But in the moonlight, with my body aching and her silent sobs breaking the crust of my hostility, they became false. Her tears spoke to a different part of me. A part I had no control over. A part I hadn't known I had. A part of me that she'd been prying away since the minute I met her.

Tick-tick-tick.

Sure as I was that she was too emotionally guileless to break my guard down intentionally, I was also sure I could put my battle gear on again tomorrow.

She tried to get control of her breath, and covered her face with her hands as if she didn't want me to see her crying. I gently turned her until my face was at her shoulder and we were spoons.

I barely heard her whisper, "You don't have to be nice to me."

"I know." I held her. I knew she was awake from the way her eyelashes brushed my arm.

Tick-tick-tick.

Johnny making that bet while I was too drunk to remember. The gears and watch guts on his table. My dealer getting a "cheap" Langematik from a guy he'd never met before.

"It was my watch, wasn't it?" She didn't answer, but I was sure she knew what I meant. "All this time I thought... my God... it was me. I was bringing the transmitter in and out of the cage."

"Johnny thought you'd notice the watch was slow before we got all the data."

"Who tells time with their watch?" I stroked her arm. I was the weak link. I was the one who'd had to have the sweetest mechanical piece. It was my ego that had brought the whole thing crashing down. "Who else is in on it? The whole town?"

"Just me and Johnny. Butthead with the spray paint. They wouldn't... they'd freak out if they knew. Johnny's the only one who believes in karmic social justice. That because my father owned this town and destroyed it, I'm the one who has to fix it."

"Do you believe that?"

"It doesn't really matter, does it?" She wiggled and turned around until she faced me. Her hands were folded flat under her cheek. The sobbing had abated. "I used to believe in forgiveness. I used to read

Sherlock Holmes because they were such good puzzles. When I got to
The Blue Carbuncle—"

"Is that the one you left in the comments? With the geohash?"

"Yes. Did you finish it?"

"No." I'd skimmed for more clues once I knew what they looked like,
but I hadn't read for story. Ego again. I'd thought I knew what the hacker
was trying to tell me, so I'd ignored the rest. A stupid, sloppy mistake.

"This regular guy steals a valuable gem. It's famous. Everyone wants
it. People have died to own it. Holmes says…" Her tongue flicked over
her lips, and her eyes went to the side as if thinking. "'Every facet stands
for a bloody deed.' He, the thief, hides it in a goose and gets caught. But
when Holmes figures it out, well, the guy wasn't a lifelong criminal. He
was terrible at it, actually. Holmes realizes there's no use in turning the
guy in. He lets him go."

I touched a half-dried tear with my thumb. "He hid his treasure in
a goose?"

"Yeah. And Holmes ate it. He broke the spell," she continued. "By
forgiving a thief, he changed someone's world."

"So it's not karmic justice or cultural social whatever?"

"No. It's different. Not that it matters. I'm the one who can do what
has to be done. But I like to think that my father is forgiven. Someday my
family will be off the hook."

"There's no hook, goose."

She spoke again after a few deep breaths. "Then why can I feel it?"

Her shoulders shook, and she sniffled. She was going to cry again,
and I couldn't take that either. Crying women scared me. They made me
feel as if I was on a boat in the middle of the ocean, sun up at the top of
noon, without a marker to know where I was.

But I had to steer the fucking boat this time. There was no grown-up
to make it all right. That was me. I was the grown-up, and I had to
commit to a direction.

I held her as tightly as I could without crushing her, but I wanted to
crush her. Hard. Into a tight ball I could tuck away someplace safe.

"It's okay." My words were stupid and ineffective, but they were all I
had. "You're going to be all right."

"I want to accomplish something. I just want to win again,
you know?"

Seeing her weep for validation punched a hole in the world. She was
brilliant and compassionate. She worked hard for everyone around her.
I'd never met such a genius in my life. Things were supposed to be easy
for people like her. She was supposed to have the world at her feet. How
could this be true? How could it happen?

"I surrender. You're going to win this. I'll do whatever you need
me to."

Her nod was so slight I barely felt it against my shoulder.

I was only human. I was ambitious and callous, but I wasn't any kind
of sociopath. She'd hurt me, opened me, then asked for sympathy with
her body against mine.

Of course I dragged my lips against her throat then her cheek. Of
course they sought out her breath and her voice. And when I kissed her,
of course I wanted to get inside her.

I didn't want to seduce her. I didn't want to relieve myself and move
on. She was neither project nor prey. She was Harper. Just Harper. She
had hands that clawed and a mouth that groaned into mine. She had
hips that pushed into me when the line of my cock was against her. She
took my control and wove it into desire.

"Fuck!" I snapped as I pulled away. "I said I wouldn't."

She was under me, breathing from deep in her chest through parted
lips. "Yes, but we can."

She wanted to. She'd said yes. What the hell else did I need? An
engraved fucking invitation?

"No transactions."

"Okay," she said with a sharp nod and locked her hands behind my
neck. "No trades. Just sex."

"No." I gently took her hands from my neck. "It would be a trade.
Every time we touch each other, it's a transaction. I can't. You didn't
come down here for that. And I'm not going to pretend I understand it,
but I'm fucked in the head when it comes to you. I'm not going to take
my fucked-upness about it and relocate it to you." I kissed her because
that crease in her lip needed to be kissed very badly.

One of her eyelids drooped a little, narrowing her focus. "You have feelings for me."

"I said I didn't understand it." I got up on my knees and nudged her to her side. "It must be your powers of seduction."

"I'm amazing," she said with a smile.

I fit my chest against her back and pushed one arm under her neck, spooning her again. "You are. Now go to sleep."

I didn't expect to sleep. Sleeping with another person in the bed was impossible—until that night. Her breathing got even and shallow against me, and her shoulder went limp. I planned on holding her until the sun came up, but soon after, my mind went into the weeds then cut to black.

XLI

I was on the boat again, but I was sitting alone on the stern. My watch was ticking as if it was pressed right up against my ear. Sharks circled the boat. I couldn't see them, but I knew they were there, and I knew they were hungry.

I wasn't scared. I was irritated. My tailbone itched. When I reached behind to scratch it, I pulled back a wiggling salmon. What to do with it? If I threw it back into the ocean, the sharks would eat it, and I didn't want that. I had to save it.

I threw it in a water-filled red bucket. It splashed and swam the perimeter.

My tailbone tickled again.

Another salmon.

Plop, into the bucket.

It was crowded in there, but they'd be all right.

But then, another prickled my tailbone.

Still, I couldn't let the sharks eat it. Couldn't. These were my fish. I was responsible for them.

When I dropped it in the bucket, all three fit comfortably, then four fit, as if the bucket grew bigger on the inside but not the outside.

A fifth appeared with no sign they'd ever stop, and the five-gallon bucket increased its interior size.

"Stay still."

Harper's voice cut through my dream. I was on my stomach with my watch to my ear, and the pitching of the boat had been her shifting weight on the bed. She held me down when I tried to turn, and I let her because whatever she was doing to the place where my back met my butt was kind of nice.

"What are you doing back there?"

"Code number three."

"I thought we weren't being transactional."

"We didn't have sex. So it wasn't a transaction." With the click of the pen cap, she checked her work by counting on her fingers and checking notations in a little pad, then she nodded sharply. "Done."

I twisted around. "How am I supposed to see that?"

"Tricky problem." She took her cell from the night table. I was immediately jealous that she had her connection to the wider world while mine was cut. "I can take a picture, and you can call from here. You don't even have to get out of bed."

"No." I said it more harshly than I intended.

"I promise to not post your butt on the internet."

"I'm not worried about that. My partner already located the house when I called from the landline. I don't want him to locate your personal phone."

"You know I'm cloaked, right?"

"Don't test him."

"So how you calling this one in? Smoke signal?"

I stood. "I already called from the kitchen phone."

She followed me down the hall. Downstairs, Catherine hummed to the *whoosh whoosh* of a broom.

I stopped in the middle of the stairwell. Harper couldn't get past me if I didn't want her to, and I didn't. "You don't need to come."

"You're reading the code on your butt?"

"I was going to use a shiny teapot or something. Hack life, Harper. Not just computers."

"I'll make a note."

"Yesterday. About Everett."

"You apologized already."

"It's a shitty plan. But I understand it. It's not about money. It's about maintenance."

"Yes."

"And also, you're cute when you lie. Your nose turns up just a little."

She tapped my nose from the step above and whispered, "You don't know the whole plan."

I was a pawn in a chess game, and I should have been worried about being used without consent. I should have wondered when I was going to be sacrificed. But I was just curious how much bigger this thing was.

She wasn't going to tell me. I would have to play along until I could figure it out myself.

I unblocked her way, and we went to the kitchen together. Catherine was nowhere in sight, but her presence was felt in the hissing coffee pot and the two mugs she'd left in front of it.

I picked up the phone receiver.

Harper ran her finger along my waistband and shifted it down. I was glad she couldn't see my boner from behind.

Deepak was on the phone in two minutes. "What do you have for me, my friend? It's getting fucked up over here."

"What kind of fucked up?"

An important question since the person holding me hostage was stroking my lower back with her fingernails and it was driving me crazy.

"Your devil investor's AWOL. I liked it better when I could see what he was doing."

"He'll be happy when he gets back. You ready for decryption?"

"Ready."

Harper read the characters to me, tracing each one with her finger. "124 131 064 040 164 150 145 040 163 160 157 157 156 163."

"Done," she said then whispered, "It's octal, by the way."

"Who's that with you?" Deepak asked. "Is that Harper Watson?"

In other words, *are you sleeping with the enemy?* Which, technically, I was.

"Can you just keystroke, please?"

She continued, and Deepak read it back, which I repeated back to

Harper in the oldest game of telephone. I decoded the octal in the translations.

I looked over my shoulder as she flipped her hair, inadvertently exposing her ear. I didn't mind the missing diamond. She looked better without them. More naked.

"You're welcome."

She smiled. The octal converted into "Thank you for the spoons," and she was very, very welcome.

"Yeah, no," Deepak said. "I'm getting nothing. Can I have it again?"

"Can you call it again?" I asked Harper.

We did it again.

"No." Deepak's voice was soft with dread. "And I'm getting a new message at the prompt."

Standing straighter, I turned to Harper. I must have been pale or something because she put down her coffee cup and grabbed for the phone. I shooed her hand, but she pulled my arm down until our ears shared the receiver.

"What message?" I said.

"Enter decryption code to boot OS, colon, backslash, then this: 'System will lock after two more failed attempts.' Then the prompt."

"No." Harper snapped the receiver away. "That's not right. I didn't put a lock against a brute force attack. I didn't have to. I'm generating codes on the fly."

"That makes no sense."

"Random is built into quantum trinary. Selective decryption is—"

"It's you!" Deepak shouted "Put Taylor on!"

She gave me the phone. I held it between us so we could both hear.

"It's me," I said.

"Have you lost it, brother?"

"I can hear you," Harper said.

"She can hear you."

"This is bad," she said with a shaky voice. "I didn't set that up."

"You've done enough." Deepak sounded as mad as I'd ever heard him sound.

"Deeps, listen—"

"Keaton did it," he and I said at the same time.

"He's been hooked up to the sys on his own machine for days."
Deepak's cool, sweet charm was dissolving under the stress. Harper
leaned away from the phone and crossed her arms, looking into the
middle distance and biting her lower lip while Deepak continued his
rant in my ear. "Fucker. Fucking evil-ass motherfucker said he was trying
to crack through. He was locking it. Next time, Taylor, get a goddamn
bank to invest all right?"

"Where did he go?" I asked. It was the last calmly thought-out
question I had. My last hope that all this was some kind of mistake
Keaton could clear up if he was around. Maybe he was developing a
workaround and had to put a layer of encryption over the Harperware to
finish. Maybe this was simple. Maybe I could just hold the ocean in a
five-gallon bucket if I stayed calm.

"How should I know?" Deepak's voice shook. "Jesus. Fucking.
Christ."

Calm broke under pressure from chaos. Jesus fucking Christ was
right. The world went a little whiter, as if it went under an overexposure
filter, washing in white and yellow. Details got warmer before my eyes,
dissolving into bright fury.

"Know, Deepak. Know. Find out. Don't panic without a reason. Don't
go code black over what you *think* is happening."

I slammed the phone into the cradle. It made a sickly yet satisfying
little ring from inside the case. I picked it up and slammed it
down again.

"Taylor?" Harper had her phone clutched to her chest like a buoy on
the open sea.

"What?!"

"How could he talk to QI4 if it's not binary?"

"My guess?" I leaned into her, and she backed up against the
doorframe. "He's hooked up to your fucking poison pill."

As she still clutched the phone to her chest, her pupils dilated just a
little as if taking in extra information. Or because I cast her in shadow.

I put my hands up, not touching her, but extending the moment
before I did.

I was so mad at her I couldn't even think. I was clouded with hot red
rage. It latched on to every emotion I already had, all the affection and

warmth, filling all the places where I'd let her in. All the empathy I had for her. My anger found purchase on those and grew to infiltrate anything decent.

Her butter skin. Her lips. Her dark-to-light lashes. Hurt it. I wanted to hurt it so my anger had a place to go. If I didn't eat her alive, I was going to digest myself in my own acid.

And that phone to her chest, like a black monolith from deep space. I wanted to rip it away and throw it in the thorn bed then shred both our bodies wading to it. We'd be one thing. A single monster made of anger, blood, and brutality.

I wasn't even thinking straight. I'd lost a battle with sense and patience. Logic had jumped to its death rather than be in the same room with what I'd let in.

The little boat rocking on the flat circle of horizon. The pressure. The physical compression of my infinite speckness. I needed a lifeline to a point in the distance. Any point. I needed to know I wasn't cut off, because if this went on much longer, I was going to lose my mind.

"Can you get to him? Keaton? Can you—"

"Not without my phone." I put angry emphasis on the last word, filling it with all the blame and regret I could get into one syllable. "Fuck this."

I pushed away with the force of everything left in me that was civilized and decent. It wasn't that hard a push. It had just enough torque to get me away from her, turn me, and propel me toward the back of the house. To the bed of thorns that covered my phone.

"Taylor?" she called from a miles-long tunnel.

I heard her but kept my pace to the back of the house, slapping open the screen door and heading into the chilly, humid late morning. The clouds were low and oppressive. I opened the shed, and the stink of mildew and rotting wood hit me square in the face as if it could stop me. I plucked a pair of rusted, scissor-shaped hedge clippers from a nail on the wall.

When I turned back to the door and tried to walk out, Harper appeared in a goose-down vest the color of rust.

I reared back, almost stabbing her. "Jesus! Harper, get out of the way."

She moved. "I'm sorry," she said as I unlocked the blades. "I'm sorry this happened. I'm sorry it was my pill. But let's figure it out."

"Sure." I gripped the handles, but the hinge was loose and they flopped and waved. "That's great. Positive attitude. I had it all under control but no fucking problem." I tried to twist the little screw holding the two halves of the scissors together, but I couldn't narrow my attention. "Everything. I had everything. Knee-fucking-deep in money. I had the legs of every credit card company wide open, and I walked away to go straight. For this."

The nut came off the clippers and the halves split. I caught one as it fell. I held them by the handles like giant pointer fingers. I must have looked like Edward Scissorhands.

"For *this*." I pointed a blade into the horizon. The direction of QI4. "This useless hunk of code. And if you think it's anything better than useless right now, you're not thinking. It's been hacked twice. Twice."

I held up both rusted blades at the grey sky, and as if in answer, a rumble of thunder came from far away. A raindrop fell on my forehead.

"What do you want?" I asked the sky. The wind picked up in answer. "Tell me what you want out of me!"

"We don't have long," Harper said from a million miles away. "Your phone's going to get wet."

Of course. Because everything was fucked up. Because every single lucky break I'd gotten my entire life, from my first steps off the brick stoop when my father caught me before I smacked my head to the sweet parking spot in front of Anglioni's, was being paid back in spades right now.

And what had my life been but a series of fucking lucky breaks if I couldn't tolerate a few bumps in the road?

It was a lie. All of it was a lie.

I choked out the shortest expression of what flooded me, throwing the blades into the bushes. First one, then the other, disappeared with a rustle as if swallowed by the ocean.

"I am worthless."

"You're not," she protested.

I didn't want to hear it. Not a word of it. I hadn't said it so she could make me feel better. That would have been needy. Taylor Harden was a fuckup and a lie, but he wasn't needy.

Harper stepped toward me as if she was going to hug me or some shit.

I put my hand out like a crossing guard. "Don't. Don't get all girly and squishy on me. Don't expect me to cry on your shoulder while you pat my back and say it's going to be all right. It's not going to be all right. I don't need a fucking hug."

She looked at me as if I was made of shit and chicken liver. "I wasn't going to hug you."

This woman.

"What then?"

She approached again. Came right up to me. Took half a pause and slapped me in the face. "Snap out of it. Everyone's worthless. Don't be such a baby about it."

My wrist went to my stung left cheek. I was stunned she'd slapped me and equally surprised that it had worked. The mantra of worthlessness that looped in my head stopped and was replaced with complete attention to the moment. The situation. The stillness of the air. The faraway rush of the polluted river.

I didn't know what I looked like to her, but I wasn't frightening enough to scare her or sad enough to melt her into empathy. She was waiting like a blank page. I could write whatever I wanted. She was doing that for me. Like the slap in the face, her openness was a gift, and I could open it…or not.

I lived in a world of butting heads and chest-beating, dick-slinging competition.

And here, Harper had slapped me and left herself exposed. She hadn't slapped me to win. She was trying to help me.

"Huh." My utterance was the breath of a pressurized jar popping open.

Her eyebrow twitched with curiosity. She was utterly fearless.

I was so fucking crazy about this girl. I was losing my mind, and I didn't know how much longer I could fight it. I wanted to save myself, sure. But I wanted to lift her up. Show the world what they'd missed out on. Present her like a jewel in a box then keep her for myself.

But I had nothing.

I was a loser.

That wasn't going to do her any good, now was it? She deserved better. She *needed* better. She needed a win, and I was going to get it for her.

I went back into the shed. Adjusted to the darkness of the places under shelves and behind busted doors. Found another pair of clippers that wouldn't even open. Tossed them. Found the best tool for the job.

A chainsaw. The gas gauge was at the quarter-full mark.

"I'm nobody. I'm just a kid from Jersey."

"What are you doing?" Harper asked when I came out.

I yanked the cord. The engine coughed. "We've both been fucked." Yank. *Cough.* "And you want Fitz. I can get you Fitz." Yank. *Cough cough.* "I'll suck his dick myself. But you're not sucking it. Put your last dollar on that." Yank. *Sputter. Cough.* "I lost everything. I'm not losing you."

Yank. *Roar.*

The rain thickened to a fine mist that swirled around the chainsaw blade. Harper had her arms crossed over her tits and her mouth set into a line. I waited a second with the chainsaw held up. She knew what I was going to do, but she didn't stop me.

I reached over the little white fence and slashed at the thorn bush bed. Shards of wood flew up, stinging my cheek as I cut away the branches.

Harper put her hand on my back and pointed at the scraps of tangled shrubbery. She had on gloves and goggles.

I nodded.

She reached over the fence and pulled up an armful of bushes. I cut a crooked umbilical cord and she hauled the bunch away before throwing it to the side.

Space had opened up inside the fence. I stepped over it, into the little circle of dirt, and cut that fucking shit right out of the earth, slicing at the trunks, squinting to protect my eyes. I thought a raindrop fell from my forehead, but when I wiped it away, it was blood.

Harper barely paused, and I only stopped when I had to get the chainsaw out of the way or risk taking off one of her limbs.

"I think you have to go a little left."

I followed the angle of her arm. "Yeah."

I sliced the bushes. We'd gotten about a third of the way to the center of the bed when the thunder was coming less than three seconds after the lightning. The raindrops got fatter. The chainsaw was running on fumes when it hit something hard and snapped the chain. The motor kept on with a *whirr*.

"What was that?" I put the chainsaw down and pulled the tangle of branches away from the hard object that had broken the blade. It was a marble tombstone.

EARL BARRINGTON

1945 - 2010

B/LØX\ D FATHER

There was nothing notable about the stone except the chips and cracks in the word *beloved*.

"Harper?"

"I forgot to mention." She was right behind me. "There are gravestones from this point on to the edge of the fence. It's the family plot."

"This your father?" I pointed at the headstone that had broken the chainsaw.

"The one and only. May he rest in peace. Or not. Whatever. Can we keep going?"

"Who added the extra carving?"

"I got a little drunk." She slid the goggles up to the top of her head. Her hair stuck out from around the elastic like a crown. "He was nice to everyone's face. Played at being their pal like a phony baloney, and they fell for it. I'm sorry, but they were suckered." She waved at the factory over the horizon. "Even Catherine. He kept laying people off and dumping the extra work on whoever was left. Long hours. No overtime. They did it with these big proud smiles because they felt like they were special, you know? 'Sure, I'm overworked and got my health insurance cut. And well, of course he fought Fred McGee on his worker's comp. That's just business. But I'm special because I got to stay.' He was a shit. Acted like he was one of the guys. Then he'd throw all his employees a picnic and make it potluck. What a bag of goods." She kicked the headstone, but the density of the thorns behind it kept it from falling. Not to be thwarted, she rattled her throat and spit on the grave. It dripped then rerouted into the carved letters. "Fuck you. You fooled everyone. You never fooled me."

"Don't hold back, Harper. Tell him how you feel."

She slid her goggles back down. "This is why she let the bushes grow. Hiding my vandalism."

"I like your vandalism."

With a thunder crack, the rain came harder.

"Shit!" we cried at the same time.

The phone was going to get drowned. I crouched, bending to see under the bracken. The earth was still dry—but not for long. Harper got to her belly and crawled forward into it.

"I can see it," she called.

I pulled on a thick, thorny joint, opening the tunnel a little wider. She crawled, disappearing to the waist. Thorns grabbed her vest, shredding it. When I wiped my face with my wrist, it came back bloody. Great. I didn't care if I got a little cut up, but I didn't want Harper to bleed. Not to get my phone.

I was about to tell her to forget it. We'd cut back more or tarp the thing and wait for the rain to clear. I wanted the phone, but I didn't want her to get shredded.

"Harper?"

"So close."

"Come back."

"Almost... ow!"

That was it. I hooked my hand in her waistband and pulled her out. She slid on the dirt, vest shredding, light as a feather, pants moving below her sexy ass. When her head was free, she twisted and faced the rain.

My phone was in her bloody hand.

"Ha! I got it!"

I pulled her up by the wrists and flung my arms around her, kissing her as if my life depended on it. Her scent mingled with the rain as two parts of the same nourishment. Ozone. Water. A life in latency.

She put the phone in my front pocket and got her arms around me. The rain fell between us, catching some of the blood from my cut, going into our mouths. It tasted like copper pennies. It tasted like her. She was falling from the sky.

I could have taken her right on the ground. Let the loose thorns and splinters cut our skin. Let the rain soak our hair to flat masses and our fingertips to prunes.

Not this time.

Bending, I kept one arm around her waist, put the other behind her knees, and lifted her.

"I can walk." Her eyelids flicked against the rain. She licked sky water off her lips.

"I know."

I carried her out of the thorn bed, up to the porch, where she opened the screen door with an outstretched hand and I kicked it open. Squeaking wet shoes left a trail on the wood floor. Up the stairs, I walked by feel and habit. She laced her hands around my neck. I couldn't take my eyes off her.

The goggles were still pushed up on her head, and dirt speckled her cheeks like freckles. She was so perfectly flawed, so precisely herself, the sum total of all the meaningless moments in her life leading up to me taking her down the hall to my room. She was the cement holding events together. The darkness after the lightning and the thickened silence before the thunder.

It was rainy-day dark at the top of the stairs. She leaned hard to the left until I let her go. Once she was on her feet, I couldn't keep off her. Lips first, I pinned her to the wall. She wrapped her legs around me, and I drove against her until I felt her heat. She grabbed at my shirt as if she wanted to shred it, and I pulled hers up so I could get at her skin.

We took unsure, turning steps to the room I called mine, with hands everywhere. I got under her bra. Her hard nipple was like a completed pilgrimage. The pressure at the base of my cock was unbearable, and for the first time since I was fourteen, it threatened to relieve itself without my say so.

"Hold on," I said.

"No, no." She reached between my legs. Thank God the sweatpants cut the sensation, or she would have pulled back a sticky mess.

I took her by the wrist and kissed her hand. The back of it was scraped as if she'd gotten into a fight with an alley cat. "You poor girl." From wrist to elbow, I kissed her wounds to the crack of thunder. "You got scraped up for me."

The wind slapped the balcony door open, unleashing her hair. She touched my face. It stung.

"You look sexy with a little blood on you." She pulled my head down and kissed my forehead.

A feather floated to the floor at her feet. It blew across the worn wood, getting stuck on the bed leg.

I put her hand against my chest. "I want you. I haven't known what to do with how you make me feel. But I feel…" I shook my head. "Like the world is bigger with you."

Her eyelids fluttered, and the tightness of her smile told me she wanted to hide it but couldn't.

"I want to take care of you. Everything is going to go your way. Do you hear me? You're a queen, and everyone's going to know it. No one's going to treat you the way I did ever again."

She put her fingers on my lips. "Hush. You can't promise that."

"I can." I pulled on the shoulders of her vest. "Starting with me, right now."

She put her arms down, and I slipped the vest off her. The shredded back panel leaked feathers. They blew in the wind like snow. I held it up. The thorns had ripped clear through. I closed the window and tossed the vest in a corner.

"Come." I held my hand out and led her to the bathroom.

The light from the window was enough. I pulled off her goggles before I kneeled at her feet and tapped her boot. She picked up her foot, and I slipped off the boot. Then the sock, kissing her instep before moving to the other foot. She giggled.

"Sorry," she said. "I'm ticklish."

"I'll make a note. Arms up."

Standing, I lifted her shirt over her head, revealing a plain white bra that was half off where my hand had intruded. I reached around to unhook it. She winced. I went around her and moved her hair to the front. A three-inch gash was drying between her shoulder blades, and a half dozen little ones surrounded it. Her jeans were ripped at the top of her butt and the backs of her thighs.

"The thorns got you good," I said, going around to her front and slipping off her bra.

"That thorn bush always hated me. It was waiting for the day it could get at me."

"We should cut it down." I kissed between her breasts, kneeling to get my lips on her belly.

She put her fingers in my hair as I undid her jeans. "It's my sister's. It's her way of protecting the family plot. It's nice when it blooms."

I pushed her jeans down slowly, trying to keep the fabric from rubbing where she was hurt. "Step out."

She picked her feet out of her pants, and I pushed the jeans away. I could smell her. She was so close. A big part of me demanded I take her right there, any way she'd let me. But the smaller part, the part that seemed as though it had been dormant my entire life, demanded I take care of her first.

The medicine cabinet was full of shit. Expired, half-used, dried-up bottles of vanity goop, amber bottles of medicine, bandages, makeup. No alcohol. No gentle astringents. I found a brown bottle of hydrogen peroxide and a few loose cotton balls in a Dixie cup.

I sat on the toilet with the bottle and cup between my legs. "Come. Let me see your back."

She stepped forward, spun on the ball of her foot, and swung her hair out of the way. "Thank you."

"I haven't touched you yet." I tipped the brown bottle over a cotton ball. "I might suck at this."

"It doesn't matter."

I touched the cotton ball to the deepest gash. She sucked in a breath.

"Told you." I dabbed around it before going for the raw parts. "I need practice."

"We'll have to get in more adventures."

I stretched a Band-Aid over her shoulder blade cut and worked on the backs of her thighs. "More adventures?"

"Yeah. Like wrestling alligators in Florida."

"We could take a dog team across Alaska."

She got one Band-Aid across the long cut and a circle on a particularly deep one.

"Percy needs to be on the back with us. We can take pictures of him and send them back. Like people do with the lawn gnomes."

I kissed the place where her back met her ass and turned her to face me. "Whatever you want."

"I like the sound of that."

She ran her fingers through my hair, and I took them away so I could see the damage to her hands. It wasn't too bad, but I wanted to heal every wound she'd gotten for me.

"You know what though? I'm going to kibosh the dogs and the alligators and every other animal. Not even a kitten," I said.

"No?"

I put the bottle and compressed cotton ball to the side, looking up at her naked body with my hands gripping her elbows. The rain hadn't let up a bit, but the thunder had gotten farther away. "Not until you swear you're giving up on Fitz. The whole plan. Get him here by getting Badger to promise tax breaks or whatever. Show him how committed you all are. But he can't have you. You're mine. Only mine. And I know you care about this town. I'll give up everything to save it if it makes you happy. But I cannot let another man touch you. Do you understand?"

She didn't answer. She didn't nod or give me a signal. She picked up the wet cotton ball. "Stay still."

"That's not an answer."

She dabbed my forehead. It stung. She moved the cold pad to my cheek then my chin. The pain followed. It was bearable against her not answering.

"Well?" I asked.

"It's complicated."

"No. It's very fucking simple."

She tossed the cotton ball onto the vanity. "Taylor Harden, I thought I could just keep hating you. I figured you'd help me then go away. I swear to you, on everything I love, that you opened a door in my heart and walked right in. If I knew how to unlock that damned door and throw you out, I would. The way you act. The way you treat me. You're too big in there, and it's uncomfortable."

"That's. Not. An. Answer."

She swallowed hard. "There's no one else. Not after you."

She bent her knees and straddled me. I pressed her down against my erection. She swayed a little, rubbing herself against the length.

"Swear it," I said with my lips on her collarbone. I couldn't kiss the entire surface of her body fast enough.

"On a stack of Bibles."

I kissed her mouth between words, and she kissed me between syllables.

"I'm going to be your first." I stood, holding her. She wrapped her legs around me as I carried her to the bedroom. "Right now."

"Yes. Be that."

"I want you to come your first time. I want it to be good."

I laid her on the bed. She was so fully naked. All cream skin and smooth perfection in the light of a rainy day.

"I'm a mess," I said, pulling my sweatpants down. "I should shower."

"If you shower, I'm going to put my clothes back on and make lunch."

Crawling onto the bed, I hovered over her. My dick weighed a ton, dropping against her belly as if her body were a magnet and I were iron.

"You will not."

"Don't test me, Beeze. We were both out there."

My lips ran down her neck, landing on a sweet, pink nipple. "You smell like the roses. I smell like the thorns."

When her back arched into me, I gave up on a shower. I took her breast, her belly, the sensitive places between her thighs with my mouth. I tasted the nectar between her legs. Gently, I circled my tongue at her opening, tasting the tight ring I was about to break. She dug her fingers into my shoulders, and I backed off. I didn't want her to come, but I wanted her to be close.

"I hate to do this," I said, reaching for the night table. I grabbed my wallet and flipped it open. "I need to take care of you."

I put the condom in my teeth and tossed the wallet on the floor.

She snapped the packet away. "I got this." She ripped it open with her teeth, spit the strip, and took out the condom. Would she ever stop making me smile?

Yes. When she stroked my cock, she wiped the smile right off my face.

"That's good?"

"Yes." I was lucky to form a coherent word.

I helped her roll the condom on. That was one thing I didn't want a first-timer to be in charge of, though I felt like a first-timer myself. When she spread her legs wider and lifted her hips, I was overwhelmed by her needs and mine.

I ran my finger over her clit once more, then I pressed against her opening. Her lips parted. The rain pounded the windows, and the drops cast moving shadows on her cheeks.

"Say good-bye to this."

"Yesokaygood-bye."

One finger inside. So tight. I was stalling. I didn't know how I was going to last.

"Fuck me," she squeaked. "God, could you just fuck me?"

"Is that how we ask for something?"

"Please. Fuck me, *please*."

My cock throbbed in my hand as I put it against her. She put her hands on my cheeks and mouthed *please* one last time before I pushed forward.

I felt the break immediately, and the arousal on her face twisted into pain.

"You okay?" I didn't move. Couldn't. One stroke and I'd be done for.

"Yeah."

"I'm going to go slow. It's going to feel good. I promise."

She nodded as if she trusted me because she had no choice. "I want to do it right."

"You're beautiful, goose. You're perfect." I could see that wasn't what she needed to hear. "And you're doing it right. Very right."

I moved inside her, taking it slow and easy. I kissed her frequently. Reassured her constantly. When she seemed less pained, I reached between us and touched her clit with my thumb.

She gasped.

"Is that a yes?" I whispered.

"Yes."

"Does it still hurt?"

"Only a little. Oh, God, but not when you do that."

I pushed deep inside her and circled her clit with my thumb. The pressure to come was building, but she had to come first.

Her legs shuddered. Her knees spread wider. Lips parted, letting out a soft groan, eyebrows knotted.

I wanted to take that moment and live it forever. That second before her fingernails dug deep into my back and her spine twisted. But it was eaten up by her orgasm and my need to keep my thumb on her clit.

When she moved my hand away, I leveraged my knees and fucked her faster, getting as deep as I could and letting go.

Nothing had ever felt that good. Nothing except falling on her and burying my face in her neck, drinking in the scent of infinite possibilities.

XLII

J hadn't curled up with a woman like this since the first week of college, before Soo and I had been too hosed to fuck or even see each other outside study group.

When I woke, very early in the morning, Harper still slept on my arm, still naked and probably so sore she wouldn't be able to walk. My phone wasn't broken. It was charging on the chair seat, silent but flashing. I'd woken to the glow half an hour before, but I didn't have the willpower to let Harper go. Somewhere in Silicon Valley, my life was falling apart, and the umbilical cord to that clusterfuck was calling.

I wished I'd put the phone in another room so I could live in a bubble. Just for one full night, I wanted to take in the smell of her, the satin of her skin, the sound of the rain, and the whoosh of her breath.

A man has to make a choice at some point. Either do great things or enjoy half sleep in the rain in the arms of a woman. I'd chosen a long time ago to do great things.

There was always the possibility I could do both. I'd been wrong before. I had been wrong about the type of person behind my destruction. He wasn't a sociopathic criminal, and he wasn't even a he. He was a she, and she was as warm and bighearted as could be.

I had been wrong about my immunity to women like her, if another one even existed on the planet. I thought about that for what seemed like a long time.

"Can you get that please?" she mumbled. "It's making me crazy."

"It's not even on vibrate, and you're facing the other direction."

"I can feel it flashing."

"Fine."

We untangled. She dropped back onto the pillow, and I sat up. The sky outside was opaque grey, and the sunlight said five o'clock. My watch disagreed by four and a half hours. It was nine thirty.

Jesus. I hadn't slept that late in years. And it was before work hours back home.

Still naked, with a streak of blood on my thigh, I picked up the phone. Harper rolled out of bed and trotted into the bathroom, clicking the door shut behind her.

Deepak had been trying to get me.

<I'm not asking where you are anymore.>
<There's a clause in your contract.
You become incapacitated, control of QI4
reverts to your main investor.>
<It's been triggered.>

"Shit."

I called Deepak.

"You need to get back here," he said without a greeting. "Now."

"Where is he?" I sat on the edge of the bed. "Let me talk to him."

"Are you kidding? I'm not going in there. He wants to know where you are. Please tell me your phone is cloaked."

Harper came out of the bathroom, naked as a Renaissance painting. Fuck. I'd been doing everything except what I was supposed to be doing.

"Of course it's cloaked. What's he doing?"

Harper kneeled behind me on the bed and put her hands on my shoulders. She rubbed them and kissed the back of my neck. I was crazy about her, but I wasn't crazy. I knew she was listening.

"Once he locked the system? He made phone calls. Dozens. Jack found him on a Tor forum offering to make QI4 boot sector open source—"

"What? No!"

"If anyone could get past the lockdown. There was a feeding frenzy. He's stirring the pot. He's connecting to Wi-Fi and opening the cage in six days for day one of GreyHatC0n."

He couldn't do that. There was no coming back from the system becoming open source. Anyone could use it. Anyone who wanted to be a star could build an OS on it. It would flush everything down the toilet.

"Has anyone talked to him?"

"Once he got off the forums, he was gone. We all tried."

"Don't go code black. We'll fix this." I said it to myself more than Deepak. I had to believe it. I had to talk myself out of a meltdown. The OS had been the easiest part to build. Anyone could do it.

"Fix it? Tell me how!" he shouted loud enough to hurt my ear.

"The quantum circuits are still ours."

"Until someone reverse engineers them."

"It's six days until the convention," Harper said.

"Is that her?" Deepak asked.

"Yes. Have you checked—?"

"Fuck you, bitch!" Deepak shouted to Harper.

"Deeps, do not—"

"Then fuck you too, bro."

Harper tapped my phone to turn on the speaker. "We fix it the same way I broke it. Does he have a company credit card?"

"Yes," Deepak and I answered together.

"Does he use it?"

"It's a Grand Cayman bank," I objected.

Deepak chimed in. "It's totally cloaked."

"Gentlemen." Her eyes met mine and were so clear that if I'd thought she'd need help standing or doing anything, I was wrong. "It was a yes or no question."

"Yes," we answered in unison again, like busted third graders.

"Can you see purchases from the past few days?"

"Raven has that stuff," Deepak said. "She's probably stuck on 101 right now. She'll be here in half an hour if there's no traffic."

"Do you trust her?" Harper asked. "Yes or no?"

"Yes," I said without thinking.

I didn't have to think. I trusted Raven. She didn't need the job, but she stayed and it wasn't for the sex. She was the only woman in an office of men. She was oft-maligned, the butt of jokes, well-paid, overworked, and underappreciated. Plenty of other jobs waited at other companies, yet she stayed.

I shouldn't have trusted her. She was a woman and an unpredictable entity, but she'd put a lot of faith in QI4. She deserved it back.

"We find out if he's ordered anything online," Harper said. "We can intercept it at the distro center."

"Is that how you hacked our monitors?" Deepak asked.

"Yes."

"Call us from her desk when she gets in," I said before I could be questioned.

I said "us," not "me." I didn't know if Deepak or Harper noticed, but I looked at the unintentional pronoun as if it were a wedding crasher.

"Okay?" I said urgently. "Deeps? You got it?"

Deepak didn't answer. The silence on the other end of the phone was deafening.

"Are you there?"

"Consider this my resignation," he said. "I'm done being your sidekick. I'll get you a letter in an hour."

The connection went dead before I could try to talk him out of it.

Shit. I put the phone to my forehead and looked at the space between my knees. I trusted Deepak's competence and loyalty completely. Apparently he didn't trust mine.

If I lost Deepak, what else had I lost? Who would follow him out? How many of the guys were halfway out or fully gone? Was I operating a shell of a company? I didn't even know. Deep's resignation was a deep wound I had to sew up, but I couldn't from Barrington.

"I have to go home," I said.

"I think you do." She rubbed my shoulders.

"This isn't about the system anymore. It's about the people."

"Yes."

"I need to get to the airport."

"I'll drive."

I looped my fingers around her wrist and pulled her into my lap. I couldn't imagine being separated from her for a second. She'd become a part of my life. "Come with me."

She smirked just enough to give away a deep distrust of something so simple because it was simple but powerful. "I'm not letting him smoke me out." She tapped my chin and stood. "He knows where I am, but he's waiting for you to deliver me."

"I can protect you. I got this."

She sucked in her lower lip just a little, trying to keep her face expressionless. Every twitch of insecurity was magnified. "Get in the shower. I'll pull the car around. If we go now, we can take Route 34. The interstate is gross."

She spun on her heel and left the room as if her decision to get on the plane was the last to be made.

It wasn't. She was coming with me. She just didn't know it yet.

The airport was 145 miles away. At sixty mph, I had about two and a half hours in the car to let her know that I wasn't leaving her. She was coming with me. I needed her support, her body, and to a large extent, I needed her brain. She was too smart and too devious to leave behind. She was too sexy and warm to do without.

We were ten minutes out of Barrington, with farmland stretching in all directions. I was driving the shimmymobile, swearing I'd get her a new car as soon as I had a minute.

"So he tells her, on his goddamn deathbed, 'Make sure my daughters marry the right kind of man.' To her face." Harper was in the middle of a story about her father. "Then she tells everyone, and they all decide no one in town qualifies as the right kind of man. What kind of self-loathing is that? How much do you have to hate yourself to take orders from a guy who paid his contractors half what they billed? Because they 'didn't do a good job'? And then agree your children aren't good enough for his?"

My phone dinged. It was lodged in an empty space in the front console, and I could just catch the preview in the sliver of visible glass.

It was Fitz. I pulled out the phone.

"At one point, I wanted to fuck someone just to… hey, there's no texting and driving."

She reached for the phone, but I pulled it back. "Nope."

"No. Texting. And. Driving. I'll read it to you."

She was right. But I needed to see the text.

"Easy does it, goose. There's no one on the fucking road."

I leaned the phone on the steering wheel and read it at seventy-five mph. I don't recommend it. Especially if the text freezes the blood solid in your veins.

—Sorry about QI4, bro—

Fitz was a bro all the way, and come to think if it, he was a week late with condolences. He was secretive and eccentric, but he wasn't cheap with support.

—Sailing around Horn of Africa.
Back in 2 days. Talk then.—

Harper had no trouble getting the phone out of my hand at that point. As a courtesy, she shouldn't have read my texts, but I wasn't surprised that her curiosity bulldozed her manners.

The logic and timing took a second to sink in but no more.

Of course, Fitz could have been bullshitting her the whole time. He was a bullshitter and a filthy, kinky fucker, but he didn't have to lie about buying a factory.

Harper tucked the phone away without commenting. The road went straight to the horizon, disappearing into a pinpoint at the end of the earth.

"It was me, wasn't it?" I asked. "You were after me. Just me."

She turned on the radio.

I turned it off. "You went to a lot of trouble to get me here, and it wasn't just revenge. Maybe you told yourself it was. But it wasn't revenge at all. You were after *me*. Say it. Just say it."

"I don't know what you want out of me."

I slammed on the brakes. Blue rubber smoke billowed so thick I was sure I'd blow a tire. The car skidded to the side of the road.

"Jesus, Taylor!"

"You didn't bring me here to help you with Fitz. He's not coming."

"Maybe he lied to me."

"No. No, you're fucked if you think I'm believing another thing you say. You were after me. You knew I was making my own boards. You want me to buy the factory. You hacked me, and you set this whole thing up so I'd fall in love with you. Right? Say it."

"It's not that simple." She took a breath so deep her chest expanded.

"Were you using him to teach you what I wanted? Or to make me jealous?"

"I was in contact with Fitz to get him here, then he went sailing. But I never thought we could get him. We needed an unproven company that was going to have a growth spurt. You were the most likely mark, but any of the other outcomes was acceptable."

Funny how she ran right into talking as if she had a laser pointer in her hand and a PowerPoint presentation behind her. Strategy and tactics. Straight outta Barrington.

"And revenge? Don't forget revenge for not hiring you, right?"

"Unexpected upside."

I leaned over to her and draped my arm over the back of her seat. "Stop. Lying."

"Fuck you." She got out of the car and slammed the door.

"Oh no. Fuck *you*." I got out.

She was walking back toward Barrington. Fifteen miles in cowboy boots. I should have let her go. Just taken her fucking car, driven it to the airport, and dumped it there. But I had a score to settle.

I took her by the elbow and spun her around, letting go as soon as she was facing me. A truck blew by. Gravel smacked my cheek, and she turned away from the road as if slapped.

"Who's in on it? Catherine?"

"Never."

"Johnny. Butthead? Who else? How did you get them to clean up the factory? Tell me. Is it the whole town? Are all of you in on it?"

Eyes on the ground, toes pointed inward, arms crossed, her body language was guilt. The white heat of my anger was directed at her and back at myself for falling for it. The rage burned through my tenderness but didn't consume it. And that made me angrier.

"You know what? You're right." I held up my hands. "It doesn't matter."

Leaving her, I walked back to the car. Another SUV went by so fast the car was lifted a little from the ground. Fuck these assholes. Fuck this town. Fuck Harper Barrington. The Watsonette. Goose.

She didn't make a sound behind me. I was going to leave her on the side of the road. Let her figure it out.

You're not leaving her anywhere.

Maybe not. Maybe I was going to turn the car around, put her in it, and leave her at Pat's grocery store, where I found her. And I was never going to see her again. I was going to leave her there and not even kiss her. Then I was stealing her shitty car and leaving it in long-term parking. Because—

"I can't let you leave," she said from behind me. Closer than I left her. She was a stealthy little goose.

"Good-bye, Harper." Three steps from the trunk of the car, I waved without looking. Just to hurt her. Just to pay her back for the lies. I wasn't leaving her on the side of the road, but I still wasn't done with the lava burning my guts.

The car's lights flashed, and the horn tooted. All the locks clacked.

I spun around. She had a little handmade remote control in her hand.

"I'm sorry," she said. "I can't let you go."

"Are you out of your mind?" I was in her face in three steps.

"We have to fix QI4 from here." Her voice was steady as a boat on a mirror-flat sea. "I can't let you leave. You'll never come back."

"You know what kind of parasite kills the host?" I picked up a rock from the side of the road. She could lock the doors all she wanted. "An extinct one. If I don't fix this, I can't buy your fucking factory." I lifted the stone, tossing it up a few inches and catching it again as if I were Mr. Nonchalant.

"I know, but—!"

I threw the rock through the passenger side window, then I reached in to unlock the doors. They clacked. She ran to me and grabbed my arm, hair blowing all over her face when a truck passed. She had a desperation I'd never seen before. Putting my hand on the door latch, I kept my face hard and cold, or I was going to be her bitch, and I was no woman's bitch.

"You can't leave," she cried. "Please. I love you."

In a flash of a second, I went from a stretched, bursting bag of hot rage to a brittle shell around an empty cage. My brain went dark. Neurons stopped firing. My heart flatlined for a beat while I absorbed the shock. She was the first woman to tell me she loved me, and she'd caught me in the defenseless state between coherent thoughts.

As if sensing an opening, she put her hands on my chest, looking up at me with her blue/brown halo eyes. I filled my lungs, my heart thumped, neurons fired. She wasn't lying when she mouthed it again.

I love you.

What a brave little psycho she was. What a reckless woman. What a fierce and sensitive warrior.

Somewhere in the conflict of my admiration, a voice cut through.

You're not leaving.

I was leaving. I was taking the car and going back home to salvage what was left of my life. Her love was irrelevant.

You're staying.

I could come back. I could deal with this whole Harper mess later.

You're staying with her.

The voice was correct. I was staying. Every other bit of coding in me resisted what I knew was true. I was staying to make her happy, and I wasn't pleased with the choice. I'd been perforated between what I'd wanted before I met her and what I wanted after, then she'd ripped me in two.

I grabbed the hair at the back of her neck. She closed her eyes and sucked air through her teeth. She went liquid.

I pushed her against the car, grinding my erection into her. "You love me?"

"Yes. From that day in the cafeteria that you forgot. And over the conference room table when you ignored me. All the other reasons, they're real, but they're not true. I hoped you'd help us in a hundred ways, but that's not why I hacked you. I told everyone here something half-true and you something half-true, and I had my own truth. I know I'm crazy. The whole time I was trying to make this work, I knew I was out of my mind. That has to count for something. It has to because I'm admitting it."

I lifted behind her knee to change the angle of her body so I could press against the heat between her legs. She groaned and dug her nails into my arms.

"Say it."

"I brought you because I loved you."

Pushing harder against her, I demanded more because I believed it. For once, what she said had the ring of truth. For once, it was exactly what I wanted to hear.

"Again."

"I loved you."

"I'm going to show you what you love. What you want to keep here. I'm not going to fuck you like you were a virgin yesterday." Another hard thrust. She squeaked. "You're getting fucked like a woman."

"Do it."

I opened the back door and flicked away the few shards of glass that had flown that far. She bent to sit in the backseat. I got in and closed the door, crawling over her like a predator.

She put her face close to mine, but there wasn't going to be any kissing.

Kissing was for women who didn't hold me hostage.

"Show me your pussy." I unbuckled, unbuttoned, unzipped.

"I think we can hack the system back," she said, wiggling her pants down to her knees. "If you have his number on your phone."

"He's not keeping anything on his phone." I fisted my cock. All my frustration flowed into it. "Turn over. Show me your ass."

She paused. Started to turn. It was tight in the backseat. I couldn't straighten all the way, and she had no room to flip comfortably.

"What's the way in?" She asked it without irony.

I turned her over the rest of the way. Her waistband was right above her knees, and her ass was oval and flawless, with a dark, fuckable seam in the middle.

"I have to talk to him." I put three fingers inside her. She was wet.

Very wet. "That's the only way in. Friendship." I twisted my hand and pressed my thumb to her clit. She groaned. "You like that?"

"Yes."

"You like three fingers in you?"

"Yes. In the meantime, we can look for a kill switch. Or a flaw in his lockdown."

I pulled my hand out and slapped her ass. "He doesn't do flaws." I put my dick to her opening, letting it hover there while I spread her thighs apart. "We have to persuade him to unlock it."

I shoved myself into her hard and deep. She let out a long sound of surprise and pleasure.

"I'm going to fuck you like you fucked me." I twisted her hair in my hand and yanked her head back. "And you're going to take it."

"Yes."

She couldn't finish the question when I thrust into her so hard I thought I'd break her. But I didn't. She looked over her shoulder at me. I pulled her hair until she looked forward.

"This is mine," I said, fucking her hard and fast. Pulling her hair to keep her still while I pounded her.

"Fuck yes. Yours."

I bent over her and put my lips to her ear. "This is what you get for keeping me here. Now I own you. Your tight little cunt is mine. You happy now? You wanted me to fuck you like an animal?"

She grunted. She was so hot. I put my fingers in her mouth so I could feel the vibrations of her groans.

"Answer me. You want it like this?"

She couldn't talk with my hand in her mouth, and that was part of the pleasure.

"Touch yourself." I slammed her as if I could snap her in two.

She let go of my arm, leaving a line of red marks, and put her hand between her legs.

"Make yourself come."

I held back the explosion that built inside me and watched her back arch. She went stiff and tense, yelling in a language that didn't exist.

When she moved her hand away and took panting breaths, I pulled out of her and kneeled, facing the side window.

"I think we can backdoor him," she said.

"It needs a social engineering component. Turn around."

She turned halfway. I took her by the hair again and looked her in the face. She was dewy and loose. Her tongue flicked over her lower lip.

"You're going to suck my cock now. Any objections?"

"No."

"Open your mouth."

She did it, and I pushed her head onto my erection. She took what she could, and my hand demanded more. When I let her off, she sucked air.

"Is he on Chaxxer?" she groaned.

"Yes, but you aren't anymore. Finish sucking me."

Looking up at me, a mischievous smile crossed her lips as if she'd just had an earth-shattering idea.

"What?" I asked, thinking she had a hack on her mind.

"Nothing." She went down on me, sucking like a champ, using her hand with just enough expertise to get me off and just enough clumsiness to be one-hundred-percent Harper.

I didn't correct her. I wanted her exactly like this.

I came in her mouth with the back of my head on the backseat window. She took it like a good girl, looking up at me again with that mischievous glint in her eyes. When I was done, she closed her lips and swallowed.

She straightened her back, and I pulled her up. I wasn't squeamish about kissing a girl after I came in her, especially Harper, who deserved to be kissed long and deep and without a second of hesitation.

I thrust my tongue past her lips, holding her head as if it was precious, and I tasted the sharpness and felt the thickness of bathroom cleaner. "Ugh!"

When I pulled away, she started laughing. She still had a lot of my cum on her tongue. It dripped off the crease in her bottom lip.

"Fuck!" I said, reaching into the front center console, trying not to close my mouth or open it wide enough to drip all over me. I found a napkin and spat into it, then I wiped my mouth and let myself laugh. "You're in trouble, goose."

She was still laughing. I couldn't help but smile with her. I pulled out another napkin and held it in front of her mouth. She closed it and tried to swallow but couldn't stop laughing long enough to gulp.

"Okay, come on." I held the napkin under her chin, but she was holding her belly and laughing. Tears streamed down her hot, pink cheeks. I had to control myself enough to wipe her face. "Stick your tongue out."

She managed to do it, and I wiped it down with the napkin.

"Oh, my God." She ran her wrists over her eyes. "That was… oh, my God. You should have seen your face."

"What was it?"

"It was like…"

She made a face that crossed horror, shock, distaste, and wounded pride, and we both fell into laughing fits. She fell into my arms and made the face again. Then I made the face, and she shook her head because I'd gotten it wrong. We were cracking up and trying to form words. Failing.

"Okay, seriously," I said. "Can I pull your pants up?"

She was lost in it. She seemed to be making up for a few years' worth of missed laughter in the backseat of the Chevy. I pulled up her pants, and she arched her back so I could get them in place.

My mouth tasted like Mr. Clean, and she delighted the fuck out of me.

XLIV

"That's it?" I asked from behind the shower curtain. "You think he's going to fall for that again?" She was using the closed toilet as a chair.

"You fell for it last time. Not him."

"Thanks for the reminder." I stuck my head under the water.

"Anytime."

"But he knows your exploit probably better than you do at this point."

"The problem with you guys is you think it's not going to happen to you. You think you have your bases covered. The more direct we make it, the more likely we are to get through."

"You think he ordered something from Amazon, coming through your distro center, and he's going to bring it to the office and just roll in and out of the cage with it? Because he didn't learn from me?"

"He doesn't know it was your watch that had the transmitter."

Her voice was clearer, louder, with a more defined echo. I opened my eyes. She was naked in the curtain opening.

"You like what you see, goose?"

"I like what I see." She stepped into the shower, getting under the faucet as if she was entitled to the flow. "Why is this freezing?" She turned the temperature up.

I soaped her shoulders, running my hands down her back. "The distro center's going to be a red flag. It's a loser."

She turned to face me and bent her head back to soak her hair. "Don't worry about the distro center." She pressed her lips together and shut her eyes as water poured down her face.

I ran the soap over her. Her body was slick and soft, with hard places at the bones and nipples. "Worrying's my job."

She opened her mouth to get water in it and closed her jaw so it came out in a gentle fountain. It was the kind of unthinking, unplanned gesture we all made in places where we were used to being alone.

"Worrying isn't a job," she said, opening her eyes. Her lashes were black and stuck together like thornless bushes, and one particular water droplet was centered exactly around a pale freckle on her cheek. I rubbed it away. It was too perfect.

"Your plan has so many holes it could drain spaghetti," I said, pushing my dick against her.

"That sounds delicious."

"Are you wondering what it's like to fuck in the shower?"

"A little."

Taking her by the backs of her thighs, I pulled her up and leaned her back against the tile. "Fucking in the shower is as American as apple pie." I held her slick cunt against my length.

"What do I have to do?"

"Spread your legs around me."

"Like this?"

"Tell me what you want. Say it exactly."

She sucked in her bottom lip. "I want you to put your dick… no, cock inside me. All the way. I want it to hurt a little bit when I feel you hit the end. I want you to do it hard so I can feel everything."

"Let me hold you up. And use the wall as leverage. You ready?"

"Yep." She looked down at where we were about to be joined.

She was slick when I thrust inside. Two strokes to get the whole thing in. I grabbed under her thighs, holding her up and keeping her legs open and still. She was still looking between us.

Her curiosity was so hot. I looked with her as I pulled out and went back hard.

"Like that?" I asked.

"Yes."

"God, you're in for it now."

Holding us together, I fucked her as hard as I could, using my body to rub her clit when I was deep. I wanted her to come without my fingers. Just my cock and us and the dripping hot water. To get the most friction, I pulled her to me until she couldn't see between us. There would be another time for her to watch our bodies couple.

In the shower, we were better positioned for a fingerless orgasm. Her mouth opened. Water dripped from her nose onto her lip.

"How's it feel?"

"Yes." Her voice cracked on such a short word. "More."

I gave it to her so hard I grunted with the force. I wanted to crawl inside her and live. Peel her open. Surround myself with her.

Her throat let loose a series of short *ahs*.

"Are you going to come?"

She nodded. I didn't slow down or speed up. I wanted her there.

"I can't hear you," I said.

"I'm going to come."

"Look at me."

The effort to keep her gaze on mine and her eyes open was all over her face. I held her by the jaw to keep her toward me. Always thrusting. Always pushing. Something in me was loosening. The valve was turning, and when it spun, it was going to fly open.

I couldn't come inside her.

But I couldn't stop before she had hers.

I thought about anything. The exploit. Qubit structure. Her name in base64 encoding.

The muscles of her face tightened.

"Look at me," I demanded again to keep my mind off my pending explosion.

Her eyes narrowed to slits but stayed open. I wasn't going to last. Her back tightened, straightened. The muscles in her thighs tightened. She cried out to her creator, scratching the skin off my back more effectively than a thousand thorns.

When she removed her fingers from my skin, I pulled out and held my cock. It was lubricated and swollen. "Jesus, I—"

The valve blew, and I came on her belly, jerking myself like an adolescent. By the time I was done, the shower had mostly washed her clean.

"Thank you," I whispered.

"No, thank *you*." She turned off the water.

She tried to get out, but I blocked her. "I mean it. Thank you. Not for the fuck. I mean, yes, thank you for the fuck. But thank you for…"

For what? I put my fists against the tile and lowered my head. Our feet comingled in the draining tub.

"For kidnapping me."

"I didn't kidnap you."

"You did."

She slapped my shoulder playfully. "Did not."

"Well, whatever you did, it was worth it."

"We'll see." She dodged me and stepped out of the tub.

"You're a once-in-a-lifetime person, goose." I followed her out.

Taking a white towel out of the cabinet, she let it fall out of the fold. "Yeah. Sure."

I took the towel away and wrapped it around her. "I can't explain what you've done to me. I want to take care of you and hurt you at the same time. I shouldn't trust you, but I do. I'm willing to crash to find out if you're trustworthy, and I don't care if you're not. It was all worth it to have you. Everything was worth it."

She stepped on my feet, and I lifted her to kiss her.

XLV

The trick was to get past Keaton, who would have protections on his devices. I was sure he had scripts that he'd coded himself and never released, making them impossible to test.

The sun set at a deep angle through Harper's third-floor window. She was in a tank top and shorts, her butt in her desk chair and her feet on her desk. I'd moved a few boxes of circuitry to stretch out on a beat-up love seat. In the previous hours, she'd looked through the exploit apps on my phone, I'd looked over her shoulder at code, we'd searched Tor for pieces of usable malware, and finally, she'd sat me at her desk so I could look for Keaton on the dark web.

Letting me fuck her was trust. Coming back into town with her was trust.

But probing each other's devices, especially knowing what we knew about each other, was intimate beyond imagining.

"Can we plant a transmitter on Deepak?" she asked. "You'd have to refuse his resignation and make nice first."

"I don't want to get anyone else involved. He and I fighting works right now. Keaton's got a thing about revenge. If we break him and he comes after anyone, it's going to be me."

"Or me."

"Yeah. No."

"He's going to find me," she said. "I'll deal with it."

She thought she was strong enough to survive anything, but I wouldn't leave her long enough to test the theory.

"I'm not trying to scare you, because none of this will happen," I said.

"Oh, this should be good."

"He's loyal. That doesn't make him a nice guy. He has this code he lives by. If you're in, he'll kill for you. If you're out, he'll kill you."

"'Kill' meaning commit actual murder?"

"Mostly cyber stuff. I don't know if he's capable of actual murder, but he knows people who have the same code. They all live by it. And the rest of these guys? I've met them. I can't say for sure they haven't buried any real bodies."

She'd gone bedsheet white. "I'm the enemy."

"No. Not yet. Just trust me. I'll take care of it."

She cleared her throat. Nodded.

"So." I changed the subject. "We transmit from inside the cage. And he takes the transmitter in and out, like you did with my watch?"

"Yeah."

"How are we going to get him to fall for that?"

"What's he keep in his bag?"

"His bag? Lunch?"

"He brown bags his lunch?"

"He's a cheap motherfucker. And he's picky about his food. He only uses this one kind of mustard made by French monks. It's disgusting. It tastes like asshole."

"But he wouldn't carry a whole jar of asshole mustard in his bag."

I leaned back, stretching the backs of my knees over the armrest. What did he carry around? What had I seen him take out of the leather bike messenger bag? Laptop. Keys. Wallet.

She tapped at her keyboard so fast and hard it was no wonder she needed to tape her knuckles. "I don't know why I didn't think of this before."

I got up and looked over her shoulder, brushed my lips along her neck, then looked again. She was inside a deep web database.

"Is this the distribution center?" I asked.

"Yeah. I cracked it months ago. We don't need his credit card. Do you know his home address?"

"He's not going to just order stuff from Amazon, goose."

"Yeah, that's what everyone says. What they don't know is half the small businesses in this country run fulfillment through four major distro warehouses. One of them's right off the interstate." She pointed north. "Unless the owner's writing addresses in Sharpie at the kitchen counter. Can I have an address?"

I gave it to her. She tapped it into fields faster than I could speak. Nothing came up.

"Wait." I rubbed my eyes, trying to remember the address he had everything forwarded from.

"You're very cute when you're thinking."

"And when I'm not thinking?"

"You're dazzling."

I kissed her and gave her Keaton's forwarding address.

A recent order came up under Lupine Alfa. What my friend and silent partner had in malicious intent, he lacked in imagination.

"British hand cream and deodorant," I muttered. I couldn't believe she was right, but there was the order—in full color LED. "So much for being an international man of mystery."

"It's at the distro center now. Shit. Stuff to California goes out on the night shift because it buys them an extra day. Turning of the earth and all. I'm only scheduled for a morning on Tuesday."

She and I were silent for a minute. She stopped typing and tapped the table.

As calm as I'd been on the surface, I'd been covering a deep well of panic that this town, this house, this woman was a snare designed to hold me squirming forever. The panic revealed itself in its decline. I was still unnerved. Still anxious. But as I leaned on the desk and looked over her shoulder with my arms on each side of her, I could see a way out. The tunnel was long and dark, but at the end was the tiniest and dimmest of lights.

It was the possibility of a social engineering hack that let some of the anxiety go. Hacks always revealed themselves in time. It was Harper. Her partnership. Her knowledge. Her loyalty.

I put one of my thumbs over her tap-tapping fingers. "I say the hand cream."

"I say we have room in the deodorant container." She crossed her fingers over my thumb.

"Both then."

"We need to work fast. I can only hold it in distro a few hours before there's a flag. Everything moves out in twenty-four hours, even if it's five-day delivery."

"I'm not going to have time to fuck you, am I?"

She turned to me with brutal efficiency in her eyes and sex on her lips. "Not if you want to get this done, Beeze." Back at the computer, she opened a field and dropped down the delivery time. "Johnny's on the night shift. He can do the switch. It should be in his mailbox in… I'll upgrade the package delivery now."

"No," I said. "He'll notice. And he's a cheap motherfucker."

"You want to wait an extra five business days?"

"Split the difference."

"Fine." She put him on four-day delivery.

"I code," I said. "You make me some pretty transmitters."

"You think I'm going to let you sit at my machine unsupervised?" she purred.

I kissed her neck. I could die happy with my lips on her jaw, tasting her passion and her panic. "Yes. I do."

She sighed, and with that sigh, she surrendered.

XLVI

Catherine didn't ask questions when Harper sent her miles away to get the nearest deodorant stick that matched Keaton's taste. Harper said she'd done plenty for her sister without asking questions.

The hand cream wasn't as accessible. There wasn't a jar of Moxie's shea butter at retail in a one-hundred-mile radius. So Harper filled out a form saying the distro center's jar was broken, buying us another day. Johnny would grab the unbroken jar from distro and deliver it the next night before his shift.

"We do it all the time." She waved at me as she got off the phone with Johnny. "They log everything, but if it breaks, you fill out a form and it's done."

"Fucking criminals. All of you."

She locked her hands around my waist. "You mad, bro?"

I kissed her and returned her hug. "Yes. Raging mad we have to finish this before I can fuck you again."

She pushed me off her and picked up the legal pad that had our notes and flowcharts. "Let's get 'er done."

Though we'd conceived the plan without words, we'd worked out the details with lists, on paper so nothing was missed.

We would place tiny transmitters, much like the one Harper had built for my watch, into Keaton's toiletries. One or both would (hopefully) end up near his cell phone, where it would keylog from his Tempest emissions. Every tap on his phone would be transmitted to us. He might not bring his phone into QI4's Faraday cage, but we'd have access to his laptop through the Bluetooth connection and could figure out how he'd put a layer of encryption over Harper's. Then it was a matter of time before he connected his laptop to the poison pill. Which would give us access to QI4.

A hundred variables bounced around the plan. This was why I didn't like social engineering hacks. They were too dependent on human behavior, which was unreliable as shit. Openings in code were openings in code. You could depend on code to do exactly what it said. No more. No less. That was the beauty and downfall of pure code.

Harper's machine was safe when I coded what we were planting on the transmitter. She showed me her QI4 hack so I could use pieces of it, and I was lost. It strung together pieces of what she assumed was there, looping them together like a drawstring bag and tying them tightly with layers and layers of encryption and exploitation code she'd designed.

"You really wanted to get me," I said, scrolling through it.

"I guess I did." She reached up to the top shelf of her closet for a clear plastic box. The muscles in the backs of her thighs tightened when she went onto the tips of her toes and just touched the bottom of the box, slipping it half an inch forward.

I got behind her and grabbed the box with one hand and her waist with the other. "How long did it take?" I shook the box before I gave it to her. It was full of circuitry scraps.

"Lot of hours. But…" She shrugged, embarrassed. "Anger's a motivator, I guess."

"No shit, goose." I kissed her forehead and gave her butt a little spank. "No shit."

"You really forgive me?"

I hadn't used the word *forgive*. It was too heavy and serious. Too high on itself. It meant something had been broken.

In her little room, with her in my arms, I didn't have to forgive her for what she'd broken. By smashing her way into my life, she'd made it whole.

"I have no choice," I said. "I love you."

We didn't have time to fuck, but we had enough time to kiss as if the future was a done deal.

XLVII

Out in the deep parts of the country, the horizon's different. It doesn't disappear behind buildings or get lost in a haze of light and particles. It's not a line graph of mountains. It's cut straight all around, like an ocean of land, and at night, it's marked by the line where the stars end.

"Why don't you get Orrin to fix the steering on this thing?" I asked.

It was hard enough to keep the shimmymobile on the road in daylight. With visibility at zero outside the cones of the headlights and the wind whipping the plastic we'd used to cover the window I'd broken, I'd almost run into a ditch more than once. She took deep breaths whenever the car went wide, digging her fists into her sweatshirt and tying her face into knots. It was cute and unnecessary.

"He won't take my money. I won't let him do it for free, and if I go to another mechanic, he'll never forgive me. And I like it that way. It's like a horse I tamed myself."

"You're all crazy. Down to the last one of you."

"You've mentioned that. Pull over here. I see him."

I didn't see shit until she pointed toward the right and the headlights caught a flicker of reflective red. His truck was parked behind a bush between the road and the train tracks.

"I love the whole cloak-and-dagger thing you guys have going."

"Yeah, well, if Pat knew, she'd have a fit."

"She'd be right." I pulled up in front of the bush and cut the engine. I'd never known stars could be bright enough to see by, but there was a lot of shit I didn't know.

The deodorant with the transmitter was in a paper bag at Harper's feet. We'd opened the deodorant from the bottom so it wouldn't disrupt the seal and put the transmitter under the base. The other transmitter was in Harper's pocket, protected by clear kitchen wrap.

Harper pulled down the plastic over her broken window. I turned on the dome light. He leaned his elbows on the top of the door. "Well, hello, Mr. Harden. Harper. What happened to the window, here?"

"Taylor happened."

He shot me a dirty look, and I shrugged like a man driven to madness.

Harper handed him the paper bag. "The order number's on the inside of the bag. Do you have the jar?"

He looked at Harper, then me, then back at Harper. There was only one interpretation for that look. *What the hell is this guy doing here?*

"He's all right," Harper said, holding out her hand.

"First, you're going to tell me what you're up to."

"Trust me." She took the jar from him and spun the cap off.

"I trust you. And I like the gentleman in the driver's seat well enough to shoot pool and throw back a few. But trust is a different thing. I'm not risking my job for some rich, excuse the term or don't, asshole. No offense."

"None taken," I said. "But you put the plant in my watch. So consider this more of the same."

"That's what I thought." He dropped the bag back in Harper's lap, stepped away from the car and into the darkness.

"Johnny!" Harper opened the door.

I reached over and closed it. "Stay here."

"Why? What—?"

Grabbing her wrist, I gave her my full attention for two words. "Trust me."

I grabbed the bag with the deodorant and got out of the car, where the road slanted away. I almost fell. Gravity pulled the door closed. As I went around the front, Harper's face went to stone as she shut off the dome light.

No dummy, that girl. She could see us and not be seen if the dome light was off.

No dummy. Unexpectedly smart.

Why unexpected?

Say it.

To yourself, you can say it.

Say, "I always assumed pretty girls weren't that bright."

"Johnny!" I called, running into the bush. I found him with the clack of a zippo and the pin light of a cigarette. "Hold up."

My eyes adjusted to the starlight. We were right next to his truck. He leaned on the bed.

"I'm holding up." He held a pack of cigarettes out for me. I declined. "Good move. These fucking things killed my mother." He took a drag as if testing mortality. "You want me to do you a favor. I know I don't have much to lose, but it's all I have."

I leaned on the cab. He had a house. His wife had a barely profitable business. He had kids in school and a truck. No, it wasn't much. And who was I to jeopardize it?

I had no right to ask him to do me a favor, but I had no other way to save myself. "Tell me how to make it worth your while."

The smoke billowing from his lips was blue in the starlight. It dispersed when he shook his head. "I helped Harper with… what did she call it? Her *exploit*. A few of us did. Desperate people take risks. It was a stupid idea, but you showed up, right on time. It looked like it was working. You, then we were going to work on the Irish one. Fitzgerald. Then Catherine says you're holed up in a room at their place. I had to practically tie Butthead down."

"Why?"

"Because she's ours. We protect her and her sister, and they protect us. That's how it goes. And now I'm seeing… I don't know what you got going on with her. I'm not making assumptions. I mean, I know well enough. It's your intentions I can't seem to figure out."

"My intentions? What were your intentions bringing me here? You talk like you're so clean. You ruined my life so you could squeeze me. And for what? You think I have some endless well of cash? I'm nobody. I'm ten years away from buying a factory."

He threw his cigarette down and smashed it with the ball of his foot. A car passed, casting moving bush-shaped shadows across us before fading away.

"We'll be here," he said.

"Why?" I only said one word, but a lecture's worth of questions was inside it. Why stay if it's so miserable? Why risk everything for a town that had abandoned him already?

"We got nowhere to go. I wanted my children to raise our grandchildren here, but they're in all corners of the country. Maybe three times a year Pattycakes gets one to show up. Maybe. My daughter, did you know she's an artist? She can't ever come back here. For what? So she can be alone? There's no opportunity here for her to be more than a mother, and she can do that anywhere. My son, the one in law school? Who's he gonna represent here who can pay him? I raised them to do better than we did. I didn't know that meant I'd never see them. I miss them. I miss my children. And you can buy that factory and hire all of us at twenty-five an hour, but my kids aren't coming back. It's me, my wife, and this town. It's all I got."

That was that. I couldn't offer him his life or the company of his children. His home wasn't a place; it was a time in his life that all the money in the world wouldn't bring back.

"I'm sorry." I didn't have any words of wisdom.

"Things were supposed to get better." He seemed to speak to the dirt, the stars, his broken heart.

Jesus. I was turning into some kind of pussy. What was the difference? There were winners and losers in this world. We sank or we swam. Complaints were for whiners and failures. Change. Grow. Learn. Get it right the hundredth time if you had to.

I felt the truth of all of that, but I couldn't say it out loud, even in a supportive, managerial way. It meant accusing Johnny of not trying hard enough, not getting lucky enough. It meant accusing him of being complacent, which wasn't fair even if it was true.

My worldview was having a head-on collision with the world.

"I got you." I switched the brown paper back from my right hand to my left and held the right out to shake. "Harper and I will figure it out."

He clasped my hand and shook it. "Sorry I went girl on you."

"Speaking of girl." He let my hand go, and I pointed at her shitty car. "Harper."

"Yeah?"

"I'm not playing around. I love her. You don't have to believe me, but it's the truth."

"You take care of her then. She's the gem of Barrington. You can't break her, but you can lose her if you know what I'm saying."

"Sure." I started back for the car, but Johnny came for me and grabbed the paper bag.

"I'll see what I can do," he said. "No promises."

"None expected."

He got in his truck and turned the ignition. The rear lights turned the greenery black and the ground red.

Harper was behind the bush.

"Is he taking the jar?" she asked when Johnny's truck pulled onto the road.

"I don't want to use him." I passed her. "We'll figure something else out."

I got into the driver's side, and she slid in next to me.

"What happened?" She slammed her door closed.

"Life happened." I turned the ignition. "It's one thing to risk your job for your own good. But this isn't for him or Barrington. It's for me. I can't ask him to lose his job for me."

"Get out." She pushed my shoulder as if we were fighting on a playground. "I'm driving."

"Fine. You drive this shitcan."

"It's not a shitcan. It's a choice. Like you giving up."

She had to scream the last part because I was already out of the car.

Note to self: this was a girl who didn't like to change plans.

"Officially," she said when I got in, "we are not speaking."

She wasn't cute when she was mad. I'd have been crazy to minimize her ferocity. She was formidable, and it was a massive turn-on.

"Unofficially," I said as she made a U-turn to go back to Barrington, "I'd like to kiss you."

"Fuck off."

"Is that a smirk? Are you smiling?"

"Smiling doesn't mean I'm not mad."

"Letting Johnny off the hook doesn't mean I'm giving up."

She let that hang between us on the empty road, and I didn't follow up. I watched the starry horizon change and let the *thup whup* of the seams in the road lull me. How many days had gone by? How many more until Keaton turned the boot code into open source? How long did he have to crack the rest of the Harperware? We had no time, and we had too much.

Five days.

Code laced like a drawstring bag.

Harper turned down the tight little dirt road to the Barrington house. The car did shimmy less when she drove. When I bought her a new car, she probably wouldn't know how to make a left at all.

The contract.

The contest.

The con.

She stopped in front and cut the engine. Didn't get out. Didn't open the door. Said nothing. We sat in the dark together, listening to the grass crackle.

My chain of thought wasn't disrupted.

Cut the cord.

To the anchor.

And drift toward the horizon.

The lights went off on the bottom floor and clicked on upstairs. Catherine wouldn't cry tonight. I didn't know how I knew that, but I didn't question the truth of it.

The system is closed.

Until it's not.

Then...

"GreyHatC0n's in less than a week," I said.

"If you want to go, you should go."

"You know how Bitcoin works, right? The information blockchains?"

"Yeah." She slid down in her seat in a resigned slouch. "Transparency creates honesty. If everyone can see the transaction history, it can't be falsified, et cetera."

"Documentation of every Bitcoin transfer ever made is available on the blockchain. What everyone sees becomes the truth."

She faced me. "Yes?"

She was so beautiful I didn't think I could ever live without her. I was so far ahead of myself I was living in two mental time zones.

In one, she was mine.

In another, I'd lost her and everything I'd worked for to the consequences of my bad decisions.

"If I tell everyone the contest is on, then it's on, whether Keaton wants it to be or not. He has to unlock it, or he looks stupid. He looks like he's not in control."

"If *you* tell them? How are you getting online?" She spoke softly, as if there were more on her mind than the elegant social engineering of my plan.

"You're going to have to turn off your signal scrambler. If you dare."

"I dare."

I opened the door, and the dome light went on. She squinted.

"I want you to win it, goose."

WITTER

@Beezleboy363636
None of you bitches are ready for QI4.
GreyHatC0n # QI4

@hackerbitch
Look who's back. Still pwned?
Change your handle to
@BreachBoy. # QI4choked

@Beezleboy363636
Five mill says you can't get in.
But bring what you got.
GreyHatC0n # QI4 # IT_Solid

@git-up
You patch that RU hack?
Nyet? I got money on you shitting

your pants. # tool # douche # QI4choked

@anon_00110001
Bro. You find the dude who hacked
you? You fuck him good? Or did
41ph4_W01f break his kneecaps?
 # BeezeIsBack # QI4rulz

@J0k3r_K1Ng
Oh, shit. It's on.
 # GreyHatC0n

@BeezleBoy363636
Wasn't a dude.

@anon_00110001
Bot? AI?

@BeezleBoy363636
Girl. Female.

@hackerbitch
ALL HAIL KARMA.

@anon_00110001
Yeah… no.

@shelly-code
And you haven't literally died of
shame yet you fucking sexist douche?

@BeezleBoy363636
Can't talk now. Eating crow.

@hackerbitch
(dies)

@anon_00110001
Dude. Seriously?

@BeezleBoy363636
Bump in the road, people. You need to
have a little faith in the early fail.

@shelly-code
I'm buying tickets to #GreyHatC0n
just to see you eat shit.

@engadget
The QI4 Challenge is back on. bit.ly/4nfw8rfS

@Wired
EXCLUSIVE: Sources say QI4 code still on
lockdown but ready for a 5-million-dollar
exploit. bit.ly/7bfw9sfW

@gizmodo
Show us the money. Five-mill challenge to
hack QI4 is back.

@hackeropz
Buckle in. #QI4 @BeezleBoy363636 &
@41ph4_W01f are mid-stunt.

JUST LIKE I knew he would, Keaton came on a private thread like a
gopher popping his head out of a hole.

<PRIVATE @41ph4_W01f >
What the fuck are you doing?

<PRIVATE @Beezleboy363636>
My damnedest to get QI4 back on track.

<PRIVATE @41ph4_W01f>
I HAVE IT.

<PRIVATE @Beezleboy363636>
I've secured my end. Just make sure
it's unlocked in time. Out.

XLIX

I leaned back in her chair. She was on the love seat with her feet tucked under her, watching the hacker forums and Twitter blow up.

"It's happening," she said, eyes big. Was she pale, or was it the light?

"Hell, yes. And Keaton's going to have to go along or eat his shirt. He's got pride where most people have sense, so I'm pretty sure he'll go along."

"I don't know if I can."

I spun the chair to face her. "What? This is easy. You hack in. Then you get the five mil and do whatever you want with it. Pay the taxes on the factory. Buy everyone Oxycontin."

"Not funny."

I dropped to my knees in front of her, wedging myself between her thighs. She put her arms around my shoulders.

"What are you so nervous about?" I asked.

"This is so big."

"You've done it before."

"That was different. I locked it from the outside. I didn't get in and crack it. I got QI4 to run my code. And I got a ton of lucky breaks. This time, once I decrypt—"

"*Your* encryption. Harperware."

"I'll be up against everyone. The best."

"You know how to talk to QI4. You're already ten steps ahead." I leaned forward, elbows on her thighs. I wanted her to know I was serious, but I couldn't touch her. She needed to believe it without the sex. "I built this to withstand the attack. I'm not worried about anyone at the conference. Just you. And you can take that money and pay the back taxes on the factory. Then you can sell it, give it away, break it up into luxury condos if you want."

She turned her hands over in her lap and rubbed her palm with the ball of her thumb as if she wanted to change the lines of her fortune. "He won't let me win."

My phone buzzed.

Keaton. Right on time.

I squeezed her hand and dashed down the stairs, picking up when I was in the only enclosed, private space I could think of. The kitchen pantry.

"Hello."

"I don't know if you're a genius or an idiot." Keaton was as calm as ever. "Baiting me to unlock QI4 like that?"

"I'm not baiting you."

"Describe what you're doing."

"Letting everyone know the hack is fixed and we're going on as planned."

"Is it? And are we?"

"It is. Once you open it up, we'll decrypt the lock. The flaw was in the supply chain. That's rectified with line inspections. We are a go."

"What about the hacker? Who are they? That house you called from—"

"I can't reveal that."

"—is occupied by women."

"I promised to keep it secret."

"What does she want? She humiliated us for a reason."

"Relax. We opened it up for hacks to test it."

"In a controlled setting." Keaton's voice shredded in his throat. "That was the deal. This was an attack. A direct attack timed for the most attention. It was meant to kill the demand for a product that was set to revolutionize computing. And we do not sit still for it."

There was only one way to deal with Keaton when he had vengeance in his voice. Calm authority.

"We are sitting still for it because we see the big picture. We don't get revenge because we're butthurt."

"We will discuss this when I see you."

"When are you unlocking it?"

"When I see you." He hung up.

Harper was outside the pantry door, looking more frightened than I'd ever seen her. If she was scared, I wasn't doing my job.

"They say Alpha Wolf is a military contractor," she said. "They say he's a sociopath."

"They say a lot of bullshit."

"He already knows I'm here from the landline call."

"No. He knows I'm here—and possibly the hacker. If we cloak right, and we will, he won't know you and the winner of the challenge are the same person. Once he unlocks the system, we'll open up the Harperware. He won't find you."

She didn't believe me. Not one hundred percent. Twenty percent. All I had to do was fill in the other eighty. I took her hand and led her back to my bedroom, where we wouldn't be interrupted.

"Do you know why I took Keaton's money?" I sat on the bed and took her hand.

She stood between my legs. "He offered the most?"

"No." I counted on my fingers, index to pinkie. "It was in Bitcoin. He's Alpha Wolf. It gave me dark web credibility. It gave the impression I was watching hackers as much as they were watching me. Which…" I made a fist and dropped it. "That's half the story. The other half is weirder."

"Oh, I'm intrigued now."

"Let me tell you a story. I was once a teen hacker who grabbed what he could. I could have gone the rest of my life like that, until one day, Keaton and I cracked Luhn's formula. I was conflicted about it, but Keaton was already setting up a route for secure wire transfers. Then the FBI ended up in my parents' living room."

"I didn't know that." Her eyes widened, and her posture leaned forward slightly. She held onto the edge of my shirt as if she didn't want me to leave until I finished the story.

"They took me to a secure interrogation room where I told them it was me, all me. They knew someone else was involved. Someone with ties to US Intelligence."

"Keaton?"

"Yes, but no. Maybe his parents. Point being I didn't flip on him. I said it was just me. And because I hadn't taken anything, I could convince them I was white hat. Which made even more trouble. Because then I had to *be* one. They tried to recruit me, and you know, I thought, sure. Whatever. Could be cool. But my mother didn't want anyone to decide anything for me at that age and flew into this…" I pressed my fingers into my eyes and let out a nervous laugh. "God, she could be scary when she wanted to be. She had a constitutional lawyer in the room in two hours. They fought hard, man."

"They were going to forgive the other exploits?"

"If they could take me to Quantico right there, yeah. After two days, the lawyer cut a deal. Show them how I turned the credit card company's formulas against them, stay clean, and stay available if they needed me. I covered for my friend. My father never spoke to me again. The FBI comes around every once in a while with some easy shit to help with and a job offer with shitty pay. But Keaton's walking around because I didn't flip on him, and that counts for something. He owed me, and he still owes me. If he finds out it's you, I'll call that favor the fuck in." I kissed her just enough to let her feel me. "You're safe. I'm going to fuck you every day between breakfast and lunch. Then I'm going to eat you for dinner."

She turned to straddle me. I slid down so my erection met the damp crotch of her pants. I pushed her against me, and she let loose a breathy *ah*.

"That's it?" she asked.

"And teach you how to think in quantum trinary."

"I already hacked quantum trinary."

"Without that poison pill it's going to be ten times harder. I can help you. There's plenty you don't know about QI4."

"That's cheating."

I moved her body against the length of me. Hotter, wetter, harder. My dick wasn't going to stop until it was inside her. "You want to win or not?"

"I want to win."

I pulled her T-shirt over her tits. The tips were hard and pink, bending under my thumb, salty on my lips. I yanked on her waistband.

"Off." She stood and pulled her jeans down, and I took out my cock. "Turn around."

Hesitantly, she turned her back to me. Stroking her ass with one hand, I got a condom out of my wallet with the other and cracked the package with my teeth. I spit the edge and rolled it on.

"Tell me…" I guided her onto me and put downward pressure on her hips. "Tell me how much you want to win."

When she was all the way down to the base, I reached around and opened her legs.

"Ah. God," she groaned. "I want to win."

"Everything. You want to win it all." I moved her up and down slowly.

"I want to win it all."

"No matter what it takes."

"Yes. I'll do whatever it takes."

My hands ran over her inner thighs and landed between her legs. I opened her, exposing her clit to the air. "Fuck me, goose."

She moved faster. "Like this?"

I touched where our bodies met and rubbed her hard little clit. "Like you mean it. Fuck like a winner."

She took two more slow strokes, and I ran two fingers over her pussy.

"Yes," she said as if understanding for the first time. She moved her hips hard, deep, in a quick rhythm.

I kept a hand between her legs and took a fistful of hair in the other to steady her. She slowed down when she started coming. I tightened my grip on her hair.

"Win, goose."

She sped up through her orgasm. Her guttural *unf*s went with the rhythm of her thrusts until I gave in to the pressure and came right after her.

She collapsed against my chest, and I held her steady, staying inside her as long as I could.

"You're going to get everything you want." As she turned to face me and put her arms around my shoulders, I held her on my lap. "You're not going to know what to do with yourself. Success is trickier than failure."

"You going to help me with my success problem?"

"Once I solve my own, yes."

She laughed a little. Just enough to keep steady on my lap. She put her head on my shoulder, and we stayed like that for a while.

I'd been called a genius and a game-changer, a harbinger of the future and a once-in-a-generation mind. I'd walked in the halls of power, met with titans of industry, had my name mentioned in the same sentence as historical figures.

Yet holding this woman was the greatest honor of my life.

I was losing my once-in-a-generation mind.

L

The first time we came downstairs together during daylight hours, Catherine was on the couch, facing the rain-soaked windows with a blanket over her legs. She glanced up from her sewing or needlepoint or whatever the fuck long enough to say hello, then she looked back down. I caught a little smirk. I didn't know if it meant she approved or if it just meant she knew.

"There's a pot of soup on the stove if you're interested," she said.

"Thanks!" Harper bopped off to the kitchen with her ponytail swinging and her ass swaying in a pair of little pink shorts. She already had the lid off the soup when I joined her.

"Bleh," she said, putting the lid back on. "Chicken."

"You don't like chicken soup?" I took the lid off. It looked fine to me. "What kind of person doesn't like chicken soup?"

"She puts peas and carrots in it. Frozen. It's gross."

Catherine's voice came from the doorway. "If you want to chop carrots and shuck peas all day, you're welcome to."

"No thanks. Complaining's easier." She lifted a corner of foil from a covered plate. "Is this cookies?"

Catherine slapped her hand. "For church."

Then she turned to me, and I was caught between guilt at looking at Harper's ass and the awareness that her pussy was still on my lips.

"Are you coming?" Catherine asked.

"Uh, where?"

"Church," Harper said, getting the spoons out and knocking the drawer closed with her hip.

"Sure." I said it without thinking. I wanted Catherine to like me. I was fucking her baby sister in her house and eating her food. Saying yes was the least I could do.

Harper's reaction was immediate. "God, no!"

"God, yes," Catherine said, opening a cabinet. "It won't kill you. And now you have to go, or Taylor's going to have to listen to the sermon without you." She pointed at an empty shelf. "Where are the bowls?"

"We can use the white ones," Harper said, opening another cabinet.

"Harper," Catherine scolded, "did you hide them?"

"Maybe."

"I told you I wasn't going to sell them. Where are they?"

"Can't we just use the white ones?" She handed me three white bowls and the spoons.

"Where are they? I need to know you trust me."

"It's—"

"Tell me." Catherine's voice dropped an octave. "Where are they?"

Harper cleared her throat. Catherine crossed her arms. I stood there with a stack of bowls in one hand and spoons in the other.

"They're gone," Harper whispered.

"Where?"

"I'll tell you later."

Later? Later meant "when Taylor can't hear" as far as I was concerned. I put the bowls down and held my hand over the soup pot so she couldn't open it. "Now is good."

Harper crossed her arms and ankles, rolled her eyes, and put her tongue in her cheek. "Johnny pawned Taylor's watch and so I got it back. It's not a big deal, and if you make a big deal about it, I'm going to knock this soup all over the floor." She snapped up the spoons. "Do you want to eat or not?"

I moved my hand from the pot, and Harper slid a ladle out of the drawer.

"Those were really expensive bowls," I said.

"He's a lousy pawn broker. And I might have had a bracelet I didn't like hanging around." She pressed her lips together as if holding back what she wanted to say, then she said it anyway. "I couldn't get your laptop back. That was a straight sale."

"My laptop?"

Catherine gasped. "That was Taylor's?" She held her hands up, looking me with raised eyebrows and a half-open mouth, the words "I didn't know" written on her tongue.

"It got sold to a guy in Florida."

I didn't care about the money, and I was way past needing it to break a hack. But if the wrong person found out it was mine and they took enough time and energy, there was QI4 code inside I didn't want to fall into the wrong hands.

"Tell me you cleared the hard drive."

"I nuked it." Harper looked me in the eye when she said it, and even though I believed her, she held up her right hand. "Swear. It was clean. And I'm sorry for that and all the other things."

"Is that the last of it, goose?"

"What other things?" Catherine asked as she sifted through a rack of envelopes.

"The other things. Now." Harper bumped me with her hip. "Get out of the way."

I moved and let her ladle out the soup. She did it carefully, making sure we each had the same.

Catherine looked up from stuffing the envelope.

"You better ask for forgiveness at church," she said, licking the flap. "For whatever it is."

"I will." She lowered her voice. "I'll make it up to you. I don't know how, but I will. If I have to sell my own machine, I'll give you back what I took."

I was silent. An inconsequential speck on a tiny boat surrounded by continuous horizon, humbled in the sea of her generosity. I'd felt that insignificant before, but for the first time in my life, I didn't fear it would crush me.

We ate the soup, I tried to teach her some tricks coding within QI4, but as soon as I got to anything she couldn't learn on her own, she put her hand on my dick. I used my last condom on her. I didn't mention the bowls or the watch or the mystery bracelet she didn't like. I'd buy her bracelet and her grandmother's bowls back and raise her up on a throne for her selfless kindness if it was the last thing I did.

L I

fter showering and finding my best shirt laundered and ironed on the doorknob, I got into the passenger seat of the shimmymobile and let Harper drive me to church.

She pulled up in front of the grocery store where I'd first met her.

"What?" I asked.

"Condoms. Go."

I started to get out but stopped myself when she made no move to join me. "Are you blushing?"

"Shoo," she said, checking her face in the rearview.

I kissed her pink cheek and went into the grocery store. I was the only customer, and Pat wasn't working. A bored girl sat behind the counter, reading a full-color newspaper with red headlines. She cracked her gum as if it were her job, and maybe it was.

Produce took up the center aisle. Tomatoes. Bananas. Oranges. Apples. Iceberg lettuce. The basics. Five other aisles of prepared foods. The personal bullshit section was all the way in the back, and there wasn't a birth control method in sight.

"Hey," I said to the girl at the register.

"Hey." She smiled and closed the celebrity rag. "Sorry. Not much else to read around here."

291

"Yeah. I hear you." I jerked my thumb toward the back wall. "I was looking for condoms."

"Trojans? Sure." She got up from her chair. "How many you need?"

A billion. "Twenty-four pack would be great."

"We don't have any ribbed in a box of twenty-four."

"That's fine."

She peeked her head up. "We do have the ultra large, if you need it." Her voice was thick and syrupy.

I leaned on the counter. "Do you know I can get my whole arm in a regular size without breaking it?"

"But it's tight, right?" Her eyelashes fluttered. They were fake. So much effort to work in a grocery store. "On your arm, I mean."

"I don't need to show off."

She stood with a twenty-four box of regular lubricated. "Fourteen ninety-nine." She rang it up as I took a fifty out of my wallet. "You're staying at the Barrington place?"

The bell above the door rang. It was behind a wall of chips, so I couldn't see who had come in. Did I want to answer truthfully in front of someone I couldn't identify? Or at all?

"Can you break a fifty?"

She plucked the bill from my fingers. "There's a bedroom with a painting on one of the ceilings." She opened the register and made a production out of checking the bill's authenticity. "Have you seen it?"

Not everyone who had ever seen the painting had fucked Harper Barrington. It seemed like a safe truth. "Yes."

"My uncle Reggie painted it." She flipped the fifty under the drawer and counted out the change.

"Is that the same Reggie with the trucker hat? And the reddish hair?" How many Reggies could there be in a small town? Plenty. The Reggie I'd met didn't seem like much of a pink peony kind of guy, but hell, I'd been wrong before.

"That's him! He worked so hard. Showed us all the sketches he did before. I was twelve, and I thought he was the best artist in the world."

"It's a nice painting."

"Uncle Reg sold paintings sometimes but nothing as big as that ceiling. Mr. Barrington paid him five thousand dollars. It was, like, wow.

That was so much. I thought Uncle Reggie was famous and rich, but he never painted another big room like that." When she handed me the change, she touched my hand. "I'm glad it's still there. I thought it must be gone by now."

"Still there."

"I'd love to see it again."

I folded the money and put it in my wallet. "I'm sure Harper or Catherine would show it to you."

Harper's voice came from behind me. "Oh, please." She stepped out from behind the wall of chips and smacked her hand onto the condom box. "Cynthia saw it at my birthday party in last December. Remember, you were smoking weed up there with your boyfriend?"

"Oh, right!" Cynthia faked a memory jog.

"Right." Harper picked up the box as if the shame over the condoms was nothing compared to the desire to shove the box up her friend's ass.

"Nice to meet you." I pulled Harper out of the store. Once we were in the parking lot, I took the box from her. "What was that about?"

"She's a famous boyfriend stealer."

"Okay, one"—I held up a finger—"I'm not your boyfriend. I'm half of your binary pairing."

She pushed me so hard I had to take a step back or fall over. "You're the one to my zero?"

"I'm your mate. A boyfriend can be stolen. A mate can't." I held up a second finger. "Two, she's not my type."

She crossed her arms and leaned on one hip. "Is there a three?"

"Three." I made a W.

"Knew it."

"You need new friends if you can't trust the ones you have."

"Did you text the kettle to tell him he was black, Mr. Pot?"

I laughed. She tossed me the box. I caught it, and we went to church.

Keeping my hands off her in the house of God was no easy task. Everyone turned when we came in, and by the time we slid in next to Catherine in the third row, people had stopped singing to stare. Harper held her head high. I nodded to Kyle, who nodded back as if he approved. Butthead wore a black shirt that pulled at the buttons. Orrin nodded but didn't seem to appreciate my wave. Johnny wasn't around, but Pat didn't even look up from her book.

"I didn't know there were this many people in town," I whispered.

"Shut up." Harper handed me a booklet.

"I feel like I'm on display."

"You are."

"Do I look all right?"

She looked at me. Really checked me out, up and down. "Very fuckable."

She said it loudly enough for the older lady in front of us to shoot a glance over her shoulder. Catherine subtly whacked her sister with her hymnal.

The song ended, and everyone sat.

"What are you doing?" I whispered while pretending to follow along with the readings.

"Praying." She elbowed me, eyes on the reading.

I tried to focus on my booklet but couldn't find the words. Harper sighed and flipped the page, pointing at the right place.

"Thanks," I muttered. I'd missed half of it already.

We didn't get two more lines into it before her hand was on the inside of my thigh. Turning toward her, I let her know she was out of her fucking mind by moving her hand and twisting my face into a scowl.

She was unfazed.

"Praise be to God," she said with the rest of the congregation.

Another reading started. More words. More songs. Harper kept trying to rub against me, and I kept trying to stay churchy. I had a boner that barely fit in my slacks, and at some point, we were going to have to stand and sing. There were about a hundred fifty people in the room with their heads bowed over Corinthians. If I got up now, all those heads were going to unbow themselves. I was going to have a tent in my pants for the Virgin Princess of Barrington, the girl the entire county had protected because they loved her dead father.

"Praise be to God." The congregation's voices rose in the dead, flat tones of churchly responses.

Shit rustled and banged as people stood. Harper put her hand on my ass. I moved it. She did it again even while singing the first verse of the song.

It was arousing, sure. I wasn't made of stone. But it wasn't normal or smart. And yeah, Harper wasn't normal, but she was fucking smart. She was using me as a fidget toy for a reason.

"Can you show me the bathroom?" I kept my voice low but audible so we had a public excuse to be out of the room together.

Of course, Harper got flirty as she pulled me out of the row, practically skipping down the center aisle. We exited into a courtyard with a fountain and gardens of dying flowers.

Once the door shut behind us, I took the lead, guiding her around the back of the rectory to a narrow space between the building and a fence. The ground was scraggly and weedy. A kid's yellow sand bucket lay on its side three feet from a broken orange shovel.

She went right for my belt.

I pinned her wrists against the wall. "What is wrong with you?"

"Nothing."

"Everyone sees you grabbing at me."

"So?"

"So you and your dirty little mind belong to me now, but the people in this town think you belong to them." I let her wrists go. "You have to let them get used to you not being sweet Miss Mary Jane."

"Fuck them."

She took me by the collar. She was aggressive, passionate, as intense as any woman I'd ever met, so I let her wrestle with my damn shirt. I put my arms around her and drew her close.

"I feel free," she said in a low roar that went right from my ears to my spine. "I feel like I can do whatever I want. Really be myself. God, Taylor, I know I trapped you, but you turned around and saved me. I'm free, free, *free*. I feel so… God, I feel so good. I can do anything."

She could, but not because of me. Because she was Harper and brilliant and crazy enough to try the hardest things because she saw the big picture. I kissed her, pushing my tongue past hers to touch the core, throbbing Harperness.

Pulling her shirt and bra up in one motion, she revealed tits that made me ache. "Fuck me. Right here. At church. Before they finish with communion."

She laid her hands on my crotch like a kid in a candy store. Not just any kid. A kid who had never tried candy her whole life then gone bananas at her first taste.

"Harper. Goose."

My tone got her hands off my pants, but she unsnapped her own fly. "Beeze?"

"You're a little crazy."

She slid her hand past her panties, wrist deep. "I'm so wet."

"I bet you are. And you're reckless."

She groaned. "I can't even think. I want your dick all the time. I can't sleep I want to fuck so bad. Is this normal?"

I leaned into her until I felt her arm move out of her pants. I grabbed her elbow and pushed it back down. "Nothing about you is normal. Go ahead. Make yourself come."

"I should?"

"Show me how you look when I'm fucking you. Move faster. Three strokes on your clit, then back to your pussy, then… yes. That's my goose. I love it when your mouth opens like that. I want to bite that lip."

I took her lower lip in my teeth and sucked on it. She exhaled, hot on my skin. Her nipples were hard, and when I pinched one, she nearly came off the floor.

"Hush," I warned her.

She came quietly, frozen in a muted cry, leaning on me to keep from falling.

I took her hand and sucked on her wet fingers.

Music came over the courtyard then voices.

"Shit." She stood straight, whipping her hand from my mouth, and buttoned her pants.

I laughed and helped her pull her shirt down. "You didn't care in the damn pews."

"Pressure's off, I guess. Do I look presentable?"

I took her hand. "You look like a nice girl from the heart of America."

"Let's go around the garden side. Then we can fade into the crowd."

Holding her hand, I let her lead me through the slit of space and onto the brick path leading to the garden.

Dirt tasted the same in Barrington as it did in Camden. I'd eaten more than my share of the ground in elementary school. I'd been thrown down, stepped on, had my face pushed into asphalt, grass, dry soil, snowpack, and puddles. By far, the puddles were the worst.

"Uncle!" I shouted before I spit the dirt. There had to be five guys on me, and if any of them weighed less than two hundred pounds, I'd have eaten the football under my stomach.

"Give me the ball," Kyle grunted.

"Fuck off!"

"No cursing on Sunday!" a female voice came from the sidelines.

Hands tried to flip me and strip the ball, but what I lacked in body weight I had in tenacity.

"Ref!"

The whistle blew, and the reverend's feet came into view. He was youngish and wore combat boots with his collar. "All right, guys. Get off him. That's a touchdown!"

Once the weight was off, I rolled off the ball.

Butthead helped me up. "That was some run, brother."

"Thanks." I brushed myself off.

The rest of the team high-fived me and clapped me on the back.

Orrin's two high-school-aged sons and his father. Damon's brother. Pat's half brother.

"Butthead would have blocked for you, but he's too fat to keep up with you," Orrin said after he gave me a clap.

"You're pretty quick for an old man," I replied.

A can of beer had materialized in my hand. It was ice cold, and it still tasted like chemicals and bad breath. By unspoken agreement, the game was over. Or there had been an agreement beforehand, years ago, when these boys learned to play park football from their older brothers and fathers.

"What do you mean you never played football?" Damon said from across the food table. "You wear dresses too?"

Trudy shot him a look. I couldn't tell if they had something together, but he seemed less aggressive around her.

"I'd shut it if I were you," Orrin said to Damon. "Darcy'll flay you before you have a chance to say another stupid thing."

"Who's Darcy?" I asked. "Do we need to disarm her?"

"Him," Damon grumbled.

Trudy poked him. "She's my sister if she says so, and if you want me to be nice later, you'll follow along."

"Whatever you say." He didn't look convinced.

"Try the mushroom salad." Orrin pointed his fork at a bowl of canned mushrooms with unidentified beige squares. "My wife made it. Everyone loves it. Go on. It's going to be gone in ten minutes."

"My Orrin's too nice." A woman in her forties with poufy brown hair and glasses I hadn't noticed before patted his arm, and he kissed her on the lips.

"He is," I said as she put a scoop of mushrooms on my plate. "Thank you."

"Uh oh," Harper's voice came from my left. She had a plate with a burger and potato salad. "He's going to want to bring a five-gallon drum home to California now."

I got out of the table line to stand next to Harper. "Is it good?" I whispered.

"Try it."

I forked a couple of mushrooms and stuck them in my mouth. I didn't chew. I didn't think I could. My tongue rejected the super-sweetened, ultra-salty, rank buttbuds completely. I stepped out of earshot and Harper followed.

"No good?" Harper asked around a mouthful of burger.

I swallowed without chewing and gulped the beer. Shook my head hard.

"Is she getting them from your bathroom wall?" I kept my voice low.

She covered her mouth so she wouldn't spit her burger.

I poked at the slippery beige cubes. "What are these little things? Chopped asshole?"

She couldn't laugh. She couldn't swallow her burger. Her face was red.

"It's really not that funny."

A tear fell down her cheek.

I wasn't the funny guy. I'd never gotten a girl because I could make her laugh. They all said they wanted a sense of humor, but I'd gotten by all right without one.

Watching Harper get ahold of herself while I tried to find another mushroom joke in me, I wondered how I'd gotten the girls I had. Around her, I was different.

"You gonna eat that, mister?" A voice came from below, where a little girl of about five stood in a dirt-rolled dress, wielding a white plastic fork.

"This?" I pointed at the potato salad.

"This one." She pointed her fork at the mushrooms.

I hadn't known that many kids, but rumor had it they generally didn't like mushrooms.

"Here." I gave her my plate. "You can have it."

Her eyes went wide, and her mouth opened in joy.

Catherine rushed over. "Lori!"

"She's all right," I said. "Really."

"If you turn your back on your plate, she'll take it."

"She asked politely." I jerked my head at the girl, telling her to get out of Dodge before the narcks got her.

A mistress of subtlety, Lori ran to the table with the other kids.

Catherine watched with longing in her eyes. She touched her nose as if it had suddenly filled up.

"Hey," Harper said to Catherine. "Snap out of it."

"Sorry." She smiled, and I remembered I hadn't heard her crying behind the walls in the past three nights. "Wally!" She ran to the children's table, where a kid had barbecue sauce all over his shirt.

"She's like Momma Barrington," Harper said.

"I haven't heard her in a few nights. Or have I just been distracted?"

Harper wiped the last of her burger across a palette of condiments. "She got a letter from her long-lost love."

"The guy? The one who left?"

Romantic? Sweet? Fucking crazy?

"She told you about him?"

"Not much. But that's...wow. Good for her."

"I know." She neatly placed the rest of the burger in her mouth then chewed with one cheek so she could talk. Her every move was graceful and efficient. Mostly, every gesture was honest and part and parcel of who she was. "Been years and boom. He's coming."

"When?"

"Friday. Had to squeeze it out of her. She really doesn't tell me shit, if you want to know the truth. I had to threaten to kick Daddy's grave over before she told me."

Catherine kneeled in front of Wally's shirt as he wept, and a woman in a sleeveless denim shirt who looked just like the barbecue-stained kid ran to them with a roll of paper towels. When his mother reached him, Catherine stood up, getting out of the way.

She backed up, looking wistful, longing. She looked just like Harper, but a little taller, older, with unruly hair. I never wanted Harper to have that look on her face. As if she accepted a world of things that would never be.

"We have to fix her room," I said.

"Excuse me?"

"Her long-lost love is coming, and her room is moldy."

"It's not. It's... wait. You mean the master suite?"

"She can't bring what's-his-name into some shitty bedroom. Come on. While you're mastering qubits, I'll do the walls."

"You?"

"I'm from a line of contractors. And the guys'll help. Where's your romantic spirit?"

"It's my sister. I don't want to think of you creating some romp room for her."

"I've been banging you right under her nose, and she hasn't said shit."

"To you, she hasn't."

I got between her and the eyes of the town. "What did she say to you?"

She shrugged and wiped her mouth. "My sister's not exactly a chatterbox, if you haven't noticed. She has a way of asking how I slept that's pretty much asking how big your dick is."

"What did you tell her?"

"I said, 'He's hung like a watermelon, and he fucks like an animal.'"

"You said that?"

"No, dork. I said 'fine,' but I said it as if I was talking about your dick, and I know she heard what I was thinking because she blushed."

I pinched her chin between my thumb and the bend of my index finger. "Let's get back and make some noise while we can."

She took my arm, and we went back home.

LIV

Once, when we were on a demolition project, my dad had told me that mushrooms are never just mushrooms. In the case of the Barrington master suite, he was right, as usual. The mushroom in the bathroom had eaten the wood behind it, and the more plaster I removed, the more mushroom appeared. There was an entire ecosystem back there.

The day after church, I woke up early, went to the shed to get the sledgehammer with half a handle, and called the lumberyard with an order. My phone was jangling and beeping with messages. Media. Employees. Friends. I reassured my mother, who was worried after the call with Gram, and texted a couple of friends. I didn't want to talk to anyone else. I wanted to fix the damn bedroom.

Harper picked up a shift at the distro center. I kissed her before she left as if I actually lived there with her.

The moment the sledgehammer touched the plaster and I started breathing lead dust, I let the physical activity take over. I was sweaty, stripped down to my undershirt, filthy everywhere. I'd dug sneakers and jeans out of my bag, moved and covered the bed with a tarp I'd found in the shed, and made a really loud, big fucking mess.

"Oh my Lord!" Catherine was at the door in a robe and bare feet.

"Good morning."

"What… what are you doing?"

"Don't come in!"

"But—"

"There are nails."

She bent at the waist, peering into the room. Half the walls were down to the studs, and mold, mildew, and fungus had left much of the busted plaster black on the back side.

"You won't have the mushroom again. The mold isn't safe to breathe."

She looked at the ceiling.

"And that? I looked behind it. It's clean."

"I want to say something." Her voice was as grave as I'd ever heard it. Not black in its tone but a serious shade of grey.

"Yes?"

"I own a gun."

"Okay?"

"I know how to use it."

"Cath—"

"Don't let anything happen to the painting."

I nodded slowly. "Yes, ma'am."

"And thank you," she said more lightly. "It'll be nice to sleep in here again."

She walked away without saying more.

By the time I got the last bit of plaster down, a flatbed from the hardware store arrived with a dumpster in tow.

Butthead got out of the truck with Florencio from the factory and Jorge, who came to the door while the other two slid drywall off the bed.

"Where you want it?" Jorge asked.

"Dumpster in the back. The rest of it can go upstairs."

He called back to the two guys in Spanish. They pulled the flatbed around back. I followed it.

"The dumpster should be right under that balcony, right there." I pointed up at the master suite.

The three other men looked up.

"That the room with Reggie's painting?" Butthead asked.

"Yeah."

"What are you thinking of doing?"

"Fixing it."

"Who? You?"

"Me." I slapped his chest and went to help Jorge unhook the dumpster from the flatbed.

He called out to Butthead. "You gonna help us, or are you gonna chitchat like an international man of leisure?" Jorge's thick accent made his command of the language funny, and he seemed to know it.

Generally, pallets of drywall sheets were raised into an open window by crane, but the windows weren't big enough, and the balcony doors couldn't be used without risking the railings. I didn't want to warn Catherine that her house could be destroyed before the first nail was driven in, so the supplies had to be brought in via the stairs.

We worked out the route around corners and up stairs, padding the corners and moldings.

I jumped up on the flatbed to help Florencio with the top slab of drywall.

"Oh, Jesus. Is Cali-Boy's going to pick up heavy things now?" Butthead hauled himself up.

"The store ain't payin' worker's comp if you blow something, man," Florencio said to me with a grunt. "Trust me on that."

"I'll keep your broke ass in mind when I visit you in the hospital," I said.

We carefully turned the drywall sheet on its side.

"Who's doing this with you?" Florencio asked as we angled the panel through the back door. "Better be somebody good."

"Just me."

"Come on, man. Nobody's stupid enough to do this alone."

"That's me. Nobody."

It took him a minute to get my joke, and he only acknowledged it by shaking his head in irritation. We were angling a seventy-pound sheet of drywall around Victorian-sized doorways.

The stairs were narrow, and the boards were wide and heavy. Jorge turned out to be Juanita's husband, and Florencio made it a point to let me know he was single and Jorge was an idiot to have gotten married. Butthead said that not having any options was easier, but I didn't believe him.

Covered in dust and breathing heavily, the four of us stood among the piles of debris in the master suite. I showed them the black mold on the plaster and the damage to the beams that had to be scraped away and reinforced.

"What's the ceiling?" Florencio asked.

"Enamel on tin," I answered. "The mold couldn't damage it, but I don't know what's going on behind it. You might be back with two-by-fours to replace beams."

"Dude," Butthead stated, punctuating a final word. "You are not doing this by yourself."

"What the fuck is this?" Jorge picked up the half-handled sledgehammer. "You didn't even order a new handle?"

I opened my mouth to answer, but I had no excuse.

"And, wait," Butthead said. "You did all this with that?"

"Don't you assholes have somewhere to go?" I said defensively. "I have shit to do. Come on. Get out of here."

They had a clock to punch, so they left me alone to bag old plaster and throw it off the balcony into the dumpster.

"Do you know how loud that is?" Harper said from the door. She had on her polo and lanyard. The bright yellow set off the fact that she looked exhausted.

"So? You don't have neighbors."

She ran her fingers over the lath. "Three days to GreyHatC0n."

"Three days until you win five mill."

"I'm going to enjoy taking your money."

"It's my partner's. If it was mine, I'd just give it to you."

"I wouldn't take it."

She put her arms around my waist, and I held my hands away from her. "I'm a sweaty mess."

"I don't care."

My shirt stuck to me when she laid her cheek on my chest. I flipped my gloves off behind her back.

"Lead paint. Seriously. Mold. You're breathing it."

"So are you." She didn't let go, which made the next part of the conversation more difficult.

"I need something from you."

"What?"

"The decryption for the object code." She pushed me away, but I kept her close.

"Keaton has to unlock his."

"It's an act of good faith to give him your code first. I think we're past me teaching you how to fuck anyway."

"Very past."

"Keaton's been nagging me about it. I almost wish my phone was still in the bushes. But he has a point. They really need to check it over before we open it."

She took a folded-up scrap of paper from her back pocket. "I figured you'd need it." She handed it over. It had a teddy bear in a Santa hat on the top and the code written in blue pen.

4e 2d 2e 20 6d 20 2e 2d 2e 20 4d 2e
20 4e 20 6e 2d 20 2e 40 4d 20 2e

"Hex?"

It wasn't a message when decoded. Just nonsense letters and punctuation.

She put her hand over it. "Nope. Don't decrypt it yet. It's for after. You'll like it, I promise."

"You're asking a lot."

"I deserve a lot."

I put my thumbs on her shoulders and pushed her away. "Be naked when I get out of the shower."

She tried to kiss me, but I wouldn't let her. Her ass was so sweet as she walked out that I had to slap it.

I took a picture of the code and the Santa bear, then I called Keaton. "Hey, Keat."

"I preferred when you were the face of this company," he said. "Everyone's asking for you."

"Where are you?"

"New York. Where you should be. Now. Immediately."

I was knee deep in moldy plaster and promises. I couldn't leave the house looking like a construction site, and I couldn't leave Harper to hack QI4 alone. "Can't. Still stuck."

"I will send you a car."

"No. I'm doing something."

"I don't want to be here. This was not the deal. It's your job to talk to the media and the stupid people."

"Just be dark and mysterious. Brood and growl."

"Tay—"

"I have the object code decryption key."

I could practically hear tires screech on the other side of the country.

"Now, listen," I said, walking onto the balcony. Below, the thorn bush still had our path to the center cut through it. "I can give it to you at 8 a.m. on Thursday. But I know you want it unlocked now."

"You should too, don't you think?"

"I do. I need you to promise me something first."

"I'm starting to wonder where your loyalties lie."

"In more than one place."

"That's not possible."

"Promise you won't come after the hacker."

For a few seconds, all I heard from his side was the indistinct voices of a public place and his breathing. I assumed he was thinking about it. Barrington had made me into a civilian.

"I promise nothing," he said. "But thank you for the code."

"What?" I looked at my screen. The picture of the paper was on it. He'd hacked me, the motherfucker. He'd used our cellular connection to hack my phone.

"I hope to see you Thursday," he said and hung up.

LV

*H*er upstairs room was actually a little suite with a full-size bed behind a door. She'd been as naked as a jaybird when I got upstairs, and we twisted around the sheets for a while, fucking as if our lives depended on it.

I thought about going to New York then pushed it away. Then considered it again. I could leave for a few days. I could come back and finish the bedroom. Come back to her. She'd be here. It wasn't so long.

But no. It wasn't that simple, if I was being honest with myself. Even after she cracked QI4, I was convinced I wouldn't come back to Barrington.

I shut my phone off, and she set up her center monitor to pick up TV, opening the door so we could see it from bed. She even had a remote she'd built from an old TV version. Answering a few messages, I knew tension was building for GreyHatC0n. I knew everyone was in New York, working their asses off to get it set up, and I was in bed with the enemy. I had a twinge of guilt that stayed with me even after Harper brought up a bowl of grapes and put her knees on the bed.

"Is today Monday?" she asked.

"Yeah."

She muted the TV signal. Crickets. Rustling grass. The hiss of her

309

processor fans. The squeak of the weather vane turning in the wind above us. In the spaces where it all went silent, I could almost catch the sound of the river flowing.

"Do you hear it?" she said.

"Hear what?"

"Catherine cries on Mondays."

"I didn't realize there was a schedule." I took the grapes and put them on the night table before gathering her in my arms.

She twisted my wrist to look at my watch. "She should be going by now. I know she's in her room. I heard her in there on the way back up."

"Maybe she's not sad today." I turned the sound back on. Commercials. I didn't even know what we were watching. "We should throw her a party."

Harper sat bolt upright, back on her knees in a ribbed tank top that rode up, exposing the space between her tits and her pajama bottoms. "Oh my God!"

"I was joking."

"Her birthday is Thursday. I almost forgot."

"Harper. We have—"

"And the room? Is it going to be done? We can make that a big gift! We can invite everyone!"

"GreyHatC0n starts Thursday," I said with the flat affect of fact.

"So? It's still warm enough for the backyard. Maggie can make a birthday cake."

Harper dropped to her hands and knees and put her lips on my chest. I got hard before she even moved down.

"Who's Maggie?"

"She lives over on Dandelion Road."

I twisted my fingers in her hair as she got closer to my dick. "Every time I think I know everyone… oh, you little tease."

"You'll meet them at the party."

"You have to crack my code, and I have to be on the phone to make sure you don't. Or that everyone sees when you do. And the drywall…"

She ran her tongue from the base of my cock to the tip.

"We don't have time to plan a…"

She sucked lightly on the back of the head.

"Ah, that. Perfect."

Not much could distract me from my cock disappearing into her face. Not the news, which contained the usual reports of everyday malfeasance, faraway violence, and maps with overlaid swirls of cloud cover.

Except Keaton's voice from the television.

"Quantum code was just a theory."

I sat upright so fast Harper nearly choked.

"Sorry."

I didn't have to apologize. She wiped her mouth with her wrist and stared at the screen with me, watching the stone-cold confidence of Keaton Bridge.

"In three days, it becomes a reality."

The black ball of the mic popped out of the frame while the female reporter asked the question. *"We understand the system was hacked just eleven days ago?"*

"It was an encryption overlay, and it exposed a flaw in our supply chain. The system itself hasn't been touched. It is still the most secure system in the world. We challenge anyone in the world to hack it."

"What if there's more than one hack? Will two people get five million dollars?"

His knowing smirk could have frozen the deep blue sea. *"Sure. Why not?"*

"You do not have ten million dollars, you fuck." I didn't realize I'd said that out loud.

"He's showing how confident he is," Harper said.

"He's going to bankrupt himself."

She leaned into me, and I put my arm around her.

"He believes in it. And you," she said. "He's handsome."

"What's that supposed to mean?"

"Are you jealous?"

"No. Fuck that."

The reporter had broken from Keaton to talk to some of the attendees outside the con, make some partially informed comments about hacking, and come back to the "biggest challenge prize ever."

"He's a criminal," I continued. "And I think he was wearing makeup."

She pulled away far enough to look at me. "You *are* jealous!"

"Just saying." I pulled her closer so she wouldn't see that, yeah, I was jealous.

The reporter took up the center of the screen to close out.

"She's a total fluff-piece reporter," I said.

"Yeah, she does the after-the-weather stuff."

"She's not a tech journalist. It's insulting. I mean, it's one thing to not know shit. It's another to be proud you don't."

"The QI4 system will be online from 8 a.m. to 8 p.m. Eastern this Thursday. Get your keyboards ready! The IP address will be posted on the QI4 website. The prize is awarded worldwide for any…" She made a show of looking at a piece of paper. *"Invasive malware, adware, worms, DDoS, virus, or Trojan horse."* She put the paper down. *"But according to everyone I've spoken to here, only a zero-day exploit will work."*

"And can you help us non-tech people? What is a zero-day exploit?" The guy in the left-side box smiled as if he knew damn well he'd forget the answer to his question before he finished his second Cosmo.

"It's a hack invented from scratch, and apparently they're worth five million dollars. So you better get to work!"

I shut off the screen.

"You should go to New York," she said.

"No."

"Why not?"

"What if you need me?"

"You need to get over that right now. I'm not asking you for help. And you have your codes. Did he open the system?"

"Yes."

"You need to go. This is a big deal for you."

She was thinking of me. I didn't deserve her. Brushing her hair away from her face, I wanted to crawl into her skin and love her unpredictable, brilliant soul from the inside.

"What kind of attack were you thinking of doing?" I asked.

"I was going to just put something in the comments to taunt you."

I clamped my lips together. I didn't know how to do the hack she wanted, one where she'd be able to edit the code, but I knew the mountains she'd have to climb because I'd built them. I could have easily defined those obstacles and cut her work in half.

As if reading my mind, she put her hand over my mouth. "Don't. Even."

"Mmph."

She took her hand away.

"You can do it," I said.

"I just locked your system. I didn't crack it. This is a code-only hack. I can't plant transmitters in your office. This is the real shit. I want to do it."

"Do you promise to let me know if you're having trouble?" She started to object, and I held up a finger. "Not right away. But if you get to the end and you haven't done it."

"Can I just suck your dick now?"

"I don't know how to hack it. If I knew, I would have built a way to avoid it. But if you're close, I can tell you what you're up against. It's still up to you to figure out."

"Lie back." She pushed me down and straddled me.

"When you get in there, you're going to be shocked."

She shifted down until her mouth was on my dick again. "I won't be shocked. I'll act bored." She ran her tongue along my length, curling it around the curve of it.

"It's different down to the motherboards."

"So you say."

She took me down her throat and sucked on the way out. I wasn't going to be verbal much longer, so I just spit out the last sentence I could.

"I want you to win."

LVI

Thank God for Barrington, USA.

If I'd had two solid days to hang, tape, and spackle drywall and another half a day to paint it, I still wouldn't have gotten done in time. That became apparent a few hours into the project.

But Barrington showed up. Men who knew how to "do things" came and went through a revolving door, picking up pieces of the job bit by bit. They kept the site clean, did a better-than-average job, took the sink and toilet out so we could hang behind it, and went to get more stuff so often I started to wonder how much fell off a truck on the way to the distro center.

As far as my time went, I was useless forty percent of it. Calls kept coming. My coders, double-checking and rechecking that the system was correct. Keaton complained about my absence. My mother called to see if I was excited. The venue called to make sure they had enough broadband for the traffic.

Harper stayed locked in her room, working. Late at night, we fucked and collapsed.

The morning of the party, Harper got out of bed before the sun came up.

"Hey," I muttered. "It's not even five in the morning."

"It's ten after five." She kissed me gently. "You need to get a watch with a battery."

I slid back in the bed until my back was to the wall. "Are you ready?"

"More than you. You haven't even painted yet."

I grabbed her, pulled her onto the bed, and rolled on top of her. She giggled when I tickled her.

"Stop."

"Take these pants off before I rip them off."

Laughing, she pushed me away. "Taylor! Really!"

"Really?"

She made her voice steady and solid. "Really. I just… I want to be at my best, and I want to be on the forums early in case anyone has any genius ideas. I don't want to get behind."

She rolled over to get away, but I grabbed her by the wrist.

"Taylor!"

"One second."

"We're not having sex now."

"No sex." I let her go and sat on the edge of the bed.

"You won't even get hard?"

"I won't. Give me your hands."

She held them out. Her right index and left middle fingers were taped. I kissed each of her palms.

"These hands are going to do good work."

"Yeah, yeah." She tried to pull them away, but I yanked her back. Her hair crisscrossed her face.

"You have two minutes, goose."

"Fine."

I kissed every one of her finger joints. "No typos from you. No slipping off the keys from you. No cramps from you." She giggled, and I continued to address her hands. "All of you will show up for work two Mondays from now, whether you're counting money to five million or not." I pressed them together and looked at her. "Your brain has to show up too."

"You're hiring me?"

"Yes. I'm sorry it took so long."

"Taylor."

"Name your price."

She put her hands on my face, one on each side, as if she wanted to hold me still. Even as skin pressed against skin and her warmth mixed with mine, her face was down a long, dark tunnel.

"Harper? I mean it. You're coming on with me."

"You're hiring me because you're sleeping with me."

"I got to know you because I'm sleeping with you."

Her hands fell down to my shoulders. "Did you ever want everything to be fair?"

"Sure." I pulled her down so she straddled me. "But it's not. Nothing is. You were born brilliant. That gives you advantages. Take it up with God."

"God didn't make me sleep with you." She bit her lip as she did a grind into my erection. "Even though I see Him when I do."

"You get credit for good choices." I pushed my hips into her and pulled her down. "You want to see God before you go upstairs?" My fingers ran up her shirt, finding a pebble of a nipple. When I gently pinched it, she tilted her head to one side, parting her lips. I had her. "I'm not going to beg you to let me lick your clit."

I got on my back and spread my arms. When she got up, I thought she was leaving, but she peeled her pants off.

"You drive a hard bargain," she said, crawling over me.

"Wait until you work for me. I'm a real pain in the ass."

She didn't answer in the affirmative. She didn't answer at all, which didn't bother me in the moment.

In the moment, I wanted to taste her as she kneeled over my face. I wanted to suck her hard enough to get her close then let her hover on the edge until she exploded over me, grinding on my mouth.

She came so hard she almost rolled away. I had to hold her tightening thighs down so my tongue could reach her, and even then, she tried to get away.

LVII

"*I*'m fine! Go away!"

It was ten in the morning, and Harper hadn't moved from her desk. When I poked my head in, she was bent over the keyboard, tapping lines of code or scouring the Tor forum that was put up just to share theories about QI4's GreyHatC0n challenge.

"Are you hungry?" I asked.

"Go away." She turned away from the screen, a deadly focus in her eyes. "I'm not kidding."

The system had gone online right on time. Jack had developed an app for the team that counted the number of break-in attempts and fails.

ATTEMPTS: 34,989

FAILS: 34,989

At times, the attempts column was higher, and my chest twisted, hoping it was Harper. I bolted up the steps twice, but the app caught up a few seconds later, and I got back to painting Catherine's walls with the rest of the guys.

She'd chosen a warm off-white that looked good with the ceiling mural and a pure white for the moldings. We finished right before lunch.

"Harper," I said after I knocked.

"Go away!"

That was my cue to open the door obviously. "Your sister is going to see her room finished. Do you want to come—"

"No." She didn't stop her fingers for even a second.

"It's important."

"Not now," she hissed. "She knows I'm busy."

I'd done a lot of coding in my day, and there was nothing harder than tearing yourself away when you were on to something.

ATTEMPTS: 89,084,172,651,097

FAILS: 89,084,172,651,097

The guys from the cage were on a chat inside the app, discussing the numbers, considering updating the app to count DDoS attempts separately, and crossing their fingers until they broke.

Two guys were missing: Keaton and Deepak. Keaton was an antisocial shithead, but there was a big hole in the conversation where Deepak should have been.

Juanita and Mrs. Boden called gift time, blindfolded the birthday girl, and led her down the hall.

"Is Harper coming down?" Pat whispered to me.

I gave her the official excuse. "She's not feeling well. Trust me, you don't want her coming down."

Juanita removed the blindfold, and everyone shouted, "Happy Birthday!"

Catherine stood in the doorway with her hands folded at her lips. The room stank of paint, and the floor wasn't done, but she looked happy. Really happy.

"Don't touch the walls," Kyle called. "Not yet."

"Thank you," she whispered, turning into the crowded hall. She held her hand out to me. "Taylor."

I took her hand. "Let me show you what we did."

I showed her the smooth walls, the moldings, the way the painting was completely intact, the updated bathroom, the place where the mushroom used to be, and the reglazed French doors to the balcony. The barbecue smoke from the backyard obscured the view.

"That's all we could do," I finished. "But the floor needs to be done, and you need new pipes and a rewire."

"Can I sleep in it?"

"Paint should be dry by tonight."

Her cheeks turned eighty-five shades of pink, and she looked at the floor. She hugged me and got pulled out of the room by one of her many, many friends.

"Chris is coming tomorrow," Pat whispered to me as Catherine went into the hall.

"Is that her old boyfriend's name?"

"More like secret love. Only love, if you ask me."

ATTEMPTS: 127,054,836,201,916

FAILS: 127,054,836,201,916

I kept my attention on the third-floor window through conversations about cars and sports, a smattering of politics, and gossip. Harper's excuse for not being there floated without trouble. In a way, it was the truth. She was indisposed, trying to save everyone from the changing world by disrupting the tools of the change.

When she got in, would she cheer? Would I hear her from the ground? Would she text me? Call out the window? Announce to everyone? Keep it to herself?

I went upstairs with a plate of mushroom salad and a burger. "Open the door, Harper. You know I can pick this lock."

It clicked, but she didn't open it. When I did, I found her working. Almost all of her fingers were taped. The roll sat next to the keyboard, its brown core exposed, hanging on to the last inch of white tape.

I put the burger down and looked over her shoulder. "A Plone CMS. Good idea but—"

"Shut it!" She spun toward me, cutting me off with the look of death on her face. "First of all, you're seeing about ten percent of this script, and second of all, I'm doing this fair."

319

I stole a kiss. It was supposed to be a short peck, but I kept it going until she yielded, just a little.

"I'm going."

She had four hours.

LVIII

The sun got lower on the horizon. The challenge was going to end about half an hour before sunset, but I still kept my eyes on my inaccurate watch. Jack had updated the app with the countdown, but they couldn't figure out how to isolate the DDoS attacks, so the numbers were exponential.

ATTEMPTS: 389,491,610,776,287
FAILS: 389,491,610,776,287
T-MINUS: 02:12:34

Party guests came and went, their jobs and kids determining how long they stayed. I met so many of them I lost track. They shook my hand and thanked me for saving the mural.

I'd had no idea what the house meant to Barrington. Kyle and Johnny were talking by the thorn bushes, waving their arms at the thorns and shouting words drowned out in the white noise of the party. Pat and Jorge shook their heads at whatever suggestion Johnny offered up. Reggie and three others I'd just met listened but didn't seem to have much to add.

They cared about the house as if it was their own.

Harper's not leaving.

She was leaving. Maybe we'd have a long-distance thing for a while, until she figured out how to put the five million to the best use. I could take it.

I was walking toward the thorn bushes to see what the argument was about when I got a message from Deepak.

<*You're almost there.*>

<*Two hours.*>

<*When are you coming back?*
You can write your own ticket.>

<*...* >

I looked up at Harper's window glowing blue from the screens.

<*You are not a sidekick.*>

<*I hope you keep that five million.*>

I didn't. I wanted Harper to have it, even if it meant my own failure. I started to type a bland response. Something on the order of "We'll see." But Deepak shot back a message.

<*You're going to need it to pay me.*>

<*Yes, dude. That's...* >

I laughed at how excited I was to have him back. I'd almost agreed to pay him five million dollars.

<*too much, TBH, but I'll promise*
this: you get paid the same as me.
Salary and bonus.>

<I want a team. >

<Yes>

< My own projects.>

<Yes>

I heard something from Harper's window. A clap and a shout.

ATTEMPTS: 710,887,019,611,003
FAILS: 710,887,019,611,003
T-MINUS: 01:54:12

I might have been mixing the sounds up with something else, or misinterpreted what I'd heard, but I bolted up the stairs and poked my head through Harper's door. She'd left it unlocked.

"I'm not coming up here again."

Silhouetted against her triple screens, she shook her hands out at the wrists until they blurred. "I'm fine. I think I might have it."

"Really?" I stepped into the room fully.

"Yeah. It's… I'm not going to explain it yet. It's a combination. Zip, then boom, then right under."

"Can I see?"

"Not until it works."

"I love you, Harper."

"I love you. Please get out," she said absently.

There was something nice about that. To be loved habitually. Thoughtlessly, almost. Being so deep in her heart that she could say she loved me without thinking too hard about it.

I closed the door behind me. She had this. It was happening. She was going to get the money, save the factory, and who even knew? Stay in Barrington? Run it? She'd have to turn a shell into a manufacturing business. QI4 didn't have the capacity for an operation like that. We had neither the money nor the demand yet.

So if she ran the factory, she couldn't work for me back at QI4HQ.

But she had to.

I couldn't stay in Barrington. She had to come back with me. And she wasn't working for the competition, which was everyone at this point. From retailers to software giants to hardware manufacturers, we were about to disrupt all of it, and she couldn't work for any of them. She was mine. I'd found her. She was going to sit next to me every goddamned day to share her beautiful mind at work and her beautiful body at home.

"Hard-on!" Butthead called upstairs. "You got someone here!"

"Me?" I stood at the top of the stairs and pointed at myself.

"You know another Hard-on?"

Before I could answer, a man in black jeans and a jacket stood next to him.

Keaton.

LIX

I hadn't seen Keaton in the flesh in a long time. He kept to the shadows, where he was comfortable, disappearing in crowds, hiding where anyone could see him if they looked.

In Barrington, they watched him in clusters. Young girls giggling and pretending not to look. Groups of men puffing out their chests or singly standing between him and their wives. The primal posturing was unconscious and pretty much standard operating procedure whenever Keaton was in a room full of strangers.

"Nice to see you," I said when I got to the bottom of the stairs. "Just passing through?"

"On the way to certain victory." He held up a bottle of Dom Perignon. "Do they have buckets of ice here in… where are we?"

"Barrington." I took the bottle, and he followed me to the kitchen.

"Well, hello." Catherine wiped her hands on her apron.

"Catherine, this is my partner." I coughed back his name. I didn't know how he wanted to present himself out here.

He held out his hand to her. "Marcus."

"Welcome. It's so nice to meet a friend of Taylor's."

I held out the bottle. "Do you have a bucket?" I asked before she could mention Harper. I had to tell her he was here. Had to warn her to stay upstairs even if she won it all.

Especially if she won it all.

"Cathy!" a voice came from outside. "We need you!"

"I'll take care of it." Mrs. Boden plucked the bottle out of my hands. "Dom. Nice stuff. Real nice. Had it once in Paris when I was in nursing school."

"You lived in Paris?" Keaton asked.

"After the Second World War." She slid a silver ice tray out of the freezer. "I cut more metal out of muscle than a butcher at a hunting ground, but I needed 'more training' to practice in the States." She smacked the ice tray on the counter.

Keaton crossed his arms and leaned on the counter. "Paris after the war must have been—"

"Complicated." She pulled the lever on the tray, releasing the shattered cubes.

Keaton could talk to old people for hours, especially women. Where men tended to clam up as they got older, he found women gave less of a shit about who thought what as they greyed and made more interesting conversation.

He wouldn't ask about Harper, and even if Mrs. Boden mentioned her, it would be in an innocent context. I backed out of the kitchen. All I had to do was get up the stairs and tell Harper that no matter what happened, she had to stay in that room. Cheer into a pillow. Celebrate her first hours of victory alone, or my partner would figure it out.

Then shit would get really random, really fast.

A hand gripped my bicep and yanked me away. Keaton had broken Mrs. Boden's magic spell long enough to grab me and pull me into the backyard. The discussion around the thorn bushes still raged, but with Catherine at the center of it.

Keaton let me go and held up his phone.

ATTEMPTS: 1,032,234,165,777,029
FAILS: 1,032,234,165,777,029
T-MINUS: 00:43:34

"I don't understand what happened to you," he said, pocketing the device. "What you're doing here. Why you dripped the decryption out the way you did. I checked everything in your past. Even called your mother—"

"You called my mother? Are you fucked in the head?"

"Excuse me? She was a part of my childhood too. In any case, she says you have no connection to this little town as far as she knows. I found your rental car trail. Not pretty. Intercepted your wireless bill. No calls. No data usage. Found some activity at the lumber yard, a few drinks at a bar in the middle of a parking lot. It's not much, but you weren't even trying to hide. Not really. I couldn't figure out what your game was. How you were trying to screw me. Then it came to me."

"Taylor!" Butthead cried from the porch. "Did you not give your friend a fucking beer?"

A small, hard projectile came toward me at speed, nothing more than a displacement of air in the near-dark. I reached my hand out and caught the can of beer without realizing what it was until I felt the wet cold against my palm.

I handed it to Keaton. "Just hold it. You don't have to drink it."

Another launched then slid off my fingertips and succumbed to gravity with a groan from Butthead.

"I'm dying to hear what came to you." I picked the can out of the dirt, faced away from my partner, and cracked the top.

Orrin pulled a silver canister from the back of his truck. It looked like a keg in the twilight, but it had a hose on it. Behind him, Damon lugged two red gas containers.

"What are they doing?" Keaton asked.

"No fucking clue." I slurped the carbonated slurry and made a face.

"They bottle that shit in Mexico," Damon said as he passed with his gas cans. "That's why it tastes like piss."

"They used to bottle it in the factory over that way," I said to my partner.

Ignoring my recommendation, he took a swig of the beer. "I was trying to figure out your game. Then I thought, maybe you aren't playing a game. Maybe you were being honest. Stupid, probably. But honest. The only way to know was to come here, look you in the face, and ask you what the fuck is going on."

The porch lights went on. They didn't illuminate much, but the way this conversation as going, I preferred the twilight.

"What's going on," I said pensively, looking toward the side drive, where Harper's light fell onto the trees. "It's stupid."

"You found the hacker. Obviously. And you're protecting them. Don't deny it. I thought, up until a minute ago, that they were related to this girl."

"Which girl? You assumed there was a girl. I never said shit about it."

"Please give it a rest. There's a little…" He held his beer hand up at me, tracing the shape of what he wanted to say. "Softening around the edges? And it explains a lot. Why you're protecting her friends. Why you stayed here. Why you weren't hitching on the interstate to get home. Why we got the decryption in pieces. She's really got you on a leash."

The suggestion that I was on a woman's leash was meant to get a reaction out of me, but it didn't. What made me tense up was how close he was to the truth.

"She's not related to our hacker."

With a manner calculated to minimize my reaction, he held the can to his lips and stated a fact as if in passing. "Because she is our hacker." He swallowed with a gulp. "And you love her."

Deny, deny, deny…

I hid behind a sip of beer, looking away from the light so he couldn't see me. I couldn't tell too many lies. I couldn't even go direct opposite because lies in direct opposition pointed 180 degrees directly to the truth.

The drink went down like a pair of loaded dice. "You're fucking crazy."

"We know that's true. But you're a shitty liar."

She was going to win, and he wouldn't let it happen. He wouldn't turn over the money because he'd never believe I didn't help her do it.

"Maybe."

"Maybe?"

Fuck it. Fuck the shit out of it. Fuck it to hell. If I was going to bring her back and make her a part of my life, I was going to have to love her in front of the world, starting with my childhood friend.

But I didn't have a plan to hide QI4's hacker in plain sight. So I could talk about me but not her.

Don't forget who he is or what he is.

He was loyal to me, not Harper. Not to anyone I was protecting. He could act like a normal friend when it suited him. Ask normal questions. But when it came to business, the alpha wolf would shed the sheep's clothing in a heartbeat.

"She's not why I stayed. She's why I'm coming back."

"Is she here tonight?"

I looked at everything but the light coming from Harper's room.

"She's working."

He laughed in disbelief. "Anyone that good doesn't *work*."

Orrin was spraying the contents of the silver container on the thorn bushes. Damon was at the end of the path Harper and I had hacked, dumping gas on the bracken. Orrin's participation made me think whatever they were doing might not be a bad idea, but even the wisest men get a little reckless after a few beers.

"I lost," I said. "She played me, and I lost."

A gaggle of children ran past us like a wave crawling onto the beach.

"If you lose," Keaton said, "I lose. And I don't lose."

A whoosh, a burst of light, and a blast of heat came from my right. I put my arm up in an inadequate gesture to guard against it.

The thorn bushes were on fire.

Keaton barely squinted. The children cheered. The adults around the bonfire whooped and hollered. Damon got close to the flames, an unlit cigarette dangling from his lips. What a knucklehead.

"Once this is over," he continued, "we'll deal with her."

"No," I said. "We won't. We're going to drop it."

"Oh, Beeze." Disappointment dropped from his lips. "You can be the doormat. I'll take care of it."

I was going to throw him off by calling in a favor, but that was playing by his rules.

His rules, our rules, the rules of the underground? They didn't scale.

"You won't. Let me tell you why." I faced him so he paid attention to me, not the fire. "If you want to go bigger, go better, go more public, this hacker mafia bullshit has to stop. We're going to be under scrutiny like never before. A thousand people might care about whether or not we get revenge, but a few million are watching to see if we keep our noses clean. Don't fuck this up with petty bullshit."

He nodded slightly. I could never read him before, but that changed in the firelight. His code scrolled across his face.

He was afraid of the big time. He didn't know the rules.

"If we walk away from tonight with a secure system," he said, "I'll walk away from retribution. I won't indulge in 'petty bullshit.' If we're still a struggling startup in twenty-one minutes, I'm burning her down."

He held up his phone.

ATTEMPTS: 1,332,871,552,921,972
FAILS: 1,332,871,552,921,972
T-MINUS: 00:21:04

If Harper lost the challenge, she'd be mine.

If she won, he was going to hunt her down until he found her right under me.

I didn't know what to wish for. Both options were losers.

If she won, we were over. For her own protection, I would have to shield her by leaving her behind.

The threat hung in the air like lead. What was Harper waiting for? The last minute? To ensure no one followed her into QI4, was she waiting for the last possible second?

Twenty-one minutes and counting. That was how long she was mine because she was going to crack it. She was too good not to.

The fire hit the back side of the bushes, catching on the gasoline and whatever Orrin had sprayed. The flames rose to the height of the house. Harper's room on the third floor was on the front and side, but if the house caught, she'd be stuck up there at the top of a single staircase.

"Who in the hell thought that was a good idea?" Keaton sipped his beer as if he was watching a movie.

He seemed awfully calm, but everyone was backing away. We were in the moment when a fun thing turns into a dangerous thing. That moment when decent, relatively intelligent people start to wonder if the method they'd implemented to clear yesterday's bad idea was becoming today's tragedy.

And Harper was a sitting duck. Stay back here and try to put it out? Or run upstairs and grab her?

Nineteen minutes.

I stepped forward. Water. The green garden hose wouldn't do much, but if I doused the house? Would it deter the flames from taking the whole thing?

Leaping for the hose, I twisted the valve. Water shot out of the seal between the threads and the nozzle, but it held.

A man came from the back door. I didn't recognize him, and I would have dismissed him as yet another Barrington citizen I hadn't met yet, but he stood out in a jacket and slacks.

He carried a fire extinguisher canister in one hand and the hose in the other.

"Chris!" Catherine cried.

"Stand back!" he shouted, jumping off the porch and spraying the flames.

With those two words, Orrin jogged to the shed. Kyle ran for his truck, which was parked in the back and blocked in by what must have been Keaton's black Mercedes.

I doused the porch, sending Trudy and her friends running.

Orrin and Kyle retrieved fire extinguishers, and the thorn bush bed was reduced to a smoking mass of brambles in no time. I loosened my grip on the nozzle, and the flow slowed to a drip. I couldn't let it go. I wasn't ready to drop the safety net.

Reggie was the first to laugh. Then Kyle. Then Trudy and her friends.

"You." Johnny, who I hadn't seen, pointed at Orrin. "I expect better from you. This was some bonehead shit if I've ever seen bonehead shit, and I've seen some boneheaded shit in my day. Je*sus*."

Damon was blind with laughter. Orrin had his head between his knees, and his shoulders shook with it. I stood there with the hose dangling from my fingertips.

Keaton's voice came from just behind me. "People in dark times do dark things."

"I didn't see it coming."

"Tension's released for now. Danger's like scratching an itch, isn't it? Life's shit until you try to make it worse."

I dropped the hose.

Laughter had taken a backseat to deep breaths and relieved chattering. With a red fire extinguisher, Damon fogged the smoking center of the thorn bed using the path Harper and I had made, a lit cigarette drooping from his lips.

Catherine, who had the most to lose from the foolish attempt to clear the bushes, had her back to the scene, her hands balled into fists and placed on her hips. Chris, the guy in the jacket, stood lover close, brows knotted in irritation.

That must be the guy. A day early, and it didn't look as if it was going well.

I hung up the hose and realized I hadn't dropped my beer.

Fuck it.

"Waste not." I tipped my can toward Keaton and drank.

He slid his thumb along the glass of his phone. "They created the worst danger they could then avoided it," he said, turning the display to me. "Just like a certain technology disruptor."

ATTEMPTS: 2,007,911,945,365,018

FAILS: 2,007,911,945,365,018

T-MINUS: 00:00:00

I stared at the numbers.

They were the same.

Every digit matched.

And time was up.

The chat from the guys was in all caps with strings of exclamation points.

"You did it, you crazy bastard." Keaton was happy. Joyful. I'd never seen him with a genuine smile that wide, but when he clapped me on the shoulder, he was a proud big brother.

My heart was on the third floor of a house that had almost burned down.

Had she stopped because of the fire? Had she simply not made it?

What had happened? I'd thought she had it. She'd thought she had it. What had gone so wrong that everything had gone right?

"No one got in," I muttered, checking my own phone. Same numbers. Same time. Same chat thread.

WE DID IT!!!

WE WON, WE WON, WE WON, WE PWNED THEM!!!

CHAMPAGNE AND A BLOW JOB!

"You're their leader," Keaton continued. "Do you have something to say?"

"Yeah." I looked at the trees that had been lit by Harper's window, and they were dark. "I do."

> *Gentlemen. We are now the*
> *proud owners of Silicon Valley.*

The responses poured in, scrolling faster than I could read.

You're the KING!!! Motherfucker!

Pwned!

I'm pissing myself.

Keaton's trunk smacked shut, and he walked toward the porch with the rest of the case of Dom Perignon. He was a cheap motherfucker until he wasn't.

Dude, THANK YOU!

I'm calling Deepak, man.
I MISS THAT CURRY-EATING FUCKER.

HAIL TO THE CHIEF!!!

I had to go to Harper. We had to make another strategy. Figure out another way to get her the win she needed. I had to deal with the guys fast and go to her.

> *Deepak's coming back. If you're*
> *interested in being on his team, fill out a*
> *form with Raven.*

The responses were fast and in the enthusiastic affirmative.

YESSS!!!!

Deepak's return wasn't exactly what I'd wanted to talk about. I didn't want to get so wrapped up in their joy that I brought it upstairs to Harper. She didn't need to see that.

> *Guys.*
> *Keep it together.*
> *Make sure the cage stays closed. Celebrate*
> *now, take a few days off. Monday, we need*
> *to analyze the attempts and see who got close.*
> *Then we need to act like they breached*
> *because the next person will.*
> *And as a company, we're going to do*
> *better. We've already made the best product*
> *in the world. We need to be the best*
> *company in the world.*
> *See you Monday.*

I LOGGED OUT. Took a deep breath.

She was my queen, but what was I king of? Technology? History? What was I supposed to do with that shit? I couldn't live off people's adulation. But her? I could eat and drink her. She was made of the food of life. She nourished me.

My job was to nourish her in her time of crisis.

I hopped up the steps to the porch and was about to run through the kitchen when I saw the black blur of Keaton out of the corner of my eye and heard the *pop* of champagne.

My mind was up the steps to Harper's door, but my body had stopped walking before I hit the other side of the room.

Keaton was indeed popping the champagne over the sink, though he hadn't lost a drop of foam. Harper stood next to him with paper cups pinched between her fingers, four to a hand, tape on all the joints that had taken the worst beating.

"Hey," I said. "I was just..." I pointed upstairs.

"I felt better, so I came down," she said. "Your friend told me what happened. Congratulations."

She wouldn't look at me. Just at the champagne falling. I needed to see her face. Read her expression. Hear her words.

"This guy you're talking to, right here?" Keaton filled the little cups as he spoke. "Taylor Harden. You're going to tell your grandkids you met him, and they won't believe you."

Mrs. Boden swooped in holding three cups in her bent fingers. She pushed her bangly red bracelet farther up her arm. "Just a splash, young man."

"To remember Paris," Keaton said, moving the flow of bubbly to her.

Harper paced to the backyard with her four cups in hand and her face down. I tried to follow, but my business partner put one hand on my arm and held up his champagne cup with the other. Mrs. Boden put champagne in my hand.

"That's the girl?" He didn't wait for me to confirm. "She's stunning."

"I know."

I didn't want to be with the man whose support had made tonight's victory possible. I wanted Harper, who'd almost crushed that victory once and who, by all rights, should have beaten me on the second try.

He held up his cup. "She's victory number two tonight. Well done."

I didn't tap my cup to his. She wasn't a conquest. She wasn't a tool for disruption or a mountain I'd climbed.

"Harper!" I went outside after her. My paper cup disappeared from my hand, and I let it go. I didn't want to drink champagne to celebrate. I wanted to drink Harper's disappointment to relieve her of it. I threaded her fingers in mine. Her skin was ice, and her taped joints were rigid. "I'm sorry."

"It's fine." She still wasn't looking at me.

"No, it's not."

"It was fair."

Fair.

Fuck fair.

Fair was a pipe dream. Fair was different for everyone. Fair couldn't even sit at the same table with justice.

I pulled her close and snarled in her ear, "What's the point of it being fair if the outcome is wrong?"

She pushed me away, gently at first, harder when I resisted. "There is no wrong. There's only what is. Don't make this about something it's not."

"It's about us then. It's a speed bump. It won't stop us."

"Taylor." With a little shake of her head, she took a hammer to the crust around my illusions. Just a tap. I felt the vibrations from inside, but the shell didn't crack.

"Come home with me," I said. "Work with me. We'll find a way to save Barrington. Together."

The party was hitting a fever pitch around us. Damon had a near-empty bottle of Dom in one fist as he pounded his chest with the other. Harper shot out a laugh.

"Harper." My tone was sharp.

"What?" She was sharp back, eyes focused on me, her chin a degree or two higher. The little crease in her lower lip was shallow from tightened muscles beneath.

"This is important."

"Okay, so?" She went from frown to smile with a glance at Damon, who was pretending to put out a smoldering patch of bush with invisible champagne. He was getting big laughs.

"I'm trying to tell you something, and you're being entertained by the biggest jackass in town."

"You know what? Stop trying to tell me things."

She walked past me to Trudy and a few girls, brushing me aside as if I wasn't even there. No. Worse. If I'd been invisible, she'd have had a good reason to turn her back on me.

I was less than that. Smaller. More inconsequential than a man she didn't see right then.

The insistent pressure of my insignificance crushed air from my lungs, weighed my shoulders. It bore down with an exponential force of gravity.

I couldn't continue to exist.

"Harper!" I yelled with all the air my squeezed lungs could hold.

Conversations stopped. In the periphery, faces turned my way, but the person at the end of the tunnel of my attention didn't show me her face.

No moment would happen after this one. There was this. Only this. Then a short, painless blinking out before the void.

The only way out was the tunnel.

I chased her to the end of it, touching her shoulder, curving my fingers, pulling.

"Get off me!"

She kicked me down the tube. It was dark, and the only sound was sucking.

"I love you." Grappling for the edge.

"I know. And I'm sorry about that." Her voice had a clang, as if she was talking inside a soda can.

"No. You love me."

"I'm sorry, Taylor. I don't. I used you. I did a shitty job, and I didn't get what I was trying to get. But that doesn't make me your charity case, and it doesn't make you one of us. It makes you done, just fucking done around here. Go home."

"You're lying. I can see it in your nose." I must have reached for her again, even though I didn't remember making a decision to, because she slapped my hand away.

"I've *been* lying. This is the first time I'm telling the truth. I don't even like you."

The pressure of the air coalesced around my arms in the shape of fingers and hands, gripping, pulling me away.

"You sold the bowls to—"

"I didn't want to owe you anything." She was a little flustered, raising her voice and jamming her hand at the air between us. "I didn't want you to have a reason to come back here."

"You're mine."

"No, I'm not." Her creased lip quivered. Was she crying? Was it sadness? Guilt? Tension? Or did she love me?

"You belong to me. I didn't even exist until we met. I wasn't a man before you. I was an idea. I don't want to be an idea anymore. I want to be real. I can't be real without you." What the hell was I saying? "And you? Living half your life in the shadows? No one in this place knows you. They have no idea what you are. You're going to live and die a stranger."

"Fuck you! This is who I am!"

I couldn't see anything outside her. Couldn't hear anything but her denial. "No, it's not."

If I could just grab her the way she liked, by the base of the back of her neck, pulling the hair tight, she'd be mine. She'd realize I gave her something she needed. She'd know she loved me.

I went to make that grab, hand out with fingers in tight hooks, snarling to take what was rightfully mine.

Someone moved in front of my vision, cutting off the sight of her. That tunnel between us was my breath. I was pulled and pushed in a dry riptide of forces. I fought as if I was drowning. My feet went from under me. I kicked, struggling for the surface.

I knew people, men, were taking me away. Physically. They were increasing the distance between my and Harper's bodies, but the proximity of my attention never wavered.

"Harper! You're mine! No matter where I am! You're mine!"

She was the bowl of the sky above, and I was screaming for her in a glassy ocean.

A loud *hup* preceded the darkness.

LX

My hand hurt, but I kept pounding the window. The back doors were locked from the outside. The keys weren't in the ignition.

The men watched me, lined up between her and me, facing the black Mercedes like a wall between us.

I knew she was out there. Waiting? Sobbing? Laughing?

Keaton got in the driver's seat and started the car. Flinging his right arm over the front seat, he backed out of the driveway. "I've never seen you like this."

I put my cheek on the cool window to keep my eyes on the yard. The wall of men broke up. In a flash of blond between the side of the house and the edge of the car window, I saw her run toward the back door.

"Let me out."

"No."

Was that the last time I'd see her? That flash of blond hair jogging to the back porch and out of sight? Was that the end of the script?

I snapped the door handle. Still didn't work.

Keaton swung onto the road and peeled out as if he was being chased. He wasn't.

"What is wrong with you?" he asked.

339

"How much gas do you have?" I leaned over, figuring if he had to get gas soon, I could get out.

"Always full. Have you lost your mind? Is this what happens when you succeed? You turn into a raving lunatic?"

I threw my body against the back of the seat, sliding down until my knees hit the front seat.

"You went code black back there." Keaton jerked his thumb in the direction of the house we'd left behind.

"She's trying to protect me. She thinks she'll drag me down."

He turned for a split second to look at me, then he put his eyes back on the road. "She said this? Or you're making it up?"

"I know her."

We blew by the gas station and got onto the interstate. A yellow stick-of-butter truck went by, and the distro center slid in and out of view. As I got more distant from her, I got more distant from myself, moving at seventy-five miles an hour and as stagnant as wet summer air.

"Okay, let me explain something to you," Keaton finally said. "Women are not subtle. If they're not one-hundred-percent crystal clear, it's because they don't know, not because they're being elusive or enigmatic or call it what you will."

The bar where I'd lost my watch came into view and left my sight in an instant.

Gone.

I checked the Langematik. It was wrong. I went for my pocket to check it against the phone. I came up with a piece of paper. I opened it. The last code.

4e 2d 2e 20 6d 20 2e 2d 2e 20 4d 2e 20
4e 20 6e 2d 20 2e 40 4d 20 2e 0d 0a

Hexadecimal. But random—no message because the text decoding left so many dots and dashes.

N-. m .-. M. N n- .@M .

"You were stupid to trust her," Keaton said. "Have a tantrum over that."

Stupid? How could he say that? He didn't know her.

I was drained of the ability to be offended.

He'd never had much to say about women until that day. I was the one with the deep distrust I'd never admitted to until I trusted the wrong woman.

"Never trust a woman who hacks you." Keaton pointed upward as if the truth came from God.

I nodded. She had been wearing tape when she held out four paper cups of Dom Perignon. "Yeah."

"But you didn't help her get into the system."

"She wanted to do it fairly. On her own."

He shook his head. "Fucking myth. No one does anything on their own." He made eye contact in the rearview. "That saved her life. I swear to you. If she'd gone in, after what she already did, I would have made sure this entire town burned."

The will to resist him couldn't overcome my exhaustion. I didn't have energy for arguments, even in my own head. I only saw my mother's old car against the backdrop of Jaguars and Mercedes in the Poly parking lot. The feds letting me go if I just showed them how I'd used Luhn's formula against the banks. Having a best friend with the money to invest in my ideas.

I ran my finger over the paper with the last code.

Dots and dashes started with two. I was an idiot. And a bunch of even numbers should have been enough to clue me in to the fact that the message was *all* dots and dashes if I just broke apart the larger numbers.

2e 2e 2d 2e 20 2d 2d 2d 20 2e 2d 2e 20 2d 2d 2e
20 2e 2e 20 2e 2e 2e 2d 20 2e 20 20 2d 2d 20 2e

It was so simple I broke it down in my head.

..-. --- .-. -- .. ...- . -- .

A simple request in Morse code.

Forgive me

I pressed my knuckle to the window where the land met the darkening sky and whispered to myself, "I don't know what to do."

Fields sped by, the perpendicular rows visible one at a time then disappearing into a bicycle-spoke blur. I was the hub of it. The tiny center of a circle larger than the circumference of the horizon.

LXI

*S*teve Jobs. Bill Gates. Jeff Bezos.

What does it take to change the world?

Mostly luck and a support system and timing. Secondarily, a person's talent has to fit into the surrounding puzzle of the era, their opportunities, and the willingness of the people around them to smooth the path. Most pieces don't fit on all sides, but when they do, the entire world hears it all click into place.

I didn't feel guilty for being a guy who could make things work with quantum theory at a time when quantum theory was ready to become things. I hadn't turned down favors or hands up. I'd had plenty of both.

Rockefeller. Carnegie. Ford.

Even Fitz seemed to know already, instinctively, who he worked for and why.

Luck + opportunity + talent + other people. There were no shortcuts. We ascended the throne because we fit the puzzle on all four sides.

Decades from now, they'd crown a new ruler. I'd be no one or a myth or forgotten. I might be a footnote or an afterthought. It didn't really matter.

What mattered was my life now.

What mattered was the wrong question anyway.
Who mattered?
That was the question. Who mattered?
A woman who wouldn't speak to me. I was a footnote to her.
Her name was Harper.

LXII

$\mathcal{I}$ emailed her once in a language I could write and she'd understand.

```
<script>
var person = {firstName: "Taylor", love: };
var person = {firstName: "Goose", love: math.random};

IF (Goose: love> 0) {
execute phone call = 669-555-2280 ;

ELSE IF (Goose: love < 0) OR (Goose: love = 0) {
execute memory = thorn bushes ;
execute memory = lessons ;
execute memory = spoons in bed ;
execute memory = taste ;
execute memory = voice ;
execute memory = laughter ;

THEN
execute phone call = 669-555-2280 ;
```

```
</script>
```

When I didn't hear back, I texted. I messaged. I found a stagnant Twitter account and DM'd it. I wrote the entire thing in Sharpie and sent it in an envelope.

She never responded.

LXIII

SIX WEEKS AFTER GREYHATC0N

SHE WAS BRILLIANT. She knew it too. She wore I-don't-give-a-fuck pumps and told me exactly what I was doing wrong.

"You rolled out the software before you had the capacity for hardware. You disappeared at a critical time for the company. You let a bunch of media take pictures of that monochromatic coding team you got in there." She leaned forward when she spoke, elbows on the table, fingers laced together.

Her last employer had said she was "bossy," "demanding," "shrill," and lastly, after a few drinks, "a bitch."

"I have an HR director," I said, mimicking her posture. "I have a media person and a business manager. You're not here for any of those jobs, so your observations may be correct, but they're not useful."

"This is my fifth interview—and my first one with just you." She indicated the empty room, the shut blinds, the closed door. "What do you want? I was COO of RKD for four years. It started smaller than QI4 and wound up ten times the size."

Interviewing men was easier. I had a better sense of them from a handshake and a nod. We spoke and read the same language. I felt crippled talking to this candidate, but I had to go through whatever this language barrier was. I couldn't go around it anymore.

She was the best for the job. End script.

"Can I be frank? About your reputation?"

"Oh, here it comes." She leaned back in her chair.

"I'm traveling a lot. So is Keaton. Deepak's around, working on the monitor design and his own projects."

She shifted her jaw to the side a little in defiance, as if girding herself against what I was going to say. I'd run it all through my head. She thought I was going to question when she intended to start a family, whether or not she was going to be "a bitch" when I traveled, or if she could handle all the testosterone-flinging.

"You have a reputation as a maverick," I continued. "A DIY hands-on outlier."

Her face changed. She hadn't expected me to go there.

"They needed a shark at RKD before they got rigor mortis."

She smiled.

"We're growing fast. You know, we talked about it last time, we just secured a huge infrastructure investment."

"And rumor is another's coming?" She raised an eyebrow.

She kept her ear to the ground. I liked that.

"The rumor is right." I wouldn't have told her that unless she was hired, and she knew it. "We're different, but I want you to bring here what you brought to RKD. We don't have time for timid or CYA. I want you to make mistakes fast and fix them faster."

She held her palms up in a half shrug. "I don't know how to be any other way."

We shook on it.

As if reading the vibrations in the air, Raven came in with paperwork. "So glad to have you on board, Ms. Friar."

"Gwen, please."

Raven turned to me, every word loaded with things she knew that no one else did. "Mr. Harden, Mr. Fitzgerald is on the way to the airport."

LXIV

FOUR DAYS AFTER GRAYHATC0N

I WAS OBSESSED WITH HER, and four days after I got back, Raven caught
me at it.

To the world, I was completely in control. I took interviews, accepted
adulation and awards. I met with real bankers about real money, not
Bitcoin. When I went out, I brought my mother or my sister because I
was obsessed with Harper Barrington and no other woman would
come close.

I attacked the obsession in my off hours as if it was a second job.
Harper's daily movements. Harper's internet presence. Harper's past.
Harper's thoughts, feelings, and emotions.

Raven caught me hacking into Barrington Christian High School my
second day back.

"Who's that?" Raven asked as she sneaked up behind me. I had
Harper's third-grade picture on my screen.

"Niece." I closed the window, lying as if I wasn't the boss. Maybe

349

because I was tired and it was after work hours. Maybe because no one else was in the office.

She'd brought things to sign. New hires. Resumes to look over. Checks. Invoices. A flood of the mundane.

"Taylor," she said.

"Raven."

"Are you all right?"

"Not really."

"Can I be honest?" She sat across from me as if I'd asked her to.

"No. Please. God, no."

"You're a mess." I almost objected, but she got her first words in edgewise. "You're in this office more than you've ever been. You shut windows like a kid caught looking at porn. Your traffic is almost constantly—"

"You're monitoring my traffic?"

"I monitor everyone's. It's my job. And the activity on yours shows certain patterns."

"Patterns?"

"You're hacking."

"That's my job."

"Who is she?"

I hadn't been in the mood, and I would have loved to shut her down, but I couldn't. I'd changed, and I couldn't just tell her to mind her business. "Rave, what we had—"

"Was convenient. We were friends, as much as Taylor Harden could be friends with anyone. And as a friend, I'm telling you, you're a mess. You have dark circles under your eyes. You haven't brushed your hair in two days. Do you want me to go on? Or do you want to tell me?"

"Neither."

It was late. I'd just seen a young, fresh third-grade genius I eventually loved. I wanted to go home and stew. I was still raw from being dragged away in a rented Mercedes. I slid my jacket off the back of my chair. "I owe you. For putting up with me. For staying professional when I wasn't. For everything."

"I was horny," she said. "And I was coming off a bad breakup. Yes, I can sue your ass from here to Disneyworld. But you got lucky this time."

"Turns out I'm a pretty lucky guy."

"Don't push it."

"Thanks, Rave."

I'd been on my way out, but she had to get a few more words in as she collected the checks and papers off my desk. "Did you know there are cameras all over the distribution center outside Barrington?"

"Excuse me?"

"Live feed. Deepak and I were looking for you, and we came across it."

"Thanks."

Again. I'd gotten one foot out the door when she spoke up.

"And the Barrington post office is using Windows 3.1."

"What?"

"Just saying." Her smile hadn't been joy. It had been pure mischief.

"Motives. Spill," I said.

"You guys with your underhanded crazy 'exploits' and the way you see things other people can't. It's always been intriguing. When I was working with Deepak to figure out what was going on with you, I... well, it was fun."

"Fun?"

"Yeah. Fun. More fun than video games."

"You're a gamer?"

"Yes. And I want you to teach me how to hack."

Her breathing was sharp, and her face was flushed as if she was turned on—but not by me. I knew when a woman wanted me, and she'd moved on from my body to my knowledge.

"Have you heard of Chaxxer?" I asked, pulling a chair out for her.

This was going to take a while.

LXV

We couldn't get into Harper's wireless. She was too good for that. She'd never open a phishing link or download anything unknown. The only way in was around.

In the weeks between secretly partnering with Raven and before my flight with Fitz, Harper had been doing the following things:

1. Turning away the most appealing Chaxxer profiles Raven could come up with.
2. Lurking, but not participating, in dark web hacking forums.
3. Quitting the distro center.
4. Buying groceries with her credit card.
5. Applying to college.

We'd tapped into every security system in town, from the distro center to city hall to the police dash cams. I tracked her credit card to see when she pumped gas, then I watched her do it on station's security video. Raven suggested we tap into the wireless at Barrington City Hall to see if anyone had taken phone video of the council meeting. I showed her how to breach it, and she learned so fast I could barely keep up. She would have been a formidable criminal.

Harper was at the city council meeting to discuss the sale of the factory. Someone had indeed taken video, and it was automatically uploaded to the cloud, where I watched it so closely and so many times I dreamt about it. She was tiny, but it was her. When she pinched her bottom lip, I inspected the video for signs of tape on her fingers. There was none. When she raised her hand and stood to speak, I could hear her clearly but failed to read her mind.

She and Catherine were going to meet Fitz at Barrington Glass Works. She didn't know I knew that.

LXVI

It was easy to sleep on Fitz's private jet. The whole thing was designed for rest and work. Raven was already dozing, and Deepak was pounding away at his laptop as if he was playing Whac-A-Mole with the keys. Fitz's team buzzed around a set of blueprints.

I wasn't tired, so I listened to Fitz practice his speech. I never mentioned the identity of the girl he was dirty-talking from his sailboat. The Watsonette was mine, and as far as I was concerned, she was talking to Flow_ro to get to me. End.

"Overpopulation is the single greatest problem we face." Fitz was putting on his "TED Talks voice," which was infuriating in close quarters. Good thing he was my friend, or I would have punched him. "Why? Not because we're running out of space or oil or ways to dispose of our waste. But because there's one resource people need to live that depends on an environmental balance that's being disrupted right now. Water."

Fitz was about to continue, but I interrupted. "That's the longest sentence ever."

"It's two sentences," Fitz said, pointing at the screen. "Look. There's a period right there."

I should have been sleeping, but I was too nervous. "You can't just make one sentence into two by putting a period before a conjunction. That's a bullshit fake period."

"It tells me when I need to pause." Fitz had a manly face despite the red hair, but when he was full of shit, he sounded like a teenager trying to get away with something.

"You paused after 'but,' not before."

"You think your speeches are so perfect?"

"My speeches are awesome." They were. I'd pitched QI4 hardware and software all over the world, selling triple our projections, building the choke on supply I was counting on.

"Then why don't you do it?"

"Because you need the practice."

Fitz knew I was lying and closed his laptop.

"Ladies and gentlemen," the pilot called over the intercom, "we're starting our descent. It's a short strip, so if we don't make it the first time, don't panic. We should be landing outside Barrington safe and sound in eleven minutes."

LXVII

*I*f I rubbed my palms on my pants one more time, I would leave sweat marks. I clutched a handkerchief instead, switching it between my right and left hands like a fucking neurotic. When I'd met the prime minister of the UK, my palms were as dry as her sense of humor. When I'd asked Fitz if he was interested in a partnership an hour after he got off a sailboat, I was half-drunk and easygoing. I'd taken calculated risk after calculated risk in the past month and never lost sleep over it.

Now, in the limo with Fitz, Deepak, and Raven, my body was in complete revolt.

I wasn't able to eat, and I felt as though I wanted to puke. My mouth was dry, and my skin was wet. I couldn't sit still.

"Keaton's meeting us there," Raven said, swiping her finger across her phone. "They want to know if we need anything."

"We" included Fitz's team, who rode in the car behind us. They'd seen the factory floor, drawn the plans, moved the money, negotiated the zoning, and brought in the utilities at the speed of Everett Fitzgerald's signature.

"Water," Fitz said, projecting without shouting. "The coming water shortage is a global risk that must be addressed immediately. You, people of Barrington, are at the cusp of rev—"

"Cusp?" I asked. "You're really saying 'cusp'?"

"What's wrong with cusp?"

"It's weird," Deepak agreed. "'Edge?' Can you do 'edge'?"

"I can't. It needs to be cusp."

"It amazes me," I said, "that you can invent and commercialize a system that combines hydrogen and oxygen molecules but you can't replace the word 'cusp.'"

"When you buy me out," Fitz said, "your speech can have all the words that make you happy. But at this moment, it's my signature that got us the money to buy this monstrosity, so I'm—"

"I paid the back taxes."

"Oh my God," Raven said. "Here we go."

"I'm going to use the word 'cusp,' the word 'boondoggle,' and I might throw a 'natty' in there to pretend I'm English." He straightened his jacket cuffs. "Actually, since you'll be squatting on half this property, you should give half the speech."

"Squatting?"

"Until you pony up."

"And you get the hell out."

The plan was for H(two)O to develop the commercial water creation system in half of the Barrington space then move to a bigger location as the operation expanded. By then, the theory went, QI4 would need the entire building. I'd buy him out—with a shot in the arm for interest.

"Keep it clean on your side," I said. "It's mine."

"Squatter."

"Guys," Deepak interjected, "really?"

I could see the roof of the Barrington mansion as we pulled up to the gate in front of the factory. The arm was up, and the parking lot was full. Bickering with Fitz had passed the time, but as soon as I was forced to pay attention to my location, my heart started pounding again and I had to switch my handkerchief to the other hand.

The car stopped, and the door opened immediately, as if someone had been waiting.

"Holy shit," Kyle said when he saw me. He was in a cheap suit jacket and jeans like the rest of the welcoming committee. "Does she know you're here?"

I got out, straightened my jacket, then straightened his tie. "No."

She doesn't know.

Because she doesn't want me.

And she hasn't answered my letters.

Or calls.

And she doesn't need me.

The air brought me back a month to her ozone scent. The memory of infinite possibilities.

"I think I ought to tell her," Kyle said.

"Aw hell!" Butthead's voice boomed, and I was almost knocked over in an embrace before I realized who it was. "Where you been?"

"All over," I said. "Trying to figure out a way to buy this shithole so you can get a decent suit." I flicked his tie.

"Harper's gonna flip."

Was she?

Was that good or bad?

He was smiling, so maybe it was good?

I was the only one with an unplanned, dedicated two-man greeting committee. The rest of the party, including Fitz's team, was already being guided by what I'd have called "everyone else," which included Damon, Reggie, Juanita, Pat, and Johnny, looking like a sourpuss even from behind.

"Why didn't you tell us you were coming?" Kyle asked. "We coulda set something up."

"Told the sisters at least," Butthead broke in.

"You don't like surprises?"

"Man," Butthead said, "the last time we saw you…" He shook his head.

I patted him on the shoulder. "I'm not going to flip out on you again."

It was a statement. Not a promise. I had no idea what I was going to do when I saw her. I had some words I'd put together. Nothing with random periods or the word "cusp," but something just this side of begging.

The yard was clearing out as people went inside. There was going to be a ceremony, a handover, a lunch with handshaking and greetings, and last, a speech where Fitz promised a ton of shit I really hoped he could deliver.

The events would take all afternoon, and I couldn't wait that long. My need to see Harper broke through my worry over what she'd do.

"Where's Harper?" I asked.

"Funny you should ask." Kyle ran his fingers through his hair.

"Yeah," Butthead added. "Today of all days."

Between the shore of seeing her and the bank of not seeing her was a river. I was getting pulled away in it. "Guys. Where is she?"

"She had to go today—" Kyle started.

"Or she wasn't going to make the…" Butthead snapped his fingers at Kyle as if he couldn't remember but his friend might.

"Trimester—"

"I think they're on quarters."

"Semester, maybe?"

"Where?" I shouted.

"Stanford," they answered together.

"Who the hell gets a midyear acceptance to Stanford?!"

From their shrugs and expressions, they had no clue.

"Is she there yet?" I could take Fitz's car back to the airport right then and haul ass to Stanford.

"Leaving today."

"You might catch her." Butthead pointed over the reeds toward the Barrington house.

She was here. I could run. Catch her. Bury my face in her neck in the next ten to fifteen minutes.

I grabbed Butthead's cheeks and kissed him on the lips.

"Jesus," Kyle laughed.

I heard Butthead behind me say, "Is that blueberry ChapStick?"

But I couldn't answer because I was already on the path through the reeds. Four steps from where the toxic stink began then hopping the chain, hauling ass over the bridge, through more reeds, trees, grass— Jesus, was it always this far?

The thorn bushes were gone except for a few charred rose bushes around the edge of a little family cemetery. I didn't have time to take in more than that. I threw myself against the back door.

Locked.

"Harper!"

Down the steps and around the side. I pulled on the screen door and yanked the handle of the wooden door.

Locked.

"Harper!" I looked up at her room, backing to the other side of the side drive. No light, but it was afternoon. "Harper, are you there?"

Her car was in the front, but she was flying out, so she wouldn't take her car. Everyone was at the factory, so she couldn't get a lift.

"Harper!"

Gone. Was she gone?

Up the front porch to the door. Locked, of course. I pounded on it. Jammed the doorbell repeatedly.

They didn't even lock the doors on a regular day. Why were they locked now?

Because she was inside.

That was why.

I leapt off the porch and stood in the middle of the front yard where I could see a third-floor window. "Harper! I know you're in there!"

A green-and-white car came down the driveway.

Car service. And luck of all luck… a Middle Eastern dude with a short beard leaned out the window.

"Hey," he said. "I remember you. Going to the airport this time?"

"Ahmed."

"Yes, yes. I can help you with your bags."

He started to get out, but I put my hand on the door.

"Listen"—I took out my wallet—"I need you to wait at the end of the driveway, on the main road." I gave him two hundreds.

He took them. "How long?"

How long would it take to know if she'd come back to me?

I was sure I'd know right away.

"Half an hour."

"Okay." He rolled up the window and backed out.

"Hey!" a voice came from above. Harper, leaning out the window from the waist, the heels of both hands on the sill. Golden hair draped on either side of her face. Thrust forward like a woman who wanted things and was going to find a way to get them. "Stop!"

Ahmed had closed his window all the way against the early-winter chill and didn't hear her. Or two bennies had made him hard of hearing. Her eyes swept over the front yard, and she saw me.

I tried to look confident and attractive. Like a guy she'd want to come back to or a guy she hadn't wanted before but maybe, just maybe, she could want now if she was interested in a man who felt humble and insignificant most of the time.

"Hi," I said.

She went back in the room and slammed the window closed.

That wasn't an answer, and I needed answers. I stood on the porch between the steps and the door. I would wait for half an hour. Then Ahmed would return. She'd see him and have to go through me to get out.

I'd let her go—but not without trying to stop her first.

Half an hour didn't pass. Sixty seconds went by before the door opened. She stood on the other side of the screen. My Harper. Even seeing her veiled by the screen, my purpose was clear. She was the last piece of my puzzle.

"Taylor, did you send the cab away?"

"It's nice to see you."

The screen was a sensory barrier. Did her cheeks flush? Did she swallow hard? Take a breath?

"It's..." Her hand went to her lower lip, folded it, then snapped back. "I want to say it's nice to see you too."

"So say it."

Her lips disappeared between her teeth. "I knew you were coming."

She wasn't supposed to. My involvement had been hidden so she couldn't avoid me.

Which was exactly what she'd tried to do, wasn't it? That hurt. I had to call Ahmed and get him back, but...

"How?"

"I hacked you."

"Of course."

"And I found out you bought the factory too. With Fitz."

"That was a secret."

"Why?"

Why indeed. She was still behind the screen door. I could have punched through it and ripped it to shreds. I could have ripped it off the hinges.

"Come out here, and I'll tell you."

"No." Her answer came before I even finished the sentence. She snapped the lock.

"If you knew I was coming, why did you hide? All you had to do was answer an email and say, 'Sorry, I still don't want you. I never wanted you and never will.'"

One of her hands pressed against the screen, going white, bubbling like the bottom of an eggshell carton. "I couldn't." Her voice cracked, and she pressed her lips between her teeth again. "I saw what you were doing, and I knew why. I knew you bought the factory to reach out to me, but Taylor, I'm not for you." She choked back a sob. "I'm always going to be connected here, and you're going to..." She couldn't finish.

I went to the door.

"No!"

I stepped back. "Harper, please..."

"I'm going to drag you down. You'll never be what you want as long as I am who I am. I'm a loser. You're not. My God..." She was fully crying, and I couldn't get near her. "Please tell me you didn't blow everything on that pig of a building. You can't lose it all for me."

"Open this door."

She just sniffed, crossing her arms.

Fuck it.

I pulled the screen door handle. Once. Twice. The third time, the little lock snapped apart the jamb and the door swung open.

The screen had hidden the extent of her anguish. Her face was red and slick with tears. Her shoulders slumped. I went to put my arms around her, but she dodged me.

"I'm protecting you, you dumb shit!" she choked out.

Halfway in and halfway out of the house, I knew something for sure that I hadn't known before. Maybe it was her vulnerability or the weakly guarded posture or seeing her with fresh eyes.

"You got into QI4," I said. "You won the challenge."

"Don't be stupid! You would have seen the breach."

"You were close. Close enough to know you could."

She didn't answer but cried harder.

"You backed off."

I was right. She didn't look at me. Didn't shake her head or wave her hand to deny it.

"Why?" I asked.

"I wanted you to win."

She took a folded piece of paper from her pocket. It flopped halfway open to reveal the code I'd mailed to her.

"This?" She held it toward me like a weapon. "I read it every day, and I remembered everything you ever said to me. I used you again. This code gave me the confidence to apply out of here." She opened the paper and read from it. "'Execute memory = thorn bushes ; lessons ; spoons in bed ;' God, Taylor, the spoons… when I needed you, you were there, and I threw you away. I said, 'Don't call him, don't call him.' Because you forgot the last *IF* function. If call script runs… if I call you and you come to me, you fail. Do you understand? There are things bigger than us. And if I'm with you, you won't have those things."

"Harper." I put my hands out and went toward her. "Harper Barrington, you are working with so much bad data." I got closer. She didn't back away. "Sorting it out is going to take me a lifetime of loving you."

"How are you breaking me down?"

"I'm irresistible. Can you come here, please? Admit defeat, and let's get on with it."

She fell into my arms as if she couldn't hold herself up for another minute. She shook and cried while I held her as tight as I could. We collapsed on the foyer floor together. I wiped her face with my crumpled cotton handkerchief. She took it and wiped her nose, holding it close as she leaned back on my chest.

When the car came around front, she was just about slowing down.

"Are you going to Stanford?" I asked after Ahmed tooted the horn.

"I got an early decision for fall."

"That's in eight months."

"I figured I'd get a job." She looked up at me. "I just couldn't face you."

"You're lying." I touched her nose.

"No—"

"All the schools in the world? Stanford? It's in my backyard."

"Your damn ego."

"You wanted to be near me."

"They accepted me. No one else did."

"You applied because you were hoping to see me. You know it. I know it. You would have been in QI4 reception before the year was out."

"I'm not working with you. You're a jerk, and I'm getting a business degree."

I kissed her forehead. "Can I send the cab away without you?"

"Yes."

Gently, I got up to deal with the car. She sat on the floor with her knees bent, wiping her face and pulling away the hair that had stuck to her eyes.

"This smells like you," she said of the handkerchief.

"I'll wash it."

"Never."

Outside, as I approached the cab, I could hear the celebration and announcements at the factory.

"Thanks for coming back," I said, leaning in the open cab window.

"You need me?"

"Nah."

"Let me give you the money back."

"Keep it," I called over my shoulder.

When I got back in the house, she was standing by the staircase. Her elbows were bent, and her head was tilted a little forward. Her weight was balanced on the balls of her feet.

She looked ready to spring.

The innocent sexual enthusiast was gone. She was a fearsome and majestic animal.

We leapt at each other at the same time, lips crashing, hands clawing, fabric ripping. My tongue ran along hers, tasting salty tears and sweet hope. Our fingers explored places that hadn't forgotten each other. She was soft, yielding, insistent, and when her hand touched my cock, skin to skin, I pulled away before I exploded.

"Harper."

Her hair was a nest, and her voice was practically a growl. "What?"

"I love you, and I always will. But I'm only going to fuck you if I can keep you."

"If you don't fuck me now…" She pulled off her shirt. "You can't keep me."

My brain was hardwired for those bubblegum-topped tits. I bent her back and sucked them. Not sticky sugar. Salt and sex and the blood rushing through my veins.

She leaned back too far and fell against the wall, pulling me down with her. We wrestled with her pants, tearing her underwear, working my clothes away just enough to get my dick out.

When I slid two fingers inside her to make sure she was ready, she gripped my shoulders, opening her mouth and throwing her head back.

"God," she said through her teeth. "Fuck me. Please."

I thrust my dick inside her, and she squeezed me tight.

"Look at me. I want to see you."

She gasped over and over, and with each thrust, she was more mine, spreading her legs wider so I could go deeper.

"Say you're mine," I demanded.

"You're mine."

I pounded her hard for that, and she shouted in pleasure.

"Say I'm yours, goose."

"I'm yours. I'm yours."

With those words, the pressure became almost unbearable. She tightened around me again and let out a long howl, arching her back for me. I held her down while I let go, exploding with her.

We stayed on the floor for a minute, just breathing together. When the wind blew the right way, the sounds of the ceremony drifted over the house, churning with the sounds of our breathing, the pops of our kisses, and the warm words of our love. Her home was settled. Her family had the chance they needed. She'd made her own decisions, and

I'd made mine. We'd succeeded, failed, and come full circle back to each other.

Our boats were lashed together, swaying on the endless sea. We were dots, specks, insignificant blinks under the weight of infinity.

I was not afraid.

EPILOGUE

She wanted to get there early, which meant I had to fly back from Virginia early to bring her. I was relieved, actually. I wanted to see how Deepak was doing with the monitor display production line before Keaton came in to see the protos.

"You could have met me there," she said with a wheeled crate banging down the stairs behind her.

"What's the fun in that?"

"Okay, well, fine then." She slid the crate next to luggage, boxes, and storage containers. Her eyes lit on each one as if she were counting.

I tucked a length of hair behind her ear. "I had your classes checked. Your stats professor—"

"What kind of checked?"

"Asked around town." I held up my hands in innocence. She'd made me promise not to have her professors hacked to collect old tests and data on grading. "She's looking for tenure. So if you need to make trouble—"

"Taylor!"

"It was totally aboveboard."

"Don't check on people for me!" She hit my chest to make her point.

She meant it—for the moment. But I was going to keep asking around for her until she was on her feet. And probably afterward.

A car crunched and rumbled down the driveway.

"Don't eat at the campus café." I picked up a box. "They failed a health inspection this summer and passed just a week ago. That's not about a person, so you can't get mad."

"I'm going to eat at your place." She grabbed the handle on a wheelie suitcase. "Did you send the factory car?"

"Yes. What's in here?" The things in my box shuffled when I moved.

"Nothing. I thought the factory car was a Mercedes?"

The top flaps of the box bent. I could see inside. "You're taking a box of cables?"

"I always need cables."

I dropped the box and bent to see inside one of the containers. "This is full of circuit boards and…" I popped the top off it. "Coding manuals? Harper."

"What?" Her arms were crossed. I'd agreed to not interfere, but she was making it hard.

"Did you bring a toothbrush?"

She pointed at the smallest bag, which was tucked under a foyer table.

In the month since her birthday, a lot had happened with Catherine. She had enough money to buy furniture for her beloved house.

"My clothes and stuff are in there," Harper said.

"All your clothes are in that tiny thing?"

"Can you stop? Please?"

"Goose—"

"Don't 'goose' me. Just…" She stepped back and put her hands out. Her face scrunched. "I'm scared, okay?" I shut up while she took a deep breath. Then another. "I'm scared no one's going to like me and I'm too old, and I'm scared I'm not smart enough."

"Seriously? You're smarter than every last one of them."

I peered past the front curtains at the Range Rover sitting at the end of the drive with the engine running. I couldn't see past its tinted windows. Ahmed, who we'd hired as the factory driver, should have gotten out by now.

An ugly feeling brewed in my gut. Something was wrong with this picture.

"What's with Ahmed? Is he sick in there or something?"

Harper was still on the same train of thought. "I'm afraid I won't fit in. I'm afraid they'll find out about us and think I'm coasting."

"You're going to coast because of your brain. Not because of me." The Range Rover was still idling. "Maybe we should take the Caddy," I said, referring to the car I'd bought her to replace the shimmymobile.

Harper came to the window with me and bent back the curtain.

"Maybe someone's looking for the factory and got lost? Used to happen all the time."

"Stay here," I said, opening the front door.

The porch creaked under my weight. Something wasn't right with this car, and I needed to get between it and Harper.

The car locks clacked. Harper was right behind me as if I hadn't told her to stay inside. She was going to be a real pain in the ass to take care of.

The driver's door opened, and a woman stepped out. My age or a few years older in a black suit and stilettos. Red lipstick. Black hair two inches above the tits. She didn't carry a bag but a leather folder in her manicured fingers.

A guy who looked like a Ken doll got out of the passenger side and buttoned his jacket.

If Harper sensed what I sensed, she didn't show it. My goose stepped in front of me as if it was her house, which it was, and as if she was perfectly capable of greeting newcomers, which remained to be seen.

I put my hand on her waist to stop her. It didn't work.

"Hello?" Harper said.

"Hello." The woman had a deep, throaty voice and an air of entitlement I recognized from dealing with empowered people.

"Afternoon," the Ken doll replied.

"Can I help you?" Harper crossed her arms.

"Are you Catherine Barrington?" The woman asked.

"I'm Harper, her sister."

"Harper." She smiled wide and almost... *almost* genuinely. The guy just stood next to her. He seemed wildly competent in his silence. I just didn't know what he was competent at yet.

"If you're looking for the factory—" I said.

"No." She cut me off, eyes landing on me as if I was what she was looking for. "You must be Taylor Harden."

"Who's asking?" Harper folded her arms as if she was ready to stand between me and an army of Range Rovers.

The woman smiled again and walked to the edge of the steps. She took a flat wallet out of her breast pocket.

"I'm Agent Cassie Grinstead. FBI." She flipped it open with her fingers and held it up so we could see the ID card and badge.

"Agent Ken Romig." He held up his own little wallet and I had to check to make sure his name was really Ken. It was.

"What do you want?" Harper sounded as if she was about to tell the agents to get the hell off her property.

The agents flipped their wallets closed and put them away in perfect synchronicity before answering. I realized it was because they knew they might need their hands free.

I got in front of Harper. I didn't think they'd start shooting, but she was on her way to Stanford to start the life she always deserved and nothing, not these people and not the federal government…were getting in her way.

"Well?" I asked. "What can we do for you?"

Cassie answered.

"We're looking for Keaton Bridge."

</book>

THANK YOU FOR READING! I hope you enjoyed Taylor and Harper.

Keaton's story is told in the standalone *Prince Charming*.

Raven's story is told in the novella *Prince Roman*.

Catherine and Chris's story is told in the novel *White Knight*. I put a chapter in the back if you want to check it out.

SOCIAL MEDIA

Follow me on Facebook, Twitter, Instagram, Tumblr or Pinterest.

Join my fan groups on Facebook and Goodreads.

Get on the mailing list for deals, sales, new releases and bonus content -
JOIN HERE.

Follow Taylor on Twitter.

My website is cdreiss.com

PRINCE CHARMING

CASSIE

I trust men I'm attracted to about as far as I can throw them, which is surprisingly far if I have good leverage and mobility in my lower body, but not far enough to give them the time of day or half a chicken sandwich.

You don't have to like it, but I'm not going to argue with at least four generations of family history. Once I feel that little buzz in the sexual part of my brain, it's a four-alarm fire in there. Klaxons. Red flags. Lines in the sand. The guy can be a crown prince anointed by the good Lord himself and there's nothing he can do to get more than a few months out of me. It's not his fault. It's mine, and I'm all right with that. It's gotten me pretty far.

Then this morning happened.

We intercepted Keaton Bridge at a factory he's opening in the next town over and took him in for questioning. When he looked me in the eye, I went to DEFCON One. Code Red. My body began staging a bloodless coup while my mind lost its flank support.

He has the body and the eyes of a predator, silken movements and a churning, twisting mind that calculates ten steps ahead. I can feel it working, and it turns me on.

I don't know him. Nobody does. Trust isn't on the table, but I'm drawn in his direction as if the earth suddenly tilted and all the water of my attention is flowing downhill, toward him.

He's seen things, but no one's ever proven he's done anything.

He knows things, but we don't know exactly what.

He's immune to bluffing apparently. We've had him in interrogation for two hours and he hasn't even asked for a lawyer.

Most black hat hackers have confidence deficits they cover in layers of bling and swagger. They compensate for social awkwardness with tough-sounding names and facility with numbers. Some have a talent for the long con until they have to look someone in the eye. Some are straight up sociopaths.

When we picked up Keaton Bridge—a.k.a. Alpha Wolf, though no one's proven it—I'd profiled him as the latter. He and his partner, Taylor Harden, are opening the first quantum-chip manufacturer in the world. The risk is enormous. Either his guts are made of stainless steel or he doesn't have a sliver of human emotion.

Then I met him. My name had barely passed my lips before I knew he wasn't a sociopath. He had emotions, tons of them, and they were complex, real, and intense.

I watch Ken interview him through the mirror. Both men are in profile.

Bridge waits two full seconds before answering any question. His hands rest flat on the table in front of him, and he's perfectly still. It's as if he knows any movement can be a tell, so he makes none at all.

Those emotions I sensed? He has control over them. His self-awareness is frightening and exhilarating. His voice has a British lilt that's masculine, confident, educated without being snotty.

The dimples in his cheeks are a trick. The smile lines are a hoax. His voice, his looks, the leathery scent that filled the car on the way in; all of it is a long con game.

"I haven't a clue," he says over the speakers in the dark observation room.

"But you are Alpha Wolf?" Ken replies, referring to one of the three most powerful figures on the dark web.

One-Mississippi.

Google can't find the dark web. The only browser that will take you there hides your activity in so many layers of encryption, you can peel them like an onion and never find the center.

Criminals trade credit card data, guns, drugs, people.

The FBI has a presence there. We use it to speak to informants and assets. Journalists use it to contact anonymous whistleblowers.

Two-Mississippi.

"It's quite funny, that."

"That what?" Ken asks.

One-Mississippi.

There's no official or provable connection between Keaton Bridge and Alpha Wolf. But that's the thing about covered tracks. Cleanliness has its own stink.

Two-Mississippi.

"That stupid fucking assumption."

Between Ken and Keaton Bridge, one of them is a federal agent. One of them has the power in the relationship. And one of them is making stupid fucking assumptions.

"Are you the same Alpha Wolf who maintains a relationship with Keyser Kaos?"

One-Mississippi. Two-Mississippi.

"You're a very insistent chap."

Ken opens a folder. It looks like a complete dossier, but in fact, it contains cherry-picked items from a two-terabyte hard drive on Alpha Wolf and Kaos. "Is this you?"

One-Mississippi.

Bridge glances over the paper Ken hands him. It's not a photo of a person. It's a screenshot of a post on a dark web onion thread.

Two-Mississippi.

The screenshot Bridge looks over is a normal Keyser Kaos / Alpha Wolf chat about how much they'd charge to dox a female gamer. This is the least of their infractions, and he knows it.

It's proof of nothing, and he knows it.

Bridge puts the page down, then leans back. He and Ken share a moment in profile.

Three-Mississippi.

I'm in the observation room because I asked Ken for a change in strategy. I wasn't convinced I wouldn't be railroaded by my body's reaction to Bridge or that my mind's alarm bells wouldn't distract me. Now I'm not sure I did the right thing.

Four-Mississippi.

Though Keaton was intimidating at first sight, with his perfect suit, open collar, broad shoulders, and chiseled jaw, he wasn't cold. He saw me before he saw my badge, as if he'd whipped away my cloak of invisibility.

I hadn't felt naked. I'd felt noticed.

Then Keaton had glanced to my right, where Taylor Harden stood. Without saying a word, he apologized to his partner.

Fascinating. He was fascinating.

Five-Mississippi.

Through the mirror, Bridge turns and looks straight at me. His eyes are the color of the seven o'clock sky and they can't see me, but they do. He sees everything. He sees how I tap my fingers to count the seconds. He sees the lint on my jacket.

I can't move. I am sealed in my rigid skin. Joints locked. Muscles frozen. He sees the spit dry on my tongue, the callouses on my hands, the tightening of my jaw. He sees the nights I was up with firearm fist, and the mornings Mom counted my night's haul.

He hears the cacophony in my head.

Six-Mississippi.

He sees so deep into my loneliness that a *huh* escapes my throat, then he speaks.

"Won't you join us, Agent Grinstead?"

CHAPTER 2

KEATON

$\mathcal{A}$gent Rotter won't let it go. He thinks I spent sixteen years covering my tracks to be intimidated in a little room by a little fucking prat.

"You're a very insistent chap."

Rotter opens a folder and flips through the pages. It's all for show. I don't look at what he's flipping through because he has fuck-all on me.

He spins the folder to face me and taps the page he's found. "Is this you?"

I will not be rushed.

I will not be coerced.

I will not be strong-armed into risking QI4.

I don't care about the company itself. Don't give a flying fuck about quantum mechanics or changing the world blah blah blah. I don't even give a shit about money anymore. They can have it, the whole rotten lot of them.

I push away the folder. This entire drama's put me off my lunch. Agent Rotter's bloody smirk is going to get him a mouthful of fist one of these days.

But not today.

I promised Taylor I'd be there today, and I will be.

Taylor could have turned over on me a hundred times. But he didn't. And when I told him I was looking to go straight, he partnered with me, knowing I was a risk. He could have gotten plenty of investors.

I'm not going to be late thanks to the rotter here. But for the bird? Where is Agent Bird?

Someone's on the other side of the mirror on my left, and if I'm any judge, the woman who helped drive me here from Barrington is watching five feet away, on the other side. She's distractingly beautiful and gloriously proud. As soon as I saw her, I had a vision of her atop a mountain, ruling the world, and a second vision quickly followed. Her under me, begging, with my name on her lips, over and over, pride shattered.

I feel her watching from the other side of the mirror. It's not an unpleasant feeling. It is, however, inadequate. I want to see her again. I want to see if I saw something that wasn't there. I want to regain control of the situation.

Turning to the mirror, I make my request. "Won't you join us, Agent Grinstead?"

Agent Rotter clears his throat. On the other side of the mirror, we hear a door open, then close.

Taylor's going to get on my arse for bringing the FBI calling. I'm going to have to convince him they were jagging off into their little files, trying to get me to turn on Keyser Kaos. They brought me all the way to Doverton to see if I have a death wish.

When the door opens and she comes into the interrogation room, I smell her perfume. It's lavender, calming, and I know the scent isn't to calm her but to lull me.

I'm not lulled. I'm physically aroused in a way I have no control over.

"Mr. Bridge." She stands astride the FBI action doll of a man.

No, I was right. She's proud, but not arrogant. Her accent's American. They could have flown her in from anywhere.

Thirty-ish. Five-eight.

Freckles on her nose the makeup doesn't cover.

Grew up outdoors.

A few grey hairs at the root.

Fingernails trimmed, clean, unpolished.

A bare left ring finger.

Does she have a lover?

That releases a flood of mental imagery I have no time for.

"Why hide behind a mirror, Agent Grinstead?"

She looks me in the eye without shame or fear. It's a frontal attack I'm not ready for. Her hair is the black of silk sheets, and her eyes are the grey of London's early morning fog.

"We were giving you a little space."

She's blindsiding you.

It's true, but I'm not turning away. She can come at me all she wants.

I can tell there's no love lost between her and Agent Rotter. As soon as she's in the room, I know she cares a bloody ton more about this case than the Boy Scout.

Which is good. I can use that.

"That answer's beneath you."

"If you have someplace else to be," she says, tilting her chin toward the dossier, "you know the quickest way out of here."

I lean forward. My answer should shake her a little, but not too much. I think about her response two seconds and formulate my own. "We're in the middle of a promotional event. The mayor's there. The press. The Lord himself is looking down on the Barrington factory, and you expect me to believe you want to give me space."

"If you want less space, that can be arranged." Her voice is so crisp, it's seductive.

Walking confidently in six-inch heels, she steps from her position and gets behind me. Her calves are shaped for my hands. If I want to see her, I'll have to twist all the way around. If I face forward, she has the benefit of speaking without me watching her reactions. This puts me at a disadvantage, technically. But without seeing her, I don't have to be captivated like a schoolboy, getting me back a fraction of the leverage I've lost.

"Is this where you move from implications to accusations?" I say. "Maybe pull something else out of this little folder here? Reveal your narrative of crimes? Make a sincere but manageable threat, close the walls in on me, then show me a singular way out? Yes? A little Reid technique?"

Ken looks over my shoulder to her.

"A plea bargain. Maybe you want me to flip on someone?" I push the folder back toward Ken. "Keyser Kaos maybe? I read an article in the *Intercept* about him. Quite a character. According to the article, of the thousands of people on the dark web offering assassination services, he's the only one who can make good on them."

She speaks from behind me. "We have a trail that connects you and Alpha Wolf."

"No." I turn slightly, so her blur is in my peripheral vision. I can smell her with more clarity than I can see her. "No, you don't." I turn back toward Agent Rotter. Even in the corners of my vision, Grinstead is distracting. She takes up way too much room in my attention. "You could just tell me what you want."

Rotter's watch tick-tocks. The air conditioning snaps off. I hear Grinstead breathe. Otherwise she is immobile behind me. I know she and this plastic version of a man are talking with looks and hand signals.

"Two years ago, you invested in QI4," Ken says.

"My friend Taylor came to me with an opportunity I had the resources to take advantage of."

Such a flat answer for such a thick web of motivations. Taylor's a genius. I wasn't surprised when he cracked quantum computing. Anyone would have invested, but I did because it's the right way to thank him for his friendship and loyalty before the rest of my plans go into motion.

"You and Keyser Kaos have been partners for years," Rotter says. "We've tracked everything, and now you're claiming to be legit? How could we not follow up?"

He shrugs as if this is just procedure. He's going to be the good cop now. The role reversal is standard in Reid technique interrogations. I feel as though I'm the only audience for a play that's been put on every day for a generation.

"When did partnerships become illegal?" I ask.

"When their purpose is to launder money," Grinstead says, and I like her as the bad cop. She's got a slick competence for wickedness that intrigues me.

"Maybe not?" Rotter's like a teddy bear at this point. "Or maybe you never intended to finance QI4 with laundered cash and it's Kaos with the baggage. It's Kaos who lied to you. Maybe you're just getting caught up in his malfeasance."

I wait for her to go bad cop and say something refuting this soothing fairy tale, but she doesn't.

After a few breaths, I say, "I'm sure that you think you have something in that folder that proves I'm Alpha Wolf, or that I launder money through cybercurrencies. But I know you don't. There are no recordings, no screenshots, no nothing of Kaos communicating with any persona you can prove is me. This is a parlor trick, and a particularly bad one."

I lean back, knowing I'm right. They have fuck-all. I know what exists in my world and I know what's been erased, and by whom.

"Thank you, Mr. Bridge," Grinstead says, coming back around the table. She's quite a sight, and I wonder why a woman that beautiful would want to be a federal agent. She must be ever so much more than she appears. "We'll spare you further exposure to our parlor tricks."

She walks out, taking the air out of the room with her.

CHAPTER 3

CASSIE

"What were you thinking?" Ken's look of incredulity is cartoonish on his generic handsomeness. "He's not flipping."

We're in the lunchroom of our field office with our boss, Special Agent in Charge Cesar Orlando. His shaved head has flat parts, leaving a dark arc connecting his ears every few days. His tie is loose and his suit is too wide at the shoulders, but that's normal around here.

A black-and-white poster of our ten most wanted hangs on the fridge with a curling note taped to it:

Don't be like these guys.
Eat what you bring.

By the side of the sink, mismatched mugs stand on their heads. Locked grey cabinets hide cleaning supplies. Crushed-cornered boxes of who-even-knows pile under the window.

"We have an established pattern of racketeering," I reply.

"Onion site chats aren't enough to bring him in," Ken argues. He's believable and passionate now. He's most animated when disagreeing.

Orlando stands against the counter with his arms crossed, silent until he has something to say. We're chasing a white supremacist cell, one of many across the country with plans to start a race war with coordinated, simultaneous attacks, if we could just find them past the chatter. This is Orlando's chance to validate the existence of our tiny office.

"This guy doesn't spook," I say, pointing out the door in the general area of the unflappable Keaton Bridge. "He's slipped past the cyber division a dozen times, and now he's trying to go straight. He's in transition between Alpha Wolf and…I don't know—"

"I agree," Ken adds. "We need real-life leads, not digital creeps behind a screen."

I continue without acknowledging the comment because it's the only way to be heard. "This QI4 thing he invested in? It's huge, and from everything we can trace, it's above board. If we don't flip him now, before he's too well-known to hide, we've lost him."

"He's not taking the bluff, and he's not a white supremacist. There's a slim chance he's useful."

"He knows every corner of the dark web. That's where they're organizing."

"I agree," Ken snaps, not agreeing at all. "If he's Alpha Wolf, he's useful."

I cross my arms. "Do you want to get into Third Psyche or not? Because I do. And I want to do it before they take up arms."

"They're not that organized." He shoots a look at Orlando. "Not yet."

I'm waiting for Orlando to chime in and agree with Ken. I'm waiting to be erased. But it doesn't happen. It's on me to convince him through Ken.

"Are you willing to be the guy who heard chatter about a synchronized multi-state armed takeover and didn't follow up?" I ask.

"We can follow up without that guy."

I'm about to answer when Orlando chimes in. "He's a good lead right on our doorstep. But Ken's right. He's not flipping, and odds are against him even having the intel."

I don't know why I don't buckle. Maybe because—for a second—when Bridge saw me, he really saw me. Maybe I want to feel that again. Or maybe I'm just sick of taking a backseat.

"Let him go, then give me half an hour," I say to Orlando before I turn to Ken, wishing I'd said forty minutes. "I'll have something. Maybe not enough to put into Delta, but something."

Orlando will say no, but I've said what needed saying. I'll fight another day.

"Take forty," Orlando says. I'm shocked, but I keep my composure. "You've got the best shot. I think he liked you."

CHAPTER 4

KEATON

*T*he air is thick as London's. Wet and foggy. A nip of cold. It's early evening, and though I have control over my appetite, my stomach grumbles.

That whole interview was a fishing expedition with a barbed hook. She must be their closer. I don't trust my attraction to her. It's coupled with a compulsion to speak to her, tell her things, break promises I made to myself.

I want to tell her how important that company it is to me and why. Not Agent Rotter, not the FBI, but her. I cross the car park, closing my jacket and knotting my scarf as I walk over the wet concrete. I can resist the compulsion to see her, but even as I deny it, the pressure vibrates the webbing of my thoughts. I want her to understand me.

Doverton's a small city about twenty miles from the two-horse town of Barrington, where I need to be. I stayed at the Doverton country club on a few previous visits, so I have the lay of the land, more or less. I'm not lost or disoriented. I'm just slightly angry, very impatient, and deeply concerned.

"Mr. Bridge!"

Her voice cuts the mist with the accompanying clap of her high heels.

Even at a half-run, she's steady in them. Her hair is wet at the ends, and the grey corner of a laptop peeks out from the front of her coat. She cradles it to her chest as if it's a baby.

"I have to go," I say. "If you want to arrest me—"

"No." She stops short in front of me. "This isn't like that."

The misty rain is running the hell out of her mascara, enlarging the charcoal-colored ovals around her grey-fog eyes. Compared to how she came off in the interrogation room, this federal agent in front of me is the vulnerable version of herself. She's not broken, but bending.

Half-sodden, she's still captivating. What would it take to break a woman like her?

"What is it like?" I ask.

"Can we get out of the rain?"

I scan the car park. There's no quick shelter. I check my watch. I don't like being late, even for Taylor, but this version of Agent Grinstead in an uncontrolled environment is dangerous. I want to ask her what's wrong. What has she given up on to run out after me like this? It could take all freaking night. Late is late, but too late is too late.

"I don't have time." I walk, and she stays put.

"I need your help."

I turn and look at her. Is this the same person? "What's your game?"

"No game. My laptop's getting wet."

I let her get rained on, resisting the urge to hold my coat over her. "Your shoes are getting wet too."

"I have an extra pair in my desk." She indicates my feet. "Do you?"

I do not, and my shoes aren't built for standing in the rain.

She shivers once, quickly, then stills her body. That moment of vulnerability seals the deal. I figure Taylor can handle the pleasantries with Beaver.

"Ten minutes," I say.

"My car is over there," she says, turning and pointing at a black Buick without extending her arm enough to drop the computer.

"Your car or a company car?"

I'm not getting into an FBI fleet car. They'll record everything and collect DNA after.

"Mine."
"Show me the registration."
"It's in the glove compartment."

CHAPTER 5

CASSIE

I'm already soaked through when I pluck the registration card out of the glove compartment. I hand it through the window. He unfolds it with his hands inside the car so it stays dry.

His hands are six inches from me. They're tendon and bone, calloused at the tips from hitting keys. They're the hands of a man, and I want him to put his fingers in my mouth.

Are you serious? Stop.

He checks my name and the license plate. "Cassandra."

"That's my name."

"Do you know the Cassandra complex?"

"You're getting wet."

He hands me the registration. He must have memorized everything already. "Cassandra was an ancient Greek woman with the power to see how the world was going to end, but no power to stop it."

"Let me guess. No one would listen to her."

He smirks and crosses in front of the car, touching the hood with the graceful tips of his fingers as he cuts the turn around it. I hit the unlock button. When the passenger door slaps shut, he and I are in a tight space. Was the car always this small? Was the roof this low? The seats this cramped?

He slides the seat all the way back, but the length of his legs isn't the issue. He's fine. The car is suddenly too small for *me*. His presence fills the space between the dashboard and the back window, floor to ceiling with a sense of thick menace. He's as stationary and lethal as a bullet in the chamber. As perfect as a polished barrel shining in the moonlight.

Without the protection of my badge, the two-way mirror, or the buffer of a threat, I am small and vulnerable. I am made of alarms and denials. I'm water being poured into a container shaped like him.

"So," he says. "How is it you can be in the field office parking lot with me?"

I close the windows and turn on the heat. Everything turns to steam. The air gets heavy, weighing down my eyelids in a way I know will be construed as seductive. I'm conflicted about giving that impression. I'm pretty sure there's no way I can hide how beautiful I find him.

"We have nothing on you. That doesn't mean we aren't close."

"I don't know you, Agent Grinstead, but if I were a betting man, I'd bet entrapment was beneath you."

I look him in the eye, and the force of his gaze silences me. I feel powerless. Like cornered prey. The thickness of the air delivers his smell directly between my legs, which reacts with a sudden throb that's almost painful, as if an unused delivery system is asked to do too much, too fast.

I point out the half-fogged window, up at the light posts. "Those cameras?"

He's looking at me, not in the direction I'm pointing. I'm about to trust him with a piece of information. It's easy negotiation calculus. I have to expose myself if he's going to expose himself.

I continue. "Out here in Doverton, they put them up, but they don't have the resources to monitor them. Some work. Some don't. That one in particular hasn't worked in three months. That one over there." I point behind him, but he doesn't turn. "Couple of high school kids hit it with a rock and it points at the sky. It works if you want to know the weather."

"It's raining."

"Yeah."

"It bothers you that they don't work."

For a guy who makes a living hiding behind a computer screen, he sure can read people. Now, in addition to feeling turned on to the point of being liquid, I feel naked.

"It bothers me. If you're going to do something, you should do it. If they don't want a field office in Doverton, they should close us. Don't do this half-assed shit."

"Are you from here?"

"I'm from Flint. Just outside Detroit."

"I know where Flint is."

Of course he does.

After clearing my throat, I say, "So you're wondering why I asked you to come into my car."

He smiles. He has great teeth. Not fake. Ever so slightly uneven. I notice the canines aren't any longer or sharper than a normal person's, then I wonder if that's a trick to make his prey relax.

"Not really," he says. "I can work it out."

"Oh?" My apprehension gives way to curiosity. I turn off the heat, cutting the ambient noise so we can hear the *pit pat* of rain on the windshield.

He taps his finger on his knee. His trousers are a nice tweed. He was on his way to the Barrington bottling plant for a celebration. He's missed it, and I don't feel bad about that at all.

"You're an open book, Ms. Grinstead." He adjusts himself in his seat, looks away from a beat. He turns the heat back up, drowning out the sound of the rain.

He waits.

"You're testing me," I say. "I turned the heat off. You think it might be to unmask our voices because the car is wired? You don't know."

"Now I do. You didn't react when I turned it back on."

"The car isn't bugged."

"It's not." He turns to face me with more of his body. "You're taking a risk. You knew you had nothing on me. This meeting we're having here isn't planned. Maybe it's personal. Looking to get information on an ex-boyfriend perhaps?"

I huff out a laugh. My most recent ex-boyfriend, Doug, is harmless to the point of invisibility. If I want information from him, all I ever have to do is ask, except there's nothing in his brain I want to know.

But Keaton Bridge? Sitting so close to him, pressed against his presence like a raisin kneaded into cookie dough, I realize I want to know everything in his mind.

"It's not personal." I pull my laptop out of my jacket. "But the bureau won't let me be direct about it until you're an asset."

"Ah. I have no intention of getting entered in your little database of informants."

I start to tell him that I know, but stop. I shouldn't agree. I should ask him how he's so sure, but I trip on the response. I wonder if I'm having the same effect on him as he is on me. Is he turned on to the point of distraction? Does he have an ache between his legs? Everything about him is distance and control.

Imagine cracking through that.

Imagine him losing control.

Stop.

I lay the laptop on my knee, and as I'm about to open it, he holds the top down. "Don't open that." He spreads his beautiful hand over the top. I look into his twilight eyes. "Tell me first."

"There's an onion site."

"There are many."

The dark web is larger than the web we can see. No one knows how much larger, except maybe 4lph4_W0lF a.k.a. Alpha Wolf, the king of the underworld who is rumored to be Keaton Bridge.

"I know, and I know Alpha Wolf—"

"I didn't say that was me."

"He was one of the ones who took down New Peanut Butter."

New Peanut Butter was a site for the utter destruction of innocence, like putting a knife into a new jar of peanut butter. They were taken down and unmasked to law enforcement by an anonymous group of hackers.

"Good for him," he says.

"So you're a moral person. On some level, you're not evil."

"Thank you for your vote of confidence."

His answer doesn't have a denial inside it. Is that calculated? Or did it slip?

"I do know some of friends of his"—I use the third person as a buffer for his non-denial—"were in a white supremacist forum that moved a few months ago. I need the link."

That isn't uncommon. There's no Google of the dark web. You have a link or you don't, and the links are randomly generated alphabet soup. Once a moderator gets a whiff of infiltration, he'll send a new link to people he trusts and the forum will be left with a bunch of outsiders banging around in an otherwise empty room.

"There are no friends on the dark web," Keaton says.

"Fine. Associates. The forum went dead, and I have no idea where it moved. It's called Third Psyche."

"If you think I keep company with Nazis, you have something coming."

The rain gets heavier. *Pat-patter* on the windshield turns into the whoosh of rapid fire *pah-pah-pah-pah*.

"So you've heard of it?"

"I never claimed to know nothing."

"Are you going to help me?"

"*Me*? Not *us*?"

"Are you going to help or not?" I repeat without the pronoun.

He hesitates. It's not a pause. It's indecision. Maybe the forwardness of the question has shocked him. "No."

"We may have nothing on you to arrest you today, Mr. Bridge, but we're working on it."

"Call me Keaton. We're old friends now."

"Your identity is out. We're going to prove it."

"Back to *we* I see."

"*We* know the money you invested in QI4 was laundered, which makes the entire company subject to asset seizure."

He leans forward and puts his hand over mine. It's dry and warm. I never knew I had nerves that went directly from the skin on my hand to the glands inside my thighs, but now I do.

"You have nothing. The money is untraceable, and it was made honestly, taxed honestly, and used in an honest venture."

I hear a car pull up behind us. We both look. His cab.

When he takes his hand from mine, the skin goes cold. He opens the passenger door. The muffled clop of raindrop sounds get sharper and more urgent.

With one foot out the door, he stops and looks me in the eye. "If you want out of Doverton, you should try catching a criminal, Agent Grinstead."

"Call me Cassandra."

He smirks and slaps the door closed. The cracking rain goes back to muffled tapping. I am alone with plenty of room in my car, the air thin enough to breathe.

In the rearview, I see him canter across the street and get into the taxi.

It's not until he's gone that I wonder what just happened.

CHAPTER 6

KEATON * FOUR MONTHS LATER

I couldn't forget the FBI agent with the raven hair and the fog-grey eyes. I'd promised myself I wouldn't look into her background, but I'd lied. I distracted myself with work for the first week, then in a moment of weakness, I uncovered whatever I could, devouring information so I could build a woman out of meaningless details.

I stayed in San Jose until I couldn't anymore. As soon as I crossed into Barrington, I knew I would see her again.

I'm worried about how intrigued I still am by her. She's as harmless as wolfsbane, with its innocuous-looking purple flowers. Touching it with a paper cut can kill a man. Or not. It's a risk I'm not willing to consider. She can derail everything.

I'm not worried about the feds. I thought about moving out of the dark long before the FBI connected Keaton Bridge to Alpha Wolf. I'm prepared for the switch. Nor am I worried about her threats. They have the hollow ring of a prop sword on fake armor.

I won't mistake Cassie's vulnerability for weakness or her silence for lack of interest. She hasn't gotten what she asked for. She'll make sure she comes for me to get the link. I'll find a way to give her what she needs without giving her what she wants.

The taxi speeds over the empty road, rain splashing everywhere. The layer of water on the windows marbles everything into a moving grey mass, but the driver speeds along as if he can find Barrington by smell.

I've dissected my last contact with Cassandra dozens of times since leaving. She'd turned skittish in her car, like a tamed horse who only remembered her wild past when cornered. Her domestication cracked, and something unruly seeped through. Something sexy and musky. Her sweet steel smell and the soft sound of her voice is stuck to my senses, latching on like a puzzle piece.

I'm sure I'd fancy getting the girl with the long sable hair to scream my name. I'm sure her sexual obedience would be more satisfying than any other woman's.

By the time the cab pulls off onto a long road, the beating rain has slowed to a thick drizzle. The factory's details are shrouded by the mist and the setting sun. Three cranes surround it, ready to remove the roof so the equipment can be dropped in.

The guard at the factory entrance sees me in the backseat and knows the driver because everyone knows everyone here. We're waved past the gate and navigate the delivery trucks, then a flatbed with a ten-meter-high wooden box with QI4 stenciled on the side.

I pay the driver and hop up on the loading bay. I know the man with the clipboard and the woman operating the forklift. I know the name of the architect who points at the doorframe. They wave or nod, but they're afraid of me. They don't ask questions and I offer nothing. I'm a ghost, and I like it that way.

The room is cavernous. It's a fucking circus. Forklifts and boxes. Drones stringing cables across the ceiling. Robots being assembled by robots. Sparking arc welding behind screens and the shouts of men and women with clipboards as they check their punch lists.

A male voice breaches the din. "It's done!"

"Yes!"

That's a woman's voice I recognize, and I hitch my attention to it. Harper Barrington sits on a wheeled dolly, staring into a screen. Headphones arc over her blond hair, and six of her phalange knuckles are wrapped in white hacker tape.

I hop on the dolly as she pushes headphones off her ears.

"Hey, K," she says as Taylor Harden hops onto the dolly in trousers and a jacket. They high-five and kiss longer than I find appropriate.

"Hello, Alpha," he says when he's done.

"Hello, Beeze."

Harper shuts her console. "We can do the second half tomorrow."

"Does she even work here?" I ask. "Shouldn't she be in school?"

"Get someone else," she says. "See if I care."

"Winter break." Taylor hops off the platform and calls to me, "You have to see this."

I join him as he takes me across the concrete floor. It's been sanded down and shined. Masking tape outlines the equipment and wall placement.

"We're doing it," Taylor says. "When I saw this, I said damn. We're really doing it."

He bursts out onto the loading dock, where a forklift picks up a pallet of nondescript boxes. It's already cold, but colder air comes from the open back of the truck. SysCo is printed on the side.

"This is it!" Taylor's breath is smoke and his jacket flutters open in the wind. "This is when I said *holy shit*."

"It's a refrigerator car? A food delivery?"

"When I dreamed about making it, I thought about this. Being so big we needed a cafeteria."

"We need a cafeteria because you wanted to buy a factory in the middle of nowhere."

He doesn't even hear me. He's lit up like London Bridge.

A crane lowers a pizza oven onto the dock. We jump to ground level. He knows me well enough to walk toward the river, where there's less noise and confusion. We stop under the shelter built to protect equipment from the elements.

I make him nervous. His life is built on quantum circuits and the software that makes it feasible. If the law finds something on his partner, his life's work is in jeopardy.

"The FBI," he says in a more somber tone. "Have you heard from them since they brought you in?"

I'd told him about the interview, and he hasn't brought it up since. Now he has to. This is why we're by the river.

"I would have mentioned it."

"Not comforting."

He doesn't believe me. Or more accurately, he believes I'm telling the truth, but doesn't believe the truth is mine to tell.

"They were fishing," I say. "I don't have what they want. I told you this."

He looks away, then back at me. "Okay, listen. Here's the thing. I can't…" He takes a deep breath. "I can't take risks right now."

I cross my arms, trying not to laugh at him. He was never half the risk taker he fancied himself.

"Is Harper all right?"

"She's fine. Thanks for pretending you care."

"I do care." I have to jump in front of this, because this idea that I don't care about him, and the love of his life by extension? It bothers me. "Tell me what you're off about, would you? I don't have all day."

"We have a cash flow problem."

"How much?"

"Hundred."

He means a hundred thousand. It's not much in the grand scheme of our investments and liabilities, but moving that amount around to cover it won't be easy.

"Don't we have accountants?" I ask.

"They can't pull it off a money tree. All our shit's tied up."

"I'll take care of it."

"With what? Bitcoin? No." He can't look at me, or he won't. He's doing it on purpose.

"Why not?"

Finally, he looks me in the eye. "Dude."

"Wanker. I set you up clean." The end of each word is clipped, but I keep my voice low. I don't want to alarm him, but he needs to trust me on this.

He closes his eyes for a second as if gathering his own patience. "I know, but… Harper says there's hacker chatter about you. Kaos's people aren't happy you've gone legit. And on the one hand, fuck them. On the other hand, it creates a vulnerability we have to shut down."

"They have no idea who I am."

"Dude, *I* don't even know who you are."

Taylor used to be an impenetrable wall of ambition. Once he met Harper, he started saying what was on his mind whether it serves his goals or not.

"We've been friends since you got your first boil," I say.

"You dropped into New Jersey from nowhere."

"London's hardly nowhere."

"Do you remember the time Mrs. Denver was calling your name in the cafeteria? She kept calling and calling and you just ignored her? Everyone turned around but you and the girl you were talking to. Denver was just, 'Keaton! Mr. Bridge! Keaton! Keaton Bridge!' I had to kick you."

"I was obviously distracted by the bird."

"No, I thought about this a lot. There were other times. The time you had to sign out of class early and you wrote a D instead of a K."

My throat closes. There are some things I don't talk about. Not with my best friend. Not even with those in my family with the same secrets. There are things that are off-limits, but if I tell him that, he'll know by deduction. Taylor's no dolt. In fact, he's brilliant enough to get me killed.

I step out of the shelter. The rain's slowed. "Reliving the glory days has been fun."

"You didn't know yourself by that name," Taylor continues. "Keaton Bridge isn't your name. It's what it is, bro." Taylor's words come from far away, and I hang on every syllable. "It's cool. You're a mystery man. Cool. But maybe the FBI showed up here for a reason."

"You have nothing to worry about. The fed will never be a problem. Ever."

"And Kaos?"

"He's not your concern."

"That's not comforting."

"I'm not here to comfort you."

"Why are you here?"

I answer by putting a hand on each of his shoulders and looking him in the eye. I'm here for him, but I can't say that. He'd never believe it.

"I have this," I say.

He looks at me in a way meant to threaten. I love him, but he's a knob if he thinks he can scare me away from disappearing.

CHAPTER 7

CASSIE

The club restaurant is crowded with Doverton's élite. Heavy silverware clinks, and voices are dampened by the damask curtains with a rose pattern.

The busboy takes our dinner plates.

Frieda has one eyebrow that fades in the center of her nose but doesn't disappear. Where most women would remove the connection, my friend owns it. She tweaks the shape of her brow to beautiful, subtle arches, and can raise one or the other to express a question or doubt, but with the dark line connecting both sides, every expression comes with an undercurrent of strength.

Her dark brown hair is pulled back and parted in the middle. Her gold hoops swing back and forth when she shakes her head. She's a year behind me at the bureau, and the only other woman agent in the office.

"You see that factory? They're building so fast." She slides her thick black glasses to the top of her head and picks up the check.

"Barrington loves it."

"I don't trust these California guys." She puts down the check and picks her bag off the back of the chair. It's basically a leather sack Santa would find quite roomy. "Of course, you knew. You're always so on top of it."

It's my turn to pick up the check while her hand is frozen in her bag as if she's found a a prize at the bottom of a cereal box.

"Yeah. Besides being one of the absolute worst, I mean *best*, hackers in the world, he's so cocky about it, I want to slap him with an indictment just for smirking."

My wallet's out before hers. We drop our credit cards on the tray and the waitress whisks it away.

Frieda puts her elbows on the table and circles the air with a finger. "What was this that happened to your face just now?"

"What?" I have no idea what my face did before she asked the question, but it's turning red once she does the circle-thing.

"This glint when you say 'smirk' like you have a picture in your head."

"Of course I have a picture in my head."

"And you like this picture?"

I shrug, but she knows me. She raises that one gorgeous eyebrow, one side higher than the other, and tilts her head.

"Whatever," I say. "Where are they with that check?"

"Tell me something about him."

"There's nothing to tell."

"Anything. Just to pass the time."

I'm not going anywhere until the check comes, so I might as well just spill it. "British."

"Oh, and an accent?"

"Yeah. But he's been living here since he was sixteen."

"Some people don't shake it so easy. Tall? Short?" She slams the last drop of cola and places her glass in the condensation circle on the tablecloth. "Tell me."

"Tall, I guess? Six four?" I slide my own wine glass onto my own grey circle, matching hers. I don't know why I'm equivocating. "Really, really beautiful, to be honest. Like a jaguar. Not the car."

"I like this picture you're painting."

We get the check back and sign on the dotted lines. I'm uncomfortable talking about how I felt around Keaton.

I stand and grab my bag and coat. "I like the picture of him having information I can use to get one up on Ken."

Frieda snorts and throws her twenty-pound bag over her shoulder. "I like that picture too. Ken is one hundred percent *bro*." She drops *bro* like most people drop *shit*. "And he has a sneaky face I don't like."

"His face suits him. And he's going to be the one moved to CID unless I can find something to leverage to my advantage."

CID is the FBI's Criminal Investigative Division. My dream job. I've been passed over four times.

"Can you leverage Mister-Not-The-Car?"

"I can't," I say right away then stop, because I'm flooded with distracting pictures of ripped sheets and knotted bodies. "He's an asset. Off-limits."

"Ah. Well, then. The cat must disappear back into the jungle without you."

She yanks one handle of her hobo bag over her shoulder and opens it, digging for her keys as we walk through the bar. She spends half her waking hours with her arm buried to the elbow. She stops in front of me in the middle of the half-empty, post-dinner-seating bar area to rummage for her keys. There's a football game on the TV, cheers and groans in the air, laughter and clinked bottles. Our team must be winning.

I know exactly where my keys are, but I wait with her, watching the TV as the next play is set up.

In the tense silence, a voice breaks through, and I'd know it even without the British accent. I scan for Keaton and find him when the guy in front of me leans over to talk to the woman next to him. The British businessman/tech giant/hacker sits at the corner of the bar, ordering a drink.

Keaton looks calm, almost serene, more the threatening villain than I ever thought possible.

"Got them!" Frieda exclaims to a jingle of keys.

The play completes. The crowd cheers. Keaton's drink arrives.

She pulls me forward. "Let's go."

The man next to Keaton gets up, and our eyes meet. Keaton looks right at me, picking up his glass and tipping it in my direction. I'm frozen still, shot through with hot steel.

I can't turn away. He's half in shadow, one foot on the floor and the other tensed against the rail of the stool, holding me still with his gaze where most men would have bored me already.

Frieda snaps her fingers in front of my face. "What are you looking at?"

She follows my stare to him just as he puts his drink on the bar as if he's not relieving his hand of weight but making a statement about who he is and what he intends. Everything about him is calculated and deliberate.

"Let's go," I say.

I don't want Frieda to see him. She won't approve, and I'm just not in the mood for it. She'll ask me to make sense of the way I feel around him, and I know I don't have an answer for it.

What do I want out of Keaton? He'd refused to get me into Third Psyche four months ago, and he won't do it now. He's not going to do anything but make me feel unsure and vulnerable. He's going to set off alarm bells and a war between heart and head.

Nobody. No one needs to be all liquid under their skirt. No one needs to feel their heart pound or feel the air press up against them.

A guy in full team regalia tries to sit in the empty stool but makes the mistake of looking at Keaton first. I can't see what passes between them, but the guy, who has tattoos up his arms and a goatee, holds up his hands as if he's sorry for causing offense.

Keaton puts his fingers together and points all four at the seat as if to say, *Are you sitting or not?*

"Are you coming on or not?" Frieda shouts over the growing din before the next play.

Who needs to feel as though they're being devoured by a man's seven o'clock eyes, a four-course meal for a hungry jaguar. Who needs to be touched by a man shrouded in mystery? To fall into the music of his voice?

I am a federal agent. I have a law degree. I worked my ass off to get this far and I'm not jeopardizing it with an untrustworthy businessman.

Do you want to go to CID or not?

If I want to get this done, I'm going to have to stretch my values thin.

Frieda's looking at me as if I have lipstick on my teeth. "Is this Mister Smirkypants?" She jerks her head in Keaton's direction. Her voice is flirtatious, as if she's trying to pack a hundred syllables worth of *yowza* into one word.

"How did you guess?"

She draws the same circle in the air as she did over the dinner table. My face gives me away apparently. Somehow, that's enough for me to know I've already made a decision.

"I'll see you later," I say.

"You going to be all right?" *Yowza* off. Concerned friend on.

"Yeah."

"Call me." She holds up her fist, and we bump.

"I will, my sister-in-the-law."

She hugs me and heads for the exit.

Taking a long, deep breath, I stride over to Keaton. That happened so fast, I have to take my steps slowly before standing by the barstool he's saved for me.

His eyes take a quick, almost imperceptible tour of my body. I'm in sensible work clothes and naked at the same time.

I'm wary. He senses it.

I'm turned on. I'm sure he senses that too.

"Fancy meeting you here," I say.

"I stay in the club when I'm in town. The suites are quite nice."

Is that an invitation? Am I supposed to answer that with a yes or no?

He doesn't wait for my response. "You'd better sit before I have to kill a man to save it for you."

"I want to be clear," I say. "And honest."

"I expect no less."

"I'm not sleeping with you."

"Indeed."

He indicates the stool again, and this time I slide onto it. For the first time, I wonder how this will look. The patrons seem like regular folk from Barrington and Doverton. The Doverton customers have the smack of wealth. I could separate them out if I had to, but I don't. I'm not interested in who's from where. I'm concerned with being seen. I don't see anyone from the bureau in the bar, but you never can tell.

"Are you looking for a boyfriend who might see you with me?" Keaton asks.

"No."

"Then who?"

I don't answer. He knows damn well.

"What are you drinking?" he asks.

"What are *you* drinking?" I touch his half-empty glass with its pale fizzy liquid and mint leaf.

"Bitters and ginger beer."

I think that's non-alcoholic. I don't want to drink around him. I already had a glass of wine, and that's my limit if I want to keep my wits about me.

"I'll have one of those," I say, hoping I'm right.

He orders it with a tilt of his chin and a flick of his fingers. The bar is packed but the bartender gets right on it.

"Wow," I say. "I would've had to wave a twenty at her for half an hour."

He shrugs as if he doesn't know the reason for his superpowers. I've noticed no one with them knows where they come from.

"How have you been?" he asks.

"Fine."

"Did you ever get where you wanted to go?"

"No," I say with regret and a little shame. I tried and failed the forums while Ken and I followed other leads.

"Do you like puzzles?" he asks.

"Actually, yes."

He leans forward, elbows on the bar, closer to me than I expect but not as close as my body wants.

"To your left," he says, pointing at the couple next to us. His limbs are so long he could wrap himself around me. If I turn, my nose will brush his neck, and that's exactly what I want/don't want.

I look at the couple. He's young, with a short haircut and a clean-shaven face. She's got long curly brown hair, a skinny-strapped, over-the-shoulder bag, and a giggle. She likes him, and he's trying to impress her with a bar game. He's set up drinking straws in a tic-tac-toe pattern, and he shakes a little stack of coins in his closed fist.

The crowd groans at something on the screen, but these two don't care. He hands her the coins.

"Six coins," Keaton says. "Place them so that they don't make a line of three."

She places the first one in the middle.

"She's already lost," I say.

"Really? You know this one?"

"Four sides and two corners. You don't have to know the game to win."

"But you do."

"I know them all."

He leans back. The bar has settled into a murmur. It's the halftime show, and no one cares about dancing girls.

My drink arrives. He gets a refill without asking.

"Let's make a bet," he says.

"I don't make bets I can't win."

"If you show me a pub game I don't know, I'll answer any question truthfully. If I show you one, you'll do the same."

"I can't give you any classified information. Anything I know from the bureau."

"Personal information only."

Is his connection to Alpha Wolf personal? Can I ask, and will he answer?

Is that the question I want answered?

I want more, somehow. I know he's Alpha Wolf, but I can't prove it. A verbal confirmation is meaningless. I want to know about *him*, who he is, what he does, what he likes. I want to know things about his past that I can't find in a dossier, and things about his future outside the newspapers.

"Deal," I say.

"Let's make it even more interesting."

Spoken like a true gambler. Interesting means riskier.

"How?"

"We'll each mention a pub game and answer a short question if the other knows it."

"Fine. But that's as interesting as I'm getting tonight."

He nods. Reaches for bar straws. "Front-facing dog."

I stay his hand, then pull it away. "No need to demonstrate. Pivot the nose so he's looking back."

"Yes. Your question?"

"Are you single?" It shoots out of my mouth before I even filter it. "Still not sleeping with you," I add when he looks at me. His eyes don't wander away from mine, but I feel naked again. "Just asking."

"I am single. And I promise, you won't do much sleeping."

My cheeks tingle. I'm glad it's dark because my face must be beet red. I rush to the next game. "Dime in a shot glass. Remove it without touching it."

"Blow on it. Hard." When he takes a drink, he moves the straw to the side and sips from the edge of the glass. He puts it down before his question. "Are you single?"

"Yes." My face tingles. I don't know if he can see it in the dim light of the bar.

He reaches behind the bar for two brandy snifters. The bartender shoots him a look but lets him get away with it. Being seen, caught, and walking away is its own superpower.

He drops an olive on the bar and covers it with one of the snifters, leaving the other face up. "Move the olive—"

"Please." I hold up my hand. "Allow me."

I rotate the down-facing snifter against the bar until centrifugal force pulls the olive into the deep part of the glass. I pick it up and drop the olive into the upturned one.

"Very nice," he says.

Without the football game on, my trick has gotten us some attention. The couple with the tic-tac-toe quarters is leaning forward with the guy explaining the trick to the shoulder-bag girl.

I hold out the snifter with the olive in it. "Want it?"

"No, thank you."

"Are you Alpha Wolf?"

"*Want it?* is a question." He smirks. "But I'll change the answer." He plucks the olive out of the glass and pops it in his mouth.

"Fine." I put down the glass. "Let's make this more interesting." The tilt of his head is a show of respect, and I let it warm me. "Let's play a lying game."

"As opposed to this dance we're doing now?"

"If you don't know the next trick, you lie to me for as long as it takes the trick to complete. If you know it, I'll lie to you."

"You're on."

I get the bartender's attention. "Can I have a shot of whiskey and a shot of water? Fill both to the rim. And if you have a playing card?"

"Yep." She pours out the whiskey.

"Do you know this one?" I ask him. I haven't done this trick in years. I almost hope he knows it.

"Nope. Spent a lot of time at the pub, have you?" Keaton asks.

"My mother taught me."

I swallow the rest of the story. How she practiced on me. How she told me her cons, testing the tricks to see if they were easy enough for a child to figure out.

The bartender places the two shot glasses and a joker card on the bar.

"I'm going to move…" In the middle of the sentence, I stop, because I'm not invisible. A dozen sets of eyes are on me, not the least of which are as blue as the deep side of twilight. "I can switch the whiskey and the water without dumping either glass out."

He stares at the glasses and the playing card. Glances at me as if the instructions might be written on my face, then turns back to the tools of the trick. "You'd better start the trick."

"And you'd better start lying."

Placing the card over the water-filled shot glass, I turn it upside down and place it over the whiskey so that the rims would touch if the card wasn't there. It stays. Everyone in the bar gasps, and Keaton leans forward so only I can hear him.

"My lies are facts." His shoulder is an inch from my lips. I smell the tweed and the remnants of the morning's aftershave. "I'm a black hat hacker trying to establish an honest career."

Turning away just enough to finish the trick, I tap the card. Nothing. Tap harder. It shifts.

What does he mean by his lies being facts? I keep tapping while Keaton keeps talking.

"I have a long list of criminal activity I've covered up. I have no morals. No ruler except money."

The tapping moves the card enough to open a space between the glasses. The bartender gasps, but there's no need. Because both glasses are full, they create a vacuum and there's no spill.

Keaton continues. "I'm a cold, empty person and I don't want you." I hold my breath, watching the whiskey swirl upward like a marble cake. "I don't wonder what you taste like behind your knees, inside your thighs, or where your cunt is soft and wet."

"Keaton."

"That's my name."

I turn my head slightly, and he's turned his. Our noses are so close, I feel his breath on my lip.

"This isn't what I had in mind," I say.

"I haven't thought about holding your arms behind your back while I fuck you from behind. Taking you by the hair and pulling your head back until I see you breathless when you come."

I sit back with my hands clutching the seat. My face is frozen in a rictus of shock, but my body's melted into a puddle of desire.

He smirks. Without taking his gaze off me or moving away, he says, "I think your trick is complete."

"You knew it," I say without even looking at the glasses. The lying is over. The football game has started again. I can see the green mass around the line of scrimmage in the mirror behind Keaton.

He shrugs. "There are some lies that need telling."

The spell is broken, but the damage is done. I cross my legs, but I'm engorged and it sends a shot of pleasure through me.

Snap out of it.

Holding the card in place, I flip the whiskey, losing only a few drops.

"Now you know." I push the whiskey toward him. "I'm driving."

He picks it up and drops the liquid in one of the brandy snifters he took for the olive game, swishing it around. "What do you want, Cassandra? No games. What do you *want*?"

I want a reason to touch you.

"I want a lot of things."

"What do you want badly enough to invite me into your car?"

One glass of wine isn't enough to affect my judgment. I sip my drink, thinking of what I want and how much of it I can tell him. "I want to get reassigned out of Doverton. I want to say I'm Special Agent Grinstead with CID. But I'm not part of the old-boy network. I don't get invited out. I don't get mentored. I'm not good at cozying up to my boss. So I need to do something big enough that someone notices. Something they can't ignore."

"And getting into Third Psyche will do that?"

"Yes." I'm so sure of it that there's not an ounce of doubt in my voice.

He drinks the whiskey in a gulp. "I think you're beautiful and sexy. But mostly, you are fascinating."

"That was a cute trick you just did." I put a ten on the bar for the whiskey. "But I'm not available for you, and I'm not fishing for compliments."

He pushes the ten back toward me. "I have a tab."

"Leave it for a tip then." I slide off the stool and shoulder my bag. "It's been nice hearing your lies. Bring your A-game next time."

He helps me get my jacket on. It's silly to think so hard about how he does it, but I have time, because his motions are efficient and languid. The sleeves are placed perfectly. The satin lining is cool against my skin, and when the coat drops on my shoulders, I feel the weight folding around me as a comfort.

Which is a completely pointless thought process, but I can't help it. Being around him is like stepping into a world where every part of my body is sending data to my brain.

As I tie the belt around me, he grips my shoulders from behind. My hair flicks against my ear when he speaks. "Come upstairs with me. Like I said, we won't be sleeping together. You don't have enough fingers to count all the times you'd come."

I'm red. For the record, my cheeks don't tingle. I don't get flushed. I started perfecting my poker face in third grade. Sure, the unexpected sex talk is enough to make any girl tingle, and he delivers it with a matter-of-factness in his English accent that only accentuates how damn sexy it is.

"I can't."

I finish tying my belt, and his hands slide down my arms. When he's no longer touching me, I feel my attention turn back to the room, the sound of the game, the placement of my body as it relates to the world, not to him.

"I'll walk you out," he says when my silence is long enough to tell him how far off course he's thrown me.

"No." I'm too curt. I blink hard. Soften. Impulsively, I take his hand and squeeze it. "Just let me go. I had a really nice time."

He brushes his thumb along the top of my hand, and it feels so good, he might as well be drawing his tongue along the seam between my thighs. My cheeks tingle all over again.

"Me too," he says, bowing slightly. He lowers his head further and brings his lips to my hand, kissing it.

He's chaste and respectful, but those lips on my skin will be the end of me. Every nerve in my body goes dead so my brain can process the softness of their touch and the firmness of their intent.

I pull my hand away.

"I hope I see you again," he says.

"I hope it's not at the field office," I reply, leaving open a door I shouldn't. I should cut this off right now. Tell him not at the field office or anywhere. I have to get my shit together. He's a potential informant. A person of interest. Maybe a target.

Backing away, I wave at the statuesque man against the backdrop of a busy bar, then I use every ounce of my willpower to spin on my heel and walk out.

I can barely breathe.

CHAPTER 8

KEATON

The strands of my plans are like strands of yarn waiting to be woven into a fabric. In the dark, I ask myself how much I'm willing to unravel for her. For one night. Two. A fling. A relationship that takes its course.

When Cassie turns, she takes a bit of my willpower with her. When I first arrived in New Jersey, tired and dirty, blood boiling with adolescent desires, America seemed like a dangerous jungle. Once I had the lay of the land and the jungle lost its danger, it was boring. The newness of everything wasn't posh. It was flat. Dull.

Until her.

I have a plan to fold myself back into a world built on facts and realities, leaving this name behind. I will disappear. I will turn my back on her because I don't know her. I don't love her. I owe her nothing and she owes me the same. By the time the FBI has enough to get me back into an interrogation room, I'll be—

I need to make a mark on her life. Now.

How long are my feet nailed to the floor before I run outside? Too long. She's in her car. She's pulling along the drive.

I can hack her. I can get her phone. Email. Address. I can have her social security number on the tip of my tongue, but that's not the kind of intimacy I crave.

The cold air is dry tonight, cutting through the thin fabric of my shirt and snaking along my open collar as I run across the club's drive. She's stopped at the sign, but not for long. The car starts forward. I bang on the boot. The car jumps when she hits the brake.

Her window is half open when I get around the car.

"What is—"

But I cut her off. Rude. My mother would have my head. "Special Agent?"

Once the window is all the way down, I put my hands on the top of the door. She's incredulous, beautiful, her nose red at the tip from the cold.

"What?"

"You want to be a special agent with criminal investigations. Yes?"

"Yeah? I mean, everyone wants that."

I put my elbows on the bottom of the window and fold my arms together. "If you get into this forum you asked me for?"

"Third Psyche?"

"Will you get the promotion?"

"Maybe? I mean, I want to get in to stop what's happening in there. Or what we *hear* is happening. That's first."

"And second?"

"They won't be able to ignore me."

Her sentence is loaded with disappointment and isolation. "They" have ignored her for the last time, the blind buggers.

"Go home and sleep," I say, standing. "I'll do what I can."

She doesn't move, looking up at me from the open window. Her breath clouds and dissipates, as does mine. Our streams do not meet. There's a discontent in the early disintegration.

She jumps when a horn blasts. I find the source. The car behind her. I want to punch the driver for giving her a fright.

"Thank you," she says. "Do you know how to get me? If you find it?"

"I do." I step back, giving the twat behind her a dirty look, as though I can shove that horn right up his arse.

When I look back at her, she's pulled onto the road, left indicator on. She makes a turn into the darkness and is gone.

CHAPTER 9

CASSIE

ana's up watching QVC. The sound is off, and the diamond solitaire that fills the screen gets rotated by disembodied female fingers so it reflects the spotlights over and over. When I got stationed in the Doverton field office, she came with me from Flint "to take care of Cassie." It was the only way to get her to join me here, but it's pretty clear to me who's taking care of who in the Doverton suburbs.

"Hi, Nana," I say, hanging up my coat. "Were Fredo and Carol over?"

"Just left." She points at the screen. "I bought you that ring. It's perfect until you find a man to marry you."

I'm not insulted by her anymore. She's my nana. She can say whatever she wants about me. The purchase of a four-thousand-dollar ring would be a concern if her payment method was more than a Fisher-Price version of a credit card with a twenty-dollar spending limit. I set it up specifically for daily QVC emergencies. They take her orders over the phone and it declines the next day when she either regrets the purchase or forgets about it. I have the sneaking suspicion she knows the card won't go through but plays along to please me.

"Thanks. I'm not looking for a man, but I like diamonds."

I sit next to Nana. She's four-foot ten. Seventy-three and counting. My mother's mother. In front of us is a one-third-complete thousand-piece puzzle of the White House in spring. The outside edge is placed just fine, but the "completed" parts of the inside look like a shingled roof after a storm. Pieces are jammed in sideways or forced together. Some pieces have their blanks choked by ill-fitting tabs, or little slivers of open space between pieces when the tab is too small.

"I don't think these two go together," I say as if the problem is with two pieces and not with eighty percent of her decisions.

"The perfect's the enemy of the good." She says it as if it's the first time she's dropped this nugget of wisdom on me. It isn't. "You smell like a man."

I'm about to smell under my arm to see what she's talking about but stop myself when her meaning clicks into place. "I do not."

"English Leather. Had a boy like that once. We drove to Woodstock together in his Buick Skylark. Ran all 350 horses into the ground. Big backseat too."

Nana's from Detroit. She knows her cars and she knows her backseats. She knows what a man smells like, and she'll call me Agent-Pants-On-Fire for a week unless I come clean immediately.

"If I smell like English Leather, then you smell the guy I was talking to at the bar."

"Knew it."

I gently take more of the puzzle apart. Nana puts on her glasses. She doesn't like wearing them even though she's so farsighted she can't see an inch or three feet in front of her face.

She leans into the puzzle. "You're making a mess out of this, Cassandra." She joins me in taking apart the jammed-together pieces.

"Sorry. I'm not good at puzzles." I say it with the same tone I used to convince her I needed her to come to Doverton with me.

"I'll say. Tell me about English Leather. Should I return the ring?"

She never wore a ring on her left hand that she didn't buy herself, and no man ever wore a match to hers. I'm from a long line of single women. I figure I'll be single my whole life too. I've stopped calling it the Grinstead curse. Now I call it the Grinstead blessing.

"I'll cancel the ring," I say.

"So it's serious?" She looks at me above the frames as if that helps her see. I'm not sure that it does.

"No. No, it's not. It was just a conversation. I'm not interested in getting involved right now."

"Not gonna get easier when you move us to Quantico, you know." She snaps a piece into place. It lays flat. "Got the ring in a size six. That okay for you?"

"I don't like square cut."

"Carol noticed all the rich bitches at the club have square cut."

"I'm neither rich, nor a member of the club."

"Ha!" She slaps my knee with her paper-skinned hand when she realizes I didn't deny being a bitch. "You're too good for them, my girl." She pats my cheek. "Every last one of them. Get their smell on you but don't let them own you. Never trust them."

"Darn right, Nana." I put down the pieces I've pried apart. "Are you going to bed?"

"In a bit. I'm going to watch that guy." She waves at the TV. "The one with the moustache who doesn't wear a shirt."

I stand. "I'm going then." I kiss her cheek.

"I love you, Cassandra," she says absently, looking over her puzzle.

"I love you too, Nana."

I GET through brushing my teeth and putting on pajamas. I even make it to bed, more or less. My butt is on the mattress but feet are still on the floor when I can smell him as clearly as my grandmother did. I feel him where his hands and lips touched me. I put my hand under my clothes and slip them inside my seam. I'm throbbing like a teenager. His words. His touch. The lies that revealed truths just as the game intended.

He could be a dark web madman, but maybe not. Maybe I'm wrong. Maybe we're all wrong and he's just a legitimate businessman.

That was one of his lies.

Four fingers deep, with the heel of my hand jerking the surface of my nub, I consider the possibility that he is a decent man. His integrity must be battered raw with insinuation. He's beautiful, prideful, and falsely accused. He's a good man doing good things.

He has a magnetism. It's almost frightening, but I never—not for one second—felt fear. The danger of him sends me to new heights. The idea that I was walking some kind of edge at the bar sends shivers to the base of my spine.

I haven't even drawn the duvet down and I'm on my hands and knees, rubbing myself in the dark, remembering the look he gave the driver behind me.

I come so hard I have to bite back a scream that might scare my grandmother.

CHAPTER 10

CASSIE

*I*n the first days of my training, my hands weren't strong
enough to discharge a weapon with speed. After three rounds,
pain shot through my palm. I worked at it until I could empty a
magazine, but the recoil and vibration were so intense, my hand wasn't
agile enough to change the magazine afterward. I dropped it and
everyone laughed. I went to bed with a hand stiffly curled into a claw.

Now, the shooting range clears away the fog of my emotions. After
the emergency meeting today, I need a lot of head-clearing. The gun
pop-pop-pops.

Ken's uncovered a lead into Third Psyche's plans, and they're a doozy.

Orlando called him out for great work in front of everyone. I'm
jealous and pleased at the same time. But more than that, I'm not getting
promoted unless I do what he's done.

Pop-pop-pop

I need to make rain.

I review Orlando's speech in my head.

Ken's lead is flesh and blood. This was good, solid investigative
work. Old-school. We cannot do this all online.

Of course that was the issue. Online leads meant looping in the cybercrime division. I'd been too stupid to see that Orlando wanted all the credit. Once another division is on the case, we go back to being a sleepy field office in the middle of nowhere.

We're getting together a team to head up to Springfield. The subjects are operating out of a strip club, so ladies, you'll be giving us backup from here while we talk to the asset.

Pop-pop-pop. I shoot until my hand hurts.

You mean stuffing dollar bills in g-strings.

Tito believed they were going for better-looking strippers. As if. Ken has a smooth fucking lump where his dick should be, but he plays such a man to the crowd.

It's a sacrifice I'm willing to make to serve my country.

Lolz. Fucking rolling on the fucking floor you assholes.

This FBI thing is going nowhere. I have to find another path, but where? To do what?

I don't know how to quit. Ken or no Ken, I don't know how to just give up, even when I should.

I squeeze the fourteenth round into the target's chest. Chamber the last one. Pop a new magazine and empty my anger into the target.

Pop-pop-pop.

"Grinstead!"

It's Shadow Horse Brady, the guy who runs the field office's tiny firing range. He's in his thirties, built like a football player, with a long black braid over each shoulder. FBI agents don't usually have long hair, but they're not usually Sequoia tribesmen either.

"Yeah?" I take off my earmuffs.

"Someone left you a note." He holds out his hand. A yellow Post-It is stuck to his middle finger. It's blank on top.

"Thank you." I take it off, flip it. There's a phone number on the back. "Did he just walk in and leave this?" The range is pretty secure, but maybe not as secure as I thought.

"It was here when I got in. Is it civilian?"

"I don't think so. Just asking."

"Nice shooting." He points at the poor black silhouette I've left with a nearly hollow chest.

"Missed three." I point at the three holes in the white area around the target.

"Perfect's the enemy of the good, Agent."

"So I hear."

I PULL the car to the side of the road and call the number on the back of the Post-It. The two-lane road is thinly lined with trees, newly paved, with a sharp double yellow in the middle that goes straight a long way before disappearing into a single point.

"Keaton," I say when a ring cuts off and I can hear someone breathing. "You left this number."

"I have something for you." He's clipped and businesslike. I thought I'd never hear his demanding British voice again, and when I do, I catch myself smiling. With Ken outrunning me, I needed the help, and the package it came in made my nerves vibrate.

He continues. "It might be of use."

"Might?"

"I believe—"

"You believe?" I tap the steering wheel as I decide how much more to tell him, and how, because it will determine how much I want from him. I open my mouth to carefully ask what "might" might mean. That's not what comes out. "I don't have time for 'might,' okay? Or 'I believe.' I'm getting steamrolled over here. Actually, if I come in with something 'you believe might' not be exactly perfect, I'm going to get laughed at, and I have to tell you, getting laughed at is going to put me over the fucking edge."

I should be ashamed of my behavior in front of a man I barely know, but here's the rub. I'm not ashamed at all. As a matter of fact, I feel a little relieved to have it off my chest.

"I like the fight in you," he says.

"I don't like having to show it."

There's a silence that's kind of comfortable, kind of tense. I can't discern where he is from the background buzz.

"Cassie?"

"Yeah?"

"I want to see you again."

He doesn't mean he wants to wave from the window. That's for sure.

"Is that a good idea?"

It isn't. He knows it. For better or worse, once he passes me information on an active case, he's an asset. I don't know what kind of trouble this can land him in with the players in his world, but for me it's a no-no.

"It's a terrible idea," he says flatly.

I smile and look at my lap. He said it as a fact, and in stating it as a fact, he made it somewhat less terrible and completely unavoidable.

When I ask the next question, my voice sounds softer and lower than I intend. "When?"

CHAPTER 11

CASSIE

While Ken, Orlando, and a couple of the guys are in Springfield questioning an asset at a strip club, I'm standing over my bed in my underwear. My phone lies next to the dress I've laid out. Frieda's voice comes through the speakerphone.

"Is it business or pleasure?" she asks as I rummage through my closet.

I haven't told her what Keaton and I are meeting about, and as friends who work with sensitive material, we're used to giving each other half-stories.

"Business," I say. "But I can't ignore the overtones."

"Well, do you like the overtones? If you like them, you wear something sexy. If you don't, then you wear work clothes."

I throw a blue pantsuit on the bed. It looks like a cloak of invisibility. "What if I just wore a sneakers and jeans?"

"Then you are neither business, nor overtone, but you'll be able to run fast."

I laugh. "I don't think I'll have to run. At least not fast."

As soon as I see Keaton in the supermarket parking lot, I wish I'd chosen the invisible pantsuit. What was I thinking? I'm leaning against my car with the dress safely under my coat, but when he pulls his car next to mine, he rolls down the passenger side window and leans over, looking at my stocking-covered calves. It's as if he knows I have on a sexy dress.

"Hi," I say.

He gets out but doesn't shut the engine. "You found the one dark parking lot in the state."

He's right. We're in a dark corner that smells of piss and Dumpsters. The only light is from his headlamps. The rest of the lot is bathed in floodlights, as is the one for the Home Depot across the street.

"I don't like being seen," I say. "I assumed you felt the same way."

In the dark, he's no more than an outline of a man. What's inside the framework? Does it show in the light? Or am I only seeing a scaffolding?

"You deserve to be seen."

Is he made of kind words and compliments? Does the rhythmic accent hide truths or lies? Is he empty inside the outline? Or is he made of skin and muscle?

"Maybe," I say. "Do you have it?"

"Not with me."

What is the silhouette filled with? Kindness or cruelty? Life or death? Keaton Bridge or Alpha Wolf? Both? Neither?

"Not with you?" I say. "That's such a cliché."

"Too much American television as a kid."

He opens the passenger door. When the dome light comes on, he is rendered in three dimensions again.

I don't have to get in. I can just go home and wait for my team to get back from Springfield and tell me what happened.

I step forward. One step closer to the car and one step closer to him. "Where are we going?"

"Little place I know."

There's no "little place" in Doverton or Barrington. There are box stores and mom-and-pop shops that are already closed. There's a bar off the highway and a twenty-four-hour sandwich place. There are plenty of nice places to go and good places to sit, but none match his cozy implications.

I get in the car, wondering if I should have worn my sneakers.

CHAPTER 12

KEATON

It's twenty-two miles to Barrington. The highway is dry, and the air is cold and crisp. I go the speed limit and no more, as is my habit. I don't risk exposing myself by getting tickets.

"It is too cold?" I ask as she rubs her hands together.

"No, I'm fine."

"Do you like Doverton?" I ask.

She laughs a little. A short, sharp thing meant to say more than words can. "It's fine."

"Fine?"

"It's small." She shrugs. "Catty."

"Bigger than Barrington. Some people in Doverton say they inbreed."

"Like I said." She looks at me just as I'm looking at her. She is just stunning. "Catty."

I have to look back at the road. "How long have you been here? From Flint?"

"Can we stop this?"

"Stop what?"

"You know everything about me."

I know what she means, and I'm not going to waste time denying it.

"And have you not looked for me in your records?" I shoot back.

She looks straight ahead, lips pressed together. Up ahead, lights dot the sky at the factory roof and on the very tops of the cranes. I pull off the highway.

"What did you find?" I ask.

"Nothing."

"That's disappointing."

"Not a stub. People whose families immigrate usually get a stub. But you? Nada."

There had been an FBI stub as recently as six months ago. In a way, knowing it's gone is comforting. It means they've started.

In another way, it's chilling.

"Where are we going?" she asks.

"You know the factory?"

"That's a great place to murder someone."

"Not if you want to get away with it. Half the town descends on it at seven a.m."

"Are you on schedule to open?"

"Yes." I don't offer more because I don't want to talk about the fucking factory.

The service road is rutted and bumpy. We'll clean it up after we bring in the heavy stuff. For now, the car rocks like a boat on a stormy sea.

"How much do you know about me?" she asks.

"Not much."

"Please. If you don't know my social security number and the name of my first pet, I'll eat my shoe."

She thinks I'm lying. She doesn't trust me, and she shouldn't. My anger is in inverse proportion to how much of her trust I've earned.

"If you need salt, I'll allow it."

I stop at the factory gate. A guard sits in the little house. He's not an ounce under three hundred pounds. His name is Bernard, but everyone calls him Butthead.

I roll down the window. "Bernard."

"Mr. Bridge."

"Keaton. Please."

"Sure." He peers into the window to see Cassie. "Ma'am. Can I see your driver's license?"

"She's all right," I snap. Worse than Cassie's distrust is her seeing someone else not trust me.

"Mr. Harden says."

"I practically invented corporate espionage," I say, losing patience. "I daresay this lady won't pull a trick I can't see coming."

Cassie reaches one hand over me with her wallet stretched open with her fingertips. She's closer. I can smell her. Vanilla and gunpowder. My God. She's made of candy-coated bullets.

Bernard takes one look at the FBI ID and opens the gate. Cassie leans back, but I caught a whiff of her already, and it's enough.

"You invented corporate espionage?" she says. "That was exculpatory."

"Not really. It's a quote from *Gizmodo*."

I drive through the gate. The hulk of the factory grows larger as I approach. The windows on the first and third floors are lit with low-wattage LEDs. I pull into my spot and put the car in park.

"Want to make a wager?" I say.

"Again?"

I look at her. She's leaning forward, genuinely interested. I like her curiosity mirroring mine.

"I bet you can surprise me."

"I'm really boring."

"That would surprise me indeed."

I get out of the car.

CHAPTER 13

CASSIE

*K*eaton opens the door for me. The parking lot is in crappy condition, and even though my shoes aren't too high, my heel lands on half a rock and I lose my balance. He has me by the elbow before I even realize I'm falling. His hand is strong and gentle. He lets me go as soon as I'm on my feet.

"Thank you."

We walk along the side of the building. Dim lights on the ground floor glow through the web of scaffolding, cross-hatching the ground in front of us.

"We can take the lift," he says.

"I'm not afraid of a few stairs."

"Really?"

"I can make four flights in under a minute and a half, carrying a firearm and spare cartridges."

He reaches into the darkness and clicks something. A light goes on to reveal an elevator car built inside the scaffolding. It's for construction, with a wood plank floor and a big orange lever. We get in, and he slides the gate closed. With a tap of the lever, we move up.

"Don't be afraid," he says.

"I'm not."

He flicks a switch and the car goes dark.

"Oh," I gasp.

The lights over Barrington are visible, and behind it, Doverton glows just in front of the curve of the earth against the navy sky. The stars are a pin-poked wrap over the earth. We stand in silence, our perspective changing as we rise ninety feet and stop with a jerk.

Keaton slides open the gate on the factory side with a clatter and slap. He holds out his hand and I take it. Pause. His face is in shadow. His expression as we touch is hidden from me, but as his thumb brushes the tops of my fingers, I don't need to see it to know the contact is intentional and sexual.

I step onto the roof. He follows, laying his hand on my shoulder. Touching. Again. I'm conscious of how disproportionately carnal the pressure and placement feel against how tame they really are.

"Here," he says, leading me to a little café table with two folding chairs surrounded by outdoor heat lamps.

The floodlights clack on when the motions sensors detect our bodies, making the roof both bright and black. The table is in a trapezoid of shadow. There's a pitcher of water and glasses. I glance quickly into the glasses. Dry from what I can tell. Good.

Keaton pulls out a chair and I sit, noticing a square yellow Post-It stuck to the center of the table. He sits across from me and pours water in my glass first.

"Not trying to get me drunk, I see."

"If I had wine, would you drink it?"

"No."

"Why not?" He pulls his glass closer to him.

I touch mine. I'm thirsty, but don't pick it up. "It's hard to hide drugs in water. Easier in alcohol."

"You think I'm the kind of man who needs to drug women?"

"To get laid?" I go right for the point. "No."

"What then?"

"You might drug an FBI agent."

He leans forward, into a patch of light. His brown hair's brushed back, but a curve of it escapes and falls against his forehead. His left ear has a thin gold hoop tight around the lobe, hinting at a history I can only guess. Gorgeous, yes, but the promises of secrets, knowledge, depth are what make me throb between my crossed legs.

He's breathtaking.

"There's no need to drug you or any agent. If I want something from the part of you that carries a badge and a gun, I can take it without you even knowing it. I can own you. I can own your job. Your family and friends are safe because I choose it."

I'm tricked by his looks. His promise. The timbre of his voice. I've been lulled. He is what he is and has always been. And here I am—alone on a rooftop with him.

"So are you Alpha Wolf?"

"I can neither confirm nor deny any digital persona is linked to me."

"You don't scare me."

His smirk is devilish and comforting, as if mischief has a charm all its own. Then he leans back and drinks his water as if he knew I was waiting for him to go first. He puts down the empty glass. "Good."

I sip my water.

"So," he says. "You heard there are plans being made on an onion site."

"Third Psyche."

"The link's written on the back of that Post-It." He flicks his fingers at the yellow square stuck to the center of the table. I reach for it. With an efficient but languid gesture, he covers my hand as it's over the paper. "Not so fast, Ms. Grinstead."

"Cassie's fine." There's a snap in my voice. I don't care if he knows I'm annoyed.

"Cassie. First you tell me why you want the link."

"I told you."

"I believe you. But there's more. No one wants a promotion for the sake of one."

He's touching me. Skin on skin. He doesn't move his fingers across mine, but if he does, I'm going to melt into the chair. I can stay like this all night, until he tightens his palm and puts downward pressure on his fingers. It's encouraging. A barely perceptible invitation to speak what's in my heart.

It's all I need at a time when I would have denied needing anything.

"Because I want to catch criminals. I can catch bigger and better from CID."

I don't take my eyes off the way his hand covers mine. Not as I speak, nor during the long silence after I'm done.

"Small-time crooks don't cause enough trouble?"

"Maybe."

"Or do you have too much empathy for them?"

I snap my hand away. "What's that supposed to mean?"

"Oh, the lady doth protest too much. You have to know law enforcement attracts a criminal element."

I will my lips shut, but my mind simmers, then boils. "You can go to hell then." I wish I could get up and walk away, but that yellow Post-It is calling.

"I will. I'm sure of it."

"Said the black hat who's going straight."

"We have more in common than I thought."

"My record's clean." I lean back. "I don't know what you think you saw or where you saw it, but it's fake."

"I didn't say you were guilty of anything. Your mother was obviously a petty reprobate by choice. You were dragged along for the ride. Yet I saw a little flicker in your eyes when you said your record was clean." He points at each eye as if trying to recall the little glints. "You're proud of not getting caught."

I have to divert this conversation before I get sucked into it. "You were the king of the dark web. You were making millions in hacked accounts."

"I was."

"Guns."

"Yes."

"Drugs."

"No. Never. No drugs, no people."

"Every thief has a code." I know that all too well. "Why leave it?"

"Taylor needed the money."

"Are we done here?" I ask.

"As you wish."

I reach for the Post-It again, and again he puts his hand over mine. I let it stay. With everything that was said and revealed in the last five minutes, that pause before I shake him off is the moment I let myself like his touch.

He slides his hand away, and I curl my fist around the paper, snapping the glue off the tabletop.

"The link comes with a warning," he says.

I turn over the paper. The link is written in pencil. "A warning?" I fold the Post-It and put it in my pocket. "Are we enemies now?"

"No, but I don't want you to make any." He looks at the sky, apparently thinking. "You're not callous. If you have to believe you are, I understand. And working in law enforcement, you'll get callous or die. But not you. Not yet. But…" He laces his fingers together across his belt. "When I went looking for something to put on this piece of paper, I might have been noticed."

"You?"

He knows what I'm asking. Was Keaton Bridge noticed or was Alpha Wolf? I don't go further because I know he's not going to answer.

"It's not my intention to expose you to danger. If I had my way, you'd toss that paper in the rubbish and forget the whole thing. But you're too far gone. So take it. Catch the bastards." He leans forward now, putting his elbows on his knees. His head is only slightly lower than mine and he's dead serious. "Do not speak to Keyser Kaos. Do not speak to anyone who knows him. If you're wise, don't speak to anyone whose identity isn't known."

His voice is so even that I shutter any thoughts of disobeying him.

"Are you going to be all right? Are they going to come after you?"

He starts to say something. Stops himself. Leans back.

What have I done? I tuck my hands into my sleeves. The heat lamps only do so much to chase a chill.

"I wouldn't worry about it," is his final answer. "I want you to have this. I want to do something for you."

The link could be a setup. He could be a beautiful trap. But he's not. I can't know the results of his gift, but when he says he wants to do something for me, I believe he's telling me the entirety of his intentions.

"Why did you decide to go straight?"

His look is quizzical, as if he's revving up to deflect.

"Surprise me. I know you want me to surprise you, but you gotta meet me halfway here."

"How do I know you won't use it against me?"

"You don't."

I figure it's over after that. We're at some kind of stalemate. This isn't a guy who gives up a piece of information without a fight. He knows its worth too well. His eyes flick across my face as if he's reading me, but that's not what he's doing. I know it as well as I know when a mark is just distracted enough to think she's not. He's calculating the value of his story.

"I went straight, as you call it, because there are some things I can only do with a name, and a face, and a history in this world. I needed to do those things."

"You needed to invest in QI4? Why?"

"Some things can't be written and explained in a tight little fable. The short version is—I did it for friendship."

The alarm bells that bark when I'm around him shut down for a second. That wasn't the answer I expected. The fact that he'd make a sacrifice for a friend clues me in to the existence of a complex, layered person, not just a sexy, secretive criminal.

"I'd like to hear the long version some time."

"There won't be a long version."

Won't be?

He says it as if the story is still being written and it's about to be cut off.

CHAPTER 14

KEATON

The yellow Post-It is folded between two fingers. She's rubbing the paper against itself as she looks outward, at me, and inward, dissecting every word I've said.

"You're planning something," she says.

"Nothing that should concern you." I lean forward. I want to smell her. Feel her warmth. "How do you feel, now that you have what you want?"

She casts her eyes down. The lashes cast shadows on her cheeks. "Honestly?"

"Of course."

"A little scared of what I'll find."

She's so proud and so honest. I admire the way she couples strength to vulnerability, beauty to humility.

"You're smart to be scared. But you know how to do it."

I mean, how to stay invisible in the forums. Set up a fake profile behind a data wall. They'll find the FBI eventually, but they won't tie the discovery to a particular agent.

"I do know how to do it."

Her smile is confident, cocky even. I like that too.

She stands and puts out her hand. She wants me to shake it. And what am I supposed to do? Shake it and let her go? I don't know a thing about her. Sure, I've dug up plenty, but I want to hear her story from her mouth.

Her hand hangs in the cold air while I decide how I'm going to keep her.

"Thank you," she says.

I stand and take her hand. "My pleasure."

The word "pleasure" rolls out of my mouth on eighteen wheels with a payload of meaning behind it. Even if I want to keep the word clean, I don't have a choice with her.

She looks down at our clasped hands.

"Let me walk you out," I say.

"You're a real chivalrous guy."

"I'm British. It's a default setting."

She lets go of my hand and turns away. "I like your default setting."

I turn off the heat lamp and catch up to her. She takes my arm when I offer it, letting me guide her into the lift.

I get in and press the red button.

The car jerks downward. I want to kiss her in this tight little space, but her hands are in her pockets. She won't look at me. She's not ready or she doesn't want me to.

The lift bounces at the ground floor. I slide open the gate with a clatter that shakes the silence. I step aside so she can go first.

What do I want out of her? I want to fuck her, but that shouldn't be surprising. She's an attractive and intelligent woman. She's also dangerous at this point. Not because of her job, but because of the way I react to her. I lock up the lift, letting her walk ahead.

She's a siren, pulling me toward this burdensome identity when all I want to do is get away. She's halfway to the car, hands jammed in her coat pockets. I trot to her. I bridge the distance in six and a half steps. The last half-step to seven puts me between her and the car. I can't read her expression, but I caption the picture anyway, telling the story of a woman who wants to go home and blow dry her hair or rearrange the jumpers in her wardrobe.

Just as I catch up, her ankle bends when she steps on a rock. She tips.

I catch her because I don't want her to fall, and I feel in my gut that she's my responsibility.

I don't know why I care, but I do. If I don't connect now, there's no future and I don't know why it matters but it bloody fucking does and if I could just—

So I kiss her.

CHAPTER 15

CASSIE

The deal is done. I can have the guard call me a cab and wait for an hour, or I can let Keaton drive me back to my car. Either way it should be fine, but his little café table setup on the roof was romantic. His trade gives him no weapon against me. He wanted to know why I needed the link, but the knowledge is useless. There are no rules against trying to get a promotion.

He wants me as much as I want him, and that scares me. It means I have to make a decision, and either choice could have a terrible outcome.

He's just about admitted he's Alpha Wolf.

A criminal.

What has he done? What evil has he fomented? What goes on in the dark web?

Drug-trade-human-trafficking-hacking-whistleblowing-cheese-pizza-slavery-war-guns-murder-for-hire-revolution.

I'm a few feet from the car when my heel catches a rock. I slide my hands from my pockets to reweight my balance, but he's got his hands under my arms, holding me up.

Holding me still.

The list of crimes that happen on the dark net bounces through my brain as he holds me. Is he going to kill me? Strangle me right here in the parking lot of his own factory? Maybe he wants to try. He's well-built, but I'm pretty sure I can take a computer nerd in hand-to-hand combat. I just can't let him get the jump.

He goes for me.

I'm surprised and prepared for it at the same time. I didn't actually believe he'd try, but I'm reaching to block an attack while he's leading with his head, which is weird, but I got this.

When his lips smash against mine, my body is a split second ahead of my brain. It's processed the list of dark net violence and thus completes a series of moves to bring down a frontal attack.

Even as I'm using his weight against him by holding his arm still while I swing him, letting his high center of gravity do all the work of stripping him of his balance, my mind processes the kiss. Because it was a kiss. A real soft-lipped-slightly-open-mouthed-I want-her-to-like-it kind of kiss.

By the time those nice thoughts register, I'm slamming him up against the car. I'm a little disappointed that I can't take back my counterattack. I would have let him kiss me a few more seconds before taking him down.

His eyes are open wide and the breath's knocked out of him. The thump of his body against the car door fades into the night.

"Why did you do that?" I ask.

He looks at me as if I asked him why he pees standing up. Brows knotted. Arms out. Mouth half open as if he can't contain the sheer number of answers he could give me right now.

"What?" He says it like *whot* and it's endearing and haughty at the same time. Damnit. I should have taken that kiss and not gotten all black belt on him.

"Don't sneak up on a girl like that." I sound like a brat.

He straightens himself out, pulling his cuffs down and realigning his jacket. "I'm going to pretend you didn't just do a very impressive judo throw and tell you, out front, that I'm going to kiss you. First, I'm going to put my hands on your face, because I would like to feel your mouth move when I do it. Then I'm going to tilt my head to the right, so please, you should also tilt your head to the right." He waits for me to nod, and when I do, he comes close to me and lowers his voice. "I'm going to wait a second once our lips touch, just to make sure we're both appreciating this first contact. When I open my mouth a little, I want you to do the same. You need to accept my tongue in your mouth." He puts his hands on my shoulders. "Is that enough of a warning?"

"What happens after that?"

"It's unwritten."

He moves his hands up to my jaw, laying his thumbs against my cheeks. He strokes them and I lean forward.

He kisses me just as he said he would. His tongue tastes like ice water, and his lips curve into the shape of mine. The adrenaline in my veins blends with something newer and warmer. He slides one hand back and tugs my hair, which sends fluids and sensation and pleasure and all my attention between my legs. I push against him just so I can feel him resist. I need to fight him as hard as I want him.

He's rigid and yielding all at once, turning us around until I'm the one with my back against the car. I shove him away, and he separates from me with a sharp intake of breath.

He doesn't say a word, still holding me by a fistful of hair. The cold clouds of our breath mingle between us. He's a predator, a criminal, and a mistake. But his jaw is tight and his nostrils flare when he breathes. He's all those things and a bull charging for the red cape.

"Push me away again," he says finally, "and we're done here. And I know for a fact that's not what you want."

I am the red cape, and I need to be yanked away as much as I need him to charge at me again and again. "When I want you to stop, I'll say so."

I shove him again, and he smiles before laying a kiss on me. It's not a kiss I fight. It's a kiss I want. He pulls his mouth away as if giving me a second to tell him to stop, but I don't. I don't push against him until our mouths are locked again. His hips grind into me. I feel his erection through our clothes.

I'm clutching his coat without any sense. I want to tear away every stitch of fabric. I push and pull with equal ferocity. I want to spread my legs, but my coat's too long. I want to punch him. I want that hard dick stretching me and I want it to hurt. My mind is wiped clean of everything but need. I don't have a job or a career. I don't have dreams built from childhood. I don't have a name. I'm just a pillar of desire. I'm reduced to movement and hunger. I want his body inside mine. Nothing else.

"Hey, uh…"

Keaton snaps away from me at the sound of the security guard's voice. My body wants him back, but my mind fills up again.

"Yes, Bernard?" Keaton has on a full British jacket of *what-could-you-possibly-want-now?*

Bernard looks as embarrassed as I should be. I pull on my coat ties as if they could be any tighter.

"Just wanted to let you know my shift's over in ten minutes and I'll let Trey know—"

"Thank you," Keaton snaps.

Bernard nods and backs away. Keaton turns back to me as the guard's boots crunch against the loose gravel. We don't say anything until the footsteps disappear.

"Well," Keaton says, inviting me to begin the mindful part of this thing we started—whatever it is.

"Well. That was…" I swallow. Was it great? An eye-opener? An earth-shattering beginning to something that will stop my ambitions dead in their tracks? "Complicated."

"It doesn't need to be. I don't live here. There's no threat of permanence."

I know what he's suggesting. This can be very short, very simple, and very pleasurable. It's tempting. He moves a swatch of hair from my cheek, letting his fingers brush my skin.

"You'll be back a lot to manage this." I wave at the factory.

"They need me in California. This"—he waves at the factory, mirroring my gesture—"it's not my area of expertise."

"But you will be back. And I can't… getting caught having an affair with someone like you? It's not—"

"It's now or never." He brushes his finger along the length of my throat. I'm collapsing like a house of cards. "By the time I come back, you'll be in Quantico making the world safe from people like me."

He's close again. I can smell his aftershave cutting the cool air. His lips are on my throat, flipping me like a switch.

"What if I'm not?"

"We'll ignore each other."

I know that's not possible. His hands are on my jaw and his mouth is on mine. My body has never responded to a man this strongly. I've never felt so little control over it. I won't be able to ignore him when he comes back or when he's away.

But the logic is manageable. I use it to shut up the klaxons enough to hear my screaming inner child.

She's telling me I could lose everything. She says I need to be safe. For once, I need to feel safe and Keaton Bridge is anything but safe.

I soothe her. I promise her the adults are in charge. She doesn't believe me, but she trusts me. She was always foolish. She trusted the men she brought home. Trusted Mom's word that the piles of wrapped dollar bills on the coffee table were from a greeter's gig at Wal-Mart, not the results of a long con.

I'm thinking about those bills when Keaton reaches behind me and opens the car door. The pulsing beep of the open door alarm matches the thrum of my heart. I'm thinking about how I believed her because I wanted to. The bills meant food and maybe a month of cable TV. They meant comfort, and I wanted comfort more than the truth. They never meant a different life.

I'm grown up now and my comforts may have changed, but my inner child's excuse-making hasn't. I'm better than that. The adults are in charge.

"Thanks," I say. "But no thanks."

With a little push, he steps away from me. I don't know what's going on in his love life, if getting sex is easy or hard for him, but the look on his face is layered with so much confidence with its contrasting disappointment that I can only assume he usually gets "yes" for an answer.

"I'm sorry," I say. "For leading you on."

"It's nothing." He brushes my hair away from my face, and I'm suddenly aware of the cold air creeping up my sleeves. "Can I return you to the only dark parking lot in the state?"

I look over the desolate nightscape. I hear the trickle of the nearby river and the buzz of the overhead lights. I don't want to wait at the guardhouse for a cab. I want to go home. "Sure."

He steps out of the way and I get in the car, relieved, disappointed, and regretful all at the same time.

CHAPTER 16

KEATON

We cross a narrow bridge in the center of Doverton, wheels clacking on the wooden boards bolted into the steel frame. The bridge has low guardrails and a thin walk on each side that's used more for fishing in the Winnepak River upstream from the factory than for crossing it. The steel-colored water runs narrow and shallow in the summer, but in the winter or during rains, it thrashes between the banks.

There is no small talk between Cassie and me. Every word is loaded. Every pause has meaning. So when we drive for five minutes in silence, I know something's on her mind.

I appreciate this, because I have plenty on mine.

"This link?" she says, breaking the silence.

"Yes?"

"The fact that you gave it to me means I have to register you as an asset. It's a totally confidential process."

I laugh. How could I not?

"What's so funny?"

"Darling, if you want to find criminals, the first thing you have to know is that there's no such thing as confidential."

She looks out the window. Was I too hard on her?

No. When it comes to this, she needs a little tough love.

I pull into the supermarket lot and make my way to the dark corner where her car is parked.

"You do what you have to," I say.

She nods. I get out and open her door for her.

She's a few steps toward her car when she turns, keys in her hand. "I have a question."

"Go on then."

"You don't believe you're protected, and getting me this link has made people mad at you. Why expose yourself like this?"

Because in the little time I have left, I want to leave a mark. An anonymous mark, yes, but a trail of good things astride the bad. I want to know people I care about are settled, and in the little time I've known Cassie, I care about her. I want her to have her promotion. I want her to get what she wants out of life.

I don't know why she's important to me or how she's weaseled her way into my heart, but the fact of it is indisputable.

However, I can't tell her that.

"I don't care for Nazis," I say.

"Yeah." She presses a button on her keys and her car unlocks. "Ain't that the truth."

I open her door for her. She gets in. She keeps her head turned away from me, signaling that there will be no goodbye kiss unless it's taken.

Getting slammed into the side of my car was pleasant in a way, but I won't take what's not offered again. I slap her door closed and watch her rear lights get smaller in the distance.

When I reach for my phone, I realize my wallet is gone.

CHAPTER 17

CASSIE

I am seven and a half the first time I slip my hands into a
stranger's bag. I am too young to know better and old enough
to be good at it. I've practiced on my mother for weeks. I've dug her
leather wallet from her bag as she leans over the kitchen counter a
hundred times. If she feels it, I get a death glare that reminds me that my
competence is important. I could be the difference between ramen and
pizza for dinner. If she doesn't feel my hand, I get three M&Ms.

I really like M&Ms. They taste like safety. They taste like approval.
The hard crunch is the glassy crackle of her disapproval. The sweet
chocolate melting on my tongue is the warmth of her love.

She's a tough critic. She does not lie. She knows I'm coming, so she is
ready to feel any jerk or pressure on her back. Both the bag and the
wallet are leather. She paired them to make it harder for me to feel the
difference between bag and wallet. The actual leather parts of the bag
have faded in the sun. The man-made pleather is bright, deep blue-
green. She holds it more tightly than our mark will. She makes it hard. It
frustrates me, but I'm not supposed to pout over it.

The first time I do it correctly, she's leaning over the kitchen counter
with a cigarette and the phone pressed to her ear. She's talking about a

TV show to a friend, or a lover, or a mark she's working on. Behind her, the cast iron pan sits on the stove with the little chunks of scrambled egg drying on the edge. Just in front of her, on the counter, sits a salt shaker like the ones you find in a diner. A chrome crown over a white gown. Little pieces of beige rice swim inside the sparkling salt.

The teal bag is unzipped, but not wide open. She never makes it too easy, but she doesn't want me choosing marks that are too difficult. I don't sneak behind her, because other people will be watching. I come from behind her and reach for the salt shaker with my left hand while my tiny right hand slides into her bag.

Of course, the wallet is wedged under a pamphlet and a pair of sunglasses. I don't hesitate. I've done this before and even though I failed, I know she's added the obstacles for my own good.

I say "excuse me," in the little girl voice we've worked on, just as I pick up the salt and slip the wallet away.

She keeps talking into the phone. She knows that when I pick up the salt, I'm supposed to take her wallet. But she's also honest, and as she's listening to whomever is on the other side of the phone, she turns around, clasps her hand into a fist, and pumps it downward, raising her knee in victory.

I did it.

Those M&Ms—one red, one blue, one yellow—taste like victory. They taste like worthiness. The sweetness of personal contribution to my own well-being.

We do it a few more times, and each time I get better. Each time she offers me little tips and tricks. Her knowledge is endless. She's a wonderful mother who knows everything that is important. I'm the luckiest kid in the world.

On Friday, we go to the zoo. Every year, if there're fewer than two snow days, schools in the Detroit area are closed on the first Friday in May. The zoo lets in all school-age children for free, but adults pay full price. The result in this poor community is that one adult in a group of friends will take the day off so the rest can go to work. The adult-to-child ratio is huge on this day. There's a sense of unending chaos, and that works in our favor.

Mom says to try to find wealthy people. There aren't many truly rich people at the Detroit Zoo on the first Friday in May. But I know what she means, and she knows what she means. Find someone who can afford to lose their wallet today.

The zoo is a two hour drive from home, so I'm motivated to get this right. This is going to be worthwhile trip.

I find a woman who takes out a few twenties to pay for three bags of Cracker Jacks. She leaves her bag unzipped. The straps fall low on her hip. Low enough for me to reach. When she takes her three children to the penguins, I follow.

The kids she's with look like her, with rich brown skin. One is my age, and one a little bit older, and the last is around two and totally focused on his sticky popcorn. She leans over the railing to point out how the biggest penguin watches over the small ones.

I lean with the children she's watching. "Which one?"

When she points, I take her wallet.

She looks back at me with a smile. "That one!"

I use the shield of her body to hide the fact that I'm putting her wallet into my bag. Her smile is warm and forgiving, and I imagine that if she knew what I had done she wouldn't mind at all.

"Who here knows where penguins live?"

The question is for the three children she's with, but I'm caught up in the moment and I join them in raising my hand.

"South Pole," I shout.

The prize in this competition is being right. The two other kids shout the same answer, but I was first. For a kid like me, it's Olympic gold.

"That's right," the lady says.

"They have wings, but they can't fly," I add. "They're flightless birds."

I should be gone by now. I should have slipped away seconds ago, and every second counts. Mom says so. Besides that, now the lady is looking at me strangely. The wallet is heavy in my bag, and I can't run away now. Not without her wondering why.

"Emus and ostriches and kiwis too!" I cry.

The kid who's slightly older than me shoots me a look. I don't imagine she knows about the wallet, but I'm encroaching on her birthright. She's supposed to be the one who knows everything in this family. The approval I'm getting from her mother was meant for her.

"Are you with a grown-up?" the lady asks.

This is dangerous. I don't want to hang around this family for another second. If she reaches into her bag for her phone to call the three-digit number grownups use for lost children, she might realize the wallet's gone. I know what to do if I'm caught, but Mom will be disappointed. This is way past M&Ms. Chocolate is nice, but approval is sweeter.

I point at a random adult by the bathroom.

"Bye!" I say before running in that direction.

I don't take a breath of relief until I'm in a stall, snapping the lock shut. My instructions are clear. Go into the bathroom. Go into a stall. Remove the money and one credit card. Leave the wallet on the back of the tank. My mother has no use for driver's licenses or identification cards. She's not so bitter that she wants to ruin somebody's life, or even their day.

I was very young when I learned about honor among thieves.

The bathroom stinks of accidents and mold. I open the wallet and am greeted with a silver shield. It shines like a diamond. I'm not frightened of it. I only want to please my mother. But that shield is too much temptation for a little girl. I unhook it from its place in the wallet and stick it in my left back pocket. The money and the Visa card are in the right back pocket.

I don't tell my mother about it. It's mine. I don't know what it's for, but it reminds me of the day I earned the approval of someone inside the system. A sheriff's deputy thought I had done a good job. I had said the right thing. Even though I stole from her, I won a nod because I knew about flightless birds.

Sometime around my fourteenth birthday, when my mother is taken away, I realize that the badge is a placeholder. A signpost to my future self that I didn't have to be stuck. I didn't have to be what my mother was. I loved and admired her, now and always. But I didn't have to be what she was. I could choose to change the course of my life.

WHEN I GET home from the factory roof, Nana is still up. I go into the bathroom and start the shower, stripping down. I pull his wallet out of my coat pocket and empty it.

Pressing the leather wallet to my nose, I inhale him. I'm sitting on the toilet naked, shower running hot, fogging up the air, and the contents of his wallet are on the tile floor in front of me. Three credit cards. One driver's license, State of New Jersey. Birth date—not surprising. He's a Scorpio. Then I notice the expiration date.

It's expired.

I check through the credit cards.

All expired.

A supermarket membership card for Alan Smithee. A card for the Library of Alexandria.

Is he fucking with me?

He most certainly is.

The money's real. Hundred fifty-seven in smallish bills and twenties, in denominational order, all facing the same direction.

I plucked the wallet out of his jacket on a whim in the hopes that I would be shocked or surprised, and I am. It was foolish and reckless, but he made me feel both of those things. Foolish for wanting him, reckless for submitting to the want. Every time I saw him and survived, I felt as if risks were not only worth it, but absolutely necessary.

I told myself he would never be fully honest with me unless I forced his hand. Maybe that's true. Maybe it isn't. What I couldn't deny was that the little sleight-of-hand specialist inside me had been sleeping for a long time and was wide awake now that Keaton Bridge was in her life.

And he'd either known I'd steal his wallet or he carried around a lot of useless shit.

Between the last five and the first single is a small yellow Post-It with a note written in pencil.

You will return this to me in two nights.

My blood turns to ice. My fingertips go numb and tingly. He knew. He tested me and I passed, or failed. I have no idea which. I pull it off the five and turn it over.

Artful Dodger.

It sounds as if he approves, at least if he approves of a master pickpocket in *Oliver Twist*. And who doesn't approve of Dickens?

In some twisted way, he wants me to know him, but he wants me to take the information from him.

That kiss. His body. The control and command of him, even when I was throwing him against a car. His hardness against me. His scent is on the collar of my coat. He's a good kisser. A fantastic kisser. In the kissing department, he's king.

I close the wallet and notice a circular worn patch, beige against brown, a size smaller than a dime. I run my finger over it. There's something in there, but I didn't see it when the wallet was open.

I never got caught before, but this time will be different. The time I had the wallet in my hand outside the airport parking lot doesn't count. I cried and claimed I found it. Mom slapped my wrist, and we laughed when the cop let me go. The law's disapproval would never weigh on me with the same force as my mother's approval lifted me.

I turn the wallet around in my hands, looking for the place where the coin sits regularly enough to wear out the leather. I find a place in the billfold where the lining isn't stitched and take out the silver disk. It's heavier than I expected, marked with raised lines that adhere to the shape of the circle. The lines are broken in places that seem random. It's like a fingerprint, a labyrinth, a code pressed into metal. The other side is the same, but with a different random pattern. I click my fingernail along the surface.

I'm going to have to answer for this, and I stop my nail.

My relationship with Keaton is impossible to define, but it's something. It exists. It's a living thing, growing, changing, becoming a part of my life whether I want it or not.

And having stolen his wallet as if this was a game? How's that going to affect it?

I may not trust him, but what have I done to earn his trust?

I question myself, naked, sitting on my toilet, with a stolen wallet in my lap as if I'm seven years old again, when my phone rattles across the vanity.

If it's Keaton, I'm going to apologize right away, even if he calls me Artful Dodger with all the respect and approval in the world.

But it's not Keaton.

<Agent down>

<Shooting>

<All agents report>

I shut the phone, turn the shower to cold, and am out the door in eight minutes.

CHAPTER 18

CASSIE

We converge on the hospital in Springfield. I'm running like a dog to keep up, collect crime scene evidence, take notes, get the story straight. With no access to a secure channel, the Post-It does no good in my pocket. I can't even tell anyone about it until I know where it leads.

The sun is just about up when we're called into a briefing. No one's tired. Our blood is infused with adrenaline and caffeine. Three agents have been hospitalized. None are in critical condition, but nevertheless, the very idea that someone shot at federal agents is not going down well.

We've taken over a small education room on the first floor of the hospital. The blinds are open onto the parking lot. The chairs are kid-sized and the walls are decorated with the letters of the alphabet. Frieda sits next to me. She's dug her notebook from the bottom of her bag, and she taps her pen on an open page.

"They're going to want to wipe these guys from the face of the earth now," Frieda says softly as I get out my own notebook.

"Any intel on how they were tipped off?"

"Nope."

You're at greatest risk of being attacked when you attack, and greatest risk of being seen when you seek.

Was it me? Everyone knows I've been trying to access Third Psyche for months. Did my single-minded pursuit of Third Psyche cause the ambush?

I turn away, looking out the window. I hear Orlando quite clearly. I catch every word he's saying, every fact he states, and take notes. But I'm completely distracted by what part I may have had in this.

A black Lexus pulls into the lot, going too fast, screeching into a spot. I'm not the only one looking out, but I'm the only one who knows who's driving before the car's in park.

I shut the blinds. "Focus, people."

Orlando nods his thanks, and I nod back. So I'm sure it looks strange when I slip out of the briefing into the hallway. When the room's door clicks shut behind me, I bolt through the double doors.

"No running!" a nurse calls as I pass.

Fuck her. I burst into the empty ER waiting room just as the doors slide open for Keaton.

He's a wreck. Shirt untucked. Hair uncombed. A wild look in his eye that's not hungry or sexual, but violent; as if he came to settle scores. His gaze lands on me and I freeze in place, watching his hands go from fists to question marks. Feeling the tension crack and break.

"Sir?"

A man's voice. To my right.

Security or police.

If he's waylaid, he might be seen, might be held or questioned.

Nope. Not today.

I reach for my back pocket and take out my wallet, flipping it open so the badge and ID show. "Federal agent." I don't take my eyes off Keaton as he takes heavy breaths, chest rising and falling as if he's run a mile. "I need a secure location."

In my peripheral vision, the security guard looks at my ID. "This way."

I tilt my head to Keaton and follow the security guard without a word. He unlocks a door to a small, utilitarian office.

"Thank you." I point at Keaton, who's two steps behind me. "Sir."

He's in. I'm in. The door is closed. Locked.

"What the—?"

I never finish my sentence. He's kissing me, and I don't have the alarm bells whistling loud enough to use a defensive maneuver. I let him kiss me, run his hands over my back, take me in his arms as if we've just survived something traumatic.

"I caught it on the scanner this morning," he says between kisses.

"What? The shooting?"

"I thought it was you. I thought they shot you."

"I'm fine."

"I thought it was my fault. I thought they saw you on the forum and came for you."

I push him off me so I can speak for more than two words without getting kissed. "I haven't even logged on yet."

"Thank God. Thank God, thank God. I would have committed murder if they hurt a hair on your head. Cassie. Listen. "

"I was looking in your wallet when I got a call. I'm sorry I took it."

"You think I care about the wallet? Jesus, woman. When I thought you were hurt… I thought I'd never see you again."

I open my mouth to ask him what's happened? What's changed? We haven't even slept together, yet his intensity has a traction I cannot resist, and no words come out.

"You don't trust me," he says.

The words come out without a thought. Instinct speaks. "I don't."

His hand goes under my skirt, between my legs, over the fabric of my underwear. He presses against me. I'm swollen and wet already.

"Should I touch you?"

"Yes," I whisper in the shape of a groan, leaning back on the desk.

He presses my legs open. "Say my name."

"Keaton," I gasp as he rubs against me.

He's fierce and demanding. His hand has one goal only. To make me feel him through the fabric. "Wrong. Tell me my name."

I can barely breathe. I don't know what he wants, but I sure as hell want to give it to him. "Alpha Wolf, a.k.a.… whatever. You have a million aliases."

His fingers swirl, gathering up sensation as if he wants to mold it around me, but he does not get under the fabric, where my deepest want lies. "My real name. Cassandra, tell me my real name."

His real name? Is that an option? He has a real name? Of course he does. Of course Keaton Bridge isn't his real name. I knew this, and he knows I know this. Is this a test? A trick? I open my mouth to ask what I'm supposed to know and how it overlays what he thinks I know and what he wants out of me, but he finally slides his hand under my underwear and touches me where I'm tender and wet. My back arches, but he only strokes gently enough to push me against my orgasm without pushing me over into it.

"Do you want me to stop?"

"No, please don't stop." I can only whine and beg at this point.

He leans close to me until I feel his words more clearly than I hear them. "You don't know my real name. And you want me to touch you between your legs?"

I look him in the eye. The twilight blue of them is almost navy in the shadows.

"Yes," I whisper.

"You want me to make you come?"

"Make me come."

His fingers move along my seam, gathering moisture. I'm so close, and so at his command, that I will say anything. I'll even tell him the truth that I haven't told myself. Slowly and deliberately, he slides three fingers inside me. I push against him until they can't go deeper.

"First, I'm going to own your pussy, then I'm taking the rest of you. Every day is precious, Cassie." His thumb brushes against my clit. "I realized today that your trust is too. I want it, and I'm going to have it."

His hand works me, pushing inside, thumb giving friction against my slick nub.

He lets me come, and he stretches my orgasm to obscene heights, watching me squirm and bite back a groan as he touches me only enough to give me more pleasure than I ever thought possible.

When I'm reduced to panting and pain, he cups his hand between my legs as if he's protecting what's under there.

"I'm glad you're all right," he says when he pulls his hand out of my underwear.

"Me too. Next time just call me."

He picks a handkerchief out of his jacket pocket and wipes his hand, smiles a little, then kisses my cheek tenderly. His lips brush the heat away from my skin and replace it with a new warmth that runs hot with passion and warm with comfort. Whatever enflamed him when he arrived had dissipated.

"What would be the fun of that?" He helps me up, smoothing my skirt.

"You have a point."

He presses his lips to my cheek, lingering over my skin. "Be ready to see me tomorrow night."

CHAPTER 19

CASSIE

I put Keaton's Post-It on my desk and fold it so I can see the handwritten link. It's been shortened. It'll report back to whoever made it. Keaton will know when I log on. I'm not disturbed. I like that he knows. I feel both protected and aggressive in a show-offy way. I want him to see me.

I set up the secure VPN so the Bureau can track my activity, but hackers can't. I'm completely cloaked when I open Tor, the secure browser that manages access to the dark web, and I carefully type in the link. It connects to the log-in page for Third Psyche.

Thank you, Keaton Bridge.

Before I can note a single element of the site, it flickers and goes to deep blue with yellow letters.

—SORRY—
THIS PAGE HAS BEEN SENT BACK TO HELL

Fuck. I'm glad I didn't open it in front of everyone, only to be embarrassed, but *fuck* just the same.

Was it shut down by hackers? Anonymous? Did they get a whiff that I was looking? Or did Keaton move the link to protect me?

I have a feeling it was a version of the latter.

So what do I want out of Keaton now that he's ripped the site from under his link? Walking down the hall to the coffee machine, I consider what he has to offer and whether or not it's the same as what I want.

The hallway is windowless, and the dull, dead institutional shade of green is the same on the floor, ceiling, and walls. The light over the utility closet has always buzzed. When I think of getting promoted, I think of this hallway. One day I'm going to see it for the last time. On the way out of here, I'm going to say goodbye to that buzzing light and that brain-dulling shade of green.

At the end, I turn left toward coffee and find Frieda's beaten me there.

"Hey, I have gossip." She blows on her coffee. "We're getting a pay grade packet next week. I'm due for a GS-12."

The packets are sent quarterly from Quantico, and include all our promotions and pay grade changes. I'd totally forgotten to worry about it.

"You'll get it," I say.

"Keep your nose clean with Smirkypants," she scolds. "At least until this is cleared up."

She knows me. She knows I'm not attracted to a guy that often and she can tell Mr. Smirkypants is different.

"Promise," I say, holding up two fingers.

She pats my shoulder and walks out. She's a good friend. Something about sisterhood flies across my brain and hooks onto my job before it's gone. It demands attention.

There's another sister in town, and she's a hacker.

*I*t's funny watching a millionaire bag groceries, but Harper Barrington was in the habit of helping the store owners before she met Taylor or went to Stanford.

She has on a masculine plaid car coat with sleeves halfway down her fingers. It doesn't get in the way of her lightning-fast cashiering, nor does the length of the line get in the way of her small talk with the customers.

"Hi," I say when I finally get to the front of the line.

"Hey." She does a double-take on my face as she moves the loaf of bread along. "I've seen you before."

"I think I met you in front of the Barrington mansion?"

She takes a split second to tap her forehead when she remembers. Behind her, a girl in her twenties comes up behind and puts her bag in a cabinet.

"Hey, Trude," Harper says to the girl before she turns her attention back to me and the groceries I've come a long way to get. "The day you came for Keaton. FBI. Agent Grinstead. You want a separate bag for the eggs?"

"No."

"I hope he didn't cause you too much trouble."

"I think I caused him more trouble than he caused me."

"Good. Twenty-seven forty-nine please."

I hand her thirty. "I was wondering—"

"Trudy, honey," Harper calls behind her, "the credit card slips are in the envelope."

Trudy and Harper go on about bags and cash and rolls of quarters as Harper plucks my change out of the drawer. I'm sure she's finished when I continue.

"Thanks," I start. "Do you think—"

"Did Johnny go to the bank?" Trudy asks, unzipping a green canvas case.

"Yesterday," Harper replies, handing me my change.

The pimply boy at the end of the counter bags everything efficiently. I decide this has gone poorly and I'm going to have to try something else after I drop the bags of groceries home.

"You got this?" Harper asks Trudy, pulling the drawer out of the register.

"Yeah," Trudy says as I head out with a heavy bag in each arm.

I'm putting them in my trunk when Harper calls me from the top of the store's steps.

"Hey! Cassie!" She clatters down the wood steps.

"Yes?" I'm pretty amazed that she remembered my name from hearing it once, months ago.

"You sounded like you wanted to talk to me?"

"I've never met anyone so eager to talk to an FBI agent." I close the trunk.

"Here's what I know. If you want to talk to me, you're gonna. I can avoid it or just get on with it. But do I need a lawyer or something?"

Does she need a lawyer? Am I buying groceries in Barrington on official business, or am I here on a personal call?

"Tell you what," I say. "If we get into sketchy territory, I'll let you know."

"You hungry?"

She indicates the hamburger joint next to the store. It had been closed for business until the previous month. Now it's a hub of activity. It's already late. I could use dinner, and I didn't buy anything all too perishable.

"Sure," I say.

Harper trots off toward the restaurant.

SHE KNOWS THE OWNERS, who are long-time Barrington residents. We're seated in the back where it's quiet. We both order our burgers rare.

"So, you go grocery shopping in Barrington often?" She pokes her Coke with her straw, letting the insinuation that I went very far out of my way for a few boxes of pasta hang in the air.

"Almost never, but you carry Standoff's Bakery. I've been curious about the cupcakes."

"Hm." Poke. Poke. "Where's the guy you came to the door with? Ken, was it?"

"Got shot last night."

She coughs as if she's choking on her own spit.

I wait until she finishes. "It's nothing you can't read in the papers."

"Here? Barrington? Doverton?"

"Springfield. He's going to be fine. Just a flesh wound."

She shakes her head. Springfield is as near to an inner city as we get. The mythology is if bad stuff's going to happen, it's going to be there.

"Gotta tell you, when I got to Stanford, it felt like I could get shot any minute. I didn't know anyone. All new faces. It takes getting used to."

"Did you feel like that at MIT?"

She'd been there a long time ago for less than a year. I mention it because I want her to know I have information, no matter how surface it is. It seems only fair.

"No. My head was up my ass. Anyway, I'm going to be honest now, since you just basically told me stuff I never told you, so you must have a file on me."

"There are a lot of files on a lot of things."

Whatever effect my admission is meant to have—mollifying her, distracting her, lying, because she doesn't have a file—seems irrelevant to her.

"Keaton, the guy you questioned?"

I try to stay relaxed, but my skin tingles at the mention of his name. "Yes."

"He needed heating lamps on the roof and a little round table last night. I needled him about it until he told me why."

"Really?"

"Really. It was fun to watch him squirm."

I can't imagine Keaton Bridge squirming under Harper's interrogation. She looks so young and defenseless as she sucks on her straw until she's getting nothing but air and ice. She's a kid, in a way, but not to be underestimated.

"So." She places the glass to the side. "Here you are this afternoon, over twenty miles out of the way for cupcakes I don't remember seeing on the belt. I figure you're going to ask me a bunch of stuff and get around to Keaton at some point. I don't know what it has to do with who's getting shot or anything, but I don't like people getting shot. Not even in Springfield."

There are rules about what to tell civilians, and I follow them to the letter.

"You hacked into QI4 before it was released." Common knowledge. Even the *NY Times* covered the hack and the revelation that a small-town girl had cracked the world's first quantum system.

"Most fun exploit ever." She smiles as her teeth bite the straw flat.

"So you're a pretty advanced hacker."

"If you say so."

"As is Taylor Harden."

"He's the best."

"And his partner."

"You know I can't say anything about that."

I take the labyrinth coin from my pocket and lay it on the table. Her gaze locks on it as I push it toward her. "Do you have one of these?"

Our food comes. We ignore it.

"Where did you get this?" She doesn't pick it up. She only touches the edge.

"I won't lie. So I won't tell you."

I recognize something brash in her at the moment. Something show-offy and cocky. Something that makes her head sway with defiance as she takes out her phone.

"I can't believe you guys don't know about this." She pokes her phone and points the camera at the coin as if taking a picture. "What do you do all day?"

"Look for crooks," I say as she watches her phone spin. The first thing QI4 did was build cell towers, but the signal out here is still terrible and she probably has seven layers of VPN. "I'm trying to find out if Third Psyche was involved with the shooting."

"Shit, no." She puts her phone face down and regards me seriously. "Those guys are no good. They're the devil."

"I know."

"I'm so glad you're trying to get them, because seriously? That's the kind of thing I can't even look at or I'm going to lose it. Did you hear about the thing last Halloween? When they tried to do a coordinated attack against seven synagogues?"

"Yep. Then they moved servers."

She slides her plate in front of her.

I take the coin back. "Do you mind?"

She picks up her phone instead of answering, holding the glass up to face me. It's a picture of Keaton looking straight at me, and suddenly I'm surrounded by the smell of him and my ears are filled with the danger in his voice.

I glance at the list of names below.

4LPH4_W0LF

X7R3M3_157

D0XX_D3V1L

There were more, but she puts the phone down before I can note them all.

Still chewing, she digs her keys out of her bag. "I should ask where you got this, but obviously you stole it."

I admit nothing. The waitress refills the drinks.

"What is it?"

"You guys." She shakes her head and ribs me. "What do you do all day?"

"Clean our guns."

She isolates a tiny charm on her keyring. The same coin with a different fingerprint. She points her phone at it. This time, the VPN connects immediately and her picture comes up, filling the screen where Keaton's was. She hands me the phone. "Scroll."

She eats her burger as I scroll through a list of avatars, IDs, height and weight stats.

"It's a verification system," I say. "A passport. And the swirls are like a QR code—if you have the software to read it."

"Right." She gently removes the phone from my hand. "Because hackers never really know who we're talking to IRL… in real life."

"I know what IRL means."

"We could meet and you could say you're anyone, unless you have one of these."

"Why did you just show it to me?"

She smirks and takes a pull of her soda. "Keaton said if you came to me with a cert kwon, I should scan it." She wipes her mouth. "You should have told me you were after Third Psyche right away. From now on, you tell me what you need and I'll get it for you. I won't try to romance you on the roof or kiss you in the parking lot…"

I nearly choke on my burger. Harper finds this delightful.

"Come on!" she cries. "Do you think Taylor's not going to look at the security video to see why he needed a heat lamp and a pitcher of water, just so? Please. He's known Keaton since he was fifteen, and he's never seen him try so hard."

I'm flattered. I'm honored.

I'm swooning, which is completely inappropriate and unprofessional.

I clear my throat to get back my bearings and take a bite of my lunch to buy time, because I don't deserve that kind of effort. I'd never say it out loud, but I'm convinced of it. I'm a regular woman in a masculine job. Men don't treat me like a queen. It's disorienting and exciting.

"You all right?" she asks.

I'm all right. Better than all right. I'm high on *never seen him try so hard.*

"I'm concerned." I sip my Coke. Swallow. I pause to feel my feet on the floor and my ass in the chair. Time to get over it. "Keaton alerted them to the fact that we were looking for them so they could ambush our guys."

"Yeah, no." She shakes her head so vigorously, her hair sways under her chin.

"He *is* Alpha Wolf."

"Whatever. I'll tell you something about Keaton that I know and Taylor would totally back me up. Keaton's interested in money. Em-oh-en-ee-why. Long-term dollars. Nazis are losers. Short-term, risky cash that's soaked in blood. I mean, the first thing he did was fuck credit card companies over Luhn's formula."

That's a slip on her part. Not because the crack was a secret. Luhn's formula is the reason you're asked for the expiration date when you buy something with a credit card online or over the phone, and why giving the wrong one leads to a rejection. The formula's used to checksum the credit card account number against the expiration date. If they don't match, the card's rejected, but if they do, the purchase sails through. Anyone who has the formula has the keys to a kingdom of wealth.

"Taylor Harden cracked Luhn's," I say, touching base with known fact before moving on to a new reality.

"*They* did it, and Taylor took the fall with you guys. Keaton didn't even get to look a federal agent in the eye over it." She wags her finger at me. "You're counting in your head. Statute of limitations is up."

Nailed it. I was indeed counting the number of years since Taylor cracked Luhn's.

Harper gathers a skein of French fries in her fingers and bites it in half, runs the raw ends through the last of her ketchup, and finishes them off.

"And then Alpha Wolf was born," I say.

"Wouldn't know anything about that."

Maybe she does. Maybe she doesn't.

"Taylor sent you to talk to me, didn't he?" I ask.

"He said if I saw you, I should say 'hi.' But I'm here because I like the burgers and I like Keaton. I want to check you out. See if you're trouble for him."

"Am I?"

"Probably. Actually, definitely."

"If he hasn't done anything, he has nothing to worry about."

She laughs as if I'm such a card she can't help herself. "Oh, I didn't mean like that. I mean he likes you and you like him. I can see it and I think it's great, but it's trouble. Every time. Especially for that guy. He's allergic to commitment."

"I'm not available for him." My voice snaps as if I'm irritated by the notion that I'd be interested in a man who has to worry about statutes of limitation. Even though I do want him, very much so, and it's that very real threat that he is lawless that piques my interest as much as *never seen him try so hard.*

"Crap," she says, looking at her phone. "I have to go." She slips her coat off the back of the chair. "Keaton's a better guy than Taylor was, that's for sure. And if you have to pretend you don't want him, you go ahead. You do you."

"I'm just doing my job." I reach for my wallet even though we haven't gotten the check yet.

"The bill's taken care of." She swings her coat behind her and gets her arms in the sleeves. "It was nice to meet you again."

She bounces off, hair swinging across her back as she calls everyone in the place by name. I'm left staring at my half-eaten burger and wondering who Keaton Bridge really is, because with the cert kwon, I know more than ever, and less of what makes me truly curious.

Taylor's never seen him try so hard.

"It's a coin about the size of a dime." I'm in the parking lot of the grocery and the restaurant, watching the edge of the sky go from orange to blue. "Heavy. Steel maybe? Check their personal effects and I'll be there in thirty minutes."

Keaton's cert kwon sits in my fist. I pretend I'm trying to decide whether to show them or not, but I decided before I even called Orlando. I'm going to tell them I know about them, not that I've seen one.

"Where did you get this intel?" Orlando asks.

"A good asset. A different one."

"If we find one on these guys, it's going to break this wide open."

"I know."

"Tell me what you think about the shooting."

"I think my asset either sold us out or revealed himself."

"There's a lot happening between 'either' and 'or,' Agent Grinstead."

"I don't think they sold us out."

He makes a weary sigh. "Who is your asset?"

I don't have to tell him. Not unless I need money to pay him. The fact that I'm under no obligation to tell him does not remove the pressure to do so. I should tell him. He'll keep it under wraps. That's his job.

And if he doesn't?

I've betrayed Keaton, and my guts twist at the idea. My reaction to revealing his name isn't sensible. It's not logical. It is not the result of a thoughtful calculation. My body doesn't want me to say his name. I won't be able to take it back.

"I trust him," I answer by not answering.

"Is this person known to you personally? Or is this an online ID?"

"Personal."

His lips are personal. His touch. The sound of his voice. They're personal, and they're mine.

"You better make sure you know exactly who they are. I don't want you or this office to be distracted by inquiries into this asset. Do you understand?"

"I understand."

"If you need to take some time to vet this person, take it. Come to me if you find out your trust was misplaced."

"It wasn't, sir."

"Prove it to yourself, then prove it to me. I'll get you Level 4 clearance to dig them up."

"Thank you," I say. "One more thing."

"Speak."

"I think the answer is online, in the white supremacist forums. And I think I might have gotten access."

"Really?"

"Yes. But I need to work on it here. I don't want to shirk my duties if you need me in Springfield, but I believe I can do more good here."

"Agreed. Keep me updated."

"Thank you, sir."

"Good work, Agent."

We hang up. On the drive to the field office, I try to remember the last time Orlando told me I'd done good work and how I felt when he did.

The first time he told me I'd done good work was my first two weeks on the job, when I'd found messages inside the comments script of a website no one could prove was behind a money laundering scheme.

Frieda and I had a glass of champagne that night, and I beamed.

But not today. Has the excitement worn off? Or has something else happened? Because I'm happiest about Keaton's trust. Not his approval, but his trust that even if I found out about the coin, I'd protect him.

I'm going to live up to it.

SUBJECT: Keaton Bridge

SEARCH TYPE: Level 4

Everyone is somewhere in the FBI database at Level 4. Having a stub isn't a big deal. Having a file doesn't mean as much as everyone thinks. Most of it is automated anyway.

But Keaton?

He doesn't have shit. For a foreign national with part ownership in a soon-to-be huge company destined for government contracts, he has less than Joe from Petoskey.

I check Interpol.

Nothing.

I check our shared data with MI6.

It was a longshot to begin with, but nothing.

My blood gets cold. My mouth tastes like the inside of my stomach. Something isn't right. I do a quick check for Taylor Harden, just to make sure the system's even working.

—BeezleBoy363636 offers Luhn's formula with bids starting at one million Bitcoin.

—BeezleBoy363636 tracked down to Camden, NJ.

—A bunch of redacted shit.

—Taylor Harden a.k.a. Beezleboy363636, a fifteen-year-old hacker with a nice family who likes to think they raised him better, flips in exchange for expunged records.

—Asset records filed in Delta show Taylor did three years of coding and hacking consultation before heading to MIT, which he quit with three credits left.

No mention of Keaton or Alpha Wolf. They lived in the same town. Went to the same school. I'm amazed at how little he's actually told me in the time we've spent together.

Why is Keaton Bridge even in the United States?

Deeper isn't the way to go. I need to search wider.

I set my VPN to London and do a broad search. I'll take anything. A picture. A school. A birth announcement. He was born just as social media was, so I didn't expect much from that, but what does come up surprises me.

—A Facebook profile with a picture of a handsome boy who looks exactly like the Keaton Bridge I know. Three posts. Fifteen friends from every corner of the UK. None with mutual friends outside the circle.

—His name and photo listed in London's Dagenham School. No clubs. No interests. No quote. He's facing slightly left. All the other students face right.

—A crystal-clear birth announcement in a small local paper.

I'm in the process of looking up William and Phyllis Bridge when Frieda pokes her head into my office.

"I'm on my way out to Springfield," she says. "You're not coming?"

"Working Mr. Smirkypants."

"Always on it." She looks over my shoulder. "Is that his birth announcement?"

"Yeah."

"Are his parents famous or something? Rich? Old money?" She leans farther, squinting at the screen. She sees what I see. Crisp digital lines from an analog age.

"Not that I can tell."

"Kind of odd to have a birth announcement then," she says.

"Yeah. Everything about him is kind of odd."

"Sister?"

"It's fine," I say.

"You know how much I admire you."

"Hush."

"Don't let him mess you up. Please. I want to call you my boss one day."

Her faith in me has eclipsed my own for as long as I can remember. She's my biggest fan, and even when I pat her hand to reassure her, I fear she's headed for disappointment.

CHAPTER 21

CASSIE

I'm exhausted when I get home. I feel like the cat not only dragged me in, but toyed with me for hours beforehand. I feel wrung out, hungry, tired. My jaw aches at the hinge from pounding at crossed t's and dotted i's, coming up empty, and starting over again.

I figure I'll sit up with Nana for a few hours and do some puzzles. She'll tell me I don't need a man out one side of her mouth and talk about diamond rings with the other.

But I can't take another conversation about men. Not with the fresh memory of Keaton's fingers in me and the desperation in his voice when he said he was scared for me. My God, I must be tired—because not only am I ranting and raving to my grandmother in my head as I step in the door, but when I see Keaton next to her on the couch, I'm so suddenly awake that by contrast, I must have been near walking in my sleep.

He's not the only one there, but he's the only one I see. Molly's there with her knitting. Fredo, who still has a head full of hair, silver though it is, has a glass of wine swirling. Carol sits next to the box wine, filling her glass. They're all laughing like old friends, which they are. All except Keaton, who seems perfectly comfortable with the geriatric crowd.

When I see him laughing with my grandmother's friends, I feel as if

I'm alive for the first time since he walked out of the little hospital office. My face nearly cracks when I smile.

And he's not just sitting. No, nothing that simple for Keaton Bridge. His legs take up half the room. They're the length of a shotgun. Nana puts a hand on his knee and pushes it because whatever he said is so damn funny, he needs to be pushed.

I close the door, and Nana cries, "Well, she's finally here!"

I'm greeted with a chorus of my grandmother's cronies.

Keaton slaps his knees as if the whole conversation is finished, finally, and he can get on with his business.

He looks up at me when he stands. "Are you ready?"

"For?"

They all laugh again as if they share a joke I'm not privy to. I don't feel left out as much as I would like to know what I'm supposed to be ready for. I give him the side eye and he winks at me.

"Did you know what they call cigarettes in England?" Carol says.

Keaton snaps up his jacket and bows to my grandmother, then each of her friends. "I have much to learn." He takes Grandma's hand and kisses it in an obsequious, British, and charming way.

Not shockingly, she loves it. She's one batting eyelash away from full flirt.

"Nana…" I hear the scold in my voice and swallow it.

"Where did you find this one, Cassandra?" Molly asks. "Have you been hiding him?"

"He does quite a fine job of hiding himself."

"All the best ones do," Nana interjects. "Now you two just run along."

Keaton can take a cue. He holds the door open for me, and with Nana & Co smiling and waving, I have no choice but to step outside with him.

I speak when we hear the dead bolt snap shut. "Don't turn around. I happen to know for fact that she's still looking out the window."

His hands are in his pockets. I suspect that's a gentlemanly show. "She's a very interesting lady." He walks me to his car. "Have you ever talked to her? She has a few choice words for your grandfather. I pity the motherfucker."

Motherfucker is Nana's pet name for my disappearing grandfather.

I point at Keaton's Lexus. "Did she see the car you drove up in? She's from Detroit. She wouldn't appreciate the Japanese make."

"She mentioned that." He opens the passenger side door for me. "The factory's in Tennessee."

He almost has me. I'm almost in the goddamn car. But I stop myself.

"I didn't agree to go anywhere with you. You can't just show up here. One, people talk. I haven't told them my source, but now you just appear on my couch, pretty as you please, and expect no one can put two and two together."

"Most people can't."

"You're not understanding me. I'm trying to protect you."

"Thank you, but I have this."

"And how did you know where I lived? Do you know that's weird? You could have called, not that I ever gave you my number."

"Is this any worse than you pickpocketing me? Or tracking down my best friend's girlfriend to get intel on me?"

"My reasons are clear."

"So are mine. I couldn't keep away. The more I learned about you, the more I wanted to see you again. And this morning, everything changed for me. So maybe it's me. Maybe I'm the one with the problem. I figure there's only one way to find out. I was going to suggest this over dinner, but since you're such an insistent little git, I'll bring it up now. I need to find out if this is my problem or your problem."

I blink at him. "Are you asking me out?"

"Apparently. I also need my wallet."

"I was supposed to return it tomorrow night."

"I need it today."

"You could've just called."

"I'm hungry now, so I'm taking you to dinner."

"Something like that."

He touches my cheek with his thumb. It's tender in the way I've never experienced. Sure, men have touched me before, and they have been gentle. It's been fine. But his thumb on my cheek is more than the results matching the intention. It's more than a simple touch. He has a complexity that is encapsulated in the place his thumb meets my cheek. He's been charming, chivalrous, and deferential. Tenderness is the revelation of another plane in a stone that seems to have more facets than I can count.

"I have never met a woman so deserving of everything being better than normal for her. And I'm sorry if my attempts to do better for you are actually worse. I'm breaking new ground with you"

I don't expect this. I'm not only surprised, I'm a little bit liquid right now. It's the danger-dash-unknown-dash-taboo-dash-dash-dash. But more than any of that, it's him. I like him. I like his confidence, but I also like the thread of unsurety that runs through it. I like his competence, and I also like the way he lets my grandmother tell him how to do puzzles.

"I'm going to have to forgive you." I take his wallet out of my bag. He holds out his hand for it. "After all, when a girl kisses a hacker, she shouldn't be surprised when she's hacked." I place the wallet in his upturned palm, and we rest there with his long fingers curling to take my hand as well as the wallet. "Just leave me something to tell you over dinner."

He steps away, pulling the wallet with him. He runs his finger over the worn circle, checking for the cert kwon. It's there as expected.

"Thank you for that," I say. "For letting Harper tell me."

He smiles and indicates that I should get in the car, which I do, letting him close the door and realizing I've hacked him as surely as he's hacked me.

CHAPTER 22

CASSIE

*H*e's taken me to one of the the nicest restaurants in Doverton. It's late, so we're seated right away. And it's a good thing too, because I'm starving. The host hands us menus and takes our drink order.

"Red wine," I say. "Just something dry is fine."

"Ginger ale," Keaton says.

The host spins off to fulfill the order. This is the second time I've seen Keaton order a drink, and it's the second time he's ordered something without alcohol.

"Do you not to drink at all?"

"Driving." He smirks as if he knows this is half an answer. "And I still need my wits around you."

I've never been more flattered by a compliment. Once my mother went away and my grandmother started raising me, I was homecoming queen, captain of the cheerleading squad, and voted most likely to be on the cover of a magazine. I've been called a long-stemmed rose, a tall drink of water, and a handful of adjectives that all meant "attractive."

But this brilliant guy saying he needs to keep his wits around me is the nicest thing a man ever said to me. I smile into my water glass, trying to swallow my gushing satisfaction.

He's reading you.

Obviously, he knows how to flatter me.

The waitress is fresh out of high school, and tucks her hair behind her ear when she talks. She addresses Keaton as if I'm not there, mesmerized by him, rattling off specials and smiling like a ventriloquist's dummy.

"I read the burgers are really good here," I say just to get her attention. "I like mine rare. And I mean rare."

"Okay, and sir?"

"She'll have the filet mignon."

"Wait." I hold up my hand.

"You want a burger more than the filet?" he asks as if what I want is an issue.

"Well, no. But it's…" I run my hand over the length of the menu. I'm saying *it's at the bottom* without saying it, which is code for *it's forty dollars*.

"Delicious!" the waitress chimes in.

"Fine." I hand over my menu.

"What do you have without meat?" Keaton asks.

"We have a chicken cacciatore that's really nice."

I'm as surprised by his question as I am by her answer.

"How about an eggplant parmesan?" he asks gamely.

"Sure thing!" She pencils it in, asks a bunch of questions about sides and drinks, and takes off with the leather-bound menus under her arm.

"So," he says, folding his hands on the table and pressing the full weight of his gaze on me. I'm distracted by the arch of his eyebrows, how perfect and expressive they are. How they seem to hint at all the facets of the stone.

"So," I say. "How long were you hanging out with my grandmother?"

He shrugs, holds his answer until the waitress is finished giving us our drinks. I suddenly wish I hadn't ordered wine.

"She has quite a story to tell," he says. "Working her way up at the plant, taking care of her daughter all by herself."

"My great-grandmother was also a single mother. Grandma understood what it would take for her to make a life."

"You must come from a long line of extraordinary women."

"We don't make it easy on ourselves." I don't want to talk about me or my mother, the kind of person she was, how she raised me, or how I wound up taking care of my grandmother. I want to talk about him. I want to see how many facets of this stone I can uncover over one dinner.

I swirl my wine. A basket of bread and a bowl of butter appear between us. I wonder if I'm in over my head.

"There are two reasons people become vegetarians," I say. "They either believe in animal rights or they do it for health reasons. Which is yours?"

"How binary of you."

"If you have a third reason, I'd love to hear it."

He regards me, the room, his bread, me again, for what seems like an hour, but is actually two Mississippis. He's leisurely about it. I can see the wheels turning as he calculates what to tell me. I hope it's everything.

"I grew up in London, right in the middle of everything. Small row house with flowers in the windows. We had a cat to kill mice and a dog to keep the cat in line." He pulls out his stirrer and finishes his ginger ale. "I had an extraordinarily ordinary childhood."

He waits, as if testing for what I already know, and I take a second to weigh the fact that he's Alpha Wolf against how his hand felt under my skirt.

"In the interests of full disclosure," I cut in, "I'm still an FBI agent. So you might want to be careful about what you tell me."

Mr. Smirkypants is in full effect. "Tell me then, what do you think you know?"

"I know the shape of a fat goose egg. Your UK records were completely fabricated."

"How so?"

Does he not know?

He knows. He has to know. He wants to know how I know, and I decide it's a fair question.

"Your school records are impeccably average for someone so smart. Your elementary school photo faces the wrong direction. Your birth announcement has the clearest edges I've ever seen in documents that predate digital inputting."

"You have a real nose for bullshit, don't you?"

I tip my glass toward him. We click, and I sip my wine.

"So," he says, leaning forward, "do you have a fact to share? Any theories? Wishes? Dreams? Who would I be if I could be anybody?"

"Dreams and wishes aren't things I waste a lot of time with. I do, however, have a hypothesis."

He leans forward even farther, as if he wants the table to fold away and disappear. As if, given the choice, he would twine his body into mine to hear what I had to say. "Spill it now."

Such is my desire to obey him that I nearly tip my glass. I blame his dead serious tone of voice, but the fact is, I've heard this tone before and not reacted this way.

"If I put together your story about decamping to New Jersey, which is a known asylum state for the United Kingdom, and if I look back at what was going on then in the international community, it's all pretty clear."

His left eye squints just a little. He's not exactly smiling. But his dimples crease a little more, as if a smirk is waiting just behind his mouth.

"I had to look it up," I say. "NATO *did* have a sort of agent protection program during that time. You went dark. Your identity was wiped clean. A new one was created for you."

He leans back. I feared, even as I told him what I'd discovered, that he'd be angry, or afraid, or worried, or that he'd act aggressively in confirmation or denial. Instead, he seems pleased. Is he pleased that I'm so very wrong? Or that I have such a vivid imagination?

It's neither of those. He's glad that I'm right. I can see it in his face, in his deepening dimples, in his relaxed smile and posture.

"I still don't know why," I add. "I can't find your father or your mother anywhere. I guess that should be a clue itself. But without something to go on, I'm not going to assume."

"Did you manage to uncover the reason we moved?"

"Your dad was in MI6 and pissed off the wrong person."

It's a shot in the dark, but he nods, finding my answer acceptable. "I'm going to tell you things I haven't told too many people. I may live to regret it. But it may also relieve me of the burden of these ridiculous secrets."

Secrets are indeed a burden. I want to relieve him. I want to be that person he can tell things he won't tell anybody else. The badge in my pocket weighs four hundred pounds at that moment. For the first time in my career, I wish I wasn't a federal agent, and I make a promise I believe I can keep.

"It's between us," I say, twisting two fingers in front of my lips and flicking my wrist as if I'm throwing away the key.

With a short nod, he accepts my guarantee and puts his elbows on the table, getting close enough to me that he can speak softly. "I haven't eaten meat since I was fifteen. Our last morning in London. Our last hours. My father was home, which was always my favorite time. He often took me out of school on a Friday for a weekend trip. We'd packed to go camping. We always brought Baron, a sheepdog and the sweetest animal you ever met. It was morning. Crack of dawn. We had a little alley behind the house with a car park. I open the door to start loading the boot. I stepped…" He stops and closes his eyes for a second, then opens them. "I'm not a squeamish man. We hunted and dressed deer and fowl. But this was different. You might not want to me to continue before dinner."

I lean forward on my elbows and hiss, "Finish the story or I'm going to give you something to be squeamish about."

He laughs softly then looks away as if checking the room, before turning back to me. "All right. I'm carrying my rucksack in my arms, so I can't see where I'm stepping. Then…" He flattens his hand, palm down, and draws it horizontal across the space in front of his body. "I slide. My feet go out from under me and I'm arse over tits in Baron's guts."

"Ugh. I'm sorry."

"I was quite fond of him."

"Do you know who did it?"

"My father had…" He pauses, wheels clearly turning. "His job made him enemies."

"Was he a prosecutor or a spy or something?"

"Yes and no. But to the meat of the question—"

"Good pun."

"Thank you. Baron was special. His insides, however, looked exactly the same as packed meat, and I thought any animal could be Baron. I was put off it completely."

"Wow." I say it with real awe, just as dinner arrives.

"Wow, what?" He flips his napkin open and drapes it over his lap.

"You really have a heart." I push my knife into my steak and twist so I can see if the restaurant understands what rare means.

"Maybe. Let's let that be our secret."

My meat is deep pink inside. Just the way I like it. I look at him. He's watching me with his dark blue eyes.

I point my knife at my dinner. "Does this bother you?"

"No. Does it bother you?"

"Actually, kind of. I feel sorry."

"It's fine. Really." He points his form at my plate. "Eat. You're going to need energy."

"For what?"

"*Bon appetit*, Agent."

CHAPTER 23

KEATON

*T*aylor knows Baron's story, as do a few relatives I contacted when it was safe to do so. I don't see the harm in telling her, and I like her. I like the way she bites into the bloody steak after I tell her I was swimming in dog guts one morning. I don't tell her I was in those same clothes all the way to America, on an unregistered military flight. I don't tell her that I didn't want to take the clothes off because I didn't want Baron to be gone forever. I don't tell her I love dogs but can't bear to get another.

Maybe later.

Right now, she's wiping her mouth, looking away, eyes flicking to the exits out of habit. Her lashes brush her cheeks when she looks down at her food, strategizing the next bite. She's gorgeous, but that's a small part of her charm. The rest is inside her, and all I want to do is dig it out.

"What?" she asks, noticing that I'm staring.

"You came with me. To dinner. I thought you were going to hand me the wallet and send me on my way."

"I was hungry too."

"After everything I said, you could have eaten out of your own fridge."

She spears a green bean. "It had a ring of truth."

"Really?"

"Because…" She takes a deep breath. "I don't understand myself either. Why I feel like… I don't know, like you take up more space in my mind than you should. Whenever I'm in a room with you, I feel like you press against the world. My world. My attention. That makes no real sense, but you make no sense."

I reach for her hand, but she pulls back.

The effort required to tell her things she's not ready to hear is monumental. Crime is folded into the fabric of society, sure. I could argue that, but it misses the point, because so is crime-fighting. Also, we're past intellectual posturing.

"Where is your mother?" I ask gently.

"She died in a prison fight." She says it as if she's trying to cast off the pain of it. As if it's nothing. But she holds onto it at the same time, like a buoy of righteousness in an ocean of uncertain morality.

"I'm sorry. How old were you?"

"Sixteen. And there was a part of me, an awful part that I'm ashamed of, that was relieved to not visit her every other Saturday anymore. God, I'm a terrible person. I wouldn't blame you for walking out right now."

She can't look at me. Her self-abuse lights a fire under my already hot sense of protectiveness. I want to protect her from her opinion of herself, but if I jump across the table and shout her doubts away I'll make them worse.

"A sixteen-year-old girl probably wants to do fun things on Saturdays. Probably has to make up a story for her friends every other week about where she's going."

Cassie nods and bites back a quiver in her lower lip.

"The part of life when we define ourselves isn't a fitting time to be lying about who we are." I take her hand, and she lets me. "Trust me. I get it."

"It was awful there. Dirty. Someone always yelling. And the last time I saw her, I was so mad at her for leaving me, even though she wouldn't have if she could have helped it. But I was so sick of those visits and her stupid advice…" She wipes her cheek with the pads of her fingers. "I didn't know it was the last time, so I was kind of a bitch. Why am I telling you this?"

"Because you think I'm an amoral criminal." I hand her my handkerchief and she presses it to her eyes. "You don't have to impress me."

She doesn't respond to the charge, but carefully wipes away her tears and dabs her nose like a lady. I wonder if her mother or her grandmother taught her manners. I wonder if she learned them from observation or a desire to distance herself from her humble beginnings.

The waitress slips a fake leather folder in front of me and slinks away as if I might bite her. If she'd interrupted, I might have.

"Are you all right?" I ask.

"Yeah. This was kind of purging."

"You look…" I search for the right words. "Unguarded for the first time since we met. Your real self is beautiful on you."

"For now, at least. I'm emotionally disinfected."

I laugh as I open the folder.

"I have that." She stretches for the bill, but I snatch it away.

"Thank you, but I have it."

"Half then."

"I appreciate you wanting everything to be even." I reach for my wallet. "But I owe you."

"For what?"

I close the leather folder. I'm about to do something I said I wouldn't do when I walked into her house, but knew was unavoidable from the time she came through the door. "For what I'm going to do to your body tonight."

The crackle and tingle of her skin is practically audible.

CHAPTER 24

CASSIE

He helps with my coat, and we walk out to the parking lot. The last time we walked out to his car, he tried to steal a kiss and I flipped him for it. Wondering what he's going to do is as far as I get, because he's quicker this time. There's not a millisecond for a defensive move before his lips are on mine and his hands are on my face and his body is so close, all my thoughts basically melt into a warm puddle.

"All night," he whispers in my ear. "I want you all night. Now until the sun. You promised me I wouldn't sleep with you, and I plan on helping you keep that promise."

Which I want. I want it badly, and I want it before I lose my nerve.

Keaton kisses my cheek. His lips pull electrical current over my skin, crackling gunpowder sparks down my spine until they all land and ignite between my legs.

I don't push him away.

"I can get into trouble." I say it because I want him to talk me into it. Give me a single, simple reason to risk my career to feel his body against mine.

"One night."

That's his single, simple reason. Odds are good we can get away with a night, but can we keep it to just that? Won't it be worse? If it's good, how will I control myself?

I can wonder about the future all night. I can regret the past for the rest of my life. His voice and his scent are a hard call to *now*. His hands are a demand that I be *here*. I can't ignore it. I can't turn away from it. In the parking lot outside a Doverton restaurant, there's not a dream or ambition I ever had that doesn't involve Keaton Bridge.

"Not my place," I say. "And not your room at the club."

He leans away. Even in the ugly light, he is beautiful, scruffy-cheeked, angular, lupine in his appetite. "We'll take my car. I'll drop you off in the morning."

It can all be solved. I can have this. I can fold into tonight and disappear with him. In the morning, I can unfold back into my life.

I give myself the opportunity to change my mind, and decide I'm going for it. I don't want to go home. Something happened over dinner that needs to be consummated. No more unfinished business.

He takes out his phone and says one word. "Yes?"

"Yes."

He taps something into the glass while we wait for the car. When it comes, he puts the phone away.

"All arranged," he says beside the open car door.

I get in, and he pulls onto the highway.

"Where are we going?" I ask, trying not to knead my hands together. They make their own sign language. Only I can understand it. They're saying, *It'll be all right. It'll be all right.* When I clamp them still, they say, *You'll regret it if you don't.*

"Somewhere so secret, I bet you don't even know about it."

"I bet it's crime-scene perfect."

He flicks his signal and leans into the turn off the next exit. "I promise no one will hear you scream."

It's pitch dark on the service road. The cone of the headlights drown out color and movement, rendering the world in two dimensions. A two-lane strip cutting through flat, overgrown trees and bushes. No one will hear me scream, that's for sure.

My nerves are dumb and blind, humming hard in the frequency of arousal when they should be generating a rational fear that will trigger a plan to get the hell out of here.

Fear of being seen in this little archipelago of towns.

Fear of being taken to the unknown.

Fear of being left for dead.

He reaches for my hand, turning long enough to look me in the eye. "You all right?"

Should I lie? Should I tell him I'm not afraid of the fact that I'm not afraid? That my confidence in him is what frightens me? "I'm good."

"Good." He slows by a sign with nothing more than the Doverton Country Club logo. It's so small I wouldn't notice it in broad daylight. He turns into an invisible driveway.

"What's this?" I ask.

"The club keeps a bungalow behind the nature preserve."

He slows before we reach the white-and-yellow gate.

There are cameras. I find them without even thinking about it. The little red lights glow like single eyes. They don't make me feel safe from Keaton; they make me feel exposed to the conflicts of my decision.

He stops the car and reads my mind. "Do you want the cameras or no?"

"No."

"Good." His phone rests in his palm. He gestures to the camera to the left and taps his phone.

The red light blinks out. To the right. Same. The camera dies.

He pulls up to the gate and keys in a four-digit code. The arm goes up. I turn as we pass. The red lights flicker back on. I face front again, breathing easy.

A cute bungalow with a short porch and garden lights appears as we turn. He parks at the front door.

"Before we get too involved," I start.

"Yes?"

He shuts the engine. It's quiet. Dead quiet. Forest creatures are hibernating, and the crickets and insects are in their winter cycles.

"I don't have any condoms or anything." Which means I insist on them, and in the time it would take us to get them, I could change my mind. I might need that space to come to my senses.

"I have some."

I'm concurrently relieved and discouraged.

He opens my door, and we walk up the steps together. The little porch is outfitted with two chairs and a table, with potted plants in the corners. The pots have the club logo engraved on them. A little home in the middle of nowhere.

Keaton unlocks the door with a code. "Are you sure you're all right?"

"If I wasn't, you'd be on the floor with your arms behind your back."

"Indeed."

He shoves the door open and steps aside. A lamp is already glowing by the couch, illuminating comforting florals and homey paisleys. Behind me, Keaton shuts the door and yanks the cord on the blinds so they close like a stack of eyelids.

We are alone.

I've never done anything like this. I realize that when the door closes. I lost my virginity at seventeen to a "nice guy" named Mark Wayburn, who I stayed with for five years. Boring sex with a boring guy had been all I'd known. We broke up when I went to Michigan Law. He was afraid I'd make more money than him. That was an actual argument I was supposed to sympathize with. Then he couldn't stand the idea of being with a federal agent because he didn't believe in the federal government. I'd dodged a slow-moving bullet with that one, and I'd never looked back. I slept with a professor for a few months, a fellow student for a year, a seven-night stand with a guy I met in a bar. That was it, and it was never great.

Since entering the Bureau, I'd been too busy, too distracted, too ambitious to date. The few boyfriends I had after law school didn't last more than a few weeks. One-night stands don't suit me. The whole process is boring and unfulfilling.

I've never just gone to a hotel room for a night. And here I am, turning so a man can see me. Unlooping my coat's belt while he watches. His eyes run over the center of my body, where the placket opens as I unbutton. The rush of fluid between my legs is so fast it hurts.

I let the coat slip down my arms. He takes it and hangs it on the wooden coat hanger by the door. I swallow. I'm not wearing anything special, just a skirt and blouse. Work clothes. The way he looks at me makes me feel as if I'm in black lace.

"Go on." He takes his coat off efficiently, popping snaps and jerking it over his shoulders. "Take it slow."

He hangs the coat, then pulls the cuffs as if he has no intention of taking it off right now. He leans on the dresser and crosses his arms, nodding as if I can start any time now.

Where is the blind passion that inspired him to kiss me in the factory parking lot? Why are his folded arms and leisurely commands even more arousing? I'm a rule follower, but I'm not blindly obedient either.

At least, those are the things I believed about myself.

I unbutton my jacket. I want to rip it off, but I'm trying to go extra slow because I'm wondering how turned on I can get. My underwear is touching sensitive skin. I feel like a bullet the moment the hammer hits the primer and the gunpowder ignites.

I reach for the fabric stretched over my hips, ready to pull down the skirt.

"Your blouse next."

His voice reaches my ears just fine, but that's not where it has the most effect. It vibrates everything below my waist, and my obedience comes not from the mind but from my bones. I fumble with the buttons. Undo two. Pull it over my head. I toss it away.

When I look at him, in my pale pink cotton bra, his arms are still crossed and the bulge in his pants is unmistakable. It's then that I know I don't need to drown this in kisses and unconscious decisions. I'm here for the night.

"You're very sexy, Agent Grinstead." He leans hard against the dresser and crosses one ankle over the other. Mr. Casual with a boner the size of a Glock.

"Thank you."

"Have you ever been properly fucked?"

"Can I get back to you tomorrow on that?"

"Get that skirt off and we'll see."

"Are you getting undressed?"

"In good time."

I pull down my skirt and kick it away. I have no idea what

underwear I put on this morning and I can't get my eyes off his erection long enough to check. When he takes a fast step toward me, I hold out my arms and get ready for a kiss. My lips are disappointed, but my mind is too busy to register the fail, because the floor disappears from beneath me as he scoops me in his arms. My lungs empty in one gasp.

Then he kisses me, laying his lips on mine as if asking for permission. With my fingers running through his hair and the movement of my mouth, I give it to him. His kiss is languid, patient, grateful. It's the prologue of the night, telling me what's inside these hours together.

The story is about us. About the outside world's irrelevance. We are two bodies existing in a time outside the troubles of our choices. He carries me through the living room to a closed door. He opens it with the hand that's under my knees.

It's a closet. We laugh.

"I'm an idiot."

"You haven't been here before."

I kiss him, and he kicks open the next door. It's the bedroom, and he lays me on the floral duvet. Slipping his arms from under me, he drags his fingers over my belly, my underwear. I put my hands on his chest as he bends his fingers around the ends of the panties, to the crotch, where he slides them underneath. I'm so wet and bursting, I nearly come when he touches me.

His breath is hard when he feels it. "My God." Curling his fingers around the crotch, he pulls down, exposing me. "I don't know where to fuck you first."

"You looking for suggestions?" Everywhere. He can fuck me everywhere.

Taking his finger from between my legs, he puts it in his mouth, curving his lips around it. He sucks me off him, then he kisses me. I taste myself, the sex, the arousal, the flavor of my musky tingling thighs.

I sit up on the bed. He undoes his belt. I quickly slide off my underwear. When I look back up at him, his cock is out in its full glory.

This erection is mine. I move his shirt tails out of the way and take it by the base.

"Have you ever been properly sucked?" I ask before running my tongue along the length of him and kissing the dot of salty juice off the tip.

He smiles down at me. "We'll tally that tomorrow too."

I hate to overpromise and under deliver. So I take him with my tongue, then lock my mouth around him, and suck on the way out. Slowly. I work him deeper and deeper into my throat, opening it for him, breathing and going in again. He pulls his shirt over his head, and I reach up with damp fingers to touch his flat stomach and grip his hard waist as I pull him in.

He groans, whispers to God, then jerks away with a gasp.

"Votes are in," he says, letting his pants drop. "I was never properly sucked before tonight."

He crawls on top of me and kisses me. My pussy can sense how near his dick is, noting its placement like a flower turning toward the sun. He pushes up my bra, kisses my tits, moves down, and now the placement of his tongue on my inner thigh is the sun and my body is a garden, focused on a moving source.

When he runs his tongue along my seam, my back arches.

"That's my girl," he says before he slides two fingers inside me and runs his tongue over my clit.

I dig my fingers into his hair, crying out when he sucks the tip. He opens my legs so wide, they hurt in the best way.

"I'm—" I can't finish, but I want to tell him I'm close.

He reads my mind, saying, "Give me what's mine."

I come in his mouth, pumping and squirming, digging my fingers into his bare shoulders. When I push him away, he kneels above me and wipes his mouth with his wrist. A condom packet sticks out between two fingers. I have no idea where he extracted it from or when he did it, and I don't care.

"I'm on the pill," I say.

His expression is a question as his hands freeze over his mouth.

"I'm not with anyone, at all," I add. "It's just that I don't want to be the latest single mother in my family."

"An abundance of caution is something I admire in a woman." He rips the packet open. "I hope you can admire it in me."

"Your hope is my reality."

In the seconds it takes him to slide on the condom in his abundance of caution, we connect not over how interesting our differences are, but in the values we share.

"Can you remember something for me?" he says as he wedges his hips between my legs.

"Do I look like a reminder app to you?"

He arches over me. I spread my legs wider for him, sighing when his weight and force press against me.

"You are the sexiest reminder app I've ever tapped."

I laugh, but I'm cut off when he enters me, and my giggle turns into a groan. I just came three minutes before, but my body responds as if it's already hungry for another. My fingers dig into his biceps. I have to be taking skin. He has to feel it. But he's controlled and slow, running his lips over my face and neck.

"Dee-seven-four-nine,' he says into my ear.

"What?"

"Repeat it, love. When you know it, I'll let you come."

"Dee-seven-four-nine." That was easy.

"Ex-four-two-two-eye."

"Ex-four—"

"From the beginning." He drives in harder, and the pleasure across his face is unmistakable.

"You're joking. I…"

The words die on my lips when he stops and raises himself so we can see each other. His bemused smirk is more telling than a hundred status reports. He wasn't joking. Not at all.

"What am I memorizing?"

"What's the fun if I tell you now?"

I'm irritated, but also turned on by his little game. I like his control, and I like his attention. He could just blow his wad, thank me, and walk away.

"Dee-seven-something… I forget." I run my hands over his chest, over the patch of hair in the center, scratching downward.

"From the top then." He relishes my forgetfulness, thrusting into me with each character. "Dee-seven-four-nine-ex-four-two-two-eye."

I repeat after him, and he gives me a push with each syllable. By the time I get to the last one, the pressure between my legs is massive.

"You're very close," he says. I nod with heavy lids. "That won't do."

He leans forward and gets his arms behind me, lifting me. When he places me on my feet, his dick frees itself. I'm not disappointed long. Gently, he guides me to the dresser and kicks my legs open. I bend over it. My face is inches from the mirror when he enters me from behind. He's deeper and I'm wider. The discomfort quells the arousal, which must be his plan.

He puts his hand on my lower back and repeats the sequence, driving slowly inside.

I get to "Ex" before descending into grunts.

"Finish."

"Four-two-two-eye."

He cups his hand under my jaw until I'm facing the mirror. "Again."

I repeat it, not knowing what or why, but loving every minute of it.

"Good girl."

"Do I get the prize?"

He fucks me hard enough to push me to the edge of the dresser. "Maybe. Keep your eyes on us, and repeat it before I tell you the rest."

I repeat it over and over, realizing he can add as many random numbers and letters as he wants to as I realize my memorization of them is the only thing between that moment and an earth-wrecking orgasm.

In the mirror, he looks down at my ass. His hands slide along my sides, my outer thighs, and work inward. He uses both hands to reach around and spread me apart.

"Very good," he says after I finish it for the third time. "Tee-six-zero-twenty-four-twelve-el."

On the third to last, one of his hands finds my clit.

"I can't," I gasp. "I-I-I…"

"Tee. Not eye."

He repeats it, and when I don't answer, his finger and his hips stop.

"I hate you," I tell him in the mirror, meaning something completely different.

"From the top."

I can barely breathe. I'm totally under his control and mad as hell.

I also love it.

I start with "dee" and he pounds me, stopping when I stop. Rubbing and fucking when I continue. When I stumble, he pinches my clit and I scream in pain and pleasure.

"Six," he says, and I finish all the way to "el."

"Again."

I know he'll let me come if I keep repeating it, and I'm right. I'm in a cyclone of pleasure, with the number sequence in the center cone, anchoring me. I say the number and letter sequence over and over. Far away, I hear him telling me how good I am. How sexy. How I've overwhelmed his senses.

I hold back until I finish a sequence and let go, shuddering under his touch, filled with him. My knees bend until my toes are holding my weight, and Keaton has to hold on tight to reach around me. I'm an automatic weapon, discharging over and over, hot in the hand, until I'm spent and empty.

"Thank you," I say.

"My pleasure." He kisses my back and holds my chin up again. We're two faces in the mirror. "Watch me."

"Yes. Okay."

I get up on my elbows. In the mirror, he straightens and takes my hips in his hands. He strokes twice, as if taking aim, then fucks me in a rhythm meant for his pleasure alone. I watch him in the mirror. Our eyes meet as he slams deep inside me. His jaw tightens. His eyelids droop. I watch him push as far inside as he can go, grabbing the flesh of my hips, pulling me toward him. He's lost control. His refinement is gone. He's lost all sense, making himself completely vulnerable inside me. There's nothing scary about him now. He's not a threat or a nemesis. He's not an asset. He's helpless.

That feeling lasts for a minute as he curves his body over mine and catches his breath.

"I think I forgot the numbers," I say.

"No, you didn't." He stands and lightly slaps my butt. "Try it."

I rattle them off.

"Brilliant." He kisses my back and steps away from me.

I turn, stand. My body aches in the most delightful way. "I'll never write the number twenty-four again without thinking of you. You might own the letter D."

He twists the end of the condom into a knot and drops it in the little pail under the vanity. His naked body is long enough to reach across half the room. "The night is young. I can give you feelings about the entire alphabet."

"That's some kind of access code, right? To the Third Psyche forum?"

"Nope." He wraps his arms around my waist and kisses my shoulder. "But you should remember it anyway."

"Dee-seven-something-something-ex-something?"

He pinches my side, and I squeak. He tickles me until I writhe, giggling onto the bed.

He kisses my lips. "Let's start over. Shall we?"

CHAPTER 25

CASSIE

The bathroom light makes a tinny sound when it's turned on. The fan whirrs. Soap, shampoo, deodorant sit on the counter in single-use containers.

Like me, stuffing feelings for Keaton into a single-use container.

I look like a hostage. I haven't slept more than an hour. I'm sore. Sticky. My hair is a rat's nest.

I've been rendered stupid and dull by orgasms. Even though I can barely put together a string of words in my head, I remember the code Keaton gave me. I turn on the shower, stretch my arms over my head to crack my shoulders and spine. Check the water. Ice cold. I get in quickly and I'm shocked awake.

That's better.

I don't rush, forcing myself to get used to the cold.

Best sex you ever had.

The clarity of the thought comes as I'm cleaning between my legs. I've been sore before, but never so happily sore.

I let the water soak my hair, freezing out the disappointment, washing away the desire for more, for things to be different, for our options to sunset later in the day.

One: He's a hacker. The FBI can't prove it today, but everyone knows it. I could lose everything I've worked for.

Two: My feelings are irrational, and I know it. I don't trust them.

Three: There is no three. Two is enough.

I stay in the shower until I'm shivering.

Three: You don't even know his real name.

I shut off the water. I don't regret last night, but I might regret it being our last night.

I get out and wrap a towel around me. It's soft and warm. The door is open a crack. I can see the front of the house through the opening. The blinds glow with the dark blue of sunrise's beginning, and the end table light is still on.

The front door opens, and I clutch the towel tightly around me. I'll let it go to spring at an intruder, but it's not necessary. It's Keaton with a tray. He's fully dressed, and nothing about him makes him look like a hostage. He looks like a man who has had a full night's sleep and just decided not to shave because the scruff made him even more handsome.

He slides the tray onto the table and smiles when he sees me peeking through the bathroom door. He crosses the bedroom and leans in.

"Does the hot water work?" he asks, not looking at my legs or my bare shoulders. Right in my eyes, like a gentleman when it's time to be a gentleman.

We'd agreed that he'd take me home right away so I could change for work, but now I want to call in sick.

"I don't know," I say. He raises an eyebrow, not understanding the answer, so I continue. "I didn't try it."

"It's freezing in here."

"I made you break your promise. I slept, but I'm awake now."

"Indeed you are." He smiles, and only then do his eyes drift. "Hurry, then. No puttering about. I got breakfast."

I quickly put on yesterday's clothes and go into the small dining room. It's ringed with tall windows overlooking a little yard and the forest that surrounds the club. One of the hotel's golf carts bounces down the driveway, back to the main house.

Eggs, bacon, toast are set up on the table.

"It's nice that they send room service out here."

"Anyone will do anything for a price." He pulls out a chair for me. "You were in there a long time. I'm surprised you didn't catch your death. Sit. Please."

I sit because I'm hungry, and because I don't want to leave this idyllic little bungalow just yet.

Keaton sits kitty-corner from me and puts eggs and toast on a plate. "I'm afraid the eggs might be cold."

"That's all right." I take the plate. While he makes his own, I peek into one of the two hot pots. Tea. I pour for him.

"Cheers," he says instead of *thank you*. Before I can get the second pot, he pours me coffee.

"Cheers," I say, instead of *I want you*.

The air is thick between us. I work backward from when I'm expected at the office and calculate Keaton and I have twenty minutes to eat.

I want to tell him he was wonderful. I can do that in twenty minutes. Outside, the winter wind flexes its muscle, knocking tree branches against each other, sending long-settled leaves clicking over the ground.

I want to tell him I'm conflicted. He's risky. *We're* risky. I don't trust him, but I want him. That code he made me memorize and won't define —it intrigues and scares me. I want him to soothe me, reassure me, clarify his feelings if he has any.

I can't do all that in twenty minutes.

The eggs are cold. I don't mind. His presence is warm enough for a few dozen cold eggs.

"So." I stab a lump in the scrambled eggs and put it onto a triangle of toast. "How long are you in town?"

The question is absurd. I feel as if I'm in a bad movie. He does me the favor of ignoring it.

"I want to see you again."

He utters the sentence as if it had gotten impatient at the back of the line and shoved a dozen other sentences aside. Yet when I look at him, he's not trying to cover up or choke back what he said. He means what he says and says what he means.

I go for the least emotional but most honest form of the truth. "I don't know how to make that happen." I'm about to take another bite of eggs, but I put down my fork. "When you gave me that Post-It, you became a federal asset."

"You mean a snitch?" He's smiling as if the word doesn't bug him at all.

"Call it whatever you want, but there's the issue of payment."

He leans back, laughing. "Please keep the taxpayer dollars."

"Not all payment is in cash."

The air goes out of the room. I can't look at him. My eggs suddenly look like yellow snot and the bacon fat is gathering in my throat. He's silent. All I can hear is my heartbeat and the *click* of the leaves in the wind. When I swallow, it's with effort.

He needs to say something, anything. Give me an opening to tell him I'm in this bungalow because I want to be, not because I'm selling myself. But my jaw is glued shut. I'm locked by inertia. I can't deny it out of thin air. I can't explain without a push.

"I'll wait in the car." He gets his jacket and bag. His movements are graceful and unaffected by anything I might confuse with tension or offense.

Does he care that I implied I had sex with him as payment? Did he even catch the inference?

Does it matter? We're a one night thing for a reason. I won't sabotage my life by getting involved with a man, only to be left by a man, but that doesn't mean I spent the night with him for any other reason but desire. If I run out there and explain that I'm with him honestly and that my concern with payment was no more than a concern about appearances, what will I achieve? Nothing. Another turn around the hotel when he comes again, more worries about how to fill out the forms, and I have to face the fact. If he gives me another piece of intel, I may not actually be sleeping with him for information, but it'll feel like it.

When I get outside, he's standing by the passenger side of the car. He opens the door.

"I didn't mean what it sounded like." I can't get into a car with him without addressing this. I'm not made of stone.

"I know."

I get in, and he closes the door. He gets in on the driver's side. He knows, but nothing's changed. By the time we're on the highway, he hasn't said a word and I'm on round three of beating myself up.

It's a TKO on the interstate.

"You know what's really stupid?" I say finally.

"What?"

"I've given you more trust than I've given any man. But you…" It would be great if I could organize my thoughts coherently. "I don't date a lot because I don't like wasting my time. If I don't like a man right away, I don't bother, so believe me, there's not a lot of bothering happening. And don't get me wrong, I didn't like you. But then I did and now I do, but the obstacles are real and that's all I'm saying."

He gets off my exit. "And I told you that I know."

"So?"

"So. You're right."

Right. I'm right. He knows I'm right and I know I'm right. He'd wanted to see me again, but in the front seat of the car, he's just a guy driving and talking. He's not looking at me. He's not reassuring me. He's not saying he wants to see me despite all of it.

So.

I'm right.

"Should I drop you on the corner?" he asks.

Because of the context, that question hurts more than anything anyone ever said to me. It means he's heard me, understood me, and agreed with me. I should be happy. I'm not. My lips have been kissed raw, and I'm so sore, I can't cross my legs. I can't shake the feeling that I've lost something I would have treasured. My mother missed only a few marks in her day. The amount of loss she felt was related to how close she came to making the catch. She said there was nothing worse than having the fish on the boat and letting it slip off the deck, unless it was already in the bucket and it tipped and slid back to the sea.

"The corner's fine."

He pulls up to the curb at the end of my street.

How close are Keaton and I to being fish in a bucket? Are we even caught? Were the muscles in my cheek ripped from the metal barb? Or had we both seen a lure and run away before getting bitten by the hook?

"I'd let you out," he says, "but that defeats the purpose of letting you out on the corner."

"No. You're good." I pull the handle and let the door swing halfway while I take a second to look at him. The perfection of early morning has worn off. He seems tired. Confident, handsome, and assured, but tired. "I enjoyed myself last night."

"I know." He lets the two words hang in the air. "I did too." There's nothing left to say, but as I shift my weight to get out of the car, he grabs my forearm. "I have to go back to California on business. When I get back, I'll be in touch."

"Is that a good idea?"

Say yes. Say yes. Say yes.

"Don't assume I care about the Federal Bureau of Investigation. Or the government. Don't assume I'll ever let the *law* come between us. I don't give a bugger about it. I don't give a shit how it looks or ethics or any of it."

"What do you care about?"

"Those things, but only because you care. I won't be the man who makes your life harder. I want to tell you something, and I'm tired enough to tell you the truth."

I lean against the back of the seat, but keep one foot on the asphalt. "Okay."

"No matter what happens, never, ever believe I abandoned you. You can forget me. I can go into the dustbin with every other man who wasn't worth you. I don't care. No matter what happens, I didn't desert you. Say you understand."

"I understand." I only say it because he asked me to, not because he's making sense.

"Say you believe me."

"I believe you, but I don't know what you're talking about."

He runs his hand along the length of my arm. "You will."

I say it because behind his words lie his intentions. He cares what I think of him. He wants me to think highly, and I do.

"When? Because you're freaking me out."

"Not today or tomorrow. Possibly never. Remember the promise that this was for one night?"

"Yeah."

"I lied to you. I never wanted this for one night. You're talking about a transaction, and I'm telling you, I've been around the world and I've never met a woman like you. You're cop and criminal. You're subtle and direct. Everything I know about you is the opposite of something equally true. You're a coin flipping in the air and I never know if you're coming up heads or tails."

"What if I have to hurt you? What if it's heads and you called tails?"

"I'm infatuated with your head and your tail, darling."

The stupid pun deserves an appreciative laugh, but it comes out sad and broken.

"I promise you," he says. "I'm going to disappoint you. I'm going to hurt you. But not today."

He kisses me, but it's not the kiss of a man who will never see me again. It's the kiss of a man promising more. I don't want more, but I do. I was lying to myself from the beginning. I was both the architect and the mark of my own long con game.

"I'm not dropping you off at the corner next time."

I nod. "Next time then."

I get out of the car and walk home in last night's clothes.

When I open my front door, I turn around, let the screen door shut, and watch his car drive away.

CHAPTER 26

CASSIE

*—Be ready 5pm on Friday. We're
going on a short holiday—*

Keaton's text comes in the late morning. The geographic tag puts him in Uzbekistan, where he couldn't have gotten to in the last few hours. He's cloaking his whereabouts.

There's a guy you can depend on.

I sit at my desk with a deep feeling of sadness. My life hasn't changed one bit from even twelve hours before. But I've changed. I've gotten stupid.

His text weighs on me. Every sip of coffee, every answered email, every time a bird chirps outside, I'm aware of the minutes that pass without me responding.

I don't know what to say. I don't know what he intends. I'm afraid that if I answer him, I'll discover another facet to him and I won't have a choice but to see if that's the last level of complexity to Keaton Bridge.

I want him. I know that. I don't know how to want him. I don't know how to let myself make it possible.

I write down the letters and numbers he made me memorize. I try a few things that fail, but after that, I don't know what to do with them, and to be honest, if I did know, nothing would change. Once I use whatever information he gives me, he's an asset and I'm cutting off the possibility of a relationship. There would be paperwork and questions. Until then, he exists in the netherworld between a problematic tryst and an ethical lapse.

—Be ready 5pm on Friday. We're
going on a short holiday —

My chest is a balloon filling, squeezing the walls of my heart tighter and tighter. I'll touch something—a piece of fabric, the silicone grip of a new pen, the smooth glass of my computer monitor—and wonder if he's thinking about me. Does he feel the creases in his bedsheets, the damp warmth of a coffee cup, the yielding inside of a loaf of bread and think of me? Because I think of him. I want to stop, but I can't. I text him back and hit Send before I think too hard.

— You're going to make it all the way
from Uzbekistan by Friday? —

—An ocean cannot separate us —

"You all right?" Frieda says as she passes my desk.

"Fine." I put my phone facedown.

"The pay grade packet's going to be late. Coming on Monday."

"Maybe they were waiting for Ken to get mobile. He'll get his transfer when they announce, I guess." I look up at her. She's clutching her coffee cup, and her one eyebrow is shorter for being knotted in the middle.

"And I'm sure you will too. One hundred percent. You earned it."

"We should have some preemptive champagne this weekend." My voice is flat, because one, I'm not getting promoted, and two, making plans with her means I'm not going to have a bag packed on Friday at five.

"Nope." She thwarts all my quickly laid plans. "I won't jinx it."

Sometimes, I wish Frieda wasn't so superstitious.

Now isn't one of those times.

CHAPTER 27

KEATON

*G*et a handle on yourself, man.

I tell myself this about every fourteen seconds. I feel unglued. I blame this feeling on the fact that she and I have unfinished business, but I fear it's *her* I miss.

I flew into San Francisco for a simple meeting with an agenda that had been set, but I needed to change everything. Every step into the stone courtyard and every click of my heels on the marble floors of the British consulate is a punctuation in the paragraph of my revised intentions.

By the time I'm in the waiting room, I'm dissatisfied with what I have done for her and with her. I'm dissatisfied with what I've taken, what I've given, and what I've sacrificed, and I don't know what to do about it. I only know I need more time to do it.

Betty, the receptionist, has a master's in political science. She knows me. She knows I'll refuse tea, but she offers it anyway and goes about her work. The leather chair squeaks under me when I shift. I don't know what to do with my body. It wants to be inside Cassie, smell her, taste her, feel her texture from the lining out. I start to consider crazy things, then stop myself.

I'm not here to ruin her life, but if I keep thinking about taking her with me, I most certainly will. She'll be separated from her grandmother, the only family she has. She'll be torn away from the job she's dedicated her life to. All the work she's put into separating herself from her mother's criminal past will be wasted.

This is not about me. This is not about what I want. This is about her. And I hate it. I hate it with a bloody rage I can barely contain. I tap my fingers on the wooden arm of the chair, cross about leaving without her, panicking about staying with her.

I remind myself that I don't panic. It's not in my repertoire.

All I ever wanted was to go home. That's all I've been driving toward for the past three years. And now I've added another contingency to something that is already nearly impossible to plan.

I'm a patient man. My plans are incremental. Long term. I am not a child.

But she makes me want to throw it all away.

"David," the ambassador says as he shakes my hand. He's a greying man with the friendly mask and calculating eyes of a diplomat. We walk toward his office. "How's the factory coming?" He closes the door behind us. "On schedule, I hope."

His office has been the same since I was a boy, with leather books, leather chairs, deep-green wallpaper, and a Persian carpet his father brought home from his days as a Field General.

I can tell he does not have good news. I sit.

He snaps a glass off the bar. "Whiskey?"

"You ask me that every time."

"This time you may need it."

"Are Mum and Dad all right?"

"Right as rain, far as I know. You should call them." The bottle clicks on the edge of his glass. "Tell me about QI4."

I sit in the leather chair I always sit in, and he unbuttons his jacket before sitting across from me.

"You know Taylor," I say. "He's not building a factory, he's building an empire."

"I trust he can take care of it."

"He can."

"Good." He folds his hands in front of him. "Because we have a change of plans."

Hope races with fear and wins, taking a victory lap before I utter the first word. "How much so?"

"There's chatter. It may be nothing. The bureau and some white supremacists got in a row?"

"With guns, apparently."

"Right. Chatter's about your involvement."

"Mine?" I press my fingertips to my chest as if I can defend the idea that I had nothing to do with it.

"Kaos thinks it was you."

With the simple utterance of a boastful Internet name, the sparks of hope sputter out and the fear catches fire. I know the real identity behind the avatar. I know that I have alerted him to the fact that I'm not who he thinks I am, or for that matter, who anybody thinks I am. This is why I'm so careful, and this is why looking for Third Psyche must have opened Kaos's eyes to what was in front of him all along.

"He's paranoid." I'm stating the obvious.

"Indeed. But you knew once you went visible with Taylor Harden, they'd stop trusting you. And now that we know Kaos runs Third Psyche, we can see just how paranoid he is."

Kaos is very dangerous. I've worked with him, so I know. But I want to get this discussion over with so I can tell the ambassador I need another month or two. I can't disappear so soon.

"The fact that I didn't sell him out to the FBI is irrelevant, I presume."

"Well…" The ambassador takes a swig of his whiskey and clicks his glass down. "It wasn't anyone. He mucked it up himself and needs someone to blame."

All I can think about is the positive. All I gravitate toward is the hopeful. In no time at all, I've become a little boy in the park throwing sticks with his dog. Everything is just roses and honey cakes. The future is all possibilities.

"Is everything still in order?" I ask.

"Yes, but we have to move the timeline."

"I need more time," I say before he can tell me where he's moving it. I don't even recognize my voice, it's so calm, so flat, so businesslike in its denial of my actual emotions. "I need to stay another few months."

"You're leaving in two weeks."

I don't have extra weeks or months or years to spend with Cassie or anybody. I won't be able to set Taylor up completely, but he doesn't need me. Not really. And if I'm being honest with myself, Cassie doesn't need me either.

What I need has changed. My hope illustrated that a little too clearly.

It's as if I've learned nothing since the morning I slipped in my dog's guts and MI6 relocated us for our safety.

"What?"

"You'll have a fresh passport. New name. Bank account. Everything as planned, but sooner. You're going to die in a fiery crash instead of drowning, if it's all the same to you. Your parents are looking forward to seeing you again."

"I need…" I drift off. I miss them.

I need more time.

I need to see if what I feel for her is real.

"You need to make sure you've done what you wanted for Taylor."

Taylor? Shit. He'll be fine.

The ambassador leans over and folds his hands in front of him. His right middle finger taps the wedding band on his left hand. "We have moles in Kaos's operation telling us he feels particularly betrayed by your new habit of doing the FBI's bidding. It's a damn near obsession."

"He and I had a lot of good times. He's leaning on them."

"If you're defining 'good times' as moving money and guns, then I don't think he's leaning on any actual warm feelings."

"Funny how I was never actually the mole."

"Maybe he's realizing what you actually were." He picks up his glass again, rolling the bottom edge on the table before taking a sip. "Be that as it may, we're working on neutralizing him."

"You haven't been able to neutralize him in twelve years. What makes you think you can do it now?"

"He's after you, and that creates a vulnerability. A sniper has to stick his head out to see his target. That's our opportunity. The plan is, you disappear for a couple of days. He'll try to find you, we grab him."

"And if it works? We push my timeline further out?" That hope again, glowing like the last coal in the dying fire. The ambassador is discussing life or death, and I seem to be guided by the unpredictable dictates of my dick. But that's not fair, not even to my dick. It's my heart that's doing the hoping.

"If you like," the ambassador replies, opening his drawer and taking out a black thumb drive. "But you know these people are like roaches behind the cupboards. Just smash one against the counter and forty more will come out when you shut the lights."

"And here I am, thinking you grew up in Kensington."

He slides the drive across the desk. I pick it up, flipping it between my fingers. It's completely nondescript.

"We've been invested in your safety since you were a lad, and we protect our investments. You have a room booked in beautiful Las Vegas for two nights."

I groan. "My God, man. Vegas?"

"Lay low. Eyes open. When you're back, we'll discuss the timeline."

I'm about to leave when something occurs to me. "Are you working with the Yanks on this one?"

"Of course I can't say, but I can tell you what you already know. Keyser Kaos is targeting agents."

I know what he means immediately. He means the shootout, but he also means future tactics. I've never seen anyone on the dark web takes things more personally than this fucking crew.

"Ruthless, these fellows. Ruthless but not reckless. We'll get them. Don't fret."

Fret. He says it as if I'm worried the milk might be a little off. Or that Manchester United might choke at the last minute. Indeed, it's his job to make everything seem as though a stiff upper lip was a cure, rather than an attitude. I'm not in the mood. I want to get back to Doverton. I never thought I'd say those words, even to myself. But I need to look at Cassie. Make sure that she safe. And not just safe, but happy.

I'm going to fret long and hard until I know that any threats against her are neutralized.

"If you don't get them, I will." I stand and pocket the black drive. "Mark my words. I know I promised you that once I was gone, I wouldn't resurface to pay any old debts or get vengeance. I wasn't dishonest but if he's a loose end, I might turn myself into a liar."

"Trust us. We'll clear this up."

We shake on it, and though I trust his intentions, I don't trust that faith, luck, or some combination of incompetence and overzealousness won't leave Cassie Grinstead exposed.

That will not do. That will not do at all.

I text her from the building lobby.

—Be ready 5pm on Friday. We're
going on a short holiday—

I NEED to figure out Cassie before I go. I need to see her away from everything. To give us time to be us, then I'll know what to do.

I check my texts.

—You're going to make it all the way
from Uzbekistan by Friday?—

She noticed my VPN server's geotag. Clever, clever girl. How long will it take me to get to the end of my fascination with her?

— An ocean cannot separate us—

SHE HAS a black leather bag that she holds in one hand. Jeans, trainers, a V-neck T-shirt that shows just enough of what I'd love to get my lips on.

I get out, pop the boot, and take her bag. "You ready then?"

"Where are we going?"

"Las Vegas."

She claps three times and almost jumps up and down. She's on tiptoes when she stops herself.

"I take it you like Vegas?"

"Never been." She's smiling like a Cheshire cat.

"Don't get knocked up!" Her grandmother waves from the front stoop in lavender polyester pants and white turtleneck with a teddy bear on it. She's wearing a down coat, slippers, and telling her granddaughter not to get pregnant.

"Not on my watch!" I shout back.

"Nice boy." She wags her finger at her granddaughter as if Cassie had told her I wasn't nice. Grandma obviously knows best. I could be brilliantly nice.

I slap the boot closed. "Your grandmother is a wise, wise woman. You should take her advice more often."

"I'm so sure." She waves at Grandma, who sits on an aluminum chair at the top of the steps. "I never asked what you guys talked about the other night," Cassie continues. "Or, actually even last night. What time did you get to my house? What did she tell you?"

"Aren't we curious?" I give her bottom an affectionate swipe as I pass to open the passenger side door.

She stands still in front of the door for a second, meeting my eyes before getting in. "We are. Mostly because you're a puzzle."

"She told me about your grandfather and how she wanted you to do better."

"I've already done better."

I have nothing to say to that. When she sits, I close the door, wave to her grandmother, and we're off.

CASSIE

"You can stay through Monday, no?" Keaton asks.

I can. I have a personal day I haven't taken from last year. "Y—wait. How did you know that?"

"Oh, please, Agent. You had your fingers all over my data. To wit—the direction of my school portrait and my results, which were quite adequate, thank you. If you can use your privileges as a federal agent to see if I am who I say I am, then I can use whatever methods I have at my disposal."

"I'm not a career criminal."

"Is that so?"

With three words, he shut me right up. My point was meant to land like a hammer but fizzled like a fuse without a firecracker at the end. I'd told him about my years of training in the arts of the long and short confidence game, and I was sure he hadn't forgotten the incident that ended with me sliding his wallet across a dinner table.

My ideas about who I am and who I was raised to be intersect where Keaton Bridge and I connect.

"Point in fact." I hold up a finger. "You're hiding something from me. I can't tell what it is, but there's something going on with you and that database. You're withholding. Omitting. Both. You can tell me now. Or I can figure it out. If I have to figure it out, I'm going to be really pissed off."

He turns toward me at a traffic light. Are his pupils dilated because it's getting darker? Or have I said something that causes a physical reaction? My skin tingles at the tips of my fingers and in the crevices between my legs. It's that dangerous side. The side I've challenged to speak truthfully. The side I've threatened with my anger. I fear this, and I like it. I want to scoop it up like a palmful of fresh water and drink from the heels of my hands as sheets of him spill down my forearms.

"Do not threaten me, my artful dodger." His voice is a little lower and as serious as a gunshot wound.

I am not afraid.

"You think you can take me in a fight?" I'm only half joking. I can take down bigger and better trained men. But I know he's not talking about hand-to-hand combat.

"If there is ever a time I don't tell you something, the omission is for your own good."

"What's that code you made me remember?"

"What code?"

I rattle it off.

"That code is everything you need to know," he says.

"Keaton!"

"Let's make a deal, love. You tell me everything that you have failed to mention. And I will tell you things you have no business knowing."

"You know I can't talk freely about my job."

"I can't talk freely about mine either. You know what you're involved with here." He taps his middle finger on his sternum. "And I'm pretty clear about what I'm involved with." He reaches for me, glancing over so he can place his fingers on my sternum.

The touch isn't sexual. It is unexpectedly tender. The startling nature of it makes my own hand react by joining his over my heart.

I'm in this too deep already. I slid down a muddy ravine into a surging river before my brain even registered that the dirt was loose. I don't even know if I ever had time to hold my breath before I was pulled away in it.

He puts his hands back on the wheel. "I have a list of things I want to do your body this weekend, and if I don't start ticking them off soon, we're going to be fucking deep into Tuesday."

His words seem heartening, but they're not. They suck. I'm not a "live for now" kind of girl. He knows that. If he doesn't, he's going to find out, because I can't visualize walking away from him, and I can't strategize a way to make it work unless he's fully forthcoming.

"Is there something wrong with fucking on a Tuesday?"

"I have a separate list for then." He winks.

I hate it when guys wink. Winks are ways to assure me that I'm not seeing the whole picture and everything's taken care of. But he's different in this too. His wink is a devilish hint, not a way to shut me up.

When Keaton Bridge promises mischief, there's a good chance mischief will occur.

I'm satisfied for the moment that I'm not going to have to walk away from him after Vegas. I'm also confident that I can chip away at his secrecy if he gives me enough time to do it. Maybe enough time to figure out if he's been in the FBI database out of more than curiosity.

As a woman—not a federal agent—I want to know where his interest in me lies. I don't know if I can ever make him believe that painful truth.

CHAPTER 29

KEATON

The commercial airport is one hundred sixty miles away. We'll get into Vegas late.

We're almost on the highway when she plugs her phone into my dashboard. I stiffen as if she's pulled a gun on me, then I try to hide it. I never plug my devices into anyone else's without the explicit intention of stealing information from it. I want to scold her for being so careless, but I don't want to start the trip on a bad foot. I also wouldn't mind acting like a normal person for a change. I wouldn't mind trusting someone. With her phone plugged in as she flicks her hands along the glass of her phone, this feels more intimate than what we did in a bungalow in the woods, or the time she threw me against the side of the car because I tried to kiss her.

What about that time she picked your pocket?

The connection between her phone and my stereo is like a mosquito bite I can't scratch. It's against every protocol I've ever set for myself out of necessity, but an equally urgent necessity drives me to shut the fuck up about it.

"I made a playlist of driving music," she says. "Actually, two playlists. One with old stuff and one with new stuff. Which would you prefer?"

I admit to being a little enchanted about the idea of driving music. Of course, I went to high school in New Jersey, where one takes long, short, and intermediate drives to Bon Jovi and Bruce Springsteen. It's not a foreign concept. But I've never actually taken a long drive to actual driving music.

The stereo is controlled by a pane of glass in the center of the dashboard. She taps it.

"Which ever one your lovely hand is stroking right now."

"You're a scoundrel, my good sir!" She says it with probably the worst accent I have ever heard in my life. No one would confuse her for British. "You get the new stuff. Cheerio!"

An anthem of guitar and vocals get the star treatment from my speakers. With the playlist going, she should be leaning back and looking out the window or making small talk. But she's not. She's playing with the screen on my stereo. What the hell is she looking for? The nuclear codes? My bank account number? At seventy miles an hour, I glance at her and she glances back for a second before I put my eyes back on the road.

"What do you think you're looking at?" I ask as casually as I can.

"I have never heard of any of this music. Is it music? You listening to books or something? Spoken word poetry? What the hell? Is this even English?" She mangles the pronunciation of an Icelandic band, and I know, just know for certain, she isn't trying to hack my car.

"I'll have you know most of the music produced and released in the world is not in English."

"Well, fancy that!" Her British accent, if at all possible, has gotten worse in the past minute. She gobbles up her vowels like a multisyllabic glutton, sticking her Ts as if there's glue on her tongue and flattening the tones with an aural steamroller.

Yet I am more than charmed. I don't want to hear her British accent ever again, as long as I live. But having heard her hideous rendition, I appreciate her natural American steamroller-vowel-gobble. I want her to talk more. I want to hear her history in her voice. All the words, but not the words. I want to hear the fingerprint of who she is inside of what she says and how she says it.

"Have you ever been to London?" I ask, stopping myself before I tell her I want to take her there. I can't guarantee her anything, but I want to promise everything.

"Nope. I haven't been much of anywhere. Virginia, Quantico for training. Ann Arbor. Dipped into Canada twice… uuh…Washington, D.C. I'm pretty boring."

"Do you want me to tell you that you're not boring? I don't usually invite boring women out for more than an hour for a quick shag."

She runs her hands along her thigh, smoothing out her jeans. I grab it and squeeze. She runs her thumb along the ridges of my fingers. This feels nice. This companionship with her on a drive.

"Where do you want to go?" I ask. "If you could go anywhere."

"Anywhere?" She looks out the window. "Like as a tourist?"

"Sure."

"I read about this place in Edinburgh. It's a whole city under the city."

"Mary King's Close?"

"That's it! I've seen pictures, and it's like a parallel universe, right under the streets. Have you been?"

"No."

She twists in her seat, forgetting about the stereo. "It's got huge rooms with stone arches and little rooms with beds where people died of plague, and a room full of dolls people leave for this little girl who's a ghost."

"You believe in ghosts?"

"Of course not." She sits straight. "But the idea of a room full of dolls underground is kind of cool. I loved dolls when I was a kid. That would have been heaven."

"I bet you were very cute with a dolly under your arm." I rest my hand in her lap and she takes it.

"When I was a baby, my mother used me to distract people while she robbed them."

"You must have been quite an adorable child."

"Yep. People literally paid money to coo at me. I was that cute."

I bet she was, and I wonder what her children will look like. A dangerous path, because there was a good chance they won't be mine.

I start by telling him the safest stories, and slide into the things I don't normally talk about. The years away from Nana were the hardest because she kept Mom honest, watching me while Mom was "working." She made sure I went to school, did my homework, ate and slept at regular times. But between the ages of seven and eleven, my grandmother lived on the other side of town. This was by design. She and my mother weren't speaking for reasons that had to do with an old boyfriend, my grandmother's unwillingness to reveal my mother's paternity past the name "Barry the Motherfucker," and probably plain old daily personality conflicts over the breakfast nook.

I don't often talk about those Nana-less years. My mother didn't abuse me in ways that were discernible. I never had a bruise, I was never raped by one of her boyfriends, she never neglected my basic needs. But there was one winter the furnace broke and she couldn't afford to fix it, so we slept in our coats. Another Christmas when she kicked her current boyfriend out for the way he looked at me in my pajamas. He tried to beat her, but she got lucky and cut his face open with a letter opener.

She's the reason I never assumed women were weak, but she's also the reason I want to fold between moments and disappear. She's the reason I came into adulthood with sins to expunge.

I try to make it all sound funny and interesting. I sprinkle in funny adjectives and make faces Keaton can't turn around to see. He doesn't judge or expect me to be ashamed when I tell him how a nine-year-old goes about picking a pocket or leading a mark to a con. He seems to appreciate that there are things my mother taught me that I never would have learned in a normal household. How to read people. How to understand the criminal mind. How to find backdoors and loopholes.

No, he doesn't "seem" to understand. He's a master at backdoors and loopholes. He's the king of not getting caught. He's a ninja at cleaning up his messes and covering his tracks. He doesn't have to tell me that, but I know it and it's more than an assumption. It's a common thread between us.

Two thirds of the way to the airport, he pulls into the rest stop to go to the "loo." It's not a bad idea. We meet on the outside of the convenience store attached to the gas station. He cracks open a fresh bottle of water and hands it to me.

The lights flood the parking lot. Everything looks yellow-green, and Keaton's eyes are a clearer shade of blue in this light. They move down my body as I drink and back up when I finish the bottle.

"Never seen a woman drink a bottle of water before?" I ask as I hand it back.

He chucks it in the recycling. "Not with such purpose."

He puts his hand on my lower back as we walk. I usually find this gesture infuriating, but I like the feel of him, the weight of his hand on me. Is this what chivalry really is? All the things that I can't stand, but from the right person? That doesn't seem quite fair, but if I tell him that I don't need to be guided across the parking lot, he'll move his hand, and I'll lose the warm security I feel when it's there.

I want to give him something for listening to me, for not judging me, for taking care of me in these small ways. I want to give him a gift.

When we're in the car, he locks the doors before kissing me. Together, we taste like water. Fresh, cold, new. He slides a hand under my shirt and I put mine between his legs. He's rock hard, sucking in a breath when I put pressure on it.

"This can't be comfortable," I say, pulling his belt through the buckle.

"It's not a big deal."

"I bet I can suck you off so quick we still make the plane."

"I don't—"

"Have to do a thing."

I have his dick in my hands. Thick, ridged with veins, so hard the skin is tight around the core.

"Suck it then," he moans, shifting low in his seat.

I bend over his cock, licking the salty drop of pre-cum away, replacing it with moisture from my tongue, sucking the end. He gathers my hair away while I work my way down him, opening my throat on the way in, giving him my tongue on the way out.

He whispers my name. "My God."

His pleasure inspires me to suck harder, picking up speed. I give my breathing a break, sliding my tongue along the length of his shaft, then with a sudden move, I take him as deep as I can. He releases a sharp *uh*, pushing down my throat.

Having him under my control, being solely responsible for his pleasure, drives me wild, and my consciousness drives to my own pleasure, where the seam in my jeans meets my core. A groan vibrates my throat.

I take his shaft in one hand and use my saliva to move it up and down with my mouth.

"Cassie." He's shuddering. His hands have stilled and now just press down. "I'm going to come."

I groan onto his cock again and come down on it, sucking on the way out.

"Wait. I'm. Going. To."

He's trying to be a gentleman, but I got this. I'm going to suck it right out of him.

"Fuck." His surrender has a beautiful sound. The sound of the wind in your ears during a freefall. The sound of jumping off a cliff with no guarantee of a net.

The base of his cock pulses under my hand as his balls empty into my throat. I taste him, bitter and sharp, sticky at the back of my tongue. I swallow and take more. All of it. All of him.

When his last drop is spent, I pick up my head. He strokes my hair reverently, pulling a single strand from the corner of my mouth.

"That was lovely," he says.

"Thank you." I sit straight.

He fishes a napkin from the glove compartment and wipes my mouth.

"Do you kiss a girl after she's had your dick in her mouth?"

He takes me by the back of the neck and kisses me deeply.

CHAPTER 31

KEATON

As we drive from the airport to the center of Las Vegas, I feel Cassie's excitement in the seat next to me. She squirms a little, leans forward as if she wants to see a little farther over the horizon.

Here's something we do not have in common. She's excited by this mess. Well, I can see that's not going to work. I can hang on that. I can engrave it into a plaque and nail it on the wall. Quote: "She likes Las Vegas." There we have it.

"I hear there's a fake Eiffel Tower," she exclaims. "And a big, fake Statue of Liberty."

"Yes. All that. And they're building a Big Ben."

"Oh! We can pretend we're in your hometown."

That is absolutely the last thing I want to do. Nothing feels less like London than Las Vegas.

"I should take you down to the shops under the Bellagio," I find myself saying. "They're quite nice. Quite posh."

What the hell am I doing? Las Vegas is hell, yet I want to give her tour. I want to show her all of the abominable sites and watch her find whatever happiness in it that she can. I just want to see her happy, full stop.

"Well, you can show me, but I'm not buying anything."

Maybe she won't, but I make no such promise.

524

CHAPTER 32

CASSIE

The Strip is amazing. I've seen crowded places and cities, but though I've seen pictures and videos, I'm totally unprepared for Las Vegas. I can barely keep in my seat. Everywhere I look, I see something I want to point at. The big stuff, sure. But it's the little things that are the most fun. The little bits of lights, the little details in the façades, the way people dress as if they're all on a permanent red carpet.

I can tell Keaton thinks I'm just adorable, and normally I'd want to punch him in the face for his knowing little smile. But he's driving, and also? The way he smiles isn't condescending. He's smiling because he can't help it. I've always tried to impress people with what I know, but here I am, charming somebody with what I've never seen.

He makes a right into a long circular driveway. Over a line of trees, an arc of water lifts into the sky as if borne by angels. Lights from underneath it renders it into a sparkling silver, and another one joins it, then another. They fall back under the tree line, surrendering to gravity.

I tap on my window. "Can we go there?"

"The fountain?"

"Yes."

"Your wish is my command."

I spin in my seat to face him. "Really?"

"I suspect I'll be sorry I said that."

Behind him, a valet in a burgundy jacket opens his door. The dome light goes on, and behind me, my door opens.

We're at the head of the circle, in front of a wall of glass doors leading into a massive golden lobby capped by multicolored glass flowers.

I get out. The crowd is a living thing with a controlled pattern of chaos. Clicking stiletto heels, sequins, silk tuxedo jackets with sneakers, cheap tourist sweatshirts fill a scene of mosaics—flowers—huge rotating glass doors in constant motion. I turn back to Keaton to share my delight, and he does. I can see it all over his face.

Our bags are already on a brass trolley being pushed by young bellmen.

Keaton leans down to whisper in my ear. "I got us a room overlooking the fountain. I'm going to fuck you while we watch it."

CHAPTER 33

KEATON

I walk slowly with her under the ceiling of multicolored glass flowers. I enjoy watching her that much. The way her eyes flicks from flashing light to flashing light, the slight smile, the way the exhaustion of the long drive falls off her body like a jacket in a warm room.

There's no way to get between the rooms and the outside, or restaurant and the bathroom, or between the parking lot and the show, or between heaven and hell without going through the casino first. The design of Vegas hotels is infuriating except when I am with Cassie. She slows down when she sees something, which is every fifteen seconds. Her lips part as if she wants to ask questions, but before she can, she moves onto the next thing.

"What's this?" she asks indicating a poker game.

"Have you never seen poker before?" I admit that I almost wish she'd never heard of the game, but it's unlikely.

"Of course I've seen poker before, you idiot."

"Sorry then, what was the question?" She looks at me slyly as if she doesn't believe that I didn't understand her. "I think your beauty has deafened as well as blinded me."

"Keaton Bridge, you are utterly full of shit."

She's right, of course. I am utterly full of shit under just about every other circumstance.

"This one." She indicates the small low-limit table to our left. I'm not off the hook to explain the game. "They remove their bets every time he shows a card. You're supposed to put money in, not take it out."

I put my arm around her and pull her close so that I can whisper in her ear. "It's for people with a soft stomach." The scent behind her ears is a garden of flowers. "You're not asked to bet on what you think you have. You show what you have and you take money away as you proceed to lose your nerve."

"What is wrong with people? Where is the fun in that?" She looks as if she's just eaten a rotten lemon, or swallowed a half a cup of cheap white vinegar. For a woman who seemed overwhelmed, amazed, enchanted, and even out of her depth, she is the mistress of this con game. She is the most artful of dodgers.

My lips linger at her throat, brushing the skin, tasting her as she tries to figure out who would want to sit at a poker table and not increase their risk. She tastes like a good bet, made at the right time, with a straight royal flush.

"What do you play?" I nip at the edge of her ear. "I'd like to know before I play you. I want to know how much of a risk-taker you are."

She turns halfway, looking at me with a sultry tilt to her head. "I like blackjack, but I wouldn't make too much of that. The hands are usually short and unsatisfying. And only a couple of cards can end the game."

A quick upward jerk of her eyebrows punctuates the entendre, and though a minute ago I wanted to watch her play cards, all I want now is to watch her come.

I slide my fingers down her arm and grasp her hand. "The tables are open all night."

"I might be as well."

That just about does it for me. I'm not waiting another second. I pull her to the lift.

CHAPTER 34

CASSIE

We get out on the top floor. There are six penthouse suites with doors at the far corners of the hall.

"I've never stayed in a penthouse," I say.

"First time for everything," he says as we step into the hall.

My skin misses him. The waters go still again, but they crave the rippling wake of his touch.

There's a door at the end of the hall. He drops behind a step, watching me as I walk in front of him. I feel his gaze appreciating me, wanting me as much as I want him. The door seems so far away, and I know that once we get to it, that look will turn into his hands and his body.

When I get to the end, he's on me from behind, pushing his body into me, his breath in my ear, his hand wrapped around my waist pressing against the fabric between my legs. "Are you ready?"

"For what?" I say playfully.

"To see the fountain from the penthouse, of course." He waves his card in front of the lock, and it clicks open. Then reaches around me and opens the door.

He slams the door, and I turn to face him.

529

I've seen Keaton look hungry before, but framed in the hotel doorway, he looks ravenous. Feral. Like a man with a single thing on his mind. And it's me. It's the barrier of my clothes and his. It's the space of the few feet between us. He looks as though he wants to tear those obstacles away and shatter them under him.

He's frightening, but I'm not scared. Maybe I am scared, but the fear doesn't make me want to run away. The fear makes me want to be captured.

I back up a step, and he steps forward. I realize I'm smiling. He must realize it too, because a mischievous grin spreads across his face.

From the window, I hear a boom and the first notes from an orchestra.

He unbuckles his belt and says, "That would be the show."

I turn my back to him and walk to the floor-to-ceiling window where the sound is coming from. The suite isn't dark, lamps are on, but I don't see a thing yet. Just the rectangle of the window overlooking the Las Vegas strip. I feel him behind me, those eyes, that feral look that has a physical presence, and hear his belt slip around his waistband.

Down below, the fountain is huge, and the jets of water stream to the sky in sync with Brahms' hallelujah chorus. It's beautiful.

The water jets boom with pressure, and his body presses against mine. He takes my hands and lays them flat against the windowpane. It's cool to the touch.

"Just stay still," he whispers, sliding his hands along my ribcage and hooking his thumbs in my waistband. "Enjoy the show."

I'm immobile only by his command, and I want to be. I want to watch the water fountain, and I want him to touch me as if I'm a pliant statue.

Reaching around to my front, he unbuttons my pants and pulls down the zipper. My stillness lets me feel every single brush of his fingers as he wedges his hands under my underpants and slides them to my mid thigh. I can barely breathe. He does it so slowly that I feel impatient, yet every single moment is a morsel to be savored.

I let out a whimper just as the chorus down below reaches its apex. The water drops to the surface in a mosaic of ripples and splashes. "Is it over?"

"Hardly."

Before he's even done speaking, another classical piece rises. I recognize it but don't know the name. A jet of water so powerful it almost reaches the top floor makes me gasp. Or maybe it's his hand running along my stomach and just barely touching the skin between my legs.

"My God, Keaton. I don't think I can really watch this if you do that."

"Believe me, there will be another show." He slips his middle finger between my folds. I almost lose my footing, and my hands slide down the glass a few inches. "You're pretty wet for a girl who wants to watch the fountain."

"Yes, I —" There's no end to the sentence, because two fingers slide from my opening to my throbbing nub and rest there.

A crowd has gathered around the fountain. They lean up against the gate on the Strip and on the hotel side. The suite is dark enough that I'm sure they can't see us, and we are on the thirtieth floor. But I like seeing them below. I like knowing that I'm doing this and they can't see me, but I can see them.

The skin of his dick pushes against my bottom. He's hard, thick. There's a brutality to his erection and how he pushes it against me that makes my eyes nearly flutter closed. The rush of blood between my legs drains the feeling from the rest of my body.

His hands run up my belly, under my bra, pushing it up until my breasts are free. He runs his hands back down and presses my lower back. "Take your bottom up, my dodger."

I do what he asks, watching the water explode with the rhythms, exposing myself to him. I feel as though I'm begging. And when he pulls my thighs apart until I move my feet, I feel as though my pleas have been heard.

"Are you ready?" He runs the head of his dick along my wet seam.

I jerk toward him as if that will make him enter me sooner. I should know better by now.

"Please." I don't know if I sound as needy as I feel, but if I do, he ignores me.

"I'm a patient man," he says, running his hands all over me, letting his thumbs fall into my crack as they make their way along my upper thighs, slowly, maddeningly, until I groan with frustration. "This is quite a lovely piece. Beethoven. 'Ode to Joy.' Do you see how they've programmed the fountain to go slowly higher as the piece gets more intense?"

He slides two fingers into me. This satisfies nothing. It makes my anticipation even greater.

"Yes." Yes to everything. I can barely keep my eyes open. My head drops when he strokes my inside wall. With his other hand, he pulls my hair back gently yet forcefully until I'm looking out the window again.

"You're so beautiful when you're like this. You, hovering between two worlds. Your mind doesn't know whether to pay attention to what you're seeing or what you're feeling. One has to win. Which one is it going to be?"

"Feeling. I'd say feeling, in about five minutes."

The music swirls. The jets of water fly upward, and as they hit a finale, he enters me.

When I cry out, it's not in pain or pleasure. It's the anticipation leaving my body all at once.

He presses his hands against mine, pushing them against the glass, which is no longer cold but warm from my touch. He thrusts powerfully and slowly. Every movement is calculated. Another concerto rises from the speakers, and like the fountain that is programmed to explode with the rhythm, so is his rhythm programmed to my body.

The music rises again, but I can barely hear it. The jets of water have turned into a blur and my attention can only focus on one thing. Him. The way our bodies slam together. The way my orgasm is about to take over my entire body. He finds my clit and rubs it for three strokes before my toes curl, my back arches, and a long, hoarse vowel spirals from my throat.

A million miles away, his voice says, "yes,yes,yes," in a drumbeat of affirmation.

He pulls out, and I'm left empty and wanting. His hands on my hips push forward left and toward him right, turning me around. My hands leave the glass reluctantly, because he told me to leave them there, and when I'm facing him with his shirt half open, his pants

around his ankles and his fist around his cock, I see his hunger
yet again.

He pushes toward me, and with my back pressed against the newly
cold glass, he spurts onto my belly, leaving a warm trail of thick
pleasure.

Below us, the music falls, dies, and the last jets of water drop to the
pool's surface with a splash. The crowd applauds, and Keaton and I
catch our breath.

He puts his elbow on the window behind me and runs his fingers
over my hair. His hand drifts to my waist, through the semen he has left
on me, spreading it over my belly. Marking me with it.

He moves his hand downward again and lays four wet fingers over
me. "You make me want to come inside you."

"I told you I was on birth control."

His hand runs over me from back to front. "I know."

I wait for him to continue, but no more reason is forthcoming. He
slips three fingers inside me and I suck breath through my teeth. I don't
know how I'm still standing. Maybe he's holding me up. But when he
presses all of those fingers against my nub again, I lose all feeling in my
legs and fall into his arms, sliding to the floor. He guides me to a chair. I
fall over the arm of it, sideways, legs spread—one over the back of the
chair with one set of curled toes leveraging against the floor—as he
brings me to orgasm again.

I can't move. Can't think. I can barely get myself to a more
comfortable position as he stands over me, one hand up with his wetness
and mine glinting in the flashing lights of the Las Vegas strip.

He kneels by the chair, that mischievous smile back in spades, and
puts his thumb to his lips and sucks it clean. I open my mouth just a little
and flick my tongue over my bottom lip. He reads my mind and puts
two fingers in my mouth. I suck us off him.

"You are a filthy little girl." He removes his fingers. "Let me get you
washed up."

With that, he gathers me in his arms and lifts me.

I put my arms around his neck. I can finally see the room, with its
flower arrangements, plush furniture, mirrors, and fireplace. He carries
me into the bathroom, popping on the light with his elbow. The tile is

glistening white, there are four sinks, a deep bathtub, a glass-enclosed shower, and Keaton Bridge.

My Keaton. Whatever his name is or where he's really from, for this weekend, he is mine, secrets and all.

I sigh softly.

CHAPTER 35

KEATON

I get my money's worth out of the penthouse by fucking her in every room, on every piece of furniture. I tell her about the fog in London (it's real) and the law that allows pregnant women to have a wee in a policeman's hat (that's false). I feed her room-service strawberries, and she washes my hair in the bath.

She is foggy weather, when the air gets so close you can feel it around you like a skin. She is the crowds flowing around Trafalgar Square with their own purpose and predictability that is comforting. She is the smell of the sea air unexpectedly coming from the south, bringing the sting of salt to the city. She is an unexpected reminder of where I stand in the world.

She's none of those things. She's not even British. She's an American woman through and through. She probably wears American flag underwear as she eats apple pie on July 4th.

I've been drifting too long. I'm fed up with drifting. It's that irritation that brought me here. It's that discomfort that led me to the ambassador's office to assure him I was ready for something different.

"I want to gamble," she says on our last morning. "Do we have time before the flight?" She's fully dressed in a flowing skirt that seems quite unlike her. I like this new, casual look. Will I ever get a chance to truly know all of the ways she can be?

I zip my bag closed. "You don't want to give this bed another workout?"

She slips her arms around my waist and looks up at me. "I'm sore."

"Giving up, are you?" I kiss her temple. I'll kiss anyplace I can reach. "Never took you for a quitter."

"I'll teach you how to count cards."

"You count cards?"

"For blackjack. I know how, but I'm not great at it." She pulls away. "Come on. Let's have a couple of hours of dumb fun."

Gambling is money wasted on manufactured risk, but I want to see her in the bright lights, doing something I can't imagine her doing. I want to revel in her competence and unexpected skill.

A call comes in, and though I've ignored my phone all weekend, I take it from my pocket and check the caller as she rests her head on my shoulder.

It's the ambassador.

"I have to take this." I hold it up with the glass facing me so she can't see.

"Do you want to meet downstairs?"

"Sure thing." I tap her backside. "Don't talk to anyone. This place is loaded with hustlers and scammers."

"I can handle it." She sticks her tongue out and slings her bag over her shoulder.

I tap the phone to answer it as I watch her go. It occurs to me that this could be a mistake. I shouldn't let her out of my sight. But nobody knows we're here, and she's a federal agent for fuck's sake.

"Hello?" The ambassador's voice comes from the phone.

I'd forgotten I answered it. Now I have to deal with time and the fact that it's slipping away from me. "I'm here."

"I'd ask you if you're having a good time, but I don't give a toss."

"Fancy that."

"There's been some chatter. I don't want to alarm you, but I want your caution."

I sit up straight, foot on the floor, leg tense so I can bolt if I need to.

"Kaos says he's coming after you personally. Got on a plane, apparently."

I'm heading for the exit before he even finishes. "When?" Jamming feet into shoes.

"This morning."

"Where did he say he was going?" I'm out the door. Down the hall. Shoes softly shushing on the carpet. The lift is light-years away.

"He didn't," the ambassador says with not a single ounce of shame. "You should go, and not back to California. Certainly not back to Barrington."

I slap the button for the fourth time. Why don't these fucking lifts show you what floor they're on so a bloke can get on the stairs if he needs to? Fucking Yanks.

I hang up as the lift arrives. He can just bugger off. If this is how he's going to manage my transition, then maybe I should just transition my own fucking self.

In the two minutes it takes to get to the casino level, I'm painfully aware of the fact that I let Cassie walk out of that room without me. Fucking stupid. So easy to get careless when I feel comfortable. She's making me soft. I liked it, but now I hate it.

The casino that delighted me because it delighted her is now a cacophony of lights, sounds, smells, vying for my attention. But Cassie isn't at the blackjack tables she promised she'd be at. I text her.

—Where are you?—

I clutch my phone at my side and wait for the buzz while I scan the casino. It's designed so you can't see across it. If you could see across it, you'd know how to get the fuck out. But the twists and turns are devised to create smaller spaces that loop passers-by into machine-lined corners and dead ends. I can't see across the room. I can't see past the next bank of glitzy machines. I don't know where she is and my phone isn't buzzing. I look at it. No message. No surprise. The signal sucks. It's intentional. It shuts out the world. Casinos are big Faraday cages.

I could be walking in the opposite direction. I check the blackjack tables, but there are blackjack tables everywhere. I check the poker tables for the low-risk gambler, but she's not there either.

Finally, a message comes in.

—I don't know—

The text is like a cold spear through my gut. She doesn't know. Does that mean she doesn't know which end of the casino she's in? Couldn't blame her for that. Does it mean she's been led away? Or taken away?

I call her, but the lines won't connect. I text again.

> *—What do you mean you don't know? What are you close to?—*

I continue scanning the casino. I walk from one end to the other, considering the possibility he knows I'm here, calculating the distance from McCarren to the Strip, how long it takes to park, whether he was a passenger on a chartered flight which means he would just have to get from the plane into a car, or if he flew the plane himself which means he'd have to park it, check in.

If he landed thirty minutes ago, he could be here by now. He could be in my room, looking for me. I hope he is. One, because I'm not there. But mostly because she's not there.

I walk from the bar to the other bar, from one stairway to another. I'm losing patience. I send another text.

> *—Cassie?—*

The cold spear through me expands, turning my body rigid and cracking my heart.

CHAPTER 36

CASSIE

I decide to hold off on blackjack until Keaton comes down.
Wandering around, I sit at a poker table. I buy some chips and
nod at the other two players at the table, a couple in their fifties. He's
wearing a cowboy hat and bolero. She's in a Vegas sweatshirt and
hairspray. They smile and nod. Nice people. I don't feel bad when I win
the first hand.

A man slides in two seats down from me. He has soulful brown eyes
and a nose that's been busted. He's not much older than I am, but they
seem like they've been hard years. I smile at him, and he smiles back.
One of his front teeth is a little chipped. I've seen chipped teeth
look worse.

"How is this table running?" he asks with a vaguely Eastern
European accent. His blink is hard and long. A tic.

"I'm batting five hundred," I say, mixing my sports with my games.

The couple doesn't give him the same warm welcome.

"I'll take those odds." He throws a few hundreds on the table, and
the dealer changes them for chips.

We play the next hand in silence. I end with a pair of nines, which
doesn't get me far. The couple leaves with a tip of a hat and a nod.

The next hand is dealt. I watch Chipped Tooth. He reacts to every card. Extra blink. Tap of the corner of the card. Shifting the cards quickly means there's something there to organize. He doesn't move any of them.

"Did you see that kid over back that way?" Chipped Tooth jerks his thumb back in the general direction of… I don't even know. His hairline is deeply receding, and he scratches right where the hair meets the edge of his forehead.

"I didn't see anything," I say, tossing ten into the pile. "I just got here."

"Young girl, couldn't be more than eight years old, caught with her hand in a lady's purse. The cops cuffed her. Can you even believe it, a kid that young?"

This has nothing to do with me. But it has everything to do with me, and I can barely finish the hand before I talk myself into getting up and taking care of whatever it is they're doing to this girl. The psychology of it is so cheap that I should see right through it, but I don't because I am justice. I was never caught, but I was lucky, and I can make another girl like myself just as lucky, and maybe one day she'll be an FBI agent too.

It's not that simple. It doesn't go through my head all that clearly. It's too fast, it's too bright, and it's too loud. But I'm standing and collecting chips before I can work through the sound, the light, or the speed.

I win the hand with three of a kind.

"Where was it?"

He scratches his head again. His fingernails are manicured. "I guess… um… I think it was by the bathrooms."

Of course it was by the bathrooms. I could have told him that. I take a few steps away from the blackjack table, scanning for the walls… are there any walls? Is there an end to this room? A boundary line along which the bathrooms would be situated?

"Hang on," Chipped Tooth says. "I'm sure I can get you there if I'm actually walking it. She your kid or something?"

"No, but I have some experience with this."

"Okay. Okay, I can take you there, but she may be with security already. Are you a social worker or something? Work with troubled kids?"

"Sure." I don't want to say I'm an FBI agent. That's just silly.

"I'm a doctor myself," he says. "I have a practice in Texas. San Antonio. Have you ever been?"

"No."

He leads me in one direction, then another, then around the bend and down a wide indoor boulevard lined with stores. The text comes in. It's Keaton.

—Where are you?—

— I don't know —

I look at Chipped Tooth. Who is this guy with the European accent? What kind of weirdly specific story is he telling? Suddenly, my instincts kick in like a stalled lawn mower engine. He's asked all the questions and every single one put me on the defensive. Something's wrong. Very wrong. Keaton warned me about con artists and I thought I was too smart to hear it.

"What's your name again?" I ask.

"John."

"Cassie!" Keaton's voice comes over the din of bells and whoops.

I turn toward it and wave to him.

When I turn back, Chipped Tooth is gone.

CHAPTER 37

KEATON

She's standing there in one piece, not a hair out of place. Panic drops off me, leaving a relief so profound, I'm left breathless.

"Hey," she says. "I'm sorry I got lost."

I kiss her long and hard. I don't have to tell her I was being overprotective, or that I thought I'd put her in danger by leaving her alone. Nor do I want to describe the sense of panic I'm still shedding. She'll want to do something about it, and I don't want to put her in danger.

I just want to kiss her. Surround her. Worship her wholeness and her well-being. I want to feed her my relief without defining it.

"What's with you?" she asks when I let her get a breath.

"Just glad to see you."

"Well…" Her eyes scan the room as if she doesn't know what to say next. She looks as if she's hiding her own secret. "We should go."

"Did you want to play a few hands?" I stroke her arms, still appreciating the solid reality of her life in the world when I was convinced it would be snuffed out.

"Nah," she says. "Let's just go if you don't mind."

"Did something happen while I was gone?"

"I won fifty bucks at poker."

I don't know if she's off or I'm off. But something's off. Maybe she's embarrassed to win money at a low-risk game. Maybe she's put off by how relieved I was to see her. Maybe, since I thought everything was getting turned upside down, my view of the world is still sideways.

I assume it's me and take her home.

BY THE TIME we board the plane, she's back to normal, from what I can see. She's lively and bright, thanking me for a wonderful weekend. I kiss her and thank her back, but my thoughts are caught in a net.

With her head on my chest and a book in front of her, I pretend I'm asleep on the plane. I need to think. I need to not just decide my future—that was done weeks ago. I need to acknowledge the decision and do something about it.

Vegas was the proof.

I can't leave her behind. Even without Kaos in the picture, for better or worse, Cassie Grinstead is a part of my life. Pretending otherwise is a fool's errand.

I'm going to have to neutralize Kaos myself.

CASSIE

Orlando stands at the front of the briefing room that morning and makes an announcement. It's over. One little Nazi in the Springfield cell had a cert kwon, and once the Cyber Crime division used it to confirm his ID, he flipped like a pancake. Federal authorities all over the country were banging on doors six hours later in secret night time raids.

And all because I told them about the little hacker coins.

Ken's shaking my hand as well as he can with a bad shoulder, Frieda's fist-pumping, and everyone at the field office is clapping.

"All right, all right." Orlando's at the podium, tamping enthusiasm by bouncing his palms at us. "You can thank her later. For now, we want t's and i's crossed and dotted, in that order. We caught these guys because of the exceptional work of one agent"—he indicates me in the crowd of agents and staff—"but we won't get them put away without the careful work of every other individual in this office."

We disperse. I shake more hands, feeling a curious emptiness. I wanted this, and yet it's not what I need.

"Grinstead!" Orlando calls as he goes into his office. I follow. "Close the door behind you."

I do it. He sits behind his desk, and I stand in front of it.

"They have psychics over in Quantico," he says.

"Sir?"

"You put in for a transfer to division?"

"CID, sir."

"That's what I nominated you for."

"Thank you, sir."

"You're being sent to Cyber Crime."

I open my mouth to tell him that wasn't what I wanted. I wanted criminal.

"I have to be honest," he says. "This is the right call. You have a razor-sharp sense of that world. And someone over there doesn't want you in CID."

"But I can't get into a division I wasn't nominated for."

"Apparently you can." He stands and holds out his hand. "Congratulations, Special Agent Grinstead. You are to report to the Division Office in San Francisco in two weeks. Case dossiers will be on your desk in a couple of days, if not sooner."

I shake his hand, eyes wide in disbelief, gratitude, and utter bafflement.

IT's midnight when I get home from the best day ever. My feet hurt, my hair is scraggly, and my suit is wrinkled, but I feel expanded, lit from within, tied to the earth and filled with helium.

> *—We need to talk—*

I send this without thinking that it might sound as if I don't want to see him again. But I figure I can clear it up quite quickly once he's in front of me. I don't know if he's in California, New York, or a mile away at the club.

When I pull into my driveway, I check my phone. Still nothing back from him. I'll compose something more inviting once I'm inside.

The flickering blue light of the TV tells me Nana's up, but when I open the door, I find her sleeping on the couch with a blanket over her, wine glasses on the side tables, and a half-complete kitten puzzle on the card table. I'm a little disappointed. I want to tell her about my reassignment. She's always wanted to go to California; now I can take her there.

The sound of creaking floorboards startles me, and I almost reach for my gun when I see Keaton coming out of the shadows, drying his hands with a dishtowel. I'm surprised. He's the last person I expected to see and the first I want to tell.

"Hello," he says.

He starts to say more, but I can't wait another second. I leap on him and smother his face with kisses. He's all leather and rainy London mornings.

"I'm so pissed at you," I say between kisses. He's holding me straight as I climb him. The blue light flickers on his face.

"Why?" He pulls my leg around his waist.

"Just showing up here? Presumptuous."

He's hard already. I feel him against me as we kiss and drag each other to the kitchen so we won't wake up my grandmother.

"Not cool," I whisper. "Bad form."

He pushes me up against the kitchen counter and I'm absolutely wild with sensation. The TV light flashes on the open door and the teacups hanging under the cabinets, drowned out by the stars I see when I wrap my legs around him.

"I needed to see you," he says. "You took the air out of the room with you."

His needy, clutching hands push up my shirt, under my bra. I don't even feel the corner of the counter biting into my back. I don't feel a thing but his lips and his fingers. I think I'm grabbing his shirt. I think I'm kissing him back.

But his softly spoken words fill the sound range. I can only hear him and feel his body where it presses against mine. "Everyone else looks flat and grey now. There's no life in anything. You carved a place in my world and everything else fell into it."

We thrust our hips together in a rhythm, the length of him flush against me, end to end.

"I think I can come like this," I say.

"What's stopping you?"

The blue light disappears and we freeze. A rustle of blankets. A creak of the couch.

"Nana?" I say.

"Where are you?" she calls.

Keaton and I look at each other. We try not to laugh. He could let me go so I can deal with my grandmother. Instead he presses me into the counter.

"I'm home." I try to sound normal.

"That nice man was here looking for you."

"I know, Nana."

There's a long pause. I wish I knew where she is, but I can't see her.

"I'll be going to bed then." She says it more loudly and deliberately than normal. I hear the floor creak and her bedroom door snap closed.

"She knows," Keaton says.

"She's old, but she's not stupid."

"Then she knows I'm going to fuck you senseless."

"Let's not confirm it for her, okay?" I whisper so low I can barely hear myself.

"The only thing that's going to be holding you straight is my cock." He bites my lower lip.

"My bedroom is past her door. She's a really light sleeper."

He takes a breath, looks around. I'm thinking a quick dash to a hotel. Maybe we can fuck in the car or something. But he opens the pantry door and leans over to check it out.

In half a second, we're crammed inside between the unbleached flour and the serving trays. The only light's coming through a tiny window above us. Below it sits a little stool for getting to high shelves. He closes the door behind him, knocking over a bowl of Halloween candy. We stifle laughter.

He doesn't waste a second, pulling his belt out of the loops and looking at my pants as if I should know better than to be wearing them at all.

I take the hint and wriggle them down, getting one leg out.

"What were you so happy about today?" He says it while he's fishing his dick out of his pants, which freezes me in place for a second.

I'm happy because I got a pay raise, a promotion, and a new title.

Special Agent. Cyber Crime division.

And here I am, in my pantry about to fuck a cyber criminal.

"Cat got your tongue?" he asks.

"There's been a change."

"What sort of change?"

He doesn't seem particularly concerned. Maybe he thinks there's a guy in my life who he's going to have to vanquish, or maybe he thinks I have my period or something. I hate doing this to him, but more importantly, I hate doing it myself. I want him. I want to peel away his layers like an onion and find the center. Or never find the center and just die trying. I can't decide this now. It's all too big to figure out while I throb between my legs and my knees feel like butter on the counter, keeping their edges while slowly softening.

"I don't want to lie."

"What an intriguing way to begin," he says, drawing his hand up my shirt, under my bra, squeezing away a few more IQ points until I am half dullard.

My brain is mush. My mouth is dry.

Keaton cups my jaw, slides his hand back, and pulls my hair until I buckle. "Maybe you'll tell me on your knees."

I drop to them. He steadies me with the hand that's not yanking on my hair until I'm looking up at him with the spot of moisture at the tip of his head an inch from my nose. I flick my tongue out and lick it off. He breathes through his teeth.

I did that. I made this beautiful man tilt his head back and suck on air as if it's a drug. And I know there's no going back. From this point on, it's only going to get harder to tell him. I shouldn't care. If he's a criminal, then he's on my radar and it doesn't matter. My job is to hunt him and people like him and my job is my life. But it's not. I don't know what my life is anymore. I care about this man. I crave his attention and his approval. I want to get to know him, and now I won't be able to. How can I not be honest with him about that, or give him the opportunity to prove to me that he won't be on the wrong side of the law while it is my job to defend it?

"I got reassigned," I say. "I'm moving to San Francisco in two weeks."

"Well done, my artful dodger!"

He seems too happy. The obvious reason is that I haven't told him the division. It seems crazy to tell him with the hard heavy weight of his erection an inch from my nose, the glistening drop of pre-cum begging for my tongue's attention.

"Cyber Crime division." I choke it out before I can think too hard about it.

I'm ready for him to step back and thank me for my time. I'm also ready for him to fuck me as though I'm his enemy, which might not be the worst way to say goodbye.

"You think you'll be chasing after me then?"

It seems ridiculous that I'd ever chase Alpha Wolf, or that I'd ever catch him.

"You tell me."

I'm giving him a chance to assure me that he is just an investor. I'm giving him the chance to surgically remove everything he has admitted and insert a same-shaped lie.

He doesn't.

He draws two fingers over my cheek and slides them into my mouth. I take them, closing my lips around the webs at the base.

"I'm going to tell you something, all right."

He smiles and puts his fingers back in my mouth before I can ask him for his reassurances. He puts them far back, as if testing my abilities. I take them, locking eyes with him above me, sucking on the way out. I want his cock. I want to show him how deep I can take it, but he only gives me his fingers. With his other hand, he reaches onto the shelf with the spilled Halloween candy and grabs a lollipop. The kind with bubble gum inside.

"I'm going to tell you when and how to take whatever I put in your mouth."

He unwraps the lollipop with his teeth, spitting out the shavings of paper like confetti. When the deep red ball is freed, he removes his fingers.

"Open up." He taps my lips with the lollipop. I open them and he slides it against my tongue, to the back. "Say *ah*, Special Agent Grinstead, and take the lolly."

Something about being called Special Agent, or maybe just *special*, floods me in arousal. I want more than anything to please the man who said it. I open my throat and the lollipop goes down it.

"Brilliant," he says softly, twisting the pop out then back in. He leaves it on my tongue, and I close my lips around the white stem. It's strawberry.

"Yum," I say around the pop.

"Indeed." He takes it away and puts it in his own mouth. "What are you going to do when they tell you to get Alpha Wolf?"

"I get him."

"I like that answer."

"Thank you."

Why isn't he worried? Why isn't he reticent in the slightest? Why isn't he denying who he is or anything he has done? He seems delighted.

"You're going to go far in Cyber Crime, dodger." He squeezes my cheeks until my lips part. "Again. Say *ah*."

My mouth is barely all the way open before he has the head of his dick in it. I take it, groaning deep in my throat when I can, breathing every few strokes. His skin is slick and soft, throbbing underneath. The lollipop is jammed into the side of his mouth, teeth tight on the stick. When he jerks away with a gasp, I know he's close.

"Bloody hell."

"What?"

He plucks out the lolly and bends to give me a strawberry-and-sugar kiss.

"You almost had me," he says, pulling me up. We're both standing, looking onto each other's eyes. "I'd love to come in your mouth, on your body. I want to mark you with me, but I can't."

"Why not?" I sound like a petulant child because I feel like one. I desperately want to be marked with him, by him. Yet I know what's stopping him. "You're legit now. Right? That's what you said."

He drops his gaze, pressing his lips together. I can sense he's keeping himself from saying the first words that come to mind.

"I know you," he says finally. "Better than you think and more than is fair. I know what I am to you. I'm a thrill for a woman who forgot how to seek thrills. But you're not that to me. I don't just fancy your ass in a tight skirt. I want you to have everything you ever dreamed, and you can't if you're with me. You understand that, right? I'll sabotage everything you're doing. I won't mean to do it, but I will. How can I live with myself? How can you live with it?"

He takes my chin and tilts my face up to his. I can smell the strawberry sweet on his breath. It matches my own. "You think you can because we're in a bloody pantry with our trousers down. How long will it be before I'm a liability? You'll be asked to hunt me down or I'll be your informant. Or someone I know will feel you breathing down their neck. And here's the rub, darling. I'll do whatever I need to to make you happy or to protect you, and they're not always going to be the same thing."

"What if I didn't take the promotion?"

Did I really mean what I was saying? Would I really refuse the transfer to stay in Doverton? I hadn't thought about it enough to know for sure, but it was a very real possibility.

For me, it was an option. The idea made him chuckle.

"What's so funny?"

"You think I'd allow that?"

"I can wait for a spot in CID."

He kisses me, but it's a consolation prize.

I gently push him away. "Don't you do this. Don't you use this as an excuse to run away from me. If you don't want me, then just say so."

His expression flares into anger and his grip on my jaw gets tight. "You think I'm standing here with my balls out to fuck with you? I want to fill your mouth and your tight little cunt with me like I want nothing else, but I can't lie to you. I can't fuck you now and listen to you talk about quitting afterward."

"I'll do as I like, Alpha."

He's as much as admitted to being Alpha Wolf, but I've never acknowledged it by using the name, and we both stiffen as if I dropped a bomb.

Clarity is a powerful thing. Clarity put into words is a sawed-off shotgun two inches from a target. It blows resistance away. It turns barriers into hot shrapnel.

"I want you to fuck me, Alpha Wolf. I want you to fuck me like you've wanted to kill every fed that ever got close. Fuck me like I'm reading you your rights."

He yanks my hair so hard, my lungs empty in a single breath. "That's a lot of saucy talk from a special agent."

"You have the right to remain silent." It's hard to say that without a smile, but I manage.

He indulges in what I deny myself, letting an evil grin spread across his face. "I have the right to fuck you unconscious."

He pushes me into the shelves. Two cans of beans clop to the floor as our hips meet. His cock is pushed up against my belly. I wrap a leg around his waist, and he holds it there with one hand while he guides himself into me with the other. I stretch, angle myself, push into him until he's buried inside me. He pulls out halfway and thrusts forward with a grunt. More cans fall. Pumpkin pie. Artichokes. Pitted black olives. The cabinets shake as he pounds me. Paper towels fall. I'm pinned against a shelf of pasta and crackers, his fingers digging in my ass cheeks. It hurts. God, it all hurts and feels so good.

"This what you want?" he growls.

"You have the right to fuck me harder."

He obliges, wrapping my other leg around him and thrusts slower and harder. Another stack of cans rattles, falls, rolls off the shelf. I'm too blind to see what they are. My body swells around him, hungry for more, more, more. I want him deeper than physically possible. So deep he wipes me into the ether, into invisibility, into nonexistence.

When I come, he covers my mouth. I scream into his palm, shaking over and over, completely lost. Invisible.

I'm made of jelly. My limbs have lost the will to function. My tears fall over my cheeks and onto his hand. He slides it away.

"Hang on to me."

I wrap my arms around shoulders, sharing the weight between them and the legs I have curled around his waist. He pulls out and with one hand, he fists his throbbing cock; with the other, he lifts my shirt. In three strokes, he's exploding all over my belly, and I think this is me. I've done this. He's so beautiful when he comes that I feel like an artist stepping back to see a finished masterwork.

He breathes his last orgasmic breath and kisses me, putting his arms around my lower back to hold me up.

I reach behind him, grabbing a horizontal roll of paper towels that's half hanging off the edge of the shelf. He sets me down, snaps the paper towels away, and unspools a few sheets.

"Thank you," I say as he cleans me off.

"The pleasure is all mine."

When I'm clean I let my shirt drop, and we both pick up our pants. The floor is littered with groceries, like flowers in a nonperishable garden. I pick up a can of beans in each hand.

"You knew," I say.

He slides a box of pasta back onto the shelf. "Knew what?"

"Don't play coy."

He doesn't play coy. He plays silent. He plays with a knowing smile. He plays a long pause punctuated with the sounds of shelf-stocking like a musical instrument.

"Keaton."

"Cassie."

He looks down at me, lit by the street light coming through the tiny window. It's a little blue in the depths, a little yellow at the highlights, cutting to black at his dimples and the ridges under his eyebrows, tilting a box of Cheerios against the edge of the shelf. He knew. He fucking knew.

"You knew I was going to be sent to Cyber Crime."

"You don't trust me?"

"I trust you. But I don't believe you."

"I came here to tell you I'll be away for a few days. Maybe a week." He slides the box on the shelf until it pops against the back wall and bounces back a quarter of an inch, then he picks up crackers and a half-eaten bag of tortilla chips. The plastic crunches at a billion decibels. "There's nothing else going on."

I take the chips and put them on a low shelf. He puts the crackers where they go with a flawless sense of order. I scan the floor. There's nothing left to pick up. There's nothing left to do in this tiny room but leave it.

He puts his arms around me, and I sink into the warmth and solidness of him. I shouldn't. I know that. But he fits into me, and I fit into him so easily that it must be law of physics that draws me close to him.

CHAPTER 39

KEATON

I said I was going to be away for a few days as if it was nothing. As if I had some easy business to manage, not that I was going to Salton Sea to track down Keyser Kaos. Not that the success of this mission would determine whether I could stay with her or not. Not that I could be killed.

All I want her to know is I won't be around, not that I'm leaving in the hopes that I'm protecting her and whatever we have together.

This woman means more to me than the goals I've been reaching for, and after the lie of omission in the pantry, the lies about her promotion won't stand. I have to relieve the pressure.

She's walking me to my car as this unravels. It's like a net coming loose. Or ropes that bound me suddenly unwinding themselves until I can move, then breathe. Soon they'll be so loose I can walk away.

Which is why I can't continue the lie.

"About the promotion." But I can't finish so fast. I've stuck my foot in it now. It's the truth, or nothing.

She is calm when she responds, closing her jacket around her, waiting a full two seconds before opening her mouth. "What about it?"

"They weren't going to put you in criminal. They weren't going to put you anywhere. And before you ask me how I know, trust me, I know because I know people. You deserve to be where you are, and you need to go where you're going. And don't look at me like that. Don't look at me like it's cheating. Because it's not. This is the way the world works for everybody. Everybody."

She opens her mouth to say something, then snaps it closed, waiting another two seconds before speaking.

"What exactly did you do?" Her breath makes clouds in front of her face, giving me the impression that she's breathing fire.

I have to answer. I'm trapped now. Trapped on this street, trapped in her gaze, and trapped in the truth.

"I know you think that you never got caught lifting wallets and being bait for your mother's con jobs. And it's true, you don't have a record. But they know. They know about your mother, and they assume that you've inherited some of her art. Criminal justice and counterterrorism is full of Boy Scouts. You'd never get in. Cyber Crime is a totally different game. All I did was move your application from a place where it was toxic, to a place where it would be seen by people who would appreciate it."

The air has gone from heavy, to heavy and wet. Cold dewdrops collect on her cheeks as she looks at the ground with wet lashes, thinks a good long time as the mist gathers on the ends of her raven hair.

"How did you do that?"

"Someday I'll tell you."

"You just hacked it and moved the application over?"

"More or less. There were other steps. You got the job based on your qualifications."

"I'm uncomfortable with this."

"You said you trusted me, but you didn't believe me." She turns away, billowing a breath, then turns back so I can look her in the eye when I answer. "I want you to believe me, but it's your trust I treasure."

Her sigh is long and profound, with a deep, sad resignation. "Will you be back before I move to California?"

"Will you be here for me?"

"Yes."

"Then I'll be back before you know it."

I expressed my hope rather than my certainty.

CHAPTER 40

CASSIE

*N*ana took the news quite well. She seemed more excited than I was, opening her closet as if she was throwing open French doors after a month of rain.

"Everyone was moving to California." She throws clothes on her double bed and tells the same story I've heard a hundred times. "All the girls. They thought they'd find nice boys in California, and maybe they did. I had Barry the motherfucker and your mother in my belly. So we went where the jobs were. Detroit, Michigan." The story took on a new, never-heard-before emphasis on the Golden State. "All the other girls were moving to Los Angeles, but me? If I had my druthers, it definitely would've been San Francisco."

Whatever druthers are, they must've been in short supply back then, and I must have plenty. I may not always be happy and I may not always get what I want, but taking her to California with me gives my life meaning.

She starts packing almost immediately and backwardly, putting the mementos away first, piling unidentifiable knick-knacks into the middle of the room.

I almost trip on a box of old bills. "We can hire movers, you know."

"Why would you do that? Something wrong with your arms?"

Midwesterners. Defining do-it-yourself for four generations.

"I don't want you straining yourself." I try to get a box out of her arms, but she won't let it go.

"It's heavy."

"Fine if you want," she says. "Put it over there and grab that red box on the top shelf if you don't mind."

"I do mind. That's the problem. Are these boxes of puzzles?" I hold up a box with a bowl of fruit. "Are you bringing boxes of puzzles you've already done to California?"

"That one's important." She snatches it away. "It's the one I was doing when you got into the academy. It goes in the keep pile."

"You moved puzzles from Flint to Doverton? How did I not notice this?"

"You used to not question me this much."

She puts the fruit bowl puzzle in the stack under the window, then attacks the pile of puzzles in the corner and slides one out of the middle with enough dexterity to keep the tower from falling.

"This one too." She hands it to me, running her finger down the stack.

I take it. It's a generic mountain landscape. "Why?" I'm practically whining.

"That's the one I was doing when you broke up with that idiot. Mark the idiot." She pulls out a slim box and hands it back. "This was the day you fractured your elbow playing volleyball."

I take it. Wild horses running over the plains. I worked on it with one arm in silence with her, passing the time I wanted to be out with my friends on small victories.

"Junior year." I run my fingers over it. Every piece snapping together made me a little less miserable.

Grandma's stacking them in my arms now. Pumpkins. Orange leaves. A cold blue Autumn sky.

"What's this one?"

"That time you weren't pregnant."

"Jesus, Nana, I was eighteen."

"And you almost killed me." She hands back a swirling mandala. "The last time we visited your mother."

As I take the mandala puzzle, my sinuses fill and my lungs squeeze tight and release, forcing out a sob. I say something I didn't know I believed, but it exits me with the same uncontrolled velocity as the sobs. "I miss her."

Grandma lays a family of bunnies on top of the pile in my arms. "I know, sweetheart. I do too. But I have you and you have me. So we have her."

She squeezes my shoulder and looks me in the eye. Hers are clear, grey-blue, darker than mine and lighter than Keaton's. They're clear. I think of her as old, but she's not. She's just got years on me.

"She taught me so much."

"She did."

"She was teaching me how to survive without her. She was doing her best."

The puzzles aren't heavy, so I let Grandma take the stack from me and lay it next to the keepers.

She hugs me as I cry. I hold her as tightly as I can, putting my head on her bony shoulder. She understands me. She believes in me. There's no replacing her in my life.

"All right," she says when I pull away and wipe my eyes with my wrists. "Let me get to work here."

"Keep them all," I say. "Every one of them."

She picks up a puzzle of the White House. "This is the one that nice man did with me."

"He's not so nice." Correcting her is completely counterproductive. Why shouldn't she think he's a nice man? The fact that she's completely wrong notwithstanding, it doesn't make a damn bit of difference, except it feels as if she's stealing from me what I find most attractive about him.

"I'm sure you're right, not such a nice boy. I was a young woman once. I understand the appeal. But I'll tell you the same thing I told your mother."

I move all the puzzles to one place. "What did you tell her?"

"I told her not to get knocked up. Fat lot of good that did."

I laugh. She loves me. I'm the product of my mother not listening to a word Nana ever said, and I know she's glad of it. We both are.

CHAPTER 41

KEATON

The trailer stinks of men. Three of us in an enclosed space, the processor tower set inside the shower stall. We're in the deserts of the Salton Sea in January, home of survivalists, meth cookers, and fugitives. We got lucky when we found Keyser in this little trailer park, but the conditions are terrible. No wireless for miles. Below freezing at night. Fuckhot in the day. Cassie's a thousand miles and a week away. I'm tired and dirty. We haven't left this tin can in six days. With Keyser and a handful of cronies in the next trailer over, we don't risk being seen in the daylight.

"I don't think we're close enough," Hodgekins grumbles, crouched at the base of the four-foot-wide, five-foot-high antenna, twisting two wires together. He's the antenna guy. Jackson's managing the satellite connection. I'm the one who knows how tempest emissions work.

I'm not here for my comfort. I'm here for my life and Cassie's. But my God, we just took the cabinets out to get the antenna closer to the trailer wall.

"We could just put it outside," I say without looking away from the monitor. Tempest emission decoders pick up delicate signals from machines in range and feed the contents of a neighbor's screen onto the hacker's, no matter the encryption or security. They're always wonky, and this setup is no different.

"Or knock on Keyser's fucking door and ask him what's on his screens." Jackson's monitoring the satellite connection, which is shite. His voice is muffled past the headphones I'm wearing to catch the aural peaks and valleys of the emissions.

"Fuck you both." Hodgekins slides out from under the antenna.

"Fine. Tonight you're my bitch," Jackson replies.

"Again?" I say. Something's coming in, so my retort isn't as sharp as it should be.

The screen sparkles with smears of color. Hodgekins and Jackson look over my shoulder.

"Is he watching…what is that?" Hodgekins asks, referring to the pristine landscape and dancing humanoid monstrosities on the screen. We don't have sound and the picture is incomplete, but there's no mistaking the show.

"*Teletubbies*," Jackson says. "The antenna's pointing at the wrong trailer."

"It's not."

"Fix it," I command.

Hodgekins gets back under the antenna.

With the satellite connected, my phone dings.

It's Taylor on our secure channel.

*<Did you hear about Cassie's
grandmother?>*

The computer screen flickers, changes with the speed of my mood. Code and panic. C++ and trouble.

<What happened?>

"That's him." Jackson seems in awe of what we've just done. Hack one of the best hackers in the world.

My awe is put to the side when Taylor texts back.

*<Harper says she's in the hospital
with a broken hip>*

"He's flipping to a forum," Hodgekins reacts to the change in screen. "Fuck. We're doing it. He's laying out the whole plan."

<She's sending flowers>

I'm breathing, but my lungs feel pinched and hollow.

Keyser is laying it out, right on the screen. He thinks I'm in California. He's got my apartment wired.

Bugger the flowers. Bugger the plan. Bugger the broad daylight. Cassie's alone. Maybe not exactly alone, but I'm not with her. I haven't been needed many times in my years, so this feeling that someone I care about is calling me without saying a word is new. It's fresh, and it's a physical urge, like hunger or exhaustion calls for food and sleep, this yearning calls for me to go to Cassie.

But if I leave now, we lose Keyser, and he's still a threat. We may not have an opportunity like this again.

The only choice is to stay and finish the job. My only option is to take the long view. Neutralizing Keyser will ensure Cassie's safety and give us the possibility of a life together. Going back to Doverton to sit next to her won't make her grandmother any better any quicker.

I simply can't go.

She'll understand.

"Gentlemen," I say, taking off my headphones, "I'm sorry, but I have to leave."

"What?" they cry in unison.

"We can't maintain the connection without you," Hodgekins complains.

I crack the door. The light hurts my eyes. We all hold our arms in front of our faces like vampires.

"I'm going for the car." I put on sunglasses. "Give a shout if the bastard leaves his tin can. And if he threatens to come to Barrington, Doverton, or anywhere near there, give a shout."

I leave them and run in broad daylight for the car. Quite possibly, I've traded my singular goal of the past few years for a few hours of comforting and supporting someone in her time of need.

For her, it may be a worthy trade.

CHAPTER 42

CASSIE

If something happens to my grandmother—and by "something," I mean if she dies—who am I?

Who cares about me? Who do I care for? Who do I love?

I understand that these thoughts are selfish. I understand that it's not about me, my feelings, my needs, or my life. But I need to wonder these things to block out the knowledge that I'm sitting in a hospital waiting room because I wanted to move to California.

If she'd been sitting around watching QVC like she's supposed to, she wouldn't be in a hospital bed. She'd be telling me to get married to break the cycle of single motherhood in my family. She'd be worrying about me, hoping for the best, pushing me toward my future while she held onto my past.

I have never felt so alone. The hospital waiting room is empty and decorated like a meal with no salt. It's so bland, so completely inoffensive that it leaves me no choice but to use my thoughts as weapons against myself.

My friends are working, what little family I have is far away, and if I lose my grandmother, I won't be uprooted so much as unmoored.

I finger my phone. Frieda is going to come by after work. Unless some new emergency pops up. Then she'll have to stay to cover for my absence. I appreciate her. She's a good friend. If I move, I lose her.

I hope Nana isn't suffering. I hope they give her all the pain medication she wants. I hope I can see her soon. I've brought a bunch of puzzles and some junk food that they probably won't let her eat.

I can't pay attention to a book. The news is depressing. There are no granola bars left in the vending machine. If Nana dies, is it my fault?

I say things to myself that make me anxious, as if anxiety is a drug that I need extra doses of. Why do I do this to myself? I'm helpless to stop it. Helpless to stop the self-bludgeoning about my responsibility and my loneliness.

I don't cry. Not until he shows up. When Keaton walks in from the hall with his travel bags and unkempt scruff along his jaw, the water main funneling my emotions cracks. When his eyes land on me and he smiles with those damn dimples, the crack snaps the pipe and I flood.

I don't know if he rushes toward me, or saunters, or jumps, or runs. All I know is that I'm blind with a sadness that I'm now allowed to express, and a joy I don't feel any guilt for. I'm in his arms, held tighter by him than by my own skin. He squeezes sadness from me, drop by drop. With sweet words, he gives me back what was hurting me, and takes away the loneliness that kept me from feeling it fully.

He leads me to a chair, snapping tissues from the dispenser on the coffee table. He presses them to my cheeks and eyes. This hacker criminal who cares nothing for anyone is caring for me. I let him put a fresh tissue under my nose and wipe away the snot.

"I'm sorry I'm so gross," I say with a sniffle, taking the tissue from him.

"What was she doing?"

"I came home from work, and I was two hours late. And I'm sorry I was two hours late, but I didn't know. She was on the floor. She's only seventy-three. She's not at the 'I've fallen and can't get up' phase. But there she was and she didn't even know how long she'd been there. But she was lying on the floor, helpless. They say she fractured her hip. So I'm glad she can't remember it, but I feel bad. This wouldn't have happened if I came home on time."

"Pretty good chance this would have happened even if you were on time."

"She's so young for this. Do you know that women who have a fall like this are five times more likely to die within the next year?"

"Do you know anything about how statistics work, Cassandra? If one woman usually dies under normal circumstances and five will break their hip and die, that's five times more likely. Something can be five times more likely and still not be statistically significant."

"My grandmother is not a statistic."

"Agreed. She will not be a statistic because she has a wonderful, competent, caring granddaughter to watch over her."

He really seems to believe that I'm instrumental in saving my grandmother's life. He makes me want to believe it as much as he believes.

"I really wish I'd been there for her when she fell."

"I know." He brushes away the hair that sticks to my cheek, kneeling dutifully on one knee in front of me as if he's at my beck and call. Maybe he is, but it doesn't even matter. "Business first. Are you thirsty? Hungry? Horny?"

"Honestly, sex is the last thing on my mind. Though you do remind me of sex."

He gets up and sits next to me, sliding down the seat a little and crossing his ankle over his knee. "Well, I'm at your disposal. We're quite good at a quick shag in the closet."

"Everyone has talents." I take his hand and squeeze it, half turning toward him so that I can look him in the eye. "Thank you for coming. I can't tell you what it means to me. No, I can. The reason I was comfortable picking up and moving across the country was that I have no one here. I have no one anywhere. I've only ever had my job and my grandmother, and the thought that I would have to choose between them made me feel like I was getting ripped in two. It still feels that way. And I may still have to make that choice. But you coming… I don't know what you had to do to get here, I don't know how you found out that I was here, and I don't care. You being here makes me feel…" I choke back another sob. "It makes me feel less empty. I feel like I belong to something, and I know I shouldn't say stuff like that this early in a relationship, but I don't know how to not speak the truth right now. I might not feel whole ever again in my life, but sitting with you here instead of alone makes me feel, damn, I don't know, half full? Five eighths? This is a crummy way of saying thank you."

I slide down a little in my chair as well, and I squeeze his hand, looking away so I can gather my thoughts. They won't come together. I'm just a mess of feeling where words should be. He's not asking for my thoughts, he's not asking for my feelings. He's not asking for anything.

I settle in with the possibility that this is exactly what I need.

CHAPTER 43

KEATON

I wish I knew how I could help her. I offered her food, water, affection, comfort. I didn't have anything else after that. So I just sat with her until the doctor came out in her knee-length white jacket and reading glasses as she flipped through papers on a clipboard.

When the doctor first appears, Cassie stands with her hands fidgeting at her sides, then folded in front of her. I don't want to impose, so I let her stand by herself, but she looks back at me expectantly as if I have a place in her family, collecting family news and sharing a family experience. Maybe she wants some water, or she wants me to bugger off. I'd get her water and bugger off at the same time, but she waves her hand a little by her hip and there's no way to misinterpret what she wants.

She wants me to come stand by her, and it still feels funny to do that even after she takes my hand. Funny, but right.

The doctor smiles and pokes her reading glasses up her nose. "So, I have some good news and some bad news."

Cassie squeezes my hand so hard, I'm sure she is cutting off the circulation.

"The good news is the surgery went fine." The doctor pauses. "The bad news is she won't be one hundred percent mobile for a while."

Cassie squeezes my hand until her arm relaxes and her exhale is so deep, her shoulders drop an inch. "I can live with that. We can do that. Yes. That's okay."

She doesn't sound as if she's trying to convince herself of something; she sounds as if she's working herself up to believing it. Digging herself out of her hole of despair. I can't help but smile.

They discuss physical therapy, prescriptions, some other shit I don't care about because the endgame is that her grandmother will be okay for a while.

"Would you like to go see her?"

"Yes." Cassie sounds as if she's been offered a chance to drive a Lamborghini.

The doctor heads toward the hallway, and Cassie follows. She tugs me along.

I resist out of surprise. "I'll wait here."

"Are you kidding? You're gonna cheer her up."

She yanks on my hand, hard, until I have to follow. On the way to her grandmother's room, I wonder if this has been wise. She's counting on me, and she won't be able to do that for much longer. She's also smart, well-connected, and curious. She'll look for me. The closer I get to her and the more I offer her, the more likely this diligent and ambitious woman will seek me out, and not only will she find me… I will want to be found.

CHAPTER 44

CASSIE

hy's he freaking out on me? He just stands there as if he doesn't know whether to do what I'm asking him to do or not.

"I don't know why you would come all the way here so that you could be with me and then stand in the hallway. Are you afraid of sick people or something?"

I thought of it as soon as I said it. Maybe he has some kind of sick person phobia. Maybe hospitals freak him out. In which case, he can stand in the hallway all he wants.

He shakes his head for a second as if getting cobwebs out. "No, no. Let's do this then."

"Keaton, really. You've done a lot by being here. If this is too much for you, you can wait in the hallway. Or in the waiting room."

"Get in that room before I pick you up and carry you in there."

I turn slowly and walk in to find my grandmother in a hospital bed with a My Little Pony twenty-piece puzzle that she should be able to do in thirty seconds splayed out on a tray in front of her. She isn't even looking at it. She's gotten half of one edge finished and seems to have lost interest.

"Nana," I say. "How are you feeling?"

"She's very tired," the doctor said. "She might not be able to talk much."

I point at the puzzle.

The doctor takes my meaning right away. "I grabbed one from the children's wing."

I sit by my grandmother and take her hand. She looks at me as if she doesn't recognize me. Or as if I actually exist somewhere in her mind but she can't place me. This is scaring the shit out of me. Have I lost her forever? I'm overwhelmed by the horrible possibilities, all the stories I've heard about grandparents who had an accident and never came back from it. Then her eyes flick over my shoulder and suddenly become awake.

"Ah," she groans hoarsely. "You're back."

I follow her gaze over my shoulder to find Keaton standing behind me with his hand on the back of my chair.

"You never finished the story about moving to Michigan," Keaton says. "I still want to kill that guy you were with. What was his name?"

"Barry. The motherfucker." Her eyes flutter as if cursing my mother's father took a lot of effort. But she's called him a motherfucker at least a thousand times in my short life.

The doctor laughs a little. I smile. Keaton puts his hand on my shoulder, and I put my hand over it. I feel as though I can get through anything with his hand resting on me.

"That's kind of how the story ends," I say. "My grandfather is a motherfucker, like the rest of them."

"He gave me you," she says, turning her head toward the window. "Even your mother, who was a huge pain in my ass. He gave me her."

"Motherfuckers can be a necessary evil." I hear Keaton smiling behind me, as if smiling had a sound. His does.

"So are you feeling all right?" I ask.

She nods ever so slightly but says nothing. I wait. We all wait. But there's nothing else. She's breathing. I see her chest rise and fall under the sheets. I look at the doctor, a little worried.

"Let's let her rest for a while," the doctor says.

When the three of us get to the hallway, the doctor seems more cheerful than I feel.

"I know this can seem worrying," she says. "But this is as good of a result as we can expect so soon. I'm actually surprised by how vibrant she looked after such an experience."

I take a deep breath. Yes. Of course. Who would want to have an extended conversation after that? She was lucid. She recognized a man she'd only seen twice. She called my grandfather a motherfucker. What else did I expect?

I put my fingertips to my mouth as if they can hold in my relief. I didn't realize how tense I was until I sensed the doctor's confidence. "So you mean she's going to be all right?"

"She's not a young woman," the doctor says.

I cut her off. "I know."

She's not a young woman.

She's going to stop existing soon.

She won't be in my life anymore. But for now, she's okay.

My breath hitches again. Crying is like drinking a bottle of wine. You can get drunk, and you might have moments of lucidity, but when you try to stand up, the room spins a little bit. So yes, I stopped crying before I went into the room. Hearing that she was going to be all right was like standing up. The tears came back like a drunkenness. Tears of relief for the present and fear for the future.

Keaton's arm is around me, tightening me in a protective vise. I hitch again, swallow, have an intelligent conversation with the doctor about my plans to get my grandmother home in a few days, sign some papers, and it's all over.

But it's just beginning.

"Keaton," I say as we sit in plastic chairs lining the hall, "I don't know what I'm asking you for. But don't leave me. Or, if you're going to leave me, can you do it right now? If you just turned the plane around to fulfill some sense of obligation or because you thought I was interesting, I totally get it and I won't think worse of you if you bail on me right now and say no thank you. Because it would be the right thing to do."

He shakes his head and *tsk*s as if I'm totally out of line. He's a good person who doesn't want me to suffer unnecessarily in a hospital hallway. But that's not what I want. I don't want to be a good person right now. I wanted him to be the bigger person.

"I don't want reassurances," I say. "I don't want promises. I want to not worry."

One-Mississippi-two-Mississippi.

"What have I ever done to make you worry?"

How funny, the pause before he answers my question with a question. Maybe I should worry that this is a technique, or maybe this is just who he is.

"Besides the usual?" I say with a smirk. "Nothing."

"There you have it."

This time, I do the counting.

One-Mississippi-two-Mississippi-three-Mississippi.

I'm not going to say a damn thing. Inside, I'm smiling from ear to ear. I can see his discomfort in the way he looks around the room and in the way he strokes my fingers.

Four-Mississippi.

"You've gotten a bit under my skin, Agent Grinstead. If that surprises you, imagine how I feel. There aren't many people who can do that. And certainly not any women I've had before. But there's something about you. Maybe it's the artful dodger in you. Maybe it's that badge. Could be the way you threw me against my car. I don't pretend to know, but I can promise you…"

He presses his lips between his teeth as if he's stopping himself from saying more. He's so sexy when he does that. The scruffy hairs around his lips stand up like porcupine spines when his skin bends to the new curve. He was so cocky that first day in the interrogation room. I can't believe this is the same man.

"I can promise you that no matter what happens, I'll never leave you willingly." He shakes his head once as if knocking a pinball in place, then stands and holds his hand out to me. "Let me get you home. You must be tired."

I am tired, but I'm also alive and exhilarated. I want to find out more about this man, who he is, and what I'll find when I peel away the next layer. I don't think I'll ever run out of layers. I don't think there are a limited number of facets to the diamond of Keaton Bridge.

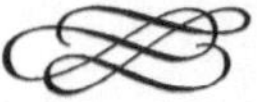

CHAPTER 45

I've stripped her down and laid her on her bed. She already has things folded, piled, packed. Her room has the look of something completely lived in, with its knick-knacks and attention to detail, but the dresser is moved a little away from the wall and the wardrobe's been half emptied.

But my focal point is her, naked on her stomach, toes pointed, the arches of her feet calloused and hard and facing the ceiling. Her eyes are closed, and her hair is splayed across the sheets. I haven't fucked her yet. First, I want her to feel as safe as I don't feel. I run my hands from her shoulders to her lower back, pressing against the skin and releasing tension from the muscles. She groans in release.

"I'm going to drive you to and from work for the next few weeks," I say.

"You don't have to do that," she grumbles sleepily.

"I know."

The fact is, I'm lying. I do need to do that. I need to make sure she's safe. I need to see her walk in and out of her office. If she leaves during the day, she'll be with other agents. I can't do more than this. Not without alarming her.

"I want to," I say, running my hands along the backs of her thighs. She's warm between them, and soft everywhere.

"Thank you for coming to the hospital." Her voice is barely a breath. She didn't sleep at all the night before.

"I will always try to be there if you need me." Again, I'm a liar. I'm voicing my desire, not my reality.

"I'll always need you."

She's killing me. Her dependence is a sugar-coated knife twisting and twisting and twisting, spooling my guts around it.

I slide my hand between her thighs. Her skin and muscle yield under me when I slide toward her core. When I touch her, she groans, already wet for me.

"Hush, my love."

She makes a satisfied hum, opening her eyes for just a second. I pull her ankles apart, not more than enough to give me access to her. I don't want her to be uncomfortable. Not this time.

"Just stay still and relax," I say. "Let me take care of you. Just for now."

Gently, I touch her and stroke in a way that isn't aggressive or forceful, but soothing. With my other hand, I hold her down between her shoulders, giving her something to push against. When she comes, her toes curl and her knees bend. She groans from deep in her throat.

I get my pants off, then her eyes flicker open, a smile playing across her lips.

"Keep smiling. I'm going to fuck you right to sleep."

I only pick her hips up as much as I need to angle myself inside her. I move slowly and deliberately, wedging my arms under her and holding her tight. I don't want to jar her out of her stupor. I don't want her to worry about her grandmother or us. I want to surround her with my love.

She grips the sheets, and when she's close, I come inside her. I want to fill her with everything I have. I want to mark myself on her soul.

I fall on top of her and let my weight press against her body. She can't see my face, and I'm grateful. Because she would see regret and loss.

I let her sleep, but I can't fall into it. My deception keeps me up.

CHAPTER 46

CASSIE

When I put in for two weeks to move, and I got it, I figured the timing was tight but I could manage. Now, with Nana in the hospital, I'm not sure if I have enough time to make sure she's well enough to even go back to the house we already live in.

I enter her hospital room and drop the toiletry kit she asked for on the table next to her, bending over and kissing her cheek. Her skin is warm under my lips. She's getting better.

"It's about time you showed up," Nana says, taking the puzzle from me. It's an idyllic seaside scene with palm trees and a beach chair. She's never interested in the picture as much as the process, but now I'm realizing I just handed her a box of California.

She hands the box back to me, and I slit the tape that holds the top to the bottom. She looks better, she sounds better. I'll be stunned if she dies in a year or ten.

"I had to find one you hadn't done already." I hand the box back to her. It's only a hundred pieces, but it's better than the twenty-piece My Little Pony puzzle she's been taking apart and redoing for two days.

"When are we leaving?" She pokes through the box for the edges.

"You have a week of inpatient physical therapy, and then—"

"They have physical therapists in San Francisco, don't they?"

"I don't think you should move," I blurt. "I don't think it's safe for you."

Her fingers hesitate for a moment in the soup of puzzle pieces, then continue as if nothing important has been said. Anyone who ever said that a hospital stay dims the mind of an elderly person never met my grandmother.

"Thank God," she says. "I can turn your room into the sewing room."

The fact that she hasn't sewn a god damn thing in years notwithstanding, she has never shown an interest in my bedroom before.

"You're not getting rid of me that easily."

"I'll put a guest bed in there. I'll make it a queen so you can invite that nice boy over."

"I'm staying. I can get a promotion another time."

She pushes the puzzle box away to the other edge of the tray. It's only two inches, but the statement is clear. "You will do no such thing, young lady."

"I am a grown woman and I can decide what's important to me. You are the only family I have. I'm not leaving you alone, I'm not moving a thousand miles away, and I am most certainly not going to put your life in danger by taking you with me."

"How is my life in danger?"

"You can't move with a broken hip. It's bad for you."

"Then you can just move the hell out of my house."

"It's my house! Give me a break."

She jerks the puzzle back, sending pieces flying. I pick them up off the blanket and put them into the box, flicking an edge piece onto the tray.

"You know," she says, "you're the first one of us who had a chance to be something."

"I am something. I'm your granddaughter."

"That's very sweet, but stupid. You know I'm not that old. And I'm not some crotchety old biddy that can't get around."

"I know, I—"

"Just go. I'll meet you there." She deliberately picks a piece out of the box and lays it flat. Tapping it twice. "You missed an edge."

I know my grandmother. My mother didn't come from nowhere, and

I inherited a bunch of genes from the both of them. She's manipulating me. She's reverse engineering the whole argument to get me to leave her alone. Or she has a point. I have no way of knowing. She's too good at this.

"I don't want to leave you." I have more to say, but they're only illustrations of those six words. "I was fourteen when you took me in. You were supposed to have a life then. All you did was make sure that I was taken care of. I didn't make the same mistakes that you made and that my mother made, my great-grandmother made. Why did you have such faith in me? Why did you love me so much?"

She rests her hands on the tray, covering a bunch of pieces we laid out. "I always knew you were special. I knew you could do anything you wanted if you just had someone to love you and teach you the right way. When I got you, I knew I could make you the best thing that ever happened to me. And you are. I'm so proud of you. So proud to know you. If you stay here because I fell like a fucking fool, you're going to ruin all of that. So go for me. Get the hell out of here for me."

I pinch the bridge of my nose, hoping she can't tell that I'm crying. But she's way too sharp for my pathetic obfuscations.

"Can you reach that little makeup kit for me?" It's the one I brought from home for her. When I pick it up, she says, "Open it."

I unzip it. Inside is a collection of old powders, blushes, eyeshadow from the 1980s. And a blue velvet box.

She points at the box. "Open that."

I snap it open and inside is a diamond solitaire. "Nana! How did you get this?"

"You mean with the Fisher-Price credit card you gave me?" She raises an eyebrow. I'm starting to think that breaking her hip has actually made her smarter. "That there is a gift from a man named Jack. He was okay. Or I thought so. When your mom went to prison and I told him I was gonna raise you, he gave me that ring. He said he'd marry me but he didn't want any children. Can you believe that? I told him to take that ring and shove it up his ass."

My jaw drops. "Wait. You could have gotten married? But you took me in instead?"

"Nothing like a crisis for a man to show his true colors. Mark my words, once he gave me that ring, he showed me who he really was. Being married is not worth that much. In any case…" She waved as if the whole thing is water under the bridge. "He told me to keep it, so I did. I kept it for you, so you wouldn't have to wait for a man to get one."

It has to be a carat and a quarter. What kind of man tells a woman to keep a ring that big?

A rich man. A man who could have made her very comfortable. A man who didn't want to take in a stray.

"Thank you. For everything."

"Might want to see if that nice British guy wants to give you one of his own before you start wearing it around."

I slowly close the box and cocoon it in my palms, one on top of the other, as if it is a powerful talisman.

Keaton is a mysterious and probably dangerous person. I haven't given much thought to him wanting to spend his life with me. It's too soon and there's too much going on, but for the first time, I allow myself to hear her suggestion.

I want him. I want him now, and I want him in twenty years. I want to know all of his mysteries and peel back the danger, the sharp edges, the puzzles, until I find the raw vulnerable place that makes him who he is. I know it's there, and I know I'm going to love it.

"Can we make a deal?"

She's poking through the box again. She's a real piece of work. My mother was more like her than I ever understood. My grandmother conned me into being my best self when I was on the path to becoming someone completely different.

"I will go to San Francisco without you. But as soon as you heal, I'm coming to get you."

"We'll see."

"We will, Nana. We sure will."

CHAPTER 47

Two weeks off work isn't actually two weeks off work, apparently. Not when there are dossiers on the desk.

I let him drive me to work because I like him. I like making him happy, and he's a nice guy to be around in the morning. He cooked me breakfast, washed my hair, took care of me in a way that is surprising, comforting, and delicious. I'm pretty confident that whatever happens with my new job, we'll figure it out. No one's proving a damn thing against him, and look, he's a legitimate businessman. Anyone can see that. I practically whistle my way into Orlando's office.

"Good morning, sir," I say. "I heard the dossiers came in."

"Live cases and assets." He hands me a thick accordion file. "They're going to expect you to hit the ground running as soon as you get there. I told them you can do undercover work."

"I won't make a liar out of you."

"I know you won't." He smiles and pats my shoulder.

I take the dossiers to the viewing room. They're on paper, which seems counterintuitive for the Cyber Crime unit, but there's nothing more secure than pencil and paper. I leave my phone at the guard station outside the door and go in, making myself comfortable at the empty desk.

The first surprising thing I find in the dossiers is that Keyser Kaos is two people. The first folder is for Keyser, who's a tall man with a round face and little glasses. He dresses as if he's seventy-five, but he's probably not older than thirty. Romanian. I memorize the rest of his stats and the particulars of the photographs of him.

The next dossier belongs to Kaos. There's much less known about him. His general age, fifties or so. Home country is Romania again. He claims to be a doctor, but it's never been proven. The only photograph is from behind. There's something surprisingly familiar about his posture, but it's hard to say.

The next surprise shouldn't have been a surprise. I should've seen it coming like a high-speed train at the end of the tunnel. Or an anvil falling from the fifth floor, set to drop on my head exactly as I passed underneath.

The presence of Keaton's dossier should have been cartoonishly obvious to me, but when I open it and see his face, I almost want to throw up. Looking straight at me with desaturated eyes and a mouth that accuses me of willful blindness, he freezes me. It's not a mug shot, but that doesn't matter. The notes swim. The details aren't sentences; they're meaningless boxes and dots. A code I can decipher if I can just push through this wall of panic. My instincts scream so loud, I can't hear myself think.

I shut the folder, gripping the edges as if I want to tear it in two.

I should want this. I should read it from cover to cover to find out who he is. Every lie he ever told me is right there, and every tiny truth might be exposed.

But it's not what I want. I don't want the truth. I want reality. Reality is his touch. Reality is his voice. Reality is him showing up when I needed him. Reality is my trust in him.

What is this folder full of paper going to tell me about Keaton Bridge, or whatever his name is, that I need to know?

I shift it aside and go through the last two dossiers. Sure, sure, sure. Catch this guy, he's done terrible things. And this lady, she's stolen more money than I'll see in my lifetime. And what about Keaton? Where does this money come from? Who can afford a penthouse at the Bellagio in

Las Vegas? Or to invest in a new kind of computing? Can't be cheap. What did I sign on for? What am I asking of myself?

As I put the folders back into the accordion and figure-eight the string to close it, I know I can be told all the truths, I can have all the facts, but I also know that what I have with Keaton is real. I love him, and it's real.

I will never trade reality for ambition. Ever.

CHAPTER 48

KEATON

I left Cassie in hospital with her grandmother to make a quick visit to the factory. Taylor's about to leave the office. I push him back in and slam the door behind me.

"What the hell, Keaton?" He takes half a step back, which gives me enough room to get by him.

"Sit."

"I have a plane to catch."

"It's a private plane. It'll wait."

"Harper's meeting me at the airport in San Jose. I don't like making her wait."

"I'm sure she'll be devastated, mate." I snap the chair around and wheel it toward him. "Or she's an adult and she'll manage."

He's going to say something, some little clever quip that'll make me want to punch him in the face. I know it. I'm girded for it. But instead, he sucks his cheeks, glances out the window, and shuts his mouth.

"You almost gave up everything for Harper," I say. "Why?"

Taylor smiles a little bit, shaking his head, giving up the fight over the next ten minutes. "I can't believe it took you this long to ask me that." He throws himself into the chair as if he's staking his claim on it.

"I figured it was your business."

"You're a strange fucking guy, you know that?"

I guess I do know that.

"The whole thing that happened with us? QI4? She broke me. I mean, she really did a job on me. And I was pissed off, but then she changed me. I saw things differently. And… I'm not trying to be a pussy, but I couldn't go on doing things the same way once I got to know her. Once she showed me who I really was and who I could be… a better guy. Okay, I'm a pussy. But I could be who I always wanted to be, all right? I could be even better with her. It really wasn't too much of a choice. Can I go, asshole?"

"Are you saying she made you a better man? You're a prat."

"I prefer it when you call me a cunt."

I can't help but laugh at him. "You know a lot of things about me. More than anyone else, but you don't know it all."

"I had a feeling."

"I'm not who I always said I was, but you were always a friend to me anyway. So I'm going to tell you something else because you really are a cunt."

"Can it be covered in a phone call?"

"That time we almost got rich together in high school? When the FBI was waiting on your couch when you got home from school? You covered for me, and I appreciated that. But it didn't work. They came to my door too, but I was still a British national."

"Are you serious?" He sits straight as a rod, the plane forgotten. "What happened?"

"I can't tell you exactly. But what I can tell you is that everything I've done since then is the result of that stupid little exploit." I take a deep breath and lean on the desk, gripping the edge. "And now all of the chickens are coming home to roost as I found my own Harper. She's changed the calculus completely. Everything I assumed I would do, every calculation I've made, every shit decision is landing in my lap. I would do anything to be with her, and I don't know how. I don't know which decision to make to have her or if having her is the worst decision I can make for her."

"You're being a little cryptic. I can't help you if you don't tell me the specifics."

"I'm not asking for your help. Not today. But if she asks for your help, I need you to give it to her. You'll do whatever you have to."

"Is this the FBI agent?"

He's not asking me about QI4. I know he cares about how my decisions will affect the company he's built his life around, and maybe before Harper was in his life, he would be demanding answers for the sake of his dreams. But now he looks as if the gears are turning in a different direction.

"Yes. You need to take care of her."

"I'm not saying I won't, but where are you going?"

I stand straight. "I'll leave it for you to figure out."

"If I put Harper on it, she can hand you your ass."

"Good luck with that. Just know that you're a fucking cunt, and I should have kicked your arse fifteen years ago."

"I love you too, dickhead."

"Go fuck yourself."

I leave before I tell him too much.

CHAPTER 49

CASSIE

Frieda can't believe her ears. I slide my folders into my briefcase, shaking my head just as she is right now. I'm shaking it because no one understands me. She's shaking her head because, yeah. She doesn't understand me.

"I can't leave my grandmother. She means everything to me." I try out my half-truth to see if I can make it sound like complete honesty.

"You've wanted this forever." Frieda is practically stomping around like a three-year-old.

But I'm confident I'm doing the right thing. One, for my grandmother. Two, for Keaton. But I can't tell her number two. I can't tell anyone. Not even him.

"I know." I shrug as if it's nothing. It's something, but not everything.

"You've wanted this forever. What did you think you were going to do if you got sent to CID? Not go to Quantico?"

"If my grandmother had broken her hip, I wouldn't go to Quantico either." I snap my bag shut. "How does it feel being GS-12?"

"Same as being GS-11, but with more money. You know, I really admired your ambition. So I think I'm taking this kind of hard. Personally."

"Yeah, look, you're not the only one who's disappointed. I really think my grandmother is going to be completely impossible to live with now. She's trying to kick me out the door. She keeps telling me that she'd have a boyfriend already if I were gone."

"Maybe she wouldn't be the only one who had a boyfriend." She waggles one side of her eyebrow, then her expression grows dark. Almost angry. "Unless you're staying for Mr. Smirkypants?"

Of course I'm staying for Mr. Smirkypants. I'm staying to protect him, not to be with him. I could be with him from the San Francisco office just as easily if being there didn't mean he'd be the object of my investigation.

"Think about it," I say. "You and I can still hang out together. We can go have champagne every time there's a pay raise. When we catch some lawbreaking douchebag."

"Sisters-in-the-law." We bump fists.

I sling my bag over my shoulder and walk out. My heels clack along the sage-green hallway. Every time I walked that hall in the past, I assumed there would be a last time. One day I'd move past this little field office. One day I'd fulfill my destiny and remember this linoleum fondly, the shade of green with warmth, the buzzing fluorescence by the utility closet with some kind of nostalgia. But none of that is going to happen. I'm here. I'm here for the duration.

Am I okay with that?

I can't say that I totally am. I'm a little sad, a little broken, very disappointed. But what choice do I have? I will not be pitted against Keaton. Truth be told, I'm not sure how long I can even stay at the Bureau and have him.

I won't give him up for anything. Not to be the director of the FBI. Not to have that silver badge linked to my name and my ID for the rest of my life. Not for all the approval in all of the world.

I only want his approval. I only want him.

There are some choices that aren't really choices. Some are really tests. This is one of them.

Out in the cold, in front of the long circular driveway between the federal building and the parking lot, I stamp my feet. It's snowing, and my shoes are completely inappropriate for the weather.

I'm five minutes early, that's how eager I am to see him.

The parking lot looks especially dismal under the cloud cover and the slapping wet snow. I pace, my heel slipping on icy crust. I right myself by grabbing a pole. It, too, is slick and cold with new ice. It's going to be a hard commute home.

When my phone rings, I'm not surprised it's him.

"You should wait inside," he says. "The bridge is covered in ice."

"Be careful."

"Winter is crap."

"Yeah."

"You won't have this in California. Not even in San Francisco. It gets cold and rainy in June, but never like this."

His excitement carries over the squeak of the windshield wipers. He wants what's best for me, to the exclusion of everything else. He has to know we have a dossier on him. He has to know he'll be a target for me once I move. He doesn't seem to care.

The snow is getting thicker. Horizontal.

"I have to talk to you when you get here."

"Tell me."

"Not while you're driving."

"You're on speaker. It's safe. I do need to talk to you as well."

"I'll see you when you get here."

There's a long pause. The wipers squeak. The rain pats his windows.

"Hello?" I say. "Keaton?"

"I love you, Cassandra."

He hangs up before I can tell him I love him too.

Ten minutes pass in the break room. I make hot chocolate and look out the window while I sip it, burning my tongue. I open the fridge and grab milk to cool it.

Outside, the wail of sirens is muted by the snow and wind. Their flashing lights move across the open fridge door. The squawk of radios, the jingle of keys and equipment, stomping feet all come from the hall, and one of the security guys pops his head in.

"You seen Nelson?"

"No. What's going on?"

"A Lexus skidded off the Winnetaka Bridge."

I drop the milk.

I DON'T HAVE my car. There's not a cab in town. No one should drive in this. No sane person would.

Apparently Nelson and sanity have not made acquaintance. I find him getting his boots on by his desk.

"Can you take me over to the scene?" I ask, not panicking at all.

"Sure. Give me half a shake. I'll be out the west gate. Green Sierra."

There's no need to run to meet him there. He's still in his office, but I hurry so I can do my very best waiting and, despite my claims to the contrary, my most efficient panicking.

I head for the west gate, which exits onto a smaller service road, and trudge through snow-thick air, turning my face against the biting wind.

What if it wasn't Keaton's Lexus? What if it was some other Lexus, or another make, or the car in front of him? What if he's coming around the front and I'm sitting at the west gate?

I call him. No answer.

I text.

—Hey, are you all right? Text any response—

I WAIT. The signal's pretty good, even in the storm, and the message is quickly marked as delivered. But there are no twinkling dots to indicate he's typing something back. He's driving in a blizzard. If he has half a brain, he's ignoring my text.

My fingers are getting cold. I pocket the phone and put on my glove.

I'm going to quickly check the front gate and see if he's there, then he can drive to the service gate and tell Nelson we're good to go.

It's a plan.

I walk across the lot as quickly as I can in these stupid shoes, head bowed against the snow, hands in my pockets, thinking it'll only take me a minute. A minivan pulls astride me. Is it a Sierra? Green? Covered in snow, with only the dark arcs of the windshield uncovered, it's hard to say. The side door slides open.

I get in.

"Can we roll by the front first?"

The side door closes, and the driver turns to me. A scarf covers the lower half of his face and a hat covers the top.

My relief at being in a warm car is swept away by the sight of a crumpled up Burger King bag on the floor and a mini baseball bat in the driver's hand.

My defensive move comes a split second too late.

CHAPTER 50

CASSIE

I hear rain first. I'm not fully capable of feeling my body outside the pain in my head, my shoulders, my hips.

I'm not quite sure I can move, even if I want to. My skin wakes. My clothes are damp. The floor against my cheek is dry. Even warm. Even soft. It's not a floor. It's a bed or a sheet or a blanket. But it's dry, belying the click of raindrops. I wonder how this is possible.

The sound of the accident is in my head, not my ears. Bangs. Whooshes. A shout from Keaton.

Keaton. Where is he?

With that panic, the rest of my senses wake up. My awareness of my body becomes fuller, surrounding the pain with the feeling of tightness in my arms. They're boxed, wrist to wrist, behind my back. Restrained. When my eyelids flutter, they scratch against fabric. A blindfold.

Where's Keaton? I can't imagine he'd allow this, and the speculation that he's the cause of this circumstance sparks and dies. No. He would never.

Is he dead? From the accident I can barely remember, or from some other crime?

I strain against my bonds only enough to test their strength. I'm conscious enough to know that I'm too unconscious to think clearly or fight off whatever's gotten me here.

Through a wall, or door, or some combination of both, I hear a male voice. Another language. Not Keaton.

I don't know if he speaks any other languages. How can I not know that?

The sound of rain is not rain. It's a crackling fire, and I realize that I'm warm even though my clothes are damp. I feel like two hundred pounds of dead, wet weight held together by ache.

I don't recognize the language being spoken on the other side of the wall. It's punctuated by a short, derisive laugh, and no other voice joins it. Whoever it is, he's on the phone. I don't assume he's alone.

Keeping my body still, focusing on my breathing and the lines, contours, and limits of my body, I move my ankles apart just enough to determine that they are not bound. I'm on my side, a flat pillow under my head.

Whoever it is doesn't want to kill me quite yet. What does that say for Keaton's life? Will they hold me for ransom to flush him out? Or are they waiting to kill me for some other reason?

I don't know what to wish for, so I don't wish for anything. I don't think about Keaton. Speculation uses too much energy.

The voice stops. There's a bit of shuffling, a bit of clanging around the kitchen. I'm desperately thirsty.

The door opens with a creak. Needs oil. The house, or room, or whatever must usually be vacant. Nobody could live here and deal with that creak.

"Wakey, wakey." The voice that had been on the phone a minute ago is slightly familiar when it's in the same room. Not quite familiar enough to pin down just yet.

I don't move. I just breathe and listen to his movements. One step. Two steps. Three steps. The distance from the door to my side. Eight feet. Nine feet, maybe.

The creak of the chair. The flick of a lighter. The thick, earthy scent of a foreign cigarette.

My blindfold is moved away. Light shoots through the veils of my eyelids. Incandescent. Not sunlight. Maybe there are dark drapes or closed blinds, but my guess is that it's still nighttime.

"Nothing broken, lucky girl."

I open my eyes. The figure sits in a chair next to the bed, smoking. My vision is too blurry to see properly, but I can see the orange pinpoint arc to his lips and I smell the smoke as he exhales it. I blink the fog away, but it's stubborn. My arms move reflexively to rub them, but I can now identify my binding as a single loop of duct tape around my forearms.

"Who are you?" And what have you done with Keaton?

"Are you warm enough?"

I'm not answering that. Hostility won't get me far right now, but I don't owe him my comfort.

I squeeze my eyes shut and move them around. Left. Right. Up. Down. Then I open them again.

He has soulful brown eyes and a nose that's been busted. He's not much older than me, but they seem like they've been hard years. He smiles at me. One of his front teeth is chipped a little bit.

I've seen chipped teeth look worse.

"Hello, Doctor John," I say with a voice that's more hoarse than I expect and a throat burns with water and grit.

"So kind of you to remember. So like a well-trained abuser of power." He reaches his arm close to me and flicks his ashes into something out of my vision. His jacket opens and I see the shoulder holster on his right side.

He's left-handed.

There's a window behind him. The blinds are open, and I can see the deep orange of the sky reflected in the snow. The color tells me that light from the ground is bouncing off the clouds. We aren't too far from the city. But the dimness of the orange hue tells me we aren't too close either.

I open my mouth to ask him where Keaton is, then shut it. I won't let him know what's important to me.

"I'm so sorry about your boyfriend." His smile turns his sentiment into a lie, but his message holds the truth about my lover.

I've lost him. Somewhere in the blackness between those brake lights and waking up here, he slipped away forever.

I swallow what little spit I have, along with my grief. Not now. Now is not the time.

"I can't move."

"I left your legs free. There's nowhere to run in a blizzard."

The lines of water pattering and dripping on the window mean the blizzard part of the storm is over, but I don't correct him.

"No, I mean I really can't move. I can't feel my legs."

He smiles, and I wonder if I've overplayed this hand. He switches his cigarette to his left side, leans toward me again, then I feel a searing pain in my heel. I jerk away, rolling over until my hands and arms are again between my back and the bed.

John pulls the cigarette back and takes a drag. "I seem to have cured you."

Now I'm wondering what he did to Keaton, or if he's still doing it. If he was sorry about my boyfriend not because he was dead but because he has cigarette burns all over him. Now I want to take his face off.

"You're a miracle worker."

"Apparently not. I couldn't save that man you were with. So now I have to use you. I'm very sorry about that. But I have some business to attend with some people. And I need a little leverage. You, dear girl, are my leverage. We're going to get along fine as long as you cooperate."

As long as I cooperate, and as long as the other side of the negotiating table cooperates, and as long as I don't fall apart. Falling apart seems like the only real choice. Grief has a way of boiling over whether you turn up the heat or not. Grief seeps through cracks in the hardest armor, and right now, I'm all cracks. I have to hold back, pretend nothing matters to me, but my eyes burn with tears I'm not allowed to shed.

"What do you want? The FBI is not going to negotiate with you. Not for my life, at least."

"Fuck the FBI." He stubs out his cigarette on the night table behind me. The glass ashtray clinks as it taps the wood.

"You were going to kidnap me in Vegas, Keaton found me first."

"He was disloyal. You would have been a tidy way to pay him back. You're not useful for that anymore, but I can embarrass his employers."

I start to ask if he's trying to get QI4 back for something, but he can't mean he wants money from Taylor. I don't mean shit to him. If he wanted ransom from Taylor, he would have kidnapped Harper.

But what sticks is the thought that Keaton had employers at all. Imagine that. A whole other side to him. The white ceiling is in shadows, with a domed overhead light in the center. I focus on it. It looks like a breast.

God, I'm losing my mind.

"I should've taken you for every dime you had at the poker table." I lick my lips. My arms are falling asleep under my back, but the rest of me is now wide awake. "You're a mess of tells."

"Your heart is too soft to stall me long enough." He puts his hands on his knees and stands over me, eyes grazing my body in a way that's objectifying but not sexual.

I can feel my clothes pressing against my skin. I'm completely covered, yet I feel completely naked.

He takes a knife from a little leather sheath at his belt and flips it open. I'm not afraid of the knife. Dead people aren't as useful in a negotiation.

He flips me over by the shoulder, and I see the other side of the room. The fireplace has no pokers, and there's a latched screen in front of the fire. I won't be able to hit him with a brass rod or throw him into the fire.

He cuts away the duct tape. My arms creak and ache when I move them. The tape is still stuck to my arms. I rip off one side. It hurts like fucking hell, but I won't give this guy the satisfaction of seeing me get squeamish about getting a little hair pulled. I pull away the other rectangle of duct tape. It takes a piece of skin. I act like I don't give a shit.

I don't actually give a shit.

I sit up straight, bending my knees to one side then tucking them under my bottom to sit Japanese-style.

He puts the knife back in the little sheath.

"For the record, you really are a shitty poker player."

"Poker's not my game."

"Of course." I slide off the bed on the opposite side so he doesn't feel threatened. "It involves actual human interaction. Not usually a hacker thing." I wave as if swatting away trivial concerns.

"Are you trying to bait me?" He tilts his head a little, brows knotting in concern, as if I'm a monkey in a cage, palming a pile of his shit. He's asking me if I intend to throw it, and if I understand he can destroy me if any lands on him.

Sociopath.

Not all sociopaths are evil. Most lead curious but normal lives. But grouped with narcissism and sadism, sociopathy is a very, very dangerous sickness.

The sadism is apparent in the heel of my foot.

The narcissism in the lengths he will go for vengeance.

So. Here we are. Standing on opposite sides of the bed.

I have this.

I trust myself.

"I'm thirsty," I say. "I'm happy to get water myself, but you're making the rules here."

"You may go." He points at the bedroom door.

One, two, three steps, favoring the burn on my foot. By the fourth step, it doesn't even hurt and I'm out. He follows me, where I can't see him. The rustic, open living space has a kitchenette, an old couch, a larger covered fireplace with no pokers. It's a log cabin, and the horizontal lines of the logs encircle the exterior walls.

I walk into the kitchenette, watching him in shiny surfaces. The microwave door. The windows.

"Glasses over the sink," he says.

I reach into the cabinet. Plastic. Can't break and slash. I fill a pink cup with a Budweiser logo. Turn. Drink, watching him over the rim of the cup.

His fingers play with the pressed edge of his jacket.

Sensory processing disorder.

When he blinks, he squeezes his eyes shut.

A tic.

"So what's next?"

"We wait. If you behave, I don't shoot you."

"Fine." I put down the cup.

His approach is swift and stealthy. He catches me in the millisecond I take to put the cup in a clear spot, punching me in the face with mercilessness and speed. My vision explodes into a thousand points of light and I drop to my knees.

"In case you're wondering who's in charge," he says from above me. "I'm not some basement-dweller. I don't need this gun to make you comply."

"Okay." I choke out as I put my forehead on the cold floor before I tip completely. My stomach twists, but I'm not puking. Nope. Not today.

I'm not standing until I have my wits back. His shoe is right in my vision.

"You were doing your job, but I trusted him. To find out he'd been spying on us all those years? It makes me look foolish."

I look up at him. His jacket is still open. His right middle finger still strokes the fabric's edge, and when he blinks, it's so hard his nose wrinkles.

My right eye throbs. "He wasn't working for us."

"I never said he was." He holds his hand out to help me up. "You were doing your job, so I don't mean to hurt you."

Timidly, I hold out my hand, and we grab each other by the wrist.

"Thank you," I say as he yanks me up.

He blinks.

I use the extra millisecond to slip my hand into his jacket like the artful dodger I am and pickpocket his gun, pretending to lose my balance so I can unsnap the holster while he's tilted.

I have it.

Not one to waste time, I pull the trigger.

The bullet hits him in the leg, and he falls backward. I stand over him. He's got his hands up, but I'm not fooled. There's no surrender in his eyes. I aim the gun between them.

I'm going to finish this motherfucker.

The roar of engines comes from outside. The flash of lights.

"You are the luckiest man alive."

"My partner's going to find you."

"I look forward to it."

The door bursts open. Headlamps. Shouts to clear the area. Only when I see rifle tips surrounding Kaos do I take my finger off the trigger and hold up the gun. It's taken from me.

I get a pat on the back. It's Ken, arm still in a sling. When I face him, he flinches.

"That's gonna bruise up nice," he says.

I touch my eye. It's heavy and tender. Orlando joins Ken in looking at my busted face.

"I had him," I say.

Orlando nods. "I know."

Ken gives orders to forensics, getting pulled away in the chaos.

"How…?" I don't finish the sentence.

A man I don't recognize walks in. He has silver-grey hair, a long wall coat, leather gloves, and a stiff upper lip.

"Agent Grinstead," Orlando says, "this is Ambassador Brookings. He alerted me that you might be the target of this asshole."

The ambassador takes off his glove and holds his hand out to shake mine. I pin his accent in the first four words. "Sorry to meet you under these—"

"Do you know where Keaton is? Is he alive?" I leave his hand hanging.

The two men look at each other, then back at me. I've obviously shown my hand. I've told them what's important to me, who's important to me, and why I shouldn't be going to Cyber Crime. I don't give a shit. The FBI can shove that job up their ass, and this British guy can go right behind. I want Keaton. I want him now.

"Tell me." I snarl those two words. They come from deep in my throat and stop right behind my teeth

"Grinstead." Orlando uses my name as a call to attention, but I don't need to be told to focus.

There are probably a dozen agents in the tiny house. Things are getting overturned, there's shouting, barking, the squawk of radios, and I don't give a shit. I don't give the tiniest little shit. I am more focused than I've ever been.

"Let's get the scene under control." Orlando doesn't know what he's dealing with as he tries to stall me, treat me like someone with no skin in this game. He thinks this is about the job for me. It hasn't been about the job since I met that man. "You'll be briefed—"

I cut him off. "You tell me right now what I need to know, or I'm going to burn this fucking place down."

Orlando looks at me as if I have lost my mind, and maybe I have. The ambassador, however, doesn't know me from a hole in the wall. Doesn't know who I am or what I'm capable of. To be honest, I don't know who I am or what I'm capable of either, but he seems to know enough about me to know that I'm not going to sit in the back of the ambulance with ice on my eye, drinking hot fucking cocoa. Maybe he's reading me like a book. Maybe Keaton told him, or maybe I have a star-spangled tell for being a woman in love.

He slowly shakes his head, turning up his hands, one bare palm one leather-gloved palm, and says "I'm sorry."

That's that then.

You don't say you're sorry unless what you're not saying is going to break somebody's heart.

I'm not going to faint.

I am not going to faint.

I am not going to fucking faint. I am, however, going to throw up. I brush past the agents coming in, run outside, no jacket, no gloves, just enough time to jam my feet in the heels Kaos left by the door. The exact wrong shoes for an ankle-deep step into the snow as I go to the side of the house. I put my hand on the log wall and bend at the waist. All I see is the snow on the ground and the top layer of white flakes vibrating in the wind.

He's dead. They killed him. He's dead. I killed him.

My stomach lurches and I try to let it up. I try to just get rid of this loop of agony in my mind.

He's dead. They killed him. He's dead. I killed him.

I want to see the body. I never want to see the body. I want to know if he drowned or banged his head in the accident or if Kaos did it. I never want to hear his name again. I want to go. I want to stay. I want to throw up, but I can't. I can't let it up because if I do, I will be expelling him from me. He is permanent. Even if I never told him that he was permanent, he changed the shape of my heart forever. He let me trust him, molding my heart into the shape that clicked into his like a puzzle piece. No one else will fit. He custom-made my love to fit his.

I will never let him go.

"I trusted you," I say to the wind. I say it to the cold. I say to myself, and I hear it.

I trusted him.

I still trust him.

The side of the building drowns in the white lights of a car, and my shadow is a cutout on it. I am the negative space, taller in the angle of the lights, tripled in paler versions of me at the edges. As the car swings to the left, my shadow swings right and disappears. I'm still here. Only the shadow is gone.

I'm going to disappoint you.

I'm going to hurt you.

I trust him.

Had he not been hinting at this the entire time?

No matter what happens, I'll never leave you willingly.

Willingly.

But the text.

An ocean cannot separate us.

And the alphanumeric string he made me memorize.

That code is everything you need to know.

What was it? I need to know *what* it is, because now I know *why* it is.

I stand up straight, and suddenly I'm not sick anymore.

CHAPTER 51

CASSIE

J've always been an ambitious person. I've always wanted something more. To be better. Do better. Go further. Now all of this energy is turned to one thing and one thing only.

Find Keaton Bridge.

The official story is that his body was lost in the river and they're still looking for it.

Good luck with that.

I have a different strategy. Find out what the code meant. Find out his real name, even though he might not be using it anymore.

I think best when one half of my brain is focused elsewhere. I'm at the firing range, squeezing off round after round after round. *Pop pop pop*. I don't even feel myself doing it anymore. I don't even feel the pain in my hand. I don't feel hungry, thirsty. Nothing.

The British ambassador in San Francisco does nothing but confirm lies. He's very sorry about my loss. He can go fuck himself. I have another stop to make, but I need my head absolutely clear for it. I need to know what exactly I want.

Pop pop pop.

I'm not going to get emotional. I'm going to do this job, then when I know for sure whether he's dead or alive, I'll have feelings about it. I practically have my breakdown scheduled.

Pop pop pop.

I leave my last bullet between the target's eyes and slide out the empty magazine. I'm out of bullets.

"What's on your mind?" Shadow Horse Brady asks. "Or do you have stock in a lead mine?"

I sign myself out. "Just trying to think."

"I hear you're moving?"

I never officially turned down the Cyber Crime assignment. It didn't seem wise, not when I was as likely to find Keaton from California as I was from Doverton.

"Can't beat the weather in California."

"Nice shiner on that eye," he says as I put my jacket on. "I heard what happened. Everyone's talking about what a badass you are." He winks at me.

"Just don't get in my way." I wink back at him.

CHAPTER 52

CASSIE

I'd opened Keaton's dossier as soon as I got a clean bill of health, minus a black eye, and after the firing range, I look at it with a clear head.

I don't know if he tried to tell me all of this before and I was just blinded by him and how he made me feel. His life was spent keeping secrets. I can only imagine how hard it would be for him to hint at anything or tell me something that had been locked away for so long.

My assumptions about him were both right and wrong.

Keaton has an asset dossier, not a criminal dossier. Cyber Crime watches him closely. Both of his parents worked in military intelligence for the British government. Low level, mostly data analysts. But his father made an enemy, and I assumed correctly that the family was moved to New Jersey to protect them. So when Keaton was busted hacking, MI6 recruited him. Unlike Taylor's work with the FBI, Keaton never quit. He had been working undercover for MI6 from the beginning, and right up until the end.

There are details on top of details about his work and his relationships. None of them more prevalent than with the two dark web hackers Keyser and Kaos.

Kaos is in custody. Keyser is not.

There's no match for the code he gave me. No indication of what it might be.

I consider the possibility that he's dead and I'm in denial. I let that option sink in, but I cannot accept it until I see either the body or some other proof.

I don't have a picture of him. I don't have a memory that's physical. An object holding my hand. The photograph of him in that dossier is all I have, and Lord knows I'm not so stupid as to try to take it with me. So I memorize it. I memorize the slopes of his body as they ran under the curves of my hand. I remember the feel of his cheeks in the morning before he shaved, the blue of his eyes that is not captured in the photograph but in the beginnings of the night sky just after twilight.

"I'm coming for you," I whisper. "Buckle in, Keaton Bridge, because I'm coming for you."

I'm NOT EXACTLY CHEERFUL, but I have a purpose. I had purpose before Keaton. Get promoted. Move up. Be better.

Now my purpose is love, and if that's not happiness, I don't know what is.

The light buzzes over the door to the utility closet. The flat green is as institutional and putrid as ever. I'll see this hallway again, and one day I'll stop walking its linoleum, but it's no more than a passage from one place to another.

"Grinstead!" Orlando calls from behind me. I wait for him. "Did you get the comm from cyber? About Keyser?"

"Closing in, sir."

"I want to make sure you're not chasing him down yourself."

"No, sir."

"Good. They have it. You should be sleeping off that knock on the head anyway. You get paid downtime for a reason."

The end of the hall is a right turn for the coffee machines and a left turn for the exit.

"I'm picking up my grandmother from the hospital."
He shakes his head slowly, "Jesus, it's been a rough week for you."
"I'll be fine. Really. Don't worry. I run faster uphill."
With a light shot on the arm, he turns right and I turn left.

CHAPTER 53

CASSIE

*N*ana and I are like two wounded warriors when I bring her home from the hospital. She's in a wheelchair, dying to get out of it, talking about how she's going to attack physical therapy as she has attacked nothing before in her life. I look as if I've been hit on the side of the head with a two-by-four, and I too am ready to attack my own healing like nothing I have attacked before.

I'd put a plywood ramp up the short steps, and I wheel her up it. The door's wide enough for the wheelchair, and with things all moved around, the living room is clear for her. I've already set up a bed and a chair that'll tip her in and out of it.

"I cannot wait to get out of this cage," she says for the hundredth time. "It doesn't even hurt anymore. I'm fine."

"You have pins in you. Do you want to sit on the couch?"

"When is the nurse coming? Don't you have better things to do?"

I help her to the couch and set her gently in her usual spot. "Someone's coming tomorrow to help you. I have to finish packing. They say you can move with me in a couple of weeks."

"Cassandra, I have to tell you something."

I fluff her pillows and lay a blanket over her knees. "Okay, tell me."

"I don't want to go to California."

"Nana—"

"I mean it. I want you to go there alone. I'm very sorry about what happened to that boy, and if you need me to be with you, I'll be there. But I like it here. I'm used to it. I have friends."

"You were so excited to go. Don't pretend you weren't."

"I thought if I went with you, it would make you happy."

"It was an act? Is that what you're saying?"

"I realized I was too old for the long con. I don't have the patience. And moving? I get tired thinking about it, and I get tired thinking about living with you again. I have to sit up and wait for you while you're off toting a gun and catching criminals. I have to worry day in and day out. And then I have to worry that you're stuck in a rinky-dink field office with no chance of making something of yourself. I moved here to take care of you, and maybe now it's time you take care of yourself so I can take care of myself. I'm a selfish old woman."

I sit next to her. "If you're lying… I don't want you to underestimate how angry that will make me."

She rolls her eyes at me. What seventy-three-year-old woman rolls her eyes? I laugh for the first time in days.

"Now that's the first time I've seen you laugh in days," my grandmother says. "Sweetheart, what happened to you makes me very sad and very angry. I mean, you can't even trust a man to live long enough to marry you."

I laugh again, dizzy with the release of my pain and sorrow. I want to rest my head on her lap. I want her to stroke my hair the way she used to. But she's too frail, and even after everything I've been through, she needs me to be strong more than I need her to comfort me.

"Eventually you're going to have to move in with me. I'll want you to. Can you understand that? I want you to come live with me when living alone is too much."

"Sure, kid."

Nana pats my knee with one hand and grabs for the remote control with the other, wincing with pain when she stretches.

"I have it." I turn on QVC, where a pair of sparkling earrings looks like the most beautiful thing in the world. "Are you settled?"

"Bernie and Grace are coming by."

"I'm going to run some errands."

I wheel her puzzle tray over to her. Half of the kittens are pieced together. I wonder if she'll remember her hip or my black eye whenever she sees this one. I'll think of how I started my search for Keaton.

Will I remember the disappointment of not finding him? Or finding out he's dead?

Or will he be by my side?

CHAPTER 54

CASSIE

I learned Taylor is in the habit of eating dinner at the Barrington Mansion—Harper's family home—right across the river from the factory. It was where we first met, the day I flashed my badge and demanded to talk to Keaton Bridge. The day I met the love of my life at the factory and brought him in for questioning.

Harper's sister, Catherine, opens the door. She is the patron saint of Barrington, selling all of her possessions for over ten years to support the people of a dying town. The house has been refurnished with new things, and she has a sunny smile when she opens the door.

"Hello," I say. "My name is Cassie Grinstead. I'm with the FBI." I hold up my ID and badge. "I'm here to talk to Taylor. Is he here?"

"Come on in," she says, standing to the side. "We're eating. Can I make you a plate?"

"No, thank you, I won't be long."

She leads me into the dining room, which is richly furnished, newly painted, and populated with two men. I only recognize Taylor. The other is a handsome man in his thirties in a button-front shirt and expensive watch.

Taylor stands when he sees me.

"Cassie," he says by way of greeting. We shake hands.

"This is Chris," Catherine says warmly, introducing the other man.

We shake also, and silence follows. In the chaos around the accident, the kidnapping, the blizzard, and the search for a body that I believed was walking on the face of the earth, not at the bottom of a river, Taylor and I have given each other condolences. But seeing him, it still feels raw.

"Can we talk in private? I'm sorry to interrupt dinner, but this won't take long."

Taylor leads me onto the back porch. The backyard is spotted with garden lights, and over the evening horizon, the scaffolding and cranes around the factory are outlined against the sky.

I don't sit, and neither does he. "I'm sorry about Keaton. Again. I know you guys were close."

I gauge his reaction carefully, because no matter how many times I say it, the wound is still fresh and his expression will tell me what he knows.

The way his face drops a little and he blinks twice quickly lets me know that he believes he has lost his friend. I can't disabuse him of this until I'm sure. Hope isn't a worthy partner in death.

"I know that you've talked to some of our agents about Keaton's death."

"The other half of that team is still at large," he says, gritting his teeth. "It's taking a lot of effort not to go hunting for them myself."

"Yeah, but I want to tell you that even though I came here flashing my ID, I'm not quite here as an agent. Not one hundred percent."

"Really?"

"Well, in one sense I am. I want them to find Keyser. That's the federal agent part. But I'm appealing to you as someone who loved the same person."

"Go on."

"Did you ever know his real name?"

Taylor shoots out a little laugh, taps his fingers on the porch railing and looks into the darkening sky. "No."

"Are you lying?"

"I'm not fucking lying. What would be the point of lying? What would I be protecting?"

"Your company? Your factory?"

"You know what, lady? Fuck this." He's about to walk back into the house.

"He gave me a code." Taylor stops to listen, so I finish. "He never said what it was for, but he said if I lost him, I should use it. He didn't say what to do with it, where to put it, or who might know what it means."

"What is it?"

"You don't have such a code?"

"No."

I can see the question annoys him, and maybe that's a good thing. I want him to be a little on edge. I hand him the code handwritten on a yellow Post-It. He takes it.

"Seventeen digits. Alphanumeric." He cracks his neck and looks at it again. "I have a list of shit it isn't. Not octal. Not hex. Obviously not ASCII."

"Obviously."

"Where did you get it? Did it come up to the top of your bowl of alphabet soup?"

"Keaton gave it to me. He didn't say what it was. Maybe it's a path to Keyser. Maybe it's a map to buried treasure."

He thinks, pressing his lips together, casting his eyes downward as he wrestles with a question I cannot imagine. "You know who you need to talk to? And I'm not really enthusiastic about suggesting this, but I promised Keaton that if you ever needed anything, I would give it to you."

To me, that's just another hint that he always knew he was going to have to disappear.

"I need this," I say. "Whatever you can do, I need—"

"You need to talk to Harper. If there's anyone who can figure out what a random string of numbers is supposed to be, it's her. But you have to promise me that you won't bring her any trouble. If anything happens to her…"

"No one outside of the bureau will know that she and I spoke."

He nods. "If you find anything out about Keaton that you can tell me, let me know. Because some days I feel like I never even knew the guy."

"You may have not known his name, but you knew who he was." I tap my sternum.

Taylor clears his throat. "Are you sure you don't want something to eat?"

"No, thank you. I've been transferred to San Francisco. I think I might take a trip to California to find an apartment."

"Good luck. You're going to need it."

CHAPTER 55

CASSIE

I see a couple of apartments, and they are utterly, ridiculously expensive. Especially because I constantly have to think about my grandmother moving in eventually, which requires space. I also have a nagging hope that there will be a six-foot-four British male in the house.

I meet with my new boss at Cyber Crime. She's tall and graceful, with a long curl of lavender hair and ears full of silver piercings. She gives me my assignment.

I give myself my own assignment. Find Keaton before I go undercover.

After the meeting, I take the train and slip into crowds so that I'm harder to follow. I don't know where Keyser is. I don't know if he's after me, but I did promise Taylor I wouldn't put Harper in danger. So when I get to Stanford, I'm pretty sure I'm alone. I check freshman classes for computer science majors, peeking my head into the lectures. She's not there. I check the second-year classes. Finally, I find her in a huge auditorium, learning a version of math I will never understand.

She's sitting in the center, away from the goof-offs in the back and the brownnoses at the front. I sit next to her, taking out a little notebook as if I'm a student late for class.

When she sees me, she seems a little startled. I'm out of context. I flip to a page in my notebook with Keaton's code written in the center and tap it as the professor runs through math functions well beyond my capacity.

She takes the book, putting it in front of her, thinking. She slides it back to me without a word, and I wait. I don't get up, and I don't give up.

The class goes on for another hour. There's a shuffle, a shouted assignment, and we're out in the hallway. I walk beside her.

"Your eye looks better." She flew out to Barrington after the accident to be with Taylor, and we saw each other briefly.

"Time's the best doctor in the business."

"What's the code?" she says, flicking my notebook.

"I was going to ask you."

"It's nonsense. Did you dream it? Did it appear in your alphabet soup?"

"Taylor didn't tell you?"

We're outside now. Harper doesn't slow down to talk, or turn, or do anything. She walks as if she's running a race.

"Taylor told me, but he doesn't know much. He said Keaton gave it to you, but he didn't tell me the circumstances. You know that's important, right?"

"He was fucking me and he made me memorize it before he let me come. Happy now?"

She doesn't slow down to be shocked. But she should be. I would be. She just laughs and shakes her head.

"All right," she says. "That means this is personal. I'm happy to help." She makes a sharp turn through a narrower campus alley. "Let's go back to my place. The fucking computers in the lab have more leaks and holes than…" She waves as if her mind is on other things. "They're not secure."

The alley spits us out into a parking lot. She bloops the alarm on a black Tesla.

"Thank you." I say.

"You kidding? Keaton was the most mysterious guy on the planet. I'm going to figure this out if it's the last thing I do."

CHAPTER 56

CASSIE

I order in for Harper and pay cash. She barely eats. She types as if she's trying to break her keyboard. She asks me to get her some white tape from the bathroom drawer. I almost ask her which drawer, but each of her bathroom drawers has tape.

She loops it around her knuckles and types faster.

Her apartment is a massive loft overlooking the Bay. The rest of the loft has such an underused, untouched feel that I can't even tell if she lives in the whole thing, or if she just lives in the path between the front door and this room. It is banked with computers on shelves that line three walls with wires and circuits and soldering irons everywhere. She has flatscreen monitors ranging in size from "I'd like to watch an action movie," to "I think I need glasses."

"Okay," she says. "From what you told me, I had to open up a tunnel through an allied nation with bad monitoring and use the protocol to—"

"I'm sorry, Harper. I know you work hard to understand all this stuff, but I don't care. Just give it to me."

"I got into an MI6 cache, and I found him."

I leap from the couch to her desk and look over her shoulder.

I found pictures of him on Google, mostly from his time with QI4, but I looked at them so much, trying to spear him into my memory, that they wore thin. This one is new. It isn't recent, or candid, but every time I see a new picture of him, my heart opens up a little wider.

Harper's not as impressed. She flicks to the next page. "It's all stuff we already know, more or less. I don't know what to do anymore"

"There has to be something. He wouldn't have given me the code for kicks."

"Have you considered it was just a sex game?"

"No. He kept mentioning it. He said it was important, and if he says it was important, then it was important."

She scrolls, and on the left, a word becomes visible. It's an evil word, rendered in bold all-caps type, as red as a bloody lip.

DECEASED

I pretend I don't see it. "His parents' names are here. Charlie and Anna Bridge."

"Hang on," Harper says.

She works on another screen. Pulls up Charlie Bridge's name, does some other crap I don't understand. A blank blue screen comes up with a white field. Nothing else. Just a white box with a blinking cursor on the left.

"What's this?"

"It's up a level of security. You can't get in without a password or a hack that's beyond me at the moment."

I lean over her and type Keaton's code, slapping Enter without pause.

The life of a family stretches before me.

A name. A place. A reason for a split-second decision to move across an ocean. It's all in front of me, including David Webber's death, which has a date.

"He's dead but the file's active?" I say.

"I have no idea if that's normal. Let me check."

"I only have a few days."

"I have less than that." She covers my hand with hers, looking at me with an expression of sharp-edged sincerity. "We'll find him." She squeezes my hand, and I believe her.

CHAPTER 57

CASSIE

We don't make it. MI6 is a dead end.

My despair lasts a few hours, but is replaced by hope. If I'm undercover, I can keep looking, I just can't expose myself. I have a week before I start, and I know I have what I need in that file. I just have to figure out where the clue is.

I'm meeting up with another agent three hours outside San Francisco. He's briefing me on the case, and we're leaving for Scotland on Tuesday to track Keyser's last known whereabouts.

I'm nervous. Nervous about starting a new job, a new city, a new life with the man I love still missing and potentially a target of the criminal I was chasing.

Trusting he could handle himself was as good as trusting he hadn't left me.

It's foggy here, just west of Yosemite. I wonder if that's intentional. A signal that I'm close.

The address here was all I had that I could use, except their real names and the real name of their only child.

I take it slow up the mountain. Redwood trees slash the sky on each side of me. The sun is just about rising over them. I'm a three-hour drive out of San Francisco.

I wonder if that's intentional too.

The location was more of a suggestion, a piece of land with a lot number, a purchase date, and a shell company as an owner.

My palms slip against the steering wheel. I'm so nervous I'm sweating. There's a driveway into the forest, and a wrought-iron gate that's locked. I pull over to the side and walk to the small opening big enough for a person. I walk a good quarter-mile on gravel winding through the trees. Finally, the house appears.

Modern. Large windows. Lights still on upstairs.

A dog barks, then another. I get nervous for a second. I'm not prepared for Rottweilers or guard dogs. But when they appear, one after the other, they're sheepdogs and they seem happy to see me.

Sheepdogs. Why sheepdogs?

Could it be?

I pick up the pace. The house seems so far away. I don't know what I'm going to do when I get there. Knock or bang on the window? Sit and wait? No way. I'm bursting through my skin. I'm like an overfull water balloon about to spill all over the Sequoia Mountains.

The dogs reach me, and I stop to pet them.

A whistle echoes over the mountains. The dogs spin and run in the opposite direction toward a man in jeans and a pale blue shirt.

He's tall.

He's as handsome as the devil himself.

The dimples in his cheeks are a promise. The smile lines are a joy. His voice, his looks, the leathery scent that precedes him as he runs toward me; all of it belongs to the only man in the world I'd lay down my heart for.

The distance between us seems miles. I'll walk it, I'll run it, I'll fly to this man.

I leap for him, arms around his neck, legs wrapped around his waist as he holds me up, lips meeting and speaking without words.

He snaps away, eye to eye with me. We're both made of breath and fog mingling in the air around us.

"Cassie, you came."

"David," I say.

"For now, until we catch or kill anyone who wants to hurt us, I'm still Keaton."

"I knew you wouldn't leave me."

"I tried to move back to London and couldn't. I had to be near you."

The dogs circle us, whipping into a barking frenzy.

I push him a little, but with the same motion, I grab his jacket in my fists. "You made me come and find you. What if I hadn't?"

He takes my wrists in his hands but doesn't pull them away. "That's why you're my partner now."

My eyes must have gone wide, because the muscles around them hurt.

"Given the choice, I would have taken care of it myself and saved you the trouble. But I needed to go back to MI6 and by then—"

"I'd been put on the case." I jerk him to me then away. I want to shake him, but he's too big.

"It's a cakewalk. Once we get him, you and I are going to get married and have babies."

"How long have you been planning this? Since the code?"

His lips curl into mischief, and his dimples are a promise that he's going to keep if only I believe in him. "The code was so you'd know what happened. I was going to become my old self, my real self, and live a normal life. This?" He puts his arm around me and extends his arm toward the house and the forest. "I changed plans after my death went so well."

"You gave up your dream in order to be with me?"

"If I'm going to be my real self, I want to be my real self with you."

One of the dogs jumps, putting his front paws on David's thighs. He loses his balance and we fall together into the grass, kissing, laughing, loving.

He's everything. I love him, and more than anything, to the ends of the earth and the end of time—I trust him.

EPILOGUE

CASSIE

*C*hris is having a panic attack, and Keaton is trying to soothe him in the middle of a windstorm of people. They're both in tuxedos, standing in front of the mantelpiece at the Barrington mansion, not that anyone could see the mantelpiece past the 744 roses it's layered with. Apparently there are supposed to be 749. It's five short.

I said Keaton. His name is David. I'm slowly getting used to his real name. Patiently acclimating to his real, gentle, giving self. He's been showing me the places he grew up, the people he knew. I met his parents, and the extended family he hasn't seen for years.

It's been a year since I found him in a house in the Sequoias. A year since he decided to live his life and commit to a place and a person. Been a few months since we nailed Keyser. But that's a story for a different book.

"I'm thinking of paper roses," Harper says from beside me. "Or just lying and telling her there are 749."

People arrive in pairs and family sets, all dressed in their best. The young pastor sets up a makeshift altar in front of the rose display.

"What's his deal with having an exact number?"

"Sentimentality. But there's not another rose in the state. So sentiment's gonna have to take a bow to math."

Chris and Catherine are finally getting married, a banner day when you consider they were high school sweethearts separated for thirteen years. Keaton glances at me and winks ever so slightly. His smirk still drives me wild, and his dimples are Morse code for happiness.

Taylor joins the two men, pointing at the rose garden in the back. I know what he's saying. You can pick five damn roses from there and none will be missed, but Chris's deal was that the rosebushes in the back stay intact. He's a stubborn guy. Handsome. Rich. Unbearably smart. And stubborn. But I guess waiting for someone that many years takes a certain kind of pigheadedness.

Keaton—no, David—peels away from the discussion and comes to me. "You need to be sitting."

"Oh God," Harper says. "I can't even with you two arguing about this." She takes David's old place near Chris and Taylor.

I'm left alone with David putting his hand on my distended belly and saying, "Doctor's orders, Special Agent Grinstead."

"My ass gets tired sitting down all day."

"There'll be time enough to massage that arse later."

My pregnancy hasn't slowed us down at all. Not sexually, at least. He's become more gentle and sweet as the months have gone on, but I can't wait for the old roughness back.

Everything in its time. I'm having a baby boy in three weeks and getting married in two. Nana and his family are meeting us in Vegas for a big, splashy wedding. I had the choice to get married in a pregnancy-friendly wedding dress or get married with a baby in my arms. Nana put her foot down. She made no apologies or excuses for being a single mother, but insisted I break the cycle.

Harper stomps to the back of the house and slaps open the kitchen door. Keaton pulls a chair around for me until its seat hits the back of my thighs. I acquiesce and sit. He kneels on the floor next to me and takes my hands, flicking his thumbnail over my diamond engagement ring.

I love when he kneels next to me, puts his hand on my belly to feel our baby kick. It's the most dominant thing he does.

"Are you sure you want to wear these shoes?" he asks.

"It's not like you're gonna let me stand up."

The screen door slams open then shut again as Harper runs in with a handful of roses. "Look! These had just fallen right off the bush. Can you even believe it?"

She hands them to Taylor, who laughs.

"That's cheating," Chris exclaims. "The entire point was to leave the rose garden in the back exactly as it is."

"No," Harper says. "The whole point is that you have a good time at your own wedding, and if you're gonna freak out over five roses that no one can even see, then you need to take the roses from where you can get them."

"You should try getting married yourself," Chris replies, accepting the roses from Taylor.

"I'm still in school. Don't push me."

"Who's pushing?" Taylor asks.

Nana trundles in from the backyard in a sparkly sequined dress. She's holding five roses. "I heard you were short some flowers. You got a ton of them out in the back."

Chris throws his arms up as if surrendering to a mighty foe. I shift in my seat, sliding to the edge so I can get up. Keaton stands with me, bracing his arms against me as if I might tip forward, which actually, I might.

"Where do you think you're going, young lady?"

"I'm going to help them set up the roses… five of them. And the other five…" I had an idea about what to do with the extra five, but it flies out of my head when I feel liquid trickling down my leg.

"What's wrong?" Keaton asks.

"I think my water broke."

I kick my foot out a little while Keaton holds me straight. My stockings are wet all the way down to the shoe.

I look at him. He looks at me.

"I don't want to ruin the wedding," I whisper. "We should just sneak out to the hospital."

He presses his lips between his teeth as if he's holding back his words.

"Just grab my bag," I say, pointing at it. "And we can—"

"Father Grady!" Keaton calls.

"Yes, yes," the pastor intones as he removes a silver chalice from a box.

"I need you to marry us right now."

"David!" I snap, using his real name without thinking for the first time.

"I'll tell Catherine!" Harper shouts before bolting up the stairs.

Grady doesn't look up from arranging the silver. "I have thirty-four minutes."

"We can wait," I hiss.

"Did you piss yourself?" Nana asks. "Or is the cake baked?"

"The cake is baked," Keaton says. "Father Grady!"

The handsome priest looks up for the first time, pushing his glasses up his nose.

"We need a quickie before this baby is born out of wedlock," Keaton says.

"Your parents," I whine. "And the party."

"We can still have the party. We need rings. Right?"

"Right," Grady answers, still looking a little flummoxed. "I think. Uh…"

"Use ours!" Catherine flies down the grand staircase with her wedding gown unhooked at the back and her veil waving behind her. "Chris! Give them the rings!"

Chris has his hand over his eyes. "I'm not looking at you!"

"Who has them?" Catherine shouts.

"The best man," Chris says from behind his hand. "Back upstairs, woman!"

I turn to face Keaton fully. He's David. He's real, and he's mine.

"It doesn't matter," I say. "Not really. Let's not take the wind out of their sails."

"We'll be gone before Catherine Barrington even walks down the aisle. And it does matter. It matters to your grandmother, for one, and it matters to me."

"I don't think you're going to leave me."

"I will never leave you. I hardly think even death can separate us." He leans his forehead on mine. "This child was created out of our love. Let's make sure he's a part of our commitment too."

He's looking out for me, and in his eyes, I see only love and care for me as a person, not the consequence of a wedding after a birth.

Chris has the rings. He hands the big one to me and the smaller one to Keaton.

Grady stands by us with an open book.

"The short version," Keaton says.

"Do you have vows? Could be quicker that way."

"No," I say.

"Yes," Keaton says at the same time. "I'll go first." He takes my left hand and isolates the ring finger.

"Make it quick," I whisper. "I'm leaking onto the carpet."

"Cassandra Grinstead. You are the partner to my real self. More than a name. More than a title. You are more than family. You are the flesh of my heart and the reason it beats." He slips the ring on my finger until it nestles next to the diamond.

"That was nice." I sniffle, running my fingers across my cheeks, clearing the way for fresh tears.

"Come on, come on!" Nana shouts. "You're going to drop it in the car."

I hold up the larger ring and isolate David's finger. In a room full of people, half of whom don't even know there's a second wedding happening, I can only see his seven o'clock eyes.

"David Webber. I don't… I can't…" Words leave me. I want to get out my notepad and read off the stupid, flowery vows I'd written, but we don't have time, and they express nothing that needs saying. I can walk right into hell alone because I know he will follow me. He can run straight into oblivion and I will be right behind him.

What I need to say can be said in six words.

"I love you." I slip the ring on his finger. "I trust you."

"By the power vested in me," Grady interjects. I'd forgotten he was there. I'd forgotten everyone in the room was there, but the volume in my head gets turned up ever so slowly. "I now pronounce you man and wife. You may kiss the bride."

David smashes his lips against mine.

That's when the first contraction hits. It's more of a twist than a pain. But still, I say, "Ow."

Nana puts my bag on my shoulder. "Get moving!"

"It'll be hours, Nana," I protest. "Take it easy!"

"So you say. My mother dropped me so quick my father barely had time to grab his hat on the way out."

"Let's just be safe." David hoists me into his arms and carries me to the door. He navigates the crowd in the living room, the porch, and to the car without taking his face off mine.

He gently puts me in the passenger seat and buckles me in.

"I have the music all picked out." I tap the screen on his stereo as he closes the door, crossing to the driver's side. When he gets in, I finish my sentence. "It's all in English too."

"It begins, my dodger. Stealing my stereo and stealing my heart."

He pulls onto the road, smiling all the while. I can't keep my eyes off his jaw and the curve of his neck. I want the baby to grow up to be just like him, with a soul so deep and layered, a lifetime isn't long enough to figure him out.

A man worthy of a woman's trust.

I'm embarking on an adventure that's been written by generations of women before me, and yet it's a story that's never been told. It's our story.

THE END

Thank you for reading! A chapter of Chris and Catherine's story, *White Knight* is stuck in the back.

If you want to know more about Taylor and Harper, you can check out *King of Code.*

Follow me on Facebook, Twitter, Instagram, Tumblr or Pinterest.

Join my fan groups on Facebook and Goodreads.

Get on the mailing list for deals, sales, new releases and bonus content - JOIN HERE.

My website is cdreiss.com

WHITE KNIGHT

PART I

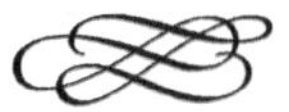

CHAPTER 1

CHRIS - PRESENT

hen I came to New York thirteen years earlier, I'd had ambition and seven hundred and forty-nine dollars to my name. My mother had tried to give me the last of what she had—a hundred forty dollars and some collector's coins—but I wouldn't take it. So by New York standards, I had nothing, which was easy to turn into three simple words years later from the back seat of a Porsche Cayenne.

I never glorified the first year. It sucked. They locked dumpsters at night. That was my biggest hardship. Locked dumpsters. Second only to not having money to take care of Lance.

Grappling for survival wears on a guy. It becomes the brain's primary function. I don't know how long it takes the average person before survival starts overriding more entertaining affairs, like the love of your life or happiness. In movies, soldiers are always in the trenches, looking at pictures of their girlfriends. I'd kept a picture of Catherine in my pocket. It turned into a ball the size of an aspirin when I woke up in a puddle.

Her picture was gone, but my one singular goal did not change. Money.

I cut flowers in the backs of grocery stores. Worked construction.

Learned to speak Spanish so I could get leads on new jobs. Finally I could afford a bike so I could courier documents and building plans.

Then Brian Cober's dog bit Lance's tail. *The* Brian Cober of Cober Trading Associates. Meanwhile, I couldn't afford a vet. I had no power. No leverage. Nothing. I was in that dog run every morning to develop a relationship with him, not to get into a conflict. Everyone on the Street knew Cober was a cold-eyed shark who hated to lose. What they didn't know, and I came to learn, was that he had guilt where his conscience should have been.

A conscience is a guide for living. Guilt can be bought off for a few bucks. Cober paid the vet bills and had me come in to try for a job as a runner on the floor of the Exchange. The interview was his payment. I was eager and humble. I got the job because that room and I were a match made in heaven. It reeked of what I wanted most.

Yes. Money.

I'd needed it to go back to Catherine. A lot of it. More than I could acquire without selling her memory. Earl Barrington money.

That had been thirteen years ago. Though the memory of her had faded into colorless snapshots taken by an innocent boy who no longer existed, the hunger for money hadn't.

Years after I stopped writing her letters, she became the girl I dreamed about sometimes. Or remembered when I caught the scent of roses from a flower cart. I wondered about her from my box at the US Open, when the *pop-popping* of tennis balls brought Doverton back to me.

I checked her address when I bought my co-op on Central Park South, and again when I bought the place in the Le Marais.

She still lived in the Barrington mansion, and she still had the same name.

I checked once before I married Lucia, my future wife's lipstick still smeared on my cock under my tux.

Why didn't I call her? Why just send one last envelope with a check inside a card? Why not pick up the phone?

I told myself she didn't want me, but the fact was, I was greedy. I was shallow. I was a shell of a man. I was a robot working eighty hours a week because... foreign markets, and money, money, money.

Which was about to change.

Ten years after his dog bit mine in the park, Brian knew it and I knew it.

The quants had gotten it wrong. The algo had found a trend and labeled it an outlier. I'd been outmaneuvered, and I was about to be the manager of an empty shell of a hedge fund.

A hedge fund's only capital was its reputation, and ours had taken a beating. It would take years to claw back to the top. I didn't know if I had it in me anymore.

Nella, my hipster dog walker from Brooklyn, called as I was assessing my nonexistent options. "Mr. Carmichael?"

"What?" I was annoyed. I'd hired her so I didn't have to be bothered while I was working, and there she was…

"Lance doesn't look good. He won't get up."

"What do you mean he won't get up?"

"He's awake, but he can't move. I think he needs to go to the vet."

By the time I got back to my co-op, it was too late.

IN BARRINGTON, the factory town where I grew up, when your dog died on the couch, you got your friends up to Wild Horse Hill and you all buried the body. But what did you do in New York City?

You sat on the arm of the sofa. You watched his body's stillness pour over the upholstery like a stain, covering the cushions, the furniture, the floor, and you, bruising the space with death and rigidity. It soaked everything. Color. Air. Muscle. Spirit. Emotion. The grip of the present seized time and perception, as the tunnels of future and past twisted closed and stranded me inside a hard candy shell.

And then I snapped out of it.

Past and future opened and I saw my life with new clarity. I put my hand on Lance's fur and knew he wasn't there.

"Good travels for a good boy."

I was alone.

I covered him with a cashmere throw and called the vet, who arranged for someone to come for him.

Grief wasn't a stranger. I'd lost my mother a few years earlier. My sadness then had been mitigated by the fact that in her last years, I'd been able to give her the life she'd always deserved. But Lance? Why did that sting more? Why did I feel as though he'd taken my identity with him?

My phone buzzed. It was one of the quants. I didn't want to talk about failed arbitrage timing.

Then Brian buzzed. He'd want to talk about survival strategies.

I'd bought this co-op because there was a dog run around the corner.

A text from Nella. *Barron's* wanted an interview. They'd photograph me in soft focus and pretend to have sympathy for my bad bets.

Ignoring all of it, I called Lucia.

"I heard, darling," she said with an Italian accent I used to enjoy. "I'm so sorry."

God, six words in and I could tell what a mistake this call was. She was talking about the fund crashing, and she had my money on her mind.

"Don't worry about your payments," I said. "They're in a separate fund."

"I'm not worried. You're a good man."

By "good man," she meant I took care of business. She meant I was responsible. But it was too close to "good boy" and Lance's body was still on my couch, an inflexible mass under a cashmere blanket.

I went into my home office. It was far away from the living room and it was all hard lines and impersonal touches.

"Christopher? Are you there?"

In the last five years, she was the only person I'd been close to, but she didn't need to know this. No one needed to know. As soon as people knew, it became real. But there it was. In the tension between my foolish need to tell someone and a more foolish need to pretend my best friend was still in the house, I said it.

"Lance died."

"Ah, I'm sorry, Christopher."

"Yeah. Bad week." An old checkbook sat on the spotless glass top of my desk. I flipped the pages of carbons absently.

"Will you have a service?" Lucia asked. "You can have something at the armory. Everyone will come."

She'd come because it would be a social event, and I'd already heard she was interviewing rich men for my old position. In normal circles, this was called "dating." I'd learned her priorities too late, and as much as they were my priorities, they disgusted me.

Money.

Maybe the fact that we shared a mutual love of money for its own sake was why I'd been suddenly repelled by her.

"No service. Not here. I just…" I just wanted to get her off the phone. "You lived with him for years. I thought you might want to know."

"Well, thank you for telling me. Will you be at the gala tonight?"

"No. Someone just came in. I have to go."

We hung up. No one had come in, of course. I lived alone.

I started a text message…

Brian—

…THEN STOPPED.

I had nothing, which meant nothing was holding me here. New York was fine, but it wasn't home. Both Lance and I were from a little town one hundred twenty miles outside of nowhere.

Lance… my last connection to Barrington was gone. Had a lifeline been cut? Or an umbilical cord I didn't need?

I'd been one kind of boy and another kind of man. I had been poor then and was disgraced now. The connections had atrophied a long time ago.

But that wasn't true. Lance had tethered me to the boy I'd been and to the woman I'd loved. With him gone, was I still linked? Or was I stranded with no family, no attachments, no one to hurt if things went south? Loneliness hung off my ribs like a lantern. This co-op. My properties. The portfolio. Built before I'd met my ex-wife, to offer security to a woman who didn't want me, and crashing with nothing to hold it up.

I needed time to sort it out but gave myself none.

Brian — I'll sell if you want it.

I TAPPED out an email quickly but didn't send it. Then I spent ten minutes looking for pen and paper.

Dear Catherine,
I will try to keep this letter short in the hope that you even remember me.

CATHERINE - PRESENT

The black garbage bag snagged on a piece of metal in the floor and ripped open, dumping a pile of unidentifiable debris all over the concrete.

I wanted to cry, but I didn't want half the town to see it.

"Let me help you." Reggie, his sandy-copper hair darkened to brown with sweat, snapped up a snow shovel that leaned against the wall. He trotted across the abandoned factory floor like a kid asking to clear my walk two months early.

"Thank you," I said, going to the long steel table in the center of the room where the roll of bags was kept. "I think we're making a dent."

The snow shovel scraped along the floor with the shriek of metal on stone, but against the backdrop of dozens of people cleaning out the space, it was barely a whisper.

"Getting that graffiti off made all the difference."

Of course he'd say that. He'd used the walls of the shuttered factory as a canvas through his early twenties, when he was as angry as the rest of the town over the closure.

The anger was still there, but a measure of the despair was being replaced with hope. The people of Barrington were working together to clean the bottling factory that had been the town's lifeblood until it closed eleven years before. The bank had repossessed the property soon after my father died and my mother defaulted on the mortgage.

Last week, a real estate agent one town over mentioned to a bartender that she was showing the factory to a Silicon Valley tycoon. The news took thirty-six hours to get to my ears. It wasn't long before the town of Barrington gathered the will to make a plan.

We needed to make the best impression. We were proud people, and that factory, my father's old factory, had been the source of that pride. I still had most of the interior keys, and the gates had been breached hundreds of times in eleven years. Only this time, we wouldn't go in to vandalize it, but to clean it.

I wouldn't see a dime from the factory's sale, but the new jobs, new people, new money would do something greater than line my pockets. It would fulfill my life's work of getting Barrington back on its feet.

Reggie scooped up a pile of junk left by teenagers and homeless adults and let it slide into the bag I held open. We filled it, tied the top, and dragged it to the open window. Florencio was by the dumpster underneath, picking up the bits of garbage around it.

"Look out below!" Reggie cried.

Florencio stepped away and we threw the bag out the window and into the dumpster with a muted crash.

It occurred to me that this was all over.

This run of despair was over. The never-ending troubles, the broken system, the exodus from a place I love—over. My trust fund had been drained, my furniture sold, my future pawned so I could keep Barrington and its people above water.

I was almost done.

That night, I cried myself to sleep as I often did. For the first time, it wasn't out of tension or habit, but fear.

CHAPTER 3

CATHERINE - SIXTEENTH SUMMER

t the Doverton Country Club, a boy, *the* boy, the one who was mine the minute I saw him, worked on the grounds. He had sun-coppered hair and strong arms. In the summer, his skin was a burnished russet that made his blue eyes otherworldly. By the second week of my sixteenth summer, all the girls at the club giggled over him. They were mostly from Doverton, but he and I were from neighboring Barrington. The town bore my name because my father and his father before him had owned the bottling plant, and that was what you did back then. If you created the town and made it thrive, you named it after yourself. Fifty years later, it was still named Barrington, we still lived there, and the folks in Doverton called it Trashington.

The town's reputation bothered my father a little... but my mother? When she heard some of the Doverton Ladies of the Court hadn't invited her to a cocktail brunch because she lived *over there*, it drove her over the edge.

"Don't you give them a reason to call you trash." She sat across from us in the limo.

Harper and I got dressed in our whites once a week for tennis lessons and once again in jeans for equestrian. Dad worked at the plant, and Mom didn't drive.

"That's the first thing." She pointed at Harper. "When you hit them with your racquet, that's exactly what you're doing. Giving them a reason to look down on you because you're a Barrington."

"I didn't—" Harper's defense was irrelevant.

"If they only knew we could buy and sell all of them."

"She didn't call me trash. She said the topspin reduced the travel distance when in fact the spin vector—"

"Harper!" Mom cut her off again. "No one wants to hear a lady talk nonsense."

I wasn't thinking of my sister or how she must have felt when Mom said stuff like that, which she always did. I was thinking of myself and how I was so much more of a lady than my little sister.

"Look!" Harper pointed out the window. "There's that guy again!"

I slid over to her, and there he was. The boy with the rippling tan skin who worked the grounds, biking up the hill in his shorts and backpack. No helmet, bronze hair flapping away from his sweaty face.

His name was Chris. He had a ready smile and full lips that I knew tasted of salt and cola.

Mom *tsked*. "That boy. He's going to get himself killed. I don't know how his parents allow him to take a *bicycle* twenty-two miles to the club."

"We should give him a ride!" Harper exclaimed, eyes wide with a brilliant idea.

"Heavens, no!"

"He only has a mother," I said. I saw him in town sometimes. Marsha had told me all about him. He was our age. Trailer trash. Invisible.

As we passed him, he waved.

Harper opened the window and cupped her hands around her mouth. "Use a lower gear uphill! It increases gain ratio!"

"Thank you!" he said with a smile and flicked his gear changer.

I got away from the window as Mom took Harper by the shoulder and pulled her to her side. The driver closed and locked the window. We rode the rest of the way in silence.

CHAPTER 4

CATHERINE - PRESENT

Upstairs, the bed creaked.

My little sister had set it up so the stairs to her attic room didn't make a sound. She didn't want to disturb me when she came down to the kitchen late at night. But though the stairs were silent, the bed made noise when she and Taylor were… busy. The day before was the first time I heard them at it.

I was in the living room on a folding chair, sewing a button on one of her yellow polo shirts. My fingers had gone numb. I thought it was a late ache from cleaning the factory two days earlier, but in the time it took my brain to catch up with my glands, I knew it was something else. My hands had lost feeling because every bit of tactile sensation went between my legs.

It was like getting slapped awake. I froze in that chair with the needle in one hand and the bag of yellow buttons in the other.

This was my sister and a man I barely knew, but my body didn't care who they were. It recognized the rhythms of their lovemaking and opened me, squeezing the breath out of my lungs and making my fingertips cold.

After putting the shirt and sewing supplies on the floor next to me, I went to the front door to get some air. The house was massive but had no rugs or wall hangings. We had very little furniture. Guests sat on folding chairs and plastic outdoor furniture that had been discarded by someone else. Our father had passed seven years before, and our mother had left with a man soon after. They'd left behind a dying town and a closed factory, so I'd sold the contents of the house to help the people in the town recover. They never did, but I employed whomever I could and sold most of what we had.

Harper went along with it because she didn't care about the furniture, but she didn't agree with my strategy. She was about "maintenance." I had no idea what she was trying to maintain.

Out on the porch, the sounds of the squeaking bed faded. I took a deep breath. The house was set back on the end of a long drive, hidden from the main road by high hedges and a long garden. Overhead, birds flew south in crooked Vs and Ws. I was alone. Finally.

But the throb between my legs didn't go away. I was going to have to walk it off.

Heading down the path toward the hedges, I thought about everything except the tempo of the creaking bed. I thought of how we used to have a staff to walk down the drive for the mail, and how, before his route doubled in size, Willy would come all the way down the drive to deliver it, just for the chance to say good morning to my mother. How many people could I hire to repave it? How many children could I feed with that small job?

I'd thought the driveway repair through before, but the money always found something more important to do. I was running out of things to sell, except the house itself. No one could afford to buy it, and those who could didn't want it. So the Barrington Mansion stayed the Barrington Mansion even though it looked like no more than a big, old confection of a Victorian.

I got to the mailbox, a green-painted cast-iron chest with a bronze slot, just as Willy drove up in the white truck.

"Morning, Miss Barrington!" His seat was on the right, like a boxy, doorless European sportster. He handed me a short pile of mail.

"Morning, Willy. How's Lara doing?"

"On the mend. It itches under the cast though. She complains like she's dying of it."

"That'll be the last time she jumps off Crone's Tree."

"Probably not. You know kids. So what's happening with that boy from California? Word is he's been hanging around Miss Harper."

My body was reminded of the bed creaking. I looked away from Willy in case the feeling was all over my face. "I think he's all right."

"How long's he staying?"

The town was very protective of Harper and me, even though we were adults. My father's dying wish was that they take care of us, and when folks here agreed, it was a solemn oath.

"Long enough for her to break his heart, I'm sure."

Willy laughed and waved. He pulled onto the road, and I flipped through my mail as I walked back to the house. A few bills. Marketing junk. An early birthday card for me.

When I got to the white business-sized envelope with my name in dark blue ball point, I stopped. Stood in place. It was an expensive buff paper. The return address was engraved in slate grey.

Him.

I hadn't heard from him since the night he left me.

Not a word.

And now… today.

All the other envelopes slipped to the ground, abandoned like old lovers.

Dear Catherine of the Roses,

I will try to keep this letter short in the hope that you even remember me. I'm not used to writing things by hand, but I thought you deserved the effort.

Lance has died. He was an old dog and he had a good life, but now I have to bring him home.

I will be burying him on Wild Horse Hill. The service is set for next Friday. You aren't obligated to come, but I would very much like to see you while I'm there.

Christopher

I read it again.

...you deserved the effort...

Did I suddenly deserve effort?

...Lance has died...

Oh, terrible. Terrible. Such a sweet dog, waiting patiently for us at the base of the tree.

...next Friday...

The day after my twenty-ninth birthday. So many years.

...You aren't obligated...

How far down the path had we come to have no obligations?

...while I'm there...

While he's here.

...I'm there...

645

HE'S COMING HERE.

...Christopher.

CHRISTOPHER.

CHAPTER 5

CHRIS - PRESENT

It was my shop, which meant I could come and go as I pleased. But it was my shop, which meant my absence was noticed.

"You're not going to Catalina." Brian sat on the other side of my desk, slouched in the leather-and-chrome chair with an ankle over his knee. He was twelve years older than me, but while I wore suits, he was a Henley-and-jeans guy. He weaponized casual. Nothing showed you were too good for all this shit like sneakers. "You're not going to Martha's Vineyard, the house on Lake Como, or the Reykjavik retreat. What am I supposed to think?"

"What you think is up to you. What you're *not* supposed to think is that I'm making side deals."

"Why shouldn't I?"

"Because you trust me."

"This might be a bad time, don't you think?" He tapped his thumbs together, the only indication that anything serious was happening. "We're in the middle of a crisis. Our investors are concerned."

"They knew the risks."

"That's going to go over like double-dipping in the latrine."

"What does that even mean?"

"'You knew the risks' isn't a way to do business if you want to continue doing business."

"I'm not going to continue doing business. I overleveraged." I pressed my hands to the desk glass. "I had a good run, but it's over. If you want it, make an offer."

He smirked. "You're so young." He leaned forward, putting his hand out to stop my objections. "It's fine. That was always your selling point. No one wants an old genius. But listen. You've never dealt with the ups and downs. Shit crashes. You pick up the pieces. It's not that big a deal."

"It's a big deal." I picked up my bag and slung it over my shoulder. Having started out as a bike courier, I never got over the easy weight distribution of a messenger bag. No one on the street used briefcases anymore anyway. "I don't know if I'm hungry enough to drag the fund out of the gutter."

He leaned back into his relaxed dude posture. "It's in your blood. If you're not hungry, you're not Chris Carmichael."

"Maybe." I left room for the fact that he could be right, but I wished I didn't have to. If I was nothing but a hunger, who was I when I was fed? And if there was more to me, what was it? "I have to get my head together."

"Don't take too long, kid. The market moves fast."

CHAPTER 6

CATHERINE - SIXTEENTH SUMMER

The first time I got close to Chris, I was a week into the summer after my junior year at Montgomery High. I was leaning on the court fence, waiting for my coach, and Chris was edging the grass with a Weed Whacker. I heard it and felt the pricks of cut grass on the backs of my calves. I stepped away from it.

"Sorry, miss."

"It's all right, I—"

My voice hadn't drifted off or gotten lost. I didn't swallow the rest of the sentence or forget what I was saying. The final words never existed. Everything before I saw him was fake, and after that moment, my life became real. Like Dorothy walking out of her black-and-white world into a three-dimensional colorscape.

My life wasn't divided into the years before that moment and the time after because he was handsome or strong. It wasn't because he was charming or interesting.

It was because he was mine.

We stood watching each other through the chain-link fence, and I knew I was just as much his. We claimed each other in those first seconds.

Blue is blue and the sky is up and the earth is down. These aren't articles of faith or belief, but knowledge. Necessity. Denying gravity existed wouldn't hurt you, because it was always the law, and up was still up and down was still where you landed when you jumped.

A yellow ball bounced behind me, skidding and clicking against the fence.

"Catherine!" Dennis, my coach, called. He could hit drunk, but speaking was harder. He slurred at the ends of his sentences. He'd always said muscle memory was more powerful than anything the brain could remember. He said your body was smarter than your mind.

He was right. My body knew this young man with the blades of grass stuck to his pants and the specks of dirt on his cheeks.

"Hey, Catherine." The boy said my name like a prayer that had already been answered.

The ball rolled by my feet. I tapped it, bouncing it under my control, until I got the string face under it and I could let it roll across. Admittedly, I was being a bit of a show-off before I replied.

"Hi, Weed Whacker guy."

"I'm sorry if the noise bugs you. I can do court seven."

"You're not bothering me."

The distance between us, the fence, the next hour of lessons, all of it overwhelmed me. Too many obstacles.

He made the first move, stepping away from the fence and saluting. "Next time then."

He took his Weed Whacker to court seven, and I hit the ball back to my coach.

I never hit so hard or so accurately. I astonished Coach Dennis, but I wasn't surprised. I was sure everything I'd do from then on out would be right and true.

When I finished my lesson, the boy with the Weed Whacker and I found each other by the water fountains, attracted like magnets. We didn't say hello or introduce each other.

Wide-eyed, he said, "Did you feel it?"

I knew exactly what he meant.

"I did. I did feel it."

We stole to the back room of the pro shop to marvel at this unnamed thing that changed everything.

"What was it?" I asked when he closed the door.

"I don't know." He touched my arm.

It felt as though two planets that had been on separate trajectories for light years had finally collided and melded. I stared at his hand, and when he tried to move it, I put mine on top of his.

"Have you felt it before?" I asked.

"No. But I still kind of... it's still there."

"Yeah. Me too. I'm..." What I was about to say had felt so trivial, I almost skipped the step. "I'm Catherine."

"I know."

Of course. In our little fishbowl, I was famous.

"I'm Chris. Chris Carmichael."

"Chris." I said his name the way he'd said mine, finally understanding how to pray for something I'd already been given. It was almost the same as praying that it not be taken away.

"I have to see you again," he said as if waking from a half-dream.

I could. I had to. I had no choice. But I couldn't agree before Irv, who ran the shop, burst in with a clipboard. He had a huge round belly, crooked teeth, and a soft spot for Barrington kids who needed jobs.

He froze when he saw us. "Carmichael, get out to court seven and finish the job." His eyes flicked to me and back to Chris.

"Yes, sir."

"And young lady?"

I held up my chin. I was an heiress and a club member.

"I believe you don't want your mother to hear back about this. So keep it quiet."

I didn't realize at the time that he was protecting Chris, but later, after I realized it, I was grateful to him.

Though in the end, no one could protect Chris but me.

His letter was folded up in my pocket. It didn't change anything right away. It took a day or so to think of Chris with a smile on my face, and another day or so to see the conditions I lived in. The patchwork of pipes and electrical work. The bare walls and barren floors. My clothes were in good shape because Ronnie was a seamstress who could repair anything, and my hair was decent because the Snip-n-Save needed every customer they could get.

I wiped down the green tile kitchen counter, seeing every encrusted piece of grime as if for the first time. A person got used to things. A bit of grime that didn't come out on the first scrub just stayed there until new eyes saw it.

Harper flew down the stairs in the yellow polo shirt she had to wear at the Amazon distribution center where she and half the town worked, her blond hair tied into a loose ponytail.

"Hey," she said when she burst into the kitchen and opened the fridge. "Taylor's hanging out here today. You should put him to work."

"Can he do anything?"

"Yeah." She pulled out yogurt. "Surprisingly, for such a nerd."

"He didn't seem like a nerd to me." I got a bowl and a box of granola from the cabinet. "He's quite handsome and confident."

She blushed a little, taking the granola and bowl. "He's all right."

Harper was a nerd herself, spending hours in front of a computer she'd built from parts. She'd gone to MIT for a year, but came home when Daddy got sick. She never went back. Staying in Barrington was a terrible waste of her mind. A brilliant, stubborn, loyal mind.

"Do you remember Chris Carmichael?" I asked. "From the country club? He gardened for us one summer. Lived in the trailer park by the station?"

"Yeah, duh." The granola tinkled into the bowl.

"He sent me a letter." I peeled the top off the yogurt container and plucked a spoon out of the rack.

Her eyes went as wide as her bowl. "Really? What did he say?"

"Lance died." I dropped a lump of yogurt into her bowl and gave her the spoon.

"Aw," she said, poking her spoon against the bottom of the bowl. "Percy's the last of that litter."

I didn't give myself a second to doubt my next question. I just spit out what was on my mind, too late to sound casual. "I was wondering if you'd look Chris up on the computer? See how he's doing?"

She put her back to the counter and held the bowl in front of her, swirling the granola into the yogurt. "Why?"

"Because I'm asking."

"Yeah, but I don't know what you're asking for exactly? Do you want to know where he works or do you want his bank account info?"

"Harper Barrington!" I scolded. "You said you stopped that!"

She shrugged. Did I like that she was a hacker? No. But I could only make her promise she wouldn't steal or cheat. She'd never promised to stop hacking. At this point, she was a grown woman and I was so ignorant of the digital world, I didn't even know what the promise meant.

Besides, she needed to exercise her mind, not shut it down.

"I don't want his bank information," I said.

"Too bad." She ate like a prisoner of war.

"What do you mean?"

She scraped the last of the yogurt out of the curve of the bowl. "He's loaded."

My heart twisted and my skin got hot. Not because he had money. She could have revealed that he was a schoolteacher and I would have had the same reaction. My body reacted to the fact that she, my sister, anyone in the same room as me, knew anything about him. It was like touching him from a universe away.

I didn't know how much further I wanted to go, but Harper wasn't one to slip through a door quietly; she burst through.

"Has his own hedge fund and a seat on the Exchange. Ex-wife but no kids."

He'd gotten married? That seemed impossible. How could what we had be replicated in the same lifetime?

"Really?" I held up my chin. I didn't want to show her that I was tripped up.

"Italian model. I forget her name. He's got a sweet penthouse on Central Park West and a net worth around—"

"Stop!"

She obeyed, washing the bowl with a roll of her eyes. My own sister was closer to him than I was. And the ex-wife…

I had to swallow a lump of jealousy before I spoke again. "You've been talking to him?"

"Hell, no!" She put the bowl in the rack. "But I've been watching, more or less. He can't see me do it and it's mostly legal."

"Mostly?"

"I won't get caught and I don't touch anything."

"Fine, I guess." I pulled a towel off the rack and dried the bowl. "He seems all right?"

"Yeah. Kinda. Healthy, wealthy. He doesn't go out much. Just big events."

"And he's divorced?"

"Yeah. Recently. She's dumb. I can tell."

I laughed a little but not a lot. The jealousy was pushing its way back up my throat. "As long as you say so."

"Why are you asking?"

I would have to tell her at some point. The minutes before she ran out the door were as good as any. "He's coming back to bury Lance."

"Wow." She shook her head a little, staring at me as if the shock kept her from averting her gaze. "We have to clean up."

"I can manage it."

"And the thorn bush?" She indicated the backyard with a flip of her fingers. "That's not going to go over well—oh." She froze as if realizing something unpleasant. "Reg."

"I keep telling you there's nothing between Reggie and me."

"But I keep hoping."

"You're sweet. But no."

With a glance at the clock, she started out. She gave me a list of things to pick up when I went shopping, including a strange men's toiletry item. I assumed it was for Taylor, and as she drove away, I felt that little bit of jealousy well up again. My sister was performing mundane tasks for a man she cared about. I longed to do the same.

I'd dated men since he left. I'd had some sex with those men, none of it memorable. There was no love like his. I'd tried to find it and come up emptyhanded enough times to give up. I'd given up on him coming back a decade ago, given up on doing more than treading water, given up on dating.

Most days, I didn't think about him at all. Sometimes when the roses were blooming and the evening wind blew the right way, I'd remember how he made me feel, but not him in particular.

I went to the back of the house and looked at the backyard and the family cemetery. It had been there before the house, when the first Barrington Father bought land by the river and died before he'd amassed enough wealth to build on it.

When I was a girl, the plot had been lined with beautiful rosebushes. After our father died, we'd let them grow over the headstones that Harper had defaced when she was angry, and as the years went on, we'd let it grow into a bed of thorns. Sometimes, in the spring, they bloomed. But the bushes were too thick to be penetrated by a gardener, so they were wild and unpredictable. We just trimmed the edges so the thorns didn't go past the short white fence around the plots.

Would Chris even care?

Would he laugh or be disappointed?

I didn't know him or who he'd become, except that he was rich and lived a beautiful life. I lived with a dense thorn bush in my yard because my sister hated our father. The weight of shame I carried got denser and heavier. I could bear it inside Barrington, but in front of Chris, it would crush me.

The note crinkled in my pocket. For the first time since getting it, I thought I should tell him I wouldn't see him.

CHAPTER 8

CATHERINE - SIXTEENTH SUMMER

On Mondays, Wednesdays, and Saturdays in the summer, Mom went into Doverton to ride horses with the Princes. She showered there, and often got home smelling of soap and perfume. Otherwise, she hovered over us like a hummingbird. She had a staff of nannies and sitters assigned to watch us during the moments she turned her back, but they were no more than moments.

Behind the rose cemetery stood a narrow band of untouched forest, then high grasses, then the river. Daddy had built a bridge over the river. He walked across it to the bottling factory six days a week and stayed there fourteen hours a day.

Soon after Chris and I met at the club, he got a job with Garden Haven. He told me later that getting a job with the company who did our landscaping was part of his plan to see me.

He rode his bike to us on Fridays to prune and water. It had a trailer with his tools. Mom had seen him caring for the roses at the club and put him in charge of the bushes in the little cemetery. She didn't like being inside the fence herself, because it reminded her that she was destined to lie there for eternity.

"He's taking a while back there," Harper said.

We were on the screened-in back porch, under ceiling fans. It was still muggy and thick. My thighs slid against each other as I watched Chris's body bend and straighten as he worked on the roses.

Harper turned her attention back to her *Complete Works of Sir Arthur Conan Doyle*. She was reading well past her grade level. It was the only respite from her painful social awkwardness. "Twenty-two percent longer, at this point."

"It's the heat."

Our meeting in the back of the pro shop was a week old. I'd seen him twice since then. His lips tasted of salt and cola, and the young body felt tight and hard under his shirt.

Watching Chris, I wasn't completely sure if it was all sweat greasing the insides of my thighs. He'd led me behind a secret fence at the back of the club. He laid a towel over a tree stump so I wouldn't get grass or dirt stains on my white clothes, and he kneeled in front of me. When he kissed me, I wanted to spend the rest of my life attached to his lips, tasting his tongue. He'd bought me a soda, and we took turns transferring a chip of ice between our mouths.

That night, I'd run my fingers over my lips to see if I could reproduce the feeling, then between my legs for the same reason. Fear stopped me from continuing to the end. What if someone saw? What if my mother's voice in my head wasn't just a voice? What if—when it burst in saying "how *could* you?"—it summoned her attention by some as-yet-undisclosed telepathic transference and she could see me?

When Chris stood and wiped his brow, I imagined how his cola lips would taste with a hint of rose on them. He turned away as if something was moving in the trees and waved. A second later, Johnny came through the forest, holding a banker's box. His son, ten-year-old Joe, was at his side.

Johnny worked at the factory as a chemical engineer. His wife, Pat, owned the grocery store by Barrington Burgers.

Harper stood. "It's Mister Dorning! Hey, Mister Dorning!"

She was twelve and didn't have great impulse control. She had a special rapport with Johnny, based on their mutual love of things I couldn't get my head around.

Johnny stood by the white fence with his box. Chris looked into it and smiled. I didn't want him smiling without me. If I was miserable and ashamed, he had to be too. I went out, pulled behind Harper as if on a tether.

Johnny put the box on the ground, and everyone looked into it.

Harper squealed with delight. "Can I have one?"

The box was full of puppies. Four of them. The bloodhounds were honey-brown and cheerful except for the smallest one. He just looked soulful.

"It's up to your parents," Johnny said.

"I like this one!" Joe said, patting a tail-wagger with her paws over the edge of the box. She licked the boy's hand.

"Me too," Chris said.

I realized he was close to me and snapped around to see him looking over my shoulder, bent at the waist so his hands leaned on the three-foot-high fence and his lips were an inch from my body. He flicked his finger against the top of my thigh and I nearly went blind with arousal.

"I like the little one," I heard Harper say from a million miles away.

Chris and I were eye-locked. I could smell his breath, his body, the heat coming off him.

"He's the runt of the litter," Johnny said.

"What's that mean?" little Joe asked.

"He'll have certain genetic disadvantages," Johnny replied.

"In the wild," Harper corrected.

Chris blinked. Licked his lower lip. I couldn't tell if it took more effort to not kiss him or to stay standing.

"If I take him, he'll have advantages," Harper added.

The voices came from a long tunnel between my connection with Chris and the rest of the world clamoring for attention and getting none.

"We're naming them after Arthur's knights," Johnny said from the end of the tunnel.

"I read *Sir Gawain* in spring." That was Harper's voice.

Johnny. "I remember."

Little Joe. "Lancelot should be the big one! And Galahad because he's the best."

Their voices melted into the density of the silence between Chris and me like chocolate in a marble cake.

"Two are girls."

"Galahad can be shortened to Gal."

"The runt is Percival and he's mine."

"I promised the runt to Orrin. He needs a beta."

"We need an Arthur and there's no girl name for it."

"We can call a girl Arthur."

"There something wrong with Guinevere?"

I shook my head ever so slightly and pressed my lips tight together.

My expression was meant to speak a few volumes.

Not here.

I can't look at you like this here.

"Harper Barrington! You put that mutt down!"

I snapped to attention. Harper had the little puppy in her hands. Our mother bounded down the back porch steps.

Johnny gently took the dog from my sister before our mother reached us. "I'm sorry, Ella. I didn't think—"

"No, you didn't."

"But, Mom…" Harper whined, and Harper never whined. "He's just a baby. He needs us."

"Your father is allergic."

"We'll keep him outside."

"No. Go wash your hands."

Harper stormed off, fists balled on the ends of stiff arms, feet slamming the ground as if she wanted to bruise it.

"I'm sorry, Johnny," Mom said gently.

"I get it."

Their eyes locked, and having just had an eye-lock with Chris, I recognized the similarity. But it didn't last. Not for even a second.

She spun to me, then Chris, smoldering like hot glass. "Are you finished?"

"Not quite, ma'am."

"I'm not paying you for the time you spend looking at puppies."

"Of course." Chris pointed at Johnny and stepped back. "I'll take Lancelot."

"You got it," Johnny replied. "You sure you don't want one, El?"

My mother was kneeling over the box, letting one of the dogs lick her hand. "Earl's too sensitive." Mom stood and put her hand on my shoulder. "Let's get in out of the sun."

I followed her back to the house, looking back only once. Chris was looking at me with his arm shielding his eyes from the glare.

When we got inside, my mother guided me to the kitchen faucet, where we washed our hands. She kept looking out the back window over the sink.

"Is this clean enough?" I asked, willing my eyes away from Chris, into the endless drain.

"Yes." She shook the water off her hands. "Come here with me."

She took me to the sun room that overlooked the side of the house. It had windows on three sides and, for that moment, was remarkable for the fact that we couldn't see the backyard from it.

"Catherine," she said, folding her hands in her lap, "are you all right?"

"Yes." I pressed my knees together, wondering if she could see what was happening under my skirt.

She wiggled in her seat as if the conversation made the cushions prickly. "That boy was looking at you."

"I didn't notice."

She sighed. "Where I grew up, in Philadelphia, we were exposed to more things. More men. I worry about you girls's prospects."

I knew where she was going, and I wanted to deflect her. "I'm not worried about me. Harper though? She's so smart."

"She'll meet a man in college."

"Maybe I will too."

She nodded with the satisfaction of a period after a long string of clauses. "Boys like the one out there will ruin your life. Trust me on that. I won't let it happen. Trust me on that too." She looked me right in the eye, one eyebrow raised as if she expected me to rubber stamp her message.

I nodded slightly, because I was sure she was right. He'd ruin my life. I just had to decide if I wanted it ruined.

"Catherine." She tilted my chin up at her. "It's hard being a woman. In Philadelphia, it was hard because you were expected to do everything. Family, work, everything. Here, it's hard because you can let a man take care of you, but you can't make a mistake. There's no coming back from them. Do you understand what I'm saying?"

I didn't. Mistakes weren't always mistakes until after they happened. "Did you make a mistake once?"

"No." Her answer was sharp, as if she was cutting off a contradiction. "I married your father and he brought me here. And now I have my two girls who I love more than anything."

I wanted to make her happy. I wanted to make her proud and do things the right way. But as she hugged me, I wondered when I'd come to where the road forked between completing her life and completing my own.

CHAPTER 9

CHRIS - LAST DAYS OF LANCE

*L*ance liked everyone. He'd even liked Lucia, more or less, though she was never warm to him and she constantly complained about his hair getting in her sweaters. She'd had a point. We had a maid five days a week, yet his stiff fur always wound up in her knitwear. She gave up on wearing anything black more than once. I thought it had been Lance's way of chasing her out.

I gave him a pat on the head and tossed him a treat. He caught it, but he wasn't jumping as high as he used to or landing as confidently. He crunched it slowly, as if his teeth hurt.

I didn't think about him getting old. I thought he'd be with me forever.

He finished the treat and slapped his tail on the kitchen tile.

Fuck it. I gave him another treat and put the box away. When I lifted my arm to reach the cabinet, I caught sight of a dog hair in my sweater. And another.

"I'm going to change."

He followed me to the bedroom.

Lucia had bought me a pet hair remover brush as a divorce present. I should have been heartbroken to even look at it, but when we split up, I wasn't hurt. I was relieved.

I never had to see Lucia again. I never had to hear her brittle, derisive laugh or be nice to her friends. I never had to pretend I was the one throwing her birthday extravaganza. I didn't have to go to another Montano Foundation event where she worked tirelessly to help children she'd never know to make up for the children she couldn't have.

In the end, it was all about money. Even if she'd ever loved me, by the end, all the love had turned into money.

So fuck me for not seeing it.

Fuck me for letting her push me into a marriage I didn't want.

Fuck me for being weak.

Lance and I wrestled around for a few minutes, but he was old and tired. He couldn't play too rough or for too long. In the end, I rolled onto my back, arms and legs spread, looking at the white ceiling.

I didn't trust people easily. Why had I fallen for her eight years ago? I had been a kid from nowhere, a little prick hotshot throwing money around in restaurants. She'd been an Italian model for fifteen minutes. She'd started a charity with millions collected from men she denied were ex-lovers. On paper, she seemed better than I could do.

Fuck the paper. Never again. She should have been no more than an aspirational fuck.

Whatever. There was no need to worry about it. I was free. I could go anywhere. I could do anything.

I took Lance by the ears and looked into his brown eyes. "You're the only one for me, ya hear?"

He licked my chin and gave me his special whine that translated to, "Go for walk."

"Okay, boy."

He leapt for the door. By the time I got there, his tail was smacking the molding and he had his leash in his teeth. I was just about to grab it when my phone rang.

"Give me a second." I checked the caller ID and answered. "Brian."

"Did you see Neville's London report? If we make the arbitrage window, there's a thirty percent return."

"Thirty?" Holy crap. That was insane.

"Guaranteed. We need to move on this now."

"And big." I'd paced back to my home office with a mind fully occupied with calculating closing times and exchange rates. We had eleven minutes.

Brian and I spoke our shorthand, moving money, calculating odds, agreeing to go big on a hunch I'd had the day before and handed to Neville for calculations. We hung up at nine minutes and I pumped the fist that held the phone with a "yes!"

A nice afternoon's work.

I came back to the front of the house whistling fucking Dixie.

Lance was whimpering, his chin on his front paws. The fur was dark and damp at the ends, and a puddle of piss spread over the floor, flowing in rivulets toward the forty-thousand-dollar Persian rug.

"Crap!"

Lance whined and gave me his guilty face, but I didn't have time. I snapped paper towels off the roll and saved the rug.

"It's all right," I said to Lance on my hands and knees. "It's my fault, but I just made a ton of money."

Lucia's voice in my mind cut through my satisfaction. "*Porque*? Christopher, what are you going to do with all this money?"

That question had come toward the end, and it baffled me. She'd loved spending my money. I'd thought she loved me, but in moments when I was honest with myself, I thought it was all about the money for her.

I squirted disinfectant on the floor and rolled off more paper towels, recalling the night I met her.

I was sure she was about the money, and I was stupid and all right with that. I liked it, because she'd have me for what I'd done, not who I was.

She'd been looking over my shoulder at Lola's. Bernie had been talking about my quant fund and she was cooing about how she didn't understand it. I'd tried to hide my phone screen because… why?

Right. I'd been looking at my checking account. Why? To prove some shit to Bernie?

Why would I call up my checking account on my phone? At dinner, no less. The most interesting transactions weren't in the checking. That was a slush fund for bills and crap.

Lucia had long nails. She'd run them along the back of my hand as I'd slid my fingers over the glass.

"You have a dog?" she asked, pulling a hair off my sleeve.

"Yeah."

"Little or big?"

She was making conversation, which you were supposed to do at a big dinner. I was agitated the night I'd met Lucia. I knew why for a while, then I forgot. Something in the checking account had been bugging me.

"Medium."

I'd been counting days.

Why? I wasn't late with anything. I had a team of people to pay the damn bills. What was it with the checking account eight years ago? And why had it mattered?

Tossing the last of the soiled paper towels, I leaned down to face my dog. "Do you still want to go out? Walk?"

Of course he did. We went around the corner. He gave what he had left to a few hydrants and I tried to pull apart that night with Lucia.

My personal checking account. *Why why why?*

When we got back, I poured Lance some water, but instead of drinking, he followed me to my office. It was hardwood and chrome, shine and windows. My weekend hideaway from the social dramas of the fashion world that Lucia brought home. Throwing open the closet doors, I rooted past the bank boxes and corporate binders on the top shelf, finding my old checkbooks.

Counting backward, I found the checks I would have written when I met Lucia. *No, no, no.* Lance plopped down in front of me and whined, tilting his head toward my desk. I didn't know if it was because of the pain in his spine or if he was trying to mention that looking at my bank account online would be easier.

"I think I'll remember better if I feel the paper, you know?" I told him.

He put his chin between his paws and watched me with his big brown eyes, as if he knew what I was about to find out.

"Something you want to tell me, boy?"

He just blinked.

"Fine." I flipped through the book.

Like most people, I used mostly online payments and bank transfers, so a carbon for a check dated six months before I met Lucia wasn't too hard to find.

Seven hundred forty-nine dollars, made out to Catherine Barrington.

My phone number was in the memo.

Yeah.

That was why I'd been looking at my checking account.

Check 3201 had never been cashed, and the night I'd met Lucia was exactly six months after it was dated. The last day it was valid.

That was the night I gave up on Catherine.

CHAPTER 10

CATHERINE - PRESENT

Dear Chris,
Your letter came as a surprise. It's wonderful to hear from you after all these
years. How they've flown by!

tapped my finger against the kitchen counter, reading the
note. The black ballpoint handwriting was fine. Neat as a pin.
The stationary was old Barrington family paper that I kept in the bottom
of my underwear drawer because I had nowhere else to put it.
Everything was fine with the note except the intent.

The soup for church was popping and boiling in the pot. The dishes
were clean, and I had nothing to do but write this note. I wished I had
something else to do.

Your letter came as a surprise. It's wonderful to hear from you after all these
years. How they've flown by!

I SOUNDED LIKE A STRANGER. Like someone who had never promised him
a thing. Even the exclamation point at the end that was supposed to
warm up the letter seemed like another line and dot of distance.

Pushing the paper's corners together, I started to crumple it and stopped. I could use it as scrap. I could write everything I wanted to say then edit it neatly onto a new sheet.

I am so sorry to hear about Lance. I think burying him at home is the right thing. I know Galahad is on Wild Horse Hill. You should get a space nearby.

WAS that all I was going to talk about? Lance? Was I going to let the subtext rule the conversation or was I going to be a grown-up?

I don't know when I stopped waiting for you.

THERE. That was closer. At least it was true. A long time ago, I'd stopped waiting without even thinking about it.

I used to cry over you, but not for a long time. Now I just cry out of habit. I cry for a release, even if I don't feel sad. It's a valve I can open and I function fine. So, thanks for the tears, I guess.

THE BEDSPRINGS SQUEAKED UPSTAIRS, and my stream of rage snapped. This thing Harper had. This man she'd met on the internet and brought home. It was strange and unprecedented and I wanted it.

I didn't even know what it was and I wanted it. I wanted it so badly I couldn't think.

To add shame to sin, the doorbell rang.

I looked through the front sidelight. It was Reggie.

"Shoot."

He worked in the distribution center off the interstate and painted small canvases of cities and spaceships in his spare time. He'd sold a few to people in Doverton, but mostly he covered them over with new ideas as they occurred.

When I was upset, my father gave me the master suite as a consolation prize. At twenty, Reggie was Barrington's resident artistic talent. Dad had hired him to paint flowers on the ceiling to cheer me up. I didn't sleep in that room anymore because of a roof leak, but knowing the ceiling was there was comforting. It was beautiful and it was mine.

My sister and every lady in town insisted Reggie held a candle for me ever since then. Even while I dated Frank Marshall and after that ended peacefully. The rumors alone put Reggie at the top of the list of people I didn't want to come inside while Taylor and Harper were making a racket.

Pressing the pedal to open the kitchen garbage pail, I gathered the top of the plastic bag. It was only about a third full, but I took it to the front door anyway. When I opened it, Reggie had his hat in his hand.

"Hello," I said.

He stuffed his baseball cap in his back pocket and took the bag. "I have that."

"Thank you." I pointed down the driveway.

The garbage pails were on the side of the house so they were easily accessed from the side door. Hopefully he'd think I came to the front to answer the doorbell, as opposed to using the garbage as an excuse to keep him out of the house and away from the sound of the bed squeaking.

He followed where I indicated without question, walking around the side with me.

"What brings you here on Sunday morning?"

"I just found out from Johnny that old Chris Carmichael's coming back."

"Really?"

"So they say."

We walked a few more steps.

"He might," I said. "But who knows?"

"Did he tell you?"

"Why would he?"

"You guys had a thing."

"That was a long time ago." I opened the garbage pail lid. "Why?"

He put the bag inside. "I was wondering how you were about it? Happy?"

"It's complicated." I let the lid slap shut. "A lot's changed. I mean, look around here. When he left, the burger place was packed every night, the factory was open, my family? We… we were big shots."

"You're still a big shot to me." He was being completely earnest. He was a trash-talking guy's guy when he thought I wasn't looking, but around me, he was warm and sincere.

"Thank you, Reg."

He cleared his throat. "So what are you going to do with that thorn bush out back? Those roses were his pride and joy."

"Hardly."

"Aw, come on. He worked twelve hours at a time on them. Pruned and mulched. I remember."

I wanted them to be nice for him, but I also didn't want to see him. I wished I could be of a single mind about anything. "I should probably make them into proper bushes again."

I walked Reggie to his car. It was the only subtle way I had of letting him know he couldn't come inside.

"If you need any help, I'm pretty handy with clippers."

"You're good at too many things, Reggie."

"I said I was handy." He flipped his hat back on. "I make no other promises."

"Will I see you at church?"

"Yes, ma'am."

"I'm making the soup everyone likes."

"I'll come hungry then."

He got into his car. We said our so longs and he drove off.

Back inside, I was glad I hadn't invited Reggie in. They were still at it. Maybe they were trying to be quiet the same way I tried to be quiet when I cried at night.

The sounds were lower by the couch. The sewing kit was on the arm because I'd sold the end tables and coffee table. The kit's lid had a hard inside surface. I opened it, put a blanket over my legs, and began my letter to Chris again.

CHAPTER 11

CATHERINE - SIXTEENTH SUMMER

Behind the courts, between the locker room and the club, there was a shortcut for members and an artery for the grounds staff. Behind that was a quarter-acre patch of grass between the fence and Route 42 which stretched between Doverton and Barrington. The entire lot was visible to the road, but there was a tree in the middle of it. A mighty oak with horizontal branches thicker than most tree's fully-grown trunks.

When Chris had a minute and happened upon the right piece of wood, he'd nail chunks of two-by-four or one-by-four into the trunk. He told me about it behind the pool house and in the hidden corners of the parking lot.

I didn't know what he was talking about until he finished at mid-summer and led me through a hole in the fence. "Where are we going?"

I was barely through before Lance bounced over to me, stopping right before he came to the end of a long chain. Still a puppy, he had big brown eyes and floppy ears with short fur the color of hazelnuts. I ran my hands over his body, and he rolled onto his back.

"Is he safe here?" I asked, crouching to rub his belly.

"Pretty safe. Irv says it's okay as long as I clean up after him and he's quiet."

Lance twisted around and nipped my fingers playfully, trying to wrestle my hand.

"Where's your ball?" Chris asked.

Lance bounced back to the base of his captivity. The tree. I stood and slapped my hands clean. Chris laid his hand on the back of my neck. I shuddered.

"I was watching you play," he whispered in my ear. "Do you know you smile before forehands?"

"You should tell me when you're there."

"Next time." He nipped my earlobe, his breath loud in my ear.

Lance dropped a sticky ball at our feet. Chris knelt and patted his head, reaching into his pocket for a new yellow ball. Lance was thrilled. Chris tossed it toward the tree and the puppy ran for it. Chris took my hand and led me to the tree.

"Put your foot on this." He laid his hand on the lowest piece of wood, at knee height. "I've tried it already. It's safe."

I dropped my bag at the trunk, and he helped me balance as I got my tennis shoe on the bottom foothold. My hands found the boards above, and I stepped up. At the second step, I pressed the back of my skirt against my bare thighs and looked down at him.

"You'll need two hands to climb," he said.

Behind him, on the ground, Lance looked up at us with his tongue hanging out.

"I think you should go first," I said.

"You're wearing shorts under your skirt. I can't see a thing."

The shorts protected my bottom from view while I ran and spun on the tennis court. But they were still really short, and he was getting a longer look.

"Do you promise?"

"Swear."

I decided to believe him and climbed until I was fifteen feet off the ground, on a bough thicker than a telephone pole. I straddled the bough and slid back so Chris could fit. He straddled it facing me. Below us, Lance protected the new ball by yipping. I could hear cars on Route 42 and the *pock pock* of tennis balls hitting the court, but all I could see were leaves, branches, and mottled sunlight.

"Do you like it?" he asked.

"I love it."

He licked his finger and chalked one up for himself. "Did you decide about college next year?"

I shrugged. I wanted to get out of Barrington. Spread my wings. Meet new people and learn new things. But Chris couldn't afford to go to college.

"Did you check out the financial aid booklet at the library?" I asked.

"There's no point."

"Well then, I'll get an Associate's from Jackson County. I won't have to move and—"

"You have to get out of here." He grabbed my hands. "I can't go, but you can."

Chris was an only child to a mother who had been too obese to leave her bed. In the past year, she'd made him proud by losing a hundred fifty pounds. Not enough to be comfortable, but enough to move around the trailer.

"Then come," I said. "I move, then you move and we meet far away somewhere."

He squeezed my hands. "Look at you. You can be anything you want. Go be it. That's all I have to say."

He looked over my shoulder, then back at my face. I knew him enough from our summer together to know I needed to wait to hear whatever he said next.

"I'll be here when you get back," he continued.

I almost lost my mind in his eyes. Almost agreed with him. I could do anything, but I didn't want to. I wasn't Harper, with her big dreams and bigger brain. I didn't have ambitions or a career in mind. I figured I'd inherit the factory and keep it going, or not. What I really wanted was a house full of people who depended on me.

"I'll think about it," I said because I wanted to make Chris happy for a moment.

"When do you have to be back?" he asked.

"Mom thinks I'm volleying with Marsha."

He brushed my knee with his fingertips. My skin felt as though it was melting underneath him and I became very aware of the hard trunk between my legs.

"Marsha's in the pool house with what's-his-face."

"Charles."

He leaned into me. "What do you think they're doing in there?"

They called Marsha a tramp, but I didn't think she was. Or maybe I thought being a tramp suited her. Or I thought it wasn't a big deal.

"Stuff."

"This, maybe?" He ran two fingers inside my thigh.

Sensation rushed behind them, to my knees, and ahead to the soft place between my legs. We'd kissed plenty in the back room of the pro shop and in the utility closet. He'd run his hands over my shirt, but he'd never touched me like that before.

"Maybe," I gasped.

I shouldn't let him run his hand up my other thigh. I should stop this right there. He was going way too fast. There were *steps* and he wasn't honoring them. But that made his touch even more explosive. My body didn't expect the speed of his advance, and it reacted by opening up all the way.

"Oh, my God." His eyes were wide and his lip was stretched behind his top teeth. When he let it go, it went from white to deep pink. "Look at you. I can't believe how sexy you are."

My face tingled. Chris wasn't any more experienced than I was, but he was so open and honest about what he was doing and what he wanted that his words made me blush.

His index finger brushed the edge of my shorts. "Can I touch you?"

I throbbed when he asked. The ache inside me was almost painful in its need.

But was it too much? Would he think I was a slut? My legs were already open, by design. Wasn't that already an invitation? I could have swung both legs to one side, but I hadn't taken the modest posture.

In the pause after his question, he kissed me, pressing his thumbs into my inner thighs. His tongue in my mouth was such a sweet violation. I wanted more. All the more.

I picked up his hands and put them on my chest. Lips locked, he ran his thumbs over my hard nipples as I reached back, under my shirt, and unhooked my bra.

He broke the kiss. I came forward to put our mouths together again, but he leaned back. "Show me."

I would have preferred to kiss while he felt my breasts so it would feel as though I was in thoughtless throes of passion. It would feel less mindful. If we were putting thought into it, pausing and stopping, appreciating every act, then I had no excuse.

Chris gently pulled at the hem of my shirt. He didn't want mindless. He wanted to see every second. I knew my nipples were hard under my bra and he was looking at them as if he was savoring the sight. His relish shamed me and made my skin tingle at the same time.

In the choice between shame and the tingle, I made my choice.

I pulled my shirt up over my breasts. The bra lifted. He ran his hands along the underside before he pulled the bra up.

He sucked in a breath.

"These are beautiful." He bent my hard nipples before he gently squeezed them.

The feeling shot right between my legs as if connected by an electric wire. My back arched, and my consciousness hid behind a wall of pleasure.

The bough slipped from under me, and his hands tightened on my rib cage.

"Whoa, there," he said, keeping me from falling.

"I'm sorry."

"Don't be. Just remember where you are." Ever so tenderly, he pinched my nipples again. It hurt a little, but the pain was part of the pleasure. "Can you put your hands behind you? On the branch?"

He guided my arms behind me. My shirt fell back down, but once I was secure, leaning back against my locked elbows, he drew it up again. I was exposed to the sky.

"Next time, I'll do it your way." He pushed my chin up so I was looking through the branches at the clouds and ran his hand down my body. "I'll go up first so you can lean on the trunk."

"Yes, okay."

Both hands landed on my breasts. "I like it when you agree."

He kissed my sternum and twisted my nipples.

I groaned.

He twisted a little harder. "Do you like that?"

"Yes. Yes."

"You smell like roses." He sucked one nipple and hurt the other in a way that brought pleasure to the surface. I was filled with blood, my insides bigger than my outside, stretching my skin to thin translucence. "I should call you Catherine of the Roses."

"More," I gasped, the word falling out of my mouth like a piece of gum I'd forgotten about.

I didn't even know what I was saying. I was losing my mind as he worked me over. Blind, deaf, dumb. My whole body was wedged between his fingers.

My face was toward the sky, a curtain of dappled orange from the daylight on the other side of my closed eyes. A frame of white-hot shockwaves flickered in my vision, and something broke in me. I stopped thinking, breathing, feeling anything but him as the world pressed in on me and I pressed out into the world.

"Jesus!" he said when I finally gasped and opened my eyes.

"Oh, my G—"

"You *came*."

Sitting up straight, I put my hands over my face. I was ashamed. I'd done that, in front of him, from nothing. "I didn't think I would!"

When I took my hands away and saw him looking at me, I yanked my shirt down.

"It was awesome!"

Awesome? I wanted to die.

Lance yipped right before Harper's voice came past the fence.

"Catherine!"

Chris looked at his watch, but I didn't need to see it. Three p.m. had come and my bra wasn't hooked. I reached behind me and grappled with it.

I had to get down and Chris was in my way. He'd made me come right here, outside, in a tree. I was ashamed and nervous, and he was pulling my shirt down to cover me. He was beautiful, with his blue eyes and the wavy fall of hair over one side of his forehead. He was inappropriate. Unsuitable. Dangerous to my future, whatever that was.

"Hey," Harper called without shouting, as if she knew I was close by.

Chris climbed up a branch to get out of my way, indicating his handmade staircase, then putting his finger to his lips.

Lance stretched his chain to get to Harper, wagging his tail like windshield wipers in a storm. She crawled through the hole in the fence to pet him while looking all around.

"Cath?" she called.

"Coming!" I shouted, scuttling down.

"There you are!" She stood while Lance sniffed around her ankles. "Mom said to go to the car."

I slung my bag over my shoulder. "Okay, let's go."

"This is Lance, right? Is Chris around?" She pointed at the tree. "Were you climbing with him?"

"I'm sure he's working."

"Is that a ladder up the trunk?" She pinched her bottom lip until it creased.

I slapped her hand down. "Stop bending your lip like that. It's going to stay that way." I took the hand I'd slapped before she had a chance to bend her lip again, pulling her to the break in the fence. "And don't even think of climbing that tree. It's not safe." She went through first, and I followed. "I'm telling the grounds crew it's there before someone gets hurt."

My muscles didn't relax until we got to the car and I knew Harper hadn't seen Chris in the tree. If anyone knew the way he'd touched me and the way it made me feel, I'd die. Literally die.

CHAPTER 12

CATHERINE - PRESENT DAY

The squeaking upstairs was done, and the pipes rattled in the walls when the shower turned on. I read the final draft of my note for the hundredth time. Beginning to end.

Dear Chris,

Your letter came as a surprise. It's wonderful to hear from you after all these years. How they've flown by!

I am so sorry to hear about Lance. I think burying him at home is the right thing. I know Joan buried Galahad on Wild Horse Hill. You should get a space nearby.

Though it would be great to see you, I'll be unavailable while you're here. Please accept my condolences.

Sincerely,
Catherine

HARPER BOUNCED down the steps in a pair of little pink shorts. Taylor was at her heels. The way he followed her was so cute I smirked a little.

"There's a pot of soup on the stove if you're interested," I said.

"Thanks!" Harper went to the kitchen. She'd say she hated it because I'd used frozen peas and carrots, then she'd eat it anyway because she was a human vacuum.

On the way to the kitchen, still holding the half-crumpled letter, something overwhelming occurred to me.

Was Harper going to leave with this guy?

Leave the house?

Leave Barrington?

Leave *me*?

She did complain about the soup, and she ate it. She argued with Taylor about a laptop and bowls and I made all the right gestures and sounds, but I wasn't really there. I was sinking into a quicksand of things that hadn't occurred to me.

I had been glad to have Taylor around. Glad Harper was happy.

But it had never occurred to me that he'd take her away.

In the middle of the conversation, the letter took on a life of its own. I pulled an envelope out of the rack. It already had a stamp and a white label over my address. The post office hadn't canceled the stamp, so I'd kept it. The seal that had closed it wasn't sticky anymore. Nothing a little tape couldn't fix. It was a gem of an envelope.

Sending the note to Chris that way would make me look cheap, or worse, poor. But I put the crumpled paper in and snapped a piece of tape from the dispenser, pressing it down with my thumb as if getting every corner flat made the decision more final.

You're really doing it?

I'm really doing it.

"Harper," I said before she left with Taylor. They were picking something up at the store before church. "Can you mail this?"

She snapped it from me as if it were just another bill before leaving me alone in the house.

For the moment.
For the morning.
Soon to be forever.

CHAPTER 13

CATHERINE - SIXTEENTH SUMMER

Playground tonight. 10:30pm.

I left him the note inside my racquet case when I took it for restringing. It had been a full week since he touched me in the tree, a week since we'd spoken or since I looked him in the eye.

I'd been avoiding him. He'd said *hi* a few times and made sure we crossed paths. Once, he stood by the opening in the fence and gestured for me to pass through with him, but I turned and walked the other way.

I'd given him more than I intended up in the tree, and I couldn't bear it. I couldn't look anyone in the eye. They'd see right into my heart and call me a tramp like they called Marsha. Mom would stop being proud of me, and Dad would be ashamed. Harper would still love me, but what kind of example was I setting?

My shame outweighed my desire for him for five days. By the end of the week, shame was feather-light and desire broke the scales. I handed my racquet through the pro shop window and walked away, holding my breath until my parents went to bed and the house was quiet. I peeled off my nightgown to the clothes underneath and tiptoed out the side door.

My bike leaned up against the house. In the dark, I rode it down the service road to the place where the trees opened to the train tracks, then I left it against a tree.

I never realized crickets were so loud until I had to wonder if they were hiding the sound of my footfalls as I kicked up leaves and needles. I'd entered the deep brush, with the witness of owls and insects. A night creature with little nails scratched and crawled over my feet and made me jump. I hit a spider web and clawed through it as if I were fighting an invisible demon.

I didn't wonder so much if the animals could see me. I wasn't that paranoid. But whenever they moved or whenever a cricket jumped, I worried that a person could detect that someone was near and they could find me. Or they could ask me why I was even on this side of town.

I crossed the train tracks, looking both ways as if the freight ran on a thoroughfare. It was a few steps to the rows of mobile homes that defined that side of Barrington.

The playground was in a little clearing just west of the center of the trailers. My fingertips were cold, but the rest of my body thrummed and pulsed so hard that I made my own heat. I told myself I didn't know what to expect from this meeting, but if I didn't know what to expect, I knew what to hope, and they were pretty much the same thing.

"Catherine!" Chris wasn't loud, but the excitement in his voice made him sound as if he were shouting.

"Chris?" I spun around, looking for him in the darkness.

And on a three-quarter turn, he crashed into me, all lips and hands, digging his fingertips into the muscles of my back as he pulled me close. I tasted the minty toothpaste in his mouth and thought *he brushed his teeth for me*. He kissed me as if he would never kiss me again. He kissed me as if this was the last kiss he would ever have in his life. As if he wanted to eat me alive. I'd given over my freedom and my choice to this thing with him, to this moment, to this stupid set of choices that would ruin me forever. As surely as the sun would rise, I was the designer of my own destruction.

I wanted to be destroyed by that kiss.

When Chris took my hand, I imagined I could feel the blood pulsing through the veins, the cells in his skin. I imagined that when my nerve endings vibrated at his touch, they connected to his somehow.

Everything felt new. I was discovering that my body had routes between one place and another that I never knew existed. I never knew that when a man touched my hand or kissed my nipples, I could feel it between my legs.

There was a click behind the tree line, and he stopped kissing me with a jerk. We froze long enough for him to smile.

"I don't want you to do this anymore," he said. "It's not safe."

"It's fine."

"I'll come to you. Please. I've been worried since the sun went down."

Behind me, a twig snapped and I jumped. "I think I just proved your point."

"Just a squirrel. Come this way."

He led me to the play structure, and I giggled as I walked up the plastic ladder. I was so big I barely even needed to hit every step. I didn't really need him to hold out his hand and help me to the top of the slide. But I took it, because his touch was the spinning center of my curiosity.

The vantage point wasn't that much better than the ground, but I felt somehow encouraged to look out over the rows of trailers. Most of them had lights on, blue rectangles from flashing TV shows, the shouts, laughs, cries of kids getting ready for bed.

His body pressed me from behind, his hands drifted up and down me. His lips brushed against the back of my neck. My eyes fluttered closed, and I sighed.

When he cupped my breasts over my shirt, I should have been ashamed. I should have run away. But I felt so safe with him. Even when he pressed his pelvis forward and I felt his erection on my bottom. I pushed my hips back against him and he breathed into my neck.

"Catherine, I want to make you come again."

Even in the tight lasso of his arms, I managed to turn around to face him. "It's your turn."

He tilted his head down a little and took my mouth in a kiss that was so much a question, not so much a permission as a demand. And I acquiesced, yielded to him completely. Our knees bent, and he ended up on the small floor, surrounded by gates, under an apparatus where a kid could change the times of day to match the sun and the moon. We barely fit on that little rectangle, but we were so twined up in each other that we didn't make any kind of reasonable or measurable shape.

"I want you," he said. "I want you so bad. I don't know what to do with myself all day. Whenever I feel rose petals, I think of your skin. I smell them, and I think of you. I stick my hands in the soil and think of getting my fingers inside you."

His words made me nervous. I'd never used words like that, especially with a boy. They seemed dangerous. He must have felt me freeze a little because he took my hand and put it between his legs. My God, he was so hard. I ran my nails along the length of him, through the fabric of his pants. I didn't know what I was doing, but I must have been doing something right because he let loose a breathy "ah."

He undid his jeans button, then the zipper, and guided my hand to the skin of him. I couldn't believe what I was doing and what it was doing to me. I felt how wet I was. The sensation at my core was going to take over and he wasn't even touching me.

I'm going to do this. I'm going to do what makes him happy.

I wrapped my hand around his shaft, feeling how the thin skin moved against the rigid core. "It's wet. Did you come already?"

"No, that's just a little bit that comes out at first."

With my thumb, I rubbed the liquid around the tip, and he kissed me so hard that my head was pushed up against the plastic floor.

"Move your hand a little bit." He wrapped his hand around mine and moved up and down. "Like that. Yes."

"Like this? This feels good?"

"Yes. Like that. You turn me on so much. I'm not going to rush you. I want to get inside you so bad."

I wanted him inside me. I wanted him to break through, tear me to shreds, open me, but I wasn't ready. I wanted to feel him in my hand before I felt him in my body.

His hips jerked rhythmically until I didn't have to move my hand so much. Still kissing me, he jerked back and forth, then he rolled onto his back with me on top of him and pulled up his shirt. We did everything with our lips still connected, as if moving away would break the moment.

He came onto his stomach. I was shocked how much there was, spurting all over him with white arcs in the moonlight.

"Thank you," he said into my mouth.

I kneeled next to him, the skin of my knees pressed into cold plastic. His bare torso was pooled with semen.

"What are we going to do?"

He dug a tissue out of his pocket and wiped it away. "We're taking care of you."

"What do you mean?"

Lazily, his hand drifted to my knee, then up my thigh and under my shorts. He pushed a little. "Spread your knees apart."

He didn't wait for me to do it. He slid his fingers under my clothes and touched me where I was wet.

"Oh." I couldn't do more than squeak.

His hand wrestled with the shorts and the underwear until he could angle a finger inside me. I exhaled sharply. I'd put my fingers inside before, but when he did it, I couldn't even think.

"I heard this isn't what works," he whispered. "Have you heard about the clitoris?"

"What?" Of course I had, but I didn't want an anatomy lesson.

"It's here, I think." He drew his finger out and up, finding the swollen nub.

"Oh, my God."

"Wow," he said in wonderment, running the back of his finger against it as much as he could in the tight space. "Is that it?"

"Uh-huh."

"Does it feel good?"

I fell back on my hands, knees off the floor, with his hand still up my shorts.

He rubbed too hard. Too fast. He was as clumsy and earnest as you'd expect from a teenager.

"I wish I could kiss it," he said.

And that was it. The thought of his lips sent shockwaves down my spine. I came into his hand.

When he pulled his hand out, he wiped his fingers with the tissue. We lay beside each other and watched the moon cross half the sky before we went home.

CHAPTER 14

CATHERINE - PRESENT

Harper confirmed she'd sent the letter. I felt a kind of relief that I didn't have to see Chris. My excuse was in the world, on the way, out of my hands.

What I did with my life now was up to me. Harper had been able to take care of herself for years. I'd drained myself of almost every asset except the house itself for the sake of the people of Barrington. I had nothing left to give them, and the town itself had nothing left for me.

I'd been waiting for Chris and I hadn't even realized it.

But now that I'd made a decision not to see him, he was everywhere.

The rosebushes that had grown wild, the creaky floorboards, the knowledge that there were still flying monkeys scratched into the back of my great-grandfather's headstone.

The space behind the beige rotary wall phone led to a pantry, and the counter nearby was stuffed with pamphlets, flyers, phone books, recipes, and any other piece of paper we didn't know what to do with.

Since I was a teenager, numbers had been scrawled on the wall around the phone. Mother wouldn't have liked it, but she did it first. And Dad, for his part, never saw any reason to update a phone that worked perfectly well.

In the ridge of molding was a number etched in quick little ballpoint lines. The dark blue had faded and the years of grease and dirt obscured it, but if I put my temple to the wall, it was still readable.

Chris's number hadn't worked in years. Not since his mother left Barrington and the trailer they'd lived in fell to the elements. I went into the pantry and sat where I always had when I wanted a little privacy—on the root box that hadn't stored a root in a decade. The peeling shelving paper had the same blue flowers, and the light hung dark and bald, kissing the silver ball chain.

For the first time since I'd sent Harper off with the letter, I felt its weight.

What had I done? If I'd been waiting for him all those years without realizing it, why reject him when he came? Shouldn't I be celebrating my success? My patience? The victory of maturity over whim?

Shouldn't I be cleaning the house and getting ready for him instead of telling him not to come? What was I supposed to do now?

I'd only done a couple of impulsive things in my life, and they all had his name on them.

It was Monday. I didn't usually cry until bedtime, but sitting on that root box, I wanted to wail my heart out.

"Catherine Barrington," I growled, "enough is enough."

When I came out of the pantry, Harper was already in the kitchen, leaning into the refrigerator. She wore her yellow shirt and a ponytail.

"Morning."

"Harper, what would you say if I went away?"

"Like what kind of went away?" She leaned her whole head into the refrigerator. "To prison or a trip?"

"A trip."

"I'd say 'have fun.'" She came out with yogurt, peanut butter, and jelly. "Where are you going?"

Where was I going? Anywhere.

"Paris." I said it as if it was the closest guess in a timed game show.

"Fancy. Nearest passport office is in Springfield. Do you need me to come?"

I didn't have a passport. If I wanted one, I would have to wait weeks to get it. I wanted to leave *now*. Tomorrow. Sooner. I wanted to go and get a new life before I lost my nerve.

"I don't know. Maybe."

"Taylor's staying here," Harper said. "I hope that's all right. He's harmless. And I only have a half shift."

"It's fine."

"I need extra cash for your birthday party." She put the containers in a plastic bag and snapped the loaf of bread off the counter without slowing down.

"What birthday party?"

"Thursday dinner barbecue." She kissed my cheek and headed for the door.

"Harper!"

The door slammed behind her. I'd forgotten about my birthday, but she hadn't. She loved me. She'd come back from college to help with Dad and never went back. She'd sworn she stayed because she wanted to, not to keep me company.

She'd lied, and I'd chosen to believe it. She and I were in this prison together. We were both going to be free.

I had to stay through the week. I guessed it was just as well. I could get a passport and take my time preparing to abandon Barrington.

Upstairs, I heard a crash that rattled the walls. Then another. I ran up, pausing in the middle of the staircase. In bare feet and a robe, I was in no condition for a man to see me. Even my sister's man.

I heard another crash. It was coming from my old room. The one after the first and before the place I slept now. The master suite Daddy gave me when he thought it would cheer me up.

The walls pounded again, vibrating top down as if they shook from fear. Taylor had asked me for tools a few days before to spackle over a mushroom growing from the bathroom ceiling. He hadn't asked for a sledgehammer.

I took the steps two at a time in my bare feet, running down the hall in leaping bounds as another crash came from the master suite. My suite. My space. The room that had been mine after Chris left, and the room I'd abandoned after a leak soaked the walls through and a mushroom grew on the bathroom ceiling.

A cloud of dust hung like a ghost outside the door. The window at the end of the hall caught each fleck of dust in morning light as they twisted and flew when I leapt inside it.

I froze at the threshold.

Taylor was in his late twenties. He was polite to Harper. He cleaned up after himself and spoke in complete sentences. Sweaty, stripped down to his undershirt, his skin was marbled with dirt and grime already. She'd said he was visiting from California, but she hadn't said he was a demolitions contractor or that he'd be plying his trade while she was at the distro center.

The bed was covered in a blue tarp, and the ceiling—which was a piece of tin painted over in pink roses—was dusty but intact. Thank God.

"Oh, my Lord!" I said when he noticed me there.

"Good morning." He had a beautiful smile for a guy I wanted to scream at.

"What… what are you doing?"

"Don't come in!"

"But—"

"There are nails."

The room seemed darker, no doubt because the plaster walls weren't reflecting the light from the French doors to the balcony. They were just exposed hundred-year-old wood. Yellow Xs had been marked on some of the beams where the wood had been damaged by mold.

"You won't have the mushroom again."

It took me a second to catch up to what he meant. The roof over the back of the house had leaked into the bathroom five years before, and since then, a long-stemmed mushroom had grown from the ceiling. We'd repaired the roof and plastered over the fungus every year, but every year it grew back stronger.

And it was gone. I was rendered speechless by his kindness.

"The mold isn't safe to breathe," he continued.

Safe. Funny word. My parents had put me in this room to keep me safe. And Daddy had Reggie paint the ceiling to soothe me while I was safe and miserable.

"And that?" Taylor pointed at the roses. "I looked behind it. It's clean."

Clean.

Another funny word. After my parents caught me with Chris, I found out what they each were obsessed with. For my mother, the issue had been cleanliness, and my lack of it. For my father, it was safety.

After all the crying. All the fighting. After I showered the blood off my leg and the sticky gunk off my belly, I could never be right again for my mother. But Daddy had done all he could to make it right, even if he did everything wrong.

When Chris left, this hadn't been my room. There hadn't been a rose-painted ceiling. Above me, two golden wings peeked out from a flare of petals, hidden cleverly by Barrington's only artist. I'd been a different person, and this room was part of a different era.

But not really.

Who was Chris? Who was I? All those years… should I sweep them away? Pretend they didn't happen? Take the tin down, roll it up, and toss it aside? Pack up and run away so I could be sixteen again as if the flying monkeys hidden in the flowers had never existed?

I'd sworn to leave a minute ago, and now all I wanted to do was stay in my house with my people, taking care of a town I loved.

"I want to say something," I said to Taylor.

"Yes?"

"I own a gun."

"Okay?"

"I know how to use it."

He must have thought I was talking about Harper, because he went from swaggering to sincere. As if I'd threaten him over her. Anyone who knew Harper knew she could take care of herself.

"Cath—"

"Don't let anything happen to the painting."

He nodded slowly, as if he didn't understand why it mattered. "Yes, ma'am."

"And thank you," I said. "It'll be nice to sleep in here again."

I ran down the hall and threw myself onto my bed.

I wanted Chris to come to me, and I'd told him not to.

I wanted to leave so badly.

And I wanted to stay.

The tug-of-war for my heart raged, and I decided I was not going to shed a tear for it.

CHAPTER 15

CATHERINE - SIXTEENTH SUMMER

My father kept the factory open even when seventy-five percent of the workers were gone and the skeleton crew didn't have much to do. He'd cut their hours, their insurance, their benefits. They understood, taking their lumps like warriors. Twice a year, on Memorial Day and Labor Day, he threw a free barbecue for anyone who wanted to come. Mom hated it because it was all Barrington people. She always invited her Doverton friends, but they turned up their noses. She claimed migraines and bellyaches, but she was expected to be there, same as the rest of us.

Some of Harper's elementary school friends were going to Montgomery High with her. She was awkward and too smart for her own good, but she was genuine. They found her tolerable because she wasn't interested in gossip and romance. She wasn't competition.

At the Labor Day barbecue, she abandoned her friends to their flirtations so she could run around with the litter of bloodhound puppies nipping at her heels. Reggie kept a booth with paintings of lightning bolts and rollicking planets. Juanita and Florencio had a booth with *pupusas*. There were more crafts and energy in that square than any other day of the year. The rock music was provided by a bunch of guys from the public high school. Bernard, who was a year older than me and worked at the lumber yard, sang in a gravelly voice that was strangely dazzling.

I wasn't as awkward as my sister, but I didn't find the girls in my grade tolerable. They ranged from rigid religious anger-bombs to Doverton kids who found me beneath them. Marsha and I spoke, but not much outside school.

I stood on the grass, surrounded by my neighbors, each of them too poor, too crass, too unseemly to associate with. Listening to Bernard sing and watching my sister roll on the ground with a bunch of puppies, I was trapped, and yet, somehow free.

Leaning on the bleachers, Chris cracked peanuts between his teeth and spit the shells. I hadn't seen him in days and it seemed like years. Every time I saw the kick of his hips and the way his lips stretched across his teeth when he smiled, it seemed like the first time.

I watched him.

He watched me.

School started the next day. We'd go back into our different worlds. Would we meet again? Would we see each other at all? We'd grappled with the question by avoiding it.

A waft of smoke from the grills came between us.

We were alone. Surrounded by people, we were alone.

He pitched his peanut bag in the trash and washed it back with a bottle of off-brand cola. When he finished, he sucked in his bottom lip to catch an errant drop.

He tossed the bottle up. It spun in the air, and with a tap of his knuckle on its way down, he sent it into the trash.

I stepped toward him, and he stepped back. Not away. He stepped back toward something, flicking his finger that I should follow.

Easiest decision I'd ever made. It was barely even a decision.

I glanced around for Mom and Dad. They were in the gazebo with Badger, the new mayor, and his staff. Harper and the kids played with the puppies while Johnny and his wife watched. Lance jaunted around the perimeter, peeing on poles whenever he could, nipping back any sibling who got too big for their britches, ever the alpha.

I tilted directions slightly toward the bathrooms, then once past the bleachers, I saw Chris peeking from an alley between the hardware store and the library. I picked up my skirt and ran toward him, cutting the corner so hard I lost my balance. Out of nowhere, his hand was on my arm, keeping me from falling over.

Finger to lips, he led me to a black iron door. He clinked through his keys and opened it, stepping out of the way so I could pass through. We were in an office.

He closed the door with a loud *clap*, leaving the window as the only light.

"Chris?"

I barely got out the S before his lips kissed his name away. He put his hands on my jaw, keeping it still so he could invade my mouth. It felt good to give it to him. My body lost all its strength, held up only by the electrical currents between us.

"Catherine," he said in a breath, keeping his lips an inch from my face as he spoke.

"Where are we?"

"Back of the hardware store. I open on Thursdays."

"What are we going to do? I'm scared."

"Of me?"

"Of not seeing you anymore."

"I'll find you."

I clutched his shirt as if I'd be swept away without him. "I don't fit in anywhere. Harper is so smart she tolerates me. The only time I feel right, like I'm part of something, like I belong, is when I'm with you."

"One more year. Then you can go to college and I'll come after. We'll be so far away, we'll forget our names. When people ask where we're from, we won't even know."

"I don't know if we'll make it a year. I feel like they see us. Even now."

I must have been shaking, because he put his arms around me so tightly it hurt. I loved the pain of his attention. It was the pain of safety, of care, of being broken just enough for release.

"Harder," I said into his shoulder.

He squeezed me so tightly I could just barely breathe, and the tension rolled off me like water.

He let his arms go slack enough to look me in the face. "We'll make it. Then I'll follow you anywhere. I'll be your puppy dog."

"Oh, Chris, don't be silly."

"Don't deny me. I'm yours." He said the last word with a gusto I'd never associated with myself. As if life was something to grab with both hands and free like a bird that could carry us into the sky.

Together, we were freedom.

The bird launched from my chest and flew to my lips when we kissed again. Not a kiss of relief this time, but a kiss of passion. Ours was a kiss that began a string of thoughtless acts.

His hands slid down my body, grazing my breasts, landing at my waist. I felt the hardness under his jeans. I should have been scared, or freaked out, or ashamed, but I wasn't. I was free.

He broke the kiss and stroked my bottom lip with his thumb. "Should we go back?"

"No." I took his wrist and put his hand on the triangle below my belly.

He gasped and his lashes fluttered. Seeing that he liked it sent my body to the edge of common sense. This was crazy and I didn't care. Being the good girl hurt, and this felt good.

"My parents have to stay at the barbecue," I said. "That's their job."

He hesitated. Swallowed hard. Pinched a bit of my skirt fabric.

I nodded.

He pulled my skirt up until my cotton underwear was exposed. I ran my hand over his jeans, feeling his erection. He seemed harder and bigger than humanly possible.

When he kissed me again, I backed into the desk, leaning on it. Chris twisted his finger around my underpants leg. His touch was pure magic, and in the milliseconds before his finger hit home, it gathered enough electricity between my legs to power the entire factory.

I didn't realize how wet I was until he touched me.

"Oh, shit." His face contorted.

I could barely breathe. Standing up straight seemed impossible, so I let the desk bear my weight.

"Rin," he said, looking down between my legs.

My skirt was around my waist and my underwear was printed with roses. Old lady roses. My underpants looked like a dinner plate and his finger was stuck under them, ready to unleash otherworldly pleasure.

"Please, don't stop."

"I've never done this before."

"Me neither." I lifted his shirt just enough to see the line of light brown hair that disappeared under his waistband.

"I don't know how to make it good. And I don't have a condom."

"My period finished yesterday." I unbuttoned his jeans. "And it's going to be good. I know it."

Was I convincing him? Did that make me a whore?

As if the sound of my mother's voice in my head was audible to him, he took his hand out of my underwear. "I love you, Rin."

I melted and relaxed. You weren't a whore if it was love. Rushing things, maybe. But not a whore. Everyone knew that.

"I love you too."

With that, I unzipped his jeans. He kissed me, wrestling my underwear off while I got my hands on the stretched skin of his shaft.

Was I even real anymore?

Was I made of skin and bone or was it all just thick liquids vibrating in his direction?

Shifting my bottom back onto the desk, he wedged himself between my legs and slid his length along me. It felt so good—better than when I did it myself. Better than anything I'd ever felt in my life. I understood why adults wanted to keep us away from this. I'd beg and steal for it. I'd break walls and set the town on fire for what he made me feel. I was weak from it, and powerful inside it.

He ran it along the hard nub at the top again and again. I came, and when he kept on rubbing, I came harder, pressing my lips together to keep from screaming.

I didn't know if I'd broken some rule of sex etiquette by having an orgasm, but when he smiled at me, I knew it was all right by him.

"You're beautiful," he said. "I'm never going to forget what you look like right now."

He'd seen me. Watched it. Shame was like a snake in the basement, ready to slink up the steps and under the door. I felt it coming. I could hold it at bay, but I knew it was there. The only way to block it was with more sex. More vibrations. More Chris.

I still wanted him. The orgasm hadn't made me want it less.

His bare head slid up to my opening as if drawn by the force of my desire. We were a gasping, sore-lipped, sweaty mess. I pushed my hips against him. Now. I wanted him to enter me immediately.

"Here goes," he whispered.

"Here goes."

He forced himself inside me. I bit back the pain. It wasn't too bad, but he stopped.

"Are you—"

"I'm fine. Go."

He didn't go. He looked confused, unsure.

"Please," I said. "If you love me, then make love to me."

Love. Always the great convincer.

He pushed all the way down to his base, stretching me as I'd never been stretched before. Slowly sliding his body into mine. Then out. Slowly. He closed his eyes and grunted deep in his chest.

I ran my fingers through his hair, pulling him down to me. He kissed my cheek and slid inside again, watching my expression. He hurt me less than last time. Maybe he could tell, because the next thrust was harder. Really hard. It pushed the air out of my lungs.

Did people talk during sex? I didn't know how.

I managed to get out a single word. "More."

As if I'd opened a gate and let a bull charge through, he pulled out and slammed into me again. And again. Harder and faster. Then slow and deep. Pleasure welled up inside me. Hard. Fast. Slow. I never knew what was coming next and it made me throb all over. His lips on my cheek, one of his hands leveraging the desktop as the other grabbed my ass, he grunted hard and pulled out.

"Wha—?" I didn't finish.

With his fist moving fast along his shaft and my naked legs spread wide in front of him, he closed his eyes and spurted on my belly.

I was appreciating the warmth and the look on his face. I was thinking about how this dishonorable thing of having my legs spread where he could see everything was actually pleasurable and freeing.

But as he was coming on me, a dog yipped outside. Lance, for sure.

Then someone rapped on the window above. A man's voice came through the glass.

"Catherine Barrington!"

I saw Chris first, looking out the window with his hand around himself, his face lit in stripes by the iron bars. Then I bent my head back.

The man at the window was Sheriff Brady, and the horrified woman next to him was my mother.

WE HADN'T THOUGHT about the blood. It wasn't much, but it seemed as if it was everywhere. We scrambled to get dressed as Sheriff Brady used his universal key to get in. Lance came in first and sniffed our ankles. My skirt had twisted, leaving a streak of blood on the fabric over my left thigh. Chris barely had his pants up when Brady threw him against the wall so hard his head bounced against it. Lance bit the cop's pant cuffs, growling like the puppy he was.

"Stop!" I shouted.

But my father, who I hadn't seen through the window, took me by the arm in a skin-twisting grip. My eyes adjusted to the light as he pushed me outside. I yanked away, but he held me tight as a bird in the hand.

"That boy's going to be sorry," my mother said from behind me. "He forced you, obviously."

"He didn't." I was sure she didn't hear me, so I looked back and said it again. "He didn't force me."

"Of course he did."

Dad loosened his grip. He wouldn't look at me.

"This is humiliating," Mom continued.

The grassy square was visible in the slit between buildings. My shirt stuck to me where Chris had unloaded, and I tried to cover the blood with my hand. My thighs slid against each other from dripping fluids. I wondered if Sheriff Brady was going to return the underwear I'd left behind or if the office manager of the hardware store would find them.

The sheriff's black-and-white car was parked up the street, its windows wide open.

"Don't hurt Chris," I said. "I'll be good. I'll never see him again."

"I know," grumbled my father, lighting a cigarette.

"We'll discuss *him* later," Mom interjected.

"Daddy?"

"Don't worry about it, Peanut."

"I'm not letting you go soft, Earl." We broke into the town square and my mother brightened, giving me a sidelong glance. "Smile, darling."

Dad shook hands with some of the guys and talked the way men talk when a bunch of them get together. I could still see the police car. No Brady. No Chris.

Mom waved at my sister. "My God, look at her. Harper, dear! Come along! It's time to go."

"Maaaaa, noooooo." Harper's shoulders dropped and her knees bent as if leaving was a grievous hardship.

One split-second look of sternness got her to wave good-bye to the puppies.

"What happened?" Harper poked the blood-soaked spot on my skirt.

Mom slapped her hand away. "Stop asking questions." She put her hand on my father's shoulder. "Time to go, honey."

"Just a flesh wound," I whispered to my sister. Was she looking at the way my shirt stuck to the now-cold slime on my belly?

Harper scrambled into the limo. Behind me, Dad dropped his cigarette and smothered it with his shoe. I stole another glance at the police car.

It was gone.

I was sure Chris was in it. I was sure he didn't have the money to get out of trouble. Whatever that trouble was, it was going to be decided by my parents. His mother could barely get out of bed to go to court. How would she defend him? He had no one. It wasn't fair. I loved him and it wasn't fair.

"Get in," Mom snapped over my shoulder.

I put my hand on the doorframe and straightened my arm, locking it at the elbow. "No."

"Catherine," Dad said softly. "Let's just get home and discuss this." He arched an eyebrow and indicated the back seat with a quick tilt of his chin.

"Promise Chris will be all right and I'll get in."

"That boy is not going to be all right," my mother said.

"Then I'm going to go find him."

"Get in this car!" Mom's face was red.

"We're going to run away together and you'll never see me again!"

"Catherine Daisy Barrington." My mother's arm was stone-stiff, extending toward the door.

"Peanut," my father said gently, expectantly, threateningly all at once.

"I'm old enough to marry him." I took a backward step toward the town square. "I'll do it. If anything happens to him, I swear I will."

They looked at each other, then at me, then each other again, speaking in the silent way married people do. I had an opening.

"Promise you'll call Sheriff Brady as soon as we get home."

"I will not—"

I took two steps closer to the square. "Promise!"

I was losing my nerve by the second. I didn't have the strength to do what I threatened to do. I had to keep Chris first in my mind. The consequences for him were worse than a bad reputation. They'd get him fired. Send him to jail. Kick him out of school. Drain whatever money he and his mother had.

"Don't hurt him." I shifted my gaze to my father.

"Can you just grab her, Earl?"

"For what?" He seemed baffled. "If she's not going to ruin her life today, she'll do it tomorrow."

Wait.

Was that a promise?

Could I get in the car before someone passed close enough to see my sticky, bloody clothes? I looked from Mom to Dad as they killed each other with their stare.

"I need satisfaction," Mom growled.

"Get it somewhere else," he said before he looked at me. "Princess, we have a deal. I won't hurt him."

"You won't get him fired from the club?"

"Oh, for the love of…" Mom threw her hands up. "Now I can't go to the club?"

"I won't go anymore," I said. "I don't like tennis anyway. I just won't see him. Ever. Never again. Just… no charges. No lawyers. Promise."

Dad answered before Mom could object. "That's a fair deal."

Mom covered her face with her hands. While she was blinded by her humiliation and frustration, I caught my father's eye.

"Thank you," I mouthed silently.

He pointed at the car.

I got in.

CHAPTER 16

CATHERINE - PRESENT

It was down to me. My decision. Stay? Go?

Chris's letter had woken me from a deep sleep, and my letter back had stunned me into a fugue. My decisions were my own from now on.

Stay or go?

Not for him. Not to wait, or to pretend to myself I wasn't waiting.

Just what did I need? What did the people I loved need?

Which master did I serve?

A half dozen little elves came to the house, armed with brooms and buckets. I knew them as Juanita, Mrs. Boden, Pat, Sally and Trudy Crenshaw, and Dina Marcus. I was shooed out of my kitchen and left to go around the outside of the house so I wouldn't step on wet floors. I wasn't allowed down the hall where the suite was because another half dozen elves were fixing it. Harper was holed up in her room on the third floor. Taylor dragged his dirty, dusty self up there with plates of sandwiches and came right down after dropping them off.

"Is she eating?" I asked.

"Shoo," he said, then kissed my cheek before trotting down the hall to the dusty suite.

The house was packed with people who loved me, but none of them knew what I was going through.

I still didn't know if I was staying or going.

Counting the days, I waited until I could be reasonably sure Chris had gotten the letter. Then I did nothing. He'd gotten it by Wednesday, for sure. Done is done. I had nothing else to say to him. That part of my life was over now. It ended not with a bang or a light, but with an exhale.

Wednesday, the evening before my birthday, I was in my old room, the one that faced the front of the house. Everything was quiet and dark. This was about the time I'd let the sadness creep in and I'd cry myself to sleep. I hadn't cried in a week, but I'd slept well.

I didn't know how to feel about anything.

On Thursday, voices from across the house and clopping footsteps along the hall told me people had arrived to work on the suite. I knew how I felt about that at least. Whether I stayed or went, I was glad to see the room taken care of.

I crossed my bedroom naked after my shower. My closet was open because I'd been looking for things to wear to my party later. A full-length mirror hung inside the door and I caught a glimpse of myself.

Most of my friends from school were in town. At nearly thirty, their bodies had been through childbirth at an early age, recovered, and done it again. My body had barely been touched.

My hands slid along my curves. My breasts, belly, hips, round and tight with disuse. All this skin was meant to be touched. It was designed to feel, to receive, to sense and interpret. My breasts were meant for children and the touch of a lover. They remained high and tight from neglect. Hardening under my fingertips, they were ready, and I was too.

I sat on the bed in front of the mirror.

This was me.

I spread my legs.

Still me. The little pink split had a function. I slid my finger there and felt the wetness that reminded me that it was ready. It worked. It could do what it was built for.

Moving my fingers along the liquid folds of skin, I quietly brought myself to orgasm without thinking of Chris until it was over.

"I'm sorry," I whispered into the sheets.

I didn't apologize to the Chris of today or even five years before, but to the sixteen-year-old boy who'd loved me. I'd let him go. I hadn't chased him. Hadn't fought for him. Hadn't looked for him or asked his mother what happened to him. And now I was releasing him with regret. But I was releasing him.

I washed my hands and dressed.

When I opened the door, I gasped. Reggie was in the hall with his fist up as if he was about to knock.

"Oh, sorry!" he said. "I was just—"

"It's fine."

"I wanted to tell you something." The paint splatter on his overalls was multicolored from years of spills and hard work.

"Okay."

Behind Reggie, Taylor carried a can of paint in each hand.

"Don't look," Taylor said to me before tapping Reggie in the behind with a can. "Come on, lazy ass. Let's get this done."

"I'm coming, Cali-boy." Reggie turned back to me. "Private."

I didn't have a place for him to sit in my room, so we went to the front porch. I sat on the swing, and he leaned on the railing. The hardware store delivery truck was just pulling away.

"What's all that?" I pointed at a stack of four moldy boxes in the corner of the porch.

"Found 'em in the crawlspace over the ceiling. You should check inside. See if there's anything you want."

I couldn't imagine anything of real or personal value in those collapsed, water-damaged, mold-covered boxes. They probably had mushrooms growing in them. I wrinkled my nose and sat back on the porch swing.

Reggie looked at the floorboards, rocking a little as if he was telling himself to get on with it. I folded my hands in my lap and waited.

"You know, I been looking at that ceiling for two days now. I musta been outta my mind."

"Why?"

"Painting roses on a tin ceiling? God, Catherine, nobody does that. You can paint it a flat color… but flowers? I bet that's the only tin ceiling mural in the United States."

"You should be famous."

"Hell, yeah. I've been telling myself that a long time now." He ran his fingers through his hair. "You know I… ah… well I remember when your father asked for it. You were sixteen and I was engaged to Carla the cheating bitch. But you, girl? You broke my heart. Like…" He squeezed his fingertips to his chest and exploded them like a starfish.

"It was a rough time."

After Chris left, my parents started the process of splitting up while living in the same house. Everyone knew it. There weren't many secrets in Barrington.

"You sure could peel the paint off with your crying." Reggie shook his head slowly with a smile. "Shit, I thought them flowers wouldn't survive with all your wailing."

I laughed to myself.

Seeing I wasn't hurt, he continued. "I thought to ask you to a job site, you know, save us some work with the scrapers." He laughed with me. "Thought we could even go international with it."

"Oh, Reggie, do you remember when I asked you to hide flying monkeys in it?"

"I thought you'd gone crazy. But your dad said to just do it."

"I loved them. I put the bed right under them so I could see them when I went to sleep."

"I'm glad. I'm really glad you got comfort from it. And I'm sorry you had to wait so long to get that room fixed up."

"I'm sorry I never asked."

"Thing is…" He looked away, then at me. "It was always something. You were real young. Then I got married." He ran through the list more quickly. "Then the factory closed and I was out of work. Then I got divorced. Then your father died. Then your mother left and you spent the next seven years taking care of everyone in this place like it's your job. It's the most beautiful thing I've ever seen. I never got to tell you how I felt about you, and now Chris fucking Carmichael is coming back and I got a sliver of a window to tell you."

"You don't have to," I said. Chris wasn't coming, which put the burden on me to refuse Reggie. He was a good man, but I couldn't lead him on. I didn't feel for him what I'd felt for Chris, and I wanted nothing less.

"I want to. I have to."

"Reggie, don't."

"I love you. I've always loved you and I don't care if you know it. I don't care if Chris comes back on a white horse and sweeps you off your feet or whatever. I'll be okay with that. But if he doesn't, I want you to know that you and me? We can talk if you want." He took a deep breath as if he'd needed to get that off his chest.

He and I didn't have anything to talk about. At least, not what he wanted to talk about. If he wanted to talk about how to get over waiting for someone who was never coming, maybe we'd have something to say to each other.

"Okay," I said, not ready to tell him there would be no Chris. No knight riding in on a white stallion. No fairy tale ending. That was my problem. Not his.

"Okay." He snapped his fingers as punctuation. "Now that we got that out of the way, I better go make sure they don't try to paint over my ceiling."

"Thank you. For everything."

"I ain't even done yet." He tapped the doorjamb twice and went inside.

CHAPTER 17

CATHERINE - SIXTEENTH SUMMER

I showered and then stayed in my room. I crouched on the floor with my knees to my chin and cried as they fought downstairs. Their voices came up the walls and into my room. I couldn't hear most of it. Phrases and words. The sun set and the room went dark. My throat was dry and my eyes throbbed.

Harper knocked and peeked around the door, letting in a shaft of light. "Hi." She stepped all the way in. "I came to say good night."

"Good night."

"What are they fighting about?"

"Me."

She sat on the bed, folding her nightgown between her knees. "Did you do something?"

"Yeah."

"What?"

"I can't say."

"Okay." She extended the last bit of the word as a launching pad into a run-on sentence. "Because I know you know everything, but it really sounds like they're mad at each other when she's calling him things I can't repeat and he's like—'well, after what you did, you have no business blah blah' and she's like 'your forgiveness is worse than revenge,' so there's that."

I put my head against the wall. "I don't know what they're mad about anymore."

"Yeah. Well. Do you want me to stay in here with you? Keep you company?"

I did. I wanted my sister's warm body kicking me all night. It would be worth it to prove I wasn't too filthy to love. But Mom didn't like when we curled up together, and it wasn't a good night to displease her.

"I think you'd better not. I'll be okay."

She kissed my cheek. "I love you."

"I love you too. Close the door on the way out, okay?"

She left me in the dark. Exactly where I wanted to be. On the floor, in the dark. When I got tired, I laid my cheek on my knees. I could have gotten into bed, but I didn't feel worthy of a comfortable pillow and clean sheets.

A cracking noise woke me.

I was on the floor under the window. The arguing downstairs was gone, replaced by crickets and the gurgling of the river. My neck hurt.

Pock. The sound came again.

It was the wall outside. I got up to my knees and looked out.

Pock.

A swoosh of yellow curved across my vision. I followed it down to the boy who caught it.

"Chris!" I didn't shout. I barely whispered, but his name echoed through me. I opened the window.

"You're there!" he said.

"What are you doing here?"

"I need to talk to you."

I couldn't see him well. I couldn't tell if he'd been roughed up or if he was upset. "Are you all right?"

Before he answered, I heard a noise in the hall. The squeak of a floorboard. Then another. I put the window down and jumped into bed, forcing myself to breathe slowly even though my heart was pounding and my lungs demanded more air, faster.

Someone came into the room and closed the door. The moonlight behind my eyes went dark as whomever it was blocked the window. Were they facing me? Or Chris?

I opened one eye.

Daddy stood over me.

"You're awake," he said, sitting on the edge of the bed. The mattress tilted from his weight. "How are you doing?"

"I'm okay." I rolled onto my back and pushed myself up, making an effort to not look at the window. "I'm really sorry about it. Today."

"Are you?" He smelled freshly showered. His hair was slicked back and his fingernails hadn't seen a day's work.

"I wasn't trying to embarrass you guys."

He sighed. "Look. Catherine. I want to ask you something, and I want you to be completely honest with me."

"Okay."

"Did you consent?"

I swallowed. If I said yes, I was a slut. If I said no, a rapist was waiting under my window. "I did."

He didn't seem shocked or scandalized. Didn't even seem bothered. "Did he hurt you in any way?"

His manner comforted me. Daddy was the kind of guy people liked just because they did, and I was no different than they were. I wanted to be honest. I wanted to please him. Mostly, I wanted to give him the answer that would get him to leave before Chris got impatient and threw things at the window again.

"I think just the normal hurt for the first time."

"Are you sure?"

"Pretty sure. It's not like I have a lot of experience. Or him either."

"It was his first time?"

"Yes."

Daddy tapped his fingertips together, elbows on his knees, looking between his feet. "I promised you I wouldn't hurt him."

I swallowed a lump of fear, going rigid with it rather than leap in front of the window to shield Chris. "You did."

"I'm glad I don't have to break that promise."

The fear went away and was replaced by curiosity.

Daddy turned on the bed until he faced me all the way. "I would have broken it if he'd forced you. I would have poisoned every part of his life. But how can I? You're old enough. You're the same age. You both agreed. The only misery here is the misery we're causing you."

I must have looked as if I saw Santa coming down the chimney, because that was how I felt. If he was admitting we hadn't done anything wrong, then he had to let Chris be my boyfriend.

"And," he continued, putting his hand on my arm as if to steady himself, "and we're going to continue to make you miserable, but in a different way."

"What kind of way?"

"The way parents do. We know what's best for you."

My heart sank. That last sentence was never spoken before good news.

"Your mother has a point. That boy is not right for you. He'll bring you nothing but heartache."

"Dad—"

"Wait. Listen to me. I want things to go smoothly for you in life. We've made sure you have an easy time of it. There are a thousand ways you can screw it up and we're here to point them out. Keep you from doing them. This is one of those ways. I've seen enough of the world to know that it's hard when you don't stick to your own kind."

"He is our kind."

He shook his head. "No, I'm sorry to say he's not."

"Daddy, please."

"Here's what your mother and I agreed to. We've spoken to his mother, and she's on board as well. You stay away from each other and everything's going to be all right. But if you don't, you'll spend your senior year at St. Thomas School."

"Where is that?"

"In Austin."

"What? That's forever away!"

"And I can't speak for whether or not he'll be able to continue to work at the club if you two are caught together again."

"You'll get him fired?"

"I'm sure it won't come to that." He stood. "I know you hate this. If you knew what your mother wanted to do, you'd be thanking me. Maybe someday you will."

I didn't answer. Didn't even look at him. I just stared at the triangles my bent knees made under the covers. When I was little and Daddy had his knees bent like that, I'd slide down them. I couldn't believe there had ever been a moment in my life when I wasn't this mad at him.

He stood there a long time. "Your mother and I are going to switch the rooms around."

I looked up at him, then at the window. Did he know Chris was downstairs? Had I already ruined everything? I needed to see him. Make sure he was all right.

"Since I work late," he continued, "we're taking separate rooms. Maybe you'd like the big suite? It has its own bathroom. I think at your age it's appropriate."

"Sure."

He leaned down and kissed my forehead. I crossed my arms so he didn't think I wasn't mad.

"You'll feel better about it in no time. And you can paint the suite any color you want."

"Thanks."

"I love you, Princess."

"I love you too, Daddy."

My arms were still crossed when he closed the door behind him. After the click, I leapt out of bed and opened the window.

Chris came out of the bushes.

I was about to call down to him. Tell him everything down the height of the house and the space across the front yard, but as he stepped forward, he was drowned in yellow light.

The porch lights. Someone had turned them on.

If he was seen there, it was all over.

He didn't need to be told. He jumped behind the bushes, and a second later, my father stepped out from under the porch roof, walking toward where Chris hid. I held my breath. I could see his hiding space clearly from the second floor, but had no idea what Daddy could see, or if he'd known all along that Chris was down there.

The porch light snapped off.

My father opened his car door and got in. The headlights bathed the driveway in light, getting smaller and smaller as he headed away from the house and turned onto Dandelion Road.

Chris didn't come out until the crickets and night birds filled the air with sound again. He was going to call to me and my mother could hear. My parents' room, the one I was about to paint any color I wanted, was on the other side of the house, but I couldn't risk getting caught.

I lifted the screen and leaned out. I wanted to say this once and I wanted to be heard. "Wait for me."

I closed the window before he could answer. I put on a robe and shoes with soft soles. I was sure they looked ridiculous with my nightgown, but I didn't want to get fully dressed.

If I had on pants and a shirt, I could leave with him right away. We could steal into the night. Never see Barrington again.

Pants. All I needed was a full set of clothing and I'd be ready.

I'd be free.

Without really deciding it, I pulled my nightgown over my head and kicked off the shoes. Jeans. Bra. Clean dark blue T-shirt that would disappear in the dark of night. Socks. Sneakers for running far away.

I stopped before I closed the door.

There was something else.

I stood on a chair to get to the top shelf of the closet to retrieve a shoebox. Inside were photos of Harper and me. A spelling bee medal. An old pearl pin from Grandma. And an envelope. Flipping open the flap, I checked the contents. Seven hundreds, each from Grandpa on my dad's side. One for each birthday I had before he died. Two twenties earned for the two times I squeaked by with all As. A few singles from the few times I thought I'd put away some money.

Seven hundred forty-nine dollars got stuffed into my back pocket.

I knew where the creaky floorboards were. I tiptoed around them. I had to go past my parents' suite to get to the stairs, but they usually slept with the door closed. I jumped when I heard a squeak and a breath from the spare room. The door was open halfway.

Someone was in there, and it wasn't Harper.

Careful.

So careful.

I got past without a complaint from a single floorboard. Now, the suite would appear and I'd have to just be quiet…

But the door was open and the room was empty.

A second parent was somewhere in the house and I was wearing jeans and sneakers as if I was ready to run away. If I'd stayed in my robe, I could have said I was going downstairs to get a glass of water or something.

Okay, well. This was going to be what it was.

I went downstairs, skipping the loose boards. I left through the side door and went to the front, where Chris was. He must have known I was coming that way, because he met me halfway and kissed me before I could get a word in.

"I've been going crazy." He stopped long enough to speak, but not long enough to listen. He was all hunger.

I had to push him away. I put my finger to my lips and pointed up at the guest room window, then at the backyard. We tiptoed to the back like thieves. He led me past the white fence, into the cemetery. Past Hubert and Edith Barrington. Past Timothy Barrington, who built the house in his old age, His young wife, Alice, and his dead child, Frieda. We crouched behind Richard, who had been buried by the river before the house was even built.

Between two rosebushes where it was dark as a cave, Chris and I kneeled with our arms around each other.

"Do you swear you're all right?" I asked. He looked fine. I touched his face and didn't feel a bruise or bump.

"Nothing I can't handle. How are you? Your eyes are swollen."

"It's horrible. Everything's just horrible. I can't take another minute."

He held my jaw on both sides and looked into my face. "You can. You're strong."

I'd never thought of myself as strong. I only did what was easiest. Doing what I was told was easier than thinking about what I wanted. Chris was the only rule I'd ever broken because once he flirted with me at the club, he was too hard to stay away from. Once he kissed me, I didn't have the strength to refuse him.

"Only because of you," I said.

"I don't want to get you in trouble. I'm sorry I came."

"I'm glad you did."

"I couldn't wait."

"I'm ready. I don't need anything. We can just leave. Right now."

He pulled away, keeping his hands on my shoulders. I could barely see the whites of his eyes in the moonlight, but his voice was clear and urgent. "No, Rin. This is never going to be right between us."

"What?"

Was he breaking up with me? Had he lied? Had I given a liar my body?

"If we run away, I'm ruining your life. We're going to be two poor kids with nothing. Living on the street. Something has to change and I have to be the one to change it."

"What are you going to change? My family isn't changing. Barrington isn't changing."

"But I can change."

"Change into what? A rich man? Here? Pruning rosebushes?" I was sorry I said it the moment the words left my mouth. They were all true, but certain truths were unspoken.

Chris didn't seem hurt. His expression confirmed that we understood the same truths. "Not here."

"Where? I don't understand. You just said we weren't leaving."

When he slid his palms off my face and folded my hands into his, I knew what he intended to do.

"You can't leave me here," I said.

"I have to. Your parents are right. I'm not worthy of you. I have nothing to offer you."

The bushes closed in on me. The sky got low, the house inched closer, the river hemmed me in.

"Yes, you do." A sob choked back the rest of the sentence. What about happiness? What about love? What about two people making something out of nothing? "What about Lance?"

"I'll take him with me."

"Me too. Take me too."

"You have to finish here. It doesn't matter if I drop out of school," he said, trying to be comforting, "but you—"

"I need to graduate?" I couldn't let him finish his lie. "For what? Why does it even matter? I'm not Harper. I'm coasting."

He squeezed my hands so hard it hurt. I cried for real, but not because of the pain. I wanted it to hurt. I wanted to be pressed so hard my bones broke and the agony leaked through the cracks.

"I'm coming back," he said. "I'll get something going and come back for you."

"When?"

"Soon. I swear it."

Soon?

Barrington was a prison. What was soon to its prisoners?

And if he wanted to go, why would I keep him here? Why wouldn't I let him save himself? Why wouldn't I want better for him?

In that, I found a little bit of strength. It came from the same place as the double-dog-dare I'd laid on my parents that afternoon. I wanted to be with him. I needed him to come back, but setting him free to become all the great things he wanted to be was a source of power.

"Chris Carmichael." The tears stopped as if I'd twisted the faucet. I pulled my hands out of his, and he looked up in surprise and a little fear. "I swear to you, right now, and I mean it, I am not going to be with anyone else. I am here the same as always. So if you go off and do whatever? Change? Get a job? Find someone else?"

"I won't."

"Shush. If you do, you'd better write me and set me free, because I'm waiting for you."

"Okay."

"Say you understand."

"I understand."

"Say you'll tell me right away if there's someone else."

"I'll... there's no—"

"Chris!" I said through my teeth. "Say it!"

"Catherine Barrington, I swear that if I lose my mind and find someone else, or maybe, like, if an army of winged wild monkeys hold—"

"Winged monkeys?" I laughed as I wiped my eyes.

"Or feral unicorns."

"How far away are you going?" I tried to laugh quietly and ended up crying. He held me tight and kissed my hair. I rested my head on his shoulder.

"If I'm insane, or trapped, or if I'm possessed by the devil, I might come across another woman who's entirely wrong for me. Before I commit to a lifetime of misery with her, I'll set you free."

"Okay."

"Okay."

What now? Was he going to walk away and leave me behind a gravestone?

I wouldn't let him. He wasn't going to turn his back on me.

I stood. He got to his feet and tried to touch me, but I pushed him away. I wanted to frustrate him. Let him feel what I was feeling before he went off to make himself into a man.

"I'm going in the house," I said. "Please stay here until you're sure I'm in bed. Wait as long as you can. Then just go."

"Can I kiss you good-bye?"

"Promise you'll take care of yourself."

"I promise."

He leaned in for a kiss, but I pushed him away. When I leaned back, I felt the stiff mass of money in my pocket. My hand shot back to make sure it didn't fall out.

"No," I said. "I don't want some last kiss you have to appreciate. You should have known the last one was going to be the last."

"You're punishing me?"

I slid the envelope out of my back pocket. "Here." I slapped his chest with it.

"What...?" He opened it and thrust it back at me. "I can't take this."

"How much do you have on you?"

"It doesn't matter. I'm not taking it."

"You are. If you fail, you don't come back. I'm invested in your success."

He wavered, then came back to his original answer. "No."

"It's been sitting in my closet."

"I said no!"

"It's my guarantee!" I hissed. "You'll come back to pay me if nothing else. Even though I don't need it, because I live in a mansion with a staff and everything, you'll get back here to pay back a stupid seven hundred and forty-nine dollar loan. So take it or I'm going to think you want to cut me out of this deal entirely."

I snapped the envelope out of his hand and stuck it down his shirt. He laughed.

"Fine. But this is a guarantee," he said. "I pay my debts. I'm coming back with the money and more."

"Okay."

"And when I do, I'm bringing you a rose for every dollar."

"Just don't take them out of this garden or Mom's going to freak out."

He smiled. "Okay, deal."

"Deal."

We had nothing left to say. I sucked my lips between my teeth to fill the vacuum where words should have been. I already felt a little more distant, a little more cut off, a little more alone.

"Stay here until I'm in my room," I said.

I stepped back but couldn't do it. Whatever strength I had wasn't enough to deny my own need to kiss him. I had all the strength I needed because of him, but none to stay away from him.

Clutching the back of his shirt, his fingers in my hair, the force of his body against mine, I thought if I could just enter him, crawl inside him, he could take me along. Maybe that dream could happen. Two people making it work despite all the odds.

When I told myself the truth—that no matter how much I wanted to be with him every second, the odds were bad for a reason—I pulled away.

"You're going to wait here, right?" I asked.

"Yes." His arms relaxed and fell away.

"I love you," I said, stepping back until I could see all of him.

"I love you too. Always."

Not another word. Not another kiss or breath. Not another sight.

He'd forever be in the back of my family cemetery with his hands reaching for me and his lips claiming an eternity he didn't own.

I ran to the house without looking back.

I DIDN'T SLEEP that night. I didn't hear him leave and I didn't check.

In the morning, the back of my great-grandfather's headstone had a crude picture of an animal with wings and message scratched into it.

Not even winged monkeys

Not even.

PART II

CHAPTER 18

CHRIS

Dear Chris,
Your letter came as a surprise. It's wonderful to hear from you after all these
years. How they've flown by!

    J'd arranged for Lance to be buried on Friday morning. The
body had been transferred. The plot purchased. A little stone
tablet would say *Lancelot Carmichael, Brave Knight. Marked territory in*
Barrington and New York City, 2004-2017.

Just because Catherine didn't want me wasn't enough reason to
insult Lance's memory. And maybe I'd find a reason to knock on her
door and see if she was home.

I flew into the landing strip outside town and took a cab into
Doverton, where the club had a car for me. I didn't tell the driver who I
was or why I was there, sure that I was as anonymous as I'd always
been. My life in Barrington had been in the shadows, behind hedges,
forgotten and never known by anyone but the girl in the tree. The girl on
my lips. Catherine of the Roses.

As we passed Barrington, I saw the roofline of the factory her father
had owned. Nothing new had popped up. No new businesses or signs.
Exactly the same.

I could have asked the driver to make the turn onto the factory service road. I could have walked over the bridge to her house or pulled right up to her front door.

I am so sorry to hear about Lance. I think burying him at home is the right thing. I know Joan buried Galahad on Wild Horse Hill. You should get a space nearby.

THE LETTER WAS SO cold I could feel her effort to contain herself inside the page. I thought about why and knew it wasn't anything as simple as another man. If there was someone, she'd invite me to dinner with him and we'd reminisce about everything but the way she gave me her body. There was more to it, and it was obvious. I'd written to her until I stopped. Those letters might have meant something to her, and I'd stopped because I needed a response she might not have been able to give. I'd abandoned her. I had no right to her. She wasn't obligated to save me from a meaningless life I hated.

Though it would be great to see you, I'll be unavailable while you're here.

SHE WAS UNEQUIVOCAL, and she had me dead to rights. It had taken me four years to get out of the gutter and another two to make real money. I could have come to her a hundred times, but it was never enough. I was nursing some old wound where I wasn't good enough. Never good enough.

So there I was. Not good enough because I'd waited too long to be good enough.

She was right there, over that little crest of land, behind the factory that had closed eleven years before.

Not waiting. I should have known. Why would she wait? It wasn't long after I left that she started dating Frank Marshall, the best-dressed kid in our grade. I should have given up on her then, but I couldn't.

I could go see her. Nothing was stopping me. She could tell me she didn't want me to my face. She owed me that.

She didn't.

Since Lance had been from Johnny's litter, I left him a message with the details. I didn't know if he'd even remember me.

The roses were being trimmed outside the club's café. An older man with a floppy hat covering his brown skin was doing an efficient and more than adequate job of it. I went in for an early dinner and took a table overlooking the bushes. A few flowers braved the autumn temperatures. Even through the glass, I could hear the *pock pock* of tennis balls.

I was a paper cutout of a sixteen-year-old boy, sloppily taped onto the page of his life thirteen years later. Or maybe I was the hedge fund manager tripping into the scene of a play he'd starred in as a boy.

"Chris Carmichael?" A woman in a navy suit stood over me with my Coke. She put it in front of me and folded her hands in front of her. She had a blond bob and fresh red lipstick. She looked nothing like the girl I'd known when I worked the grounds, but I recognized her anyway.

"Marsha!" I stood and shook her hand. She pulled me forward and embraced me. I pulled out a chair for her, and she sat. "I didn't think anyone would recognize me."

"Well, I didn't exactly," she said. "I saw your name in the registration log."

"Really?"

"I'm part owner here now, so I check it daily to make sure everything's taken care of. I couldn't believe it when I saw your name. How far you've come from biking all the way here from Barrington!"

"Yeah, and you." I indicated the breadth of the club. "Part owner?"

She waved it away. "It was invest in something or starve."

When we were kids, I'd thought people like Marsha had infinite resources, but as a man, I learned better. Anything could be lost.

"Good investment then."

She put her elbows on the table and leaned over her folded hands. "What brings you back?"

I'd come for two reasons, and both sounded ridiculous when repeated.

"My dog died. He was born here, so I figured I'd bury him here. Up at Wild Horse Hill."

"Aw, I'm so sorry." Her eyes flicked to my left hand. She was looking for a ring. I saw hers. The diamond was the size of a gumball. "My daughter buried her bunny up there."

"You have children?"

"Two by my first husband. Mattie and Oliver. You have any?"

"No." The shortness of the answer begged for clarification. I had nothing to lose by making conversation, except time. "Never got around to finding the right woman."

She laughed a derisive little laugh. "Had mine with the wrong man, but they turned out all right." She slid open her phone. "You remember Mitch Whitney?"

"That asshole?"

He wasn't an asshole. He was a solid guy who'd laugh at being called that.

"He's my second husband, and the right one. Charles…you remember him?"

I nodded. He was a real asshole.

"He knocked me up in that pool house right over there." She pointed out the window. The pool house wasn't visible past the courts, but we both knew where it was. She handed me her phone. The wallpaper was of a family on a boat with fishing poles cutting the sky behind them. Her, a man our age, and two kids. "Figured what the hell, right? Well, he was an a-hole all right. Wouldn't marry me. Said our son wasn't his up until the last minute. Took me five years to leave him, and his family made it hard. But I got out."

"And is this the new Mr. Marsha?"

Her face lit up like a Christmas tree, as if I'd brought up her favorite subject. I handed back her phone. "I met him and it was, like, I don't know. You ever play piano?"

"No."

"Well, I don't know how else to describe it, so you're going to have to live with it. You fight the metronome and then you get to this point where you feel the rhythm. And it's easy. The song flows through you like it's already there. That was what it was like the minute I laid eyes on Mitch. But you don't play music, so you don't know what that's all about."

"No, actually, I do."

"You play something else?"

"No. But do you remember Catherine Barrington?"

"I do."

It was too much to speak about. She'd nod sadly at my loss or we'd laugh about it.

"How is she?" I asked, sticking to the subject while I pretended to change it.

"Still living in that old house. Her dad closed the factory and died, I don't know, maybe ten and change years ago? Their mother took off and left those girls."

"What?" I had known the factory closed, but not the ugly personal details.

Marsha nodded. "The girls were of age and they had trust funds, but still. It was a tragedy. Catherine's like a saint now. Selling everything to keep the people in that town afloat."

Her letter got taut in my pocket, stretching the fabric to let me know it was there.

Please accept my condolences.
Sincerely,
Catherine

SHE'D NEEDED ME, and I'd let her down. I wasn't worthy of her or a warm welcome.

"It's her birthday, did you know?" Marsha said.

Did I? I knew it was in autumn because it was a few months after I left. It had taken me hours to find the right card and I'd skipped a meal to buy it. "I forgot."

"One of the Barrington guys who fixes the AC mentioned there's a party. You should show up." She winked. "Might be like playing music."

CHAPTER 19

CATHERINE

One thing you could say about the people of Barrington, they wouldn't know how to kidnap someone and hold them for ransom. They'd used one of Mrs. Boden's scarves to blindfold me and I could see right under it.

I was in front, with Juanita and Kyle guiding me down the hall and a crowd just behind them. Harper was up in her room with a headache but wished me a happy birthday from under the covers.

"I remember when this was unveiled the first time," Mrs. Boden said. She was over ninety and remembered everything from the past sixty years as if it happened at breakfast. "You cried the entire time."

I remembered too, and they weren't tears of joy.

"Okay, ready?" Juanita said.

I nodded.

The blindfold dropped, and everyone shouted, "Happy birthday!"

I was in the doorway of the room I'd occupied after Chris left, and it looked so bright and happy I had to squint. Flat cream walls. New moldings. Repaired sconces. Even the doorknobs had been polished. I looked up. The painted tin ceiling was still there, flying monkeys and all.

"Don't touch the walls," Kyle called from behind. "Not yet."

I turned to the crowded hall. "Thank you."

Two of the children were jumping up and down with tiny-toothed smiles. They didn't know why this room was significant to me. They only knew how to react to the happiness of others.

I held my hand out to Taylor.

He took it and said, "Let me show you what we did."

He showed me the new fixtures in the bathroom, the fixed and finished French doors. Mostly though, he proved the ceiling remained untouched. The monkey wings were there.

"That's all we could do," he finished. "But the floor needs to be done, and you need new pipes and a rewire."

"Can I sleep in it?"

"Paint should be dry by tonight."

My cheeks tingled because I knew they'd fixed it up because Chris was coming. I hadn't told anyone he wasn't and I hadn't told them that I didn't know if I was staying or going.

But they were happy. The barbecue was smoking, and children were playing in the yard like kittens. The dogs, including old Percy, the runt of the litter and its last survivor, nipped at their heels. The kitchen was a hub of activity with Trudy gossiping and her older sister washing the dishes. The guys joked with Taylor about his proficiency with a nail gun. I watched from the back porch as the town went about its business. It would do the same whether I was here or not.

"You all right?" Johnny asked, tipping his empty beer at me. He was in his biker vest and a long-sleeve shirt that showed the tattoos that snaked over the tops of his hands.

"I'm fine."

"You looked a little misty." He leaned into the cooler for another.

"Birthday mist." I heard the doorbell from the other side of the house. Weird. Everyone was coming around the driveway. "Let me get that."

Bernard beat me to it, opening the front door to a very tall and handsome man in a black button-front shirt. He had a bottle of champagne in his hand.

"Hello?" I said.

"Friend of Taylor," Bernard said. "I'll get him."

Rather than get him, the stranger took two steps to the base of the stairs and called up, "Hey! Hard-on!"

"Oh, I'm so sorry," I said to the tall man. "He's—"

"It's fine. I'm Keaton, by the way." He had a British accent. It was nice.

You can go to London.

"I'm Catherine. Come in."

I could go to London.

Not for long. I didn't have a ton of money. But they spoke English and I could get a job, or if I could find a buyer for the house, I'd have enough to live on for a while.

Taylor bounded down the stairs to his friend and I went outside. The sun was about half an hour from setting, and all my people had shown up after work or between shifts. They'd stay until the house was clean and the crickets were louder than the children.

I could leave them. They didn't need me. If that Silicon Valley tycoon came to buy the factory, it would again be the hub of the town. Some would work there, some would be disappointed, but the purpose of the little place would be established without me.

I looked over the family cemetery hiding under the wild thorns. Last week, Harper and Taylor had started cutting through it but stopped halfway through, at our father's headstone. I couldn't blame them. The tangle was thick and twisted, dangerous to touch, guarding the history and roots of the Barrington family.

If I left, what would happen to my ancestors?

Standing at the edge of the white fence bordering the thorn bushes, I put my hand on a thick branch. I was immediately stuck by a sharp pain in my palm. I let it cut me.

"Catherine," Reggie said from beside me, "you ain't wearing down the points like that."

"Maybe I don't want to wear them down."

"Maybe you don't."

He waited, and I drew my hand along the thorn, opening my skin. The blood falling on the branch looked black in the long shadow of the sun.

"This thorn bush," I said. "I let it grow to keep Harper from defacing the graves. And because I didn't want what was in here to be lost."

"You can talk without cutting yourself open," he said quietly. He must have thought I was going to slice my wrists on a thorn.

"I want to leave here," I said. "I want to go far away. But I can't."

"Why not? You think this whole town wouldn't put together the money for you to go where you needed?"

They would. I hadn't considered taking a penny from them and never would, but I knew they'd support me. Their wishes weren't the issue.

"And what would happen to this house if I sold it? My family's graves? My history? Harper's not going to be here much longer. There's no one. I'm the last Barrington standing. I'm trapped. I might as well be under these damned bushes. They might as well have grown over me the past thirteen years.

"I don't know how to get out. I don't know how to ask for help because it's not a thing or money in my way. It's me. I'm in my way. How am I supposed to get out of the bushes if the bushes are *me*?"

I didn't realize I was yelling and crying or that I'd attracted an audience.

"I don't want your pity," I shouted. "I love you, every one of you, but I want to get out of here now. Right. Now!"

"The bushes ain't you," Reggie said. "We're going to show you."

He walked off, passing Damon, put his hand on Bernard's shoulder and said something in his ear. They both sprang into action. Bernard said something to Orrin and Pat, who went to their cars. Damon reached under the barbecue for a can that—logically—could only be one thing.

"Now, here's what I want to tell you and everyone." Reggie popped the top off a gas can. "Catherine Barrington, get the fuck out of this shithole town." He poured gas on the bushes.

"Reggie!"

"What?" he said. "You wanna save this mess?"

Orrin waited with a silver can. Damon had his lighter fluid. Juanita hustled the kids away.

"You're drunk!" I said, referring to all of them.

"I'm asking you," he replied. "You wanna get rid of what's keeping you?"

Damon, a troublemaker since the day he was born, put an unlit cigarette in his lips, watching me like the rest of them. "Whatever, man."

He squeezed a stream of fluid onto the thorns. "These bushes are ugly and you got to go."

They wanted me to leave.

I felt a little betrayed. I understood that they wanted me to be happy, but I wanted to be wanted more than I wanted happiness.

I was backward, and for the first time, I knew it.

So I nodded to Reg. For the sake of continuing something, anything in a forward direction, I motioned that it was okay to proceed. If I wanted my own life, I had to give up being needed.

I didn't know who threw the match, but it took all of a second for the entire thing to go up in flames. I got blown back a step by the heat and light, putting my arm over my eyes. It was big. As tall as the house and bright enough to turn off the light sensor bulbs on the porch, it raged so hot that it seemed like the end of everything. Nothing could continue as it was after a fire like this burned in my own yard. No part of my life would remain untouched, unchanged, or unbroken.

I was free.

I'd said it before, but I felt it in my heart when the thorn bushes burned.

I was free.

Was I smiling?

Part of my yard was on fire, Damon was lighting a cigarette in it, and I was smiling as if I had any business doing anything but panicking.

"Stand back!"

The clap of the screen door and the voice behind me were muffled by the roar of the blaze.

Still in a calm, fixated state, I didn't jump when a man in a jacket and slacks blew past me. He carried a fire extinguisher canister in one hand and held the hose in the other. I had no reason to recognize him. No one in town wore nice clothes to a barbecue, and the smoke and clouds from the fire extinguisher obscured his face.

I didn't need to see it.

"Chris!"

As if woken by Chris's command to stand back, Orrin jogged to the shed. Kyle ran for his truck. Taylor turned on the hose and soaked the porch. Four fire extinguishers on the blaze, my house wasn't going to burn down, and I was free to go anywhere in the world I wanted.

The world had turned upside down. Everything had fallen out. I'd been ready to refill my life with new things.

Then he came back a day early and put out the fire in my house.

He turned to face me, dropping his fire extinguisher with a *clonk*.

Where was the rest of the world before the moment our eyes met again? Before I saw that boy inside the man? He barely had scruff on his cheek when he left, and now? He had little lines around his eyes and a searing intensity that a boy can emulate, but only a man can achieve.

Missing the muscle and lithe movements that defined the Chris I knew, he'd become something harder, more solid, shaping the space around him instead of bending with it.

And still, he filled me.

Everything clicked into place all over again. I only heard laughter around me, as if every tension in the universe snapped.

I was free of commitments and free of plans. Free of any kind of ambition or hope. He walked right into the space those tiny things had taken up.

Which didn't mean I wasn't mad. I balled my fists up and got ready to give him hell, but he spoke first.

"I got your note."

He came close to me. Close enough for me to smell him past the burning wood and spent lighter fluid. Close enough to see the sweat on his cheeks and the way his lashes were slightly darker than his hair.

"I told you I couldn't see you." I must have been out of my mind.

"You made a mistake." He growled as if we hadn't spent thirteen years apart. As if I'd just seen him yesterday and he was responding to a text I'd sent an hour ago. As if we even knew each other anymore.

And we didn't.

But time had folded and bent around my feelings, coming to the other side and wrapping us together again like a twist-tie. It really did feel as though we hadn't been apart at all. My experiences lied to me, and my feelings were deceptive. My senses fabricated rightness out of nothingness and what little sense I had was spun into a mess of conflicting information.

"Get out," I said, pointing at the door he'd come through. "Go through the house and out the way you came. Go home."

He tried to put his hands on me, but I curled inside myself and slunk away. If he touched me, I'd be lost.

"Catherine—"

"You can't do this, Christopher. You can't just storm in and act like you've been here for me the entire time."

A waft of leftover smoke blew between us. I blinked hard to keep it out, and so I wouldn't have to look into the eyes that felt like home.

"That's the past," he whispered.

No one came into our space, but I felt them watching. Listening. Making sure I was all right.

I wasn't all right. I was confused. I had thirteen years of hurt and disappointment built up. Crying myself to sleep had been a completely inadequate valve for what had built inside me. And the sorrow was nothing compared to the love eating it alive.

He was a mistake wrapped in relief tied with a bow shaped like everything I found beautiful.

Calmly, I walked past him, through the house, to the front door, and out to the quiet front yard where he'd stood thirteen years before and thrown a tennis ball at the wall outside my bedroom. When I spun, he was right behind me, and when I opened my mouth to speak, he planted a kiss on it.

I felt a hardness of spirit, a stern resolve against obstacles. A forward motion that drove his lips into mine, and I felt—from instant to instant— a crumbling in that rigidity. His body curved where it had been angled, his mouth went soft where it had been firm. His fingertips brushed my neck as if asking for things he'd gotten accustomed to demanding.

He was falling apart right in front of me.

We split apart to breathe. I gasped.

"Chris." I had so much to say, but only his name came out.

"I'm here now."

"So?"

"It's all over. I can fix this."

"Fix…" My face tingled, and I had to hold my hand in front of my mouth. He rubbed my shoulders. It felt so good to be touched like that.

I'd been crying alone for so long, I'd forgotten what tender company meant. I swallowed it back to speak. "Fix what?"

He threw his hand out to the dark night. "All of it. I made it, Rin! Do you know what this means? All this is over."

My body was stiff and my mind stuttered. I didn't know whether to thank him or slap him, so I did nothing.

"I can tell," he said. "I can't believe it, but I feel the same, exactly the same. It's like a light went on."

He seemed happy. Relieved even. With the moonlight on his cheek and the stars glinting off the whites of his eyes, cast in darkness, his voice carried happiness and relief. A car came down the driveway, casting his face in harsh, moving lights. He looked like a man coming home after a long journey, and I was locked down inside my new ambition to move along with a life I'd delayed too long.

"I'm still in the dark, Chris. You left me. You left and you never came back."

"I'm back now. Do you remember? Right here in this front yard? The last time I saw you? It's like yesterday."

I was shocked back to life. "It wasn't."

His mood came down a notch. "It was the best time of my life."

"That's nostalgia. It's too late. You forgot me."

"I never—"

My hand shot up and covered his mouth. His face was rough with stubble and his lips were wet from our kiss. He felt more real and concrete than anything I'd ever touched, but he was a fleeting memory, a distraction. He'd hurt me badly enough to make me disavow the reality at my fingertips.

He kissed my palm, and taking my wrist in his hand, he kissed the tender skin inside it.

"Catherine?" Reggie called from the porch. "You all right?"

"I'll be in in a minute," I called to him, then faced Chris. "It's too late to ride in and rescue me. I don't need a knight in shining armor anymore."

"Maybe I'm the one who needs to be rescued," he whispered.

"I can't do that." I pulled my arm down, and he let go. "I'm sorry. I can barely save myself."

"Tell me you don't feel anything. Just say it."

I licked my lips, looking at the shadow of his, remembering the kiss. I felt something. I felt as if a long tether between us had been stretched to the limit and was suddenly pulled back. I felt a tight shell around us, woven in the hum of destiny.

"Say it," he repeated.

If I told him what I felt, what I knew to be true, my life would click into place like the last piece of a puzzle. Everyone wanted that. Everyone wanted to find their destiny and live it—except me.

I wanted to live a life I'd chosen.

I wanted to make my own mistakes.

I wanted my own suffering. My own joy.

"Say it," he whispered again, putting his face closer to mine. The porch light flicked on, and I could see the face that was so hard to resist. "Say what you feel."

I swallowed the truth and said what needed to be said. "I don't feel anything."

Chris's reaction was subtle but unmistakable. He blinked twice, flinching slightly as if slapped. I heard the wood planks on the porch creak. Reggie had stepped forward. He'd get between Chris and me if he had an inkling that I wanted him to.

I didn't want him to.

This, I needed to do for myself. Only I could break from my past, and staying in the front yard with the man who had left me all those years ago wasn't helping. I needed to rip off the Band-Aid.

"I'm sorry about Lance," I said. "I have to go."

I brushed past Reggie to go back into the house.

CHAPTER 20

CATHERINE

Sadness and I were well-acquainted. It was a thickening cloud in the soul dispelled only by deep, genuine tears. It was a drop of oil in a glass of water that could only be thinned into tiny bubbles and, if left unchecked, would coalesce again into a slick ball of contamination.

Sadness felt like me, but a little heavier, a little thicker, a swarm of gnats I could dispel with a wave of my hand, only to find them massing around me again.

After everyone went home, leaving the house spotless and the thorn bushes charred and wet, I went to the suite and sat on my bed, waiting to feel the weight on my heart.

I didn't feel sad. Not in the same way I always had, diluting something that would concentrate again. The hopelessness was missing.

Chris had come, and I'd sent him away.

I wasn't angry at myself or him. I wasn't disappointed or let down.

Instead, I was confused. Seeing him had thrown me, not because it felt uplifting or high, but because I was suddenly grounded.

A knock at my bedroom door was followed by Harper's voice.

"Cath? You in there?"

"Come in."

She came in and landed next to me, arms around me, crying uncontrollably.

"Harper! What happened?"

"Nothing."

"Where's Taylor? What did he do?"

"Shut up, okay? Just shut up."

She cried in my lap with her face buried in my thighs as I stroked her hair. I told her it would be all right, but I wasn't sure if it would be anything close to all right. Were we both going to be stuck here? Were we just looking for men to rescue us from ourselves?

I missed him. Chris Carmichael. I'd missed him and I'd continue to miss him the same way I missed who I'd been. I was too familiar with loss.

"You know what?" I said. "I was thinking of going to Europe. London, Paris."

"What happened to Chris?"

I sighed. "I chased him away."

A snap of a laugh escaped her as if she had a lot to say on the matter but didn't. "Why?" She sniffled. "Because you don't even know the guy?"

"Oh, I know him."

My sister didn't respond from my lap. She just folded her bottom lip until it creased.

"The minute I saw him, I knew him. I can't explain the connection, but my soul says he's as much mine as my own body. It's not sensible or practical, but in a way, it is. Gravity pulls down. Fire is hot. Chris and I are meant to be. It's almost boring."

She sat up. "Then why did you kick him out?"

Why had I? Because I had pride. I was a grown woman with my own heart's desire and even if he was that heart's desire, I was in control of my actions.

"Wrong question," I said. "He left. He never picked up the phone. He never wrote me. The question is, why would I take him back?"

"Because you guys were meant to be?"

"It doesn't matter. I'm my own woman now."

She shook her head so hard her hair flew around her face. She looked as if she'd eaten a lemon and been attacked by a hornet at the same time. "What? You mean you weren't before? All this wasn't your choice? You didn't de-furnish the house and drain the bank account because it was your choice?"

"It was but—"

"But nothing." She stood, freeing me to get up as well.

"Harper—"

"You." She poked my shoulder, backing me toward the door. It kind of hurt. "What are you talking about?"

"I'm confused, all right? I'm confused!" I choked back a sob. No. No more crying. "I don't know where I fit in. I don't know what I want. No one needs me anymore. The factory's coming back. You're leaving—"

"What are you talking about?"

"I'm not stupid. I know Taylor's going to take you away."

She deflated.

"What?" I said.

Her face collapsed like a window breaking. Her expression dropped and curled into an uncomfortable, red-skinned blubber. Tears came so hard they cleared her cheeks and landed on her chin.

"Harper? What?"

She tried to speak, but just made spit.

"Did he leave you?"

My confusion was replaced with purpose, and it felt good. My blood flowed with it. As if my sister could see the chemical change in me, she shook her head violently but was lost to sobs before she could get a word out. Her pain felt like a compressed version of the months I'd waited to hear from Chris.

I was angry. Very angry.

"I'm going to kill him. Nobody hurts Harper Barrington. Nobody. Do you hear? And not just me. Oh, no. You mark my words, every man in this town is going to make it their business to find Chris and—"

Her face knotted even tighter and I shook the bees out of my head.

"Taylor," I corrected quickly. "Find *Taylor*. Whatever. They're going to find him, and if I have to use every last dollar to send them to California, I swear to God—"

She grabbed me by the shoulders, still sobbing too hard to speak, and held me tight.

"I'm sorry, Catherine," she choked out. "No one's coming to buy the factory. It's done. We lost."

I stroked her hair. I didn't ask her how she knew. Harper knew things. The end.

We lay on my bed together under the mural of roses as she cried herself to sleep.

I was still needed. I should have been both sad and worried.

Instead, knowing I was needed and nothing had to change, I felt an immediate, guilty wave of relief. I shoved it under anger, covered it with disappointment, and hid it under a mask of resolve.

But the desire to maintain the status quo was there. Always there.

CHAPTER 21

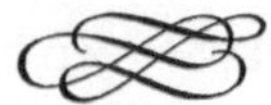

CATHERINE

Johnny's blue truck pulled into the driveway. He waved and got out wearing his yellow polo shirt. Redox slid out and came right up to the porch. The bruiser of a Rottweiler poked his nose between my legs one time to make sure it was me, then flopped onto the floor.

"Did you come for the grill?" I asked as Kyle got out of the passenger side.

"Yep." Johnny lowered the gate on the back of the bed. "Meat was pretty good last night. We nailed the timing on the evaporative cooling effect."

"Sure did," Kyle said.

My guess was that Johnny had worked out the equations to the half degree and Kyle had agreed to drink beer by the fire.

"You got coffee made?" Johnny asked me. "Been a long morning already and we have to bury Lance."

The funeral. Today. I'd told him I couldn't go and that was that.

"In the kitchen."

"Funny thing, Carmichael showing up last night."

Johnny stayed on the porch. Did he need an answer? Did he need me to say that I was skipping the funeral because I didn't want to see Chris or because I had a ton of chores to do? That I'd sent Chris away because I was confused or because I was empty? Because I was protecting myself from getting hurt again or from being happy?

"There's half and half in the fridge," I said.

He nodded and went into the house. I fell onto the porch swing, wishing this damn day would be over so I could think. Wishing Chris would disappear so I could decide if I'd made the biggest mistake of my life or dodged a bullet.

Harper was staying, at least for a while. I still didn't know the details of what had happened with Taylor, but he wasn't taking her away. At least not now. But she had to go. His presence had gotten me used to the idea that she should leave. I had time to convince her to go to college. Then once she got in, school wouldn't start until September. I could stay in Barrington a little longer.

If I wanted to.

I didn't know what I wanted anymore.

Johnny and Kyle came out with their travel cups and headed for the back. My eyes fell on the four mildewed boxes Taylor had left on the porch. I'd never bothered to take them inside. The crawlspace had not been kind to them. Maybe Johnny could haul them away on his way out.

I bent over the top box and used my fingernail to bend the flaps. Something shone from inside.

I decided to go all in. Sinks and soap were invented for curious hands. I opened the box all the way. The shine was from a glass doorknob that was probably one of the few made in the factory, along with a broken glass towel rack, a blue glass soap dish. Fancy hinges. A sconce. A door baseplate and a kitchen faucet.

I could sell some of it to the antique fixture place in Springfield. Some looked worthless. All of it was interesting. I didn't recognize any of it. It must have been Grandma's stuff from before the eighties, when Mom redid the house. Johnny would have things to say about what was in there; what had been made in the factory and what was worthless. He and Kyle were halfway down the driveway with the grill. I could ask when he was finished loading it.

I picked up the top box to lay it aside, but the bottom gave out and spilled the stuff all over. Well, that was just the kind of day this was. I got on my knees to clean up the mess before they ran over to help. I could do it myself.

A ceramic lamp base got stuck between the flaps of the box under it. When I pulled it out, the top opened. It was full of paper. Termites had made holes in the envelopes and left dust-sized wood chips all over the surface.

I put the lamp down.

The termites had eaten around the ink of the recipient's name, which was Catherine Barrington. They'd eaten around the postmark ink, which was New York, NY10005. They'd eaten around the return address label, which was a PO box in the same zip code, and of course the sender was Christopher Carmichael.

I flipped it over. The envelope had been eaten open, but the glue still hung on. It had never been opened.

Under it, another letter.

And another.

One fell apart in my hands.

Another was so black with mold, the address was unreadable.

None were opened.

All were to me, from Chris.

My hands shook so hard, I couldn't get my fingers in an envelope. I opened a folded piece of paper that fell out of an envelope. It was almost completely destroyed.

—I spilled coffee all ove—y pants I had but—you and—

I CHOSE ANOTHER. The ink had run when water hit it.

—Lan—in the dog park th—I hate to think he—nice guy. No guarantees of anything of c—and we can be together sooner rather tha— blooming because the flowers lie. You are the scent of roses—

I DUMPED the entire box on the porch and kneeled beside the pile. I went through it quickly, separating the readable from the unreadable.

—e getting used to—crowded but if you were with me b—everything—

—YOUR SKIN AND—HACKED at the tennis b—pleated skirt wa—one time in reality but in my—Frank Marsh—

FRANK MARSH—? Could that be Frank Marshall? The Christmas after Chris left, I'd started dating him. He'd begged me to, as a favor, and I stayed with him for his benefit and my own, until he finally came out of the closet. Mom had been devastated. I was happy for him.

—ny people. You'd li—used to i—re you getting these? Be—ove you, Catherine of the Roses

I STOPPED SORTING them and searched for a whole letter. I couldn't bear another minute. He'd written me and I'd ignored him. What kind of hurt had he suffered because of me already? I needed to know the exact height and weight of it so I could beat myself to a pulp with his pain.

I opened one that looked relatively whole. A picture of Chris and Lance fell out. He was kneeling next to the bloodhound, who looked away from the lens at a squirrel or a pigeon or whatever a loved dog looks at when his eyes are off his master.

The date was ten years before. Three years later, my father died, my mother took most of the money and left. Harper stayed home from MIT forever. I'd already stopped waiting to ever hear from him again.

He was a cross between the hardworking, carefree, bronzed boy I'd known that summer and the serious man who'd put out a fire in my yard. The sun angled over his face, casting deep shadows over one side and washing the other in white. His hair was cropped and businesslike and his cheeks were smooth. Whatever transition he was making had been halfway over by the time that letter came.

I sat on the porch rail and unfolded it. Most of the letters were handwritten, some were printed. This one had his pointy scrawl all over it. Had he written it at the dog park, or in the back of a cab? I smelled the paper. Past the mildew from the box, I caught a little bit of cologne, so I imagined him writing it at home, in the morning before he went to work.

Dear Catherine,

It was as bad as I told you. I got everything out before the bottom dropped, but it was a scare. I was hoping to come back for you soon, but not now. I can't give you the life we agreed on.

But—and this is a big but—I have someone interested in a hedge fund that I've been pitching around. It's based in quantitative trading and something we call market inefficiencies (totally legal, I swear). I'll explain that to you when I see you. It's so safe and profitable, I'm sure I'm never going to come that close to losing everything again.

Which brings me to the same thing I end every letter with.

I hold on to you like I'm alone in the ocean and you're the last piece of wood from a shipwreck. What we had, I've never felt before or since. I belonged. I had purpose. You haven't answered a single letter, and I have no idea if you hate me or if your parents are hiding the stamps. I don't know if you're waiting or if you've forgotten me. My mother left Barrington months ago. If I come back, it's for you, but if you're finished with me, I don't want to know. I'm not ready to let go.

I'll keep on writing, but I have a bad feeling that one day I'm going to drown.

All my love,
Christopher

I FOLDED the letter but didn't put it back in the envelope. That would be like folding Chris up and putting him away. I couldn't betray him another time.

I read it again.

At some point before Mom left or Dad died, he'd written a last letter. It was in the box, shredded, damaged, or obliterated. He'd made a hundred, maybe two hundred, attempts to reach out to me and been ignored. He'd worked harder to contact me than I'd worked to forget him.

And my mother, or my father, or both had stopped the letters. Or one had intercepted them and another had fought to keep them from being destroyed.

The only words they spoke to each other in those last years had probably been about those letters.

Was it too late to find him? Where was he staying? His mother's trailer was gone. The only hotel in Barrington, Bedtimey Inn, had closed years earlier. He didn't have any friends to stay with and Lord knows someone would have told me if he'd made plans to stay on their couch.

What was the difference anyway? Was I going to knock on his door and say, "Hey thanks for the letters," after I'd chased him away? And then what? Was I going to let him whisk me away like a knight on a white stallion? I still didn't know him. He wasn't the answer to my loneliness.

I put the photo of Chris and Lance in my pocket and looked through the two boxes underneath it.

Jesus.

More letters.

I owed him an apology, or at least an explanation. But it was too late. I was numb and I'd already sent him away. The letters would go into the trash with the rest of my mistake-filled life.

My foot landed on something soft and round. It rolled under me and I fell, dropping the box and landing on my wrists.

"Catherine?" Kyle and Johnny were loading the barbecue onto the truck, and Kyle dropped his end with a metallic clank.

"I'm fine." A yellow tennis ball rolled slowly away.

They were both off the truck. I held up my hands, but they helped me to my feet.

"You all right?" Johnny asked.

"Yeah. I stepped on a ball."

The culprit rolled to the porch step and Redox appeared, locking the tennis ball in his jaws. He came back and dropped it in front of me, sitting on his haunches expectantly.

I shook out my wrists, wiped my hands on my jeans, and picked it up.

"Yuck." It was slimy, but not everywhere. Still kind of new.

"Must be his," Johnny said. "Sorry about that."

"It's fine." I threw it into the grass and he chased it with the slow roll of a king who knows the ball isn't going anywhere. I fixed my hair and the guys went to strap down the barbecue.

With the hollowness still haunting me, I looked at my house as if for the first time.

What had Chris seen? Had he been disgusted by how I lived? The cracks in the paint, the missing shingles, the patchwork of roof tiles. I scanned the porch as Redox dropped the ball right in the letter box, as if he was done with this game. I was about to take it out, but the sad state of my house through a stranger's eyes was too horrifying to look away from.

The marks by the second floor window were still there from thirteen years ago, when a tennis ball had been thrown from the ground to get my attention.

He'd written to me. All of his feelings were lost to the elements, but he'd written to me repeatedly.

He hadn't abandoned me.

I'd abandoned him.

In a moment of vulnerability falling in a crack of time between breaths, my defenses fell away and the hollowness filled.

In that moment of opportunity created by a fracture in my armor, that old love I'd shut away saw an opening and took a chance, bursting through the fissure.

The feeling was like getting too close to a car moving at ninety miles an hour. I almost lost my footing. Emotions flooded me. They hurt like a too-rich bite of food early in the morning. It was urgent, heavy, and hot, an electrical current animating my body. Jacket. Bag. Keys. Box.

Sixteen.

I was sixteen. Smarter. More experienced. Twice as tired and half as ashamed, living from moment to moment, risk to risk, decision to decision.

Sixteen had been terrible, but the love had been real. It saturated my skin and laced my bones. His rightness. The click of the clouds and the sky locking together.

I ran back up to the porch and snapped a random letter from the nearest box, then I ran to my car.

"Catherine?" Johnny was strapping down the huge grill. "Are we blocking you in?"

"Don't worry about it." I got in and started the car. I had a quarter tank. "Johnny?" I called out the window. "Wild Horse Hill, right?"

"Yeah, we can go together."

Backing the car onto the lawn, taking down a hedge and a ceramic frog to turn, I drove around Johnny's truck and onto the driveway, avoiding their reactions in the rearview. I was sixteen again, and I only had the will to go forward.

CHAPTER 22

CHRIS

*T*he orange and yellow leaves up on Wild Horse Hill spun in cones when the wind whipped. Without close family, the holidays always approached with a certain stealth. There were no gifts to buy for kids, just sloshy parties in high rises. Glittering women and serious men returning to their true personalities under the influence of spiced drinks.

Lance had always been home for me, waiting for me to drop a tray of foil-covered leftovers in his corner of the kitchen. He'd been responsible for some of my best Thanksgiving memories.

In the front seat of the rental car, I scratched my head. A notepad leaned on the steering wheel, and I'd written only one incomplete line.

Lance, you weren't just a good boy, you were—

Wild Horse Hill was a disorganized mess of oddly-shaped tombstones from a hundred years ago to the present. The land had never been purchased for a cemetery, but no one in their right mind would buy it and dig up a bunch of bodies. The unofficial pet cemetery was behind a copse of trees. There wasn't as much of a view, but all the good girls and boys were at their master's feet.

SUCH A CLICHÉ. Everyone said that, but no one had a Lance. A car pulled up next to mine. Assuming it was the delivery guy with Lance's body, I got frustrated by the end of my time alone. I wouldn't finish the eulogy.

My irritation flipped to relief when the car's engine cut and I looked across the windows to the driver.

Catherine.

Jesus. Catherine. The girl in the roses. Not sixteen anymore, but filled out with experience and maturity. Knowledge made her even more beautiful.

Hold it together, Chris.

She got out, clutching her shoulder bag to her side, and stood at the front of her car with an envelope in her hand.

I got out. "Hi. I'm glad you—"

"I'm sorry."

"For?"

She handed me the envelope. It was desiccated and crumbling. The pale blue envelope I'd used to send resumes in had yellowed and browned at the edges. The envelope flap hung on by the last bits of glue. I looked at the front. Her address. My handwriting. We were at least joined in that.

"This was the last one I sent," I said, handing it back. I knew what was inside it.

"I didn't know," she said, clutching her bag's straps to replace her grip on the envelope. "My mother. Or my dad too. I don't know. She knew she was leaving as soon as she could, and she wanted me to be taken care of. She didn't want… me to make a bad choice. She hid them. All of them."

I looked at it again and flipped it open.

The night I met Lucia and she looked over my shoulder at my checking account, I'd been so broken about this letter.

"Did you read it?" I asked.

"No, I just pulled out one. There were boxes of them. All of them. I'm so sorry."

I handed her back the envelope. "Open it."

She took it and opened the folded paper. I hadn't forgotten what I'd written.

"Oh, Chris." She took out the check. "Seven hundred forty-nine."

I leaned over her to see my words.

We're even.

Just those two words in the center of a page. No more words of love. No more promises of one rose to the dollar or anything else. Simply an accounting.

"It was never about money," she said. "Not for me."

"I couldn't figure out what else. I couldn't believe you'd miss every single one."

"They must have hoarded them."

Catherine Barrington always saw the good in people. Thirteen years later, she was still defending her mother's paranoid psychosis. All I'd do by arguing was disabuse her of the illusions that kept her sane. I leaned on my car and she leaned on hers, the letter and the check fluttering in the wind as if they wanted to finally be free.

"If you'd read them, what would you have done?"

She looked into the wind, letting her hair blow away from her face. Her ear was perfectly shaped in a delicate swirl. The hole in her lobe was an empty comma.

"I want to say I would have run to you," she said, still looking over the cemetery. "I want to say nothing could have stopped me." When she turned back to me, her hair flew across her face like lines on a ledger. "But I don't know if I can say it. I never wanted to leave. Sometimes I thought I used you as an excuse to stay here. Then you were gone and I missed you, but would I have gone to you if I saw the letters? I don't know."

She pushed a pebble with her toe and I knew it was because she couldn't look at me. She was ashamed, and despite that, she was honest to her own detriment. With every word, she gave everything she had no matter how much it hurt her.

The distance between us wasn't more than two feet, but it was made of cold air and wind. Hard, black asphalt and the density of the years. I couldn't keep my hands away from her. I had to bridge time and the arm's length of miles between us.

When I laid my hands on her arms, she stiffened and looked at me.

"Do you want me to go away?"

"No," she whispered and relaxed into me.

I put my arms around her, and though coats and scarves and layers of fabric were between us, I could feel her heartbeat, the press of her fingertips on my back, and the rise and fall of her chest as she breathed.

"I wish I'd come," I said into her hair. "I was afraid it had been too long. But when Lance died…" I shook my head, struggling to put into words what he meant. "He was my last connection to Barrington."

"I wish I could have seen him." She pulled away enough to look at me. "Was he happy in New York?"

Was he? Had I ever asked myself that?

He was the harness that held me together. A bloodhound mutt with floppy ears and a child's love was my connection to the boy I had been and the man I'd become. He was the reminder that I'd been a different man with a different future. He was the fork in the road. The opportunity to go back. The signpost away from loneliness and cold realities. Then time blew him away and I was left on a dark road disappearing into a point on the horizon. No more forks. No signposts.

But had he been happy?

He'd needed me and I'd needed him. That was all there was to it.

"He was a good boy." I barely had the sentence out before I choked back a sob.

Catherine said nothing. I held her tight and rested my head on her shoulder, crying for my lost friend and everything he represented.

CHAPTER 23

CATHERINE

I'd held men as they cried. They'd cried for lost babies and broken dreams. They'd cried for their self-image when their wives had to work. I'd held children with boo-boos and deeper hurts that would never heal.

All of that was practice for holding Chris in the cemetery parking lot. I took in his pain and made it my own. I was strong for him for just a moment. And I did something for him I couldn't do with anyone else.

I gave him hope.

I didn't mean to, because I wasn't sure what I wanted from him, but I became his last connection and his last hope. Hope for what? I didn't know. Nor did I know if I could shoulder the responsibility of it. He felt so good in my arms, and when I thought of him weeping without me, my jaw tightened with *no*.

He was mine to comfort.

The moment I accepted that in my heart, my mind rebelled. I was freeing myself. Now wasn't the time to go backward.

But his lips on my throat. His breath in my ear. His tears had stopped and the connection between us had started something else.

He paused when we were nose-to-nose, brown eyes so close I could see the flecks of black and green.

Could I do this?

"Don't kiss me," I said. "It's too soon."

"I won't." His lips brushed mine so gently, I only felt the shifting of air between us.

His gentleness forced me to yield, returning his kiss. He was different. The kiss was different. He was a little taller and broader, holding me tighter, and despite his vulnerability a minute ago, his kiss was confident. His kiss wasn't a demand or command. It listened, and my body screamed into it.

His kiss was achingly familiar, yet startlingly new. I remembered everything that I had tried to forget. I remembered the way his hands gripped my back as if trying to find purchase in the way his tongue could command my mouth, I remembered the feeling of a new beginnings. His kiss was the start of something old. His kiss was the birth of a child we knew and loved and welcomed.

"Chris," I said when I had to breathe. "Chris." I put my hand on his cold cheek.

He turned and kissed it, closing his eyes. "Do you forgive me?"

"Never. But also, I did the minute you came back."

"I want to go back and do it all again. Every moment."

We kissed again, but we weren't gentle. Passion excluded care, mouths slipping, tongues lashing to taste every surface in each other.

Gravel crunched on the road, and we pulled apart with an inward gulp as if we wanted to suck away the last of each other's breath.

Three trucks. Johnny and Kyle in the first. Orrin, Reggie, and Percy, who barked when he saw me, in the second. The black pickup in the back was strange to me.

Chris answered my question before I could voice it. "That's the delivery service with Lance." He straightened my collar. "The guys are helping me dig."

"I'll get you guys something to eat."

"Will you stay for the service?"

I'd forgotten I'd told him I couldn't make it. "Wouldn't miss it."

"Will you stand next to me?"

Orrin got out of the truck, and Percy jumped out, a smaller version of Lance.

"Yes," I said. "I'll stand next to you."

BY THE TIME I got back with coffee and sandwiches, the hole next to Galahad's plot was four feet deep and wide. A brown leaf fell onto Lance's black crate and surrendered to the wind, clicking across the surface and away. Percy sat next to it with his tongue lolling, standing guard as if he knew his brother was in there.

The men made short work of the job. Cross-legged like children, we ate and drank in the grass.

"How long are you in town?" Reggie asked Chris.

"As long as it takes." He tossed Percy a slice of ham from his sandwich and the dog kept his post while gobbling it up.

I knew what Chris meant, and I turned my face away to smile.

Reggie glared at the place where my knee touched Chris's. "Long as it takes to what?"

Reggie was a gentle man and an artist. He was one of us. But his voice dripped with alarming hostility and suspicion. Chris was going to answer and I had no idea what the reply would be. If he wanted to prove his commitment to me, he'd say he was staying for me. Or he could obfuscate. Or change the subject. But with his companion in a plastic bag, ready to be lowered into a hole, he might be vulnerable enough to make me his reason.

"Long as it takes him to bury Lance," I scolded. "And if he wants to visit with us afterward, he's as welcome here as anyone in the family."

Reggie snorted and wrapped up the last third of his sandwich.

Johnny, who was never good at letting things slide, threw a chip at him. "Take it easy, asshole."

"I'm easy. Sunday mornin' easy." Reggie got up.

"It's Friday, dumbass," Bernard said around a big bite of sandwich.

Reggie ignored him and pointed at Chris's feet. "Got your fancy shoes dirty."

"Yeah. Thanks for letting me know." Chris stood.

I gathered his trash before he had a chance to bend down for it. "We should get started before it rains." I picked up the last of the containers.

Above me, Chris reached down to help me up, but before I could take his help, Reggie was on my other side, offering his hand.

If I took Chris's hand, Reggie would lose his Sunday mornin' easy.

If I took Reggie's, he would get the wrong impression and Chris would feel betrayed.

With an armful of containers and foil, I only had one hand free.

I tensed it on the grass and got up myself without dropping a single thing.

"Let's get to it then," Johnny said, groaning about his bones creaking.

Kyle and Bernard followed suit. They lowered the black bag into the ground. I stood next to Chris as dirt clapped off it and Lance slowly disappeared.

"I have this thing," he said, taking out a leather-bound pad. "A few words. It's not very good."

Reggie scooped dirt into the hole and watched me with Chris. Was he going to be a problem? I didn't think I could take it.

"Go ahead." I put a reassuring hand on Chris's arm. He needed me more than Reggie did. "Please."

Chris ran his fingers through his hair. I'd never imagined him feeling insecure or unsure, but the cracks in his confidence were wide enough for me to see what was inside him.

The boy I'd loved.

He looked at the paper, then back at me. I nodded, loaning him a little confidence.

"Lancelot Carmichael, you were a good boy. Always. You were always there for me, even when I didn't have food for you."

He stopped, tilting the paper. That was all that was on it, but he kept going.

"When it was raining and cold, he stayed with me." Chris closed his book. "He gave me everything. There was this one time, right in the beginning, when I had…" He made a rectangle with his fingers. "I had this much in a Chinese food container. It was all I had. I knew he was hungry, but when I offered, he wouldn't take the meat. He pushed it to me. He took care of me, even when I failed him… and… I'm sorry, Lance. I'm sorry for letting you down. Putting you second to my work. I'm so sorry."

His fingers found mine. We twined them together, and he squeezed my hand so hard I thought they'd fuse into a single gesture.

He let go and helped shovel dirt in. When it was no longer a hole but a mound in the grass, we set up the slab of stone at the head.

Lancelot Carmichael
Brave Knight.
Marked territory in Barrington and New York City
2004-2017

Chris held my hand on the way back to the car. He leaned into me and whispered, "Tonight. Are you free?"

"Lucky for you, I am."

"Can you meet me at our tree?"

I couldn't contain my smile.

Reggie watched us from the other side of the parking lot, and he didn't look happy.

CHAPTER 24

CATHERINE

I discovered the picture of Chris and Lance in New York in my pocket and inspected it. It was taken early in our separation. The background was hatched with monkey bars, blurry children running, a chain-link fence with a solid wall of red brick behind it. The ground was beige concrete. Lance was fully grown, looking away from the camera. Chris was still a boy, and very much a man. His shirt was tight in the arms, his pants were short, and he crouched next to a knapsack that had seen better days.

I flipped the picture. He'd handwritten the date and a note.

We miss you.

"I MISSED YOU TOO."

What had I been doing when this picture was taken?

Against the back wall of the hall closet, I kept a stack of photo albums. I kneeled on the floor and fingered the spines, plucking out one of the middle. Hunched in front of the closet and opened it in the middle.

My world had red brick in the background too. The factory closed.

Daddy had given notice two weeks before, and the workers had set up a "locked doors party" onsite, celebrating what they couldn't control. It had seemed like a bump in the road back then. Something to have a few beers and eat barbecue over.

I put the picture of Chris and Lance in that timeframe.

Downstairs, something shattered. I hurried to the kitchen to find Harper cleaning up a broken glass in bare feet.

"Are you all right?" I pushed her away, taking the broom and dustpan. Her hair was greasy, her eyes were puffy, and her lips were bitten red.

"I'll get over it." She hoisted herself onto the counter and got a new glass from the rack. She filled it, sniffling.

My sister didn't cry. I did all the crying for the family. Harper worked, studied, followed her curiosity down rabbit holes. Her spirit had been crushed. Something beautiful had been destroyed. I jammed the broom into the corners and edges of the kitchen as if I wanted to beat the glass out of them. My rage had its own mind, running my blood faster and hotter, contracting my muscles into tight, sinewy braids.

"Where is he?" I asked, slapping the edge of the dustpan into the trash. The glass tinkled in.

"He went back to California," she said into her glass before she finished it, looking out the window. "It's over. I have things to do now." She put the glass on the counter and saw me for the first time since I walked in. She put her hands up as if warding me off. "Whoa, Cath. It's okay."

"It's not okay."

"I've never seen you look like that."

"Like I could kill him?"

"Yeah."

"I will. I'll fly to California and find him and rip him apart." I wasn't going to kill him. I wasn't going to shred him. But I wanted to, and I could get close enough by saying it. "Look at you. You've been *crying*."

"You cry all the time."

What a sad, sad accusation.

"It's a tension release. You're crying over Taylor leaving, and I'm going to kill him."

She picked her glass up again and filled it. "It's not his fault. I broke up with him."

"Why? You liked him."

She took a long drink. "I love him." Her face scrunched as if she was ready to cry all over again. "But he was ready to give everything up for me, and I can't live with that. I can't live with holding him back."

She broke down in tears, slipping off the counter and into my arms. I took her glass and put it safely on the counter while holding her. My beautiful, genius sister. The one who was supposed to go anywhere and do anything, she felt unworthy enough to be unhappy rather than bring someone else down.

"You wouldn't have, Harper. That's..." The idea was absurd, ridiculous, unjust. I kissed her head as it shook against my shoulder. "Are you wiping your nose on my shirt?"

She nodded against me. "I have to do laundry anyway."

I gave her a paper towel. She took it and stepped into another hug. I stroked her hair and leaned against the counter while she sniffled in my arms.

"Can I tell you something you don't want to hear?" I asked.

"No."

"You need to finish college, Harper. Not to make yourself worthy, because you're the best woman I know. But because you need to be the person you were meant to become. I did it here. You can't. The world needs you to do that."

She leaned away from me, leaving me with an empty, cold place where her sadness had been. She honked into the paper towel and folded it in half so she could blow her nose again.

"The world needs you too," she said, sniffing and wiping the sides of her nose.

"Maybe." Outside, a car pulled down the driveway. "But you need to think about college again."

"I will."

We both looked out the window. Reggie's Chevy was driving so slowly into the garbage cans that they tipped but didn't fall before he stopped the car.

"What is he doing?" Harper asked.

I looked at the clock. It was only ten minutes after noon. "I think he's been drinking."

I went out the side door before Harper could reply.

Reggie got out, letting the door open so hard it bounced halfway closed again as he came toward me like a man barreling into a bar fight.

"Reggie!"

He put his hands on my face and his mouth on mine. He tasted like beer and desperation, and when I pushed him away, he grabbed me tightly so I couldn't get away.

The *klonk* was preceded by a whiff of wind and followed by Reggie's grunt. He was off me, and Harper stood a foot away with the top of a metal garbage can in her hands. Reggie had been thrown against the side of the house, bleeding from the head.

"Jesus!"

"Don't you do that, Reginald," Harper shouted. "I'm mad enough to take you out, drunk or not."

Reggie's response was a series of sharp ahs and moans. He stumbled trying to get up. "Why'd you do that?"

"If I gotta tell you…" Harper wielded her garbage can cover like a knight carried a shield.

"I was just trying to…" He took his bloody hand away from his skin. "Jesus."

"I'll get you some ice," I said, still tasting his beer on my tongue.

"It's bleeding!"

"And a towel."

"Catherine, you know I didn't mean anything by it, right?"

He came toward me, but Harper got her backswing ready, turning the shield into a weapon.

"You're drunk." I started for the side door.

"You want his money, don't you? You think he can take care of you."

I didn't have to answer him. I didn't owe him an explanation of my feelings or actions.

"Sit down, Reggie." Harper swung a plastic chair behind him. "Before I give you a concussion, sit."

He ignored her. "He can't. You know he lost all his money right? He's got nothing."

I felt a few things at once.

I was sad for Chris. I knew how hard he'd worked.

But it didn't reduce my attraction to him. It increased it.

Why?

Why would it even matter?

Leaving the side door behind, I stood in front of Reggie and pushed him gently into the chair Harper was holding still.

"Reginald, I'm sorry you feel rejected. I know it hurts. I hate that you're hurt and I hate that I hurt you, but I don't hate it enough to lie to you. Don't kiss me again. Ever. Drunk or sober. Ever. I'm going to call Johnny to bring you home."

I stomped into the house, and Harper was right behind.

Before the door closed behind her, Reggie shouted, "You're a whore, Catherine Barrington. A fucking whore!"

"Oh, fuck this," Harper started back out, but I grabbed her arm.

"Leave him be." I closed the door and locked it. "He'll regret it when he sobers up whether you concuss him or not." Picking up the wall phone, I dialed Johnny and Pat's house.

"He did, you know," she said while the phone rang.

"He did what?"

"Chris's hedge fund lost a bunch of money. Something like seventy-three point four six percent of its value."

"I don't care."

"I mean, guys like that are never totally broke. He probably has a billion hidden away."

"Still don't care."

"Hello?" Johnny's voice came over the phone.

"Hey, Johnny, are you on shift this afternoon? Reggie needs to get picked up and poured into bed."

Johnny agreed to fetch him. I hung up and prepared an ice pack.

Someone was going to deeply regret kissing me, and I wasn't sure who.

CHAPTER 25

CHRIS

*M*arsha's office was bright white, bedecked in fresh flowers and sunlight. I sat on the white-leather-and-chrome chair, and she sat across from me. Elbows on her white wood desk, she steepled her fingers. She had two huge rings on each hand and matching bangle bracelets. Her right eye squinted in my direction, and that side of her lips curved into a smile.

"We all had a feeling you two went back there," she said.

"Grounds keeping had its privileges."

"And you need it set up by tonight?"

"I'll pay for the service and tip whoever has to do extra work to get it done."

"You bet you will."

"I need access and privacy."

"We aim to please, Mister Carmichael."

We shook on it. As she led me to the door, she said, "She's worked hard for everyone else over there. It's nice to see something good happen to her."

"I may not be all that good."

"At least Harper won't have to hit you over the head." I must have taken too long trying to put her meaning together, because she explained without me having to ask. "You didn't hear?"

"I just saw her." What possibly could have happened?

"Gossip travels fast around here."

She untangled the grapevine on the way to reception. Reggie had gone to the Barrington house to make Catherine his, and when she refused, Harper had done something completely expected and bashed him over the head.

I made light of it, and Marsha promised to have the club set up for me by nightfall.

Everything was going fine, but it wasn't. It was terrible. I didn't know how long I stood in that front garden, staring through a rosebush, asking myself what the hell I was doing. I'd disrupted everything.

A bit of yellow was visible at the base of the bush. I reached through the leaves and thorns. A tennis ball. You were supposed to throw it back, but no one was playing nearby. The kid who kept the grounds would take it back to the pro shop and toss it in one of the coach's baskets.

The pro shop window was manned by a young woman in her teens. I held out the ball.

"Can you toss this in a basket?" I asked. "I found it in the garden."

"They're locked up. You can keep it or leave it here."

I put it on the counter. "Is Irv around?"

She looked puzzled. "Irv?"

"He was… who's the manager?"

"Oh! You mean the last manager? He died in…" She counted on her fingers.

She told me the year, but it didn't register. Irv was dead. The guy who'd given all the poor kids jobs. The guy who'd witnessed my first kiss with Catherine. Gone. And I didn't even know. I should have known.

"Sir?"

"Right. Well." I took the tennis ball off the counter. "Thanks for your help."

I walked back to my car in a fugue, clutching the yellow ball in my fist.

No matter what happened in Barrington, no matter how I walked away, no matter how long I stayed, or my success on a mission I couldn't even define, I couldn't leave things worse than when I came. I couldn't leave things undone, unsaid, broken.

I had to face Catherine about everything, and I had to face the town I'd abandoned.

Nothing about Barrington was the same as when I'd left, but maybe some things hadn't changed. On a Friday afternoon, payday, anyone who wasn't working would be at Walter's for burgers, beer, and pool. Or not.

I drove there on autopilot. Walter's still didn't have a sign out front, and the parking lot still smelled sour and dusty. Johnny's motorcycle with its sidecar sat in the lot out front, next to Kyle's prized Harley. I parked next to Orrin's pickup truck.

When I walked into the dark room, I felt like an outlaw riding into town. Conversations stopped, but the pool balls continued to roll and click. Faces were lost in shadow. Sunlight shot through the windows, bounced off the dust in the air, and was smothered in darkness before it could brighten the room.

I felt something warm and wet on my fingers.

Percy was licking them. I kneeled and rubbed behind his ears.

"Look who's buying the next round!" a young voice shouted. It was Damon. When I'd left, he was in fourth grade. I shook his hand.

"You don't need no more rounds," Orrin said, leaning on his pool cue.

"They still make burgers here?" I asked.

"Yeah," Johnny said from the bar. "But the fryer's been busted, so we get potato chips with it."

When I shook his hand, I saw Reggie at the other side of the bar with a rectangle of gauze attached to his forehead with a hashtag of tape. I slapped Butthead on the shoulder and gave Kyle a manly hug.

"Thanks for coming this morning," I said.

"Shouldn't be such a stranger."

I ordered a burger, and a beer appeared in front of me. I flipped a credit card on the bar and made a circle with my fingers, indicating I was indeed buying the next round.

I wished I'd worn jeans. I was casual in a sports jacket and button-front shirt, but I should have worn a T-shirt. Sneakers, not shoes. Or work boots that I didn't own, worn at the right foot, with a history of their own.

"Really, thanks for coming," I said to the bar at large.

"Had to watch Catherine," Johnny said. "Make sure you weren't going to take advantage."

"Thanks for that too." I sipped my beer.

The pool game resumed, and though I didn't expect Reggie to shake my hand or even greet me, he seemed isolated at the other side of the bar.

"What's up with Reg?"

"His head got in the way of an object at velocity. Mrs. Boden taped him up. She was a nurse in the Korean War. Didn't take no whining or crying from him," Johnny said.

"Should he be drinking?"

"A concussion woulda set him straight. But here we are."

Johnny wasn't going to tell me what happened, and I wasn't going to admit I already knew. I wasn't one of them anymore.

"Here we are," I said.

"When you going back?" Butthead asked.

"I don't know."

"We're pretty proud of you around here," Johnny said.

Butthead huffed. "He's the only one who understands what the fuck you do."

"Quantitative trading ain't that hard, asshole." Johnny turned to me. "Ain't hard to *understand*, I mean. If *doing it* was easy, this dimnut would have the scratch to drink imported beer."

"Fuck that," Butthead said. "Buy American."

"See what I'm saying? Get the fuck out of here while you can," Johnny said to me. "Place makes you stupid. I'd rather watch you make money from afar."

"What about Catherine?" I asked impulsively. I was tired of beating around the bush. "What if I took her away?"

"You got my blessing."

"Everyone south of the train tracks would shit bricks," Butthead added.

"You're south of the tracks, shithead," Johnny mumbled. "What are you going to do the next time you can't get antibiotics for your little girl? What are you gonna do when she's not here to feel sorry for your dumb ass?"

"She's done enough already. If people don't have their shit together, fuck 'em. Goes for me too."

The bravado wasn't lost on me. I'd entered adulthood with it. Walking into the biggest city in the world with a few hundred dollars in my pocket, ready to take over the world if that was what it took to win a woman I didn't understand. I'd thought money was important to her, but it wasn't. Never had been. Her people were important to her. Her tribe. I'd missed the point entirely.

I made eye contact with Reggie. He was still alone.

"I still love her," I said to Johnny quietly. "But I don't want to just come in here and cause trouble for anyone."

"Trust me." Johnny put his beer down with a deliberation that was punctuation. "We wouldn't let anything happen to her she didn't deserve one way or the other. But times are changing. Time she did too."

"What about you?" I asked as my food came.

He launched into his kids. They'd gone to college and never come back for more than holidays. One thing that came through his story was how proud he was of that exact fact. They'd moved on.

"You miss them?" I asked.

"Every damn day." With a tip of his chin, he ordered another beer. "Reg looks like he's gonna have an aneurysm."

He looked fine to me, but I had to trust Johnny on that. I took my beer and left my seat, crossing from the cool kids' table to the doghouse.

"Hey," I said, sitting next to Reggie.

"Fuck off."

There was no reason to answer him, but I wasn't walking away either. Not yet. I finished half my beer before he spoke again.

"She needs someone who isn't leaving."

"Yeah."

"Someone who appreciates her. Who isn't thinking she's someone she isn't."

"You should know."

In my complacency, he had me by the collar and pushed against the wall in a second. He was an artist and I was a mathematician, but the threat of a bloody fistfight seemed very real.

"She's not decoration," he said through his teeth. His eyes were lit by inner fire and his breath was soaked in beer.

Hands appeared on his shoulder. Kyle. Curtis. Johnny, of course. They pulled him off me, but his grip had never been the primary tools of attack. Our eyes were locked like two pit bulls in a ring. I wasn't letting him get pulled away any more than he was allowing it.

"You took your shot, Reggie," I said.

"She's not sixteen anymore. She's stronger than any of us. And your money? She's better than every single dollar you got. We all know it. This whole place rides on her back." He shook off the men holding him. They let him go but stayed close. "Well, I admit it, and I want to do for her. Take care of her. That's nothing for you, but it's something for me." He jabbed his chest hard enough to bend his finger back.

This felt like an extension of my conversation with Johnny and Butthead, but with a little more fire, a little more passion, and a single sentence that shook me.

We all know it.

I'd assumed, without thinking clearly about it, that I could take her away to something better.

But what did *better* mean?

I'd always thought it meant money, but what would have happened if I'd come for her? If I'd arrived on a white horse, rescuing her when I would have actually been rescuing myself? She wouldn't have become the woman she is. She wouldn't have been forged into the patron saint of Barrington.

I went to New York to make a ton of money, because I had to do that before I realized it wasn't important. If I'd stayed here or come back early, would I ever have understood that? Would I have come to that conclusion at Catherine's expense? Would she have come to represent everything that would have been wrong with me?

Worse, would I have spent the rest of my life chasing a dollar because that was what I'd been told I was worth?

"I fucked it up," Reggie continued, throwing himself back in his seat.

"Get up," Butthead said. "I'm taking you home."

Reggie kept on. "Fucked it bad, but that doesn't mean I'm going to just let you have her." By the last three words, he was shouting.

"It's not up to you. Or me."

Johnny put his hand on my shoulder. "You oughta go."

"You love a saint," I said, ignoring Johnny. "But she's not a saint. She's a living woman."

"You love a sixteen-year-old heiress. She's not that anymore either."

He was right. I'd come here hoping to meet the girl I'd left, but that girl was gone forever. She had been replaced by a woman of greater stature and purpose than I'd had the mind to wish for.

"I'm going to fight for her." I pointed in Reggie's face. "Don't underestimate me."

Johnny pulled me away. Reggie shook his head and let him take me outside. The sun was low in the southern sky and the afternoon wind rustled the dry grass. Everything was quiet, but nothing was still.

"Do you need a lift back?" he asked when the door shut behind me.

"Nah. Half a beer. Fuck it. Fuck it all. If I have to bulldoze over that guy or anyone for her, I will."

"Let him cool off. You'd do well to do the same." He handed me my credit card wrapped in a sales slip. "I grabbed this on the way out."

"Tell me something." I took a pen from inside my jacket and leaned on the wall to sign for the round. "Am I stealing her? Do they have something?"

"In his mind."

"And hers?" I handed him the signed receipt, and he snapped it away.

"If she says there's nothing, I believe her. She's not playing games, far as I can see."

After a shot in the arm, I was left alone in the parking lot.

CHAPTER 26

CHRIS

*a*t seven o'clock, I picked her up at her house. We exchanged ritual pleasantries and I held the car door open for her. When we were on the road, I tried to hold her hand, but they were tightly folded in her lap.

"Reggie came by today." She was turned toward the window and I was watching the road, but our attention to inattention was intense.

"I went to see him when I heard."

"You heard what?"

"That he made a pass at you and Harper clocked him." I couldn't look at her for long or I'd wreck the car, but she was worrying me. "I made sure he wasn't holding any grudges."

"Was he?"

"Only against me. Is everything all right, Rin? You said you didn't have a thing with him, but I can turn around right now if you want."

"No. There's nothing. Harper said you lost everything? All your money?"

My money? Was that what she cared about? Was she another Lucia? Was she in my car because she thought she could make a killing? Would she bolt as soon as there was a whiff of trouble?

No. Not Catherine. I wouldn't believe that of her. I was more experienced in the ways of gold-diggers than I wanted to be, but I wasn't that jaded yet.

"I lost a lot."

"I'm sorry what you worked for all those years was lost. Can you make it back?"

I shrugged. "With a lot of effort, a change of strategy, probably. I just don't know if I want start all over."

"That's terrible."

"Maybe. Maybe not." I reached for her hand, and she let me take it. "I have other things to work for now."

THIS TIME, we went to the patch of grass just outside the fence legally, through a gate on the easternmost side that Marsha had loaned me the key for.

The tree we'd climbed in our sixteenth summer was wrapped with tiny white lights, and lines of hanging lanterns were strung between the fence and the branches in smile-shaped spokes. Garland and tinsel sparkled in the light.

Catherine stood right under it in the soft yellow light, looking up into the dense branches. "It's beautiful."

Her eyes were spots of glittering glass and her smile was brighter than any electric light.

"You're beautiful." I touched her face. I couldn't help it. "Want to climb it?"

"Sure."

I led her to the base of the trunk and put my hand on the bottom rung of my ladder. The bark had grown over some of the wood slabs, making the connection stronger but more treacherous since it was harder to get a foothold. "It's higher, so I might have to help you up. And you have to be careful to make sure your foot's securely on it."

She put her hand on the bottom rung where the bark had grown over. It was chest high.

"Here." I held out my hand. "Take a step back, kick up, and I'll get you on."

She understood me right away, kicking her right foot until it reached the lowest rung. I pushed her forward and up.

She took the next rung and looked down at me. "I'm wearing pants this time."

"I didn't look up your skirt last time either."

She climbed, taking the same path she had thirteen years earlier, scooting down the thick branch so I had room to sit. She swung her leg over so both feet were hanging over the same side. I straddled the branch so my chest was at her right shoulder.

"This seemed higher up when we were kids."

"It's only about eight feet." I kissed her cheek, lingering on her smell. Roses. Still roses. When she faced me, I kissed her lips, but after a few moments, she stopped.

"How did you leave it with Reggie?" she asked.

"I told him I was going to fight for you."

She leaned away from me. A string of lights blinked off, then on again, leaving a layer of darkness on her face.

"Did you?"

I leaned away only enough to catch her perplexed expression. "Yeah, I said that."

"No." She shifted a little, putting more of her right leg on the trunk. "Did you fight for me? When I was here, by myself, holding everyone in Barrington on my shoulders? Did you fight for me?"

I was defensive and I didn't know why. "Whoa, there—"

She wasn't going to be held up. She wasn't a horse with reins I could pull back. She was a tidal wave.

"You know—" She shook her head quickly, mouth tight as if she was trying to hold back a torrent. "I thought I was okay with this but no. No, I'm not."

"Catherine—"

Her name, or my voice, broke a dam for her. "Did you come? No. Did you check on me? Did you call? You knew my parents died. You knew the factory closed. You sat in your ivory tower in New York and turned your back, and now that you're divorced and you've lost everything, you think you can come back and tell Reggie you're going to fight for me?"

"I wrote you a hundred letters!"

"I didn't respond to a single one and it never occurred to you I wasn't getting them?"

"Oh, you know what, lady—"

"You had to know something was wrong when I didn't write back!"

"You got with Frank Marshall the minute I left!"

She sat in shock. The string of lights shorted again, blinking twice.

"My mother still lived here. She told me. And it hurt, but I kept writing. When you didn't write back, I figured you married him or—"

"Frank Marshall is gay, you stupid, stupid man!"

"What? You…" I couldn't finish the sentence. I had too many questions, but I didn't want to ask them. I wanted to yell. I wanted to defend myself against her accusations.

She was wrong. She had to be wrong, because I was nursing my own hurt. I couldn't be the one who was wrong. There had to be some way to turn this around, some way I didn't abandon her.

Her voice didn't soften. Anger clipped every word. "He needed a cover for a relationship he was having. So we 'dated' and my mother stopped trying to set me up with 'acceptable' young men."

"How was I supposed to know?"

"You could have asked. You could have picked up the phone. Come around once you had enough money. Sent your number with a sympathy card when Dad died. But you didn't. You're not going to fight for me, Chris. Don't lie to Reggie. Don't lie to me, and don't lie to yourself."

She straightened her back and let her bottom slide over the branch. Thinking she was going to fall, I took her arm to steady her.

"Let go."

"I don't want you to fall."

"You were supposed to go first so I could get off first, and you didn't. You forgot." Her tears dropped like summer rain, and her chin quivered like rose petals in the breeze. I couldn't deny I'd forgotten I'd said that our first time up in the tree. I could only sit still. "So much time's passed, bark's grown over the ladder, but when you said you'd fight for me, it all came back. It's like yesterday. This raw place where I know I'm not worthy of coming back to. I'm not worth fighting for. I'm shit."

"Cath—"

She was gone, pushed off the branch, landing on her feet, knees bent, arms out for balance. Looking up at me, the dots of light glint off her tears.

"You're not shit." I wished I could eat those words, because they're the bare minimum and she deserves the maximum. They're a denial, not a declaration.

"I know."

I dropped to the ground, but by the time I hit the grass, she'd already run away.

CHAPTER 27

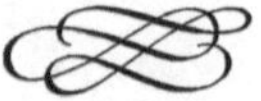

CATHERINE

I'd meant what I said about the raw place, but the words I'd used didn't do it justice. It was a picture in my head, a taste in my mouth, a deep throbbing beat in my ears. I felt that raw place throbbing pink, pulsing with anger and self-loathing. It was where I was powerless and the place I'd tried to forget all those years. The only thing that silenced the throb and washed away the taste was sealing away other people's raw places.

I was aware that made a decade of philanthropy selfish and vain, but it was the only way to soothe my own hurt.

The garden path was dotted with lights on either side like an airplane runway. I'd been defying gravity for years and I'd suddenly skidded to the earth.

I heard Chris running behind me. I couldn't outrun him and I didn't want to. He caught up, came slightly in front of me, and turned so I could see him.

"You said you hadn't thought about me in years."

"What do you want me to say? That I had? Or that I hadn't? What's going to make you feel better?"

"What's going to make *you* feel better?"

I wanted to punch him and run into his arms. "I stopped waiting for you." I articulated each word as if that would keep me from being misunderstood. "I never forgot how you made me feel."

He took half a step toward me with his hands out, assuming he knew what I meant. He didn't.

"You made me feel worthless and forgettable. And I know it was all a misunderstanding, but that was how I felt. You can't take that away from me, because I carry it everywhere. But also…" I sighed.

My words bent him. Shoulders drooping, hands retreated to his sides, he looked damaged and small with his own exposed, raw places.

"But also…" I continued. "You made me feel loved and whole. I felt passionate and alive, and no one I've met since has made me feel like that. So I don't… I don't know what to do. I want to seize this thing with you and never let it go, and I want to throw it away to save myself."

"If I'd stayed, you wouldn't be who you are. I don't know how this will sound, but who you are makes me ashamed of who I've become."

"Who is that? I don't even know."

He paused as if gathering strength to confess a sin. "A man obsessed with money, and not sense enough to be ashamed of it."

I started down the path but slowly, inviting him to walk next to me. He fell into line and we walked shoulder to shoulder.

"In my line of work, we solve problems in the stock market and we use these processes called algorithms. They—"

"I know what an algorithm is."

"You do?"

"Harper rubs off on people."

"Right. So we use them to assess risk. How much to invest. Where to invest. How long to hold, when to sell. It can get complicated, but they work until they don't."

"Is that what happened to your hedge fund?"

He took a long time to answer, walking slowly. "What happened to the fund was that I changed the weighting. I weighted the making money too far over the potential loss, and I made bets without enough data. The scale tipped. And the more I think about it, the more I wonder if I did it on purpose."

"Why would you do that?"

"Because maybe I knew I needed to be completely miserable before I came back to my roots, and you."

"It wasn't about me, Chris. Don't say that."

We passed though the garden gate, toward his car.

"I can't help but think you were the last person who loved me for me. No more and no less. I weight that pretty heavily."

"I'm just an algorithm then?" I tried not to sound as if I was accusing him of something, because I wasn't. I was egging him to talk more.

"We all are, but we kid ourselves into thinking we have enough data to run it." We got to the car, and he unlocked it. "You make me feel like a man with a chance. You made me feel like that when I was sixteen, and I feel like that right now. With you, my future is mine to write, but I need more data. And so do you."

"You sure know how to make a girl feel all warm and fuzzy."

"The lights on the tree didn't work, so I recalibrated." He opened the passenger door.

"They worked. That's why I reacted the way I did." I got in the car before he could answer.

WE DIDN'T TALK much on the drive back to my house, but as he got off at the Barrington exit, he grabbed my hand and held it. I let him, because his grip was exactly what I needed.

He walked me up the porch.

"I'm sorry I ruined your surprise," I said. "It was beautiful."

He slid his hands down my arms and linked his fingers in mine. "I should have come back. Fuck Frank."

"You can't. He's married to a nice guy in San Francisco."

My resistance was no match for his smile.

"I took years from you," he said. "We could have been together. I could have taken you back to New York, away from here and this"—he looked for the word and found it— "devastation."

His word did its job, sending pictures of Barrington through my mind. The closed factory. The boarded-up stores. Jonah Wright born with a hole in his heart and no insurance. The Bordens living in a house with a roof like a sieve. Brooke Frazier, impregnated by a rapist she wouldn't name.

I'd helped them. I gave them money, time, a ride to far away doctors. Small things.

If I'd been in New York, what would have happened to them?

"I need to think," I said. "Get data, like you say."

"Can I see you tomorrow night? At the playground?"

"It's still there," I confirmed.

"I'll pick you up at seven."

"No. I'll get there the way I got there the first time."

"No way. You are not—"

Because I wasn't getting into an argument about my safety in a town of people who loved me, I interrupted him with a kiss.

I'd never taken a kiss before, so I was clumsy. My focus on my objective overrode my passion. My lips were too stiff and my head pushed forward too hard, but once Chris gave up on finishing his sentence, he came to me, giving willingly what I took from him.

A simple, sweet good night kiss between two kids who had their entire lives in front of them and the weight of the world on their shoulders.

CHAPTER 28

CATHERINE

I couldn't sleep. I stayed up for hours, lying on my back, watching the moonlight shift over the ceiling mural.

Every option seemed like a possibility. Go to him. Risk everything. Undo the damage of the past thirteen years. It seemed so easy.

The other option, stay in Barrington. I'd found meaning in being needed and loved. The rewards of my efforts. Stay for the people who need me most. Let them take care of me.

As the night went on, shades of both options appeared. Tell Chris he had to stay here part time. Take Harper with us. Sell the last of everything and put it back into the community and split. Tell Chris maybe. Tell him I wanted more time.

Yes to all. Yes to some, no to some. I wasn't used to weighing so many options and internal negotiations. I didn't feel capable of handling it.

I AM A GROWN WOMAN.

THOSE FIVE WORDS came to me about two in the morning. I rolled them around in my head.

I AM A GROWN WOMAN.

I am a young woman.

I can do anything I want.

I am trapped.

I am free.

*I am ashamed that people will
know what he does to me.*

I am a grown woman.

I am afraid to leave here.

I am afraid to stay.

I want him.

I want him.

He'll hurt me. He's hurt me already.

This is a game to him.

This is a game to him.

*You'll give up everything you work for,
and for what?*

*Mommy and Daddy won't
love me anymore.*

They're long gone.

> *Does he still love me?*

Do I still love him?

> *What's it like to not love him?*

I am a grown woman.
I know my own mind.
I know my own heart.
I'll do what I want.
I'll take my own risks.
I will own my own failings.

> *I'm terrified.*

I can do what I want, and he
can join me in that or not.
He's a grown man.
I don't have to love him,
not now, not ever.
I can just do what I want.

> *You're scaring me.*
> *What will I do if I am left alone again?*
> *What's going to happen to me?*
> *This can't happen again.*
> *Do you understand?*
> *This cannot happen again.*

It might happen again.

> *You can't let it.*

I can't control him.

And it might not be him to
blame in the end.
He might be offering something I don't want.

Do you blame me for being scared?
Do you blame me for wanting to run away?
What if this happens again?

I'll take care of you.

CHAPTER 29

CATHERINE

My room went from black, gray, blue, to the yellow light of morning angling through the windows. I got up when I was too hungry to stay there.

Physically, I was a wreck. But mentally, the sunlight had brought a clarity that brought my emotions to heel. I had seen real human suffering, and I had seen people survive real pain. I was afraid of a broken heart, but what was a broken heart in the face of losing a child or going hungry?

A part of me wanted to run toward the risk, saying "bring it on," while opening my arms to whatever Chris Carmichael had in store for me. And the other part of me was very clear, very firm, and spoke in a voice years older.

It said I would not do a single thing that didn't serve me. If I made a sacrifice, it would be because that sacrifice would make me happy. If I made a demand of him, it would be because I couldn't live without the thing I was demanding.

I didn't know what any of that meant. Specifically, I didn't know what to demand, but when I came to it, I would know. I'd opened the door to my needs, and I trusted they would walk through when they needed to. I was not going to rely on Chris to figure this out for me, nor

784

was I going to second-guess him. I was going to take him at his word, and he was going to take me at mine.

I came downstairs to find Harper at the folding table in the dining room. She was scribbling in a notebook, and I expected to see a bunch of unintelligible signs, symbols, and codes. Instead, it was her uneven script with cross-outs, arrows, and lines across sentences.

"Good morning," she said, not slowing her pencil one bit.

"What are you writing?"

"College essay."

I looked over her shoulder and saw my name. "What's the question?"

"I have to describe someone I admire." She covered her paper and continued scribbling. "Don't let it go to your head."

I put my hand on her shoulder and squeezed it. I didn't have any words of gratitude, and I knew she didn't want them anyway. "Can I make you something to eat?"

"I'm good."

"It's nice to see you not crying."

"Same for you." She put her pencil down and cracked her knuckles. "Reggie came by last night."

"He owes you an apology. Don't you dare speak to him until he apologizes to you."

"I sliced his head open with a garbage pail lid," she said incredulously.

I put my hands on my hips. "There was no excuse for him speaking to me like that in front of you. I'll get my own apology, and you'll get yours. In the meantime, I don't want him coming around here, and I don't want him to be alone with either one of us."

"Oh my God, do you think he came here alone? You should've seen the team of assholes he was with. And I say asshole in the most affectionate way." She counted on her fingers. "Johnny. Kyle. Pat. Even Juanita came with him to make sure he didn't start calling anybody names or getting violent. It was kind of weird."

I wanted to accept his apology so that I could move on with my life, but I was still kind of mad. I surprised myself. I'd never thought I was much of a grudge holder. But maybe Chris brought that out in me.

I went to make breakfast.

"Chris called," Harper shouted from the dining room. "I left the message behind the phone."

I whipped around with the coffeepot in my hand, turning so quickly the torque almost sent coffee flying. Behind the wall phone, on a little pad we kept for such a purpose, was a note in Harper's handwriting.

> *Chris says he will be at the playground at 7 PM.*
> *Doesn't want you coming in the dark.*
> *Please drive. Or call him to pick you up.*
> *PS - I have condoms in my nightstand. Take them if you want.*

THERE WAS A NUMBER UNDERNEATH, the area code from Doverton. The club.

Reggie had apologized, and this was my town. I wasn't getting in the car and wasting gas to go a mile. I'd come and go as I pleased.

I was a grown woman.

CHAPTER 30

CHRIS

I didn't think of my efforts with the tree as a complete failure. I hadn't gotten what I wanted, which was my mouth and hands on her chest, and her promise to continue seeing me.

But I woke up feeling as if I'd gotten something. I didn't know what that was. I couldn't define it or count it. Couldn't draw a conclusion from it. But it was good, and it was enough. She'd given me the idea.

The idea couldn't be quantified or counted. I didn't have an exact string of words to describe what it was. But it involved a result, and I could build a formula from that.

Catherine would continue to be who she was. She would continue to give of herself to others. And she would be with me. All that equaled our happiness and the end of my wandering around in the wrong world.

Again, I didn't know what that meant as far as the future. She needed personal connection. She would never be one of New York's charity mavens, only partly because I wouldn't be a billionaire hedge fund manager for much longer. But after last night, I felt as if I knew her better, knew what she needed to live her life, and I was eager to provide it.

I got a text from Brian over breakfast.

— WHAT ARE YOU DOING? —

— Eating eggs and toast. —

— In Barrington USA? —

— Yes —

THE PHONE RANG. It was Brian. I'd obviously said something to piss him off. Maybe he didn't like toast.

I answered the phone and stepped outside into the rose garden that I used to tend. "What's your problem?"

"Barrington?" he snapped. "With the glass factory?"

"Yes?"

"And you don't know about the new talk over in Silicon Valley? About the Barrington factory? This is bullshit. You told me you were out, but you're just getting out to start something else. You going to just take the money and not cut me in."

"Brian, I don't know what you're talking about."

"Sure, asshole. You think I don't know you by now?"

"What's that supposed to mean?"

"Dude, you take everything and close the door behind you. That's how you operate. I never thought you'd do it with me. But you are."

"I was born and raised here. It's perfectly natural for me to show up to see the people I grew up with."

"That just makes me think you're the one who spearheaded the deal. Not cool. Not okay. And possibly a breach of contract."

I took a deep breath, then another. The fall sky was flat blue, the morning sun was shining, and I was not going to let him think I was fogging him over. "I came here to bury Lance, and I'm staying for a while. I am not here to secretly team up with some venture capitalists opening the fucking factory. Given the choice, I would burn the factory to the ground. I understand why you don't trust me. I understand why you think I'm going to take all of the money you're paying for the fund and leave. But if there's a loyal bone in my body, and there are a few, at least one of them has your name on it."

"I want in."

"There's nothing to be in on."

"There will be, my friend. If you're not stabbing me in the back, and maybe you're not, I still want in."

"Noted. But don't hold your breath."

"Noted."

We hung up, and I sat back down to breakfast. The eggs had gotten dark and translucent at the corners. The toast was chewy and cold.

Nobody trusted me. Lance had, but he'd never wanted anything from me but food and a little affection. He still gave more than he took.

I'd never betrayed Brian, but betraying him had never been in my best interests. If it had been, if some opportunity to fuck him over for my own benefit had shown itself, what would I have done?

It's business.

I would've said that. And I would've meant it. It would have been its own answer to just about any question.

Leaving my breakfast, I went back outside and called my ex-wife.

"Hello? Christopher?" People chattered in the background.

"Do you have a minute?"

"Five of them. I'm about to go into a board meeting for Montano."

The children's charity had meetings this time of year in Italy. I'd forgotten.

"This won't take long. Not if you answer honestly."

"I'm intrigued," she said in a voice laced with suspicion.

"Why did you marry me?"

"Oh, *dio mio*, Christopher. Now you ask this?"

"I married you because I thought you were as good as it got. There. I said the hurtful thing. Now you can just say what you have to."

I heard the flick of a lighter and a deep inhale. She must be in Milan. She never smoked at home. "I married you because you had potential."

"What kind of potential? Money?" I needed her to just admit it, but I knew she wouldn't. If I'd been so sure of the answer, I wouldn't have needed to call her.

"God, no. You had plenty of that, which was nice. You could have become a good man. But, you know, *que sera*."

"I didn't become a good man?"

"I don't have all my life to wait." Another long exhale.

"I thought you married me for the money."

"Of course you did. I have to go. We can talk later, okay?"

"Sure." I hung up.

If you wanted people to trust you, you had to make them money. You could be a nice guy, real prince, but if it didn't make any money, who cared? That wasn't the kind of trust I was in business for.

Some things weren't business.

My business was going to change. I just didn't know what it was changing into.

CHAPTER 31

CATHERINE

The little playground behind the old trailer park was deserted. The plastic was cracked, colors faded, and cigarette butts littered the sand. I accidentally tipped over a beer can sitting on a bench meant for watchful parents.

The trailers had been removed after my father died, leaving stumps of rusted pipes. The good pipes and the copper had been ripped out long ago and sold for scrap. Electrical wires had been dug up with spades and snow shovels in the middle of the night.

I didn't know my father owned this trailer park. Not until he died and his assets became mine and Harper's. I hadn't been able to sell the land. I would've sold it for anything, but nobody wanted it.

I heard him coming. He made no move to disguise his footfalls in the leaves behind me. I turned around, resting my arm over the back of the bench as he broke the tree line, hands in pockets, trying to look harmless.

He was anything but harmless to me. His posture drove forward in a way I never saw on the men in town, alienating my mind's better judgment from my heart's desire. He divided and conquered just by smiling.

"I didn't see your car," he said as soon as he saw me.

"I walked." I turned around. It was the only way to stop myself from running into his arms.

"I don't like you walking alone at night." He came around the bench and sat next to me, flicking the empty beer can away. "This isn't a good neighborhood. Trust me, I grew up here."

I got up, picked up the can, and put it in the lone space in the cardboard six-pack that was lying a few feet away. "There are no bad neighborhoods in Barrington for me."

I sat next to him. We sat in silence for a few minutes. Maybe it was seconds. Maybe we sat for hours, each getting used to the presence of the other again.

"I wondered if you'd come," he said finally.

"Why?"

"We have a habit of temporary good-byes turning permanent."

"I wanted to tell you something."

He sat up a little straighter. It was a defensive posture. "Tell me then."

"I admire you."

A little laugh escaped his lungs. "Sure."

"You wanted something. You spent years getting it. You fought hard. I admire that. And now you're here, which is brave. And you're looking back on what you fought for and thinking you maybe made a mistake. Maybe you fought for the wrong thing. I admire that too."

He shook his head a little, as if he couldn't accept my words.

"There was this woman," he started.

A tingle of jealousy ran through me. I had no business being jealous, but did anyone?

"Before my ex-wife and after I paid capital gains for the first time, there was this woman. She was a maybe. She looked a lot like you. She was from a small town in Georgia, and she seemed as gentle as you. Of course, I didn't realize any of that right off. I didn't realize that she and you were cut from the same cloth. So I let myself care about her without putting it all together. And then this stupid thing happened. We were getting coffee and she got there before me, so she paid for herself. And I get there just as the guy is giving her change. It's a dollar and some coins. She takes the dollar, and she takes a quarter out of the coins and puts the rest of the tip jar. And I said, 'Why did you take the quarter back?' Believe me, I could've asked about the dollar, but the quarter really bugged me. She said she might need it for laundry or the parking meter. She didn't have a car. And it's not like I didn't have someone going over there to do her laundry and her chores for her. But she took the damn quarter back. Why? What kind of person won't give a quarter? Give the whole thing because they might need it for something that would never happen?" He ran his finger over his forehead. "It took me a few days to realize that I broke up with her because she wasn't like you. I mean, she really ran down my expectations. Because no matter how much they look like you or act like you… no one was going to be you."

"I was here the whole time. But I'm afraid I would have disappointed you anyway. You had me on some kind of pedestal."

"I'm here now, at the base, looking up."

"I'm a different person now."

He smirked a little, relaxing his shoulders. "You're not the girl I took up the top of that slide, but you're the culmination of her."

He leapt off of the bench and held out his hand. I took it, and he pulled me up to the play structure. We clattered up the ladder, and I found myself laughing.

The space we had occupied as young lovers was so much smaller than I remembered, and it was littered with dead leaves and human detritus. Cigarette butts, broken glass, an empty bag of chips; none of it bothered me. There was only him, with his eyes glinting in the moonlight and the fresh smell of aftershave.

His kiss was gentle and sweet, a request for more. A door he held open for me. I could walk through or I could walk away.

My arms were bent at my sides as he embraced me, running his hands down my forearms to my wrists until he lifted them and put my hands around his waist. Only then did I yield completely, tightening the coiled springs of my muscles around his body until he was as close to me as I was to him.

We kissed as though we couldn't let go, like adolescents, afraid that if we broke for a second to speak or touch we would break some kind of spell and shame or realization of the consequences would flood us and we would have to make some kind of adult choice. We kissed as though any bond between us was between our mouths. Fighting to keep our tongues together as he ran his hands over me, I wished for more. Everything. I wanted to leave him there, spent, to take every drop from him.

His hands got under my shirt, down my waistband, and still we kissed. We kissed as he reached down so far he had to bend his knees. I lifted myself onto my toes to help him get under my underwear, his finger reaching toward where my desire had collected.

I gasped so hard when he touched me that I almost stopped kissing him. That was not allowed. The kiss must be maintained. That was the rule. He knew it. He held my head to his with one hand and his fingers dug deeper, but the other reached into me.

When he broke the kiss, my first reaction was not disappointment but the fear that he was stopping, that he was breaking his bond.

He kept his mouth close to mine and said, "I want you. I've never wanted anything as much as I want you."

He kissed me again and touched my swollen nub, stroking it just a bit. My back arched like a cat's and he had to work harder to reach me. As we bent together, angling until we were kneeling before each other, kissing, his fingers flicked me as if he could read me like a book.

"Come for me, Catherine. Give it to me."

I was confused for a moment about who was giving what to whom, but I didn't have time to sort it out, because I was giving him what he wanted and I was taking what I wanted, exploding in his hand, breaking the kiss with my cries, letting it flood me so slowly, so powerfully, that I laid my entire weight on him, flying back, reaching through his jacket to scratch through his shirt.

He finished me, letting me come down gently, and pulled his hand out of my pants.

"Thank you," he said.

"I'm supposed to be thanking you."

"When we were kids, all I wanted to do was taste you." He held up his fingers. They were shiny and slick, and I was a little embarrassed by my body. He put his finger on his tongue and licked it off. I was shocked and turned on at the same time. "You've fulfilled an adolescent dream. It's as sweet as I imagined." He stuck his middle finger in his mouth and sucked it clean. I hoped this wasn't finished, because the way his lips curved around his finger made me want to experience that mouth so much more. "Thank you."

He reveled in my shame and embarrassment, and it was exactly those things that made me want him even more. He wanted me to give him everything, and I wanted him to have it.

I was seized with fear. He would take everything from me. He would leave me a husk, a molted skin in the sun, and go away with my heart. My mother had been right—he was dangerous. Not to my standing in society, not to my finances, he was dangerous for my soul. I didn't want to be a husk. I didn't want to be left with a shell of a life.

I stood up hurriedly as if I had an appointment. I didn't know how else to act. I couldn't tell him my fear because my fear didn't have words. My fear came through my mouth, and he had already proven he owned my mouth.

A rustle came from behind the trees. The laugher of adolescents. Through the branches and trunks, flashlights bounced. Cigarette smoke stung my nostrils.

"We're about to be invaded," I said.

"We were here first." He straightened my shirt.

"Tell them that." I jumped off the play structure, landing well.

"I'll walk you." He jumped down with me as four teens broke the tree line.

I recognized Zack and Lily. The other two were in darkness. They all fell into silence. I waved. Zack waved back.

"Come on." Chris put his hand on my back and we left in the other direction, leaving the playground to the children.

CHAPTER 32

CHRIS

I could feel her arousal drying in the creases of my fingers as she sat next to me on the way-too-short drive to her house.

I knew how to seduce women. I knew I could have her on her back if not tonight, then by tomorrow. I knew that as spooked as she was, she was also turned on. My dick stretched against my pants and my balls ached for her. She might've been a little freaked out when I sucked her off my fingers, but tasting her made me want her even more.

"It looks like you need the roof redone," I said as we pulled down the long drive.

"We'll figure it out."

It had been clear from the beginning that she didn't want anything from me. I wanted to give her everything, but I also wanted to take everything.

"If you need a loan…" I shut myself up as quickly as I could, but what was said was said.

"Have I mentioned that you can go to hell?" She said it with a fine layer of the sweetest saccharin. A shell of a joke over a core of gravity.

I pulled up in front and shut the car. "You have mentioned that. But the offer stands."

I wasn't willing to hear her tell me to go to hell again, so I got out of the car and let her out. She stood near enough to me that I could smell her. The roses. I could've kissed her. I couldn't tell if she wanted me to, but I could tell that she was daring me to. And if I wanted a woman and she dared me to take action on wanting her, I usually took her up on it. There had never been a reason not to take what was given freely.

Instead, I walked toward the door, and she fell astride me. She glanced at the top floor.

"Do you think Harper's waiting for her sandwich?" I asked.

"She never asks for one, but she always eats it."

Two moths banged around the porch light, slapping their bodies against the hot glass. Now was the time for good night kisses and final gropes.

"How long are you staying?" she asked, looking at my car.

"As long as it takes." I took her by the chin and turned her face toward me. "As long as it takes." I stepped back and opened the screen door for her.

She didn't get out her keys but turned the knob and opened the front door. "Good night, Chris."

"Good night, Catherine. And thank you."

She opened her mouth to say something, but she closed it and nodded instead. She gently closed the door and I was left on the porch, watching the screen door slap shut.

I sat in the car in her driveway for too long. I couldn't move. A woman like that? A woman like that would stay beside you through lawsuits. A woman like that would wait for you while you were in jail, and she'd send letters every day. A woman like that would stand behind a man who was fucked up, using all the strength in her body to hold him straight. A woman like that forgave a sinner.

You could take everything from a woman like that. You could steal her heart, take her money, give her a life of sincerely-made broken promises.

A man could love a woman like that to death.

A man could love a woman like that forever.

A man could stand by a woman like that and watch her bloom.

Water her.

Tend her gently.

Respect the thorns. Love the rose.

A man could walk beside a woman like that the rest of his life.

I'd been at a crossroads in her front yard before. I'd made choices based on adolescent priorities, and now I felt that crossroad again. There was no tomorrow. There was no later, no taking it slow. I had now. I'd waited long enough.

The tennis ball I'd collected at the club was on the floor of the car, the yellow reduced to deep mustard in the shadows.

I grabbed it, got out of the car, and looked up at her room.

Her lights were on.

CHAPTER 33

CATHERINE

The crumb-dusted plate by the sink told me Harper didn't need a sandwich. I shut the light and went upstairs, dragging dissatisfaction behind me.

What did I want? More Chris, but how? Did I want him now or wish for the past? Did I want the broken man or the beautiful boy? Did I want him now? Later? Or never? Would the reality of him break the world I'd built for myself?

I walked right by the master suite. I didn't want to sleep under Reggie's mural. Didn't want to see it or feel its weight over me. I went to the front bedroom and flicked on the light. The bed was still made, and next to it sat the boxes of unread letters. The mattress creaked when I sat on it, and the cardboard flaps coughed dust when I pulled them up.

A parallel universe sat in a crumbling pile. A universe where I'd gotten the messages and bent my life around Chris Carmichael. A universe where I was a different woman, maybe happy, maybe miserable, maybe some shade in between. But in every iteration, I was different.

I picked up the top letter and opened the flap. The glue had hardened long ago, and the letter inside was brown at the fold.

I didn't want to be different. If I'd found the first letter or the last, I would have been a different Catherine. I liked who I was. I hadn't thought about it until I closed the envelope flap, but I'd done much with little. That alone was worth the price of every other possible outcome.

Pock.

I dropped the envelope, freezing at the memory of that sound.

Pock. Pock.

I threw open the sash and leaned out the window. Chris was in the front yard, tossing the tennis ball and catching it in one hand. The beautiful boy was purely a man, and though I was different, I was not immune to him.

"I need to talk to you," he said, tossing the ball up at the window.

I surprised myself and caught it. "Wait for me." I slapped the window closed before he had a chance to answer.

When I got out the front door, he was waiting. I took his hand, put my fingers to my lips, and jerked my thumb upward, toward Harper's room. I pulled him to the backyard, and he put his arm around me.

He pulled me closer as we walked. Strong. Secure. As real as the day we met, the thrill of his presence and his touch vibrated throughout my body. I was glad he was there because I could barely walk, but he was the reason I felt as though the earth was dissolving under my feet.

I'd intended to bring him behind the headstone where he'd left me, but the stone, and all the others around it, was covered in burned-out branches. I couldn't recreate the moment for him or myself. I stopped at the white fence. "I…"

I couldn't finish, because the realization hit me like a cyclone that started in my heart and twisted through my mind. The scene of my past was blocked by the fires of my present.

"What is it, Catherine?"

"It's not the same."

He nodded, and I knew he wasn't stalling. He nodded because he understood me. Maybe I never knew if he was having exactly the same thought.

I tore my eyes away from the web of bushes and looked the man in the face. "We're different. Things that happened, we've done things. And they changed us. We can't go back. We don't get a redo."

"But we have now."

"What if I don't love you now?"

"Are you saying you don't?"

"I'm saying I don't know."

"I think you will."

"You filled a space for me. What if I don't have that space anymore? What if it's all filled up already?"

He touched my face with a tenderness that melted the skin underneath it. I wanted him, but I didn't need him.

"Chris—" My voice broke. "What if now isn't enough?"

"My now wants your now. Come forward with me. All you've done in this world has made you the woman that would have been too much for the Chris you knew. Back then, I needed simple answers, and you gave me one. That answer, money, it isn't the answer anymore."

I put my hand on his chest and bit my lip against giving him an easy response. We both deserved better.

"It's not simple anymore, is it? Back then, you gave me reason to be my own woman, and when you left, I became that woman. I don't have any simple answers now." I felt his heart beating through his jacket. Felt the life in him fighting to get out. I wanted to see that life. "I don't know if I love you, but I want to know the man you are and I want to see the man you'll become." My tears got cold in my eyes, and I blinked them away. They weren't tears of disappointment, despair, or tension. They were tears of relief. "That's not the same as it was, is it?"

He wiped a tear away with his thumb. "It's not the same. We won't know until we try. I'm not going to ask if you still want me. You can't still want that kid. But do you want me now? Because the man I am now wants the woman that you are now."

I barely had a voice to answer, so I whispered, "Yes."

His kiss was as tender as his touch, gently greeting my lips. The greeting turned into something warmer, then hotter, as his tongue broke past my teeth, touching mine, connecting us at the mouth in a way our hands could not. I clutched his jacket, his hair, wanting to know his body as well as I knew my own.

He pushed against me, hip to hip, hitching me against him until my legs were wrapped around his waist. He carried me up the back porch. Still kissing, I reached for the doorknob and opened it. We were locked together through the house, up the stairs, and I directed him to the room at the end of the hall. The room with the made bed and the boxes of old letters. Groping him, kissing whatever piece of skin I could find, I tasted the present and the unknown future.

When he closed the door, the hall light cut off. Moonlight streamed through the windows. We undressed each other like animals getting past our prey's skin, reaching for the vital organs.

I'd never felt this before. I'd wound my entire emotional life into despair and unworthiness, and suddenly they were coins flipped to passion and desire. His body was firm and powerful and my body was melting into liquid fire, bubbling at the edge of the pot, lid tapping and rattling.

Laying me on the bed, he said, "You are more beautiful than I ever imagined."

He dropped his pants, and his erection was a singular perfection. Finally, I'd have it again. He crawled on the bed and drew his hand down my body, between my breasts, over my belly. I felt as though I'd never been touched before. Not by him. Not by this man. My body answered his hand by arching, my blood answered by closing the gap between us.

I gasped for him, saying, "Yes. Now," without making the words.

"I want you right now," he whispered with a voice as thick as the darkness. "And I'm going to have you, but I'm not rushing. We both waited too long."

"I have all night."

"Good," he sighed into my breast, kissing around the base, working his way to the peak.

He sucked until it was hard. I squirmed, but he took his time, doing the same to the opposite side. His lips worshipped my belly and hips, my thighs and my knees. He pulled them apart and ran his tongue along the inside of one, then the other. My fingers were woven through his hair, gripping tight when he got close to my center.

He paused with his mouth so close to my core I felt his breath on my wet skin. I held my own breath until my lungs hurt. My exhale was a whimper. His voice was the rustle of the grass in the wind. My name was a prayer.

His lips were reverent, soft, slow. His tongue ran slowly along my seam, not just offering pleasure but tasting me, as if the pleasure wasn't mine but his. When it reached my clit, the darkness behind my eyelids lit up with lightning and my ears rushed with my own cries. The pot bubbled over, hissing against hot metal.

And still, he was slow and deliberate. My legs opened wide for him, and my body bent and thrust with an orgasm that rushed hard and fast after thirteen years of waiting. Lifting my hips off the bed, I twisted, and he grabbed me by the thighs so he could keep his face between my legs as I flipped.

"You have to stop," I lied, pushing myself onto his face and coming again. I fell back, away from him. "Oh, my. My God."

Resting his weight on one elbow, he smiled at me with a slicked face. "I wouldn't have known how to do that when I was sixteen."

I climbed on top of him, straddling his shaft as it lay against the length of my seam. "I can't wait to find out what else you know."

"This." He shifted my hips forward then back, sliding against me.

I followed his rhythm, aroused all over again. I bent and kissed him. "Can you come like this?"

"I want to fuck you."

Sitting straight, I rode him, taking control of the pace. "You're thinking about protection."

"Yes."

"I just finished my period."

"Kismet."

I whispered in his ear. "I also got a condom from Harper."

We laughed, and I reached into the nightstand drawer. We put it on.

Lifting myself a little, I gave him room to guide himself to my entrance. I placed my weight down slowly, letting him into me, feeling my body react to his presence.

We were joined again, but this time it was without fear, without sneaking. We weren't two romantic kids against the world, but two people. No more. No less.

He pushed his body against mine, letting me set the rhythm and wrapping himself around me when I leaned into him. My lips, his lips. My heart. His heart. One breath. One moment inside of a life.

My orgasm blossomed like a rose, opening from a tight bud into a splay of petals and pleasure. I cried into his neck, and he thrust hard into me twice, then sucked in a breath, knotting his brows and arching his neck to look me in the face as he filled me.

This was what he sounded like when he came.

This was what he looked like now.

It was beautiful.

CHAPTER 34

CHRIS

When I woke, the sky was just turning chambray on the eastern horizon. Catherine was wrapped in my arms, her body rising and falling. A long strand of light brown hair lay across her cheek and over her eyes. I pulled it away and tucked it back with the rest of her curls so that I could see her face in the sunrise.

I disentangled myself to go to the bathroom, still naked and aware of Harper's footfalls in the hallway on the other side of the door. As I swung my legs over the bed, my foot hit a dusty, desiccated cardboard box. The flaps weren't sealed or puzzle-locked. I had a feeling I knew what was inside before I even peered in. From above, in the dim light, it looked like a box of garbage, but it didn't take long to see the angled seams of envelopes.

My letters.

I'd written them. I bought the paper, the pens, paid for postage. I'd licked the envelope flaps with my spit after dumping all of my heart's desires onto the pages. And yet I didn't feel like I had the right to look inside. They were Catherine's property. My heart, on a page, delivered to her. A moment in time that I thought was my own was now her possession.

When I got out of the bathroom, she was roused a little, half sitting up but still so drowsy that her body was limp.

"Good morning," I said, getting on the bed with her.

"Good morning." She put her arms around my neck. "I hate to bring this up, but I haven't really thought about it. And I think I have to."

I knew what she was going to say before she even said it. "I'm a free man. I could be somewhere else, but I don't have to be and I don't want to be."

"No one is in New York waiting for you?"

I kissed her. "They'll send out a search party at some point. Did you ever want to go to New York?"

She didn't exactly push me away, but she didn't get closer either. "I can't just run off to New York." She smiled, and a little laugh escaped her throat. "That's ridiculous. I can do whatever I want. People still need me here, but they won't for long. I was thinking, just a week ago, that I can go anywhere and do anything. I was going to go to London. The places I've never been. And I don't know why I'm hesitating with you."

She was so honest with herself and with me. I could love this woman if I only knew who she was. And I was sure—positive—that she would love me too.

"We have a gap," I said. "A big gap to fill where our lives have been. We have to string ourselves across it."

"Christopher Carmichael, I didn't know you were such a lyrical man."

"Didn't I talk some shit about flying monkeys?"

"You were a poet in the making."

"Then let me grind these rusty gears back to life."

She shifted to her side, propping herself on her elbow. "I'm ready."

I knew what I wanted to say, but not how to say it. No matter what I came up with, it was something I'd heard before or was too small in scope. I wanted to draw around us with permanent marker and show her the beauty of everything inside the line.

"We were destined. I don't want to make the mistake of saying that there's a now us and a future us. We were always in the stars, and for the past thirteen years, we were just waiting for the planets to catch up."

"That's not bad for a hedge fund manager."
"I'm not a hedge fund manager anymore."
"Really? What are you?"
"Yours."

CHAPTER 35

CATHERINE

The counter was too crowded. I couldn't fit a Dixie cup between the pots and bowls. Mrs. Boden arrived. She was over ninety and wore bangles on her wrists every day of the week.

"I can take two." She held out both her hands. I put a bowl in each.

"You got it?" I asked.

Behind me, the screen door slapped. It was Reggie, still bandaged.

"I have it, young lady," Mrs. Boden said before going out.

I should have been nervous to be alone with him, but I'd known him so long, I couldn't find fear. "Reggie, good morning."

"Morning." He jammed a hand in his jeans. "I brought the truck so I could take the big stuff." With his free hand, he indicated the food everyone had dropped off for the soup kitchen.

"I can give you a hand."

"I'm sorry," he blurted. "I called you a lie, and I knew it was a lie, but I said it anyway."

"Okay."

"And I had no business getting in your face. My feelings are the same, but I have to be a man. Just be a man about it. You're a woman of your own mind. That's the end of it. We've been friends for a long time and that's all I want from you if that's what you have to give. I'm upside down thinking I spoiled that."

I picked up the heaviest stock pot, and he rushed to relieve me.

"Thank you."

He turned and kicked open the screen door.

"Reggie."

He stopped with the door half open.

"Things are changing and you sensed that. You reacted to it. You didn't spoil it. We're still friends, but like I said… things are changing."

"Yeah."

"But not what I think of you. That hasn't changed. We're still friends."

"I appreciate that. I couldn't live with myself."

I put my hand on his arm and gave it a gentle squeeze. "You'd better get that out or everything's going to be cold."

As he walked across the back porch and I went to the kitchen to get another pot, Harper barreled down the stairs in her yellow polo.

"You're working?" I asked. "I haven't made you lunch."

"Don't worry. I got it." She yanked the plastic tail of the bread bag off the top of the fridge, spinning it in the air before catching it.

Mrs. Boden came back in. "Got room for two more." She cradled two bowls in her arms and headed out.

Harper leaned into the pantry for a jar of peanut butter.

"Are you all right?" I asked my sister.

"Fine." She snapped a shopping bag from under the sink and dropped the jar of peanut butter and loaf of bread into it. She tried to leave, but I put my hand on the door. "What?"

"You're not fine."

"I'm going to be unfine and late." I knew the warehouse shifts as well as she did, and she wasn't late. When she realized I wasn't budging, her shoulders slumped. "I'm as fine as I need to be."

"Taylor?"

"That's over. He needs to have his life. I'm not going to hold him back."

"That's awfully mature of you," I said through a haze of disbelief.

"Whatever."

I took my hand off the door and wedged myself between her and it. "How are the college applications going?"

She shrugged. "I don't see the point."

Reggie clopped up the porch to get more pots, and I pulled Harper into a corner to give him room.

"What's that supposed to mean?"

"It's, like, a hundred dollars per application."

"How many do you want to send out?"

"Three. Stanford. MIT. Michigan."

I would give it to her even if three hundred dollars meant I had to stay. "You have to become what you were meant to be."

"Oh, give me a break."

"Harper." I put my hands on her biceps. "I never thought I was meant for anything. I wasn't pretty like Marsha. I wasn't smart like you. Mom always dreamed so small for us. But she was wrong. I was wrong. I became something here. I found my purpose in my people. But you? You're never going to be your best self here."

She looked away from me, twisting her mouth into a defiant curve.

"Maybe," I added, "you'll find your purpose and Taylor at the same time."

"We're all going to find Taylor." She clopped the floor between her feet. "There's talk he's buying the factory."

"Our factory?" I exploded from the inside out. "That's wonderful news! We haven't heard a thing since… was he the one we cleaned it for?"

"No. It's…" She shook her head. "It's complicated. But it's real and you know what? I don't want to be here when he's here."

Behind her, Johnny and Pat joined the march of food-carriers.

"Do you have three hundred dollars?" My offer was tinged with hope.

She looked less thrilled. "It's three seventy-five, and I can put it together."

"Are you sure?"

"If you let me get to work already."

I hugged her first, planting a long kiss on her cheek. "I love you, Harper."

"I love you too."

She pulled away and brushed past Reggie to get out the door.

CHAPTER 36

CATHERINE

The soup kitchen closed at two. We cleaned up, distributing the pots and bowls back to their owners, and went home. I didn't repeat Harper's news and wouldn't until I knew for sure. But in that time, as I chatted with my people, exchanging smiles and hugs, I realized I wasn't needed anymore. I didn't know whether to feel free or lonely.

Chris's rental car was in the front yard. Inside, the dining room sconces glowed and a beat-up wooden table stretched from entry to egress. He sat in one of the plastic folding chairs from the back porch.

"Hi," I said, dropping my bag by a table leg. It had been scratched to the raw wood by an army of cats. "This is… big."

"Biggest I could find."

We stepped toward each other as if we were molding the space between us.

"I'll bite. Why does size matter so much?"

Fingertips touching. Palms pressed flat together. Bodies against each other.

"We have a lot of stories to tell and I don't want to run out of space."

I glanced at the tabletop. A hundred rings marred the wood, but there wasn't a story on it that I could see.

With my head turned, he laid his lips against my cheek and kissed it, breathing deeply. "You smell like paprika."

"I need to wash up."

"I'll go with you."

"Tell me what the table's for first."

"It's the distance between who we were and who we are."

"No wonder it's so big."

In one smooth motion, he picked me up, then carried me upstairs. We didn't make it to the bathroom. By the time we were at the top of the stairs, we were kissing as if we wanted to eat each other alive, clawing our way to each other's skin.

Half-dressed, he propped me against the wall outside my bedroom and peeled off my pants. I unbuckled and unzipped him, feeling the throb and heat of his arousal in my fist. I'd never imagined how much I'd want it, and I'd never imagined I'd ever feel so empowered to take it. My boldness shocked and freed me.

Holding me up by the legs, he pushed toward me and I guided him so he could drive into me with the force of an animal. I grunted. He exhaled.

"I'm having you in the shower too."

"And on the table?" I gasped as he thrust hard.

"Table's not for that."

Angling his hips to put pressure on my clit, he took me faster. I was aroused beyond all thought, but it was hard to concentrate against a wall.

As if reading my mind, he took my hand from his shoulder and guided it between my legs. "I want to see you make yourself come."

I started to object. That would be too shameful. Too embarrassing.

"Show me," he said, deep inside me.

My reaction to his intensity wasn't in my mind or heart. My spine vibrated and I nearly came from his command.

Any thought of shame was drowned and washed away. I rubbed my clit as he fucked me, letting my orgasm wash away any idea of shame. With him, I was fully myself.

"Yes," he hissed and thrust harder, grabbing the flesh of the backs of my thighs, slowing as if savoring every thrust. He buried himself in me, pinning my hand between his body and my clit. I felt his pulsing as he filled me.

When he was done, he gathered me in arms that never seemed to get tired and carried me to the shower, where we made love again.

CHRIS PULLED our one comfortable chair in from the living room and placed it at the center of a long side of the table. His hair was slicked back and he smelled of spicy soap.

"Stay here," he said before kissing my forehead.

"Okay?"

He was already on his way up the stairs, taking them two at a time.

He wouldn't discuss where we were going or what we were doing. He had some kind of future for us on his mind, but had made it clear he wasn't interested in bringing it up yet. I was relieved, because though I wanted to discuss our future, I feared I wouldn't like the results of the conversation.

Because how could this work?

I needed to find a new life, and he already had one. He was based in New York, and though I might travel, I didn't know if I could ever really leave Barrington.

Chris came down more slowly than he'd gone up, taking his steps carefully, looking around the three boxes stacked in his arms.

The boxes of his letters.

He placed them on the table and pushed the stack to the center. "Our story is here."

"Oh, Chris. Didn't you see? I'm so sorry, but most of them are impossible to read."

He slid off the top box. It landed on the table in a poof of dust. "I'm here to fill in the gaps." He opened the box and grabbed a handful of envelopes. "Upper left corner is the day I left. Bottom right is the seven hundred and forty-nine dollar check. We'll go horizontally. If I calculated it right, we should have enough space for all the letters folded into thirds."

"I don't get it. You want to…"

"Lay it all out. My entire story." He plucked a letter off the top of the pile and took out the paper. It was water damaged and all the ink had run. "This is on letterhead." He flipped the envelope over so he could see the postmark. "Right. So it goes about…" His eyes flicked from one edge of the table to the other. "Here." He laid it two thirds of the way to the right, letter tucked under the envelope flap.

I picked the next one off the pile. The postmark had crumbled away. I slid the letter out, unfolding it. Letterhead again.

"'—time I moved to Park Avenue.'" I read what hadn't been washed away. "'—aller than I'd like for Lance, but zip—'" I scanned to the bottom, where a few more words had survived.

"Zip code matters," he said. "I had a place on the Lower East Side that was fine. All the roommates moved out and I just took over the lease. But Brian, my partner, was pretty adamant that I was always going to be a second-rate player below Fourteenth." He shook his head as if getting the dust off. "Street. Fourteenth Street runs east-west. There's below it, where the creatives live, and above it. He said I needed to have a Park Avenue address, even if it was big as a closet."

"How big was it?"

"It had a two-burner stove and a sink as big as that postage stamp." He took the envelope and laid it next to the first letter. "But I had Lance, even if he was miserable in that tiny studio."

"How could you tell?"

"He shit in my favorite shoes."

I laughed. He took another letter off the pile.

I grabbed his hand. "Wait."

It was my turn to take the stairs two at a time. I rushed to the hallway, threw open the closet door, and gathered up as many of my photo albums as I could carry. When I went up for my second trip, Chris helped. Soon we had them all piled at the foot of the table.

He told me the year and season of his move to Park Avenue, and I located the right photo album.

"Oh," I said, seeing which era of my life it was. I pressed my fingers against a picture of my parents and me in the town square.

"That the Labor Day Barbecue?"

"Memorial Day. Daddy stopped funding it a few years after the factory closed, but it went on without him. Bernard and his band just set up. People brought stuff."

He put his arm around my shoulder and brushed his thumb along my neck. "This is a special place."

"It is. It's a dead end, but it's home."

"It's our home."

"Yeah." The album page's plastic skin crackled when I pulled it back. The photo came right off. I put it on top of the letter it went with.

"Why isn't Harper in the picture?"

"She was at MIT."

"Wait, what?"

"She didn't finish."

"Why not?"

"It's a long story."

His arms snaked around me, turning me toward him, my body tight against his. "Catherine, I need your long stories. I need to live them with you."

"It's so much."

"It is, but we have nothing but time and a really big table."

Could we bridge the years between us? Could we understand each other? Or would the exercise make it worse? Would we see each other's bad decisions and get disgusted or ashamed?

"What if you don't like what you find out?" I said. "What if I don't live up to your expectations?"

"I have more to worry about than you." He tipped my chin up so he could look in my eyes. "Whatever we did, that makes us the people we became. And I know I loved the girl you were. I'm pretty sure I'm in love with the woman you grew into."

For a split second, he looked like the old Chris on the day we were caught in the office, face cut into stripes from the afternoon light coming through the blinders. His skin folded into Ws at the corners of his eyes and his voice had grit in the corners, but he was that same boy with that same raw love.

I wanted him to love me again, because I was sure I loved him.

"Let me make you some tea and I'll tell you what happened with Harper when Daddy got sick."

CHAPTER 37

CHRIS

didn't have a timeline to complete the boxes of letters. Good thing, because there was no way we would have made it. That afternoon bled into the night. Harper came home, stopping to look at the boxes and the new table.

"I'll tell you some other time," Catherine said. "Have you eaten?"

She hadn't. Catherine fed her, then me, and Harper went upstairs.

"You were telling me about the subway." Catherine tapped the letter in question. Half a page of the most boring narration in the world. She sat in her chair and put her hands in her lap.

"It's a little dry. We can skip it."

"Nope."

I told her what was in the letter, as far as I could remember, expanding on it as necessary, and she told me about her life at the same time. She'd sold the paintings off the walls to bail Trudy out of jail for a DUI. She'd posted bond for half the town at some point or another.

When we realized it had gotten too dark to read my writing, we turned on the lights, laughing at the obvious solution. Morning came and went. We ate sandwiches and drank homemade iced tea.

We were tired, but we couldn't stop. She was fascinating, creative, driven to keep the people she loved above water. The table was crisscrossed with photographs and paper scraps when we got to the point when Errol Dannon went off to college. She beamed, eyes glittering with tears.

"He was having such a hard time with math in eighth grade. He thought he was dumb, but he wasn't. And when he went to Duke, he said it was because I drove Harper to tutor him that he made it." She sniffed, wiping away a tear.

My handkerchief was damp, but I used it to wipe her eyes.

"Thanks." She shook off the sobs. "I think we should take a break."

I tipped the box. A single envelope slid along the bottom. "There's one more." I handed it to her.

"This one's in good shape," she said, flipping to the front. Her brows knit. "No postmark? No stamp?"

"Might have been stuck in another envelope?"

She shrugged and opened it. When she unfolded the page, two tickets fell out. I put my elbows on my knees, leaning as close to her as I could without crowding her.

"What is this?"

"Read it."

She met my gaze for a second, then went back to the page and read.

DEAR CATHERINE,

This time, I'll come with you wherever you want to go.
I'll stay where you want to stay.
I am at your service from this point on.
All my love,
Christopher.

THAT WAS the shortest letter yet. She looked on the back of the crisp, white page. Blank.

She picked up the tickets and read them. "The Sistine Chapel?"

"You like paintings on the ceiling. Figured it was a good place to start."

She was still confused. "The date—"

"Enough time for me to get you an expedited passport." I reached over to wipe her eyes again, but she took the handkerchief and dabbed her eyes herself. "The tickets… it's just one thing. There's more. Paris is beautiful."

"I don't know," she squeaked.

"What don't you know?"

"They need me." She swung her hand toward the front door as if the entire population of Barrington could fit through it.

"Let them decide that."

"This is my home."

"You can still let me take you to Europe."

Her head was bent over the last letter. A teardrop fell on the paper with a heavy *tick*. She rubbed it into a gray streak.

"Catherine."

"I don't know how I feel."

"You don't have to."

She swallowed thickly. "I'm tired of crying." She sniffed, not looking up. "But I keep doing it. It's like a habit. I keep thinking everything's just going to be bad forever. And I think because if things got good, no one would need me. I wouldn't have a purpose. I'd be just…" She looked up, past me, to the ceiling, the morning light, the bare walls. "Nothing. Useless."

I gathered her hands in mine. "Your work in the world isn't done."

She tightened her fingers around mine. We sat like that for a long time. I'm not a praying man, but I prayed. For me. For her. For the possibility of an *us*.

It was her decision. I'd already made one for us. It was her turn.

The effort involved in shutting up was monumental.

Her hands loosened, but I didn't let go. I wouldn't. Not until she spoke.

"So…" She cleared her throat when the word caught, looking at me with eyes clear of sadness. "Is it cold in Rome this time of year?"

"You'll go?"

"I'd love to go. I'd love to be with you."

I leapt off the chair and held her. "Thank you," I said into her neck.

She laughed. It wasn't a reaction to something funny. No. It went on too long for that. It was a laugh I couldn't kiss through, though I tried. She laughed because she was happy, and I laughed with her.

I'd replaced her tears with laughter. I'd done much without her, and I'd done much for her. But I hadn't achieved anything until I turned her sadness into joy.

CHAPTER 38

CATHERINE

August was hot and sticky in Rome, but somehow, with the fountains and carless plazas, it was bearable. Maybe Chris made any kind of weather seem perfect.

I looked at my watch.

"She's going to be late," Chris said. "You know Lucia's always late. It's an Italian thing."

Something strange had happened between Chris's ex-wife and me. She'd had us and a few others over for dinner the day after we arrived in Rome the first time, six months earlier. We chatted over wine and I helped her shell peas. We didn't have a single thing in common except for Chris, which should have inspired me to steer clear of her. But I didn't.

I liked her.

Apparently she liked me too. The next morning, Chris got a note at the hotel, respectfully requesting permission to be my friend. I felt as if she were asking for my hand in marriage.

"I'll tell her no," Chris had said, rooting around his pockets for a pen.

"Don't you dare!" I snapped the letter away.

"What? Why?"

"She's different than anyone I ever met before." I folded the paper and put it back into the envelope. "And she thinks I'm interesting."

"If it would make you happy..."

"You make me happy." I slipped my hands under his jacket, circling his waist. "Lucia is entertaining, and I'd like to be her friend. But if it makes you uncomfortable..."

"No, no, no. It's fine. Just don't go shopping with her."

"First, shoes! Then, bags!"

Lucia and I hadn't bought anything but wine and pastry together, and yes in the six months I'd known her, she'd always been late. You could set your watch to it.

"We have to get moving early if we want to make it to Lake Como." He tipped back a tiny cup of espresso, finishing it in a single gulp, as expected in Rome.

Across the cobblestone plaza, flower and fruit sellers had set up tables. They did brisk business in single carnations and little, sealed grey boxes. A heavy door into the side of the church was chocked open. A stream of people came in and out. Some went in holding the flowers and boxes and left without them.

"But I want to go to the catacombs," I said before finishing the last of my pizza, which was a completely different thing in Italy. Just a piece of flatbread with sauce and a dusting of cheese. A snack. "And that apartment in *Trastevere* feels like home."

"You want to stay then?" Chris reached across the table for my hand, and I gave it to him.

Behind him, as people passed on the sunlit plaza, the pigeons fluttered up in a wave, cooing and dropping back to peck between the cobblestones. He'd let his beard grow in. I loved running my fingers through it when we kissed.

Chris would go wherever I wanted. He'd show me places he knew or discover new things with me.

"Harper's coming home from Stanford for break."

We'd been traveling for two months this time. Our first trip to Italy was a week in Rome and six weeks in Tuscany. Then we went home. I took care of the Barrington house. He took care of business in New York.

We were separated for two weeks, and we decided never to do that again. That was nine months ago.

"We can come back, or we can skip the *Citta Della* whatever festival in Como."

"Chee-*tah*. *Dio mio*, Christopher." Lucia's voice came from behind me.

I stood and we double-air-kissed. That had always looked phony to me, but when you actually kissed the person and touched them in some other way, it meant you liked them.

I was surprised how much I liked Lucia. I'd known Barrington and Doverton women who kept their hair and nails perfect like she did, and I knew women who put on fussy airs and cared about status. But none of them were as grounded about it as Lucia. She didn't gossip, and she didn't look down on me for my short, unpolished nails or quick ponytail. She liked that I didn't care about my social station, even as she made no excuses for the fact that she cared deeply.

"Chee-*tah*, then," Chris said, double-kissing his ex-wife, who now spent half her year in her home country.

"It's not a cat," she said, sitting next to me.

"Whatever. If I need a translator, I'll hire someone."

"You can look right in front of you."

The waiter came before she could explain. She ordered lunch in Italian, I did the same, and Chris ordered in a halting patchwork of syllables that I explained to the waiter.

"Excuse me," I called to the waiter before he left. In Italian, I asked, "What's going on over there? With the open door?"

He answered, and I thanked him.

"What was that?" Chris asked.

"It's the feast day of Saint Monica."

"From *Friends*?"

Lucia rolled her eyes and nudged me.

"They're bringing offerings," I continued. "Silly man."

"How is it that you're at your woman's mercy?" Lucia asked. "What would you do without her?"

"It was worse in Iceland."

"Everyone speaks English there," I protested.

"Two weeks." He held up two fingers. "Two. And she was talking to people. And not just ordering dinner."

"I spoke at a third-grade level and I barely had a vocabulary. Seriously. It's not a big deal."

Lucia, in typical Italian affection, put her hand over mine. "You have a gift."

"Well, whatever." I hid my face by taking a drink of water.

"No," she *tsked*, wagging her finger. "This is not to be ashamed of." The rest she said in Italian too quickly for Chris to understand. "This gift is what God gave you. And if you are ashamed of it, you are ashamed of God." She slid back into English. "God made me beautiful, and I use it."

"Indeed," Chris grumbled amicably.

"Anyway, are you going?" Lucia asked. "To Como?"

"We haven't decided," Chris replied.

"I want to see my sister."

"So you return."

"Maybe. There's a lot to see. I don't know. It's not like there's a schedule or a point." I shut myself up. I'd started to bring up my trouble with Chris. I didn't want to float around the world all the time. I loved traveling and meeting new kinds of people, but something was missing.

Lucia tapped my arm. "Come with me. *Un momento*." Then, to Chris. "We'll be back."

She led me across the plaza, not missing a step in six-inch heels on uneven cobblestone. Her bag was tucked under her arm, a gift from her current beau.

"Where are we going?"

She stopped at one of the sellers and bought a little grey box. "To make an offering."

"What's in there?"

"Porridge. Don't look like that. It's just a little."

We passed through the doorway, into the back of the basilica. The stone floor was worn smooth, and with the sun in the side of the sky opposite the single stained glass window, the little foyer was dark.

"I told you I'm not getting married again," she said.

"Have you changed your mind?"

"No. Please. Save me from it."

Through the far entry, we entered a large nave lit with ceiling lamps.

Along one side, a long table was set with candles. Celebrants slipped their carnations inside vases or laid them before the paintings of the saint and left bills and coins in gilded chests. Some prayed at a red velvet rail that ran the length of the table.

Lucia put her box with the rest, dropped cash into the box, and kneeled, tapping me to follow. "Santa Monica was Saint Augustine's mother. She followed him all over the world. Now, you can say what you like about that. But she was a mother first."

I nodded while she rested her chin on her folded hands. She was going somewhere, but I couldn't imagine a destination.

"I love children. Always. I begged to take care of my cousins. I thought I would be a mother. But God gave me a gift instead. He made it so that I had to give myself to children who didn't have someone to take care of them. I'm not marrying again, at least not soon, because my gift isn't to be a wife. Chris will vouch for that." She stood and smoothed her skirt.

I followed her to an empty pew and sat next to her.

"It has been so good to know you," she whispered.

"Thank you. You too."

"You pick up what people are saying and speak back to them in their language, but your gift isn't languages. Your gift is *listening*." She took my hands. "I'm going to make you an offer to use that gift."

"What kind of offer?"

"I need you at the Montano Foundation. It is a big organization all over the world, and it does good work. We feed children and build schools. We need someone like you, who listens and can learn a language. Who is generous. Who wants to help. Children need you."

My blood thrummed. Work. I'd never had a job. I'd always assumed I didn't have a skill worth paying for.

Lucia continued, "There will be a lot of travel, but we'll talk about it later. First, you think about it, because you won't be so free to move around when you want."

"Okay. Thank you. I'll think about it."

When we got back to the plaza, I could see the café. Our lunches were at the table, and Chris was on the phone. He invested his own money, but still loved taking risks and crunching numbers. He loved his job.

Our lives revolved around two things. My travel whims and his work.

How would a position with Montano, where I'd have to travel where and when I was needed, fit into that?

❦

CHRIS and I were alone on a small jet flying out of a private airport outside Rome, taking up two of the eight seats. The rest were empty. We'd stayed in the apartment in *Trastevere* another week, missing the Como festival. I'd been too wound up to take the short hop to Tuscany. I spoke less, got lost in thought mid-sentence, stared out the window for too long.

I hadn't told Chris about Lucia's offer. I wanted to think about it first, but I just kept thinking.

Would I be separated from Chris for weeks? Months?

How could I ask him to prioritize my work and his at the same time?

What did the future look like if I did this?

We were in the air before he spoke. "Catherine."

"Yes?"

"When we get home, is this over?"

"What?" I was too shocked to make a whole sentence. How could he think that? What had I done?

"Just tell me."

"Wait…" I twisted in my seat to face him. He'd shaved off his beard, and his eyes were soulful and honest. Had he looked this mournful since I spoke to Lucia? How hadn't I noticed?

"I want you to be happy," he said. "But you've been saddish."

Saddish? I'd been thinking about my life, for sure. Who I was. What I wanted. He'd turned that into me wanting to leave him, and that wasn't going to work.

"Christopher Carmichael." I grabbed the front of his shirt. "You are a piece of my happiness." I tugged the fabric. "You are the love of my life. Do you hear? Do not ever imply this is over unless you want to end it."

"Then what's on your mind?"

I let go of his shirt and smoothed it down. "I wanted to think about something before I told you."

"Well, you've thought enough. We're partners. You don't get to think that much without me. Out with it."

Lucia had put the official offer in an email. I got it up on my phone and showed it to him. His expression went from mild irritation (probably with his ex-wife) to deep consideration, to a sharp nod as he handed the phone back.

"You taking it?"

"I don't know. I want to, because I'm bored. Not with you," I said quickly. "Not with you at all. Not with traveling or the new places. I love all the people. I love seeing things I never thought I would, and there are so many things I never even imagined. Northern lights. Pompeii. So much. But I'm bored with myself. I don't have a purpose. I'm not fighting for anything. It's like…"

I'm dead inside.

But that was too harsh and unfair. He'd breathed life into my heart, but there was only so much he could be for me.

"It's like you need to become the next version of yourself."

"Yes."

"And you're not going to get there globetrotting."

"Right!"

"But you're afraid you'll lose me if you have your own needs."

He'd hit the bull's-eye, and he knew it. I couldn't look at him.

He unsnapped his seatbelt, then undid mine. He looked down the aisle to the front of the plane. The attendant was tapping on her phone in the galley. He craned his neck to the back of the plane, then stood and held his hand out to me. "Come with me or I'll carry you."

I laid my fingers in his palm, and he pulled me to the sleeping quarters and snapped the door shut, cutting us off from the rest of the plane. We were alone with a tiny bed and a standing shower. He unbuttoned his shirt.

"Chris, really?"

"Really. I don't know how to make you believe me." He shrugged off his shirt and made short work of his pants. In seconds, he was as naked as the day he was born. "Do you see me?"

I took in the beauty of his naked body, but when I laid my hand on his chest, he moved it away. "I see you."

"I have nothing." His voice was cut through with resolve and hunger. "This is me with nothing. I came in this way, and I'll go out this way. This body? It has needs. I need food, water, and sleep, okay? That's how it stays alive. I have a brain. It comes with the package. It needs to work and to figure things out. If I'm not doing that, I'm dead, because it's here, in the skin. And I have a heart. When I'm naked and all the other shit is gone, it's part of me. It needs you. You."

He was making my point for me. I nodded, about to explain that I understood. He needed me and if I was doing something else, his basic needs wouldn't be cared for. But he took my shirt at the hem and pulled it over my head.

"Chris, I—"

"Give me a minute. I'm not done." He stripped me down until I was naked and vulnerable in front of him. "You come with this package." He looked at all of me as if cataloging. No lust. No lingering on the most feminine parts. "It needs food, water, sleep, shelter. Your heart needs love, and that you have covered, by me. But the mind?" He took my head in his hands and kissed my forehead. "It's been neglected long enough."

When I blinked, tears fell onto my cheeks. I swallowed hard, took a hitching breath, and tried to thank him, but I couldn't.

He went from my forehead to my temples, my cheekbones, my jaw, my chin, and hovered over my lips. "I won't allow you to die. Not any part of you."

I couldn't hold myself back. I threw my arms around his shoulders and kissed him with everything I had, and he let me. He leaned back and sat on the bed, still connected to me at the mouth. I felt his erection between us, and my entire body—with its need for food, water, and sleep—needed it. My heart, with its need for his love, needed it. My mind, with its yet undiscovered needs, needed it. I lifted myself on my knees and he guided himself into me.

"I love you, Catherine of the Roses."

"And you. I love you."

I moved against him in a rhythm that gave both of us what we needed, together.

EPILOGUE

CATHERINE

*H*e'd planned his proposal with the care and patience of a lawyer arguing before the Supreme Court. He'd had the ring, the place, and the time.

Unfortunately, my flight out of Sri Lanka had been delayed. He'd spent the first week with me, then gone back to New York. I was supposed to follow, and he was supposed to propose at the top of Freedom Tower. Instead, he'd met me at the airport, carried me upstairs half asleep, and put the ring on my finger while I was dreaming.

Of course I'd said yes. I may have been crazy busy, but I wasn't crazy.

And now, here I was under a tin ceiling painted with roses in a designer wedding gown my fiancé's ex-wife had commissioned. It was gorgeous. The veil was set in my hair with roses. My nails were done, and my lipstick softened my face.

Lucia was behind me in a pink business suit, hooking the back of the dress closed. Marsha was pinning and repinning my hair.

"I love it," I said.

"Of course you do," Lucia replied.

"Chris is going to fall in love all over again," Marsha said. "He hasn't seen you yet, has he?"

"Not for a week."

We'd been separated for that long before. We had been apart for three weeks when I was setting up a school for girls in Morocco, but this week had been the hardest. He had stayed with Johnny while I stayed at the house, planning everything with Lucia and Harper. And Taylor, of course, who'd found his way back to Harper. But that was another story entirely.

Outside, I heard kids playing and guests laughing. Everyone was coming. The entire town, the board of Montano, our friends from New York. Everyone.

There was a commotion downstairs, in the living room. Someone was calling for Father Grady. I wasn't supposed to go down. Chris had promised a surprise.

Harper banged up the stairs and threw herself into the room. Her sentence was one long word. "Cassie-the-pregnant-FBI-agent-her-water-broke-so-they-need-to-get-married."

Cassie the Pregnant FBI agent was with Keaton the Handsome Brit in the Dark Shirt from my birthday party.

"Okay?"

"She's trying to leave. She doesn't want to take the wind out of your sails."

"Nonsense." I gathered up my skirt.

"Can't they have the baby first?" Lucia objected.

"I don't know!" Harper said. "It's a thing!"

"Americans are such prudes."

Whatever the reason, it wasn't for me to judge why they felt as though they had to get married first. I flew down the stairs as a voice with an English accent floated over the confusion.

"We need rings!"

"Use ours!" I called as I was halfway down. Father Grady was putting on his stole and flipping through his book of sacraments. "Chris! Give them the rings!"

Chris spun around and put his hand over his eyes. "I'm not looking at you!"

"Who has them?" I shouted, then froze. The mantel, the wall, the entire side of the room where we were to be married was crammed with roses.

"The best man," Chris said from behind his hand. "Back upstairs, woman!"

I couldn't back away. Couldn't turn from the roses. "Chris."

Johnny came in from the back in a long-tailed tuxedo jacket and bolero tie. "I got it."

The clamor went on as people shifted and took new places. Taylor was Keaton's best friend, so he acted as best man for the moment.

"The roses," I said.

Chris had given up on not looking at me and laid his hands on the bannister. "You're beautiful."

"So many."

"Seven hundred forty and, well, we were short five. Now we're up five."

I searched his face for a moment, trying to place the need for over seven hundred roses.

"The garden's down ten though. I promised I wouldn't cut from there, but we have some helpful people around who did it anyway."

THIS IS A GUARANTEE. *I pay my debts. I'm coming back with the money and more. And when I do, I'm bringing you a rose for every dollar.*

"I REMEMBER."

"I kept my promise."

"You did."

"Except about the garden."

"You kept your promise, Chris." I went down the stairs, and he met me at the bottom. "You kept promises you didn't even make. You made me whole."

"You made you whole. I just watched it happen."

The impromptu ceremony ended with cheers as the groom kissed the bride. Taylor kissed Harper. Couples I barely knew kissed.

And Christopher Carmichael, the lost boy who'd become a man, the persistent letter writer, owner and friend to a puppy named for a knight, looked at my lips in their sweet pink hue and leaned in.

"No!" Harper shouted and wedged herself between us. "You waited thirteen years. You can wait another ten minutes." She pushed me up the steps. "Go go go."

"She's not even hooked in back!" Lucia shouted from the top of the stairs.

Chris kissed my hand before it slipped away. "See you in ten minutes, Catherine of the Roses."

"See you forever, Christopher Carmichael."

I went back up to my room, and under a ceiling of roses, I prepared to spend the rest of my life becoming who I was meant to be.

THE END

THANK YOU FOR READING! I hope you enjoyed Chris and Catherine.

Harper and Taylor's story is told in *King of Code*. I put chapters in the back if you want to check it out.

Keaton and Cassie's story is told in the standalone *Prince Charming*. I've put a few chapters in the back. if you'd like to sample them.

SOCIAL MEDIA

Follow me on Facebook, Twitter, Instagram, Tumblr or Pinterest.

Join my fan groups on Facebook and Goodreads.

Get on the mailing list for deals, sales, new releases and bonus content - JOIN HERE.

My website is cdreiss.com

ALSO BY CD REISS

The *New York Times* bestselling Games Duet

Adam Steinbeck will give his wife a divorce on one condition. She join him in a remote cabin for 30 days, submitting to his sexual dominance.

HIS DARK GAME

Monica insists she's not submissive. Jonathan Drazen is going to prove otherwise, but he might fall in love doing it.

COMPLETE SUBMISSION

Fiona Drazen has 72 hours to prove she isn't insane, just submissive. Her therapist has to get through three days without falling for her.

FORBIDDEN

Margie Drazen has a story and it's going to blow your mind.

THE SIN DUET

Her husband came back from the war with a Dominant streak she didn't know he had.

The complete Edge series

EDGE OF DARKNESS

CONTEMPORARY ROMANCES

Hollywood and sports romances for the sweet and sexy romantic.

Shuttergirl | Hardball | Bombshell | Bodyguard | Only Ever You

www.ingramcontent.com/pod-product-compliance
Lightning Source LLC
Chambersburg PA
CBHW030353200726
48286CB00014B/1269